Hearts of Steel

Peace & War in the Royal Navy 1918 to 1941

Jim Carter

Published by New Generation Publishing in 2022

Copyright © Jim Carter 2022

First Edition

The author asserts the moral right under the Copyright, Designs and Patents Act 1988 to be identified as the author of this work.

All Rights reserved. No part of this publication may be reproduced, stored in a retrieval system or transmitted, in any form or by any means without the prior consent of the author, nor be otherwise circulated in any form of binding or cover other than that which it is published and without a similar condition being imposed on the subsequent purchaser.

Paperback: 978-1-80369-631-7
Hardback: 978-1-80369-632-4
eBook: 978-1-80369-633-1

www.newgeneration-publishing.com

 New Generation Publishing

For Mike, Robyn, James & Georgia

Contents

Preface 1

Part 1 – 1900 – 1939 7

Chapter 1 – The Senior Service – Part 1 7

       The Senior Service – Part 2 20

Chapter 2 – H.M.S Effingham 1925 – 1927 The East Indies Station & The East Indies Squadron 41

Chapter 3 – H.M.S Hawkins 1932 – 1935 102

Part 2 – H.M.S Nubian 139

Chapter 4 – Tribal Destroyer 139

Chapter 5 – TOTAL GERMANY 162

Chapter 6 – Eastern Mediterranean Fleet Destroyer 232

Chapter 7 – Illustrious 267

Chapter 8 – Relentless 288

Chapter 9 – Operation Judgement 311

Chapter 10 – Operation Excess 7 – 23 January 1941 340

Chapter 11 – The Battle of Matapan 27 – 29 March 1941 379

Chapter 12 – Strike Force Malta 'Our job is to nip out and attack the Tripoli convoys by night' 419

Chapter 13 – Operation Demon, the evacuation of Greece 452

Chapter 14 – Crete – 1 May to 1 June 1941 459

Chapter 15 – 12 days in May 1941 469

Postscript 500

Appendix I – Awards – Battle of Tarigo Convoy, 16 April 1941 511

Appendix II – Casualties H.M.S Nubian 26 May 1941 514

Appendix III – Abbreviations 516

Sources 519

Bibliography 520

Preface

2014 was the 100th anniversary of the beginning of World War 1 and as one of the acts of remembrance many villages across the U.K. set up projects to research the lives of the men listed on their war memorials located in churchyards and town squares throughout the land. This was of particular interest to me as I had always wondered who were these men, what were their backgrounds and where had they paid the ultimate sacrifice for their country? In many cases, families never knew what had happened to their loved ones killed in action. Indeed, there may not be a grave they could visit to pay their last respects and even if there were, it may be in another country and outside the means of a family member to make such a long, expensive journey.

At this time, I lived in the village of Great Shefford, in West Berkshire and I volunteered to help in our project to investigate which units 'our' men were serving, where they were fighting and perhaps, what were the circumstances around their deaths. The power of the internet and the resources that can be used to tap into vital information cannot be underestimated. It led me to the on-line War Diaries of the Royal Berkshire Regiment looked after by The Rifles Berkshire and Wiltshire Museum in Salisbury, to as far afield as Australia for information on No. 1 Squadron RAF.

I realised that whilst these men no longer had a voice, in most cases, there was little written personal material either. However, I could connect the 'where, why and what' they were doing with the experiences written or spoken by men from the same regiments, squadrons or ships companies. These accounts, by individuals who were not necessarily known by our man, but who were there, sharing the experience with him, must surely provide a window into the sights, sounds and conditions experienced collectively by all those present? A fascinating and at times moving exercise.

Around the same time, my mother gave me a four page document detailing the naval career of my Great Grandfather, Herbert Leeder, who was born in

1900. He joined the Royal Navy in the summer of 1918, having had a hard upbringing in the workhouse and on the railways as an engine cleaner. Like many young men joining up, he signed on for the maximum term of 12 years. With little prospects back in his home county of Norfolk and the country at war, what else could he do?

What immediately struck me, was not only the longevity of his service (1918 to 1945), but the number of ships he served in, some 22 different vessels in total, mainly destroyers and cruisers. His career included two long term tours on the East Indies Station, based out of Trincomalee in Ceylon, each of a duration of almost two and a half years. Time away from his family with almost no means of communication other than the written letter, a situation that is totally alien to us in the age of internet access and real time video calling. However, Herbert was experiencing the Navy at a time when its size (certainly in comparison of the Navy today) and technical capability was still unprecedented. For example, at the 1937 Fleet Review for the Coronation of King George VI, there were 10 lines of ships, stretching 10 miles across the Solent and he was there aboard *Iron Duke.*

I was very fortunate to visit the Royal Navy Library at Portsmouth Naval Base one cold and wet November day, the cobbles of the dockyard glistening black from a recent shower. Having walked through the Unicorn Gate, where my great grandfather and so many men have passed before, the *Victory*, that constant presence at Portsmouth came into view. Once the cutting edge of warship construction, *Victory* was backdropped by the latest and largest ship ever built for the Royal Navy, a huge slab of steel and purpose, the aircraft carrier, HMS *Queen Elizabeth.*

I had already sent in a copy of Herbert's S.459 form, in a hope that I could shed something more tangible around his career. On arrival the curator showed me to a desk where she had laid out several books which she said was all she could find relevant to his service document. My heart sank a little, but then she pointed to a small, but thick hardback book, entitled *HMS Effingham 1925 - 1927.* This book was a written account, compiled by some of *Effingham's* crew, describing their deployment to the East Indies Station and this was indeed one of the commissions that Herbert sailed with. I flicked through the book and whilst I could not find any mention of Herbert in person, I quickly realised that he would have been familiar with some, if not most of the men and tales described within the pages.

Once back at home, I went to my computer and searched for the book online. Behold the power of Amazon, for there was a copy. I brought it immediately. I then considered whether there was a similar publication relating to his second deployment to the Far East aboard *Hawkins*. I did a search and there it was. 'Nil Desperandum' was the title of the publication detailing the commission of HMS *Hawkins* when Herbert was aboard between 1932 and 1935. I purchased this too.

Whilst his time abroad would have been a wrench from his family, he was experiencing travel on a scale and variety that for the working man, was unheard of at the time. A ship of war on active duty clearly had a military purpose and projected the power of the British Royal Navy, but it also had a diplomatic role to play. When the warships entered a port, they were representing the King and Great Britain. They were platforms to entertain the rulers, dignitaries and businessmen of overseas friends, partners and occasionally potential foes by organising on board parties, concerts or functions ashore which included putting on film shows or arranging military tournaments.

To maintain morale and cohesion, a crew needed entertainment and activities that kept them bonded together, not only as a fighting unit but as a small and thriving community. This included trips ashore to see the local sights and sounds, dances, plays, fishing and of course, sports. Sports fixtures including, Cricket, Football, Rugby and Shooting to name but a few were the norm when a ship put into port, whether it was just between sections of the crew, another ship's crew, a local garrison or perhaps a civilian team.

On returning to England in 1935, Herbert would have found the Navy being modernised to counter the threat posed on European, indeed world peace by the rise of the Nazi Party in Germany under Adolf Hitler. As touched upon earlier, the Coronation Fleet Review in 1937 demonstrated the might of the Royal Navy and included some overseas visitors, which included the Japanese Navy and notably the German Navy, represented by their most modern Battleship, *Graf Spee*.

In 1939, as World War 2 was about to break, Herbert signed on for a further 12 years at a time of uncertainty and, as we all come to discover, a gradual realisation of one's own mortality and the responsibilities that come with being head of a family. This particular time of his life would be the culmination of his career as a crew member of a brand-new Tribal Class Destroyer, H.M.S *Nubian*. She would go to war crewed by a mixture of the Navy's most experienced men who would mentor a crew brought up to strength by reservists and youngsters who had joined up for King and Country and were classed as 'Hostilities Only' personnel.

Nubian gained 13 battle honours during her career, with 9 of these won between her commissioning in December 1938 and May 1941, the period when Herbert was aboard. However, despite such a career, she gains meagre attention by historians and writers, who have concentrated on destroyers such as *Jervis, Kelly,* (Commanded by Lord Louis Mountbatten) and *Hotspur,* plus of course the larger Warships, *Warspite, Illustrious* and *Hood.* During the second war, *Nubian* saw action in the Norwegian Campaign before heading to the Mediterranean where she took part in the battles of Calabria, Matapan and operations such as, Judgement, Excess and the evacuations of Greece and Crete. *Nubians'* involvement may not always have been front and centre, but she was there, often playing a vital role of one sort or another. As there is little written about her operations in detail, I have sought to rectify this. As a result, one finds many individuals, ships and instances that although perhaps only loosely connected to her, help give an overall picture of how important her role was. Some of the operations *Nubian* was involved in have been described elsewhere before but I hope that their retelling may spark an interest to investigate further, for those who perhaps are not so familiar with such events.

Herbert remained an Able Seaman throughout his career and whilst the lowest of ranks in the Navy, one must remember that a ships company is not just made up of Officers, it is a team of men, some are leaders, some have a particular skill set and some carry out the day-to-day routines that keep the ship working. Without the whole, the ship cannot function, and will have no soul. Roger Hill was Commander of the destroyers *Ledbury, Grenville* and *Jervis* (of which we will become acquainted with later in the narrative). Hill was an outspoken and forthright commander, who won a D.S.O whilst commanding *Ledbury* during Operation Pedestal (the resupply of Malta by convoy) and a D.S.C on *Grenville* following a successful U-Boat hunt in the Mediterranean. He wrote of his crew in his memoir 'Destroyer Captain'.

> The average age in *Grenville* was twenty-four and less than twenty in a hundred had been to sea before. It is these young men who run and fight the ship. The Captain of a destroyer in World War II was a think box into which radar, radio, and sight reports were fed, and out of which were triggered response orders (reactions), some of which were considered decisions and some wild guesses. Mine were lucky.[1]

So, this book does not focus on a particular campaign, operation or individual. Whilst Herbert's career provides the thread of the story, it is the ships, their crews and characters that really form the core of the narrative from a time of peace, the rebuilding of the reputation of the Royal Navy after Jutland, to perhaps both its own 'finest hour' and 'darkest hours', during 1940 and 1941, when it was arguably at its most powerful. A Navy of a size that we will not see in our lifetime, or perhaps anyone else's. The few ships that have been preserved from both world wars do serve as a reminder of the hardships and the conditions that the men served in to protect the shores of Great Britain, but the men that fought and died on the sea have no recogniseable battlefield that one can visit. They have no gently rolling countryside, forests or beaches dotted with memorials to specific regiments or actions, just a constant horizon and the rolling swell of the sea.

Hearts of oak are our ships,
Jolly tars are our men, we always are ready.
Steady, boys, steady!
We'll fight and we'll conquer again and again.

Chorus from 'Heart of Oak' – Official march of The Royal Navy.
Words: David Garrick 1759
Music: Dr William Boyce (1716 – 1769)

Jim Carter, Dorset, June 2022.

---

[1] (Hill, 1979)

I would like to thank my old friends Ian & Carolyn Spreadbury for their editing skills & advice and my wife Louise for her support and patience during this project.

Part 1

1900 – 1939

Chapter 1

The Senior Service – Part 1

Workhouse

'Mother don't let them take me! Please!' The young man snapped awake with a start. He blinked and looked around him in one of those moments between sleep and full awareness when you have no idea where you are. A man in a suit was regarding him through black rimmed glasses over the top of his paper until their eyes met and he looked away. Herbert Leeder sat up and looked out of the window, a greasy smudge betrayed where his head had been whilst asleep. The countryside slid past bathed in a hot July sun on ripening wheat bordered by dark green hedgerows. The train clattered over a level crossing where a gang of men were working on a road leaning on their rakes watching a steam roller belch a puff of smoke as it lurched forward. Herbert became aware of the rhythmic sound of the carriage crossing the sleepers and a drowsy stuffiness that smelled of warm dust which was somehow comforting.

Herbert's mind processed this in moments before contemplating his dream that had ended so abruptly and so vividly. His unconscious state had taken him back to the day when his family had been admitted to the workhouse. The day had started quite well, his family walking up to the gates of the imposing Walsingham workhouse with their meagre belongings and little Gertrude Eliza snuggled in her pram. Walsingham was known as 'Thursford Castle' to the locals. It was an imposing Victorian brick building, built by the Walsingham Poor Law Union in 1836 on a budget of £5600, intended to be the home for 250 inmates in 54 rooms (which included the staff accommodation), and of a design whose purpose was to deter anyone thinking this was a pleasant place to aspire to. Octagonal in construction with a central administration 'hub' around which there were 4 accommodation wings that segregated the men, women, children, able bodied, sick or infirm and pensioners. Each wing had its own exercise area, again, segregated. The entrance to the building was from the road to the east, with a Porters lodge, board room, various offices and a small chapel.

They were met by the Porter, Harry Board, and his wife Eliza who was known to the family and had helped Herbert's Parents, James and Mary arrange their first interview with Charles and Harriet Barret who were Master and Mistress of the workhouse. This interview was an important step in gaining admission (which was voluntary) and its purpose was to understand the applicants personal and financial circumstances. The decision to enter the workhouse was a difficult one and obviously carried some stigma, as well as consequences.

Herbert's father, James Herbert Leeder was 37 years old and lived in the Norfolk village of Swanton Novers. He was a brick and tile maker like his father had been, in the yard owned by Lord Hastings of Melton Constable Hall. He was in a relationship with Mary Hutton, a widower from the nearby village of Fulmodeston. Mary was a similar age to James and had two teenage daughters, Alice and Mildred.

James lived in Giles Road, but it was not his own home. It belonged to another Leeder family who, had rented him a single room. Then Mary fell pregnant. In July of 1900 their banns were read, and, on the 10 August, they were married in the church of St Edmunds. James signed his name in shaky handwriting, Mary signed with a simple X, she could not read or write. On the 3 November 1900, Mary went into labour and Herbert William was born. It must have been very difficult living in the single room with a small child that not only applied pressure on their marriage, but on the relationship with their landlords too. Then, to make matters worse Mary fell pregnant again and, on the 26 January 1904, Gertrude Eliza joined the Leeder family. Poor little Gertrude was the catalyst that led them to the gates of Thursford Castle.

Herbert shuddered as he recalled the moment when John Bacon, the Boys Caretaker, had taken his hand, kindly but firmly saying, 'Come along with me Herbert.' At that moment Herbert realised life would be very different from now on. Mary looked down at him with distress in her eyes, James looked on the verge of tears. By submitting to the workhouse, the family were being split up and there would be little contact allowed between them until they left. Herbert began to plead with his mother in the manner that had awoken him. He was taken away to the children's wing where, sobbing uncontrollably he was given a haircut, issued with some house clothes and a bed in a dormitory with the other children. There were 23 children under the age of 15 at Thursford Castle. They were provided with an education from 7 onwards as per the 1834 Poor Law Act which required the workhouse to provide at least 3 hours tuition per day. This included *'reading, writing, arithmetic and the principles of a Christian Religion and such other institutes as may fit them for service, and from them to habits of usefulness, industry and virtue.'*

Gertrude was taken by a nurse to be looked after in the children's wing whilst Mary and James were taken to be bathed. The clothes they arrived with were removed, cleaned and stored, in readiness for return should they ever leave and were replaced by workhouse uniforms. James received a pair of trousers and a jacket made to last rather than for comfort and a bowler hat. Mary was issued with a nondescript dress of blue and white stripes. Either way, the clothes they now wore managed to identify where the person wearing them had come from and resulted in either pity or distaste. Able bodied men and women were allowed to obtain work outside of the workhouse or remain in any current employment if they already had work. James continued at the brick works once the family had been admitted.

Of the 107 inmates at Thursford the majority were made up of the elderly (over 60) and infirm. Their backgrounds varied, Farm Labourer's, Horsemen, Fishermen, a Soldier, a Master Mariner, Draper, Painter and Decorator, Organ Grinder and of course James as a Brick maker. The majority of inmates were in good health, however there are some with infirmities such as the Deaf & Blind, Feeble minded, Paralysed and one who is described as an 'Imbecile.' In today's terms, these would be classed as Learning Difficulties or Disabled in levels of severity.

Workhouse welfare from the 1900's had clearly improved from the conditions described by the likes of Dickens. There appears to be a genuine will to care for the elderly and educate and prepare the young for some form of work. Indeed, the diet in some of the workhouses was not as plain and meagre as one would expect, with Workhouse Unions developing a number of diets and menus that included 'treats' such as Batter Pudding or Roly Poly.

The man across from Herbert dropped his paper once more and asked, 'So where are you off to young man?' Herbert sat up a little straighter in his seat, rubbed his eyes and answered with some pride. 'I am travelling to Portsmouth to join the Navy.' 'Good show.' Replied the man, which seemed to end the conversation just as quickly as it had begun. Herbert wasn't really in the mood for small talk anyway and he returned to his gaze out of the window.

It had been June 1910 when life took another turn for Herbert. Summer had come to Norfolk early with beautiful long, hot sunny days for what felt like weeks on end. He was allowed to visit his mother who was bed ridden. No one, not even the doctors knew what was wrong with her. He had looked at her pale face and sunken eyes, his 10-year-old mind not really comprehending what was happening, but he knew it was not good. It was the last time he recalled talking to her properly, before she fell silent for good. She said to him, 'Young Herbert, promise me you will learn your letters and numbers, don't be like me. Work hard and escape this place otherwise you'll be like the rest of them, working in the brick yard. Go and make something of yourself.'

On the 23 June, Herbert was called to Mr. Barrets office. His father was stood opposite Mr. Barret, he was holding his bowler hat and was looking at his feet. Mr. Barret had a hand on his father's shoulder which seemed to Herbert to be jumping up and down. Herbert did not need to be told. Mary had died. She was just 48.

Kate Spencer was the Industrial Trainer that looked after the welfare of the girls at Thursford. However, she took a shine to Herbert and helped him with his studies when she could. Herbert had an interest in machinery and especially engines. She encouraged him to think about what he would do when he reached the age of 15, for this was when he could decide whether to remain or leave the workhouse. This was not just out of the kindness of her heart however, as it was the duty of the workhouse to encourage people to get out of the system and reduce the numbers of people in their care.

The First World War was in its second year, enthusiasm had dampened as the casualties began to mount, the talk of 'It'll be over by Christmas' was lame on the lips of all those who had uttered it. Kate had managed to secure an interview for Herbert with one of the foremen at the Melton Constable Railway Works which he attended the day after his 15th birthday. He gave a good impression, arriving early on the old bicycle that Mr. Barret had given him. He was told to report the following Monday to begin work as an Engine Cleaner.

The village of Melton Constable had risen up out of nothing since the Midland & Great Northern railway had begun to build the Melton Constable Railway Works. It was a large Maintenance and Production facility with many buildings including a turn table for the positioning of the engines for maintenance. It required a large workforce and so the village expanded with housing built for the railway workers. The speed of growth is clearly illustrated where the population grew from just 118 in 1881 when construction began, to 1157 in 1911 (the site was closed in 1964 as a result of the Beeching act, it is now an industrial site, but there are some original buildings still in use).

Herbert was deep inside the bowels of an engine's boiler, covered in soot and ash wondering if a job at the brickworks may have been preferable. It took seven men to fully clean and prepare a steam locomotive for work and it was the young lads who got the worst jobs. Herbert was tired too; he had been up at 4:00am on that cold February morning. Wispy clouds were being driven over a half moon by a breeze that cut through you like a knife. His hands were frozen as he pedaled that old bike to Melton Constable where he had to awaken one of the Firemen, then head to the Engine Drivers house to get him up and then to the yard to begin a full day's work.

A shout from the foreman beckoned him out into the light. Blinking he placed his blackened hands around the welcoming warmth of a mug of tea that steamed in the cold. 'Got news that a couple more lads got killed last week. Poor buggers.' The foreman said quietly. Herbert looked at him, without really comprehending where this was going to lead. 'You'll need to start thinking about what you are going to do if this war keeps on going. My advice, don't join the PBI.' 'The what?' asked Herbert. The foreman shuffled his feet. 'The Poor Bloody Infantry. Look, you're a good lad Herbert. Have a good think about it. Perhaps the Navy would be a better bet.' It was a statement not a question.

The poster from the Great Yarmouth recruiting office had struck a chord with Herbert. It specifically targeted Stokers (ships engineers). Surely, ships workings including engines, could not be far removed from the work he was doing at the railway? The poster had some key points that will no doubt have been of interest for a young man who had spent time in the Workhouse. Free kit and bedding, free board and lodging, good pay and good prospects for those who wanted to get on and extra pay for good conduct. The base pay on joining was 9/11 (equivalent to £29.25/week in 2018) for those joining on a 5-year Special Service or 11/8 a week (£34.41) for a 12-year Continuous Service signing. The poster showed men on leave, playing football and travel to the China Station. It would have been a real leap of faith, a complete change of life from the sleepy Norfolk countryside and the sooty grime of the Railway yard, a big adventure with travel that was almost unimaginable.

The platform at Melton Constable was quiet on the July morning of 1918 that Herbert left. It would be the first time he had ever ventured outside Norfolk. His little suitcase was at his side, but there was little in it. His heart was racing with fear, excitement and the unknown all mixed together. Mrs. Barret had given him a clean shirt, tie, Jacket and some new trousers to 'make a good impression', his hob nailed boots were polished so he could almost see his reflection. He was not alone though, for Kate, his father and Gertrude had come along to see him off. With a few hugs, some tears from the girls and a rough slap on the back from his father, Herbert stepped aboard the carriage with a glance up to that "somewhere" where his mother was now. He would not be back to Swanton Novers, and he would not miss it either, he had made his escape.

Herbert's eyes opened for a moment, had he dropped off again? He glanced around the carriage. The man had finished his newspaper, or he had tried to. It lay open on his lap, his head was tilted back, mouth open and he breathed deeply in his sleep. His glasses were precarious in his hand. Herbert rested his head against the carriage window again and with that, he too succumbed to the rhythm of the railway once more.

1918

On 14 January 1918 at around 22:55 a star shell illuminated the night sky over Great Yarmouth. 3 German destroyers fired around 50 random shells at the town which caused damage to homes and the school. Two elderly civilians and two merchant seamen were killed. The 14-inch gunned Monitor, HMS *Roberts* was in port at the time but did not retaliate, most likely due to the torrential rain, wind and poor visibility that night. The shelling demonstrated that Germany could still bring the war to the doorstep of the people of England.

The 21 March 1918 was the start of what is known as the Spring Offensive by the German Army. The opening battle was named 'Operation Michael' and started with an Artillery barrage across some 150 miles of the front.

The attack was aimed at dividing the British and French armies and to hit hard before the Americans could join the war. Progress was swift and furious, the Germans deploying Stormtroopers; lightly equipped fast moving and hard-hitting fighters. Their advance was helped by dry but misty conditions that helped conceal the advance and add to the confusion and element of surprise.

Over the first few days of the offensive much ground was taken, and the Germans managed to break the Allied lines in many places causing fragmentation of the line and near collapse and disarray. However, the allies withdrawal was marked by fierce rear guard and holding actions.

By April, the allied situation was dire, and Field Marshall-Sir Douglas Haig issued what was to become known as his 'backs to the wall' order to all ranks of the British Army that included the following paragraph.

> There is no other course open to us but to fight it out. Every position must be held to the last man: there must be no retirement. With our backs to the wall and believing in the justice of our cause each one of us must fight on to the end. The safety of our homes and the Freedom

of mankind alike depend upon the conduct of each one of us at this critical moment.

The advance continued and the Germans re-took Passchendaele later in April and crossed the Marne in May. But the speed of the German advance was to be their undoing. To move great distances and hold them successfully, the re-supply of troops with the basic requirements of food and water as well as ammunition and the accompaniments of warfare are crucial. The Germans failed to back up their light troops with essential supply, exacerbated by the fact that the terrain they were taking was barren 'no mans land' and had been the subject of the 'scorched earth' tactic the Germans had deployed earlier in the war. The attack ran out of steam.

Moreover, the Germans had lost over a million men in their efforts and of these men were their most experienced officers and fighting troops. They could not sustain the effort any longer and with the might of America now 'in the fight', the end was coming.

The allied counter offensive began in August 1918 and rolled back the Germans beyond the Hindenburg line. The armistice, as we all now know, came at the 11th hour of the 11th day in the 11th month of 1918.

Navalism

Right up until World War 1, Great Britain and its empire was gripped by Navalism. As an island country there was only one way that it could trade and support the empire and other nations; by the sea. Therefore, it was imperative that the British Royal Navy was at the foremost of government spending. The Navy came first.

In 1900 the Royal Navy was extremely elitist, living off the memory and exploits of its greatest commander, Lord Nelson. At the turn of the century the Navy had moved away from a tradition of encouraging the raising of its commanders from the ranks, preferring instead to turn to a perceived quality over substance. That quality was the 'station' that wealth brought; an ability to purchase very smart uniforms and a focus on spit and polish over fighting spirit.

The figure to change this was Admiral John Fisher, a man who was to oversee the modernisation of the Navy through technological advances that were introduced at breath taking speed. He was responsible for and oversaw the production of the first modern battleship, HMS *Dreadnought*. He was an advocate of submarines and their particular form of warfare that changed Navy tactics almost overnight and of course hand in hand with submarine warfare came the use of torpedoes. Alongside these key components came wireless communications that would become so valuable in understanding an enemy's movements and relaying instructions to the fleet and between ships in action. The distance and accuracy that shells could be fired was improved exponentially with the introduction of rifled barrels.

However, it was HMS *Dreadnought* that captured the imagination of the general public and their enthusiasm for the Navy. *Dreadnought* personified the Great, in Great Britain and the countries technological and industrial prowess. Built in just a year, with her modern steam turbines, this ship could sail faster and sustain that speed further than any other ship. This one ship (and those that followed), was something that had never been seen before and gave the country an unprecedented ability to project power. It was akin to the nuclear weapons of today and made all ships before it immediately obsolete.

Winston Churchill was the Liberal Home Secretary at the time and his ears would have been ringing with the public cries of enthusiasm 'Dreadnought, Dreadnought, Dreadnought' and 'We want eight and we won't wait' referring to the number of ships that they demanded. Churchill famously commented, 'The Admiralty had demanded six ships; the economists offered four; and we finally compromised on eight'.

The introduction of the *Dreadnought* sparked an arms race with the Germans, who craved for military parity. They too began the development of new battleships and so began a rapid spiral towards war. As that war approached, Churchill made a decision that was to have a profound effect on the development of ships. His quest for a 15-inch gun platform was fulfilled, however the size of these guns meant the ships became larger and consequently slower, below a requirement of 25 knots. The answer was to change from coal fired engines to oil. Oil burned hotter, had a better calorific value, it left little residue and was far easier to transfer and refuel ships both in port and at sea. But Britain did not produce oil and so there came a reliance on the Middle East for supply, most notably Persia (Iran). In 1914, Churchill purchased for the Crown a 51% controlling interest in the Anglo-Persian Oil Company for £2.2 million.

Running into World War 1, the Royal Navy was at a strength and size never been seen before, or since. The public were in awe of the Navy and were hungry for a decisive victory of Trafalgar proportions. They expected the Royal Navy to blow the Germans to pieces, but they would have to wait until May 1916 for something like that to happen. The Navy policy was, in fact, to ensure that British trade and troop movements were fully protected and in particular the supply of materials for the war which clearly included the supply of oil. The wait for a decisive naval action was long and the desire for action was exacerbated by an incident that enraged the public who angrily questioned why the Royal Navy had failed to protect Britain, let alone act. On the evening of the 16 December 1914, the Imperial German Navy, slipped through an early morning mist to arrive off Scarborough and began shelling the town. Hartlepool, West Hartlepool and Whitby followed resulting in 592 civilian casualties.

Despite the shelling of Scarborough and the Hartlepools, there was a reluctance for the Imperial German Navy to venture out of port to meet the Royal Navy and provide that decisive encounter. This finally came on the 31 May 1916 at the Battle of Jutland, but the outcome was not as expected, indeed it was quite difficult to determine who had actually been victorious. In reality the result fell to the Royal Navy, not through a mass of sinking and burning ships, but a German Navy that scuttled back to port and was never to set sail again for the remainder of the war. A very strategic victory. On the other hand, the Royal Navy lost three of its Battle Cruisers, *Indefatigable*, *Queen Mary* and *Invincible*, some 6000 crewmen went down with these ships.

The public were not impressed, and the opinion was held that the Navy had been defeated. The Navy was far too slow to realise how damaged their reputation was, and it took an unprecedented amount of propaganda to counter an opinion which did not return in the Navy's favour until the late 1930's. As the war ended, the defence reviews began, and the treasury had their eye on the Navy for cuts. A country during peacetime does not require a force of equal size to that in wartime, and so the cuts began. The perceived failing of the Navy during World War 1 meant that the public took little interest or notice. Indeed, there was a view that the Naval arms race with Germany was a major contributing factor in starting World War 1 and there was no appetite for another.

The beginning of change came when Prime Minister Lloyd George commissioned Lt. General Jan Smuts (a South African who had requested to join the cabinet) to write a report on air defence and strategic bombing. The outcome of the Smuts report in August 1917 was to facilitate the forming of the RAF as an independent fighting force, with all air warfare activity taken from the Navy and the Army. As a consequence, military spending moved away from Navalism and concentrated on air superiority. The Fleet Air Arm would not be reformed until 1939.

Lord Birkenhead, who was a friend of Winston Churchill, once observed, 'When Winston's right, he's right. When he's wrong, well, my God'. One of these 'my God' moments surely must be the Ten-Year Rule, which he suggested in August 1919 when he was the Secretary of State for War and Air. Under the Ten-Year Rule, the armed forces should base their strength 'on the assumption that the British Empire would not be engaged in any great war during the next ten years'. The rule became self-perpetuating in 1928 (again under the lobbying of Churchill), which meant that Britain was never, militarily, any closer than 10 years from another war. The rule was eventually abandoned in 1932 although there was a caveat to its demise, defence spending should not accelerate once more in light of the current financial crisis that was, the Great Depression.

The National Treaty of 1930 saw restrictions in ship building and a number of conversions to existing ships to meet these requirements. One of these was the conversion of HMS *Iron Duke*, Admiral Jellicoe's flagship at Jutland, to a gunnery training ship and one in which Herbert would eventually serve.

Finally, and directly affecting the likes of Herbert, were the public sector pay cuts as a result of the Great Depression from September 1931. The Royal Navy imposed a 10% pay cut on Officers. For junior ratings, a new basic rate of pay had been introduced in 1925 for new entrants. Anyone who had joined the Navy prior to 1925 was to be put onto this wage which in real terms meant they had a pay cut amounting to 25%. The result was something that had never been seen before. Industrial action by over 1000 sailors in the British Atlantic fleet that became known as the Invergordon Mutiny (15 - 16 September 1931). The situation was so serious that it caused a run on the stock exchange and forced Britain off the Gold Standard on the 21 September 1931.

The inter war years saw a contraction in numbers of both Ships and Men from the signing of the Treaty of Versailles in 1919 and then a gradual program of rebuilding and re arming due to a number of re negotiated Naval strength agreements before a rapid re expansion, indeed all out arms race, due to the rise of Nazi Germany that will be discussed later.

One constant at Portsmouth throughout has been the ever present Royal Navy icon, HMS *Victory*. When Herbert joined the Navy in 1918, the *Victory* was still afloat at her mooring off Gosport. Whether anyone paid much attention to this most famous of ships at the time is not documented, however she was of importance as she was still a Flagship and remains to this day the oldest naval ship still in commission. At the turn of the century her fate was not guaranteed. Admiral Sir Edward Hobart Seymour wrote in 1886, 'A more rotten ship than she had become probably never flew the pennant. I could literally run my walking stick through her sides in many places and her upper works were covered by a waterproof coat of painted canvas'.[2]

On the 1 February 1901 the *Victory* fired a salute to Queen Victoria, 64 years after firing the salute at her coronation. The Queen had died at Osborne House, the Isle of Wight on the 22 January. Her body was brought from Cowes into Portsmouth on the Royal Yacht *Alberta*, closely followed the *Victoria and Albert* that carried the new monarch King Edward VII, behind which was the *Hohenzollern* with the Kaiser. Admiral Andrew Cunningham, of who we will meet more during our narrative, was a young Lieutenant at the time. 'It was a most impressive spectacle which I shall never forget-a dark, lowering afternoon with occasional shafts of wintery sunlight, and all the ships 'manned' by long rows of seamen with guards and bands on their quarterdecks. Ensigns and jacks were at half mast, and these, with the red

---

[2] (Fenwick, 1959)

tunics of the Royal Marines Light Infantry, and the conspicuous white hull and yellow funnels of the *Hohenzollern*, provided the only red splashes of bright colour. The whole fleet fired minute guns and the bands played the funeral march as the *Alberta* and the yachts moved slowly onto Portsmouth.'[3]

Victory was almost finished off for good on the 23 October 1903. The old ironclad battleship, *Neptune*, was being towed away when her wire tow broke, and she was swiftly carried by a strong tide. She collided with HMS *Hero* before striking the *Victory* and damaging her so badly that she began to sink. Some quick thinking and superb seamanship saw her into one of the dry docks before the worst could happen. Having been repaired and returned to her mooring off Gosport once more, World War 1 came along and the ships wellbeing was neglected. So much so, that by the end of the war her condition had once more deteriorated alarmingly and in January 1922 she was brought into No. 2 Dry Dock where she remains to this day.

Preserving *Victory* would not be without its challenges. The Admiralty could not afford the cost of restoration, and this had to fall, in the main, to private enterprise. However, preserved she was, and work was begun on restoring her to a state that Nelson would have been familiar with.

Through World War 2, *Victory* was stripped of her masts and rigging but remained in service as accommodation for Navy Servicemen. The Luftwaffe claimed to have destroyed her during a raid on Portsmouth during the night of the 10 and 11 March 1941. Fortunately, this was not the case, although a 500lb high explosive bomb had struck the bottom of her dry dock, bursting 24 feet aft of her port bow, resulting in a huge 8 x 15ft hole in her keel, and a 20ft gap in the docks masonry. She was lucky it was not an incendiary device. But *Victory* survived this war too. Interest, affection and enthusiasm for the ship continued as soon as World War 2 ended, and in 1946 she was re-opened to the public with over 19,000 visitors in that same year.

---

[3] (Cunningham, 1951)

The Senior Service – Part 2

Stone Frigates

The Royal Navy has always required land-based shore establishments to be used as Training, Research & Development, accounting & logistics as well as accommodation for sailors when not assigned to a ship. These establishments are known in the humorous tradition of the Service as 'Stone Frigates'. During World War 2, broadly speaking, these were clerically staffed by women of the WRNS (Women's Royal Navy Service) which inevitably earned this branch of the Navy the nickname Wrens and were overseen by male senior Staff Officers. The assignment of a sailor to one of these establishments is recorded in his service record. If the sailor is attached to a ship associated with the shore establishment, then the name of the ship is shown in brackets.

In most cases, RN shore establishments took on the name of a 'real' ship, HMS 'Vernon', for example, was a 4th rate ship originally attached to HMS 'Excellent' before the Torpedo establishment was created and split from the gunnery school, whence the shore establishment of 'Vernon' was created. HMS *Victory* is clearly the most recognisable and is the name given to the general naval barracks at Portsmouth or elsewhere. Indeed, shore establishments dotted about the globe with the same name were distinguished apart by a roman numeral. Quite often the original ships served as the accommodation for the training establishment, hulks from a bygone age that no longer served a useful military purpose. The figure head that once stood within 'Vernon' is today a centre piece of the Gunwharf Keys shopping centre in Portsmouth and was originally from HMS *Marlborough*, which was used as accommodation for the sailors attached to 'Vernon'. The Fleet Air Arm in contrast, used the name of birds (e.g., HMS 'Heron') to name their own shore bases.

Herbert was posted to several shore establishments during his career, and indeed attached to ships associated with the respective shore bases. Examples of these within Herbert's records being *Tara*, an 'S' Class Destroyer attached to 'Vernon' and the old Battleship *Iron Duke* attached to 'Excellent'. Each of the establishments played a clear roll in forming Herbert's overall career and indeed life within the service and therefore the key establishments are worth sometime within the narrative to look at a little more closely. Despite a lack of evidence in respect of Herbert's training records, he did spend quite some time at both 'Vernon' and "Excellent', which would suggest that he was trained in Torpedo and Mine laying (at 'Vernon') and Gunnery (at 'Excellent'). It is quite probable that this long service, experience and training contributed to his selection to become a crew member of HMS *Nubian* at the beginning of World War 2, that we will focus on later.

'Victory'

Often mistaken for the ship of the Nelson era, 'Victory' was also the name of the barracks at Portsmouth, currently known as HMS *Nelson*. When a seaman completed his time aboard a ship, he was either transferred immediately to another or assigned to 'Victory' until another position became available. In addition, 'Victory' was the name given to a number of locations where Naval Accounting took place.

'Excellent'

Leaving Portsmouth on a cross channel ferry and looking to Starboard (out to the right!), one will notice a group of buildings located on a small island. This is a partly manmade island, created in the mid 1800's bringing ashore the gunnery school, HMS *Excellent*. Percy Moreton Scott was the man responsible for ensuring that 'Excellent' would become the first shore base for the Royal Navy and it was his efforts to persuade the Admiralty that the island should be created that prevailed. This is Whale Island, and whilst 'Excellent' is the name of the shore establishment, it has always been known by sailors as 'Whaley'.

The soil excavated from the new basins being dug in Portsmouth dockyard was used to create the island with the labour provided by convicts. These were men who had committed crimes that did not warrant the death penalty but of a severity that ensured they would never be released. They worked in gangs of 25 and were watched over by twelve sentries with rifles. 400 men against twelve would appear quite good odds if one wanted to make an escape, but if caught, especially if a sentry was attacked and killed in the process, the death penalty would almost certainly have followed. However, those of a more devious character would goad a prospective hothead into such an attempt, giving assurance of support if they went through with it. Just as the escape was in progress the assailant would find that it was to the aid of the guard that his 'partners' came. They knew, that by foiling an escape attempt and especially protecting a guard would likely earn a reprieve.

The concept of a Naval Gunnery school was brought about by two men, Captain Sir John Pechell and Commander George Smith in 1830. Both men were concerned that British Naval Gunnery had become woeful. The origin of this state of affairs came almost unbelievably from the times of Nelson, when each Captain was responsible for training and gunnery aboard his ship, and the tactics (where guns had limited range and very few had sights) were 'get in close!'

At the end of the Napoleonic wars the Navy (in what is the perpetual yoyo of strength versus politics and funding) faced many cutbacks in ships and men. The wars with the United States bore out the fact that the Royal Navy was lacking in gunnery skills, so much so that Sir Thomas Hardy, who was due to become the senior member of the Board of the Admiralty; '…now admits that had he taken the *Victory* head on to a line of American long gunships the result of Trafalgar might have been very different.' [4] Hardy was the Captain of *Victory* at Trafalgar and was beside Lord Nelson when he was fatally wounded.

---

[4] (Captain John G. Wells, 1980)

Pechell and Smith proposed that a ship would be equipped with all types of guns currently in use within the Navy, and that the ship would be fitted out and maintained as if it were fully operational, but it would be permanently moored so that it could fire these guns safely across the mudflats of Portsmouth. Its purpose would be to train the Navy in all forms of current (and under development) gunnery practices and that at some point all sailors would at least spend some time at the school.

The plan was approved, and George Smith took command of HMS *Excellent*. By the end of 1830 his vision had become reality. *Excellent* was by now 43 years old, a 166ft, 74-gun ship that was laid down in 1787 and had seen action under Captain Cuthbert Collingwood in the Battle of Cape St. Vincent. This particular ship was broken up in 1834 and replaced by the *Boyne* a 104-gun ship of the same design as *Victory* and this ship was renamed 'Excellent'. There followed a succession of ships and trawlers that took the name 'Excellent' up until World War 2.

The development of ships and armaments, as we have seen, changed at a spectacular rate from the late 1800's leading up to World War 1 in 1914. With the appearance of *Dreadnaught* all before it, became obsolete. This leviathan had guns that could fire at distances of up to 10 miles, but there was a problem, and a very big one at that. What technical solution was available to direct their fire onto a stationary target, let alone another ship at sea?

Fortunately, there were some great thinkers who were putting their intellect to the problem, a Lieutenant Dumaresq being one. He invented a mechanical computer that could, by inputting the estimated changes in range developing between a ship and its target, calculate the 'Dumaresq Deflection', or in other words, the predicted fall of the shell fired from the gun.

By World War 1 the Dreyer Table was in use within Fire Control Rooms. Developed by Gunnery Lieutenant Frederic Charles Dreyer, this mechanical computer incorporated the Dumaresq Deflection. Range finding and bearing optics provided the distance and direction of the target from the ship. Wind conditions, changes in bearing and speed could be input into the 'table' which would output a trend in the range onto a moving paper plot. From the changing information the operator received in respect of bearing, range etc., the table would provide the angle the guns needed to be elevated and the deflection angle to compensate for the movement of both ships based on cartesian measurements.

By observing the fall of shot, an input of left or right to compensate for the speed of both ships (in knots) could be input, whilst Up or Down inputs re-calculated the predicted fall of shot, taking into consideration the movement of both targets whilst the shell was in flight. For the layman these are mind boggling calculations.

In addition to the technical capabilities, the working and firing of the ships guns in co-ordination had to change too. These new warships had individual gun turrets with crews who needed to be coordinated properly to lay down effective fire. Therefore, a centralised fire control room or Transmitting Station (TS), evolved where information on the target was collected from a number of sources, given to the Gunner who is in charge of the TS, who then inputs this information into the mechanical computer that worked out the range and deflection which was then fed back to the guns. When the guns are ready, green lamps come on in the TS and the Gunner can then press the fire gong, which is a loud bell, whence the order to 'Shoot' is give and the guns are fired.

The Dreyer Table was superseded by the Advanced Fire Control Table (AFCT) in Battleships and Battle Cruisers by World War 2, whilst a simplified version, the Advanced Fire Control Clock (AFCC) was fitted in Destroyers. A fine example of and AFCT can be seen in HMS *Belfast* moored on the River Thames by London Bridge.

For the majority of men aboard a warship at sea, especially when closed up for action with hatches and watertight doors closed, there would be an assault on the senses that could drive the bravest to the brink of madness. A human beings most precious and reliable sense is sight. Hearing and balance are not reliable, so when confined they can cause confusion of the senses. One can lose perspective of whether being up, down or turning left or right. Couple noise, confusion with little or no information around what is actually happening, can lead to panic, and being in a warship in battle the potential was acute. None more so than the confines of a sealed gun turret or in the bowels of the ship. In order to counter these most basic of human instincts the instilling of discipline was a key element in the training at 'Excellent'. Whilst at times a most unpleasant aspect, it was essential in ensuring that a ship would continue to fight in the direst of circumstances.

This discipline came to the fore during World War 1, and clearly demonstrated by two Victoria Crosses awarded to gun crew members. Major Harvey of the Royal Marines, who despite receiving mortal wounds from a shell that hit the 'Q' turret of H.M.S *Lion* during the Battle of Jutland, managed to order the closing of the doors to the magazine thus saving the ship, being one. The other, awarded to 16-year-old Boy 1st Class Jack Travers Cornwell, mortally wounded, with his gun crew dead and wounded about him, he remained at his gun until ordered to stand down. In what is probably one of the most poignant of moments during the Battle of the Denmark Strait in World War 2, German sailors aboard the *Bismark* noted that just after HMS *Hood* blew up and the great ships bow began to slip beneath the sea, her forward guns continued to fire[5].

Whilst there were great steps forward in the use of the large and medium calibre naval guns, the training and use of Anti-Aircraft gunnery did not come to the fore until almost too late. There are several reasons given for this being the case. During World War 1 there had been no attacks made by aircraft on a ship of the Royal Navy and there was a view held by some, that a capital ship was more than adequately armed to repel an attack from the air. The Fleet Air Arm (FAA) had by then, been disbanded and absorbed into the Royal Air Force until its reinstatement in 1937. Even then, the FAA would have their

---

[5] (Konstam, 2019)

hands bound in the selection of aircraft, most of which proved totally inadequate for air to sea operations or even training for that matter.

That is not to say that the threat was ignored, some who would have positions of seniority in the Navy were, from quite early on, considering the threat of air power. First Sea Lord, David Beatty wrote to his wife when a Rear Admiral in 1913; 'The Germans are fairly setting about creating a formidable Aerial Force, and it behoves us to move rapidly and provide the means of defeating them, and I am busy preparing a scheme for the defence of our ships which at present are absolutely at their mercy, a little matter that has been overlooked in the past.'[6]

Not long after the end of the Great War an exercise was scheduled whereby a group of 8 Torpedo armed aircraft attacked the ships of the 2nd Battle Squadron of the Atlantic Fleet whilst moored in Portland Harbour. Unable to manoeuver, the ships presented easy targets and 7 of the practice torpedoes hit their targets. Afterwards, Admiral Sir Charles Madden made a comment that unbeknown to him, foresaw the tactic of aerial delivered torpedoes so successfully demonstrated at Taranto and Pearl Harbour by observing that, even at its present state of development, the torpedo plane was the most dangerous form of torpedo attack upon heavy ships.

At 'Excellent' work began on developing Anti-Aircraft weapons and their use. This proved most challenging, developing cutting edge technology with no previous experience of anything like attacking a fast moving aerial object. The result was the 2-pounder pom-pom, who's ammunition was belted together, much akin to a very large machine gun. It suffered from many stoppages amid curses from the Gunners.

It was not until 1935 that a 'true' Anti-Aircraft Department was set up, but adoption of any form of intelligent sighting equipment was slow to come into use and in many ships, the Anti-Aircraft defences could not elevate any more

---

[6] (Captain John G. Wells, 1980)

than 45 degrees, even right up to the start of World War 2. In any case, 5.25-in. guns were adopted for long range use whilst the unreliable, 8 barreled pom-pom with its frequent blockages and the 0.5-in. machine gun were continually adapted for close range work.

The art of targeting with these new guns proved equally challenging, with complex mathematics required to resolve the problem. For most boys and girls at school through the years and I'm sure even today, the use of sines and cosines generates the comment 'whoever uses these things anyway?' There was a gunsight designed called the 'Woolwich Approximating' or 'Cosine sight'. Whilst being taught the intricacies of this device one Able Seaman asked, 'Please, Chief, what's a cosine?' 'Now, my lad, that's not for you to know. There's only one on the Island and that's kept in the captain's safe.'[7] Clearly no further explanation is required.

Aircraft were not just to be seen as an enemy; they would have their own valuable uses to the fleet. Obviously, there was the development of the aircraft carrier, with its projection of force into theatres where airbases had not yet been established and for the protection of the fleet. However, a further use of aircraft was a reconnaissance role, effectively increasing the range of the eyes of the fleet and to assist with the spotting of the fall of shells from the heavy guns of the Capital Ships. Cruisers and Battleships had catapults installed which could launch float planes for these purposes. The single engine Supermarine Walrus and the Fairey Swordfish were most common and there was room made aboard for a small hanger where the aircrew could work from, stores and spares were held and perhaps one or two more aircraft stored in crates. Once launched and their mission complete, the aircraft would either fly to the nearest base, or they could be recovered by the parent ship with the use of a crane, re installed on the catapult and made ready for the next sortie.

With an increasing certainty that war with Germany was likely once more, unrest throughout the world indicating conflict was not far away, Britain

---

[7] (Captain John G. Wells, 1980)

began to re-arm and prepare for war. In the mid-thirties 300 Officers and 2000 men qualified in various courses at Whale Island annually. Anti-Aircraft courses were at last the norm, but time was running out. Then came the Munich crises and soon thereafter the whole fleet, including the reserve, was mobilised. By September 1939 when war was declared, 'Excellent' had, however, done its job, and the Navy was prepared.

Great Britain stands out as the country that does ceremony not just well but is the benchmark, for the 'rest'. 'Excellent' has its own unique place in the Funeral arrangements for England's Monarchs. Queen Victoria loved her Navy and its smart attire, in particular. As we have already touched upon, the Queens body was brought into Portsmouth in 1901 and was taken by train to London, where men of 'Excellent' were providing the Guard of Honour. It was a very cold February day, and there was a delay in pulling away the Royal Artillery Gun Carriage upon which the Royal Coffin was placed. Horses are not ones for standing around for too long, especially when there is tension in the air, of which they are most attuned. Whilst the Officers in the precession could occasionally trot in circles to keep their mounts occupied, the horses attached to the gun carriage could not be afforded the same respite. They became restless, and despite the attempts by their handlers to calm them, they became fractious to the point where it looked like they would tip the coffin from the gun carriage.

Prince Louis of Battenburg was behind the carriage with King Edward VII, the Kaiser, and the King of Greece. Prince Louis approached the King and whispered to him. The King then ordered the horses to be taken away and the Carriage pulled by the Seamen instead. Form thence forth, it has been Seamen who have pulled the monarch on their final journey.

'Excellent' is now the home of Navy Command Headquarters, HMS Phoenix for Damage and Fire Fighting and a Navy Diving school which has its roots on Whale Island from as far back as the 1920's.

'Vernon'

As previously described, 'Vernon' was originally a 'component' of 'Excellent' for Torpedo experimentation and training. As an individual entity 'Vernon' split away from "Excellent' in 1876 and eventually became a shore base in 1923, occupying the land that has been re-developed and is now known as Gun Warf Keys in Portsmouth. 'Vernon' was closed in 1996.

'Vernon' had a flotilla of ships, established during the 1920's that included 5 or 6 Destroyers and a number of small mining tenders and trawlers. These were utilised for Torpedo and Paravane running and control, Minesweeping and laying for both training and experimental purposes. Torpedo running was carried out initially off Stokes Bay (Gosport), however the volume of shipping soon created operational difficulties and Torpedo running was split between Weymouth and Stokes Bay. To put the amount of activity into some perspective, the Navy was carrying out around 5000 Torpedo runs per year at this time. The adoption of Motor Torpedo Boats (M.T.B.s) by the Navy began at 'Vernon' in 1936. Initially there were 6 craft, designated the 1st M.T.B. Flotilla associated with 'Vernon'. Tactical and Weapons deployment were developed over the coming years.

The Development of Mines, their detection, destruction and indeed disposal became one of the most important aspects of 'Vernon' and this was especially so in respect of the German Magnetic Mine. Whilst Herbert was not directly involved in this, as he had been assigned to *Nubian* by then, the work that the men at 'Vernon' did to reveal the secrets of this weapon and the subsequent countermeasures and protection afforded to ships certainly was a benefit to all sailors both merchant and navy during World War 2.

It had been suspected that a magnetic mine was being deployed by the Germans as shipping losses due to mines began to mount, despite the minesweeping efforts of the Navy. Actually getting their hands on one of these weapons was proving difficult, the appalling weather conditions were not helping, for one. However, in November 1939 two mines were spotted being deployed by aircraft, their parachutes dropping them into shallow water at Shoeburyness near Southend.

In the early hours of the morning on the 29 November 1939 (low water being at 04:00hrs) Lt. Commanders J.G.D Ouvry and R.C. Lewis, along with a group of Soldiers, a photographer and Commander Maton (a Naval Experimental Officer) made their way across the mud flats under flashlight. It was cold, very dark and raining. In the estuary a number of ships were anchored awaiting the removal of these devices so they could proceed upriver.

Eventually they came across the first of these, a large, black, cylindrical device that looked every inch a diabolical weapon of war. Commander E. E. Webb describes the mine in his book 'HMS 'Vernon''. 'The mine was cylindrical in shape and made of some aluminum alloy, with tubular horns on the nose and a hollow tail containing a massive phosphor-bronze spring. There were two unpleasant-looking fittings near the fore end. One of these was evidently a hydrostatic valve and the other seemed likely to harbour a primer and detonator and was secured by a screwed ring.'[8]

It clearly takes much courage to tackle a device such as this, when one false move would end in instant oblivion. However, these men did, and one cannot underestimate the complexities of the design of this particular mine and their skill in rendering it safe in the cold and dark of that morning. Safe they did make it, and they also managed to recover the second device as well.

As a result of the subsequent examination of the mine, methods in tackling its deployment through detection and countermeasures were developed. In detecting the devices, a sweeping pattern (called an 'LL' sweep) was developed using two ships that towed a floating cable which was magnetised. In order to provide enough current to make these effective, very large generators were required although it was the problem of enabling the cables to float that proved one of the most difficult to achieve.

---

[8] (R.N., 1956)

Degaussing coils were installed in ships as countermeasures that proved most successful, and by May 1940 some 2000 merchant ships and 1704 warships were protected in this manner. The recovery and investigation into the mine was not only vitally important, it took much courage and fortitude to achieve. Both Ouvry and Lewis were awarded the D.S.O. as a result.

Portland ('Osprey')

Anyone travelling by car from Dorchester to Weymouth cannot be anything but moved when the road crests the ridge of downs and there, spread out before you is the bay of Weymouth, Portland Bill and its extensive harbour. On a fine day, the view is breathtaking. It is little wonder that not far away, atop the downs overlooking Chesil Beach, Portland and Weymouth the family of Sir Thomas Hardy (Captain of H.M.S *Victory* at Trafalgar) had a tower built in his memory that was originally used as a landmark for shipping.

The concept of Portland Harbour first arose in 1795, however the decision to build the first breakwater, using stone quarried from Portland Bill, was not taken until 1844 by the Commission of Enquiry into Harbours of Refuge. There had been much debate over the suitability of Portland Roads[9] as a refuge for shipping during which Admiral Dundas asked the following question to most of the witnesses: 'In time of war, in the present state of Portland and Weymouth Roads, could a fleet of men of war and armed steamers rendezvous there in all winds and weathers, or would it be beneficial to the objects I have stated to have a breakwater made in Portland Roads?' [10]A Lieutenant Marshall responded to this question which was echoed by many of the respondents: 'I think that, as at present they would run a risk, a breakwater would ensure this object at all times'[11].

---

[9] In nautical terms, a Road (or Roadstead) is a natural body of water close to shore where ships can safely anchor away from adverse seas, currents and weather.
[10] (Carter, 1987)
[11] (Carter, 1987)

Indeed, the evidence that Portland Roads was a safe haven was borne out by several witnesses including Lieutenant Marshall. Mr. Joseph Read who had witnessed 'sixty to seventy vessels in Portland Roads during south westerly gales.'[12] Mr. Robert White, who had been employed in the Packet Service declared that during the Napoleonic era he had seen as many as 140 vessels in the Roads at one time.

The Commission found in favour of the construction of the harbour which resulted in the Portland Harbour and Breakwater Bill of 1847. Work soon began and in August 1872 the then Prince of Wales laid the final stone with the following inscription: 'From this spot, on 25 July 1849, His Royal Highness Prince Albert, consort of Queen Victoria, sank the first stone of this breakwater. Upon the same spot, Albert Edward, Prince of Wales, on 18 August 1872 laid this last stone and declared the works complete. These are imperial works and worthy of kings.'[13]

Portland Harbour became home to a number of Naval developments, including Torpedo research, development and manufacture. Submarine warfare was a natural progression as well as a rendezvous for the fleet. Indeed, it was at Portland that the fleet gathered before dispersal at the beginning of World War 1. Ships were loaded with victuals and stores from a multitude of small craft and vessels. At night the lights of the fleet could be seen from the Esplanade along Weymouth beach. Then, as if by magic, the fleet was gone, and it was noticeably dark at night in Portland.

During the inter-war years, the development of Submarine work expanded to that of anti-submarine warfare. In 1924 the anti-submarine school was formed, HMS 'Osprey', Captain S. D. Tillard being appointed in charge. He identified that the research and development aspect of anti-submarine warfare was too dispersed and sought to bring all under one 'roof', in which he succeeded. As with any Submarine Warfare, even today, there was much secrecy surrounding these activities, especially with the development of

---

[12] (Carter, 1987)
[13] (Carter, 1987)

ASDIC, the underwater sonar detection system that was eventually fitted to warships. This device, simply put, sent out a sound wave that when it hit a solid object an echo would be returned in the form of a 'ping' sound. As the sound wave could be directed quite accurately, and the time for the returning ping recorded, a bearing and distance from the contact could be ascertained and an attack commenced.

Training in anti-submarine warfare and in particular ASDIC operation on both surface ships and submarines began at 'Osprey', including the R&D of tactics and use in adverse conditions, such as rough seas. Working up Surface Ships for Operational duties became a key role at Portland, and one aspect of this was Submarine detection. Nicolas Monsarrat was working up one of his ships (from 'Three Corvettes') when he afforded the opportunity of seeing the action from the submariner's perspective: -

> I thought I would be conscious of being underwater, and possibly nervous – indeed, at the very beginning I had been mortally afraid of turning claustrophobic, and possibly disgracing myself; but at no time was it possible to realise that we *were* submerged. The occasional noise of the hunting corvettes, sounding oddly like goods trains, passing overhead, was the only indication that we were under water: otherwise (save for the cramped space) it was no different from being, say, in the forrard mess-deck of a corvette. And it was amazingly quiet: there was no vibration and no engine noise, and orders were given almost in a whisper, instead of the wind-quelling shout we had to use on our own bridge.[14]

Monsarrat comments on the slick, professional and orderly operation of the submarine in cramped conditions, but conditions that fermented an exceptional camaraderie amongst the crew. On leaving the submarine, he took the opportunity to take a look through the periscope; '…I noted that the view of the surrounding surface craft through the periscope was distressingly sharp and clear.'[15]

---

[14] (Monsarrat, 2000)
[15] (Monsarrat, 2000)

However, the descriptions that Monsarrat can give us on the anti-submarine exercises are minimal, which he explains is due to the secrecy surrounding the development of the equipment and tactics, but what he does tell us is that during the initial training, when the ship's crew are new to such work, the target submarine would tow marker buoys, called 'buffs' that would help reveal the targets position.

In 'The Cruel Sea' there is quite some time spent on describing the working up of 'Compass Rose', the Corvette and its crew whose actions are described in the first part of the novel. Clearly this is from Monserrat's own experiences and ones that many a ships company will have experienced at Portland. The work was hard and repetitive in bringing the ship and its crew to readiness.

Daily we exercised everything, with a wild sense of crisis. We abandoned ship, we repelled boarders...we closed up action-stations against the stop watch...'[16]

There was gunnery training and depth charge exercises that included live ammunition which resulted in an explosion that; 'killed half a dozen guillemots which must have been diving nearby.' But in the end the crew was brought together; 'we emerged as a ship's company instead of a crowd of individuals...[17]

Portland remained in Navy hands well after World War 2. Never a popular posting not only because the work was hard but because it was a remote and rather inhospitable place to work. In addition to the surface ships, helicopter operations began in the late 1950's, teaching anti-submarine tactics. The base was finally closed to the surface fleet in 1996 with training being moved to Plymouth and the Air Station was closed in 1999.

---

[16] (Monsarrat, 2009)
[17] (Monsarrat, 2009)

Nozzer

'It is a picked service; of four ratings who present themselves at the recruiting offices the Navy accepts only one.'[18]

Lord Moran; The anatomy of courage.

Herbert arrived at Portsmouth with a group of other hopefuls and taken to a specific accommodation block where their new instructors would initiate the recruits into the rules and procedures that would now be expected of them in Military Service. They were taken for a severe haircut and then de-loused which reminded Herbert of his first days in the workhouse. Kit was issued, Blue clothes, White clothes, Jerseys, Overcoats, Trousers, Dress and Working Jumpers, Canvas Jackets and Overalls (Duck suits), Flannels, Caps, Cap Covers, Towels, Handkerchiefs, Boots and Shoes and finally bedding. Herbert was given a wooden stamp with 'LEEDER' written in capitals. All of the kit was to be stamped, white for dark clothing and black for light, however Herbert also received a sewing kit and a 'ditty box' to keep it in, as well as his personal effects, and he was taught to sew. For the next month of training, each recruit was required to stitch their name into each item of uniform. Any kit that was found lying about was collected up and put in a Scran Bag. As the manual of seamanship states 'It is the custom of the Service that a piece of soap is necessary to redeem the article.'

And in regard of the stowing of all clothing; 'A waterproof canvas bag will be issued to every boy on his leaving the training ship, with his name stamped on the bottom of the bag. He will retain the bag until it is worn out or until he leaves the Service.'

Herbert had become a 'Nozzer', the Navy's term for a trainee sailor.

Volume 1 of the Manual of Seamanship was issued to all recruits, and the first chapter is dedicated to detailing how every piece of clothing and equipment should be marked, and how they should be presented for

---

[18] (Moran, 2007)

inspection. The hammock was of key importance. It was the place where the recruit would sleep, it could be used to shore up any holes or breaches in the ship's hull to stop the ingress of water or become the occupants shroud should they be unfortunate enough to die and subsequently buried at sea.

Respect of rank is recognised in the form of the salute, the correct manner being 'by bringing up the right hand to the cap, naturally and smartly, not hurriedly, with the thumb and fingers closed together, elbow in line with the shoulder, hand and forearm in line, with the palm of the hand turned to the left but inclined slightly inwards.' The manual lists all who should receive a salute which includes the Royal family, all Officers either in uniform or plain clothes and flags, or Colours of the Royal Navy, Regimental Colours of the Army. It must be noted by all that; 'There is no excuse for not seeing an officer, or for not recognising an officer in plain clothes, who either on account of his rank or the fact that he belongs to the same unit as the man, should be known to him.'

In order to make it perfectly plain to all, the manual then describes in detail who should salute whom and when, or on what occasion. It includes all the insignia of rank of all the armed forces, so there was no excuse.

Physical exercise came in many forms, most notably swimming, and the compulsory swimming test that was taken at the local swimming baths in Portsmouth. Two lengths of the pool were swum in two sessions, one clothed in the canvas 'duck suit' the other naked. Boxing, gymnastics and team games such as football and cricket were encouraged. Equally testing physically was the scrubbing of decks with the 'holystone' or as it was known, the 'holy bible'.

A sailor's career was recorded within his 'Certificate of the Service' in the Royal Navy, otherwise known as form S.459.

If studied carefully there is a wealth of information about the man within this document. It is of 4 pages and covers personal information and description, including next of kin. A list of the ships or shore bases that the sailor was connected with is documented and when he started and ended that association. This includes the rating at the time, his position in the Royal Navy.

Attention was given to conduct and an assessment every twelve months (on the 31 December in respect of character and ability, signed by the Commanding Officer). When beginning research, it is worth noting the Port Division (on Page 1) and then an association can be made with the ships that use that port as their home base, and the shore bases used for training and general duties.

Herbert volunteered on the 26 July 1918; he is recorded as being 5' 4.5", a 36' chest, brown hair and eyes. At the time he had no visible scars, marks or wounds but this would change over the course of his career. Naturally any professional sailor would acquire tattoos over a long career in the Royal Navy, and Hebert is no exception. On leaving the Navy he is noted as having tattoos on his right forearm, 'Indian & Feathers, Hands across the Sea. Full rigged ships', and on his left forearm, 'non-descript picture (perhaps a pattern) and a small scar wound on the inner arm'.

Classed as a boy seaman he was assigned to the training ship HMS *Powerful*, a pre-Dreadnought cruiser that had been involved in the relief of the South African town of Ladysmith in 1899 during the Boer War. Guns were transported across country from both *Powerful* and her sister ship *Terrible*, to aid with breaking the siege. The 12-pounder guns were placed on special carriages that weighed around a ton each and were man handled over rough terrain to the town. Every year since 1909, the Field Gun competition between the services has been run to commemorate this action. Indeed, as part of a sailors training, there was a drill called 'Seamanship Rivers' which was a competition between two teams to disassemble a field gun, traverse a suitably difficult or awkward obstacle and then re-assemble it, which no doubt led to the Field Gun competition itself.

By 1918 *Powerful* was looking very dated. She was a big ship for her time, at 538ft long a beam of 71ft and displacing some 14,000 tons. The 4 funnels provided exhaust for the two, four-cylinder steam engines each driving a propeller shaft that gave her a speed of around 22 knots from 25,000 horsepower, but she was, by 1918, obsolete. Fore and Aft were a pair of tall masts, that the trainees were required to scale, without safety ropes or nets. Not for the faint hearted.

Coinciding with Herbert joining the ship, the second wave of the Spanish Flu epidemic broke out. This deadly pandemic resulted in the deaths of 228,000 in the UK, so called because the UK, France, Germany and the US suffered the effects of the pandemic, whereas Spain did not. This gave cause for the perception that Spain was the source of the disease. Conditions in this time of war, concentrations of people, malnutrition and poverty, contributed to the spread of the disease, which was fast and devastating. If you caught it, you almost certainly would die. The first wave early in 1918 was bad enough, but the second wave was the biggest killer from between October and November of 1918, whilst the third wave in 1919 was more lethal but less widespread. The symptoms were alarming to those treating it. Fever coupled with shortness of breath contributed to a blue tinge to the victims face from lack of oxygen. The lungs would haemorrhage, violent nose bleeds and vomiting would follow, and the victim would literally drown in their own fluids.

The disease was unusual in that it was most prevalent in the summer months, and especially attacked the fit and healthy, those between 20 and 40 years old. With the conditions in the training ships perfect for the spread of the disease there were many young boys who succumbed to Spanish Flu. But Herbert avoided the illness, and, on the 3 November, he was raised to Ordinary Seaman (Later to become Able Seaman) and this date was logged in his S459 as his commencement in the Royal Navy. On the 10 November Herbert was posted to his first ship *Centurion* (a King George V-class Battleship) and the following day, at 11:00, World War 1 ended.

Centurion was another big ship, much bigger and more modern than *Powerful.* Lightly tested in World War 1, *Centurion* played only a minor part in the Battle of Jutland and was very much held in reserve for most of her career. Decommissioned in 1932 and then recommissioned in 1935, used as a target ship and eventually as a block ship before being scuttled during the D-

Day landing as a breakwater to protect the Mulberry Harbour off Omaha beach.

After 4 months aboard *Centurion* there followed a further 5 years of moving between the 'Victory' barracks and a number of ships based out of Portsmouth. A mixture of 'S' Class Destroyers operating within HMS 'Vernon' (Torpedo training) and HMS 'Excellent' (Gunnery training). Herbert was gaining experience and becoming a valuable and dependable member of any crew, gaining his first 'Good Conduct' badge aboard HMS *Merlin* on the 3 November 1921.

Whilst ashore at 'Vernon' sometime after release from *Tara* in 1922, Herbert met Kathleen Lucy Bowles. Kathleen was working as a domestic servant and lived with her parents at 41 Nelson Road, Southsea. They were married at Portsmouth Registry Office on the 1 June 1923. None of Herbert's relations appear to be present, although Kathleen's father (a member of the Coastguard) signed their marriage certificate. It is unusual that Herbert was permitted to marry, as he was 23 at the time. The Navy strongly forbid anyone below the age of 25 to marry and there had to be a very specific reason for permission to be given. The reason is most likely their daughter, Doreen Lucy Leeder who was born 13 February 1924. It would appear the courting had been passionate, and Herbert had to approach his Commanding Officer for permission to do the honorable thing, marry Kathleen.

Whatever their personal and domestic situation, Herbert had signed on with the Navy for 12 years, and therefore he had no choice but to continue with the service and it would not be long before he would be posted to another ship. Just 5 days after Doreen was born, this was indeed the case. Herbert was ordered to report to HMS *Hermes* on the 18 February 1924 (she was commissioned the following day). *Hermes* was the first purpose-built aircraft carrier constructed for the Royal Navy, and by the time of her commission she bore a resemblance to the aircraft carriers of the future that included an 'island' accommodating the bridge and flight control. Aboard were Fairey IIID reconnaissance biplanes that were used to conduct flight trials before

Hermes was posted to the Mediterranean. *Hermes* went on to serve during World War 2, but was sunk in April 1942 by the Japanese, with the loss of 307 men. As *Hermes* sailed on her first deployment, Herbert was detailed to report to "Excellent' before assignment for his first overseas tour of duty.

Chapter 2

H.M.S Effingham 1925 – 1927

The East Indies Station & The East Indies Squadron

We take for granted the fact that travel outside of the U.K. is both affordable and available at (almost) a moment's notice. In the 1920s this was definitely not the case. One means of travel without considerable expense was to join the armed forces. In the Royal Navy this could mean an overseas deployment of two and a half years (not reduced to a year until the 1950's).

The purpose of the Royal Navy's presence in the Arabian Sea and Indian Ocean (or the East Indies Station) was to protect trade with England and in particular India's outgoing and incoming trade from Burma and Java which was predominantly made up of rice and sugar. The Station extended from Mauritius to Rangoon and covered 3 million square miles. The more important ports were visited annually by one of 3 cruisers of the East Indies Squadron, and often accompanied by supporting ships of the Navy. The Naval ports of Trincomalee and Colombo in Ceylon (now Sri Lanka) were central to operations. Trincomalee was of particular importance as this was a natural deep-water port and the Navy had undergone extensive work to ensure that it could support any sized fleet from a refeulling and victualling perspective.

Herbert was settling into married life with Kathleen and little Doreen was already walking and saying her first few words. Having spent 5 months at HMS "Excellent' (September 1924 to February 1925) and the past 5 months at the 'Victory' barracks, life was becoming a routine, as far as a routine goes in the Navy. The posting to HMS *Effingham* and its impending deployment to the Indian Ocean came as a shock that was both exciting and daunting ahead of an enforced separation of over two years for a young married couple and their baby daughter. Herbert was to report for duty on the 2 July 1925 with an expected departure for the East India Station in August.

It is hard to project forward in time how long two and a half years is in a lifetime. However, cast your mind back, to what you were doing two years ago. Remind yourself, what were your thoughts and aspirations then and you just might get a sense of how long that timespan is. It is a long time. Herbert had to rely on Kathleen to maintain a job, look after Doreen and their home and remain faithful that he would be home, in time, and that they would pick up their life together on his return.

Herbert's emotions were no doubt torn between excitement that he would be visiting places he had never dreamed of when living in Swanton Novers, the prospect of some danger and action, with that of sadness at how long he would be parted from those he loved. How would they cope without him? What would Doreen look like when he came back, would she remember him? Would Kathleen still love him?

Herbert had signed up for a portrait of himself in his white Navy tropical uniform. He is captured in confident pose, sat cross legged, hands resting on thighs. He has greased, short cut dark hair, black lace up boots, a single good conduct stripe on his left arm. Leaning against the chair is a white pith helmet with HMS *Effingham* embroidered on a band above the rim. Something for Kathleen and Doreen to remind them, of him.

Despite there being no personal correspondence available, there are two valuable sources that we can draw upon for this particular posting, and of Herbert's second assignment to the East India Station later in 1932. These have been the private publications put together by members of the ships crew that provide a summary of the posting. 'HMS Effingham 1925 – 27' is a hardback publication completed and published in Colombo just prior to the ship returning to Portsmouth. There is no accredited author, and whilst there are contributions from many members of the ships company, the authors of these pieces have purposely been omitted. 'Nil Desperandum' (Never despair) is a similar publication detailing the posting of HMS *Hawkins* to the East India Station from 1932 to 1935. It is somewhat different in that it is more of a narrative written by the ships Chaplain Walter Edgar Rea.

August 1925 was a dull and humid month. Two days of continuous rain preceded the morning of the 25th, some 60mm had fallen, the most in a 24 hour period since 1905. On a warm day, with scattered clouds, the 605ft Hawkins Class Cruiser, HMS *Effingham*, freshly painted in white with light yellow funnels and masts, awaited the days activity at the South Railway Jetty. She was prepared and ready to head off to the East India station as Flagship of the Squadron.

Effingham had waited 8 years for a posting. Initially a bunch of spars when laid down on the 2 April 1916, the ship had been partially constructed and placed into stocks by 1917 and there remained for a number of years, becoming a familiar landmark in Portsmouth harbour. She was eventually launched and then moved from basin to basin 'covered in red lead and rust'. On joining the ship for the first time, one of the officers remarked 'her quarter deck was piled high with everything from railway line to a dockyard monkey's tool chest'.

As work began to prepare her for her first commission the dockyard foreman was asked: -
'When do we commission for trials?' 'April.' said he in bold reply. 'What year?'
'This year.'
'Never looked like it'.

But, indeed, it was to be.

Effingham was officially commissioned on the 2 July 1925 and by that time the ship had gained the nickname 'Methuselah' as had the ships cat. On the firing of her engines for the first time, *Effingham* became a living entity and no longer a dormant landmark. Sea trials began around Portsmouth until the 4 August and on the 5th, whilst attempting to enter No. 15 dock, she managed to collide with the dock wall. It was then found that her propellers were terribly pitted, possibly due to inferior materials, and these had to be replaced. On the 17 August she once more took to the sea for final testing which included some exercises with torpedoes described as; 'a little game of strewing torpedoes about the ocean like cigarette ends in a public bar.'

Effingham had been designed to counter commerce raiders and was the largest sized cruiser permitted under the Washington Treaty. Her oil-fired engines produced 65,000HP which propelled the 9770 tons of ship to 30 knots (34 mph) across the sea, although according to her engine room she was most economical at 12 knots. To steady her at mooring there were 3 anchors in the bow weighing 5.5 tons each and a smaller one at the stern.

The crew consisted of 50 officers and 700 men, who were all fed by the most modern galley in the Navy. It had the latest electric mincing machines, bacon slicers and meat cutting machines and included oil fired ranges for cooking. She even had her own bakery which was capable of making 1300lbs of bread a day. But she was not a floating hotel, her purpose was warfare and as such she was equipped with 7.5-inch main guns that could fire a 200lb projectile some 10 miles. For air defence there were three, 4-inch quick firing semi-automatic guns and two, 2lb auto pom-poms. Salutes were fired by 3-pounder guns.

There were 5 torpedo tubes, one under the waterline and four above. To assist with visibility at night there were four, 36-inch searchlights clustered around the aft funnel which had a range of around 3 miles. There were 5 smaller searchlights that were used for signaling, situated on the lower bridge. Additional communication and signaling was carried out using flags and flashing semaphore whilst long range communications were facilitated by wireless Morse code. Internally the ship was served by some 200 telephones.

By 10 o'clock a large crowd was gathering at the dockside, Kathleen had brought Doreen along to see the ship off. Doreen was not particularly aware of what was going on, Kathleen was all too aware, and she had a very hollow feeling in the pit of her stomach. She wished this were not happening, but she must not show it. Joining her in the crowd were many other wives and sweethearts as well as crews from other Royal Navy ships and the dockyard 'Matey's' of which, no doubt, a number had been involved in building *Effingham*.

There were 194 Royal Marines on board *Effingham*, one Major, a Captain, 75 NCO's and Men in the detachment and 15 musicians. At 09:56 on the 25 August 1925, the bow ropes were slipped, and the band of the Royal Marines began to play 'Good-bye-ee' as *Effingham* slowly moved off to get under way. The crowd began waving and cheering as the band continued with 'Nancy Lee', 'Rolling home to Merry England' and then 'Auld Lang Syne'. The sun shone and glinted off the golden funnels and warmed the faces of the ship's men lined along the decks as they waved back at the crowd, no doubt it dried one or two tears too.

Effingham glided slowly but majestically out of Portsmouth as the crowed swarmed and moved with the appearance of liquid trying to follow her progress and catch that one last look. *Effingham's* engines increased in power, she picked up speed and headed out to sea before pausing to swing ship and check compasses. Then she gradually disappeared over the horizon, just a black smudge left from her smoking funnels, heading for Gibraltar and into the Indian Ocean.

The sailing to Columbo took *Effingham* just over a month to complete, having called at Gibraltar (the first time many of the crew had set foot on foreign soil), Malta and then Port Said. Here a pilot was taken aboard for the passage through the Suez Canal. A trip that was uneventful but there was a distinct lack of shipping, which was attributed by some of the crew to the Chinese Revolution. The journey was made more difficult by a strong following sea and high winds through the Mediterranean and Arabian seas. The ships passage was uncomfortable due to the swell that rolled her about and the heat was oppressive. There was no air conditioning present in a ship of this era, relief was provided by rigging canvas baths filled with sea water on the upper decks.

At this stage *Effingham* was commanded by Captain Cecil Nugent Reyne who had taken the ship through her commissioning, sea trials and passage to Colombo. On the 26 September, *Effingham* relieved HMS *Chatham* and the flag of the East Indies Squadron was transferred across whilst Reyne (who was to take *Chatham* back to England) was replaced by Captain Noel Frank Lawrence D.S.O. The ships Chaplin, Rev. A. Turner completed his first service in front of the ship's crew the following Sunday where he took the opportunity to remind the men of their responsibilities to be 'examples of British Christians in distant parts of the Empire'. He begged the men to also remember their promises to write home regularly to their loved ones. To quote, a promise 'which we all make and so easily forget…'

Colombo was the refitting base of the Squadron, so *Effingham's* stay was brief. The crew cheered off the *Chatham* before leaving for her final destination, the deep water base of Trincomalee. There followed gunnery and torpedo exercises and when back in harbour there came the opportunity to check out the sporting abilities of the crew; 'a series of inter-part games brought forward promising recruits for cricket and football teams. In addition to the facilities for organizing games which exist there, the rifle range, sailing picnics, bathing and the naval canteen help to make a week spent at Trincomalee a time to which we look forward to'.

Now it was time for the Commanding Officers to make an appearance. They arrived aboard the S.S. *Orama*. A 19,000-ton twin funneled cruise liner, built in 1924 by Vickers Armstrong, she could accommodate 1700 passengers. Her ultimate destiny was to become a troop ship during World War 2. But not for long, as she was to be sunk by the German High Seas Fleet on the 8 November 1940 during the Norwegian campaign with the loss of 19 lives.

On this occasion she carried the newly appointed Commander-in-Chief (C-in-C) of the East Indies Squadron, Rear Admiral Walter Maurice Ellerton

C.B. and Chief of Staff Captain Roger Mowbray Bellairs, C.M.G. who took command on the 29 November 1925. One must note that these men were highly experienced in command, and they had both seen action. There were a number of officers and in particular Captains, that had been amongst a core of officers active during World War 1. To attain their current position, these two men were no doubt the best of the best.

Ellerton was born 5 August 1870, the son of John Ellerton who was the Vicar of St Michaels, Crewe. Walter was educated at Sherborne School in Dorset before he joined the Senior Service as a boy in 1884. He saw much change in the Navy during his career; there came the transition from sailing vessels to steam (coal) driven ships before their change to oil. His second ship was an *Emerald* (Ellerton refers to her as a 'Gem') Class Corvette, the *Turquoise*. She had three masts and a bow sprit, but she was also propeller driven with one single funnel between the fore and main mast which was telescopic whilst the propeller could be lowered or lifted as needed. Ellerton wrote that they seldom steamed the ship, except in cases of urgency preferring to 'Down Funnel and Up Screw'. *Turquoise* had been refitted in Bombay when Ellerton joined her, and he spent some time in the East Indies so the experience gained during this time may well have been contributory to him eventually being appointed C-in-C.

Ellerton had his roots clearly in another age as far as the Navy was concerned, he comments 'Suffice it to say that all my service as a midshipman was done in ships with masts and yards, and that only in the last 5 months of that time was I shipmates with a breech-loading gun.' In addition, he saw the advent of wireless communications whilst Captain of the Destroyer *Sunfish* at Devonport. Here he was witness to Admiral Sir Henry Jacksons trials of ship-to-ship communications, 'going in and out of harbour in *Defiance's* tender which was rigged up with an extra-long mast and a lot of wire streamers.'

On the 8 December 1914, Ellerton was Captain of the cruiser *Cornwall* in the South Atlantic which was refuelling in Port William on the Falkland Islands. He and his crew were on the verge of some serious action. The Navy was still in shock, having lost two ships, *Good Hope* and *Monmouth*, at the Battle of Coronel. Rear Admiral Sir Christopher Cradock, who is described by Admiral Cunningham as 'always being immaculately dressed, with a pointed, neatly trimmed beard, which reminded one of Sir Francis Drake', had taken on the might of the German East Asia Squadron. This consisted of the armoured cruisers *Scharnhorst* and *Gneisenau* and the lighter cruisers *Leipzig, Dresden* and *Nurnberg*, all under the command of Vice Admiral Graf Maximilian Von Spee.

The two Royal Navy ships were outgunned, they had 6-inch guns, the Germans had 21-inch guns. Speed and determination were no match for the fire power aimed at the British and both the *Monmouth, Good Hope* along with Cradock and 1600 men were sent to the bottom of the sea. It was a massive blow to the Navy.

Revenge for the Royal Navy came on the 8 December and began with the signal at 08:00, 'A four-funnel and two-funnel man-of-war in sight from Sapper Hill, steering northwards.' This was Von Spee's East Asia Squadron. Lying in wait in Port William were the *Kent, Invincible, Inflexible, Carnarvon* and Ellerton's *Cornwall*. In Port Stanley, lay the *Glasgow* (escaped relatively unscathed from Coronel) and the *Bristol*.

In the 1914 equivalent of a racing start, the ships fired up their boilers and got underway. Soon all 5 ships from Port William were accelerating through the relatively calm waters to their maximum speed. 5 huge ships, engines thundering, bow waves hissing, bearing down on their enemy. On the open bridge of *Cornwall* binoculars were raised, braced and jammed by the owners' bodies against the superstructure to steady their view. Orders were coming fast and then there came the general signal 'Chase'. It was clear that the enemy's light cruisers were splitting from the *Scharnhorst* and *Gneisenau,* and so *Cornwall, Glasgow and Kent* were ordered to give chase to the cruisers. A South-South-East course was set and chase given at 22.75 knots.

At 16:17 *Cornwall* opened fire on the *Leipzig* at a range of 10,500 yards, a response was not long in coming. The seas and weather began to deteriorate but the chase and action continued. By 18:50 it was observed that the Leipzig was slowing and there were fires fore and aft. A period of cease fire at 19:16, before the final exchange began at 19:55, ending around 15 minutes later at 20:11. *Cornwall* closed on the mortally wounded *Leipzig*, and came to a stop a safe distance away to lower boats to pick up survivors. At 21:23 the *Leipzig*, ablaze, turned over on her port side and sank. The boats deployed from the British ships to rescue survivors picked up just seven officers and 11 men. Ellerton had been in command of *Cornwall* in what was to be known as the 'Battle of the Falkland Islands'. It was retribution for Coronel and saw the end of Von Spee and his East Asia Squadron with the loss of *Gneisenau, Scharnhorst, Leipzig* and *Nurnberg*.[19]

After the war, Ellerton was first appointed Director of Training at the Admiralty and then became the Senior Naval Officer in Gibraltar prior to becoming the C-in-C of the East Indies Squadron. He retired from the Royal Navy in 1929 and lived at first in Chippenham and then Kington Langley, Wiltshire, where he and his wife Gwendolin built their own home, Shipways Leaze. He was an active local Councilor and he supported both the British Legion and Toc H organisations supporting ex-military servicemen. He clearly retained a love for Tennis and was on the committee of The Society of Wiltshire Archers, a tennis club whose roots were planted in Archery!

Admiral Ellerton died after a short illness on the 27 November 1948. His love for the Navy and the Comradeship of service is summed up in his own words from his contribution to the *Effingham* publication describing the advances the Navy had made since he joined.

> But the men are the same. I mean the spirit of loyalty, the comradeship which permeates them is the same. Life in the Navy is a good life, and whether you are grousing over prickly heat in the Persian Gulf or a

---

[19] Battle of the Falkland Islands - Sources ADM53-38657 & London Gazette No. 29087 – 2 March 1915

frozen nose in the Arctic circle matters not. It is a life for a MAN, and after 43 years of it I would not have changed it with anyone.[20]

If ever there was a qualified 'right hand man' then Roger Mowbray Bellairs was that man. Both his father (Lt. Gen. Sir William Bellairs) and Grandfather (Sir William Bellairs 1793 – 1863) had been Army men, his grandfather having served under Lord Wellington in the Peninsular Campaign and at both Quatre Bras and Waterloo during Napoleons resurgence in 1815.

Bellairs was born on the 4 August1884, joining the Royal Navy in May 1899. At Britannia Naval College he excelled, passing out as a Midshipman and head of his term, quickly being promoted to Lieutenant having gained 'firsts' in all subjects. He was noted as having 'a clear analytical brain, and a remarkable capacity for rapidly grasping the whole of a complex problem, forming a balanced judgement on it and working out a logical, workable and well-balanced solution'.

During the 1914 – 18 war, Bellairs served on the staff of both Admiral Jellicoe and Beatty in the Grand Fleet and became a Commander in 1915. He saw action at the Battle of Jutland in *Iron Duke* where he was commended. After the war he became Naval Assistant to Lord Beatty at the Admiralty and Captaincy came in 1920, when he was 35.

After his position as Flag Captain within *Effingham* on the East Indies Station, Bellairs was at first Director of Plans for the Navy before taking up one of the most prestigious jobs within the service as Captain of the Battleship, *Rodney* from 1930 to 1932. However, it was at this point that his career suffered. He clearly was much respected by the men under his command, and this does indeed show through within the private publication *Effingham* that is largely built upon reflections from the crew of their time on the East Indies Station. However, loyalties, no matter how well earned or strong were stretched where pay was concerned, and it was the Invergordon Mutiny that was to affect the remainder of Bellairs career. *Rodney* was part of the Atlantic

---

[20] (Unknown, 1927)

Fleet and about to carry out exercises from Invergordon with *Nelson, Valiant, Warspite, Malaya, Hood, Repulse*, four cruisers and a host of escorting Destroyers. En route, the crews had picked up from wireless reports that pay cuts of up to 25% were coming, rumours were rife within the fleet by the time the ships arrived. The result was unprecedented in naval terms. Many of the men decided to literally 'down tools'. As a result, exercises were cancelled, with both *Warspite* and *Malaya* being recalled to port having left for gunnery practice. In general, the Officers were sympathetic with the men's 'cause' and did not interfere with proceedings. *Rodney's* crew were similar to the other ships within the fleet, in that some took part in the mutiny, whilst others remained ambivalent.

Days passed and there were suggestions that the mutiny would escalate. Vice Admiral Tomkins, who had overall responsibility for the fleet, wrote several letters to the Admiralty (generally in the men's favour) and the government's Cabinet reviewed the situation. The fleet was ordered to disband with ships returning to their home ports and thereafter the pay cut was reduced to 10%.

A number of men (some 400) were discharged from the Navy as a result, both Tomkins and Bellairs lost their jobs respectively. Bellairs did not command a ship thereafter, he was promoted to Rear Admiral, placed on the retired list and was then employed within the Admiralty in advisory capacities. He died in 1959, aged 74.

Both men carried great responsibility during their time on the Station. They were representatives of both the armed might of the Royal Navy and Great Britain as well as ambassadors hosting many important social gatherings that would include government officials and local dignitaries. In addition, there were ceremonial duties to perform as well as military exercises that sometimes included combined operations with other services and countries armed forces.

Backing up the Commanders were, of course, the crew of the ship. As we will see, the East Indies Station was a very hard place to operate, not only for the men of the ship, but on the ship itself. Intense heat, humidity as well as (at times) extreme climatic conditions made operating a ship in this era a challenge. Therefore, the wellbeing and morale of the ship's crew was of utmost importance and the success of this is reflected in the words of the crews as well as their humour.

The Officers claimed to be 'an awfully nice lot', their modesty knowing no bounds in usual tongue in cheek fashion. 'All the ships company are devoted to us…' They also claimed, 'We have to know an awful lot. We must be able to say 'carry on' when addressed at any time and things of that sort. Then if a man says, 'I thought….' One must say 'well don't think;' on the other hand should he say 'I didn't think….' one must say 'why don't you use your intelligence?' It's all so amazingly tricky.'

For the Seamen, the initial impressions were not favourable. On joining the ship there was much clearing up to do; 'Everything was in a state of rubbish. That meant but one thing – 'We' had to clear it up. 'We' did.' So, it was the general duties aboard ship would be carried out by the Seamen for the duration. However, relief came in the form of organised sports and occasional sightseeing trips as well as 'Camp' ashore around halfway through the commission.

The Torpedo Party had a rough time to begin with, getting used to some experimental torpedoes and a new bow tube that 'had a nasty habit of gorging itself with 'fish'. After which there came a period of inactivity as the ship cruised to its station, during which the Party became known as 'The Idle Rich'. The arrival of a Lieutenant Commander MacLean saw the fortunes of the Party improve and the accuracy of their 'fish'. Managing a hit on their intended target had the added bonus that the torpedo would sink to the bottom. A miss meant the wayward 'fish' would have to be located and recovered by boat.

There were supposed to be 22 Signal Staff, however *Effingham* sailed with 20, but later they managed to 'thieve' replacements from *Cairo* and *Emerald*. The Signal Staff considered themselves to be the most important branch of the service; 'No ship can be without its 'eyes'. Signalmen are called the 'Eyes of the Fleet.' Incidentally we are called many other things also, but I do not propose to mention them here.'

Effingham had a Wireless Department of 25 men, headed up by The Fleet W/T Officer Lieutenant Gairdiner and the Commissioned Telegraphist (Mr. Balfour). They looked after 11 Transmitting sets, 10 Receiving Sets, 7 W/T Offices, a Hydrophone Set and 5 other 'Action positions' around the ship for communications during any hostilities. In normal operations there was a twenty-four-seven watch on 3 sets whilst the main set remained operational almost throughout the whole commission. The main set was used nightly to communicate back to Whitehall in the U.K whilst arguably the most important task of the Wireless Department was (and for many, apparently the sole duty) to obtain the football results every week and post them on the ships company notice board some 10 hours before they were transmitted from England!

With such a small compliment, the Wireless Department could not muster up the numbers to compete in arranged team sports, and so they regularly joined forces with the Signalmen. However, the nature and commitment of their work meant that quite often key players were unavailable being on duty. Indeed, duty was most difficult as their offices were deep within the ship where temperatures often reached 102 degrees (38 degrees Centigrade). 'Join the Navy and see the world in comfort is a phrase somewhat misapplied to the W/T Department of a Man-of-War in a tropical climate.'

If the Wireless and Signal men were the eyes and ears of the ship, then the Engine Room Department was clearly the heart. In equally if not more adverse conditions the work would have been arduous. The first main job of the Engine Room was to get to grips with the various compartments and machinery that propelled *Effingham* through the water and gave power to her electrical systems. Many were cramped and confined, which coupled with the heat was most uncomfortable to work in. Propulsion was not confined to the Main Turbines as *Effingham* was equipped with Cruising Engines used on most voyages where there were no special manoeuvers or exercises planned. Main Turbines were used for manoeuvering in and out of the confines of port, but once in clear water the ship was brought to a stop and the cruiser engines then connected for the next stage of the voyage.

There were many challenges for the Engine Room to overcome during the commission. In April 1926, whilst at sea, a major steam leak was discovered, and a new casting had to be shipped from England and replaced whilst still at sea. Later, in Colombo, some 6350 tubes linking the engine condensers were replaced in 16 days.

The Royal Marines detachment within *Effingham* not only supplied the Band, who played out the ship on departure from Portsmouth, but they would have manned one of the turrets when in action, in addition to Guards of Honour, Boarding Parties and provided a fighting force as required. As one would expect from these very fit and athletic young men, they excelled at the sports put on for the men of the ship. Marines Metcalf, Mann and McBride excelled in Boxing, the RM team won the Inter-Part (Ships Crew) Soccer tournaments (there was one each year of the commission) and they wiped the floor in the Tug-of-War with the 130 stone team remaining undefeated.

During November and December of 1926, the Marines from *Effingham* combined with the detachments from *Emerald* and *Enterprise* were involved in exercises within the Janjira peninsular just south of Bombay. These exercises were combined operations with the Royal Indian Marine (now the Royal Indian Navy) and Native Troops. This included a night beach assault and the 'putting down' of a local 'insurgent' group known for the duration of the exercise as 'Jinjars'.

For two nights and a day, the battle raged, the heat of the tropical sun, trackless ground and jungle, steep ascents and descents and very little water, making conditions very severe.

There was no rest or sleep for anyone, from 11p.m. on the Tuesday until 9p.m. on the Thursday morning, as the Jinjars retired to the mainland, and were brought to submission on their own territory.

The ships Band having been front and foremost in *Effinghams* departure from Portsmouth were soon pressed into helping work the ship up to a fighting capacity during her first voyage to Colombo. Their next engagement of a musical nature being at the transfer of the Commander-in-Chiefs flag from *Chatham* to *Effingham*. Bands of the Navy were not supplied with any string sheet music and only a meagre selection of ceremonial music on departure. Indeed, string instruments were only 'loaned' to Officers who had to pay a rental fee for their use. However, *Effinghams* band managed to purchase a good supply of music from *Chatham's* band, before her return to England.

The Band's numbers were not really large enough to provide a marching compliment and were slightly too big in numbers to turn out for parties and dances. The climate and temperatures proved a challenge once again as the instruments would not tune well (or loose tune very quickly), coupled with the poor acoustics found in a Man of War. Jazz was at the forefront of the popular music scene in the mid-twenties, so the forming of a Jazz Band was almost a prerequisite. However, like the sheet music and strings, the instruments required to form a Jazz Band were not Navy issue and they had to be either already owned by band members or purchased out of their own pockets. Nevertheless, a Jazz Band was formed.

Daymen were those members of the crew whose duties were carried out in normal working hours. They were made up of Cooks, Victualling Staff, Sick Berth Staff, Writers and Ordinance Artificers. During voyage out to Colombo *Effingham* picked up 7 'Seedies' who were included as daymen aboard ship. A further 21 were eventually transferred from the returning *Chatham* later.

Seedies were African, mainly Muslim men who were employed by the Navy to carry out the more menial tasks aboard ship.

The cooks gained particular mention, being described as 'Super-Men' for living with not only the heat of the climate but that coupled with the heat from their cookers. 'But of course, cooks are super-men or else they would burst into tears when they emerge from the galley dripping with sweat, only to get abuse hurled at their heads.'

Christmas (1925) and New Year were to be spent in Calcutta before heading to Madras for the Naval, Military and Air Force Tournament in March. It was whilst en route on the 19 December, at 17:30, that a derelict ship was spotted off the port bow. A derelict is a vessel and its cargo that has been deliberately abandoned either because it is floundering or is in peril of sinking. It can also be a vessel that is registered however the owner has relinquished responsibility, perhaps for instance, the ship has broken moorings and drifted off, but the owner does not think it is worth recovering.

Cairo was ordered to investigate the ship, which turned out to be a sailing vessel called the *Dehli*, that had been reported missing several weeks previous. By some careful and skilled seamanship, the *Dehli* was taken in tow for Trincomalee. As a result of their efforts, the crew of the 'Cairo' later received prize money after *Dehli*'s cargo was sold. Able Seaman receiving £3.00 each.

The Hooghly River ran dirty brown into the sea, as it does all the time, when *Effingham* anchored off the Eastern Channel Light Vessel on the 22 December. A Pilot was embarked, a highly paid and skilled one at that, for due to the strong currents the river bed was continually moving. So much so that the Pilot had not only to possess all the necessary pilot qualifications, he had to be an expert marine surveyor.

The following day, *Effingham* pulled alongside a purpose built jetty near Princeps Ghat, the Greek Palladian style building by the river that was built during the mid 1800's by the British Raj. Close by is Fort William, another

British built fort, most famous for its 14' x 18' guardroom, or as is known by the British Army, a 'Black Hole'. In 1756 Fort William had been besieged and eventually overrun by the troops of Siraj ud-Daulah (the Nawab ruler) of Bengal, who was incensed by the activities of the East India Company. Actual numbers are somewhat unreliable, but around 100 prisoners were confined overnight in this minuscule space, just over 20 are reputed to have survived. Asphyxiation and shock having killed the rest. So came about the 'The Black Hole of Calcutta', a phrase that has remained ever since to describe the most unpleasant of places.

These were, however, happier times, and no sooner had *Effingham* berthed than preparations began in earnest for Christmas and New Year. The contrast in December climate will not have gone unnoticed by all those who had not travelled to tropical climates before and there was much discussion on the subject. If it was not surreal enough to have a state-of-the-art warship daubed in Christmas decorations, the heat and humidity simply did not fit with the visions of 'deep and crisp and even' snow that the men were so fond of imagining during this festive time. As one man remarked; 'Christmas recalls to most minds a scene of heavy snow, warm clothing and a blazing fire; with tables laden with tasty 'goodies' and a general giving and taking of presents. To our English ideas a Christmas spent in glorious sunshine, like an August Bank Holiday, seems totally wrong.'

On the special day itself breakfast was served, followed by a service for all on the Quarter Deck. Afterwards a tour began, headed up by 'The Funny Party' made up of about a dozen men and boys in all manner of fancy dress, props and musical instruments. They made their merry way around the ship, entertaining as they went, followed by the C-in-C, Mrs. Ellerton and the Officers to all the mess decks to wish everyone a Merry Christmas.

In between Christmas and New Year there came a stream of visitors, dinners and receptions for a number of dignitaries, including Lord Reading, the Viceroy of India, the Governor of Bengal, Lord Lytton and a group of 500 children before 1925 turned into 1926.

1926

New Year's Day (1926) – Calcutta

Was awakened at midnight by ships in the harbour greeting the New Year with sirens and foghorns…. Ship open to visitors at 1-30pm. Large numbers arrived of all nationalities. Wore a pair of boots out assisting ladies down ladders. Wore a pair of eyes out watching ladies go up ladders.

So begins a short excerpt from the diary of a Signalman. Humour is most prevalent, and of a type that is somewhat familiar. It is that brand of humour that came from the military services and found its way into such famous comedy shows such as 'The Goons' and 'Around the Horn'. A smattering of travelogue, parties, ladies, a healthy dose of alcohol and some mention of life aboard ship are captured over the months of January and February 1926. What a pity it is that because there are no credits to the submissions to the publication that we cannot identify the individual. What we do know is that during this period he received his second 'Good Conduct' (GC) Badge or Stripe. This was a black wool chevron that was sewn onto the left upper sleeve of the man's working rig uniform. The first GC badge was awarded after 3 years of service, the second after a further 5 years and the third and final GC following another 5 years, or 13 years total to receive all three. Pay was incremented with each GC awarded.

Saturday 2nd January

Proceeded ashore at 4-30p.m. with some letters to post, first proceeding to the Bristol Hotel for necessary moisture with which to affix stamps to letters. While there, made acquaintance of a Mr. C. A…. had enough moisture to drown letters. Was invited to Mr. A's home together with two chums. Returned on board at midnight – and so did my letters.

Sunday, 3rd January

Mr. A, his wife and daughters came onboard after dinner and were shown around the ship. Afterwards they invited us to a farewell dinner to take place on Tuesday night, 'Effingham' leaving Calcutta on Wednesday morning. Proceeded onshore at 4-40 with my two chums. Found the Bristol Hotel in the same place. Played two games of snooker and got beaten. Was informed I came aboard at 11 p.m.

Monday, 4th January

Helmet appeared to be much smaller this morning.

Tuesday, 5th January

Officers held an 'At Home' on board. Proceeded onshore at 5-30pm to keep Farewell Dinner engagement at Mr. and Mrs. A's, arriving there at 5-50 by taxi. Commenced music straightaway and had a jolly good time. Dinner at 8 o'clock-more fun afterwards. Leave was up at 11 p.m. but we conveniently forgot about that, there being a larger number of ladies to bid good-bye and plenty of mistletoe loafing. Said good-bye eventually (as it should be said) and returned onboard happy – but adrift 30 minutes. Commanders report in the morning.

Wednesday, 6th January - At Sea

7 a.m. Opened my eyes but still couldn't see much. Oiled my interior regions with several cups of tea and felt almost normal. 8 a.m. Girls and family arrived to see us off for Rangoon. Telescopes well to the fore and eyesight fully restored. Dirtied one of my dozen-minus-eleven handkerchiefs waving good-bye and ship proceeded down the river to Garden Reach to await tide. Left G.R. about 11.30 for Rangoon. General impression – Calcutta very, very nice place and roll-on Christmas 1926. Commander kindly awarded us one day's pay and leave stopped for our 30 minutes bliss. It was worth it. Sea Calm. Thank the Lord from whom all blessings flow.

Saturday, 9th January Rangoon

By putting the clocks forward on a quarter of an hour some more sleep was stolen from us. Ship arrived at the Pilot Station at the mouth of the Hlaing River and took in cargo of pilots…. Ship secured to Barr Street Buoy. Temples look very nice, being gilded and at night electrically illuminated. Pea soup for supper, very appropriate for this climate! Temperature today 92 degrees in the shade.

Sunday, 10th January

Walked miles in finding places of interest. Splendid temples, pagodas and two Cathedrals. Returned on board. Opinion: Rangoon looks much better than it smells. Indian snake charmers onboard. Snakes charmed with an instrument almost as bad as bagpipes. Ship open to visitors.

Saturday, 16th January

Was detailed for decorating the Jubilee Hall for the boxing between the Navy v. Burma Police. Had dinner at Sale Barracks, and tea with a Mr. R….. one of the Police Heads. Returned onboard after tea and proceeded onshore at 8 p.m. to witness the boxing. Very good show, which finished at 12.30 a.m.

Sunday, 17th January

Landed at 9 a.m. to undecorate the Jubilee Hall. Much easier pulling flags down and was testing drinks in the Police Sergeants' Mess by 11 a.m. Tested quite a few and returned onboard for dinner. Mixed my tot with the Policemen's samples. Dead till teatime. What a swede (head). Admiral gave a farewell dinner. I gave another display of decorating. Very pleased when bedtime arrived.

Thursday, 21st January – Port Blair

Large number of sharks observed in the harbour, not exactly conducive to good health to fall overboard at present. Football team played the Gharwharl Rifles and won by a very narrow margin, a mere 10 – 0.

Friday, 22nd January

Landed at 3p.m. with about 70 others for a climb up Mount Harriot. A retired Sergeant Major, his wife and family live at the summit which he now cultivates…Very beautiful place and well worth losing a stone and a half to reach (1193 feet above sea level)…partook in a coconut hunt, capturing several. Caught a boat back to the ship at 6:30 p.m. Ship partially illuminated in preparation for Madras. Bangers for supper. Very, very nice.

Monday, 25th January. At Sea

Unmoored at 4p.m. and sailed from Port Blair for Madras. Clocks were put back 14 minutes at 5 p.m. – very good idea.

Tuesday, 26th January

Ocean still our own, nothing having been sighted all day bigger than a flying fish (bloater with wings on). Clocks put forward 14 minutes at 5 p.m. – ridiculous idea.

Friday, 29th January – Madras

Was detailed duty at shore signal station after dinner. Not much work, but plenty of rings on 'phone from N….

Saturday, 30th January

Landed at 7 a.m. for duty at signal station. Much ado about not having breakfast beforehand, but that was due to cookie's inability to capture the sausages in time. Ring from N…. Went down to see her, and now she wants to show me round Madras. Saw Captain at 11-30 and was awarded second Good Conduct Badge....on board at 11 p.m. Much excitement caused by a rat which I managed to catch with a broomstick – bayonet fashion. Shook his tummy up and caused him to lose all interest in this world. Gave him a watery grave and turned in.

Sunday, 31st January

Discovered the Madras Port Social Club – 6 annas per pint. Relieved from duty at 7 p.m. and returned onboard. Passed remainder of evening dancing on the upper deck. Made the acquaintance of P.... & Co., three more telephone girls, who came up to the signal tower for a chat. Real dusky beauties.

Monday, 1st February

Landed for duty at 7 a.m. at S.S. (Signal Station) and had a very busy time till 2 p.m. when I was relieved. Not so busy that I could not find time to reply to rings from N.... Pleased I did not arrange any meetings as she takes her mother with her.

Thursday, 9th February

First day of the Naval and Military Tournament which according to report was a great success... Landed at 7 p.m. Found a very talkative (?) young lady on the telephone at 7-30 and had a short conversation with her till 10-30.

Sunday, 14th February

The last day at Madras...Many sad faces at the S.S. at the thought of our departure. Telephone girls all using large size handkerchiefs. Mr M... (in charge of S.S.) arranged a small party in my honour. Got very convivial and returned on board at 10 p.m. after bidding many sad goodbyes.

Monday 15th February

Broken hearts in Madras, busted pockets on board[21].

The Naval, Military and Air Force Tournament neatly completed this first period of the commission. The Effingham's had worked hard to help facilitate the tournament which proved a huge success. It not only brought together the three services, bonding and strengthening their military co-operation, but also sought to bring the local population closer to their protectorate fighting forces.

The tournament was held between the 9th and 13th of February. It included an athletics competition that was normally an Army only affair, however Officers and Men of both *Effingham* and *Cairo* were permitted to enter into the games. A tug of war competition was organised, *Effingham's* Royal Marine contingent defeating the team from the Royal Artillery in the final.

A pageant, billed as one of the headline events, harked back to the days of musket and sword and then brought the spectator up to the present day. The pageant began with the Royal Artillery, Cavalry with Horse and Foot Regiments in scarlet and blue, including an Indian Prince atop an Elephant. It was then that the rousing sound of the band of the Royal Ulster Rifles brought in the modern forces followed by the Royal Artillery, an armoured car and the pipes and drums of the Highland Regiment. Finally, to the pride of the men of *Effingham* came their Royal Marines representing the Royal Navy.

Demonstrations included the Navy Field Gun teams hauling their guns and gaining many bruises in the process, the Artillery screaming around the parade ground with their 6 horse drawn pieces culminating in taking a 20-yard gate at full gallop whilst in the skies the Air Force performed fly-past's and aerobatics finishing with a demonstration of air power coupled with troop manoeuvers.

---

[21] (Unknown, 1927)

In appreciation for their efforts, the East Indies Squadron was presented with two cups at the close of the tournament. The Rajah of Bobbili gave the Royal Navy a fine cup for their efforts during the tournament (know thereafter as the Bobbili Cup) and the Tournament Committee gave a cup (the Madras Tournament Cup) for the Navy's organisation of the tournament.

Effingham was made ready for a return to normal duties, returning to Colombo with *Cairo*. On the way they carried out torpedo and battle exercises before heading to Trincomalee via Colombo. Whilst stopping over in Colombo the liner *Otranto* arrived in Port on the 26 March. There was much excitement as the Australian Cricket Team were aboard, making their way to England for the 1926 Ashes tour which was to begin in June. The Australians played a single test against the Ceylon National team as was custom at the time, winning by 37 runs. As for the Ashes later in the year, the first four Tests ended in a draw before the decider was held, as is traditional, at The Oval. To ensure there was a result this was to be a 'Timeless' match, that is it would continue until there was a result. The English weather played its part, and with the help of Jack Hobbs, England prevailed and regained the Ashes.

Meanwhile, *Effingham* received orders to proceed to Bombay. Ceremonial duties were on the agenda with the Commander-in-Chief and his senior officers required to welcome the new Viceroy of India. There would be an inspection of some of the crew and musical accompaniment by the Royal Marines band. The Army being represented by another guard of honour from the South Staffordshire Regiment.

So it was that on the afternoon of the 1 April that those invited to the Gateway of India waited expectantly for the Viceroy's arrival. A breeze ruffled the palms and the clothes of those gathered. There was an air of excitement and a burble of conversation and then a murmur that he and his wife were about to arrive.

Lord Irwin, Edward Frederick Lindley Wood, was replacing Lord Reading as the new Viceroy. He was 45 at the time, stood tall at 6' 4" which made him an imposing figure who carried himself with a slow and stately manner that reflected his social standing. His receding hair and thin face gave him a somewhat solemn look, fitting for a man who was a devout Anglo-Catholic. Born with an atrophied left arm and without a left hand he would either wear a glove attached to his sleeve or a false hand. He would later enter politics within the Conservative party and become Lord Halifax. As a member of Neville Chamberlains government, he would be involved in meetings with Adolf Hitler, associated with the pacifist movement and the 'Peace in our Time' agreement. However, he did push for war if Germany were to invade Poland, which indeed occurred. Halifax was expected to become Prime Minister after Chamberlains resignation but instead declined and made way for Winston Churchill to take England through World War 2.

For now, as Lord Irwin, he had work to do in India but first he would be greeted and sworn in as the new Viceroy. He was certainly dressed for the occasion. The 1920's saw the emergence of designer fashion, especially in men's clothing. Lord Irwin wore a white pith helmet style hat, long 'frock coat' sharply creased grey trousers and dual tone, black and white shoes for the occasion. He was accompanied by his wife Dorothy as they boarded the little white steamboat *Elsie*, complete with white canvas awning that provided ample shade for the passengers for their short trip to the Gateway to India. *Elsie* passed by *Effingham* whose crew, who were not attending the ceremony, were lined along her decks in their smart white tropical uniforms, hailing their passing with a resounding cheer. On command, *Effingham* fired a 31gun salute.

Elsie's Red Ensign fluttered and flapped its approval as she drew alongside the jetty. Lord Erwin stooped his tall frame from under the awning and stepped onto the stone steps. A shepherd's crook style stick over his withered left arm, a glove disguising his missing hand, he turned and helped his wife from the boat. She handed away her umbrella as they climbed the steps to meet the awaiting dignitaries.

The following day, the ceremony was almost performed in exact reverse as Lord Reading and his wife left his post of Viceroy and India, for England.

The East Africa Cruise

From mid April to June 1926, *Effingham* was deployed down the East African coast visiting Mauritius, Mombasa, Zanzibar and the Seychelles. Just prior to leaving, communication was received from King Neptune. His scouts had informed him of *Effinghams* course and speed which would result in her passing his domain. The captain responded that this was indeed so and asked permission to proceed. King Neptune duly agreed and replied that he expected to be received aboard on the 16 April.

At 09:00 on the prescribed day a hail came from the Port Bow. The captain was informed, and he ordered the ship to be stopped. King Neptune and his court of Royal visitors were lit up by a searchlight that helped guide them and their Guard of Honour to the Bridge accompanied by a band. Many members of the crew were gathered on 'B' Gundeck and the Focastle to witness their arrival, the Officers and the ladies being on the Bridge.

The 'Crossing the Line' ceremony has been going on for hundreds of years and is primarily a means of bonding a ship's crew together, all those who have not crossed the equator before, or do not have a certificate to prove it, are subject to the ceremony. Selected members of the ship's crew play the roles of King Neptune (Chief Stoker Pomfret on this occasion), his Queen, Amphitrite, The Chief of Police and his staff. Then come the Bears, the Barber, and Doctor. All are dressed up for their respective parts.

The ship's crew are interrogated for proof of being a 'Shellback' (having been initiated by King Neptune before). If no proof is forthcoming, they are charged with various crimes the following day during the ceremony and punishment is served, which would include a shave from the barber, or a soap pill administered by the doctor before a dunking in sea water. Any resistance was dealt with by The Bears, who were responsible for rounding up those who were charged with attending court and woe betide anyone who displeased these fearsome creatures or tried to escape. On completion of their punishment, each man (or woman) was given a certificate that would give them safe passage across the equator in future, i.e., through King Neptune's domain and more importantly, avoid being rounded up by the Bears and another ducking in sea water.

The 'problem' that King Neptune faced on this particular occasion was the number of novices aboard ship. The King asked, 'How many nincompoups are on board'? Captain Bellairs replied, 'about 750'. Despite the enormity of the task at hand the Police and the Bears appeared very pleased with the prospect of some fine sport and without delay they were granted permission to seek out the 'nincompoups' at which they began to swarm over the ship rooting out those who had not paid homage to King Neptune before.

First thing the following day, shipwrights built a stage and a pool from an awning that was filled with sea water. A ducking stool was mounted above the pool on 'Q' gun deck. They also built a car out of a torpedo trolley that would carry Neptune and his Queen from the bow to the ceremony. Before long the crew began to assemble and either claim a seat or suitable vantage point from where to watch the proceedings. King Neptune sported a huge beard and as one would expect, carried a trident. His Queen wore a sea green frock; however, she had some difficulty sitting down as her tail got in the way. The Police were snappily dressed in their uniforms, however the Bears left something to be desired their coats decidedly moth eaten, most of the 'fur' ending up in the pool by the end of the day.

Court was duly in session. King Neptune gave an appropriate opening speech and then called before him any who he had met before. The Commander-in-Chief and Commandeer Walker were presented and awarded the Order of the Red Herring with 10 bars and the Order of the Old Sea Boot respectively. The ladies came next, being shown the appropriate courtesy by the Bears who looked decidedly sheepish, if not slightly embarrassed at having to act so meekly. However, this was short lived as next came the novices.

Captain Bellairs was the most senior Officer presented to Neptune. He was swiftly dealt with and following his immersion in the pool was immediately awarded the Order of the Inverted Kipper. The Bears now got to work in earnest and little short of organised pandemonium ensued aboard ship as the Bears rooted out their victims, beginning with the Officers and working through the ranks. No one was spared, and any resistance was futile. Indeed, the number of novices aboard meant that a break was scheduled between 2pm and 4:30 pm by which time 450 novices had been accounted for. The mayhem resumed and by 6pm, the bedraggled Bears were clearly flagging whilst the Chief of Police had almost lost his voice. All the same, 750 novices had been brought before the King and with that he brought proceedings to a close whence he and his Queen retired to their watery home.

The party atmosphere continued, and any of those who played instruments or could sing were encouraged to join in a concert that carried on until 11pm. Gradually the ship fell silent as tired bodies found their bunks. There remained the hum of machinery and the odd 'professional' conversations resumed between those on duty. Many of the crew were fast asleep as the engines were engaged and *Effingham* got under way once more.

21 June 1926. *Effingham* is moored up within Port Victoria in The Seychelles. The sky is full of bright white fluffy clouds and the sun reflects brightly off her paintwork as the aquamarine sea laps against her hull. However, there is a stillness over her, she appears to be languishing somewhat and to the mariner's eye it can soon be determined why this is the case. Fluttering in the gentle breeze she flies a yellow flag (Yellow Jack), indicating that the ship is diseased and in quarantine. This certainly marks a low point in the commission that developed soon after King Neptune had visited the ship.

Effingham proceeded first to Mauritius. The weather during the crossing the line ceremony had been bright warm and fair, however this soon changed into something more lastingly unpleasant. A cyclone had passed Mauritius just two days previous. It was strong and slow moving (just 3 knots), causing the sea to develop a most unpleasant swell that caused discomfort for those of even the strongest of stomachs and was unforgiving on anything that was not duly tied down. On the island itself there was much damage caused especially to the sugar plantations and other crops.

Arriving on the 23 April, one man described Port Louis as 'dreary, unhealthy and without interest'. This was upheld when some of the crew met with the men of the Army Garrison at Vacoas, who explained, 'We vegetate in Mauritius for 50 weeks in the year, and long for the other 2 weeks, when the Navy comes and play games with us.'

The Garrison at Vacoas was 14 miles from the port and home to a 2000 man strong army contingent that had been established soon after England re-took the Island from the French in 1810 (called at the time, by the French, Isle de France). The 'original' Dutch name of Mauritius was then re-instated. *Effingham's* crew were invited to send teams to play Rugby, Cricket, Football etc. and to assist in facilitating this the local government provided free rail travel to and from the venue.

At the end of the layover (6 May) a party aboard ship was given to the children of the garrison. The following day *Effingham* sailed for Mombasa, stopping for 5 days at the island of Reunion. However, there was little opportunity to visit as an open anchorage meant *Effingham* was laid off shore and too far to be practicable to allow a suitable 'ferry service' to be organised.

Onto Mombasa where the rainy season took hold in earnest. The time spent here was humid and very, very wet for those who remained there to provide local ceremonial duties and entertain aboard ship. *Cairo* was already in port, the Rugby and Boxing teams of officers and men from her and *Effingham* were invited to take the 300 mile train journey to Nairobi where a series of matches were held. A week later they returned to *Effingham* to begin the cruise to the Seychelles, via Zanzibar before returning to Ceylon.

In Zanzibar some of the men made a pilgrimage to Grave Island to visit the War Graves of 24 Officers and Men from the Cruiser HMS *Pegasus*, which was sunk in Zanzibar harbour on the 20 September 1914. *Pegasus* had been in harbour to carry out some repairs when the German Cruiser *Konigsberg* made a surprise attack on her. Unable to move or effectively defend herself, the ship was abandoned before being sunk.

The continuous wet and humid conditions began to affect the crew. Colds and then influenza manifested itself and crew became sick in numbers. Just prior to departing Zanzibar, Leading Seaman Arthur W. Hawkins was admitted to the European Hospital but died on the night of the 13 June. He was buried the following day and the ship sailed with heavy hearts aboard on the 17th.

Royal Marines Musician and Bandsman Albert J Elsdon played 'Goodbye-ee' with the band at *Effingham*'s departure from Portsmouth. He would never see England or his family again. At just 20 years old, not noted as the strongest of individuals, he was one of the men who caught the flu which developed into pneumonia. He died aboard ship on the 19 June. Two deaths in such a short time came as a blow to the crew. *Effingham* was brought to a full stop at 9:30am on the morning of the 20 June, and after a short service, Musician Elsdon was buried at sea.

On arrival in the Seychelles, the Port Health Officer visited the ship and with the crew's condition reviewed, she was placed under quarantine. The influenza pandemic that had manifested itself in 1918 was still untreatable and therefore an outbreak aboard meant the crew had to be contained aboard. A serious threat to the operation and fighting effectiveness of the ship and a very worrying development were the virus to take a firm grip upon the crew. A situation that is not unfamiliar to our modern way of life during the Covid-19 pandemic of 2020. There being little point in remaining in port, *Effingham* weighed anchor two days later, heading back to Ceylon. The outbreak would not develop and there would be better days ahead.

Camp

Effingham arrived back in Colombo on the 29 June where preparations began for a period of rest for the crew at 'Camp'. Normally during the two-year commission there would be two such periods.

Camp allowed the crew approximately a month ashore at the Royal Navy Camp at Diyatalawa which was a 12-hour train journey to the east of Colombo, situated in the Kandy Hills. Diyatalawa is at an elevation of some 4000 feet above sea level and therefore has climates that are much cooler than lowland Ceylon, with average temperatures around 16 degrees and during the winter months frosts can occur. A welcome break for the men from the heat and humidity aboard ship in climes that resembled England.

Diyatalawa camps origins were as a concentration camp for Boer prisoners during the Boer war. Whilst this type of camp creates an image of suffering and cruelty, it appears that internment here was relatively comfortable, despite there being approximately 5000 inhabitants at its peak. After the Boer war, the Navy took over the camp and it became a place where the crews could rest up during postings to the Far east.

One ship that paid a visit, and left a permanent reminder of its crews stay, was the old *Astraea* class cruiser, HMS *Fox* (laid down in 1893) which had a reprieve from the scrap man and was posted to the East Indies Squadron. In 1913, the crew were resting at Diyatalawa when they came up with the idea to create the image of a fox on the side of one of the downland like hills nearby. Possibly inspired by the ancient chalk horses of the British Isles, the crew began to carry white quartz stones up the hillside (as clearly these were not chalk hills) to build the fox, and labelled underneath with the year (1913) and HMS *Fox*. Afterwards, visiting crews organised a cross country race that included a run up to the fox before heading back to the finish. Today, running shoes are replaced by motor cars and motor bikes in the annual 'Fox Hill motocross', on a purpose made track below the hill, which still sports the image that the men of HMS *Fox* created over one hundred years ago. As for *Fox*, she saw much action in the first world war despite her obsolescence but was finally scrapped in Watchet harbour (Somerset) in 1920. She remains the largest ship ever to enter Watchet harbour in England, but never leave.

Diyatalawa remained a RN Station until 1949 when the Ceylon army was formed and took over the base to train 'Other' ranks and Non-Commissioned Officers (NCO's). All Officer candidates were sent to Sandhurst in the U.K. for their training until 1968 when a policy of an indigenous Officer candidates became the norm and Diyatalawa began an intake of Officer cadets. In the early 1980's, all training of ranks below Officer were transferred elsewhere and

Diyatalawa became a Military Academy for Officer Cadets, which it remains as such to this day.

Returning to the 1920's, the running of *Effingham* had to continue during the camp period, so the crew was split into two parties. The first leaving for camp on Thursday 8 July, returning on Tuesday 5 August, the second leaving on Friday 6 August and returning on Thursday 2 September. Camp was not purely for fun and frolics. It was a continuation of bonding the crew as an extended family and as a key element in the Officer Cadet training process. Seamen and Stokers were split into groups, or 'Platoons' which would be commanded by a Midshipman or Warrant Officer to give them experience in command and making sure the wellbeing of the men under their command was catered for. They were, of course overseen by one of the ships Lieutenants for continuity, however they were generally left to their own devices with as little interference as possible.

Before the first group left for camp, there was some unfinished business to attend to. Two concerts were organised to raise money for the families of Leading Seaman Hawkins and Bandsman Elsdon. Despite having little time to advertise and the very wet weather on both nights the concert was well attended and quite a sum of money was raised.

The mood following the last cruise, and the death of their two shipmates had clearly had an effect on the men. None of them had been on camp before and all they had heard about the experience was second hand and not inspiring. As one put it, 'we were inclined to be apathetic about the whole matter.' However, this soon changed after the overnight journey to within a few miles of the camp began again.

At five o'clock in the morning we were roused from sleep at Nanu Oya, where hot tea, sandwiches and hard-boiled eggs were issued to us. On waking we discovered that the morning was cold – an amazing discovery. By the time the train started again it was daylight and we could see the view from our carriage windows. All thought of further sleep was instantly abandoned.

The train wound its way through the tea plantations, catching far reaching views that excited and intrigued the men whose initial apathy dissipated, and they became like excited children on a school outing.

As we wind slowly up the hill, with the train frequently in the formation of a letter S, and with the two engines puffing and blowing like two stout women catching a bus, we can picture something of the romance of this wonderful railway.

The men were billeted in the corrugated buildings that had been built when the camp housed the Boer prisoners, they had white painted walls and green roofs. With morning duties such as housekeeping and inspection complete by 10:30am, the men were then free for the remainder of the day. There was plenty to do, for those who were not in one of the rifle shooting teams (who went off to practice). Swimming, tennis, football, and cricket on a 'fast scoring cricket ground, on which many exciting matches were played' as well as a nine-hole golf course, which was 'bad, but so were most of the players',

For those of a less sporting nature, dances and whist drives were held twice weekly in the Church Hut (which also held services every Sunday of course). With little restriction on where you went, walking in the area to take in the scenery was just one more of the less demanding physical activities, so long as you took 'a snake-bite outfit, a stick and a well-chosen companion'.

At the end of the camp period, having played against the Army, the Ceylon Defence Force and local plantation teams in various team sports, there was a final sports tournament. Included in this was the cross country run around Fox Hill.

Clearly this period of downtime was a big lift for the crew and a most enjoyable one at that. On one dance evening at the Church Hut, Mrs. Ellerton who was dancing with a Marine, talked about the second camp trip scheduled the following year. At one point the Marine remarked, 'oh no, this will never happen again.' Mrs Ellerton asked why this could not be, to which he replied, 'Because this is much too good ever to be repeated'.

He was to be correct on this matter, as *Effingham* would return to the U.K. early and therefore, apart from a small contingent of men, who the senior officers felt needed a rest, the crew would not revisit Diyatalawa during this cruise.

Whilst camp was in progress, *Effingham* remained in Colombo for what was to be some time as the work on her Condensers began shortly after the camp period was over. In the meantime, as one would expect, there was much to offer in the way of entertainment both on board with visiting local dignitaries and the coming and going of other ships visiting the port. This included the Cruiser, H.M.A.S *Melbourne,* which was returning to Freemantle after visiting Portsmouth, the Dutch Navy was represented by two gunboats, Soe*mba* and *Flores* as well as several Royal Navy ships transiting to either the Far east or returning to England. An interesting inclusion in these comings and goings was the arrival of the Japanese Navy in the form of their training squadron which included the Light Cruisers *Izumo* and *Yakumo* under the command of Vice Admiral Yamamoto (not the Admiral of the same name who orchestrated the raid on Pearl Harbour). Incidentally neither of these ships were built by the Japanese. The *Izumo* was built by Armstrong Whitworths in England and the *Yakumo* in Stettin, Germany. Which leads nicely to the arrival of the German Cruiser *Hamburg* which paid a visit to Colombo on the 19 November.

The arrival of the 3rd Destroyer Flotilla on their way to China delayed the departure of *Effingham* for exercises as there was clearly some serious entertaining to be catered for. *Effingham's* Officers and men went out of their way to look after the men of the flotilla which remained in Colombo for a week. In addition to the Destroyers, the aircraft carrier *Hermes* paid a 48 hour visit to the port, during which time one of her aircraft took the Governor of Ceylon for a scenic flight.

On the 24 October the news reached the crew of the sinking of HMS *Valerian* off the coast of Bermuda on the 22nd. It remains one of the largest losses of RN personnel in peacetime. *Valerian* was an Arabis type Sloop of about 1200 tons with a single screw that had just completed humanitarian duties assisting victims of what had been a catastrophic hurricane season in the Bahamas. She was returning to HM Dockyard in Bermuda when she was overtaken by a Hurricane and foundered in seas. Admiral Cunningham, by now having risen to Flag Captain of the America and West Indies Station, was at the time aboard the 4000-ton Light Cruiser *Calcutta* and he gives us some idea of the strength of the storm in his memoir, 'A Sailor's Odyssey'. *Calcutta* was berthed at the small port of Ireland Island of which the Station Orders made plain that on the approach of a Hurricane all ships should depart for an alternate safe anchorage. Cunningham admits that he was of the opinion that this was not necessary and was soon to learn the error of this judgement. The high seas began to break over the stone jetty's filling them to the brim with water. The high winds then tore at the *Calcutta* and rolled her against the masonry of the dock whilst visibility was reduced to nothing. The eye of the storm brought some calm and then the winds turned and increased. 'The strength and the noise of the wind were unbelievable, and we were told afterwards that the anemometer ashore registered 138 miles an hour and then gave up the ghost. A tin hut abreast the ship took wings and vanished. I saw our wireless aerial, four strands of wire, disappear like a cloud to leeward. I clawed my way forward to the forecastle to see how the hawsers were standing the strain and arrived just in time to see them snapping like string.'

The situation became worse when *Calcutta* broke free from the dock completely and was only held by her anchor which began to drag. Cunningham feared they would be pushed broadside onto the jetty and dashed to pieces. With engines at full revolutions *Calcutta* managed to gain some headway and ground herself with some damaged sustained in order to be saved.

Valerian had reported her position not 5 miles to the south of Bermuda at 8am on the 22nd, but the sea state was treacherous, visibility down to nothing and there were no clear navigational landmarks. She had to head out to sea to weather the storm. Despite being radioed again and again, this was the last anyone heard from *Valerian*. HMS *Curlew* and *Capetown* were dispatched to search for her, meanwhile Cunningham and his Navigating Officer looked over the charts and using all the information they had on *Valerians* last position plotted a search area for the two ships to begin looking for survivors. It turned out to be correct as a Carley life raft was found with 19 survivors who reported that 80 men had managed to get away from the ship only to be swept away. Nothing else was ever found. Some 80 officers and men were unaccounted for. Cunningham presided over the enquiry that exonerated the crew from any blame. Cunningham's personal view was that the ship had actually touched a reef which had resulted in her capsizing.

Effingham's crew arranged for a dance to be held at the 'Public Hall' in Colombo, with proceeds in aid of the 'Valerian Relief Fund'.

Cairo returned to take up duties with the Squadron, however she developed some serious issues with her propulsion systems and had to repair to Bombay. Having undertaken a refit she then returned to Portsmouth to be paid off. However, both *Emerald* and *Enterprise* arrived back at port and so commenced a period of the autumn exercises out of Trincomalee that included gunnery and torpedo practice. Indeed, the shooting of the guns was a live firing exercise and the gunnery teams put some pressure on the Torpedo party to perform and they duly rose to the occasion. It is with a remark of some surprise that it was noted, 'and they replied a fortnight later by scoring two actual hits on the *Emerald*, one torpedo sinking as a result'.

The Battle of Janjira

Some 40 miles south of Bombay, near the entrance to the Rajpuri River, a pair of lights shone from the old Mahratta forts of Kansa and Janjira. The men manning the lights had been deposited there some days before in preparation for the landing of an amphibious force on the Janjira peninsular to suppress a local uprising. At 22:00 on the 7 December, the sea conditions were not ideal as the men crowded on the decks of the Royal Indian Marine ships *Pathan*, *Baluchi* and *Elephanta*. *Effingham*, all lights extinguished, was stood off a little distant, the command ship of the landing force. *Emerald* and *Enterprise* shielded the landing ships as best they could from the swell, but the cutters and launches bobbed mercilessly up and down making embarkation of the men in full battle kit not only difficult but incredibly dangerous. One slip, and a heavily equipped soldier would sink like a stone. However, all were embarked without loss and the force headed for the beaches close to the town of Dighi.

The troops disembarked were members of the Northland Infantry Brigade, made up of 1st Btn. South Staffordshire Regiment and the 1st Btn. 4th Bombay

Grenadiers. They were supported by the Brigade Signal Section, Field Hospital and Divisional Train (baggage, victuals etc). The force was landed, with the exception of the Divisional Train by 05:00, with no resistance, despite a red flare being fired.

The opposition forces were encamped in the nearby forest covered hills, named by the attacking force as Conical and Dighi Hills. With the bridgehead consolidated the troops advanced inland with the Stafford's taking up the lead. The Janjir opposition were fighting a rear-guard action. Spotting that they were about to be outflanked by the Grenadiers they were pushed back further into the hills, and by the end of the first day the attackers had reached their first objective, taking the ridge of Conical Hill.

Pickets were placed and the Stafford's and Grenadiers settled down for what was a peaceful night, apart from the bugs and the heat. The following day the force advanced further, encountering some resistance across the broken terrain. The Janjirs were being forced back and appeared to be consolidating a position on high ground in front of a secluded beach from which it appeared they were to make an enforced evacuation. Stiff resistance was encountered as the attackers pressed home their attack on the ridge, and by the evening of this, the last day, the Janjir force was stranded on the beach with no means of escape. Capitulation was swift as they realised that their position was hopeless.

The Battle of Janjira was a swift affair, but one that saw a coming together of a combined forces operation including the Royal Navy, British and Indian Armies and the Royal Indian Marine. It was indeed just an exercise, and the Janjir defenders were none other than *Effingham's* contingent of Royal Marines, who had been dropped off in the area the week before. In attendance had been Commandant, Officers and Students from the Staff College at Quetta. All agreed it had been a success and so buoyed with self-congratulations, the force re-embarked for Bombay taking in a short stay at Karachi which was notable in the fact that it was the only time during their deployment that the crew wore their blue uniforms.

Christmas was spent in Bombay and like the previous festive period the ship was once again 'decorated with garlands and flags, until unrecognisable even to the owners.' Breakfast was served early before all hands changed into their best whites for inspection and then proceeding to the quarter deck for a Christmas service. The 'Funny party' once again assisted the Commander-in-Chief, Captain and their wives and daughters with a tour of the ships mess decks before all of the ships company massed on the quarter deck for a photograph. Then to dinner and a truly traditional Christmas feast that resulted in 'sighs of contentment mingled with clouds of smoke from innumerable cigarettes and cigars.'

The Boy Seamen of the ships company were given the following day off. A small steamer pulled alongside *Effingham* in the morning and the boys were embarked for a trip to visit the Elephanta Caves with their carvings that are reputed to have been carved some two centuries before the birth of Christ. They returned by the Bombay YMCA and having discovered a piano in the building, a suitable pianist from the company was persuaded to play whence singing and dancing commenced until it was time for dinner and a return to the ship.

On the 28 December the Officers threw a very large dance for the people of Bombay, whilst final preparations were being made for a rather special occasion. The ships Concert Party had written and were about to perform their first Musical Comedy, 'Honk! Honk!'. The cast were made up of a mixture of the ship's crew from all departments and ranks (a cast of 29 in total) and included Miss Bice Bellairs, who performed dance routines[22]. The music was supplied, as expected by the Royal Marines. Invites were sent out and the performance was given ashore at the Excelsior theatre on the 30 December.

The Concert Party had performed a number of variety shows but in the autumn of 1926 they decided to be a little more ambitious and by October rehearsals for 'Honk! Honk!' had begun. There were many challenges, not least trying to rehearse in a cramped, hot and humid man of war! Many of the cast had not performed before at all, and over the months Lieutenant Commander Lever, the 'Producer' worked up his performers; 'He encourages,

---

[22] Bice Bellairs clearly had a lasting passion for the theatre was one of the founders of the Guildford School of Acting (GSA), which originated as the Grant Bellairs School of Dance and Drama formed in 1935.

cajoled, bullied and entreated the performers as necessary, until chaos was reduced to order and stage-fright was replaced by confidence'.

Back stage, Stoker Meader, Signalman Cole, Able Seaman Floyd, Barton and Yeoman of Signals Worlock provided scenery, lighting and set building which included getting all of the paraphernalia of a mobile theatre company off the ship and onto shore wherever the performance required.

The performance in Bombay on the 30th was the first of several during what was remaining of the deployment, at Rangoon (at the 'Mission for Seamen', where 1800 Rupees were donated to the Mission), Port Blair and Trincomalee.

Before departing on the 31st for Colombo there were a number of changes to the ships company. It was quite common for Officers in particular, to be transferred out or into a ship depending on the requirements of the service. The most commonplace transfer was that of the Midshipmen. These young Officers in training would be assessed aboard ship and at an appropriate time would be transferred out to another posting to further their careers.

6 senior midshipmen left *Effingham* for new postings at this time. In normal circumstances they would have remained aboard for a further 3 months, however it was decided that with the forthcoming gunnery exercises scheduled it would be more beneficial for them to make way for a new group. Midshipmen Rowell, Rylands, Hill, Irven, Reynolds and Hopkins came aboard, one of them would not be returning home. In addition to the midshipmen, there was a change in the ships surgeon and then came a number of half year promotions which were also a trigger to move these newly appointed men to senior positions required on other warships.

1927

Effingham sailed from Bombay on the 31 December, proceeding to Colombo for a few days before leaving for Madras where the previous year the ships company had been involved in the Military Tournament. The visit this year was much less strenuous, indeed for those cricket enthusiasts amongst the crew there came the opportunity to watch the MCC team play. It was also at this time that the Commander-in-Chief announced that there would be a change in their orders and that rather than tour the Persian Gulf they would return to the ports that the ship had visited the previous year. Whilst on the one hand this was a disappointment it was recognised that whilst prickly heat and the humidity would be replaced with cooler climes, there would have been less in the way of amusements and less leave to be taken. The compromise was met favourably.

Effingham secured to a buoy off the Barr Street Jetty in the muddy waters by Rangoon on the 21st January, due to remain there for about a month. An atmosphere of cultural enlightenment had manifested itself aboard ship from when the ship was at Madras. The Chief of Staff had been taking a walk near Fort St George and whilst pondering the historical relevance of the place hit upon the idea of starting a series of lectures. The men were invited to come forward and give a talk, once a week, on a particular place and its historical relevance. These proved most popular with the crew and were always full to capacity.

A cultural expedition upriver, away from the ship was organised and the services of a paddle steamer made available to the crew. So enthusiastic was the take up, that two trips had to be arranged and so at 9:00am one morning the first of the trips embarked and set off along the Twante Canal, out of the city and into the countryside. 'Here and there we would pass a native village, occasionally a rubber plantation, sometimes bare wilderness, and now and again a small portion of jungle.'

Passing native villages, the tourists were given a glimpse of rural life in Burma, which they reflected, was like a trip into the past. 'The huts with walls cunningly woven from weeds and bamboo, the bamboo poles that hold the hut clear from the ground and the complete absence of chimneys, all tend to remind one of the times when the lake tribes inhabited Britain'. In respect of the inhabitants, it was noted that 'the women wearing just a sarong, then men a loincloth and the kiddies a smile.'

The canal gave way to the Irrawaddy River where the water quality improved and although still a little muddy was more inviting to those who liked a dip. They sailed past the town of Morbein (Maubin) and anchored for the night a little further upstream where they 'whiled away our time playing cards and dodging all manner of insects.'

The following day the party was split into three groups with a trip to a local market where 'the vendors were dressed in a myriad of colours, the majority being women who wore so many brightly coloured rings on their fingers that their hands were barely visible. They also wore huge earrings whilst their hair was beautifully cut in styles that would be the envy of any 'civilised' country. The vendors tended to all manner of stalls that would be familiar in any marketplace anywhere in the world, Greengrocers, Butchers, Bakers and toy stalls. The crowds gathered around the stalls where the women energetically haggled causing a human traffic jam 'until some big, brawny coolie came barging his way along and left a channel through which the more timid could pass.'

Curiously the tour included both a Police Station with its own Gaol, which was empty at the time, and a 'wooden cage like structure within which were a number of native prisoners who were chained hand and foot. They were engaged in turning a kind of capstan which, according to the guide, was nothing more than a pump that drew water from the river.' It was assumed these were the normal inhabitants of the Police Gaol. The tourists returned to *Effingham*, 'feeling all the better for the trip and for two days away from the ship and its routine.'

Whilst the excursions were away there occurred the usual entertainments such as concerts and suppers attended to either aboard ship or by invitation ashore as well as various sporting fixtures including cricket of course. The ships Boys were well cared for, being taken in groups by motor car out to the Royal Lake where they swam and took out small boats. 'And was there ever a Boy (sailor or not) who did not love mucking about in a boat? If so, we have not met him.'

Effingham left Rangoon on the 10 February with a wholly different air of expectation and excitement, not unlike a senior year at school entering their final weeks before breaking up for good. For whilst at Rangoon word was given that their commission was to be cut short. *Effingham* would return to Portsmouth in August for paying off and a refit.

Sailing back to Colombo, *Effingham* visited the tiny coral island of Car Nicobar. By all accounts, this was the first time a British Warship had visited the islands whose inhabitants were clearly impressed by the men dressed in pure white who came ashore to visit them. *Effingham* was anchored close offshore in the clear blue island waters, and it was not long (by lunchtime!) before the inhabitants came around to the fact that this large vessel was one of opportunity. They rowed out to *Effingham* in numbers that besieged the ship, bartering for ships biscuits and the most sought-after commodity, white bread.

The crew clearly found the island and its inhabitants fascinating. 'The Nicobarese house is shaped like a large beehive on legs, with sixteen inches of thatch to keep out the heat and the rain. The entrance is up a narrow ladder through a hole in the floor, and the actual flooring is made of a criss-cross bamboo, allowing the air to come up and the dust to go down (most hygienic!).'

In respect of the people, their lack of clothing came as somewhat of a surprise, the lack of money a little bewildering, their belief in devils quaint and unusual but overall, 'everything is scrupulously tidy and neat, and the children are well nourished and the people happy looking and care-free.' On an island where entertainment has to be created it was noted that bathing and fishing from homemade canoes were most popular. Some of the canoes were large enough to carry 40 men apiece, which occasionally they raced. "And what is the prize for the winner?' they were asked. They looked puzzled. 'Prize? Winner?' they echoed. 'But no one wins – we just race!"

The time came for the ship to depart. A crowd of locals had gathered on the red sands as the remainder of the crew gathered in readiness to row back to the ship. Some were happily munching on their white bread. Suddenly there was a commotion, and the last boat was held up as the final member of the landing party came huffing and puffing up the beach having almost been left behind. Between gasps of breath, he remarked 'This is the place for me, Bill. You couldn't ever be late here. Why, there isn't a single clock in the whole blooming island!'

During the passage to Trincomalee *Effingham* slowed to 12 knots and two strange, aircraft looking devices were suspended from derricks and swung outwards from both sides of the ship. These devices were in effect an underwater 'glider' called a Paravane. This, torpedo shaped equipment incorporated a 'tail' and short, stubby wings that 'flew' the Paravane around twenty feet under the water and some 200 feet from the side of the towing ship. Each Paravane had a unique registration number stamped on the side, where even numbers meant the Paravane was configured to run off the Port side of the ship and odd on the Starboard.

The purpose of the Paravane was to snag the anchor lines of a sea mine with its towing cables. These would pass down the anchor line, the Paravane cutting the mine loose to float to the surface where it could be dealt with by gunfire. Alternatively, the Paravane would come into contact with the mine detonating it at a safe distance from the ship.

For anti-submarine warfare, the Paravane could be loaded with a suitable warhead and towed at some speed (around 25 knots) in order to make contact with a submerged submarine. The war head would either explode on contact or could be triggered electrically from the ship, most likely from the bridge. *Effinghams* Paravanes were deployed in an almost flat calm sea and despite being over twenty feet from the surface could clearly be seen and indeed photographed. Ahead of the Paravane the sea was a mass of flying fish, leaping and bursting from the surface as they were charged down by this metallic grey monster.

The day after arrival back in Trincomalee on the 19 February several groups of men were sullenly drawing paint pots and brushes from stores. Described as a 'long forseen tragedy', the instruction had come from the Admiralty to paint *Effinghams* distinctive yellow funnels and masts Service Grey. The sentiments of the crew were aptly described. 'Shall we be court-martialled if we say that the originator of this crime must be a soulless Philistine?'

The 'end of term' feeling continued as there was another bout of transfers in and out of the ships company including a batch of Midshipmen who had just completed their Seamanship examinations attaining 4 First Class and 2 Second Class certificates. Commander Walker had been amongst the group of Officers who brought *Effingham* out of hibernation and worked up through Commissioning to departure for Trincomalee all that time ago. It just did not seem fair that he should be leaving the ship so close to the end of their commission and paying off. In his own words he wrote, 'The fate of one who leaves a ship towards the end of a commission abroad is indeed a sad one. One is deprived of many 'perks', such as witnessing the paying-off pendant being hoisted after Colours on the Sunday morning before sailing for Home, and the band playing Rolling Home (from your own ship) for the first time – to say nothing of actually leaving the base with all hands at cheer ship stations, with other ships cheering you out of harbour: that certainly is the time when the 'matelot' can cheer.'

The ship then commenced Naval exercises, including torpedo practice and gunnery on the 7 and 8 April which consisted of the smaller calibre guns on the 7th and full calibre on the 8th. In normal circumstances a Navy Tug (or hired tug) would tow either a 145ft or 200ft long Battle Practice Target some 1200 feet from the stern. However, as no tug was available, *Enterprise* was utilised as she was about to re-deploy to the China Station. The target was in effect a large raft with a wooden, slatted target along its length. It could be towed at around 12 knots with a maximum turning of 4 points of the compass. One of the challenges in towing such a target being the length of cable used, as if the target were not towed at the correct speed the cable would soon sink to the seabed. This invariably caused snagging and even the breaking of the cable where the bottom of the sea was rocky.

Target practice over *Effingham* returned to Colombo with departure for Aden scheduled for the 19 April. The atmosphere in the dock was stuffy and many of the crew began to suffer from colds and sore throats. Some of the crew were identified as needing a period of rest, mainly the midshipmen, the Boys and a few Officers and Men. They were packed off to Diyatalawa for a bit of rest, whilst the remainder of the crew stayed with the ship and had to grin and bear the situation.

There were few dry eyes during the farewell party that Mrs Bellairs hosted on the 19 April as *Effingham* was preparing for the last cruise of the Commission, beginning with the sail to Aden. Some 280 people attended the party that included varied entertainment preceding supper and ended in a dance. Chief Petty Officer Telegraphist Lapham closed the party with some words of thanks, and the cheers as a result conveyed the affection that was held of Mrs Bellairs and her family. *Effingham* sailed on the 26th amidst a huge downpour during one of the thunderstorms that had become commonplace every evening of the previous week.

Some days later, having left Aden behind, *Effingham* arrived at the tiny port of Berbera on the Somali coast. There were only 12 English people inhabiting the port at that time, the remaining 26 had moved about 40 miles inland to the town of Sheikh where the climate was somewhat cooler at this time of year. However, men were landed ashore, and games of cricket and football were played.

One afternoon a group of torpedo men gathered together and declared that they were going fishing with explosives to blow up all the fish near Berbera. The galley was duly prepared in readiness for the hoard of fish that would feed the crew on their return. At 16:30 the torpedo men clambered aboard a small boat and headed out to sea armed to the teeth with explosives. The first two and a quarter pound canister, loaded with guncotton and a safety fuse was dropped over the side. The men waited. Nothing. A second canister was duly prepared and once more, dropped over the side. Nothing. A third went over the side. Silence. So, it would be down to the grand finale. A sixteen pound, electrically triggered canister was launched over the side and the team repaired some safe distance before setting off the charge. The resultant wrenching and heaving of the sea in a great roar and torrent of water was spectacular to all and the sound echoed and rolled across the water before subsiding in a gentle hiss. Expectantly the team headed towards their extensive catch in the dingy. A total of five suicidal fish had ventured too close; the galley was not impressed. 'What can you expect from tin fish men?' came the retort from the crew.

The explosive theme continued as *Effingham* carried out depth charge firing for an hour after leaving Berbera for a short visit to the Seychelles. En route the ship hove to and welcomed aboard King Neptune and his Queen and entourage for the second 'Crossing the line' ceremony of the commission. On this occasion there were just 60 lubbers for initiation, and therefore the proceedings were upon 'B' gun deck. There was to be an informal sing along afterwards, however the heavens opened, and the enthusiasm was dampened. *Effingham* got under way once more for Mauritius.

HMS *Renown* was, on construction and with her sister ship *Repulse* the fastest Battlecruiser of her size. A majestic warship of almost 800ft in length, she had been refitted recently to accommodate The Duke and Duchess of York on their tour of Australia and New Zealand. At 09:30 on the 1 June, *Renown* entered Port Louis and *Effingham* fired a 21gun salute with the shore battery of Fort St. George. On the quarter-deck a Royal Marine Royal Guard saluted the Royal Couple as they passed by, whilst at the aft end of the quarter deck those Officers and men not required for duties were fallen in. Indeed, the majority of the ship's crew were ashore. A Royal Guard of Seamen were formed up at their landing place, accompanied by the RM Band. In addition, some 170 men lined the streets along the route the couple would take to the Governors House for a reception that afternoon.

The duke was taken stalking with the Admiral the following morning. The Admiral shot two stags during the 'Chasse' however the duke was not as fortunate and came away empty handed. In the afternoon the duke visited *Effingham* and inspected the RM Guard and shook hands with all the ships officers, whilst the entire ships company marched past, each saluting in turn. There followed a demonstration by the gun crews and an inspection of the upper deck. The Duchess joined the ship at 17:00 and the couple remained aboard with Admiral Ellerton and his wife until sunset. They then left for a dinner party aboard *Renown* before she sailed on the next stage of her voyage at midnight.

On departure there was an exchange of signals, with the following from the duke.

From – H.R.H. the Duke of York
To – The Commander-in-Chief, East Indies

It was with great pleasure to me to see your Flagship to-day and I was much impressed by her smartness and efficiency. The Duchess and I wish you all success and we hope that the Captain, Officers and Ship's Company will have a long and enjoyable leave on their return to England in August.

Stoker Albert Edward Watts (K65436) had just turned 24 on the 26 May. He was a fairly short young man at 5' 3" with auburn hair and light blue eyes. He originated from Towcester, beginning his working life as a labourer before joining up in November 1924 and signing up for 12 years in the Navy. *Effingham* was his first ship.

It was on a clear, sunny, warm day that he, one of the officers and 20 other young men assembled on the Customs Jetty where 5 cars awaited them. One was a private car belonging to one of 3 gentlemen (Messieurs Pezzani, Fouquereaux and Le Breton) who had invited the men on an excursion that day to visit Cap Malheureaux, the remainder were hire cars.

They set off with the private car taking the lead, through Pamplemousse, where they made a brief detour around the Botanical Gardens; 'although the trees were all named on boards on their trunks, our French did not run far enough to make the names even pronounceable.' Wrote one of the party afterwards.

Returning to the road they travelled through seemingly endless miles of sugar plantations until they came to a road by the sea which ran parallel to the beach for some time. Then they drew up next to a small row of houses that were just a hundred yards from the aquamarine sea that looked so inviting that some quickly stripped to their trunks and ran into the calm waters for a swim. The water was clearly quite chilly and before long they all returned to the shore and quickly changed into their dry clothes, whilst trying to persuade the others to 'go in'. 'These hardy people were unable to inveigle anybody else to go for a swim, even after repeated assurances of the warmth of the water, for chattering teeth are not good testimony.'

The men retired to their hosts house for some tea, and they chatted until around 17:00 when they began the journey home. Their hosts all clambered in the lead car and quickly sped off leaving the others behind. The competitive spirit and youthful exuberance of the sailors led to a race. 3 of the cars sped through the countryside at breakneck speed, and on occasion when one managed to pass the other there was much honking of horns and yells and cheers of derision and mirth.

The race ate up the miles and before long the first three cars entered Port Louis and some calm was restored before they pulled back onto the Custom Jetty. The remaining cars soon arrived, one of them had suffered a puncture and it had taken some time to fix it. They all returned to the ship around 18:15

talking loudly and enthusiastically about their adventure that day. Later an impromptu dance was organised aboard ship and a letter of thanks signed by all the men was given to their host.

Albert was on duty for *Effinghams* departure for Zanzibar the following day, 9 June. At 16:00 sharp the ship slipped its moorings and headed out to sea. The next few days were going to be busy ones as the Commander-in-Chief was due to carry out the annual inspection of the ship. This would include full speed trials, Cruising Stations, Night Action Stations, inspection of the Mess Decks and Storerooms, Upper Deck and Ships Company. This would take 3 days to complete.

Two hours after leaving port, Albert was at the ready, stood on a grating in the engine room and awaiting the order to turn the master valve that would connect the cruising turbines. The engine room was the hottest and most confined space aboard ship, the conditions unbearable as Albert waited patiently for the word. He was sweating profusely and began to feel nauseous. He tried desperately to remain upright, but the heat became even more oppressive and finally it overcame him. A warship is an unforgiving place, the metal surfaces bruising to even the slightest knock. Albert lost consciousness and fell; the back of his head struck the ship with some considerable force.

His fellow stokers came rushing to his aid and he was quickly and carefully carried to the sick bay, but he remained unresponsive. It transpired that he had fractured the base of his skull and he never regained consciousness. He died at 21:20. The following morning *Effingham* came to a full stop and the men gathered together in silence; 'we sorrowfully attended the always impressive ceremony of a burial at sea.'

Zanzibar was a favourite destination for the crew and it is interesting to note that the following words come from 1927, a time that many historians and commentators attribute ignorance and bigotry to the general population. 'The cosmopolitan population of Zanzibaris, Indians, Arabs and Europeans show a tolerance which we have often found wanting in other places: religious bigotry, class hatred and colour bars cannot apparently thrive in that balmy air. We enjoyed ourselves in Zanzibar.'

A week later a group of volunteers took a ferry out to Grave Island (Chapwani Island), which they had visited the previous year. On this occasion they took with them some paint and made good the names on the crosses. It was a good day's work and the men left satisfied that they had done something for their fellow sailors who had given everything. It would be interesting to know whether the inscribed copper plates that some of *Effinghams* Stokers made and took to the island on a visit by them and the Commander-in-Chief a week later remain there. The cemetery certainly is still there today and is under the protectorate of the Commonwealth War Graves Commission.

A group of sailors took the ships cutter out for a picnic one Sunday. They arrived at a small beach and were settling down for a comfortable afternoon in the warm sunshine when a most extraordinary sight came into view. A young Zanzibari, dressed in a scarlet uniform approached them and in a hushed voice said, 'Master say will you come up to the house as you are and the beer is waiting.' Clearly this kind of invitation is not given up by ever thirsty sailors and they made their way to what turned out to be a magnificent house, originally built by Sir John Kirk (Botanist and friend of the explorer Dr. Livingstone). The house, it turned out, was owned by a big game hunter, who was apparently famous for having shot a Lion and a Leopard with a right and left from his shotgun!

The picnic party duly found that they had been proceeded, 'We thought to have arrived there first, but some folk have long ears and we found a number of sailors already comfortably settled in the house.' The momentum gathered as, 'after washing the salt of the sea from our throats in excellent beer, we lifted up our voices in song…' Soon the party broke up and they had to leave but they promised to return the following Tuesday with a larger compliment and many more musical instruments, which they did!

Not to be outdone, 80 sailors made their way 7 miles up the coast from Zanzibar as the guests of the local Ladies Committee. They travelled on the little railway that ran the distance at a very slow pace. By all accounts it appears the railway had been closed to the public in 1922 and was used by the time *Effingham* arrived to transport stone. Whatever, the Regulating Petty Officer describes, 'We entrained at the jetty in the Zanzibar Express – a roaring express- which travelled at a speed of about one mile per hour.'

On the beach there were those who went bathing whilst the remainder played coconut shies. The Ladies challenged the sailors to a contest, which they duly won by 9 nuts to 7. However, it was noted that the sailors nuts had been nailed to their posts! Eventually they all sat down to tea which was washed down with Beer and Cigarettes, accompanied by much laughter and singing until the time came to return to the ship, most content.

Cricket games and tournaments were organised, but the football games played during their stay were most popular drawing crowds of around 5000 spectators! Paymaster Lieutenant Glenister was their hero and became known to the natives as 'Makaniki' as he always wore a blue jersey and shorts when playing, which resembled the long blue dress commonly worn by Muslim women. It is remarkable to think that so many turned out to watch the matches played during the *Effinghams* commission, and a sign that to the people of these countries, these were very special and enjoyable spectacles. Indeed, when *Effingham's* football team were invited to play the Army Garrison side in Mauritius, they estimated a crowd of 15,000 in attendance.

At the end of June, *Effingham* arrived for her second visit to Mombasa, and her final lay over before returning to Colombo and then home to Portsmouth. The May of the previous year they had arrived in pouring rain that continued almost without pause, however this time the weather was warm and pleasant. As has been the case during the previous visit, a special train was laid on to take a party to Nairobi. Fifteen officers and some fifty-seven men departed Kilindini for the long journey. The party included the Rugby, Soccer and Tug of War teams as well as the Concert Party in order to perform 'Honk! Honk!' at the Theatre Royal.

Tragedy was set to make one final appearance to the commission. Three midshipmen, Henry Copinger Hill, along with Rylands and Hopkins were involved in a motor accident in Nairobi. Rylands and Hopkins were injured, but Hill was killed. The games scheduled for the next few days were cancelled, and the funeral arranged for the morning of 3 July. Hill was buried with full military honours, the firing party provided by 3rd Battalion, Kings African Rifles commanded by Lieutenant Colonel Davies. Back at the ship, the news was conveyed to a stunned crew and a memorial service arranged for the following day whilst *Effinghams* ensign fluttered in the breeze at half mast.

Hill was just 21, the only child of Henry and Ethel Copinger Hill, a brass plaque to his memory is located in St Mary's Church, Buxhall, Suffolk.

Homeward Bound

9 days in Colombo, that was all that was left of the Commission to the East Indies before heading back to Portsmouth on the 26 July. It would take a further 9 days sailing to Aden for refuelling, 5 days to Suez and then through the canal to Port Said. 4 days to Malta and refuelling again with a break of 2 days before a 2 day run to Gibraltar, an overnight layover and then the final hop to Portsmouth arriving 9am on the 25 August. That was the plan.

In the meantime, there were farewell parties and many goodbye's to be made. This included a fond farewell to the Commander-in-Chief who had proved to be most popular. He would remain until the 1 December when his flag would be hauled down and he would be replaced by the incoming C-in-C, Rear Admiral Bertram S. Thesinger, C.B., C.M.G.

Back in England, Kathleen was preparing for the return of her husband. The Portsmouth Evening News regularly reported the movements of Royal Navy ships during peacetime, and on the 10 August, it stated that the *Effingham* was at Port Said. More news on the 22 which was not so good. *Effingham* was required to take a dredger in tow from Malta, and this would delay her arrival in Portsmouth. But Herbert was getting closer to home and Kathleen could begin to think about travelling to the dockyard to meet him.

Friday the 26th, and the excitement in Portsmouth was building, especially for those with loved ones coming home aboard *Effingham*. The Portsmouth Evening news was read with great expectation, and it did not disappoint. 'East Indies Flagship Due at Portsmouth Tomorrow' was the headline. 'Due to arrive at Spithead at 8:30am tomorrow. The Cruiser will in all probability proceed straight into harbour and be berthed alongside the Boat House jetty.'

Kathleen took Doreen to the main gates of Portsmouth Naval Base early on the morning of Saturday 27th. A large crowd had gathered and there was a hum of excited chatter and an air of expectation. Word spread that 09:30

would be a reasonable time to expect the ship to arrive, but that came and went, and by 10:30 the chatter had died down. Then came the news of a further delay which temporarily dampened the spirits, but these were lifted once more when the news came that *Effingham* was expected between 14:00 and 15:00.

The return of a warship from deployment is still a special event to this day, and the scenes at the dockyard would not be unfamiliar now. Families travelled from far and wide to welcome home their sons, husbands and fathers. There was much chatter and merriment, flags waved whilst women and children beamed with excitement. Then, almost like magic *Effingham* appeared and the cheers began from all over the harbour as the ship, almost silently but graciously glided through the harbour entrance. From her mast fluttered her long, thin, Paying Off Pennant. Traditionally as long as the ship, it may have been made from various pieces of material gathered up by the sailors.

The bands played 'Rolling Home to England' as *Effingham* came alongside and the gangways were pulled up fore and aft. The call of 'All Engines Stop' was relayed and *Effingham* was silent, and home, after travelling just over 500,000 miles during her travels to the East Indies.

Rolling Home

Call the hands to man the capstan
See the cable run down clear
Heave away and with a will boys
For old England we will steer
And we'll sing in joyful chorus
In the watches of the night
And we'll sight the shores of England
When the grey dawn brings the light.

Rolling home, rolling home, rolling home across the sea
Rolling home to dear old England
Rolling home, dear land to thee

Having been away from home for such a long time it has to beg the question of how the sailors would re-adjust to home life? With a compliment of 750 men there would no doubt be some (amongst those married of course) who's wives had either left them already or would do so later. For the wives that remained with their husbands, how would they now readapt after so long apart with quite possibly little correspondence with their husband since the ship departed almost two years previous? To some, it must have been like a stranger invading their home, and no doubt it would take time for a family to re-adjust and relationships to be reformed. Let us not forget, that for some of the families, their boys were not coming home at all.

For this crew of *Effingham*, it was time to disperse. Herbert was to remain attached to the ship until the 6 October when he was transferred to duties at the 'Victory' barracks and it wouldn't be until the following January before assignment to another ship. Clearly, he and Kathleen did cope with being re-united. If anything, their family life was cemented and re-enforced rather than damaged by their separation.

For the reminder, they too were re-posted. Having been a part of one big family, with all the camaraderie, shared experiences both good and bad, their time together would no doubt have forged lasting friendships. As one man put it; '…but when all the shouting is over, will there not be the slightest regret that another Commission is nearly over? Sailors are dreadful sentimentalists: we grouse at the moment, but we always maintain that there is no ship like our last ship, no commission like our last commission. And so, at Portsmouth, although naturally happy to be home once more, we may look back with other sentiments than disgust at the places we have just left.'

A glimpse of sentimentality comes not from one of the sailors, but from one of the Commander-in-Chiefs daughters. Surely the following description would have been appreciated by all those who sailed with *Effingham* during her Commission to the East Indies, between 1925 and 1927.

> 'The palms are swaying gently in the breeze; beyond them is the harbour, across which little swelling waves are chasing each other till they gently break upon the shore. The *Effingham* lies in the rippling water with a background of hills stretching away into the distance. The sun is setting. Now the sky is changing colour – from a bright blue it is turning to a flaming red shading into orange; the water is reflecting it in softer hues, and pinks seem to chase yellow and reds across the

harbour. The sun has nearly set. The sky is now turning dark blue, streaked with light pink and yellow; over all is a transparent green, but gradually even this disappears. The sky and the water merge into each other, the *Effingham's* lights shine out in the darkness, and she stands alone in one vast space'.[23]

Portsmouth & Home waters – 1927 to 1932

Like the once yellow funnels and white livery of *Effingham*, the memories of those two years away from Portsmouth were soon replaced with the realities of the present. It may have seemed like a punishment, rather than reward that Herbert found himself assigned to HMS 'Fisgard'[24]. The location was almost Dickensian, and indeed harked back to a time when French prisoners of war were held captive aboard the rotting hulks of once proud warships. Life in Fisgard was tough, very tough.

A group of hulks lay lashed together in Fareham creek, interconnected by gangways, with corrugated structures perched on the upper decks whose soot blackened chimneys belched forth dark smoke when work was being undertaken. The hulks were vaguely familiar. Old Iron clad ships from that time between sailing craft and the Dreadnoughts, like *Powerful*, on whom Herbert had begun his career in the Navy. They looked out of date even before they were commissioned. This motley collection made up the 'shore' training establishment of 'Fisgard'.

The great Admiral John 'Jackie' Fisher had proposed the creation of a training school for Boy Artificers, those who would go on to become senior engineers within the Royal Navy but holding the rank of a non-commissioned officer. The scheme got under way in 1903 and within two years Portsmouth, Chatham and Plymouth were conducting courses, which now included Electrical and Ordinance Artificer training to maintain pace with the developing technological advances in these fields. However, the growing 'trend' in Navy spending cuts materialised so that by 1920, only Portsmouth remained.

---

[23] (Unknown, 1927)
[24] (Association, 2022)

Aboard the hulks conditions were oily and dirty, an environment that went hand in hand with the trade that was being taught in the Blacksmiths shop, the Foundry or either the Boiler or Fitting shop. Clearly it was in these departments and the day to day manning and supporting of the training establishment that Herbert was to be involved in for a year and a half between January 1928 and June 1929.

Whilst there is no real 'normality' in service existence for a family, even to this day and certainly not compared to civilian life, clearly there became something of a routine for Herbert and Kathleen over the next 5 years. It was a time when their little family put down some firm roots with the arrival of Dorothy in October 1929 and obtaining their own home in Woodmanscote, near Emsworth. How far the boy from the workhouse had come.

June 1928, an escape from the hulks and a return to the sea. H.M.S *Flinders*, a survey ship named after a man who has largely been overlooked by Great Britain. But he is well known in Australia and his link with the 20th Century is both intriguing and worthy of a deviation from the current narrative.

Matthew Flinders was born in Lincolnshire in 1774 and destined for the sea, joining the Royal Navy at 15 years old and serving with the infamous, but most accomplished seaman, Captain William Bligh on one of his expeditions to Tahiti (not the one of the famous mutiny) in 1792. During this time his interest in cartography was kindled. Then to 'Billy Ruffian', officially known as *Bellerophon*, and action at the battle of 'The Glorious 1st of June'.

5 years later, Matthew is in Sydney (or Port Jackson as it was then) and assigned to *Reliance*. He strikes up a friendship with the ship's surgeon, George Bass with whom he makes several surveying expeditions which included the discovery that Van Diemen's land is actually an island, later to be renamed Tasmania. Most of their surveying was from the single masted, 20-foot cutter, *Tom Thumb.*

On return to England, Matthew lobbies to carry out a detailed survey of the coast of 'New Holland'. Despite England being at war with France and the navy's resources very limited, HMS *Investigator* was placed at his disposal for the forthcoming expedition. Haste was required as the French were also embarking on a similar quest under the leadership of Nicolas Boudin with two ships, the *Geographe* and the *Naturaliste*. In some ways peculiar to the time, both men were provided with 'Passports' that allowed them to carry out their expeditions, despite their countries being at war with one another, so long as their aims were scientific and not military.

*Investigato*r, just 100ft long, purchased by the Royal Navy as a Survey Ship was an old ship and a very leaky one at that. Despite the risk of sinking the compliment departed and sometime later, still afloat, the coast of the 'New Holland' land mass was mapped. During this time, Boudin and Flinders 'met' whilst mapping the southern coastline, some 60 miles from what is now Adelaide. Flinders called this 'Encounter Bay'.

Matthew Flinders had to return to England with his work and quickly as Boudin had already left for France with his own survey and map of the continent. Flinders took command of the *Porpoise* and made haste up the west coast only to be wrecked on the Great Barrier Reef. The majority of the crew made makeshift camp on a sand bar whilst Flinders took a small boat and light crew to sail the 700 miles back to Sydney, fetch a rescue team and return to recover the remaining crew without loss. Not dissimilar to Shackleton's exploits about a hundred years later.

Flinders then took command of the *Cumberland* and attempted to return home once more, but fate would have it that they had to find a port due to the poor condition of the ship. *Cumberland* landed at Port Louis on the Isle De France which at the time, was still 'French' and Britain was still at war with France. Matthew was imprisoned as a spy because his passport declared he was the captain of *Investigator*, not the *Cumberland* and so he remained on the island for a further 6 years, during which time he wrote in detail about his voyage of discovery.

On return to England Flinders consolidated his work, and his map was eventually published in 1814 with the title 'General Chart of Terra Australis or Australia', along with his book, 'A voyage to Terra Australis'. Both of which coined the name of the continent that he described as, 'Australia'. However, Flinders was not well, he had kidney disease and died aged 40, the day before his work was published.

Captain Matthew Flinders was buried in St James burial ground, and it appeared his final resting place was lost forever with the building of Euston Station on the site. It was believed that his grave lay beneath one of the platforms. In 2014 a statue of Flinders, and his beloved ships cat, 'Trim' was installed outside of the station. Then in 2019, with the construction of the HS2 Rail Link and during excavations of the burial ground, archaeologists found a coffin, that unusually, had a lead breastplate fitted which stood the test of corrosion. It stated that it belonged to Matthew Flinders. It is fitting that his remains will be reinterred with the rest of his family in the Church of St Mary and the Holy Rood, in his hometown of Donington, Lincolnshire.

Digression over and it is back to some fairly routine work at Portsmouth. An assignment to 'Vernon' in March 1920 during which time another daughter, Yvonne was born in May. Then returning to sea for just over 12 months with two Scott Class Destroyers, *Montrose* and *Campbell*. These were quite large and fast ships, of some 320ft in length and with a top speed of around 36 knots. Built towards the end of World War 1, they were just too late to enter active service. However, both *Montrose* and *Campbell* were very active during World War 2, mainly on convoy protection in and around the waters off Britain. Both ships were present during the evacuation of Dunkirk and the D-Day landings later in 1944. *Campbell* went to the breakers yard in 1948, whilst *Montrose* was effectively written off when she collided first with a cargo ship and later with a Landing Craft and was broken up sometime soon after disposal in 1946.

In between ships, Herbert was back in 'Victory' barracks, where he gained his 3rd Good Conduct badge on 3 November 1931. Then came a very short spell aboard another Survey Ship, HMS *Challenger* during March and April 1932, just two weeks in all, before a 6-month spell again at the 'Victory' barracks during which time Kathleen gave birth to their 4th child, a boy they called Herbert.

Summer came and went, with barracks life taking on some form of routine and the family settling down in their new home. For the wife of a Navy man, a posting is always an inevitability and with it the potential of having to fend for oneself for long periods when their husbands are at sea. Breaking the news to young children that enforced absence of their fathers is imminent cannot be easy, but this was the case for Kathleen and Herbert. *Effinghams* sister ship

Hawkins was being prepared in Portsmouth as Flagship of The East Indies Squadron and would be departing on a two-and-a-half-year commission. Herbert was to report for duty on the 21 September with departure expected 11 October.

Herbert Leeder in tropical rig prior to joining HMS Effingham, 1925.

HMS Effingham

Effingham returns to Portsmouth from East Indies 1932.

Fleet review 1937. Graf Spee with battleship HMS Resolution and battlecruiser HMS Hood

A Fairey Swordfish dropping a torpedo over Stokes Bay

Chapter 3

H.M.S Hawkins 1932 – 1935

Portsmouth Dockyard can be a draughty place, and on the 21 September 1932, there strode a man in frock coat and top hat towards the gangway of HMS *Hawkins*. This was the Reverend Walter Edgar Rea, being assigned to his first ship, and first commission. The sun was shining but it was a windy day, and as he turned a final corner a strong gust caught his top hat and removed it from his head whence it skitted and spun across the wetted cobbles from an earlier shower. It finally lodged itself in a puddle. Retrieving the unruly hat, Rea ascended the gangway and up to the Quarter Deck, where he almost bumped into his new captain, who although short in stature, gave every appearance of command. The captain struck out a hand to welcome his new Chaplain; the Chaplain, in somewhat of a fluster, went to salute, forgetting his top hat, which he promptly knocked off his head.

Having gained his composure, Rea headed to his cabin and then to lunch. He sat next to what he thought was the Surgeon Lieutenant but was in fact a Stoker. There was an awkward silence between the men, and Rea thought that perhaps he should strike up conversation; 'Have you done for anyone yet?' The Stoker was clearly unimpressed and simply replied, 'Is this your first ship?' Rea, once more returned to his cabin, and decided to stay there for a while to regain some composure.

Rev. W. E. Rea was tasked with writing up the journal of the Commission of HMS *Hawkins*, the result of which is the private publication, 'Nil Desperandum' ('do not despair' or 'Never despair') published by 'Butler & Tanner' of Frome. It is an entirely different approach to that of *Effingham* that is dealt with earlier in our narrative. Rather than drawing on a number of experiences of crew members, with contributions from all ranks, the first two thirds of the publication are from Rea's perspective, the final third a rough timeline of the commission. Rea is somewhat self-indulgent in that he takes up a chunk of the book describing his personal journey to Madras following *Hawkins* arrival in Bombay. He requested leave from the ship to visit friends, and promptly describes his 'holiday', which one must assume was of little interest to anyone but himself. Perhaps this is disingenuous.

Rea's writing, is however, quite humorous and self-deprecating on occasion. He is good at recounting a tale, he enjoys fishing and plays golf. Indeed, later in his career he represents the Navy in Golf Tournaments and boasts a handicap below 10. He also suffers from sea sickness, certainly in the earlier stages of the commission, when during periods of rough passage, he can be found taking air on the Quarter Deck. It has to be assumed, that Herbert had some contact with Rea, not only during religious services that were attended by all the crew, but simply as a member of the crew of *Hawkins*.

Almost inevitably, the bulk of the writing concerns the activities of the officers and senior NCO's aboard *Hawkins* during her commission but there are a number of tales that are worth revisiting so that in the spirit of association and the close knit community of the crew there is no doubt that these stories were circulated amongst all those whose 'home' and 'family' resided in *Hawkins* and Herbert is certainly included in this broad 'brush'.

There were of course many parties and social functions during *Hawkins* commission, but whether it was because of his Chaplain Status or because he was a senior member of the crew the book is more workmanlike. The publication suggests a more 'professional' approach to the commission, as opposed to the almost 'Boy Scout' description of *Effinghams* deployment. There is an impression that the earlier commission was much more fun with the roaring twenties shining through. This time, with the rise of fascism in Germany and Italy, as well as Communist Russia in the background, it 'feels' more measured. Great Britain was losing, and would lose at an increasing rate, its grip on the Empire, but there was still time for amusement and there remain many such instances in the publication. Whilst there is a quaint naivety in some of the humour that does not stand the test of time some episodes and comments certainly do.

Captain Thomas Spenser Vaughan Phillips (Tom, or as he signed himself T S V Phillips), whom Rea had met on his first visit to the ship, was appointed to command as Flag Captain of the *Hawkins*. Being a short man, at 5' 4", shorter than Nelson, he had gained the nickname of 'Tom Thumb'. He had served on destroyers in World War 1 in the Mediterranean and the Far East, being promoted to Lt. Cmd in 1916, Commander in 1921 and Captain in June 1927. In 1928 he took command of the destroyer *Campbell* until 1929. At the beginning of 1939 he was made Rear Admiral and eventually Chief of Naval Staff, becoming a close advisor to Winston Churchill, who promoted him to Vice Admiral in 1940.

In 1941 Phillips questioned the validity of the report on the sinking of HMS *Hood*, pointing out that of the 3 survivors, only one had been interrogated and that every individual who witnessed the explosion should be interviewed too. He commented that 'It may be that in years to come our successors may wish to look back at the records of the loss of the *Hood*.

Having been considered by many as a desk admiral, it was with some surprise that he was appointed C-in-C of the China Station. He was at the time the youngest Admiral at 53 years old. He took command of Force Z, aboard the Battleship *Prince of Wales* with the remaining force consisting of the older *Repulse* and four destroyers (*Electra, Express, Tenedos* and HMAS *Vampire*).

Force Z sailed from Singapore on the 8 December 1941, the day after the Japanese attack on Pearl Harbour, with the initial intention of intercepting a convoy and then to oppose Japanese landings on Malaya at Kuantan. The aircraft carrier, *Indomitable* was supposed to have been on hand with a compliment of Sea Hurricanes and Fulmars, however she had run aground in the Caribbean and had to sail to Norfolk, Virginia for repairs.

Flt. Lt. Tim Vigors, a thoroughly experienced pilot who had fought in the Battle of Britain was now commanding 453 Squadron equipped with the rather odd-looking Brewster Buffalo fighter. He had put together a plan to provide air cover for the fleet which would utilise forward bases and ensure there were 6 aircraft over the ships during the hours of daylight. The squadron would need some notice when the ships were due to sail in order to deploy effectively so long as the force remained within 60 miles of the coast. Vigors was invited aboard the *Prince of Wales* and met with Admiral Phillips' Staff Officers. The plan was well received, resulting in the agreement of radio frequencies to be used as well as call signs and operational procedures.

However, as the fleet were preparing to sail Vigors was somewhat perplexed that no request had come for his plan to be put in action, and he received news second hand that indeed the ships had sailed already.

The Task Force was shadowed by Japanese reconnaissance aircraft, but still no request came for Vigors to put his plan in action, and on the 10 December, after being picked up by enemy reconnaissance once more the bombers arrived and there followed a very accurate high-level bombing which caused some initial damage to *Prince of Wales* that affected her steering. Soon after intense attacks by massed torpedo bombers materialised and the fight was brief. Despite manoeuvering like a nimble destroyer and avoiding some 18 torpedoes, *Repulse* was finally hit and was the first to sink. *Prince of Wales* was hit soon thereafter, her sailors taking to the water to join the survivors of the *Repulse*.

By now 453 Squadron, who had been at readiness since the ships had departed was called for. Vigors led the squadron as fast as he could to join the fight. There was a chance that they could do substantial harm to the bomber and torpedo force as they were a long way from their bases and would not have their own fighter protection, but when 453 arrived on the scene, the skies were clear and the damage had been done. 'As we drew nearer, the full scale of the disaster gradually sunk home. The first thing that struck me was that there was no sign of *Repulse*, but a large patch of oil spreading over the water suggested where she might have been.'[25]

Prince of Wales was clearly in trouble. One of the Destroyers was close in, taking off the crew. The Battleship was well down at the stern and listing to port. Vigors had by now slowed his aircraft down and could clearly see the end of the great ship. 'Suddenly her bows rose in the air, nearly knocking over the destroyer. Then, like an enormous whale she started to slide backwards beneath the gentle waves that were lapping at her side.'[26]

The Destroyers picked up many survivors from both ships however some 840 men were lost. Phillips was last seen, with his Flag Captain, John Leach on the bridge of the great ship, just before she sank. Despite being implored to leave, they remained there, and both went down with the ship. Phillips was the most high-ranking Naval Officer to be killed in action during the Second World War.

Vigors came down to fly low over the water, it appeared that the men were waving at him, but it later transpired that they were shaking their fists. They believed they had been let down by the Air Force once more, when in fact it had been their commanders who had not taken advantage of the air cover that his staff had carefully arranged with Vigors. In that moment, it became clear that no matter how powerful capital ships had become, the old beliefs that they were invulnerable to air attack were sunk along with the *Repulse* and *Prince of Wales*. Vigors comments wryly; 'It appears that Admiral Phillips never called for our support. It was the Captain of *Repulse* who broke radio silence as his ship was sinking. That signal, sent to Naval Headquarters in Singapore took nearly an hour to reach me, sitting in readiness, in my Buffalo, 3 miles away.'[27]

---

[25] (Vigors, 2008)
[26] (Vigors, 2008)
[27] (Vigors, 2008)

The Commander-in-Chief assigned to the East Indies Station for *Hawkins* commission was Vice-Admiral Sir M. E. Dunbar-Nasmith, V.C., K.C.B. He arrived in Bombay on the 25 November 1932 and his flag was transferred from the *Enterprise* to *Hawkins*. Dunbar-Smith had shown exceptional skill and bravery as a Lt. Cmd in Submarines during World War 1, where he earned his Victoria Cross

> ...for most conspicuous bravery in command of one of His Majesty's Submarines while operating in the Sea of Marmora. In the face of great danger, he succeeded in destroying one large Turkish gunboat, two transports, one ammunition ship and three storeships, in addition to driving one storeship ashore. When he had safely passed the most difficult part of his homeward journey, he returned again to torpedo a Turkish transport...

This came about when he was in command of HM Submarine E11 at the age of 32, operating in the Dardanelles. Having penetrated the defences which included avoiding patrolling Turkish gunboats and minefields, he manoeuvered E11 into the Sea of Marmara. Here he ensured the destruction of a gunboat, two transports, an ammunition ship, three store ships and four other vessels. However, this was not all, on his return journey he was informed that a large cargo of coal was inbound to Istanbul from the Black Sea. Turning back, having realised that the coal would be essential for the besieged city and the moralee of the people, he waited for his moment. There was a large crowd gathered to watch the ship arrive, including many dignitaries, eagerly awaiting the arrival of these vital supplies that would keep the water, electricity and railways operational. The ship came to a stop and berthed, and then, to everyone's surprise, E11's torpedo salvo blew it up in front of their eyes. Nasmith extracted E11 but continued operations in the Sea of Marmara for another 3 months.

Nasmith had a long career in the Navy, he was invested as Knight Commander, Order of the Bath (K.C.B.) in 1934, and during World War 2 was Commander-in-Chief, Plymouth and Western Approaches from 1938 to

1941 and from 1942 until his retirement in 1946 he was Flag Officer in charge of London. He died on the 29 June 1965, aged 82.

Hawkins was worked up for Commission from the 21 September 1932, out in the Solent and the Channel, going through numerous drills before re-birthing at the South Railway Jetty to prepare for departure. Before sailing each crew member was given a Commissioning Card. The Commissioning card detailed which Division he had been assigned to and where his action stations (Quarter Bill) or emergency station would be and as an aside would help the Officers to identify an individual and their responsibilities before they had become familiar to them.

The running of a Royal Navy Ship has developed into an incredibly ordered and structured organisation that assists not only in the day-to-day operation of the ship but its effective means of fighting whilst maintaining discipline. A crew is divided into groups to allow a continuous, twenty-four-hour operation that is known as the 'Divisional System'. The ship is divided into three or four parts: Forecastle, Top and Quarterdeck or Forecastle, Foretop, Maintop and Quarterdeck. The crew is then equally divided into these Divisions and each Division is therefore responsible for tasks within these areas, such as cleaning and evolutions (a task that required some organisational effort, such as replenishment of stores or armaments or taking another ship in tow).

In respect of manning for Action Stations, the Divisional System is followed once more. Ships with four gun turrets, for example, name them in order from bow to stern, 'A', 'B', 'X', 'Y'. In the Divisional organisation, the Forecastle would man the 'A' turret, the Topmen 'B' turret, the Marines 'X' turret and the Quarterdeck, 'Y' turret.

The men from each Division mess together and may be divided into smaller companies or platoons for other duties such as landing parties and therefore the men of each Division work, eat and live within the same group. The men within the Division come under the command of either a Lieutenant

Commander or Lieutenant, who is responsible for discipline, training, organisation and clothing of the men.

In order to keep the ship running full time, an around the clock watch system is used, with the Divisions providing two or three watches, known as Starboard and Port or Red, White and Blue. Again, these would be equally subdivided to provide the required manning of the ship all of the time. As such, the 24-hour day is divided into seven watches which include two shortened (Dog Watches) at the end of the day. This odd number meant that the men had different watches every day.

0000 to 0400	Midnight to 4 a.m.	Middle Watch
0400 to 0800	4 a.m. to 8 a.m.	Morning Watch
0800 to 1200	8 a.m. to noon	Forenoon Watch
1200 to 1600	Noon to 4 p.m.	Afternoon Watch
1600 to 1800	4 to 6 p.m.	First Dog Watch
1800 to 2000	6 to 8 p.m.	Last Dog Watch
2000 to 0000	8 to midnight	First Watch

To signal the time of day, a bell is struck every half hour. The 1937 Manual of Seamanship's description, cannot be bettered.

> One stroke of the bell at half-past four, half-past eight and half-past twelve, one more stroke being added for each half hour until eight stokes of the bell, or eight bells are reached at four, eight and twelve. The dog watches are different, 6.30 p.m. being one bell, 7 p.m. two bells, and 7.30pm. three bells, but eight o'clock is always eight bells. 'Little one bell' is a light stroke five minutes after the beginning of a night watch, and calls the watch to muster.

There were of course various tasks aboard ship that had to be carried out continuously and these were undertaken by 'Duty Men' who maintained their own Divisions. Examples of 'Duty Men' being the Quartermaster, who supervises the steering of the ship at sea and the Boatswains Mate, responsible for the conduct of the ships routine and issuing of orders.

There are some tasks that fall under the responsibility of the Duty Men that can be performed by any of the seamen and therefore these are covered by ratings detailed to the task from the watch on deck at the time. These are called 'Tricks'. These duties were often split during a Watch, often being two hours in duration. Duties included, for example, Helmsman, who's duty it is to steer the ship, under the supervision of the Quartermaster and Lookouts who by day are located in the mast head and by night, either side of the bridge. They are tasked with looking out for other shipping, land, lighthouses, shoal waters, wrecks or anything out of the ordinary. They would report the bearing either being Red (Port) or Green (Starboard) off the bow and the relevant compass bearing. Look-outs were relieved every hour.

Herbert was now 32 years old, had 14 years of service in the Royal Navy and three stripes on his arm to indicate that he had maintained Very Good character (as marked in this Navy Record every 31 December from his Captains review), which remained the case throughout his career. A long serving and capable sailor within a crew was invaluable for helping bring on the younger and less experienced men, and it was often the case that 'Boys' were paired with older hands for this reason. Having a career seaman such as Herbert, who had already been out to the East Indies, in a ship almost identical to *Hawkins*, experienced the physical conditions, sea states, homesickness from being far from home, for so long was indeed priceless currency.

Underway again.

The 10 October finally came around and to set the mood the weather was intolerably inclement. Kathleen and the children were wrapped up in their raincoats as the low, dark clouds mercilessly dumped torrents of rain on them and all those who had come to watch *Hawkins* depart. The Royal Marines band played from the Quarter Deck with numbed fingers and sheet music that was sodden and dripping to an audience bedraggled and drowned in the sadness of the moment as *Hawkins* cast off. As Rea comments, 'It was indeed heart-rending to watch that mass of humanity soaked to the skin waving handkerchiefs till growth of distance outstripped vision.'

The first official port of call would be Bombay on the 8 November following the usual outbound route via Gibraltar, Malta and then through the Suez Canal. The passage was not without its moments, especially for the sea sickness prone Rea, whose first experience of a rough and rolling sea came one morning in the Bay of Biscay. He awoke to a very loud bang and looking down at his feet noted; 'To my amazement they were rising, rising rapidly, and I could not prevent them.'

His feet shot towards the ceiling and with that his head banged painfully on the bulkhead behind him. He was now wide awake and took stock of the situation. 'I looked at my carpet and there I saw all my belongings – books, brushes, boots, hats, jug and water bottle – indulging in the frivolity of leapfrog.'

By gripping the wash basin with one hand, Rea managed to shave and prepare for the day, before making his way to breakfast. 'In due course I rolled onto the quarter-deck, where with hypnotic interest I watched the side of the ship – up; down; up; down. Why could I not look away; why did it insist on rolling; and why did I not like the thought of going to breakfast?'

Between Gibraltar and Malta, Rea was to experience a 'following sea', where the direction of the waves was the same as the ships heading. A strong wind brought stinging rain that coupled with the spray managed to soak anyone who ventured on deck. However, it was on deck that Rea found himself as he headed to the Wardroom. He sheltered for a moment behind a gun and then, at the prescribed moment, moved off again only to have his cap snatched by the wind and tossed into the sea. Rea looked aft, '…the stern heaved, then dipped. Before I could gain my balance, I was sprawling on the deck with the water percolating through my waistcoat. By Gosh, it was following us; and overtaking us too!'

Rea made his way to the Poop deck at the rear of the ship, where he watched the waves race up from behind and attempt to overtake her. However there came a change in the resonance of the engines and gradually *Hawkins* began to surge forward, faster and faster. 'The *Hawkins*, as graceful as a bird, flashed along, churning up the foam all around her. It was great; it was thrilling – but why?' The answer was quite simple, *Hawkins* was carrying out a high-speed trial which took her to 28 knots, surfing the following sea.

For the remainder of the commission, it appears that conditions were relatively calm however later, when sailing from Mauritius to Durban, *Hawkins* was tossed like a toy on a southerly gale that increased to such an intensity that the bows were continually plunged deep into the waves. The resulting spray lifted so high that it engulfed the bridge and anything that was not firmly lashed upon deck was carried away which included one of the ships cutters. With each 'dive' the ship was felt to judder with the forces at work. One huge wave, 'completely smashed in the Admiral's Day cabin, the Commander-in-Chief was discovered with a razor in his hand, barricaded behind his floating furniture…'.

Hawkins left Bombay on the 5 December 1932 for a tour of the Persian Gulf, spending Christmas in Basra before heading to her new home port of Trincomalee arriving there on the 24 January 1933. The crew were allowed a day ashore to rest, and on the 25th, James Robinson, one of the Stokers, was returning from a day out most likely with a group of others when he was involved in a tragic accident. According to the 'Sunderland Daily Echo and Shipping Gazette', published on Friday the 27th: 'James Robinson, one of three first-class Stokers belonging to HMS *Hawkins*, of the East Indies Station, was drowned in Trincomalee Harbour as he was stepping into a canoe says Reuters Colombo correspondent. A companion attempted to rescue him but was forced to release his hold on the drowning man owing to the violence of his struggles.'

Not mentioned within 'Nil Desperandum' is the Court Martial on-board *Hawkins* of one of the other two 1st Class Stokers aboard, John Roberts. He was brought before the Court on 8 April charged with 'Wounding with intent to murder' and under the Naval Discipline Act (1860) he was found guilty and given a 7-year prison sentence. At the time, (as reported in the Hampshire Telegraph, Friday 19 May 1933) it was one of the heaviest court martial sentences of the post war years. He was detained in a Colombo prison until he could be transported back to England on HMS *Suffolk*, whence on arrival at Portsmouth he was escorted by the Portsmouth Dockyard Division of the Metropolitan Police to Winchester prison where he would complete the remainder of his sentence. Whether this is connected with the drowning of James Robinson is an intriguing possibility.

Naval exercises of torpedo and gunnery were carried out during the period before the cruise southward for the East African Coast was begun on the 4 April. Then on the 1 May the equator was reached, and the 'Crossing the Line' ceremony took place. The number of men crossing for their first time was far less than that when *Effingham* had done so on Herbert's previous cruise but there were still some notable crimes committed. For example, 'Melody Mills', was charged with endangering the ships companies hearing on Easter Sunday by 'playing five different hymns, each in a separate key, simultaneously.' His punishment being made to 'sing the five hymns solo – the last four under water.' Clearly 'Tubby Blunt' was of some considerable size, noted as having the rank of 'Spherical Seaman' and charged with hazarding King George's Ship *Hawkins* by shifting his weight from one foot to another. His punishment: 'To be totally immersed, if practicable in the bath, and have administered to him slimming pills until the level to the water returns to normal.'

As we have seen in the cruise of *Effingham*, there are a number of crew members who come and go during the two and a half years away, and it is noted that on the second cruise along the African Coast the following year, another 153 men were charged with various crimes when 'Hawkins' crossed the line once more.

On 4 May, *Hawkins* dropped anchor after 4 days at sea to give the crew a break, just off Peros Banhos, one of a small set of Islands that today makes up the British Indian Overseas Territory and contains Diego Garcia, a joint US/UK Military facility. That evening the Paymaster Commander J. Dent and the C-in-C came on deck, each carrying a large chunk of meat that had clearly turned rather nasty and gave off a somewhat awful stench. Together, to the amusement of those who looked on, they attached the meat to large hooks and line, and then tossed them overboard. All who saw it thought the men had lost leave of their senses, however after dinner there came a shout from the Paymaster 'Got him! Got Him!'.

News travelled fast around the ship that something was happening and before long a large number of the crew were peering over the railings at the rather bizarre site of the captain, squatted down at the foot of the accommodation ladder, attempting to lasso the snout of the 12 foot shark that had taken the C-in-C's bait. Above, one of the officers covered the captain with a pistol. The Shark was finally hoisted aboard and weighed in at 500lbs. As with all professional fishermen, the size of the fish was in due course doubled.

At Diego Garcia, another lay-over and another opportunity for some fishing. This time there were many lines in the water around the ship and there was much success. The catch was varied in species and size, a good number being presented to the cook who discarded most as inedible. One evening, Rea was lying on his bunk, reading a book after a long bath, when he heard a curious splashing noise from beneath his scuttle, followed by a flapping sound. Looking up towards his porthole, 'I saw a fifty – pound shark gazing in at me…', however a moment or two later; 'But alas! Just as the beast was raised another few feet the line snapped. Splash, below; and above, a cry as of pain.' Ask any fisherman, and he will concur, the loss of a good fish is like losing a loved one.

650 miles south of Mauritius is the small volcanic island of Rodriguez (sic), which Rea remarks is almost 'Scotch like in appearance'. They stayed but a few

days between the 12 and 15 May. Port Mathurin with its rather narrow entrance for a warship of *Hawkins* size was a challenge and required some quite robust manoeuvers to depart safely without grounding. It was 06:00 when *Hawkins* slipped her berth, many of the officers were in their cabins asleep, with scuttles open to create some respite from the heat. As *Hawkins* gathered pace, she was turned quite hard to starboard, at which all the scuttles on that side dipped below the water. The result was dramatic: 'Schoolie (one of the officers who ran educational classes for the men), conscious of a sudden roll, jumped up to close his scuttle, but a wave of water smiting him on the tummy, almost stunned him as he fell from his bunk; Mr. Doughty still in the bliss of his slumber, was not only deprived of his bed but actually knocked out through his cabin door…' When the water was finally drained from the aft end of the ship, a set of false teeth were found. However, the owner never did come forward with his bar of soap to claim them from the Commanders scran bag.

The first East African stop on the cruise came at Kilwa Kisiwani, a once thriving Swahili port and one of the three main trading centres with the Arab nations along the east coast that included Mombasa and Zanzibar. The word Swahili can be translated into Arabic as 'people of the coast' indeed the Swahili people were very prolific and successful merchants and traders as far back as the 9th Century and reaching out as far as India and China. Of the three ports, Kilwa was quite likely the most important of the three, and there are no less than three ruins there that trace its history from the 10th Century and Arab influence, the Portuguese and finally Omani influence in the 18th Century.

Hawkins arrived on the 7 June 1933 in one of the many short stops made up and down the east coast during this phase of the commission. Time to sample some hunting which was arranged by the District Officer, in particular a shooting party, the quarry being practically anything that moved. The bag included a Kudu and a Bush Buck, however the most prolific of species that habited the wide mangrove lined river that flowed into the sea by Kilwa was Hippopotamus. 'Hippo hunting' by those members of the crew who partook the 'sport' would be highly frowned upon today and certainly would not sit well with the ethics of the modern-day hunting man. Indeed, Rea describes the act of shooting a Hippo in the water as 'a brutal and most unsatisfactory amusement', in the main because a novice in the activity would kill few but wound many. However, Rea states that although there were many splashes in the water from the shots fired, he did not think that one was actually hit!

The hunting continued with the teams firing at all manner of targets from birds on treetops at ridiculous and unattainable ranges to the snouts that occasionally broke the surface of the rivers waters. Rea soon became tired of taking pot shots at these snouts and decided to take a photograph of them instead. His fellow crew members managed to get him in a perfect spot where 4 of the beasts raised their heads out of the water. With fumbling hands, Rea brought the camera view finder to his eye and paused just a little too long before pressing the shutter, much to the chagrin of his fellow crew mates.

However, they rowed ashore and walked a little way to a clearing, whence with a mass of crashing and cracking of branches a hippo charged out of the mangroves into the open. The men levelled their weapons and after at least half a dozen rifle shots had rung out in quick succession, the hippo was down. To their astonishment their accompanying native hunter strode forward and cut off the huge head and once the task was complete, he came towards their small boat with it. The men protested that they could not possibly load the head which no doubt weighed over two hundred pounds into such a small craft. The hunter was rather crestfallen. Rea continues that the dead animal would not go to waste, 'I understand that it is customary for a band of natives to come along and encamp around them until the whole is consumed.'

Onto Mombasa and the inland trip to Nairobi by railway for games tournaments. Trundling through the game reserves everyone was up early to view the animals that could be seen from both sides of the train which included Giraffes, Ostriches and hundreds of Gazelles and Zebra. The paymaster commented that he had seen seven Giraffes standing on the line earlier, and his audience assumed that he had indeed been up earlier than the rest of them to see such a spectacle. When asked how the train managed to get past them he simply replied, and without hesitation, that it just passed between their legs.

The 'Innocents of Chicago' has very much passed into cinematic history, but in 1933 it was a very popular comedy and gangster film, starring Henry Kendall. The advent of films with synchronised speech as opposed to the silent film area had begun in the late '20's but had really taken off with the release of 'The Jazz Singer' in 1927, which was the first feature length film. This new form of cinema was known as a 'Talkie'. *Hawkins* had its own set of equipment for playing 'talkies' which were very popular with the crew (especially the 'Innocents of Chicago') and indeed to locals at all ports of call who were invited to screenings, especially on the trip up and down the east coast of Africa. As is familiar even today, some of the crew enjoyed the film and the lines so much that they recited them at opportune moments, one of the Commanders was often heard to ask his opposite number to accompany him for 'a nice, long, walk…', which anyone who has seen a gangster movie of any kind can surely relate to.

The ship returned to Colombo on the 1 August through to 3 October for the period of Camp at Diyatalawa in the prescribed manner of two weeks per half of the ships company. During the week of camp Leading Signalman John Acourt was taken seriously ill and rushed to Haputele Hospital, however he died on the 17 August and was buried in the Boer Cemetery at Diyatalawa.

Meanwhile, *Hawkins* remained in dock for refit and repair whilst as customary there were a number of functions, parties and visitors aboard ship. This included entertaining the Captain of the German Cruiser *Koln*, which was on a yearlong global tour at the time. Koln was of a similar size to *Hawkins* and would later operate with the Kriegsmarine during World War 2. She was eventually sunk whilst awaiting refit in Wilhelmshaven on the 30 March 1945 during a bombing raid by Liberators of the US 8th Airforce. However, she had one last gasp of breath as she had sunk on an even keel. Whilst her hull was submerged, her superstructure and gun turrets remained above the water line, and these were put to use as a fixed artillery battery to defend the city to the end of the war.

With camp over, *Hawkins* proceeded to Singapore via Penang, in an unusual detour to join the Flagship of the China Station for a Naval conference. *Hawkins* slipped into Penang on the 11 January 1934 and to the crew lining the deck in their finest white uniforms, the scene was definitely oriental. 'Chinese junks with old ragged brown sails through which at many spots the wind whistled cheerfully, crowded the harbour as they trudged along backwards and forwards, seemingly with one objective only, that of reaching some place, some day.'

Penang for 6 days could not have been any more different to their experiences in India, Africa and the Middle East that had been their stamping ground for over a year now. All at once it was a pronounced and welcome change that was everywhere and everything. Smells, colours, countryside, people, all wrapped up in the entrepreneurial enthusiasm that is within the Chinese people; 'There was a glow of business about the whole place.'

Rumours of war

The dockyard at Singapore was still under construction, and indeed some way from completion, when *Hawkins* was berthed in No. 10 Section, Keppel Harbour on the 18 January 1934. The Naval conference commenced on the 23rd and was held aboard the China Station Flagship. HMS *Kent*. Attending were senior officers and their staff from the Australian and New Zealand Navies. The conference lasted 4 days before *Hawkins* departed on the 29th. In between arrival and the conference *Hawkins* was once more the host of functions and visitations whilst dances ashore were organised and several tours of the new Navy Dockyard.

Whilst the stay was a pleasant diversion, Rea notes that the local press were stirring up some unrest in the population with predictions of conflict. It is the first mention in either publication from the East Indies Station that in the wider world there remained tensions amongst Britain, Europe, Germany and Japan that would gather pace towards World War 2. 'If war had broken out while we were in Singapore, I do not think that any of the inhabitants would have been at all surprised, for in this den of cosmopolitanism the newspapers are such successful scaremongers that people are absolutely full of fighting. Indeed, there were times when the less informed on board were rather uncertain as to whether it would be possible for us to get clear of the pugilistic East before war was declared on someone.' Which suggests, the articles were getting into the minds of the crew as well as the locals. So, what was the cause of this pessimism?

Whilst the Battle of Jutland's outcome has always been a matter of debate, the fact that the German High Seas fleet was effectively confined to port for the remainder of the first world war does indeed indicate a Royal Navy victory. That victory was somewhat qualified when war ended. With the job in hand complete, the Commanders of the Navy determined to ensure the surrender of the German Fleet would remind the world and more importantly the people of Britain of the might of the Navy.

Early in the morning of the 21 November 1918 the British Grand Fleet under the command of Admiral Beatty, sailed out of the Firth of Forth to once again meet with the German Fleet. Whilst hostilities had ceased on the 11th, the peace treaty had not been signed and there was a risk that the Germans may just change their minds and fighting would begin again. The German ships were required to form up 50 miles to the east. All of the German ship's crews, with the exception of the engine room were to be on deck and all guns unloaded. In contrast, the Grand Fleet was at action stations, all crews at war readiness with guns loaded and at the ready. This was Operation ZZ.

Beatty organised the fleet to approach the Germans in an almost ballet like manoeuver by forming up the Grand Fleet into two columns, one for the north and the other for the south. The northern column consisted of 19 Battleships, 5 Battlecruisers, 2 Cruisers and 13 Light Cruisers. The southern column contained 14 Battleships, 4 Battlecruisers, one Aircraft Carrier, 1 Cruiser and 12 Light Cruisers.

On reaching the German High Seas fleet (Commanded by Rear Admiral Ludwig Von Reuter) the columns made a 180 degree turn with the North and South Columns taking up flanking positions, whilst in the rear were arranged some 120 British Destroyers that made any attempt at retreat impossible. In the centre, the German Fleet of 70 ships was similarly arranged and once formed up, the procession sailed ahead into the Firth of Forth. It was and remains the largest gathering of warships ever seen. On entering the Firth of Forth the German Fleet were ordered to anchor to the east of Inchkeith, whilst the Grand Fleet remained to the west, blockading the entrance to the Firth and any attempt at escape that may have been contemplated. The German High Seas Fleet had been neutralised, was now in British hands and its internment had been a humiliation and this is important. The Fleet had not yet surrendered. They were still, technically under control of Berlin, belonging to the German Government.

The German Fleet was moved up to Scapa Flow during the following week. The bulk of the crew were taken off the ships, which were left with a small contingent of men. Meanwhile negotiations for the final peace treaty continued in Paris, which dragged on into the new year. The German crews had minimal rations, they were stuck in a location far from civilisation, interned on their ships with little to do. Discipline began to suffer, whilst at a command level, Von Reuter was only getting news updates from the British commanders and from the Times newspaper. Aboard his own ship, the *Emden*, Von Reuter prepared a letter to all his ships commanders detailing a plan to simultaneously scuttle the fleet.

In Paris, the British, French, Italians and US were struggling to come to an agreement on what to do with the German fleet. The French and Italians wanted the ships to be distributed amongst the allies. Agreement could not be reached and so the deadline of the 21 June earmarked for conclusion of the talks was extended. Aboard *Emden*, Von Reuter was made aware of the extension, and in a belief that the talks had broken down, a possibility the fleet would fall directly into British hands, and an uncertain fate thereafter, he ordered the transmission of a single signal in Semaphore or Morse via searchlight; 'Paragraph Eleven, Confirm.' It took a while for the signal to reach all of the ships, which then ran up their black German Navy Colours before the sailors went below and began to open sea cocks and smash pipework. The cold waters of Scapa Flow coursed into the hulls of the German ships, which began to settle in the water, some overturned.

It was a beautiful warm day; the water was calm and hissed from the bow of the little boat *Flying Kestrel* as it chugged through the clear waters. Aboard was a group of 160 children from Orkneys Stromness Higher Grade Public School, on their summer outing. No doubt there was much noise and excitement, as well as the teachers making sure the children behaved. What then occurred was most unexpected, another boat came past and warned the crew of the *Flying Kestrel* not to approach too close to the German Fleet as it appeared many were unexpectedly sinking. 'We watched the last great battleship slide down with the keel upturned, like some monstrous whale,' recalled James Taylor, a 16 year old from the school. 'Suddenly, without any warning and almost simultaneously these huge vessels began to list over to port or starboard; some heeled over and plunged headlong, their sterns lifted high out of the water. Out of the vents rushed steam and oil and air with a dreadful roaring hiss.'[28]

The crews took to lifeboats or other craft, immediately raising white flags, but this was an act of defiance that had to be stopped, and those of the Navy attempted to do so, some with force. Whilst none of the German sailors drowned, 9 were killed when they were fired upon in an attempt to stop them from scuttling the ships. They were the last casualties of the First World War. HMS *Revenge*, which was the Flagship of Admiral Sir Stanley Fremantle, who was charged with guarding the ships, was at sea on exercise (having sailed earlier that day, thinking all was well), when the news was received that the Germans were deliberately sinking their own ships. *Revenge* returned to Scapa

---

[28] (Museum, 2021)

Flow at speed, the site that met them was recorded by Sub-Lieutenant Edward Hugh Markham David, who wrote the following day to his mother: 'A good half of the German fleet had already disappeared, the water was one mass of wreckage of every description, boats, carley floats, chairs, tables and human beings, and the *Bayern* the largest German Battleship, her bow reared vertically out of the water was in the act of crashing finally bottomwards, which she did a few seconds later, in a cloud of smoke bursting her boilers as she went.'[29]

Edward was present aboard *Revenge* when Von Reuter was brought aboard and presented to Admiral Fremantle. Whilst Von Reuter wrote of this meeting in his own memoirs, it appears that Edwards is the only other source to write down the conversation.

At first there was a pause, the German standing at the salute then the following conversation –

Fremantle: I presume you have come to surrender?
Von Reuter: I have come to surrender my men and myself (with a sweeping gesture towards the fast sinking ships) I have nothing else.
Pause
Von Reuter: I take it upon myself the whole responsibility of this, it is nothing to do with my officers and men – they were acting on my orders.
Fremantle: I suppose you realise that by this act of treachery (hissing voice) by this act of treachery you are no longer an interned enemy but my prisoner of war and as such will be treated.
Von Reuter: I understand perfectly
Fremantle: I request you remain on the upper deck until I can dispose of you.
Von Reuter: May my Flag Lieutenant accompany me?
Fremantle: Yes, I grant you that.'[30]

---

[29] (Pruszewicz, 2015)
[30] (Pruszewicz, 2015; Museum, 2021)

Edward then joined a number of men in an attempt to save what they could of the ships that remained afloat. Despite their efforts, 52 ships sank, and whilst most were refloated and scrapped, 7 remain where they sank to this day.

The reaction in Britain was one of anger and outrage at the perceived treachery in the act. The French were furious that the opportunity for their Navy to gain some new hardware was at the bottom of Scapa Flow, whilst the Germans were jubilant in a victory that slapped the allies right across the face. Admiral Reinhard Scheer expressed the feelings of the Navy and indeed of the German people most aptly. 'I rejoice. The stain of Surrender has been wiped from the escutcheon of the German Fleet. The sinking of these ships has proved that the spirit of the fleet is not dead. This act is true to the best traditions of the Navy.'[31]

In a time when these mighty weapons could have been distributed to nations with less than morale intent, there was certainly some sense in the words that Admiral Weymss quietly observed to those close to him. 'I look upon the sinking of the German Fleet as a blessing. It disposes, once and for all, the thorny question of the redistribution of these ships.' Admiral Weymss had been one of the senior staff at the negotiations of the ceasefire that signalled the end of World War 1. He was the one who had the foresight to recognise the significance for future generations of its timing, the 11th hour of the 11th day on the 11th month. He was later involved in the Paris Peace Conference that led to the Treaty of Versailles.

Admiral Von Reuter was certainly not a popular man in Britain. Especially as he stood fast in his resolve that he only did what any other Officer in his position would do. He was most probably right, but this was not an argument at the time that had any weight with the British people. This was clearly illustrated in a report in the Northern Wig newspaper (30 June 1919) about an assault on the Admiral when visiting a bank near where he was being held.

---

[31] From The Northern Wig newspaper, Monday 30 June 1919. British Newspaper Archive

'Admiral Von Reuter had an unpleasant experience at Oswestry on Saturday. He was recognised when he called at a local bank, and when he was leaving the building, he was mobbed. He was hit on the cheek with a rotten egg and otherwise assaulted as he entered his car.'

The Treaty of Versailles was finally signed by the allied powers on 28 June 1919 and would take effect from the 10 January 1920. Germany would pay a very high price, one that would in many ways result in the uniting of the nation and the rise of Nationalism. German territories were redistributed, for example, Alsace and Lorraine were returned to France whilst overseas colonies in China, the Pacific and Africa were taken over by the Britain, France and Japan.

In Military terms the restrictions on the armed forces were massive. The Army was restricted to a maximum of 100,000 men whilst armaments manufacture of armoured cars, tanks, aircraft, poison gases and submarines was prohibited. The Navy was to be but a shadow of the Grand Fleet, with just 6 battleships permitted (obsolete at the time), 6 older Cruisers (with two in reserve), 12 Destroyers and 12 Torpedo Boats (with 4 of each in reserve).

Public opinion in Europe and Great Britain was now in favour of policies that would rebuild their countries as opposed to arming them. There was absolutely no appetite for conflict. The USA and Japan, however, had not been as financially crippled by the war and they began a building program to modernise their Battleship Fleets. Sense did prevail, and in 1922 the USA, Japan, Great Britain, France and Italy signed the Washington Treaty that put a halt to the arms race that was brewing by restricting the expansion of their Navies and providing limitations to the size (in tonnage and armaments) of new ships. The building of new Battleships was prohibited. As a result, the Royal Navy scrapped 46 pre-dreadnaught Battleships and Cruisers, whilst there were similar reductions in the other countries.

Political interest and jostling for supremacy inevitably continued with all of the individual countries looking at ways of maximising the size of their Navies within the constraints of the treaty. Emphasis switched to the building of Cruisers. The Washington Treaty had set a Cruiser design specification of no more than 10,000 tons which was based on the Royal Navy's *Hawkins* Class (of which type of course *Hawkins* and *Effingham* belonged). Between 1924 and 1926, all 5 nations were planning on building a series of these 'Washington' class Cruisers, as they had become known and by 1927/28. Britain for instance, had ordered 13.

In Germany, work began in 1929 in building the *Deutschland* (later renamed *Lutzow*) which was in effect the first of the so called 'Panzerschiff' or 'Pocket Battleships'. *Deutschland* was a prime example of taking the specifications of the treaty to their limits, indeed taking them so far that her design didn't actually fit into any of the categories within the Washington Treaty! It was inevitable that the other countries would follow suit. The building of the *Deutschland* was the beginning of the new arms race. This triggered new treaties, notably the London Treaty of 1930, however it illustrated the disagreements remaining between the countries that neither France nor Italy would sign the London Treaty, despite an attempt to make it more appealing to them later.

Whilst Battleship construction was prohibited, the modernisation of existing Battleships was not, and so both Britain and the US began a program of bringing their ships up to date. Most notable in Britain was the complete overhaul of *Warspite* during 1934 which was present at Jutland and would become the most decorated ship of the Royal Navy during World War 2.

The arms race really built up a head of steam for a number of reasons most notably the rise of Nationalism. In Germany, Adolf Hitler became Chancellor in January 1933 and then in March the Reichstag passed the 'Enabling Act' which effectively made him Dictator. His grip on power strengthened with the banning of opposition parties and Trade Unions as well as clamping down on the Jewish population. The following year, in June this grip was strengthened once more following the 'Night of the Long Knives', where Hitlers final crushing of any opposition came about and in August, following the death of Hindenberg, he was declared Fuhrer.

The rebuilding of the German armed forces began in earnest in 1935. Hitler ordered the re-instatement of the Luftwaffe in February beginning Germany's defiance of the Treaty of Versailles. In March, he announced the full re-armament of Germany, conscription to the Army followed in May. However, in June, the Anglo German Naval Agreement was signed which restricted the growth of the German Navy to 35% of the Royal Navy's size. In shipbuilding terms, Germany was building some very fast and modern capital ships that included *Graf Spee*, laid down in 1932 (Commissioned 1936), *Scharnhorst, Gneisenau* and *Prinz Eugen* laid down in 1935 and 1936 respectively, (both Commissioned 1939) and their biggest Battleships of 50,000 tons the *Bismark* and *Tirpitz*, laid down in 1936 (Commissioned 1940, 1941).

Japan also began a program of Nationalist Expansion in the 1930's. With few natural resources, Japan was keen to protect and stretch her empire to include much of the Pacific from Midway to China. She needed a large Navy to do so and withdrew from the League of Nations (forerunner of the United Nations) in 1934 and renounced all Naval Treaties. In much secrecy, work began on two huge, 70,000-ton Battleships, the *Yamato* and *Musashi* which were ordered in 1937 and commissioned in 1941 and 1942.

The Italians were not to be out done, they too had a plan to build 5 battleships, of which three, *Littorio, Vittorio Veneto* and *Roma* of approximately 45,000 tons were built in the 30's. However, similar to the Japanese, these ships were designed with a full scale naval battle in mind, of the nature and size of a Jutland type engagement which would prove an error. These three ships, and the remainder of the Italian Navy were not equipped with the newly developed radar sets which would prove disastrous later in the Mediterranean theatre during World War 2.

The Royal Navy, on the other hand, had continued to contract in size, although a series of 5, King George IV Class, 45,000-ton Battleships were ordered in 1936 and 1937 which were commissioned in 1940, '41 and '42. It was almost too late. The era of the Battleship was at a high water mark, they were the equivalent of the modern nuclear arsenal until the realisation that Aircraft Carriers were the real projection of power, and in more recent times, surface to surface Cruise Missiles. Fortunately, at this time the Navy had a champion in Admiral of the Fleet, Lord Chatfield who for 5 years, up until August 1938, according to Admiral 'ABC' Cunningham (who we shall hear more of later) 'fought hard against the great difficulties and frustrations to maintain the fighting efficiency and well-being of the modern Navy...'[32]. 'ABC' goes on and does not hold back on his criticism of politicians.

> After a hard struggle he had retrieved the Fleet Air Arm for the Navy, and the Service again stood high in the estimation of the country. He had not succeeded in all he attempted. Short-sighted and parsimonious governments had refused to give him all for which he asked, and there were still wide gaps in our armour after years of unenlightened popular belief in the League of Nations which did not include the United States, and unilateral disarmament which caused many of our still useful ships to be scrapped while permitting other nations to build. A succession of naval treaties which could only be considered disastrous in their effect had caused the Navy to be whittled to the bone, particularly in its building and replacement programmes and the number of its personnel.[33]

Little wonder that the press of Singapore was beginning to discuss the possibilities of conflict in that January of 1934. It would be 8 years later, in February 1942, that the Japanese Army would inflict the biggest military defeat on the British Army in Singapore. For now, *Hawkins* cast off from her mooring and headed back to Trincomalee.

Arrival in Trincomalee on the 6 February 1934 marked the beginning of the final year on station and a period of recuperation time for the crew. Rea describes the arrival in Trincomalee as a 'very welcome sight' for it means that there would be some respite from what often seemed an incessant procession

---

[32] (Cunningham, 1951)
[33] (Cunningham, 1951)

of social engagements and entertaining that became almost wearisome. Once docked and the engines silent, the Staff Officers would pack their belongings and retire ashore with the Commander-in-Chief where they would reside in Navy House, a mansion purchased by the Royal Navy in 1810. It is set in 23 acres of ground, can be accessed by road and from the sea via its own jetty. To this day it is in use by the Sri Lankan Navy as home for their Commander-in-Chief. Many Royal Navy traditions remain in place also.

For the remainder of the crew who reside aboard ship there is plenty to occupy any free time when the working day is done. One man heads off with his butterfly net to collect local insects, one takes a small boat into the harbour with his fishing tackle (with jeers from his crewmates leaning over the rail), another shoulders a rifle to head off hunting. All of the ships motorboats are lowered and in the evening hundreds of the men go ashore to enjoy games either participating or spectating, or just out for a drink ashore. There are a few who simply stay aboard and while away their time by just doing nothing. The beauty and peace of Trincomalee 'has a wonderful way of meeting the approval of everybody.'

On the 22 March, *Hawkins* left Trincomalee for the short trip to Colombo for another refit and period in dry dock, it signalled the second opportunity for the crew to visit camp. Just over a month later, *Hawkins* was underway once more heading for her most southerly port of call during the commission, arriving in Durban on the 2 July. Two weeks later, she headed back up the East Coast of Africa, stopping once more in Kilwa Kisiwani, Zanzibar, Mombasa and the Seychelles and then 'home' to Colombo and Trincomalee at the end of September. A final short cruise during November completed the Commander-in-Chiefs time on the Station, arriving once more in Colombo to remain there between the 1 December and the 17th. A dance was given by the Commander-in-Chief and officers aboard ship on the 2nd and on the 8th the S.S. *Maloja* arrived with Vice Admiral F. F. Rose, C.B., D.S.O., who would be taking over from Dunbar-Nasmith. In the long traditions of the Royal Navy, the Station was handed over to Rose in some style on the 12th.

At 08:00, when his flag was broken in HMS *Colombo*, Vice Admiral Rose saluted Vice Admiral Dunbar-Nasmith's flag with 15 guns, fired by HMS *Colombo*, which salute was returned gun for gun by HMS *Hawkins*. Vice Admiral Rose subsequently proceeded on board *Hawkins* and took Command of the Station.

As the sun dipped below the horizon, Dunbar-Smiths flag was stuck in *Hawkins* and he and his staff then departed for England on the S.S. *Orontes*. *Hawkins* set sail for a Christmas in Karachi, however en route Midshipman Bromage developed appendicitis, so *Hawkins* increased speed to 22 knots to reach Bombay as quickly as possible to deliver the patient safely to hospital.

On Thursday 7 March 1935, the order came for all engines stop and her anchor chains rattled noisily as gravity plunged her anchors to the seabed. For those with a view, or on deck, the lights of Portsmouth twinkled in the clear, cold night. It was very calm, they were home. Almost.

The following day, Kathleen and the children were once again part of the babbling crowd awaiting the return of their loved ones. They heard the great booms rolling over the water from Spithead as *Hawkins* fired a 17 gun salute to the Commander-in-Chief (Admiral Sir John D. Kelly K.C.B.) and the 7 gun reply from the saluting battery before she sailed up harbour at 08:45. *Hawkins* was gleaming in the bright, early spring sunshine that hinted of summer to come. She was painted bright white, her paying off pennant fluttering way behind her, her crew proudly lining the decks as she wafted grandly into Portsmouth before manoeuvering alongside the Fountain Lake Jetty. Once secure, the Unicorn Gates were opened and the crowed rushed forward. Before long, *Hawkins* was filled with reunion, tears of joy, very excited (noisy) children and of course a lot of tales.

'Never mind the 56,400 miles she had sailed, or the 24,565 tons of fuel expended, what about the 3,000 gallons of beer drunk in Trincomalee during March 1933, with 312 gallons alone consumed on the 18th.'

'How about the four seamen manning the diving pump, with a diver below, when 'Stand Easy' was called. 'Stand Easy, sir?' Enquires the seamen. The Officer replies rather incredulously 'But what about the diver below?'

'Oh it's ok, he can have his when he comes up.'

'Or the Stoker who returned to ship somewhat worse for wear, stumbling up the gangway to the Officer on Watch who snaps 'Absentee, eh?' 'Sure, I'll have a cup please."

'Then there was the two stokers who in closing a heated argument shouted, 'You ought to have been twins.' 'Why' says the other blinking slightly confused. 'You're too clever for one."

'What about when we were ammunitioning in Trincomalee, alongside there was lighter and deep within the bowels were a group of Marines, stripped to the waist humping great projectiles. Finally, with much sighing and relief the last shell is loaded ready to be hoisted onto the quarter deck. 'Look out! Last one coming' is shouted from down below. 'Blimey, that's the one we've been looking for!' Comes the reply.'

'Ah, but then there was when we were sat by the railway when the ship was in dock arguing about the width of the rails, when one of us goes and measures it. Then some wag shouts, 'Splendid, Now try the other way.'

Now, those were memories.

Pompey 1936 – 1939

August 1936 and a flat calm sea on a blue Solent. The Downs of the Isle of Wight are greying in a hot haze whilst little waves lick at the side of the odd looking navy grey ship that is imperceptibly turning on its anchor in the tide near the old Stokes Bay pier. HMS *Skylark* is a mining tender attached to HMS 'Vernon', used for running paravanes, picking up dummy torpedoes, mine laying and retrieval and occasionally a diving platform amongst any other job that can be thrown her way. She is a tiny vessel in comparison to *Hawkins*, but she has been the workplace of Herbert for the past 13 months. Being a tender, she has no paymaster and does not tend to stray far from Portsmouth for long, if at all. It has been a good job, almost like being a civilian. Reporting to work on a daily basis, living at home and being able to spend time with the family.

The ship is at Stand Easy for the moment, and the small crew are leaning on the rail, having a smoke and a general chat. Herbert taps his pipe on the rail and looks across the bay off Ryde, where a little cluster of ships can be seen. HMS *Tedworth* and a salvage tug have been out there since 2 July when the submarine, L19 was towed out just to the east of Ryde Pier and deliberately sunk. Divers had been working in between the bouts of poor weather to ready her for raising in a few days time, which would be the first time such a large recovery operation would have been achieved.

In harbour, *Hood*, the largest and most beautiful warship in the Navy is in for a refit, whilst the equally but less elegant (although very purposeful) looking and distinctive bulk of *Nelson*, Flagship of the Home Fleet is also 'in' and currently being visited by a group of French Navy cadets who have arrived on a four-day visit aboard the French Cruisers, *Chacal* and *Leopard*.

For Herbert it is his final week aboard *Skylark*, as he is due to report aboard *Iron Duke* on the 1 September. *Iron Duke*, or 'Iron Duck' as she is known to her crew, is right at the opposite end of the Navy spectrum to *Skylark*. A Battleship of 622 feet in length and 25,000 tons displacement she was a very large ship. *Iron Duke* had been the Flagship of Admiral Jellicoe at the Battle of Jutland and whilst not exactly in the thick of the action her gunnery skills had landed a number of direct hits on the *Keonig* which caused some serious damage. At Jutland she had ten, 13.5-inch guns housed in pairs on the forward 'A' and 'B' turrets, a midships Q turret with another two pairs in the 'X' and 'Y' turrets in the stern. However, under the Washington treaty, her teeth had been somewhat prized away with both the 'B' & 'Y' turrets removed as well as a large portion of her armour plating. Her status in the Fleet had changed too. An old girl, but a useful one, she was attached to the gunnery school 'Excellent' as a training ship.

On 12 May 1937, England crowned a new Monarch, George VI which signalled a special Royal Navy tradition. A Review of the Fleet. The first recorded Royal Fleet Review was held in 1415, prior to Henry V leaving for France, which culminated in the Battle of Agincourt. Thereafter, Royal Fleet Reviews were held at times when there was a mobilisation for war (or a show of strength required for the benefit of England's enemies), the Coronation of a new monarch or in a Jubilee year. The last Royal Fleet Review was in 1977 for Queen Elizabeth II's Silver Jubilee, the one scheduled for her Golden Jubilee in 2002 was (predictably) scrapped due to cost although a review that included a gathering of tall ships did take place in 2005 for the bicentenary of the Battle of Trafalgar. The buildup to the 1937 Coronation Review began on the 13 May with the assembling of the Mediterranean Fleet off Spithead culminating in the review itself on 20 May.

When he was known as Prince Albert, George VI had joined the Navy at thirteen in 1909, passing out of Dartmouth as a Cadet in 1912. He then joined the training ship *Cumberland*. There followed a cruise to the West Indies and Canada returning in September 1913. He was now a Midshipman and was assigned to the battleship *Collingwood* which left for a cruise in the Mediterranean, returning in 1914 to take part in exercises with the Home Fleet before the Naval Review that same year. This particular review was, according to Winston Churchill, who was First Sea Lord at the time, 'incomparably the greatest assemblage of naval power ever witnessed in the history of the world.'

King George V was of course present aboard the Royal Yacht, *Victoria and Albert* and as required he inspected many of the ships on review. On the morning of the 19 July 1914 the fleet dispersed for exercises, the Royal Yacht anchored off the Nab. The fleet included some 54 battleships, of which twenty were Dreadnaughts, four battle cruisers, sixty-nine cruisers, one hundred and forty-nine destroyers and sixty submarines. It took over six hours for the fleet to pass the Royal Yacht. As Churchill put it afterwards; 'One after another these ships melted out of sight beyond the Nab, they were going on a longer voyage than any of us could know.' Indeed, this was the case, for just over two weeks later, the First World War began.

Prince Albert sailed with the fleet in *Collingwood* which took part in the Battle of Jutland. Albert was stationed in one of the fore turrets which housed a pair of 12-inch guns. To those who served with him it was said that he mixed well with all ranks and of course, did his duty like the rest of the crew. According to Captain Taprell Dorling, D.S.O., F.R.Hist.S., R.N. or 'Taffrail' as he was known, the Prince; 'Coaled ship, ran a boat, kept watch, and, it is said, answered to the name of Mr. Johnston.'

The Prince joined the Royal Naval Air Service in February 1918, attending Cranwell Air Station before transferring to the RAF when both the R.N.A.S and the Royal Flying Corps was amalgamated into the Royal Air Force in April. Whilst his career as a serving naval officer was over, he did remain on the active list and was appointed a Commander when he was created the Duke of York. He married Lady Elizabeth Bowes-Lyon in 1923 and as we know from our voyage to the East Indies with *Effingham* he and the Duchess departed on a world tour aboard HMS *Renown* in 1927 which brought him back into Navy life for the duration. On ascension to the throne, he was made Admiral of the Fleet and so would review his fleet during that May of 1937 from what was now his Royal Yacht, the *Victoria and Albert*.

The ships were arranged for the review in 8 lines, with the head of each at the eastern end of Spithead stretching westwards for around 10 miles beginning just south of Southsea Castle to Cowes. Each line was annotated from A to H, with line A to the north. *Iron Duke* was at anchor in an appropriate location for her past station in the fleet, 4th place in Line E, one of the two Battleship lines with *Revenge, Barham* and *Queen Elizabeth* ahead, *Hood* directly behind followed by *Repulse* and then the fledgling Carrier Fleet before a long line of heavy cruisers. Out to starboard line F included the fleet battleships, *Nelson, Rodney, Royal Oak, Ramillies, Resolution* and *Royal Sovereign*. In line G the ships belonging to the foreign visitors assembled, 17 in total. Either side of these large ship lines came the lines of smaller vessels of all shapes and sizes from submarines to light cruisers. In all, a total of 145 Royal Navy ships were present.

The foreign visitors proved quite challenging to accommodate, especially as the crews had trips ashore arranged which included days out to London. It was challenging, because some of the countries that were represented were not the best of friends and some would of course soon be most unwelcome in British waters. The *Graf Spee* represented Germany, whilst the cruiser *Asigara* came all the way from Japan. The battleship *New York* was familiar to the Royal Navy as it had been attached to the Grand Fleet during the last war, whilst the *Dunkerque* was the new French Battleship designed to meet the threat of the likes of the *Graf Spee*. The *Marat* represented the U.S.S.R.

In order that clashes of a nationalistic nature were avoided, all foreign libertymen were landed through "Vernon" at the South Railway Jetty. As Commander Webb writes in his history of that particular shore establishment. 'all foreign libertymen passed through 'Vernon', with times suitably staggered to avoid the Germans meeting the Russians and the Russians meeting the Japanese.'[34]

The uniforms, conduct and the fact that these men, whilst sailors, were simply tourists in another country is aptly described once more by Commander Webb. 'It was amusing to see the Russians landing from their drifter in the early morning, bound for the Tower of London or some other capitalist stronghold. Immediately on landing there was one cigarette all round and the air was filled with Eastern perfume. The next moment they had all fallen in and were marching smartly to the gate in their blue and white striped flannels, specially bought for the occasion and reminiscent of Tsarist

---

[34] (R.N., 1956)

days. The Germans, too, from the *Graf Spee* had a special walking-out dress, with round jackets and trousers fitting very tightly across the seat.'[35]

The King and Queen arrived by train at the South Railway jetty on Wednesday 19 May, boarding the Royal Yacht for an evening of entertaining. The following day, at 10:30 aboard the *Victoria and Albert* a stream of official visitors was introduced to the King, which included the Commanders of all the visiting foreign ships. Then at around 15:00 the Royal Yacht cast off and with the Trinity House vessel *Patricia* leading the way, followed by an entourage of ships in procession, the review began. It took over two hours to complete before the *Victoria and Albert* was safely secured at her mooring ahead of *Queen Elizabeth* in what was 'E' line. There followed a growing drone as several squadrons of R.N.A.S. Swordfish carried out a fly past before dinner was served.

Aboard *Nelson*, Lt. Commander Tommy Woodroffe had been enjoying the day with old colleagues that culminated in dinner in the wardroom. Since his retirement from the Navy, he had become a respected radio commentator for the BBC and had already covered the opening ceremony of the 1936 Olympics. On this particular evening he was tasked with broadcasting a description of the fleet illuminations, where every ship would be decorated with lights which would outline their forms in the darkness. However, by 22:00, the sun had indeed gone down well below the yard arm.

There is little doubt that in homes around the country, jaws dropped, and couples looked at each other with all manner of reactions as Tommy began his broadcast. It quickly became apparent that he was very, very drunk. For about four minutes he slurred with great regularity 'It's lit up!' (referring to the fleet) and that the scene was "like fairy land". Towards the end he declares, 'It's gone! It's gone! There's no fleet! It's…it's disappeared! No magician who ever could have waved his wand could have waved it with more acumen than he has now at this present moment. The fleet's gone. It's disappeared.' Whether the ships lights had been turned off, *Nelson* had perhaps shifted around in her

---

[35] (R.N., 1956)

moorings, or poor Tommy had simply fallen on his back and was now looking at the sky we will never know for sure. One can imagine a phone in the control room ringing, the technician picking it up and holding it away from his ear as a producer shouts at the top of his voice, 'For god's sake get him off air!' Poor Tommy and his ramblings were faded out after 4 minutes.

Leading up to that fateful summer of 1939 life no doubt went on regardless, people went to work, they took holidays, went to the pub, theatre and cinema. There was of course the Coronation to celebrate, Snow White and the Seven Dwarves was released in December 1937, the first full length colour animated film by Walt Disney. The Mallard gained the world record as the fastest Steam Locomotive in 1938 (125.88mph) and whilst on the subject of speed, the RMS *Queen Mary* regained the Blue Ribband for the fastest crossing of the Atlantic. Superman appeared in the first addition of Action Comics in June 1938, Batman the following year. For Herbert and Kathleen, the January of 1938 brought the arrival of Eileen into the family.

The last day of 1938 marked the twentieth anniversary of Herbert's career in the Royal Navy. He was 38 years old, a husband and father or four children. Kathleen was a Navy wife, she was used to him being away from home and she had endured 5 years on her own during their married life, bringing up the children and looking after their home. However, the biggest test was yet to come. Most combatants in a war are made up of the young, with little or no fear and a sense of invincibility. Age and experience temper the emotions on the one hand but strengthen on the other in particular where friendships and family are concerned. There is a realisation that where a life for oneself and loved ones has been built, it has to be protected and that life itself is a fragile gift. Herbert had to deal with the realisation that in the final years of his career in the Navy, he would most likely have to go to war, and he may not survive. No one could know how long this would last or where it would lead, but the threat from belligerent nations had to be faced. Herbert did have twenty years of training and experience behind him, and he must have had confidence in the men around him and the equipment that he would go to war with. He would need both as the enemies that were facing Britain and the world were formidable and ruthless.

The clouds of war continued to gather at a pace. Hitlers grip on power increased as did the size, complexity and strength of the German military. On the other side of the world, Japan was restless and nationalistic whilst Mussolini (March 1938) was granted control of the Italian Military. Almost too late, Britain was re-arming herself, as was the United States although her policies of isolationism would mean that it would take a monumental event to bring that country to the aid of Europe and Britain as the War took hold on the world. Austria finally became one with Germany, Czechoslovakia was annexed, Neville Chamberlain announced 'Peace in our time'. Then Poland was invaded by Germany and that, was that.

At 16:30 on the 16 March 1939, The Parliamentary Secretary to the Admiralty, Mr. Geoffrey Shakespeare stood to address M.P.s in Westminster on the state of the Royal Navy. He was there to ask for £149 million for the Navy of which £61 million would be earmarked for the continuation of the current ship building programme that would give the Navy a total of 21 Capital ships by 1943 and the modernisation of some of the existing fleet. He described the power of the Capital ship in layman's terms to his attentive audience. 'To give some idea of the power of the 16-inch gun, it is as if I went into Palace Yard where the cars are parked and picked up a car of medium size weight and threw it with great precision at St. Albans and I could throw many of them a minute.'[36]

The ship building programme that combined the current work in progress with that of the coming year was staggering. Two 10,000-ton cruisers of the *Southampton* class were almost complete. These were the *Belfast* (which is preserved by Tower Bridge in London) and the *Edinburgh*. In addition, over the next 12 months the following were predicted to join the fleet. 9 battleships, 6 aircraft carriers, 25 cruisers, 43 destroyers, 19 submarines and various smaller craft. Not only were these ships modern in design they incorporated the latest developments in fire control and anti-aircraft armaments. To give some weight to this statement, Shakespeare declared that pre war expenditure

---

[36] (Parliament)

on this kind of technology in a capital ship was £11,000; now it had risen to £200,000.

To continue the theme of confidence, Shakespeare outlined the three perceived threats to the modern Royal Navy. Firstly, a fleet action. The strength of the current Navy and with the building programme in place covered this eventuality. Secondly, the threat from Submarines. However, the previous war experience and the lessons learned in the protection of the Convoy system meant that this was also covered. Finally, the threat from air power. In a staggering display of naivety and ignorance that would come back to haunt all concerned, the threat (especially to Capital ships) was dismissed. It was argued that the anti-aircraft guns deployed would force bomber aircraft to heights above 10,000 feet which would require highly accurate bombing of which techniques had not (yet) been developed. Besides, bombing from this height necessitated a bomb release as far as two miles away from the target. Even if a bomb did find its mark, the deck armour was designed to withstand plunging fire from another warship that had far more kinetic energy than a bomb released from an aircraft. Of course, a torpedo could be delivered from an aircraft, but this was covered not only by the anti-aircraft fire but the underwater armament that was now a standard feature of the larger warships.

All the same, the Royal Navy was clearly on the front foot, with an ambitious building and upgrade in progress, and a capable experienced core of sailors that were being joined by many young men who wished to sign up. In the previous year there had been 70,000 applications to join the Navy of which 18,000 officers and men were recruited bringing the total number of men employed in the Navy to 121,000 and a figure of 133,000 proposed for the end of 1939 which would necessitate recruiting a further 19,000 officers and men.

To return to the ship building programme, Shakespeare followed up his statement that the *Belfast* and *Edinburgh* were near completion with the following: 'Equally satisfactory are the reports on our new heavily armed and fast destroyers of the 'Tribal' class, of which two flotillas are now with the Fleet.'[37] One of these 'Tribals' was His Majesties Ship, *Nubian*.

---

[37] (Parliament)

Part 2

H.M.S Nubian

Chapter 4

Tribal Destroyer

Commissioning

John I Thornycroft began building ships from the 1860s from a yard in Chiswick, specialising in the design of high speed boats and ships of all sizes and uses, from paddle steamers to Royal Navy vessels. However, as those designs got larger and bolder, the ability to sail these vessels under the bridges of London became an increasing problem. A new home for J.I.T (as its workers called the firm) was required, and in time the yard at Woolston on the River Itchen estuary, near Southampton was chosen.

Thornycroft's had won a contract to supply two of the modern Tribal Class Destroyers to the Royal Navy, the first of these to be completed was job 1138/38 HMS *Mohawk*. Earmarked as a flotilla leader it had been the centre of much attention during construction and commissioning. Her cleanliness was noted by all who visited her, a trait that was to continue throughout her life as an active warship.

The second of these Destroyers job 1139/38 was, at the beginning of December 1937, almost ready for launch, the date set to coincide with the high tide on the 21st. December 1937 began very cold with snow falling heavily in the south, so hard that on the 8th and 9th it almost cut off the New Forest by blocking local roads. But as the month progressed some milder air brought rising temperatures and fog, which lingered and barely lifted during the day.

The launching of a new ship was a very special day, the culmination of much hard work by the men of J.I.T. The ship wrights removed all the wooden supports during the morning, and the new vessel was poised on its waxed sled, ready for launch.

A scaffold rostrum was in place, the traditional rig set up with champagne bottle poised to be dashed against the bow at the appropriate moment. A Royal Marine band is likely to have played some rousing tunes as the dignitaries gathered in an air of anticipation and excitement, despite the damp and cold that restricted visibility to just across the opposite bank of the Itchen, a few hundred yards away.

The honour of naming this new ship fell to Mrs. Wake Walker, wife of Admiral Wake Walker, who later, commanded HMS *Norfolk* in the shadowing of the *Bismark* leading up to the laters sinking in 1941. Dressed in black overcoat, brimmed hat and carrying a matching handbag, Mrs. Wake Walker appears grim faced as she utters the immortal words 'I name this Ship, HMS *Nubian*', as the champagne bottle explodes when it hits the purposeful bow. The men doff their hats and there is a huge 'crack!' as the restraining wood is removed. For a moment nothing happens, then as the friction grows and the wax melts, the grease does its magic and the grey form of the *Nubian* glides down the slipway. Entering the water for the first time, *Nubians* stern throws up a plume of Itchen spray. All the vessels in the vicinity blow their whistles, horns, sirens to celebrate the birth of a new ship. Pathe news is on hand to film the occasion, the commentator addressing the microphone in the inimitable, rushed and clipped tones of the time.

> At the Woolston works of Messer's Thornycroft there is forged another link in Britain's chain of Naval re-armament. Mrs. Wake-Walker names HMS *Nubian*, second of the Tribal class of destroyers. And another 2000 tons is added to Britain's wall of defence.[38]

---

[38] (1937)

Once in the water a gaggle of small boats surround the newborn ship. Bunting is rigged from stem to stern. She rides high above her water mark as at present she is simply a shell. There is some of her superstructure in place, but no guns, funnels, engines or propellers to thrust her forward against her enemies. There is much work to do, and it will take a further 12 months before she is commissioned into the Navy with the pennant of L36.

Herbert could almost feel Christmas coming, it was the 8 December 1938, and he was stood with the steaming party on the platform of Portsmouth Station ready to take the train journey to Woolston to join his new ship, HMS *Nubian*, pennant now F36. Meanwhile, at the Thornycroft yard, Commander Richard William Ravenhill was making last minute preparations with his 1st Lt. Commander Robert Tindal Lampard and the junior officer Lieutenant John Duyland Bush for the forthcoming sea trials of their new ship which included sorting the Commissioning Cards for the men. Both Officers had been handpicked for their experience and abilities.

Ravenhill was born in Retford, Nottinghamshire in 1901 and had joined the Navy at the age of 14, promoted to Lieutenant by the time he was 22 and Commander at 35. He was a career sailor, known for being good at getting along with all types of people, most notably both senior and junior ranks. He was a big man, and despite being physically fit, he had an appearance of being portly, a trait that followed him through his career. Philip Mack, the Commanding Officer of the 14th Destroyer Flotilla, of whom we shall here much of, later, wrote an assessment of Ravenhill in March 1941, providing us a foretaste of what the men of *Nubian* could expect in the coming months.

> This Officer possesses good sound common-sense in more than his fair proportion and he combines it with intelligent anticipation and an excellent knowledge of his job. He wields a strong and cheerful influence for good. He is most tactful in dealing with both seniors and juniors and has a happy and efficient ship. He has a great sense of

humour, very good social qualities and is an excellent 'mixer'. He keeps himself physically fit although inclined to stoutness.[39]

Lampard was 2 years junior to Ravenhill. He was born in India in 1905 but his home was now in the little village of Aveton Gifford in South Devon, not far from Burgh Island, where the rich and famous would holiday in the gaudy art deco hotel. His mother and father, Percy and Ann had settled there after their time in India. Another career sailor he entered the service in 1918 when aged just 13. Most likely as part of the Selborne Scheme, which took prospective Naval Officer Cadets at 12 or 13 years of age. They spent 2 years initial training at the Royal Naval College based in Osborne House, the former home of Queen Victoria on the Isle of Wight. After this, cadets were transferred to Britannia, the Royal Naval College, Dartmouth. Once passed out, Lampard followed the standard career route of a two years at sea as a Mid Shipman with just over a year aboard *Revenge* (a Super Dreadnaught), followed by a 4-month posting to *Vortigern* (a V-Class Destroyer) before returning to *Revenge* for a further 9 months. He became a Lieutenant in June 1928. Clearly destined for the higher ranks, his service record stated that his experience and tactful handling of the men showed good leadership potential, and this would prove most useful to his new Commander in the coming months.

Bush was somewhat more volatile. At 24 he was the epitome of what a Navy Officer should be. He was fit and rather fiery of nature, which, combined with his red hair had earned him the nick name 'The burning Bush'. He was born in Bristol, educated at Clifton College, but did not excel academically. Having spotted 4 destroyers in the Bristol channel one day he decided that a career in the Royal Navy was for him, and he never looked back, thoroughly enjoying life in the service he excelled as a cadet. His first posting was on the China Station before returning to England, where he chose to serve in destroyers. He was one of 3 Officers assigned to *Stronghold*, an S-Class Destroyer that was attached to the carrier *Furious*, her job was to follow the aircraft carrier about and pick up any aircrew that ditched, she was even equipped with a crane for

---

[39] (Admiralty, 1945)

recovering aircraft. Of his time in *Stronghold*, he later commented in an interview with the Imperial War Museum, that he had the opportunity to learn much about the running of a ship as part of her senior crew. On being picked to join *Nubian* he thought her a 'beautiful ship' and commented that his Commander was a 'very good captain'. His career would lead him to captaincy by 27 and the status of Admiral at the end of his career.[40]

Both men were looking forward to their challenge ahead. *Nubian* was going to be a fine ship, it would be manned by some of the most experienced seamen in the service who would mentor and shape those who were new to the Navy. The past months had been hard work, ensuring the contractors were on schedule for the ships Commissioning. Once launched, work had swiftly begun to add in her propulsion units, consisting of 3 oil fired Admiralty boilers, whose 44,000 horsepower would propel *Nubian's* 377ft and 190 personnel to 35.8 knots (taken from her trials).

Then came her armaments. 4 main turrets ('A' & 'B' forward, 'X' & 'Y' aft) each housing a pair of 4.7-in. guns, in addition there were 4, 2-pounder guns and 8, half inch as well as machine guns. There were 4 torpedo tubes (21-inch), one depth charge rail and 2 depth charge throwers. *Nubian* was a state-of-the-art war machine. Fast, powerful and for her time, a very complex weapon.

News came to the three men that the train with the steaming party had arrived, and the crew were currently being provided with hot soup in a nearby drill hall. They would be ferried out to the ship within the hour and then, along with a contingent of contractors, the trials flag could be raised, and they could get under way.

Out in the Solent, *Nubian* forged through the swell with ease. The engines resonated through the hull with a comforting throb. On the bridge, Ravenhill, Lampard, Bush and a gaggle of contractors began to plan the exercises ahead. The trials commenced with speed tests, that would be carried out in various sea states over the next few days, starting at low power and building up to full

---

[40] (Bush, 2005)

power, taking readings from directly into the tide and at 180 degrees to it. Stopping tests, or 'Crash Ship' followed. These were again, carried out at various speeds. As the speeds built the manoeuvers became increasingly violent as the ship's engines were flung into full astern and the wheel put hard over to either port or starboard like a handbrake turn in a motor car. The distance from the moment the engines were reversed to a full stop (zero knots) was recorded.

Onto Maneuverability tests, more violent turns as *Nubian* was zig zagged and spiralled across the sea, churning it to a white foam before it was time for the more sedate endurance tests to record the fuel flow, exhaust, water cooling and speed achieved. Once complete *Nubian* returned to the traditional mooring point off Netley Roads. The team of constructors were ferried ashore, and the ship settled down to what would now be her career in the Royal Navy.

Rolling trials

HMS *Nubian* almost looked forlorn, a naughty thoroughbred who has just been broken. She sat hull down in the middle of Portsmouth's No. 3 basin, a slack hawser keeping her in position, into a light westerly breeze, the like of which at this time of year was 'lazy' and cut through anyone who happened to be standing around. Herbert was amongst 117 men stood around that day, in groups of 4, on makeshift planks across her deck. 'This is bloody ridiculous', was muttered many times from the mouths of many of the men, for what they were about to do was indeed out of the ordinary.

The days before had been spent fuelling *Nubian* to 97% of her capacity, taking on board a full complement of ammunition including torpedoes, filling her water tanks to capacity and embarking all possible stores, so that she would sit as low in the water as possible. It was bloody hard work. Then the platforms were added, the forward of which was between the funnels and necessitated the removal of the boats, their davits and the machine guns. The second plank was aft of the rear funnel, across the torpedo tubes.

Now the rolling tests that *Nubian* had been prepared for could begin. It was a quiet day, there were the odd sounds of men calling to one another in the dockyard, a clang of metal here and there, a train whistling in the distance. *Nubians* engines were silent, but a diesel engine soon rattled into life with a cough and a belch of blue exhaust to ensure the ship had lighting and the Sperry measuring equipment was powered. On the forward plank were 34 men, and on the rear, 84. On the command from an officious looking man with a megaphone, the men would run from one side of the ship to another. 'Don't forget to stop!', shouted one wag, as they all set off.

Nubian rocked under the feet of the men, gradually listing from one side to the other. A total of 6 measurements were taken, with the largest reading showing a 7.5-degree maximum angle of roll obtained. In the end, all rather inconclusive and as the men agreed later at dinner, 'a bloody good waste of time'.

A waste of time it may have been, but *Nubian* was stored and ready to depart although for the moment she had guns to fight with but no sights to aim them with. The rest of the 1st Destroyer Flotilla had already left for Malta which left the *Nubians* kicking their heels for the time being. Herbert managed to get some leave to spend with the family and was to report back the following week. The threat of war was like a dark cloud gathering towards the horizon although it was not omnipresent nor overbearing, but if your mind's eye wandered for a moment then that cloud was definitely there. As the day approached that Herbert would have to return to the ship, Doreen gave him a horseshoe for luck, he promised he would keep it with him at all times.

Returning aboard there was much to do to keep one's mind from their impending departure. Re checking the stores began under the supervision of the Coxswain, who was responsible for victualing (as well as steering the ship during battle). Water was already stored in tanks within the Lower Deck, one of *Nubians* four decks, whilst the food and perishables were kept in the Cold

Rooms on the same level. The Gunner, Frank Miller, was supervising the checking of the Torpedoes, Depth Charges and 4.7-in. shells in the aft magazines which were also on the Lower deck, whilst Chief Ordinance Officer Charles Aubrey Wilson Foreman was ensuring the 4.7-in. shells for 'A' and 'B' guns were secure in the forward magazines. In between these compartments were the fuel tanks for the boilers.

Situated in the centre of the ship were five very large compartments. The forward three housed a boiler each, of which the forward two exhausted into the larger of *Nubians* two funnels, the third out of the smaller aft funnel. Behind the boilers was the engine room aft of which came a smaller gearing room containing the main electrical switch board. The propeller shafts were connected to the gearing room and housed in tunnels that slanted towards the stern. Engine Room Artificer George Thompson Foy and Chief Stoker David Chun controlled the operation of the machinery spaces, Chun was arguably the oldest member of the crew having been born in 1892 and was the holder of the British Empire Medal. The remainder of the engine room team included ERA 3rd Class Anthony Edward Sadler and Stoker Petty Officers William Frank Knight and George Hawson Morten.

Herbert, meanwhile, sought out a living space that would afford him as much comfort as possible, with as little disturbance as could be derived in a tightly packed ship. His seniority through age, experience and respect did give him some level of choice, perhaps a bunk within the smaller forward crew area on the Lower Deck? It did not suffer from the disturbance of crew members trying to reach the canteen or the Heads as it had only the Cable Locker and the ASDIC Room co located towards the bow. Above was the Upper Deck and the larger of the Crews mess decks. The Upper Deck stretched from the Stem (the forward part of the Bow) to behind the aft funnel, with the crews mess in the forward part, the Canteen, Washrooms, and Heads to the rear. Space for the Oilskin Room, Potato Store, Fire Control and Transmitting Stations were also within the Upper Deck.

Tradition dies hard, especially in the Royal Navy and in the design of the Tribal Destroyers the Officers accommodation was, like the sailing vessels of the Nelson era, in the stern. The problem with this arrangement in a modern warship, was the aft gun crews would have to traverse almost the length of the ship from their forward quarters to man their guns. This would of course cost time in manning the guns at 'Action Stations', and could be awkward, especially if midships mounted torpedo tubes were at readiness (pointing to Port or starboard). In later designs, such as the 'U' Class Destroyers, the commanding officer's quarters were centrally located and the gun crews aft, a more practical solution.

The aft Lower Deck housed the Wardroom and Officers cabins, the Ships Office, Engineer Officers Cabin, the Wireless Telegraphy Office and the Gunners Office and torpedo stores. Above this (the Quarter Deck), was the rearward superstructure, within which the Commanding Officer had his quarters and the relative luxuries associated with his seniority. Ravenhill was afforded a hardwood panelled Sleeping Cabin, Day Cabin and Washroom with toilet and bath, he also had his own pantry. Roger Hill described the CO's quarters of *Jervis* (which would have been very similar to *Nubian's*) in 'Destroyer Captain'.

> There was a big mahogany dining-table, a large writing desk, a settee the length of the wall along the ship's side, a deep blue armchair which was so comfortable I went fast asleep whenever I sat in it, and all sorts of lights and radiators. The bunk was almost a double bed and the bathroom led off to the sleeping cabin.[41]

Next door was the Sick Bay where Surgeon Lieutenant Cooke and Sick Berth PO Frank Clifford Harvison would treat any sick or wounded. To the rear of the structure was the Engineering workshop and 'Y' turret. Above, a blast shield protected 'X' turret and moving forward the aft mast, control position (for emergency steering), the 2-pounder gun and a 36-inch

---

[41] (Hill, 1979)

searchlight. In between the fo'c'sle deck and the aft funnel were the torpedo tubes.

The forward superstructure was atop the fo'c'sle deck. It too had a blast shield to protect 'B' turret when 'A' turret (on the fo'c'sle deck) was in action. Within the lower portion of the superstructure the CPO's PO's and ERAs had their cabins, a shared accommodation for two with a bunk bed arrangement. The engineering office and drying room were also on this level. Above was the command portion of the ship with an open bridge. As one would expect the Bridge was equipped with the latest range finding and directional control for the aiming and firing of not only the 4.7-in. main armament, but the Anti-Aircraft guns too; it also had an ASDIC cabinet with a repeater display from the ASDIC Office.

Just forward of the bridge, the wheelhouse was shaped to deflect the blast from 'B' turret and the wind from the forward motion of the ship which made the bridge a relatively sheltered place to be, despite being open to the elements. The wheelhouse itself was a very confined, narrow space, the helm, telegraph gear and speaking tubes taking up much of the space, although it was bullet proofed. There was little room left for the Quartermaster (or Coxswain) and his helmsman, whilst there were just two small scuttles on the port and starboard sides and a rectangular window to the front. Placing the wheelhouse forward of the Bridge had a positive effect of lowering the overall silhouette of the Tribals.

The Signal Office, plotting table, Charthouse, Direction Finding Office and Commanding Officers Sea Cabin were accessible behind the Bridge as was the Director Control Tower, Rangefinder and Anti-Aircraft Director. A Tripod Mast with Crowsnest for lookout was positioned directly behind accommodating the aerials for the Direction Finder and Medium Frequency sets which gave the ship the capability, with a 'sister ship', to gain a triangulation fix from an enemy ships radio transmission.

George Scicluna was one of the daymen aboard ship and like Herbert had been born in 1900. He had been a waiter before joining the Navy in May 1918 and served for 12 months aboard *Ark Royal*, the second ship of that name that was originally designed as a freighter but modified to carry and launch seaplanes, which were deployed overboard by crane. He then joined *Iron Duke* until 1926, leaving the service for a short while but returning in 1927. On assignment to *Nubian* he held the position of Leading Steward and oversaw the running of the wardroom. He was particularly keen for *Nubian* to depart for Malta, where he had been born. He was busy serving refreshments to Lt. Busch and his officers, who were meeting in the wardroom having been detailed by the commander to review the watch list. George was trying not to listen in on the discussion, and soon returned to his Stewards Mess on the same deck, to await further requests.

The Officers meeting had to come up with a Divisional and Watch system so that the crew could maintain a battle readiness at any time of the day. This was to be a combined 3 Division and Watch system as required for operation in wartime where each Division had the capability of cruising and fighting the ship. When Roger Hill joined the destroyer *Jervis* in February 1944, he found the ship had been run on a two watch system, which he immediately changed, as he describes in 'Destroyer Captain'.

> I found the ship had been in two watches all the war; which meant the men did four hours on and four hours off. Over a long period they became tired and, since one went to action stations when there is any kind of alarm, I always felt it was an unnecessary strain.
>
> If the men are in three watches and have four hours on and eight hours off, they have time to sleep, wash, eat and relax, whilst I had no hesitation in pressing the bell for action stations on any alarm.[42]

Nevertheless, with a crew of 190 aboard *Nubian* this was not simple to organise, for example, the 4.7-in. guns required 11 men (each) to keep up a firing rate of 12 rounds per minute (usually more like 8 or 10 rounds in practice). The crew of each 4.7-in. gun consisted of a Gun Layer, Trainer, two

---

[42] (Hill, 1979)

breech workers, two tray workers, four shell suppliers (positions of which George and the other servants/stewards would fulfil) and a sight trainer.

Further manpower challenges came with allocation of 4 Quartermasters, made up of perhaps one Leading Seaman and three Able Seamen. Able Seamen would be provided as backup helmsmen. The Engine Room staff would of course maintain their own separate Division, whilst two or three men were required as messengers. *Nubian* had two 27ft motorboats a Whaler and a dinghy that needed crews on standby not to mention the depth charge, torpedo and anti-aircraft gunners and signalmen. It was a manpower juggling act but finally it was complete, and *Nubian* was ready to sail.

The Mediterranean – 1939

The mouth of Valetta and the Grand Harbour of Malta was not a new experience for Herbert though to his surprise *Nubian* carried on past and into the Sliema Harbour instead to her berth with the other destroyers. The voyage from Portsmouth had not been eventful, and neither had their departure which was a far cry from the bands and waving crowds that had seen off *Effingham* and *Hawkins* all those years before. They had departed on a Saturday, so the family had come to wave the ship away. Departure had been exciting for the boys aboard, as indeed there were a large number which in the early days of Tribal Destroyer deployment was the norm. For the older sailors, some mixed emotions. They were off on a cruise but that dark cloud was still there, the prospect of some form of contretemps with either Italy, Germany or perhaps even Spain in her final throws of Civil War was indeed a possibility. Whatever, there was another reason for a quietness amongst the crew, they were not sure when they would be back.

The stay was a short one, there were the Home Fleet exercises to attend. *Afridi* led the 1st Destroyer Flotilla to Gibraltar on the 23 February. *Mohawk* the epitome of spit and polish with her bands of red, white and blue adorning 'B' turret was reunited with her sister ship from Woolston. The painting of 'B' turrets with the colours of the Union Jack appears to have been normal practice at the time, and there are photographs of *Nubian* and indeed of *Warspite* from this period with the same paintwork. Its primary purpose was to clearly identify Royal Navy ships operating in the Mediterranean at a time when the lines between supposed allies was a little blurred, especially where Spanish and Italian forces were concerned. Along for the ride were *Cossack, Gurkha, Sikh, Maori* and *Zulu*. Together they powered their way across the Mediterranean creaming the blue waters into wakes that fanned out way behind them. They were a pack of happy spaniels in rough cover, crisscrossing and zig zagging their way practicing formation maneuvers.

Slowing to catch their breath the flotilla arrived in Gibraltar that was rammed with Service Grey ships of all sizes. As the Hampshire Telegraph had reported on the 17th February the fleet assembled was made up of over 100 ships. 'The ships engaged will include the battleships *Warspite, Barham, Malaya* and *Ramillies*, the aircraft carrier *Glorious*, six cruisers, 37 destroyers, six submarines, a depot ship and a net layer belonging to the Mediterranean Fleet. The Home Fleet ships taking part will be the battleships *Nelson, Rodney, Royal Sovereign* and *Resolution*, the aircraft carrier *Ark Royal*, five cruisers and 25 destroyers, three submarines and a depot ship. It was a phenomenal gathering of hardware.

The place was awash with gold braid too. Some 13 Admirals were present with Admiral Sir Dudley Pound C-in-C of the Mediterranean Fleet in *Warspite* and Admiral Sir Charles Forbes the C-in-C Home Fleet in *Nelson* commanding the forces gathered. There were two exercises scheduled from the 28 to 3 March and the 6th to the 10th.

The reward for the hard work during exercises would be a spring cruise to somewhere along the French Riviera with another ship of her class. But before that could happen, *Nubian* was called away on a humanitarian mission whilst the news reached them that Germany had invaded Czechoslovakia on the 14 March. The British government and indeed the rest of Europe did nothing, but what could be done apart from all-out war which the policy of appeasement continued to avoid that at all costs.

The Spanish Civil War was coming to a head with the Republican Army under Colonel Casado being pushed to the coast. They held around 700 Italian prisoners that they could no longer accommodate, and the Royal Navy was requested to begin the repatriation of these men through the small port of Gandia, about half way between Valencia and Alicante. The Arethusa Class, Light Cruiser *Galatea* and the London Class Heavy Cruiser *Sussex* were detailed along with *Nubian* to carry out the mission on 29 March, dropping the men off at Marseilles the following day. There was a request for *Sussex* to return to Alicante to assist in the evacuation of a further 40,000 republican refugees, however this was declined in fear that such an action would forever divide Anglo, Spanish relations. Many of the refugees were taken to prison camps, a large number committed suicide by jumping into the harbour.

In stark contrast, the holiday could begin for the *Nubians*. It had become a kind of tradition that once the Home Fleet Exercises were over the ships of the Mediterranean fleet would split into pairs and visit a number of ports in the French Riviera. *Nubian* was paired with *Zulu* making for the little French port of St Maxime. For a short while all thoughts of conflict were put aside as the sailors went ashore in their best whites to walk the sandy beaches and frequent the local bars.

Despite the fact that Italy had embraced fascism and had military aspirations for North Africa and the Mediterranean as a whole several Royal Navy ships were due to visit Italian ports. Britain, France and Italy had good relations in 1935 when it appeared they would stand together to unify Europe rather than follow the nationalistic policies of Germany. However, this gradually fell apart over the next 3 years with a number of incidents that eroded the relationship whilst bolstering the aspirations of Mussolini. No sooner had an agreement been made, Italy began moves on Abyssinia (what is now Ethiopia) by making claim to her territories. Mussolini was emboldened in his actions as Britain and France did not object. France, however, began to smell a rat, especially once Britain signed the 1935 Naval Agreement with Germany that restricted the size of the German Navy to no larger than 35% of the Royal Navy which they saw as a revision of the Versailles Treaty. It would, of course, completely unravel in the coming years when Hitler revitalised the army and revealed the existence of the Luftwaffe. France had seen the writing on the wall and began to pursue more belligerent policies towards Italy as she predicted conflict in the Mediterranean and could see clearly that Italian fascism would more likely ally with the Nazi's. For those in the Royal Navy, at the sharp end of the stick in the Mediterranean, it was becoming equally clear that this was not going to end well.

7 April 1939 provided a sharp poke in the eye for the British government. According to Admiral Cunningham in his biography, the invasion of Albania by the Italians came as a complete surprise to both the Admiralty and the Government as political and military intelligence from inside Italy at the time was non-existent. Equally worrying were those Royal Navy warships currently visiting Italian ports, and these were quickly ordered to depart. It was quite clear that the international situation was deteriorating in a way that diplomacy would make way for conflict. In the U.S. President Roosevelt had attempted to gain assurance of non-aggression and expansion by Germany and Italy, but this was rejected whilst the British government pledged to Poland, Romania and Greece that if there were any aggressive moves towards their countries, Britain would come to their aid. How that would happen, no one seemed to know.

At the time *Nubian* was in the Eastern Mediterranean with the flotilla carrying out working up exercises that put them through their paces once more. These included re supply at sea of ammunition, fuel and victualing. Then came the order for them to gather at Alexandria. Those ships closest to Malta were to refuel, rearm and re-store there and then make their way to Alexandria without delay but not too hastily for prying eyes to come to any conclusions. *Nubian* and her crew were about to become associated with Admiral 'ABC' Cunningham and HMS *Warspite*.

'ABC'

Andrew Browne Cunningham ('ABC') was born in Dublin on the 7 January 1893, but he was not Irish he was Scottish by birth. His school days began in Dublin which was not to his liking although lucky for him it seems his father was not impressed either and he was dispatched to Edinburgh Academy after just a couple of weeks. By his own admission Cunningham had thought little what he may do once his education was complete but a telegram from his father arrived one day that triggered something within the young man. It simply read; 'Would you like to go into the Navy?' and with that he replied, 'Yes, I should like to be an Admiral.'

The route into the Navy was to pass a 'Civil Service Exam for the Navy' which on successful completion Cunningham joined HMS *Britannia* as a cadet on the 15 January 1897 at the age of 14. Training included time aboard the *Martin* which was a two masted sailing ship that included a period of 6 weeks at sea. The Navy was having a difficult time of letting the past go in its training programme.

Cunningham spent some time in South Africa during the Boer War and then came his first posting to the battleship *Implacable* in what would be a long association with the Mediterranean. By 1911 he was in Command of the recently built destroyer, *Scorpion*. During World War 1 he was involved in operations in the Dardanelles and Gallipoli being present at the landing and evacuation of troops in July 1916. By 1922 he was Captain (D) of the 6th Destroyer Flotilla aboard *Shakespeare* before being asked to be Flag Captain of the cruiser *Calcutta* in the America and West Indies Station until 1928.

On return he attended the Imperial Defence College where Staff Officers began their training. Here potential Staff Officers from the RAF, Army, Royal Navy and from the services associated with the Dominions were brought together and lectured in foreign and economic affairs as well as military subjects.

Just prior to being given the Captaincy of *Rodney*, Cunningham married Nona Byatt who joined him aboard ship for what was to be a year long posting. Both *Rodney* and *Nelson* were most unusual in design with their 3 main, 16-inch turrets forward of a very large 'castle' looking bridge. Both had problems of one sort or another, but they were loved by the public for their sheer projection of power, quite possibly through their unique silhouette. One of these problems came about when the aft gun turret was trained as far aft as possible, at full elevation. Cunningham stated that you could see around ten feet down the closest barrel from the bridge when the guns were trained in this manner. So it was that his final task as her commander was to take *Rodney* out to the south of the Isle of Wight on 21 November 1930 to carry out trials with the guns in this configuration. The ship wrights had installed plate glass windows on the bridge as protection. The test was a complete failure. The guns went off and the concussion smashed the windows to pieces, showering glass shards everywhere and caused further damage to the bridge. With her tail between her legs, *Rodney* returned to Portsmouth and then on to Devonport for a refit. Her aft gun training limits (and of *Nelson*) were amended accordingly. Command of *Rodney* was handed over to Roger Bellairs on 15 December, with Cunningham becoming Commodore of Chatham R.N. Barracks in July 1931. He was made Rear Admiral, which would normally mean unemployment, however he remained in charge of Chatham until 1933 when he was made Rear Admiral (D) of the Mediterranean Fleet in 1934.

Cunningham was not a great sportsman but like most Scotsman enjoyed golf and fishing, notably for trout and salmon. Wherever he was posted he liked to try and get some fishing in. Fortunately, Nona was a keen fisher too. Cunningham describes one memorable fishing trip in his biography traveling to Yugoslavia in what is now known as Croatia. He stayed at a rather primitive but clean and comfortable hotel, where the staff and indeed the proprietor Herr Rude Bergleitner (a former Sergeant in the Austrian Army) would simply walk unannounced into their room at any time. On one occasion he came into their room when Nona was almost naked and unperturbed, he began to enthusiastically discuss the days fishing. Cunningham describes the countryside as being very much like highland Scotland, greenery being a welcome change to the sand of Malta. The rivers of Croatia and Slovenia are clear running, often aquamarine in colour from mountain meltwater, the scenery is quite breathtaking remaining a popular destination for fishermen today. Herr Bergleitner fished with them every day as ghillie, preparing lunch of skewered meats basted in olive oil over an open fire.

Having returned to England and spending time renovating their house in Bishops Waltham as well as staff appointments to various committees, Cunningham was approached to take on a temporary position as Second in Command in the Mediterranean to Sir Dudley Pound. This involved the command of the Battle Cruiser Squadron from the darling of the Navy, HMS *Hood*, based out of Malta. Cunningham describes his quarters in *Hood* as palatial when compared with the ships he was used to, 'large and airy cabins on the deck above the quarterdeck with great windows instead of the ordinary portholes. Even my cabin in *Rodney* was smaller by comparison.'[43]

The protection of British merchant shipping became a task for the Battlecruiser Squadron in 1937 with the Spanish Civil War in full swing. Franco had declared a blockade of the eastern Spanish ports, notably Valencia and Barcelona but this was not recognised by the British government. Therefore, British merchantmen began to run the blockade. There resulted some mysterious and ominous disappearances of ships through torpedo attacks that the Spanish claimed were carried out by their own submarines, however Cunningham states that there was no doubt they were actually Italian. As a result, the fleet was reinforced by destroyers from the Home Fleet and two squadrons of flying boats from Coastal Command and the R.A.F were dispatched to provide additional protection. The sinking's ceased.

The motives of the Italians, and of course the Germans, were not lost on Cunningham and his staff colleagues. The Anglo-Italian talks that had appeared so promising to the government led to a visitation and the expected entertainment by the Navy of an Italian Squadron of two battleships and four destroyers. Cunningham and his staff were unimpressed. 'Most of us in the

---

[43] (Cunningham, 1951)

Mediterranean were sceptical about the results achieved by these same conversations. Nobody was prepared to trust anything that Mussolini said or signed, and one had only to regard the reception given to Hitler when he visited Italy a week or two later to realise which way the wind really blew. As our merchant ships were being bombed almost daily by Italian bombers in and outside the Spanish ports it was not easy to work up cordiality.'

Cunningham returned to England being appointed Deputy Chief of Naval Staff to Sir Roger Backhouse who had begun to process of rebuilding the Navy and its reputation that had languished in the minds of politicians and the public since Jutland. The programme was ambitious and included the adoption of new technology, Radar and ASDIC as well as increasing manpower, ship building capacity, supply and the defence of the ports. Both the RAF and the Army were ambivalent to the requests by the Navy to bolster Anti-Aircraft protection for Naval Ports and went as far as objecting to the increase in gun numbers to protect Malta believing it a lost cause in any ensuing conflict. To consider Malta a lost cause seems almost incredulous given its strategic location and importance within the Mediterranean Sea. For example, a destroyer making its way from Gibraltar to Alexandria could not make the crossing without refuelling at Malta. But let us hear the strategic view of Captain Roger Hill, who perhaps perfectly describes the importance of Malta in his memoir, 'Destroyer Captain'.

> As long as Malta held out, the enemy supply ships flowing to Rommel's African Army had to go down to the Tunisian coast in darkness and had to be escorted by warships. The fact and threat of submarine, air and surface attack on the Italian supply ships slowed down the reinforcement tremendously. Remove Malta and anything that floated, including tugs towing a line of barges, could wander across direct to Tripoli or Benghazi at any speed and unescorted.[44]

In what with hindsight can be seen as a naïve mission, Cunningham was sent by the government with a team of staff to Berlin to meet with the German

---

[44] (Hill, 1979)

Admiralty in December 1938. The reason for this mission was to attempt to persuade the Germans to reverse a decision to rebuild their submarine force to be on parity with that of the Royal Navy. Under the 1935 Anglo-German Navy agreement this could only be initiated under specific circumstances above the prescribed limit of 35% the size of the Navy's submarine fleet. Despite a cordial and most welcoming visit, Cunningham and his team could not persuade a change in policy, Hitler confirmed that no matter what, the submarine building programme would continue.

The Navy Estimates were completed in January and February 1939 outlining the ambitious ship building programme that Sir. Geoffrey Shakespeare presented to parliament that March. Meanwhile, on the 14 February as *Nubian* was sailing between Portsmouth and Malta, Cunningham knelt before the King to become Knight Commander of the Most Honourable Order of the Bath whilst Sir Roger Blackhouse became ill, so much so that it was unlikely that he would be able to return to the Admiralty. He never did. Sir Dudley Pound was recalled from his post as C-in-C of the Mediterranean Fleet to replace him, Cunningham became an Admiral replacing Pound in the Mediterranean whilst Rear Admiral Tom Phillips took on Cunningham's old job.

Warspite

In conception she was a gamble, no ship had been deployed with guns as large as hers before. In birth she was difficult, she held onto her slipway for as long as she could, refusing to budge once the champagne bottle had shattered, until she was ready. In death she would be stubborn, foundering in a storm on the way to the breakers yard off the coast of Cornwall in 1947. H.M.S *Warspite* was a rejuvenated soul and an icon in the making. Sir Dudley Pounds flag was lowered at sunset on the 5 June 1939 and Admiral Cunningham's was raised the following morning at 09:00. *Warspite* was alone in Alexandria at the time but without delay her main engines were fired and she sailed to rejoin the fleet that was at sea.

Winston Churchill championed the *Queen Elizabeth* Class Battleships, so much so that he took a huge gamble with his career by ordering their construction before the Royal Commission had even approved the go ahead. There were to be five ships in total, The *Queen Elizabeth, Warspite, Valiant, Barham* and *Malaya*. Their main armament would be a 15-in. gun that would throw a combined broadside of 15,600lbs accurately to a target 15,000 yards away. It was just as well they did, during their trials in 1915, as at the time construction began on the ships these guns were just a dream and no one knew whether a ship could take one let alone ten of these guns! In line with the change from coal to oil, *Warspite* had oil fired boilers to propel her to over 20 knots.

At the Battle of Jutland, *Warspite* was in the thick of the action and most severely damaged. Receiving a hit under the waterline at the stern her steering gear was damaged, and she simply thrashed around in circles for some time whilst German shells rained down on her. Eventually she had to be brought to a stop. With shells still falling on and around her the crew managed to make good the steering and she limped home to Rosyth.

During the inter-war years, she and the other Queen Elizabeth battleships survived the cuts to the Navy. Both *Warspite* and the *Queen Elizabeth* were almost completely rebuilt to more modern specifications. *Warspite* was literally taken apart and reconstructed from the bottom upwards which began in December 1933. She was fitted with modern boilers that saved 1500 tons in weight, her guns modified for an additional ten degrees elevation and their range increased to 32,000 yards. She had new fire control systems that were located in a completely re designed, slab sided Bridge superstructure and her surface guns were supported by modern Anti-Aircraft batteries. A new, slimmed down funnel meant that there was room for a small hanger and catapult to accommodate up to four Fairey Swordfish seaplanes with electrical handling gear to recover the aircraft when at sea. It was normal for two to be operational with the remaining two as parts or crated as spares.

By 1937 the work was complete and *Warspite* was drafted with a compliment of 1200 men and officers. She weighed 32,000 tons, could make 24 knots, was 634 feet long and 104 feet wide, almost double that of *Nubian* (377ft long and with a 36ft beam).

Warspite and the fleet (including *Nubian*) carried out many exercises over the coming months using Alexandria as the fleet base due to the Italians presence in Albania. According to Cunningham it was not the best port from which to base operations but if war broke out, they would have to operate from there. He was thankful that he had the foresight to have requested the transfer of the floating dock from Portsmouth. There was a floating dock in Malta, but this was in a poor state of repair and could not be moved. The provision of a dock capable of maintaining or repairing a battleship was most important as the facilities at Alexandria could only cope with warships up to the size of a cruiser. There were no deep-water areas either and so work needed to begin on these too. Cunningham also reviewed the Anti-Aircraft defences of Alexandria and Port Said, both were woeful.

Britain needed all the friends she could get and there was no better way to demonstrate this than a visit from the Royal Navy. Herbert had never been to Istanbul, but on the 2 August, he found himself in best whites lining the deck of *Nubian* as she came to a stop at an anchorage off the Dolmabahce Palace. There was a shout of 'Let go' and the familiar sound of the rattling chains as her anchors fell away into the clear blue water of the Bosphorus whilst the crew dispersed to their stations that to the spectator appeared random but in an organised manner. Close by were *Cossack, Maori* and *Zulu* acting as escorts for *Warspite* which appeared every bit of the warrior queen in the bright sunshine.

Over the coming days the hospitality was outstanding but exhausting. The Turks had put on a packed agenda that included, of course, all the necessary official discussions but also dinner parties and outings for both the Officers and men of all the crews. 'We were royally entertained. Everyone seemed genuinely pleased to see us, and the sailors were well looked after, being taken out to some of the big houses on the Bosphorus. The British Ambassador set a very high standard in his entertainment for 300 sailors. The basis of it was 1,200 bottles of beer and a troupe of dancing girls, both of which were most popular.'[45] Wrote Admiral Cunningham.

On the 6 August the ships began to make their way back through the Sea of Marmora after a trip that had almost banished all thoughts of war and what was likely to come the way of these ships in the months and years to come. The Turkish people came out in their thousands, lining the beaches and coves along the way waving and cheering. The effort had been worth it as the visit did contribute some way to ensure Turkey would remain neutral over the course of the war.

Back to work. There was gunnery practice off Cyprus and then a convoy protection exercise with one force simulating the attackers against (ironically) an Italian convoy, the other the protecting force. The exercise lasted 48 hours during which all the warships were closed up for action stations for the duration. Watertight doors and scuttles were closed despite the sweltering heat and nonexistent ventilation with no air conditioning, especially in the boiler and engine rooms where temperatures soared to as much as 130° f (54°C). It was a greulling test for the ships companies who were required to wear all their flash protective clothing to add to the discomfort. On one ship there were 8 cases of heat stroke.

---

[45] (Cunningham, 1951)

Chapter 5

TOTAL GERMANY

The beginning of September, *Nubian* was at sea carrying out a routine patrol. The day was quiet, the men going about their normal routine. In his sea cabin, Commander Ravenhill was having a break and reading a book but whilst his eyes saw the words his mind was elsewhere, Poland in fact, where the German Army had invaded two days previously. There would be consequences. A knock on the door pulled him back from his thoughts, he put the book down and looked at the doorway. Lt. Bush entered and with a rather grave look on his face handed him the signal he had just received and decoded It read 'Commence hostilities against Germany'[46]. It was the 3 September 1939 and Britain was once more at war with Germany, which answered the question he had just posed to himself. It was almost an anticlimax and in some ways a relief.

As an immediate consequence, all merchant shipping, in line with the threat policy that the Admiralty had drawn up, had to sail as a convoy with protection provided by the Royal Navy. That was reinforced with the sinking of the liner *Athenia* by a German submarine on the 3 September. For those Navy ships operating in the Mediterranean at the time this was thought a waste of effort. There were unlikely to be many, if any, German U-Boats in the Mediterranean right now so surely it would be better to concentrate all efforts on anti-submarine patrols around Gibraltar?

The first months of the war were somewhat surreal with little for the Mediterranean fleet to do. Indeed, the worst-case scenario of simultaneous war with Germany, Italy and Japan had not materialised. For a start, Mussolini was biding his time and possibly waiting to see what the reaction would be to Hitler's invasion of Poland. Gradually the fleet were being recalled to Britain,

---

[46] (Bush, 2005)

with the expectation that Japan would be next and a rather misguided belief that Italy could be rolled over easily whenever Britain wanted to. A belief that was not shared between Cunningham and his staff, but as he writes in his autobiography; 'Towards the end of the year the only British naval forces left in the Mediterranean were three small 'C' class cruisers and the handful of Australian destroyers. I could not complain. It was best that every available ship should be used wherever the situation demanded, and in an emergency the Mediterranean could quickly be reinforced. Our situation was one of watching and waiting. We still tried to enforce some form of contraband control without, however, hurting Italian susceptibilities. It was clear that the longer they could be kept out of the war the better.'[47]

Contraband patrols became the order of the day for *Nubian*, including participating in screening two convoys. Back in England people continued to go to work and children attended school, the farmers worked the fields, and each day came and went much as it did before the 3 September. This period, that ran roughly between September 1939 and April 1940 is known as the 'Phony War', where to the public at large there was little to indicate the country was at war with Germany. For the Royal Navy in some parts, the war came to them much sooner.

There were those in the Admiralty that knew the fleet base at Scapa Flow was vulnerable, but the risks were deemed minimal with the channels into the natural harbour blocked, albeit in some cases only partially. On the night of the 13 October, in a most skilful and daring piece of underwater navigation, U47 and her crew, commanded by Gunther Prien managed to enter Scapa Flow during high tide through one of the blocked channels, actually touching one of the sunken block ships on the way through,

At the time there were some 50 ships at Scapa Flow, included in these was the old battleship, *Royal Oak*. Too old and ponderous for front line duties, she

---

[47] (Cunningham, 1951)

was assigned to Scapa Flow primarily as an Anti-Aircraft platform and due to her minor duties role, her crew consisted of a large number of boys.

The attack began around 01:00 with a salvo of torpedoes striking her hull but there was no explosion. German torpedoes in the early part of the war were notoriously unreliable and none of those in the first attack detonated. Prien tried a second time and missed the target. He must have been incensed, but by taking another twenty minutes to reposition the U-boat he lined up once more and fired three torpedoes at *Royal Oak*. All of them hit, and this time, they all detonated with catastrophic effect. *Royal Oak* heeled over rapidly, her progress hastened by the weight of her guns toppling over and dragging her underwater. Of the 1100 crew, 834 men and boys lost their lives.

Prien managed to extricate U-47 and return to Germany a hero. In parliament, Churchill had to announce the loss of *Royal Oak* on the 17th. It was a blow and of course the German government took this as a huge propaganda coup. However, in the grand scheme of things, it could have been worse for the Royal Navy had there been more of the modern fleet there at the time.

Mohawk had already returned to Britain with *Cossack, Maori* and *Zulu*, proceeding from Portland to Methil on the Firth of Forth to begin convoy duties between there and Norway. She joined *Jervis* which was a 'J' Class Destroyer commanded by Captain Philip Mack, who we shall meet again in the Mediterranean. The 'J', 'K' and 'N' Class Destroyers, collectively known as the 'Kelly's' looked a lot like the 'Tribals' at first glance, but they were fundamentally different. To aid with identification, their names all began with the letter of their class. The main differences were quite obvious once one took time to study their form. They had two boilers instead of three, this meant they only required one funnel which helped lower their silhouette. Whilst the 'Tribals' were gunnery orientated these destroyers returned to a more 'traditional' role of anti-shipping and submarine work sacrificing 'Y' turret to accommodate more torpedo tubes and depth charge launchers or Anti-

Aircraft defences. The torpedoes were located midships and in 4 sets of a new, 5 tube design.

Anti-Aircraft gunnery remained woefully inadequate for some time. The main armament still had a maximum elevation of forty degrees with machine guns and the unreliable pom-pom as close in protection. It was not until the Oerlikon was adopted that the Anti-Aircraft capabilities were improved.

Jervis was flotilla leader at the time. This meant that her Captain was senior within the flotilla and therefore was known as Captain (D). He would usually have his own ship, but if this was unavailable (for a refit, damaged or sunk) then he would transfer to another ship in the flotilla with his senior staff and he would command the flotilla from there whilst the 'resident' commander carried on the normal routine of commanding the ship. A flotilla was usually made up of two divisions of 4 ships (one of which included the leader) and each division divided into a subdivision of a pair of destroyers.

On the 16 October *Mohawk* and *Jervis* were passing the Isle of May when they were attacked by a bomber which was dispatched by a pair of Spitfires that appeared to come from nowhere. Jervis stopped to pick the crew up, one of whom was dead whilst *Mohawk* continued into the Firth of Forth with the remainder of the convoy they were protecting.

Mohawks crew remained at action stations, prepared for another air attack which soon materialised in the form of a JU88. It came at them with a purpose and simultaneously dropped two bombs which fell either side of her, roughly alongside the torpedo tubes behind the aft funnel and strafed the ship with machine gun fire. Both bombs detonated as they hit the water with the ensuing shrapnel and bomb parts flying in all directions, cutting down the machine gun crews, mooring party and anyone else who got in their way from the bridge to the quarterdeck.

The bridge superstructure was almost wrecked with many of the senior members of crew killed or injured. 15 men in total were killed and 30 wounded. The engine room crew rushed to provide medical assistance. As the men collected themselves together to take stock of the situation, they noticed that their commander, Richard Frank Jolly was wounded. He had a severe stomach wound that made him bend double to counter the pain, but despite this he would not retire for attention and insisted on taking the ship into Rosyth despite the fact they had around 35 miles to travel through waters that were packed with vessels. It took an hour and twenty minutes to complete.

Jolly gradually became weaker, and his orders had to be relayed by his Navigation Officer (who was also injured) to the wheelhouse and Engine room as his voice had reduced with the pain to a whisper and could not be heard down the voice tubes. Despite his wounds, as *Mohawk* sailed past the Fourth Bridge and a number of larger warships Jolly managed to stand and return their salute. Jolly was gently asked on many occasions whether he would like medical attention, however (as per the London Gazette, 23 December 1939) he simply replied, 'Leave me, go and look after the others.' At last *Mohawk* pulled alongside her berth where Jolly managed to ring off the main engines before collapsing. He was rushed to hospital but died 5 hours later. His body was returned to his wife, and he is buried in the Churchyard of St. Peters in Boughton, Kent. On the 23 December he was posthumously awarded the Empire Gallantry Medal. He was just 43 at the time he was killed.

Mohawk was taken to Hawthorn Leslie's yard on the River Tyne for repairs once she was made good at Rosyth. She was a sorry sight with her bridge in tatters. A far cry from when she left in pristine condition for the Mediterranean. She would however, meet, sail, and fight once more with *Nubian* who had in the meantime been ordered to return to Portsmouth on the 19 October.

Norwegian Convoy's - Winter December 1939 – February 1940

No doubt eyes rolled to the back of heads and there were incredulous looks and cries of 'you must be joking' when Commander Ravenhill described to the crew over the tannoy what their next assignment would be. 'You will notice some crates being brought aboard at present. These contain tethered barrage balloons. We shall be carrying out our own sea trials on Monday and then working off Spithead for two days flying these devices as a trial that if successful will be adopted by shipping to protect against low level attacks from aircraft. We shall then proceed to Scapa Flow and Rosyth, which will be our new home, to take up convoy duties.' Shades of running up and down planks during the rolling trials, but the trials were indeed successful, and balloons were used for convoy protection as a result with the creation of the 'Channel Mobile Barrage Balloon Flotilla' which consisted of a number of ships equipped to fly the balloons within convoys. These were largely successful as the presence of a balloon gave the attacking bomber crews, especially the dive bombers, a nasty aerial obstacle that had to be avoided at all costs.

The crew had returned during the weekend of the 25 and 26 November, some of them from up to 4 weeks leave ashore. *Nubian* had been exhibiting power problems for a while and the constant running of engines at high speed had resulted in turbine problems that now required attention. It was a common fault with the 'Tribals'. *Nubian* was towed away to the Woolston Works for a refit and the replacement of her turbine blades.

Early in December *Nubian* joined in her first convoy protection on the Norwegian run between Methil on the coast of Fife to Bergen. She joined convoy HN4 which was returning to Methil, arriving on 12 December. This particular route used the prefix ON for those convoys running from Methil to Bergen and HN when returning and simply incrementing in number every time they sailed. There was no Convoy number 13 for superstitious reasons alone and the last convoy was number 25 in April 1940 following the invasion of Norway by the Germans.

The following day the Royal Navy was in action, but on the far side of the world from Methil. On the 13th 'The Battle of the River Plate' occurred with the Cruisers *Ajax, Exeter* and HMNZS *Achilles* engaging with the *Graf Spee* which had been marauding in the Atlantic, undetected for some time. Assisted by her supply ship the *Altmark, Graf Spee* had sunk a number of merchant vessels whose crews were transferred and confined aboard *Altmark*.

In the ensuing action the *Graf Spee* suffered enough damage that she needed to put into port for repairs but her only option was to enter the neutral port of Montevideo in Uruguay. Meanwhile, the Cruisers remained at sea, but *Exeter* had to withdraw to the Falkland Islands for repairs as she was so badly damaged that she was barely afloat. This left *Achilles* and the damaged *Ajax* which alone would be no match for a ship with the armament of the *Graf Spee*. Through some canny deception it was made known to *Graf Spee's* Captain Langsdorf that a battle fleet would arrive imminently when in fact it was hundreds of miles away. Coupled with this fact and that he was given 72 hours by the Uruguayan government to leave port, Langsdorf decided to scuttle the ship rather than sacrifice his crew in what would be a suicidal battle. On the 17 December Langsdorf and a skeleton crew took Graf Spee into the estuary, hauled down the ships flags and set off a number of explosive charges that settled the ship onto a sandbank. Three days later, wrapped in the German Flag, Langsdorf shot himself. The *Altmark* in the meantime seemed to have disappeared, along with her captured crew.

The outbound ON5 Convoy left Methil on the 16 December with *Afridi, Mohawk* (newly repaired), *Maori* and *Nubian* as escort. They were due to meet HN5 and escort it back into Methil although the timing of the arrival of HN5 was unknown due to the events in South America. The news of the sinking of the *Graf Spee* had been a cause to celebrate a victory which gave some credence to the thought that this war would end quite quickly and in Britain's favour. But the hornets' nest had been poked and poked pretty hard too. A smarting German government may just hit back and Convoy HN5 was a juicy target of some 27 merchant ships plus their escorts. Nothing happened though and the phony war took hold once more.

During December and January 1940 Great Britain and much of Europe was hit by the hardest winter storms for 45 years. Temperatures plummeted into minus double figures, as low as -23° f (-30°C) in some places. The sea at

Bognor froze, as did the harbours at Folkestone and Southampton. In the north of the country there was snow to 60cms which drifted in an icy easterly wind. In the south there was freezing rain that coated everything in ice. So much so that birds feathers froze and they could not fly. A 'Report on the effect of the severe winter of 1939 – 40 on bird life in the British Isles' collected statements from around the country, from Evesham (near Worcester) came the following report.

> '…on January 28th 7 Woodpigeons were found stuck to boughs, their tails and flanks being held fast by ice, and many others incapable of flight were found in stubble fields. A Chaffinch was completely embedded in ice attached to a laurel leaf and various small birds lost their tails whilst a Chaffinch and Greenfinch had completely bald heads.'

For the men of the Navy life had to go on. *Nubian* found employment in a number of roles that included incoming Atlantic Convoy protection and patrols to counter mine laying by the Germans. Quite often *Nubian* was in support of *Hood* and both put into Greenock for Christmas as the defences at Scapa Flow were still being reorganised and strengthened following the sinking of *Royal Oak*. There was no home leave but there were days off on Christmas and Boxing Day before joining *Barham* and *Repulse* on patrol duty. However, the patrol was cut short when U-30, commanded by Fritz Julius Lemp (who had sunk the *Athenia*) fired a salvo of torpedoes at the two capital ships. One hit *Barham* on the port side, seriously damaging her between 'A' and 'B' turrets which caused her to list by 7 degrees. She was able to make way under her own engines but had to retire to Liverpool for repairs. *Nubian* and *Isis* provided cover. 4 men had been killed aboard *Barham* during the attack.

An escort of a different nature came when *Nubian* escorted some dummy battleships to Scapa Flow. This was one of Churchills ideas first formed in 1914 when a number of merchant ships were 'converted' by the addition of wood and canvas to make them appear like battleships. There were three built in 1939 which sailed under escort from Belfast to Scapa. One of them was made to look like Herberts old Carrier *Hermes* and later in the war 'she' did appear in reconnaissance photographs taken by the Luftwaffe. The effects were very creditable.

In early January *Nubian* assisted in towing a liner that had grounded outside the boom at Greenock. Good deed done *Nubian* managed to collide with a merchant vessel and had to spend 10 days in Dry dock for repairs. Then the *Altmark* incident occurred when Captain Heinrich Dau took *Altmark* northwards around Scotland and slipped into Norwegian waters.

3 Lockheed Hudsons took off from RAF Thornaby on a mission over Norway on the 14 February. These twin radial engined aircraft earned a reputation for being so robust against Anti-Aircraft fire, that they were affectionately known as 'Old Boomerang', for their ability to always come back. Designed from the Lockheed Electra, they had a single Boulton Paul dorsal turret mounted towards the rear of the fuselage and distinctive dual finned rudder. The aircraft duly spotted the *Altmark* and relayed the location which subsequently found its way to Captain Vian aboard HMS *Cossack*.

Cossack had been tasked with *Nubian, Maori, Sikh, Intrepid, Ivanhoe* and *Arethusa* on operations to intercept German Iron Ore merchantmen in the Skagerrak. However, notification came on the 15th that *Altmark* had been sighted. The ships split up and began the search.

Arethusa, Intrepid and *Ivanhoe* found the *Altmark*. Warning shots were fired in an attempt to force her into international waters, however Norwegian warships actually hampered the RN ships and *Altmark* managed to slip into the narrow fjord of Jossingfiord. Later that evening, Vian arrived with *Cossack*. He conferred with a Norwegian officer, who indicated that the *Altmark* had indeed been searched, but there was no sign of any prisoners on board. It was a tricky situation. Vian contacted the Admiralty and the response from Winston Churchill (at this time the First Sea Lord) was an offer to escort the *Altmark* to Bergen where further searches should be made and if refused, she was to be boarded. Intervention by the Norwegians should be discouraged and only if absolutely necessary should any shots be fired against them.

At 22:00 Vian took *Cossack* into the fjord and commenced the boarding of the *Altmark* with pistols and cutlasses drawn. A short action followed resulting in 4 dead Germans and a wounded member of the boarding party. The bridge was secured, but the *Altmark* ran aground. A thorough search was made, and it was when the hold was opened up that one of the most famous of Royal Navy exchanges began. The boarding party shouted down into the hold 'Are there any Englishmen down there?', to which came cheers, and the response was 'Then come up. The Navy's here.'

299 Merchant sailors were taken off the *Altmark*, the *Cossack* turned about and left for Leith. The Germans were left behind. The British public were heartened by a minor victory, Hitler was furious and approved plans for Operation Weserubung, the invasion of Norway. Later, when the Germans had completed their conquest of Norway, they placed a plaque in Jossingfiord, 'Here on the 16th Feb. 1940 the Altmark was set upon by a British Sea Pirate.'

Before the war, Methil[48] had been the busiest port along the northern shore of the Firth of Forth due to the coal mining in the area. The Kingdom of Fife may have a Royal Seat at Falkland Palace, but the veins of the kingdom ran black with coal. For now, Methil was used primarily to bring ashore goods that the convoys had sailed with from Norway that included Iron Ore, Pulp, Timber, Fish (including Cod Roe) and paper. Norway was not the only destination for convoys from Methil, they also sailed down the east coast to the Thames (FN/FS convoys), around to the Clyde or Lock Ewe (EN convoys) or to the Clyde (WN convoys).

Protecting the port and its visitors were a number of different vessels which were requisitioned such as the 8 barrage balloon barges, two mine observation vessels, a degaussing ship and number of naval control ships whilst two steam trawlers were used for Air Sea Rescue. The old pleasure steamer *Bournemouth*

---

[48] (Dowie, 2012)

Queen was modified for Anti-Aircraft gunnery and the MFV *Dorando* the resident D.E.M.S. (Defensively Equipped Merchant Ship) which is likely to have had a 4-inch gun in the stern and a 12-pounder up front. The gun crews were under the overall command of Captain F. A. Randall of the Royal Scots. They would be made up of Machine Gun teams or from the Royal Artillery. Some of the ships crews were trained in gunnery at HMS 'Excellent' and this often included the 2nd Mate who would be in charge of the gun teams once the ship sailed. Finally, there was a N.A.A.F.I. vessel, the M.V. *Fair Endeavor*, which the merchant ships could use for victualing and general supply when in port.

There were many merchant ships off Methil in Largo Bay on the 3 March 1940, gathering for Convoy ON17 outbound to Bergen which would take them about 6 days to complete. So many in fact that there ended up being two convoys, the first of which *Nubian* would be one of the 5 destroyer escorts along with *Gurkha, Delight, Diana* and *Ilex*. Of the 40 merchant ships sailing with ON17, 3 were British, 16 Norwegian, 12 Swedish, 5 Danish, 2 Finish and 2 Estonian.

Commander Ravenhill trudged up the road from Methil Harbour, his breath coming in great clouds due to the cold. He stopped briefly outside of HMS 'Sentinel', a grand name that didn't really fit the white building that was once the Miners Institute. He stepped slightly to one side of the doorway taking off his gloves as he did so and with a sweep of his left arm gave way to a Danish ships master who grunted as way of a thank you for the courtesy.

A meeting was held here before every convoy departed. As usual the meeting room was muggy and airless with a pall of pipe and cigarette smoke hanging above the heads of the men. Everyone was in some form of conversation whilst they waited for the briefing creating that indiscernible babble when a mixture of languages are all speaking at once. Ravenhill spotted the Commander of *Gurkha*, Anthony Buzzard and made his way through the crowd to where he and the other escort commanding officers were stood chatting. No doubt picking Buzzard's brain about the U-Boat he and his crew had managed to sink last month, thought Ravenhill.

The men attending the meeting were made up of the Ships Master and 2nd Mate from each of the merchant ships due to sail in the convoy. The Master would be handed his secret orders pertaining to the sailing whilst the 2nd Mate was provided with the latest amendments to the local shipping charts. The charts detailed the narrow lanes that gave access to the Firth of Forth which included marked shoals and minefields. The lanes themselves were only a few hundred yards wide in some places with lighted boys every 5 miles. The merchantman's Chief Steward and one of the crew were also ashore but detailed to fetch supplies from the *Fair Endeavor*.

From the Royal Navy, each Commanding Officer of the escorting ships was present with the meeting overseen by the Convoy Commander who was from the Merchant Navy. With a convoy of this size there would be a number of escort ships involved which was a comfort to the merchantmen, for if their ships were sunk, the moment they set foot in a life raft or took their chances in the cold waters of the North Sea their pay was immediately stopped until, if they were lucky enough to survive, they could find employment on another ship. On this occasion the old cruiser *Calcutta* would provide Anti-Aircraft support with the two larger cruisers *Arethusa* and *Edinburgh* as close support whilst *Hood* and *Valiant* were distant cover. Occasionally a submarine would join them and, on this occasion, *Narwhal* would provide specific cover for the fleet auxiliary ship *Greenawn* which was planned to split from the group later and proceed to Scapa Flow, *Diana* would join them as surface cover.

Misery is a bitter wind that sneaks its way around the Director Control Tower watch position and whistles so sadly in the wires of the foremast it breaks your heart. It's the almost lazy swell that twists and turns the ship doing the same to your guts whilst every now and then it throws a clod of water that takes your breath away. It's the salty sharp sting of those tiny cuts that have formed in the creases of your thumbs and the edge of your nails that hurt like hell when you knock them once more and they begin to bleed. Will they ever heal? Then there is time, there's lots of time, as the cold does its work on your mind so that even though you try and resist you can't help stealing a glance at your watch once more to reveal that only ten minutes have passed since you last looked. No matter how miserable you may feel at that moment you can, if you let yourself, sink deeper into despair when you long for it all to be over but know there is just no way out of this until your hour is up. Or of course, if you've been here many times before, as Herbert has, in all kinds of wind, rain, heat and cold, you know that it will end. It's just that this time some bastard is out there looking to kill you.

Nubian had been closed up for Action Stations as she made her way out towards the Isle of May and there the sea changed, and the wind began to blow. There were small victories though, like the corned beef sarnies that were brought up along with a hot cup of kye that you tried desperately not to spill, not a drop. Kye was simply made by melting dark chocolate in warmed condensed milk. Eventually Herbert was relieved as were the crews at action stations (with a report of Submarines in the area they had been at readiness for over 6 hours) and they headed below but needed to remain on defence stations in case the situation changed. Sanctuary was not a word that came immediately to one's thoughts when going below but for those who had been in exposed positions it was an improvement. At least today the water swilling around the lower decks was only a few inches, it had been over a foot on the last trip.

Men slumped down at the benches, lay across tables or tried to climb into hammocks. Anything just to catch a few minutes sleep. Many just loosened their wet coats and clothing, sleeping at the mess tables, there was no way of getting dry, besides the condensation that formed on the metal surfaces ruined any remote chance of that. It smelled awful too. That hard stale smell of clothes that have been damp for too long, body odour from unwashed men, piss, stale farts and sick. As the ship rolled, locker doors popped open and spilled their contents onto the floor amid curses from their owners. Some of the contents floated about or sank to provide a banana skin for the unsuspecting sailor to stand on.

Eventually it was over, the shelter of the fjords provided welcome relief and Bergen itself came into view. Still cold, but the water is calm and there is just the hiss of *Nubians* bow carving the water and the throb of her engines. Back on lookout it is almost a pleasure to behold the mountains, the snow and the other ships of the convoy, its partly the relief that it's all done for the moment and the misery has vanished far quicker than it appeared as has the sea sickness for those who suffered its torments. There is little time for rest as in not too many hours they will turn around and do it all again with HN17.

February and March 1940 were almost relentless for *Nubian* with three back-to-back trips to Bergen and Methil which included ON and HN17. On the 25 March *Nubian* escorted the Submarine *Tribune* to Scapa flow. A normal routine duty but a welcome change and noteworthy as *Tribune* featured in a Navy instruction film 'Submarine Patrol 1943' (ADM5031) under the pseudonym of 'Tyrant'. *Nubian* then proceeded to the Hawthorn Leslie works on the Tyne. She was somewhat battered and bruised from her convoy duty where the heavy seas had taken their toll on the integrity of the hull.

Refit took a week to complete, before returning to Scapa Flow on the 11 April, by which time the base was almost empty. The Home Fleet had already sailed for Norway to begin Operation 'Wilfred'. *Nubian* would be returning to Norway once more, not for convoy duty but for Operations in support of an invasion.

Norway 1940 – Part 1

Winston Churchill recognised that the Iron Ore trade, mined in Sweden but shipped out from Narvik in Norway was vital to Germany, so much so that he proposed a scheme to send a task force into the Baltic called 'Operation Catherine'. Its purpose was to stop the shipping of goods from Norway, Finland, Estonia, Latvia, and the Soviet Union, but more importantly, to cease the supply of Iron Ore from Sweden. This plan never materialised, however Norway remained clearly under the gaze of Churchill.

Hitler had his views on Norway too, in particular its potential threat as a base for Britain for a flank attack on Germany itself. On the other hand, continued supply of raw materials from Norway was quite essential and it could be used by Germany for submarine warfare too. Whatever, Germany was certainly playing a cunning hand, using Norwegian National waters (and her neutrality), to transport their Iron Ore via waters known as The Leads, before heading out into International Waters that were closer to home and more importantly, allowed protection from air cover. Clearly the British government was frustrated by this gamesmanship. Churchill advocated mining The Leads but in the time of appeasement and minimising any risk of armed conflict the government were fearful of antagonising Norway by an action that may result in their alignment with Germany. Eventually mining was approved with a task force at the ready for any German intervention.

Two plans, both with the common objective of taking control of Norway and both similar in that they would land in several strategic coastal ports. The Germans would be deploying combined forces with troops and supplies from the air as well as the sea. Further air support came from Heinkel 111 and JU88 twin engine aircraft for high level bombing and JU87's as close air support for troops. On the other hand, the British plan sought to capitalise on the reports that the Norwegians had such a dislike for the Germans that they would quickly join forces and provide artillery and motorised transportation. As Captain Donald Macintyre wrote in 'Narvik'; 'But whereas German plans and preparations were made with the meticulous detailed care which was the hallmark of the German Staff Officer and were based on the sensible assumption that the assault would be opposed, the British plan, in spite of months of consideration, wore an air of amateurish improvisation.'

The Altmark incident tipped the balance to put the German plans into action, the order to invade Norway being signed by Hitler on the 1 April, with the 9 April designated Zero Hour. The plan was to send 6 Groups of ships to strategic ports around the Norwegian coast which included Oslo, Stavanger, Bergen, Trondheim and Narvik. Ahead of the warships of the task groups were 7 merchantmen ships acting like Trojan horses, being packed with men and supplies. They were to slip into Narvik, Trondheim and Stavanger and await the main force.

As we have seen, *Nubian* was at Hawthorn Leslie's for repair when the German force sailed on the 7 and 8 April, coincidentally at the same time as the British troops were being loaded onto their transports and the minelayers and destroyers were heading towards Norway. Over the coming days the Royal Navy would be in action, suffering some losses but gaining some staggering victories too.

The campaign begins

HMS *Glowworm* was a Thornycroft built G-Class Destroyer, captained by 35-year-old Gerard Broadmead Roope. As part of the minelaying force, she was rejoining the group on the 8 April, having been detached for a short while. The seas were rough and visibility poor when she came across two German destroyers who were part of the Narvik bound enemy force. She fired the first shots of the Norwegian campaign at these two ships who managed to radio for assistance and answered by the 14,000-ton cruiser *Admiral Hipper*.

The *Hipper* caught site of *Glowworm* and fired her 8-in. guns from relatively close range that found their mark like a fist pounding an irritating insect. *Glowworm* made to run in order to flash message a report, but she would never be able to gain enough distance quick enough to get beyond the range of those murderous guns. Report sent, she turned about and, whilst still dreadfully mauled loosed off a salvo of torpedoes that simply passed by the cruiser. There was only one final course of action, and whilst still under fire Roope had *Glowworm* ram her tormentor.

Glowworm struck the *Hipper* screeching and tearing her way down one side, ripping off 130 feet of armour plating before falling away a burning wreck. Roope ordered the ship to be abandoned, the *Hipper* ceased fire. *Glowworm* was a mass of smoke amongst a boiling, white horse sea before a huge explosion finished her off. The crew of the *Hipper* lowered a ladder to allow the men, who were covered in slick black oil, to climb aboard from their carley floats or whatever else they were clinging to. Roope was one of the last to come up, but either his strength failed him, or his frozen hands could no longer grip, either way, just as he was close to the deck he let go and fell back into the sea. There were 149 crew aboard *Glowworm*, 40 managed to survive. Roope was posthumously awarded the Victoria Cross at the end of the war.

The message was most unusual, it came straight from the First Sea Lord, Winston Churchill. 'Norwegian Coast Defense Vessels *EIDVOLD* and *NORGE* may be in German hands. You alone can judge whether in these circumstances attack should be made. We shall support whatever decision you take.'

For Captain (D) Warburton Lee, of the H-Class Destroyer *Hardy*, leader of the 2nd Destroyer Flotilla, this signal gave him free rein to fight or pause. The news had reached the admiralty that the Germans had landed in Narvik, they were stunned. Initially there was little further intelligence as to the size of force, it appeared there were two or more German transports and perhaps two destroyers. Whilst numerically that seemed to favour the 2nd Destroyer flotilla the German destroyers were known to be more heavily armed. What no one in the admiralty or in the flotilla knew was that both the *Eidvold* and *Norge* were already at the bottom of the Vestfjord.

Warburton Lee decided to call on the Norwegian pilots based at Tranoy Island in the hope that they may be able to provide more substantial information. Here they learned, despite the difficulties in communicating with each other that the forces were larger than they expected, as Lt., Geoffrey Stanning from *Hardy* wrote afterwards. 'One man said that he had seen a submarine entering the ford and that he was sure that the channel was mined.

A young boy told us that he had seen six destroyers, not five as the older man claimed. They asked if we were intending to attack Narvik. I gave them a fairly vague answer. They pointed at the *Hardy* and said that the German destroyers were larger. If we were really planning to strike, then we should get more ships.'[49]

Warburton Lee reported this intelligence to which Churchill had responded directly to him. After some deliberation the operation was on and the 2nd Destroyer Flotilla crept up the fjord through snow flurries and semi darkness towards Narvik. Eventually they reached the first of the ships at the harbour entrance, they had gained complete surprise. Torpedoes were loosed off which struck the German lead destroyer, *Wilhelm Heidkamp*. The aft magazines blew up breaking the ship in two, the stern sinking rapidly. The second salvo hit the *Anton Schmitt* sinking it too. Havoc and confusion reigned down on the unsuspecting Germans resulting in two more destroyers badly damaged and 17 merchant ships sunk.

The *Hardy* began to lead the flotilla out of the fjord at full speed as it was realised that the German force of Mountain troops had been disembarked from no less than ten destroyers. Those that had not been damaged were now on the offensive. Warburton Lee sent one final signal 'Continue to engage the enemy' before *Hardy* was bracketed by shells destroying the bridge. The surviving officers managed to gain control of the ship and run her aground, Warburton Lee was barely alive, and would die shortly afterwards of his wounds. He would receive the second posthumous V.C. of the campaign.

The *Hunter* was now lead ship and she too was soon under fire. She took several direct hits which resulted in fire and smoke belching from her funnel. She turned to one side and slowed. Behind *Hotspur* came on at speed, the bridge calling for evasive action just as shells hit her also disabling both the steering and the engine telegraph systems. There was only one outcome, *Hotspur* rammed *Hunter* with such force that the two were locked together

---

[49] (Jacobsen, 2011, 2016)

for some time. *Hotspur* eventually broke free to escape but *Hunter* sank. Only 50 of her crew were picked up later by the German Destroyers.

The first battle of Narvik was over and the German Destroyers that remained, along with the troops landed were trapped and cut off far to the north of their comrades who had landed in the south. This was too much of an opportunity to pass over and so *Warspite*, returning from the Mediterranean, was re-directed to join with 9 destroyers to finish the job. These destroyers included several Tribals *Cossack, Eskimo, Bedouin* and *Punjabi* with the smaller types *Forester, Hero, Kimberly* and *Foxhound*.

Early on the 13 April *Warspite* entered the fjord her size almost overshadowing the snow-covered hills and mountains. Ahead of her the destroyers provided screening duty.

Warspites Swordfish was launched and soon reported back the positions of three enemy ships, it even found U-64 trying to get under way and managed to drop one of their bombs which scored a direct hit behind the conning tower, sinking the submarine. As for the German destroyers, they were soon overwhelmed, sunk or deliberately run aground.

Whilst the German forces ashore at Narvik were light in numbers, they no longer had artillery or supplies that had gone down with the transports. Nevertheless, they could not be easily overrun by a British force that was only equipped for an unopposed landing. The strategy had to change. By now, Bergen was out of reach, being too far south with the threat from German air attack far too great. Trondheim remained a key target having a large port and central placed to build a bridgehead.

Operation Maurice

Plans were made to take Trondheim with two forces in a pincer movement. Operation Maurice would land the 146th Brigade of British troops, supported by French ski troops, Chasseurs Alpines, in the port of Namsos about 50 miles to the north of Trondheim. To the west, a second operation but smaller in size, 'Sickle', would land at Andalsnes with the 148th Brigade and Royal Marines supported by Norwegian troops. Both would hold in readiness for a naval bombardment of Trondheim (Operation 'Hammer') which would signal them to take the port.

The crew of *Nubian* put the ship through her paces following her refit the day the 2nd Destroyer Flotilla were in action at Narvik, whilst 800 and 803 squadron Fleet Air Arm flew from Orkney to successfully attack and sink the cruiser *Konigsberg* at berth in Bergen harbour. The *Nubians* were keen to be back at sea and ready to re-join the Home Fleet but no more convoys, please! However, on arrival at Scapa they felt a little like being late for school. The majority of the fleet had already left for Norway, but there was an important job to be done.

RFA *War Pindari* was being loaded with fuel oil for the fleet and would need an escort. She was a 'War' class freighter, one of 800 ordered as a result of losses to merchant shipping during World War 1. 400 of these ships were (eventually) built of which 15 were purchased for use by the Royal Fleet Auxiliary as oilers. Every ship of the class was prefixed 'War' to identify her as one of the class.

Commander Ravenhill received orders to sail with *War Pindari* on the 14 April to Lillesjona fjord arriving the following day. Already present were two liners, the *Empire of Australia* and the *Chrobry*. The *Empire of Australia* was the larger of the two, being 22,000 tons and with a capacity to carry 5000 troops. Now painted in navy grey, she was in so many ways different to the beautifully white painted liner with a blue stripe around her hull and 370 First Class Berths that she had been in the late '20's. The *Chrobry* being much nimbler and more suitable for operations in the confines of the fjords would eventually participate in the landings at Namsos. Aboard the ships were men of the 146th (Territorial) Infantry Brigade which included the 1st and 4th Battalions of the Royal Lincolnshire Regiment, the 1st and 4th Battalions of the

Kings Own Yorkshire Light Infantry and the Hallamshire Battalion of the York and Lancaster Regiment. The man in overall charge was General Adrian Carton De Wiart.

General De Wiart almost did not make it. He had boarded a four engine Sunderland flying boat in Scotland with one of his Senior Officers, Captain Elliot bound for Namsos. As they arrived, they came under fire from a German aircraft that was involved in the bombing of the ships in the fjord but somehow managed to land in the Namsen fjord whilst still being machine gunned. The Sunderland was a big aircraft and a strong one at that. It's ability to protect itself earned it the nickname 'The Porcupine' by German aircrews. On landing the pilot deployed the aircrafts rubber dinghy and encouraged the General into it. He refused, not seeing any merit in climbing aboard a rubber craft whilst bullets were whizzing about especially with the Sunderland remaining afloat. As it was, Captain Elliot was wounded and had to fly back to Scotland with the Sunderland. *Somali* was close by and sent one of her boats over to pick up the General. Aboard *Somali* was Colonel Peter Fleming (brother of James Bond author Ian Fleming) and Captain Martin Lindsay who had been landed the previous day to reconnoiter the landing ground. Lindsay would return to England after the campaign and write the 'Lindsay Memorandum' which was a scathing report on the Operations in Norway disclosing that those who had read the report and had 'been there' suggested it 'does not fully disclose the extent of the disorganisation and incompetence exhibited.' This document initiated the resignation of Neville Chamberlain and the rise of Churchill to Prime Minister.

Captain Nicholson of the *Somali* gave De Wiart an appraisal of the situation. Namsos was a small port that was used to export timber from Norway. Like most ports in Norway, it was at the end of a narrow fjord that did not give ships of anything like the size of a destroyer much room for manoeuver. The mountains and hills that were covered in snow came right down to the water's edge whose banks were steep, wooded and rocky. As for landing, there was a single stone quay which could accommodate large ships and a wooden version too. Across the fjord at Bangsund there was a similar wooden quay. Both were open and clear targets for air attack. Indeed, as the two men met there was a bombing raid in progress consisting of high level and dive bomber attacks. This would become the norm during daylight hours over the coming weeks, that at this time of year stretched from around 4am to midnight, indeed it never really got dark at all especially with the snow reflecting the moon and starlight.

Somali was firing all the weapons she could, but as expected the inability to elevate the guns above forty degrees and having just light close-in Anti-Aircraft armament meant that the ship was relatively ineffective against the enemy aircraft. Captain Nicholson expressed the opinion that the landing sites combined with the threat from the air power that was now ranged against them meant the transports would be most vulnerable and the troops should therefore be landed by destroyer. However, without any air support of their own and therefore no command of the air over the area of operations, there was serious risk afforded to the forces deployed as well as the town itself. The landings would have to take place at night, what there was of it. Meanwhile, *Somali* had run out of live ammunition and had begun to fire off its practice shells. That was all that was left. With that, they sailed to join the troopships.

With the arrival of *Somali*, all the escort destroyers were assembled. These included *Afridi* (D4), *Sikh, Matabele* and *Nubian*. Clearly without ammunition, *Somali* was now no use to anyone, so she would sail to Scapa to rearm and therefore *Nubian* would take her place in the operation to land the troops. General De Wiart transferred to *Afridi*. The ships refueled and embarked the troops from the liners. As they completed this transaction the enemy found them. The destroyers accelerated away to full speed whilst the enemy drilled bombs into their foaming wakes in a vain effort to stop them.

The destroyers arrived at Namsos at dusk. The troops disembarked in quick time much to the delight and the satisfaction of their General who wrote, 'The troops were only too anxious to do what they were told, and to be quick about it, and it says much for them that not only did they succeed in landing, but they completely obliterated all traces of their landing. The

Germans who flew over next morning suspected nothing.'[50] Once ashore De Wiart took stock of the equipment that the soldiers had been given. Someone had thought to ensure that the cold was catered for, heavy boots, thick socks and great coats had been issued, but as De Wiart observed, '…but if they wore all these things they were scarcely able to move at all, and looked like paralysed bears.'[51] In respect of transportation and artillery, De Wiart had little to worry about; 'As far as planes, guns and cars went, I had no trouble at all, for we had none, though we commandeered what cars we could.'[52]

The troops quickly began to deploy to their positions to the south at the towns of Steinkjer and Verdal. The roads were almost impassable with snow. Apart from a railway that ran trains intermittently, these were the only means of getting about. As soon as one left the road there was deep snow or dense woodland that hampered any forward movement. The only consolation being that the Germans faced the same challenges.

The following day, the French force was due to arrive with Convoy F.P.1. This comprised of four troop ships and three supporting destroyers (*Tartu, Chevalier Paul* and *Maille Breeze*) which carried the 5th Brigade Chasseurs Alpines, a very well-trained force of ski troops. The Anti-Aircraft Cruiser *Cairo* was included in the screen.

Supporting the landing convoys were the 15th, 16th 21st and 23rd Anti-Submarine Striking Forces comprising in each 4, armed trawlers equipped with ASDIC and depth charges as well as Anti-Aircraft guns and a 12-pounder gun. Designated HMT, (His Majesty's Trawlers), they collectively became known as Harry Tate's Navy after the popular comedian, who incidentally appears to have inspired the World War 1 song 'Good-bye-ee' from one of his famous catch phrases. They were manned mainly by Royal Navy Reservists with a crew of between 35 and 40 men. Whilst their ASDIC suffered from interference from the steep banks of the fjords, they proved invaluable in

---

[50] (Wiart, 1950)
[51] (Wiart, 1950)
[52] (Wiart, 1950)

ferrying troops to and from the larger ships and the shore and they packed a punch well above their weight when challenged from the air, as we shall soon find out. One of these was the *Rutlandshire*. Her crew were to soon become familiar with *Nubian*.

The French troops were landed on the 18 April however one of the troopships, *Ville D'Alger* had to retire and with it were the mules that the Alpine troops needed to transport their equipment. Worse news was to come. Whilst they were indeed a highly trained and motivated bunch, who could carry their well-equipped 60lb packs effortlessly across the snow on their ski's, they were rendered useless by the omission of their ski bindings which had been left behind.

Unlike the British troops, they made the mistake of not obliterating the tracks and traces of their landing. The following morning the German reconnaissance aircraft could not mistake the telltale signs of a large force having been landed. Sometimes it is better not to strike out, but the French soldiers were up for a fight, and they fired their machine guns at the circling aircraft adding weight to the evidence that opposing troops were in Namsos.

As we have seen the Germans were targeting Trondheim as much as the British but were gaining the upper hand. They were rapidly pushing north from Oslo and Kristiansand as well as west from Stavanger. The troops were being effectively supported by air power and most notably the Stukas of Hauptmann Paul Hozzel's, Sturzkampfgeschwader 1 (StG 1 – Dive Bomber Wing 1). They flew the JU87-R which was equipped with drop fuel tanks for a longer range and radius of operation. The Stuka was the perfect dive bomber and ground attack aircraft seeing service right the way through the war. However, it required air superiority to operate effectively being relatively slow and therefore vulnerable to fighter attacks. It had a gull wing configuration, long purposeful nose with a dropped air intake, fixed undercarriage and a long glasshouse style cockpit. Behind the pilot was a rear facing gunner. In flight, pilots reported the Stuka a delight to fly and with a nose heavy configuration quite perfect for dive bombing operations. It had two ingenious developments for that role. Airbrakes controlled the speed of the aircraft in the dive, as described in Helmute Mahlke's book, 'Memoirs of a Stuka Pilot'.

> It was commonly believed that the near vertical dive to earth was in itself an enormous strain on a Stuka crew. Many of those who asked me how I could possibly stand it were amazed when I told them that a vertical dive was not all that different from normal flight. This was due to the fact that, with the underwing dive brakes extended, the speed during the machine's decent was kept very much to a constant and there was little or no g effect.[53]

Pulling out of the dive, which was generally at around a 70 to 80 degree angle, although it could be as much as 90 degrees, was either initiated by the pilot or by an ingenious automatic recovery system that activated when the bomb release mechanism was triggered. The pilots tended to distrust this and ensured they pulled out of the dive by their own means which invariably meant a smoother transition back to normal flight, pulling around 3 or 4g as opposed to 5g when the automatic device was initiated.

When to release the bombs, or at which height is also covered by Mahlke. 'What I found more difficult was estimating the correct height at which to release the bomb. The altimeter couldn't unwind fast enough when the Stuka was in a near vertical dive and always lagged a little behind the machine's actual height. The pilot therefore had to rely mainly on his own judgement as to his altitude – or lack thereof!'[54]

The Stukas of StG1 were operating from a number of bases and very quickly they were far enough north to be harassing the Royal Navy and the troops of both Operation Maurice and Sickle. Meanwhile the JU88's and the Heinkel 111's were used for high level bombing and quite often on shipping. This proved more annoying than effective as the ships had time to manoeuver. Indeed, it was fortunate that the anti-shipping techniques the Stuka crews

---

[53] (Mahlke, 2013)
[54] (Mahlke, 2013)

developed and used with such affect later in the war were only just being realised towards the end of the Norwegian campaign.

The Luftwaffe clearly did have air superiority and could operate almost with impunity in theatre. The effects they had are described by both General De Wiart and Brigadier Dudley Clarke (from his book Seven Assignments). De Wiart states; 'It is a most unnerving and unpleasant sensation to be peppered from a plane bearing straight down on one, and takes a lot of getting used to.'[55]

Clarke goes further. 'The German pilots flew now just as they liked, up and down that one narrow road along which everything had to move. In relays of two and three they would come out to bomb the bridges and the cross-roads and then, with the bombs spent, they would drop down on their remaining petrol for the sport of shooting up anything left in sight. The hum of engines soon became so regular that there was no more chance to stop the car and streak for shelter before each made his initial run in'[56].

He goes on; 'That first attack either got you or it missed you; and only then, after it was over, would there follow the exhausting process of tumbling out and ploughing through snow to the nearest tree or wall, or even the roadside drain, in the few minutes that were left before the next one…'[57]

Where is the R.A.F?

Herbert often chastised my grandfather (who was in the RAF during World War 2), asking him 'where were the bloody R.A.F when we needed them most.' True to say that during the retreat to Dunkirk the RAF were there but operating some way in-land to shoot down the bombers way before they reached the beleaguered troops, hence an impression was given they weren't

---

[55] (Captain Donald Macintyre D.S.O & 2 BARS, 1959)
[56] (Captain Donald Macintyre D.S.O & 2 BARS, 1959)
[57] (Captain Donald Macintyre D.S.O & 2 BARS, 1959)

present. It's also fair to say that if there were aircraft over the beaches then it was almost too late as the bombers had got through. In Norway (and as we will see later in the early part of the Mediterranean operations) there was no effective air cover but there was some attempt to get the RAF there. When they did arrive, there is no doubt about their commitment. The Fleet Air Arm were somewhat shackled with the aircraft available to them as they tried to rebuild after years or forced neglect and prejudice. HMS *Furious* was there from the beginning but she had no fighter aircraft aboard, only Swordfish torpedo bombers and when *Ark Royal* and *Glorious* joined later, they could only operate from 150 miles offshore, limiting the time over the theatre of operations and unable to provide continuous cover for the troops.

263 Squadron RAF [58] was formed in 1939 and was based at Filton aerodrome near Bristol. In the winter of 1940, it was training up its crews in navigation and gunnery whenever the harsh weather permitted. They were operating Gloster Gladiators, an aircraft that when observed closely is most definitely an inter war design that was modern but old fashioned at the same time. A biplane with a large air-cooled radial engine, part fabric, part metal construction with fixed undercarriage it was the first RAF aircraft to enter service with an enclosed canopy. Despite being obsolete almost immediately it came into service, the Gladiator was loved by pilots for its handling and manoeuverability although compared to the more modern monoplanes it was slow with a top speed of 257 mph. That meant the Spitfire and Me109 were over 100 mph faster, whilst the JU88 twin engine bomber was also quicker by some 30mph. However, it was robust, highly manoeuverable and it had a short field capability suited to operation from the tiny strips in Norway.

With this in mind, 263 Sqn was informed in March 1940 that it should prepare a Field Force Squadron with a likely deployment to Finland at any moment. This meant additional personnel, extensive firearms training as well as packing and transportation practice. With the 'go, no go' dithering that the government went through over the next month this had an impact on the squadron who were one moment meant to be running an operational

---

[58] (Squadron, 2007)

squadron and the next preparing for deployment, only to be stood down and then asked to do it all again!

Finally, they received the order to prepare to depart their aircraft on the 20 April, flying to Prestwick via RAF Sealand. The ground crews, spares and maintenance materials had already departed for Leith where they would board troopships for Aandalsnes. On arrival at Prestwick, Fleet Air Arm pilots ferried the Gladiators to HMS *Furious*. 14 managed to land but one had some form of issue on final approach and ditched 200 yards behind the carrier. Fortunately, the pilot escaped but the aircraft was lost. 4 more Gladiators arrived the following day. To compliment the 18 serviceable aircraft were the pilots led by Squadron Leader J. W. Donaldson, a 29-year-old from Sussex, and his Flight Commander, Flight Lieutenant R. S. Mills with 11 other Pilot Officers and 5 Sergeant pilots.

On a miserable mid-morning of the 24 April Donaldson was called to a meeting with the captain, who informed him that the ship would steer into wind in readiness for their departure within the next 3 hours. Grey clouds created dull, overcast conditions and on occasion there were snow showers. The deck may have been 700 feet long, but it looked awfully short, there was a big drop at the important end and if you ended up in the sea there was 27,000 tons of carrier bearing down on you. Donaldson requested that the Squadron split into two formations of 8 aircraft with each formation escorted by an 803 Squadron Skua. This was agreed, quite likely because the two-man crew of the Skua could provide more accurate navigation to the frozen landing ground of Lake Lesjeskogen to the east of Aandalsnes where Operation Sickle had landed.

In the squadrons operational record there is a note of particular interest that reads: 'For the information of RAF pilots who may be called upon to take off from a carrier in future it is pointed out that, provided take-off is made with care, there may be no anxiety for the safety of the pilot.' Comforting indeed.

The landing strip on Lake Lesjeskogen had been prepared for the aircraft by an advanced party from the squadron ground crew and with help from local people. They had formed a runway by heaping the snow to either side of the makeshift runway so that by 19:00 hours the aircraft were all safely on the ground after a 4-hour flight. However, Donaldson and his Flight Commander had noticed when positioning to land that there were bomb craters in groups spaced about a mile apart all along the road and railway line running alongside the lake. That was rather ominous.

Despite all the practice preparation over the previous months, the operation had begun to unravel back at Leith. The lorries and supplies had arrived late and much of the vital stores including important lubricants had not been loaded. There was no time to lose for now, and three of the Gladiators were set at readiness to take off should the enemy approach whilst the remainder were dispersed around the lake and protected as best as possible from attack. A sortie was flown by the section at readiness, however a reported enemy turned out to be aircraft from the Norwegian Airforce.

With all available aircraft, pilots and equipment accounted for a meeting was held to review their capabilities. Attending were senior officers and a captain of the Norwegian Air Force. Donaldson put forward that the squadron could not operate from the lake and would need to move, but he was told that there was nowhere else suitable in the area. It was now a case of practicalities, they needed to work out what they could do, not what they couldn't.

The first decision had already been taken. They were no longer capable of being an offensive unit. What aircraft and stores they had would need to be protected, so the serviceable aircraft would provide protection for the squadron, the airfield itself and to make a nuisance of themselves to the enemy if the opportunity arose. The ground crews that had arrived were not those trained to rearm, refuel and keep the aircraft flying, so these duties would have to be carried out by the pilots with the available ground crews helping as best they could. There was one armourer present but there was no way he would be able to service 72 Browning's alone.

Despite the squadron aircraft landing intact, restarting them was now a problem. In order to turn over their 9-cylinder Mercury radial engines, the Gladiator required an external electrical generator to provide initial starting power. This was connected to a position underneath and behind the engine cowling, so a man was needed to remove this after the pilot had started the engine. For safety reasons the batteries were shipped without acid, and like a lot of the fuel and lubrication oils the acid had not turned up. So, with what acid they managed to beg, borrow or steal they only had enough to run two or three generators at most. This meant that with pilots rotating flying missions combined with ground crew duties it was likely they could only deploy two or three aircraft at one time.

Captain Unwin from the Norwegian Air Force then provided a summary of the latest intelligence. The enemy bombers were operating at will and against both civilian and military targets. Paratroops had been used and it was reported that those who refused to jump were shot by their officers and some had been forced to jump at low level into snow drifts without parachutes. In cases where Paratroopers were cornered, they feigned surrender only to throw grenades when their would-be captors approached. If these reports were true, then the intelligence was indeed grim.

The morning of the 25 April began like any other in Norway, very cold and very early. Overnight the temperature had dropped to -2 and with daylight approaching at about 04:30 the crews were out beforehand to prepare the aircraft. The cold had done its work though and the controls of the aircraft were frozen solid but worse still, the carburetors were frozen too. The oil was drained and warmed, the ice scraped, and the carburetors warmed by whatever means they could find. These normal routine tasks were made all the more difficult with hands and feet like blocks of ice and the threat that at any moment they could be attacked.

The crews managed to start two aircraft that launched at 04:45 intercepting a twin engine Heinkel 115 float plane which they shot down. However, a lone

He111 crept up on the airfield and managed to drop a stick of bombs which made more noise than damage, but it was a foretaste of what was to come.

Pilot Officer Purdy, a 22-year-old Canadian from New Brunswick, put his foot into the fuselage recess that enabled him to swing into the cockpit of his Gladiator. Once settled into his seat, which he adjusted for comfort, he quickly scanned the instruments to check they were all reading as they should. Then there was a shout, not that the electrics were connected as he expected but 'enemy aircraft approaching!' Looking up he saw three aircraft in formation split to commence individual attacks on the airfield. Normally it would take a few minutes to go through his checks, but this all went out of the window now. He primed the engine and simultaneously shouted 'external power?' 'Connected' came the reply, he switched both magneto's to 'on' and the same for the third, starting magneto. He set the throttle to about an 1/8th of an inch open, checked the main fuel tank was selected for startup, expecting in that moment for the engine to cough into life. Except it didn't. A bomb exploded just in front of his Gladiator so loud and so close that for a moment he could not comprehend what had happened. Snow, ice, smoke, flame and the concussion all hit in an instant along with the noise that was so deafening he didn't hear it. The explosion ignited the fabric wings of the aircraft, pieces of which began to drop into the cockpit, he had to get out. He unfastened his harness and hoisted himself out of through the searing heat which burned through his gloves and seemed to melt his face. He hit the ground and ran for cover in the snow and trees at the side of the lake about 50 yards away.

There he met the other pilots, including the C/O who was dazed and clearly concussed. It was only 07:45 and the Germans had attacked the airfield in force. The men looked out from their hiding places, breathing heavily, trying to take in the situation and agreeing that they were lucky the bombs did not detonate until they had penetrated the ice which had somewhat softened their effect. Out on the ice, 4 aircraft crackled and burned, their exposed airframes like bones, black patches of burned material below them. The sound of aero engines returned and with it a chatter of guns. Pilot Sergeant Ernest Russell was still on the ice having been rearming the aircraft with some of the ground crew, but now he ran crouching low as he did so towards his fellow pilots as machine gun bullets hammered into the ice around him.

The men gathered together and decided that only the pilots would attend to the aircraft from now on although this meant it would take up to an hour and a half to rearm and refuel the planes. Pilot Officer Purdy was badly burned but he refused to have his wounds attended to and carried out a flight on the next patrol at 09:00 when they managed to get 6 aircraft into the air. During the patrol Flt Lt. Mills had an He111 confirmed shot down, one of a formation of 6 aircraft that Mills took on alone.

At lunchtime Pilot Officer McNamara was patrolling by the airfield when Heinkel 111 L1+BM was spotted approaching. McNamara closed in for a deflection attack and scored a number of hits which resulted in the port engine catching fire and streaming white smoke. The ground crews cheered as it appeared the aircraft spun in, when in fact the crew had managed to jettison their bombs to make a forced landing. They were duly captured, the pilot, Unteroffizier. Kurt Kern had a clipped ear and cheek.

Despite these small victories the squadron was feeling the effect of attrition and by this time they had lost ten of their eighteen aircraft through bombing. Out on the ice Donaldson and Mills were in their Gladiators with P/O Purdy who despite the pain from the burns on his hands was connecting the starter generators. Once more there was the sound of approaching aircraft as three He111's bore down on the airfield depositing a salvo of 12 bombs. The pilots rushed for cover, Mills and Purdy got behind a machine gun, Mills firing the weapon whilst Purdy fed in the bullets. They targeted the 111's which had begun a strafing run, tracer arched towards the attackers who broke off their attack. With this the three men jumped up and ran back to their aircraft. Donaldson and Mills clambered in whilst Purdy connected the generators as a lone 111 began another attack. They ignored its presence and shortly both aircraft got airborne whilst Purdy trudged back to cover, sat down and lit a cigarette, blowing out a satisfied plume of smoke as the sound of the Mercury's dwindled into the distance.

An hour and a half later Donaldson and Mills returned to the airfield from patrol, just as an He111 from KG4 was making an attack. Donaldson and Mills set upon 5J+JM flown by Oberleutnant Wolfgang Richter setting fire to the port engine which began to trail white smoke and loose height. Richter was badly injured, but he managed to crash land the aircraft. One of the crew were dead but Oberfeldwebel Ziegler and Feldwebel Augustin escaped and exited the wreck which began to burn. Locals gathered to find only the tail section remaining and the body of one of the crewmen left behind. The following day Norwegian forces found the men hiding in a farm. A firefight ensued resulting in both Ziegler and Augustin being killed, whilst Richter was taken to hospital where he turned a pistol on himself following the amputation of his arm.

Donaldson and Mills came across a second He111 and made another successful attack which resulted in the aircraft crash landing. By now they had been in the air for over 2 hours and would need to land soon. As they approached the lake Donaldson spotted two more 111's approaching in a diverse attack, one from the east and one from the west. The pair managed to fight these off but by now Donaldson only had a few rounds of ammunition left in one of his Browning's and very little fuel. He signalled to Mills to land whilst he would provide cover from about 2000 feet.

Donaldson watched Mills begin a short circuit to land, momentarily he breathed a sigh of relief and gave himself a moment to just be aware he was flying and listen to the sound of the Mercury. He checked over his oil and temperature gauges, the fuel status was very low, but he had his reserve tank and so all was well for the moment. Then he saw them. 4, JU88's inbound his concentration snapped back into place, and he accelerated to attack despite his lack of ammunition. He fired a burst that ended as quickly as it began and then his engine died from fuel starvation. He quickly reached out and flipped over to the reserve tank, thankfully the engine picked up once more. However, his intended victims had now turned on him and he had to fly like the devil possessed to be rid of them. He managed to dive away to shake off three of them, but the fourth was good and stuck with him, the both of them now at very low level with trees flashing past just below. In a last-ditch attempt to escape Donaldson, breathing hard through the excursion and stress of combat stamped hard on the rudder, pulled up and over in a barrel roll finding himself somehow behind the JU88 within a narrow ravine. The pilot of the JU88, unaware that the menace now behind him in a perfect attacking position was without ammunition, broke off the attack and headed for home. Donaldson climbed to gain height and some safety margin should his engine quit once more.

Meanwhile Mills was going through his landing checks. Brakes off, main tanks selected, speed below 78knots, flaps set for landing, harness tight, a little more power to counter the drag of the flaps and maintain 65 knots approach. He shuffled in his seat and loosened the muscles for landing, and then noticed that the ground crew were nowhere to be seen. That could only mean there were enemy aircraft about, full power applied for a go around, speed building, flaps away and re-trim for climb out. As he was doing this, he spotted them, and Donaldson attacking.

He in turn was now set upon and began evasive manoeuver's, but one particular JU88 had latched onto him and despite his best efforts to turn away it attacked time and again. As Mills made turns to evade, the enemy pilot pulled up into a steep climb gaining height and momentum and then rolling over to dive down again on to Mills. Eventually Mills decided enough was enough and turned onto his tormentor in an effort to ram him. The enemy pilot wisely chose to retire. Mills watched the JU88's go out of sight before climbing for safety as the aircraft was now flying on fumes which shortly resulted in the engine quitting. Mills set the Gladiator into a glide approach and made a forced landing at one end of the lake. He clambered out; all was quiet apart from the ticking of the cooling engine. There were a lot of holes in his aeroplane, the engine had been hit too. Then there were a lot more holes as a 111 came hurtling upon the stricken plane. Mills ran for cover as his Gladiator caught fire and burned to a withered crisp.

Donaldson, meanwhile, had gained enough height to give him some time, but he had strayed too far from the lake to get back with what fuel he thought he had left in the reserve tank. He needed to get the aircraft down in one piece. Below was Aandalsnes and he spotted a small strip on a plateau which would suffice, it should also be in friendly hands. He made his approach and successfully touched down on the 400-yard sloping strip. As he stepped wearily from the aircraft he was met by friendly forces.

A dispatch rider arrived at the lake sometime later with Donaldson's orders to prepare any serviceable aircraft left and ferry them immediately to the landing strip at Aandalsnes. All useable stores and fuel were to be gathered up in readiness to move there also. In time Donaldson arrived with a truck and supervised the packing and relocation of the squadron. 4 aircraft managed to take off, 11 aircraft were burned out from bombing whilst two were damaged beyond repair. The ground crews set fire to these before departing as the black smoke from the two burning aircraft towered into the darkening sky. It was almost midnight.

The remaining four aircraft were prepared for a reconnaissance and strafing mission the next morning. On returning to base the engine of Pilot Officer Craig Adams aircraft ceased at a most inappropriate moment. He managed to land at nearby Sundalen which remained under the control of the Norwegians. The aircraft was a write off, but Adams managed to find transport back to base.

Three aircraft landed safely, refueled and rearmed. At 10:00 the Heinkel's and JU88s began to bomb the troop positions and docks at Aandalsnes in force which continued all day long. They flew at 25,000 feet which meant that they were operating with impunity as there was no oxygen available for the Gladiators. They were stuck at 10,000 feet at most, powerless to intervene. The bombs fell, the docks took a beating, an ammunition dump exploded.

By the afternoon there was just one Gladiator serviceable. Pilot Officer Jacobsen made the final flight, claiming a probable 111. On shutting down, Donaldson came over and helped him from his aircraft. That was it, there was no fuel left. The aircraft were inspected, just in case some fuel could be found, but all were in a poor condition, none were safe to fly. The attempt to provide air cover for Operations Maurice and Sickle was over.

In the brief time 263 Squadron were operational, they carried out 49 sorties over Norway, 37 attacks on enemy aircraft and scored 6 confirmed kills, 8 probables. Squadron Leader Donaldson received a D.S.O, Pilot Officer Mills, McNamara and Purdy a D.F.C. and Sgt Pilot Russell a M.M.

Back in England the Government and the Admiralty were locked in a struggle to decide whether to initiate Operation Hammer (the taking of Trondheim). Trondheim was the prize but clearly out of reach now that 263 Squadrons brief and frantic foothold had evaporated. A landing of troops under intense and unrelenting bombardment from the air would end in certain disaster not to mention the risk to the ships of the Royal Navy. The consequences of losing an asset such as *Warspite* did not bear contemplation. The decision was made, 'Hammer' would not go ahead.

Instead, the 4000 troops earmarked for the assault would sail to Aandalsnes where they would add strength to the forces already deployed there. The freighter *Cedarbank* departed Aberdeen with the troopships originally destined for Trondheim with the 'J' Class Destroyers *Javelin* and *Jackal* providing close escort. As the coast of Norway came into sight there was a colossal explosion, *Cedarbank* had received a hit from a torpedo and rapidly began to sink. In his memoir, 'Destroyer Man', Rear Admiral A. F. Pugsley who was Commanding Officer of *Javelin* at the time recalls that the sinking of *Cedarbank* forced him into a situation and a decision that no escort wishes to encounter, that is to ensure the protection of the remaining ships and to leave the men of the sinking ship to their own fate. 'So easy to decide thus in theory. But within sight of men whom one was there to protect, drowning in an icy sea, it tore the heart to ignore them as we swept by on our search for the attacker. This was the only occasion when I had to make such an appalling decision and the anguish of it will live with me always.'[59]

---

[59] (Pugsley)

As a consequence of the cancellation of 'Hammer' the Germans were able to land troop reinforcements into Trondheim Fjord supported by destroyers. These troops were not just any troops either, they were specialist Mountain Troops equipped with skis, and this force had not left their bindings behind. Up in the surrounding mountains the British forces stood out like hares on snowy downland. The destroyers began to range their guns on them as the Mountain Troops assaulted the British positions and began to drive them back towards Namsos.

Generals and Trawlers - Namsos 19 – 23 April 1940

Back on the 19 April, as 263 Squadron was in transit to Lake Lesjeskogen *Nubian* was out to sea off the coast of Norway having finished assisting the troop landings at Namsos. The coming days would throw *Nubian* into direct conflict with the enemy and test the ship and her crew to their limits.

During the afternoon Commander Ravenhill received a signal from *Afridi* that he was to take *Nubian* back to Namsos to assist with the landing of the French forces. They parted company with *Afridi* at 18:43 and by 23:50 *Nubian* was closing on Namsen fjord, making contact with the outer sea defence in the form of the French Destroyer *Maille Breeze*.

The following morning at 04:30, out of the gloom came the returning convoy of French transports from Namsen fjord, and so Commander Ravenhill had *Nubian* position to join the convoy and to make contact with *Cairo* that was leading the convoy to deeper water, away from the narrow fjord and the threat from enemy aircraft.

Herbert was once more on watch and could not help himself spare a moment to appraise the big cruiser that was alongside and be impressed at the handling of both ships in close proximity, their boiling wakes churning between the ships that were running so close together. *Cairo* was a bit different now, having been updated to an Anti-Aircraft platform since he remembered her from the days on the East Indies Squadron. His attention was drawn to one of the men preparing a heaving line, the weighted despatches could be seen hanging down from the coiled rope in his right hand, whilst he held in his left the other two thirds of the coiled rope which combined measured about 150feet in length. With a smooth and almost effortless single movement the seaman twisted his hips to the right and then left, letting go of the rope which snaked over the water between the two ships. One of *Nubians* men managed to grab the line, detach the despatches and head towards the bridge. 'Nicely done' thought Herbert.

The orders were straight forward. Return to Namsos arriving at dusk to avoid air attack. Pass over the despatches to the commanders of the forces there, receive and transmit any that were given by return if their importance warranted a signal. They were then to sail at dawn for Scapa and further instructions.

Nubian piped to action stations for full readiness when she entered Namsen fjord at 21:30. The crew were already tired from being at a second state of readiness all day, which did not afford much rest. They now needed to be fully alert in case of attack. Ahead was an orange glow in the sky that gradually became more intense as they moved further up the fjord until it was quite obvious that the port was on fire. Commander Ravenhill later wrote, 'I concluded that the fire was almost certainly due to bombing but kept in mind the remote possibility of the town having fallen to the Germans. When the town came into view the sight was remarkable. The whole place was a mass of flames from end to end and the glare on the snows of the surrounding mountains produced an unforgettable spectacle.'

Ravenhill called for Lt. Commander Lampard to attend the bridge. 'Number One. Ask Mr. Bush and Mr. Terry to take two boats. Bush will proceed in one to the town, ascertain whether it remains in our hands and if at all possible, make contact with our forces there informing whoever you find in a position of command that we have despatches aboard. Place Mr. Terry in the other and have him inspect and report the condition of the landing facilities to include the wharves and jetties. We will continue to manoeuver within the fjord close by in case of enemy intervention.'

Later Bush returned. Within the boat, and to Ravenhill's relief there was a British Army Officer who was brought up to the bridge. Before heading to the Captains Sea Cabin to discuss the situation, Ravenhill took stock of the man in front of him. A slim but wiry looking gentleman of about 60 years of age, slightly thin faced with a full, grey moustache and a black patch over his left eye. He had a stick in his right hand, his left hand was missing. This was General Adrian Carton De Wiart.

General De Wiart would have certainly appeared a formidable character and someone to treat with the utmost respect. He had been wounded 11 times in his military career, shot in the stomach and groin in the first Boer War. In Somalia he lost his eye and his left hand. The palm and part of his wrist had been blown away; two fingers remained hanging by threads which he pulled off himself because a doctor refused to remove them. During the First World War he had been shot in the head. The staff at the London hospital where he was treated for his various wounds had a set of pyjamas made with his name embroidered inside as he was such a regular visitor. It is little wonder he had received a Victoria Cross. Some have suggested he was reckless, others that he received his wounds because he led from the front, often preceded by the words 'Follow me'.

Much has been made of his Military career and the fact that he could be forthright or rude, often swearing, especially when his famous temper overcame him. Having become a private soldier in the ranks of the British Army, where like any male dominated profession profanity is often interwoven effortlessly in conversation, it is little wonder that he continued to use such language all his life. The humour was hard, of a gallows nature and often scathing which would not have gone down well with the more sensitive of his officers.

Despite being the epitome of a 'Boy's own' professional soldier he was a man with a sense of humour that allowed him to laugh at himself. Once after being wounded in the leg in France; 'On Dover Station I was lying on a stretcher feeling extremely bad-tempered and disgusted with my last brief stay in France, when a well-meaning clergyman came up to me. Seeing the disgruntled expression on my face and my one eye, he told me to cheer up, as it might have been much worse; he said he had had such a cheerful fellow through his hands a few months earlier, a man who had lost an eye and an arm. I asked him the man's name and he said 'General Carton De Wiart' and seemed quite hurt when I lost interest in the conversation.'[60]

During the inter war years, De Wiart was posted to Poland as Second in Command of the British Military Mission. As he states, 'I went to Poland for 3 weeks and stayed 20 years.' Here he saw changes in warfare that he found difficult to comprehend. On the more amusing side, there were the women soldiers he found in the Polish Army; 'The guard of honour was drawn up at the station and whilst inspecting it I found to my confusion it was composed of women soldiers. I believe they had fought heroically in the defence of Lwow and suffered heavy casualties, but I found them an unnerving ordeal, like all women in uniform.'[61]

On a darker side he was one of the first British Officers to witness the effects of 'Blitzkreig' style warfare as the Germans attacked Poland, most notably the effective use of aircraft. The overwhelming of all before it was something that as a soldier from a time when conflict was confined to the armed forces was difficult to come to terms with. 'The same day the Germans bombed Warsaw, and with the first deliberate devastating bombing of civilians, I saw the very face of war change – bereft of romance, its glory shorn, no longer the soldier setting forth into battle, but the women and children buried under it.'[62]

Away from the battlefield he had a great love of the countryside and especially field sports. A good horseman, he played Polo but had a zeal for Pig

---

[60] (Wiart, 1950)
[61] (Wiart, 1950)
[62] (Wiart, 1950)

Sticking (hunting boar from horseback with a spear). Shooting was a real passion, but as is often overlooked and almost incomprehensible by those who do not hunt, he was fascinated by wildlife and had a great respect for the quarry that he pursued. Indeed, his view on shooting will ring true with those who shoot today, despite being written in 1950; 'Perhaps, inadvertently, I have been stressing too much the size of the bag in those never-to-be-forgotten shooting days in Poland, for to all good sportsmen the size of the bag means little, and it is the quality which counts. The quality of the day, the setting, the friends, or just the intelligent working of one's dog can make a day memorable that has heard few shots fired.'[63]

It is the love of the outdoor life that De Wiart obviously thrived upon and why, no doubt, the life of a soldier was so appealing. There is no clearer illustration of this, than when he was taken prisoner by the Italians later in World War 2. 'It was there and then, in that small bedroom, that I felt the walls close around me, shutting me in alone with the inescapable fact that I was a prisoner. Often in my life I thought that I might be killed, and though death has no attraction for me, I regard it more or less phlegmatically. People who enjoy life seldom have much fear of death and having taken the precaution to squeeze the lemon do not grudge throwing the rind away. But never, even in the innermost recesses of my mind, had I contemplated being taken a prisoner. I regarded it as the calamity that befell other people but never myself. In the ordinary sum of daily events, I seemed to have a fairly equable philosophy, but it could not rise to this, and I faced despair.'[64]

General De Wiart may have been a soldier from a different era, crossing into a new one but that did not make him any less a man for the job as he came aboard *Nubian* that day. He liked the look of the countryside, and why wouldn't he with his love for the outdoors, but he did not like the look of it for the operations he was meant to be undertaking with the inexperienced officers and men that he had at his disposal.

---

[63] (Wiart, 1950)
[64] (Wiart, 1950)

Ravenhill opened the discussion reporting that the French were ready to bring in the *Ville D'Alger* with stores and the mules for the French Chasseurs. There would be support from a further French Destroyer, *Bison*. General De Wiart was not impressed by this and no doubt his assessment of the situation would have been peppered with some deep-felt expletives.

There was simply no point in sending any more ships into Namsos with the air superiority the Germans had over the skies at present. The bombing raid that day had completely destroyed the town, of which the raging fires were testament to. Fortunately, the civilian population had managed to evacuate to safety but there would be little for them to return to, and one could only feel sympathy and sorrow for them. In managing to escape they had used all available means of transportation, so he and his men were left with very little means of getting about. Perhaps if the French had shown the same diligence as his own troops in clearing their tracks once ashore and restrained from firing at the enemy reconnaissance aircraft things would have been different. But that was not worth mulling over.

The damage to the harbour facilities was extensive, with almost all the warehouses burned, the wharves and jetties smashed. If a landing were to be made, then there was little doubt any stores brought ashore would receive the attention of air attack and no doubt be severely damaged if not destroyed completely. It would be doubtful if troops could set up their own Anti-Aircraft defensives quick enough to provide adequate cover and casualties would be inevitable.

Currently the Generals forces were in forward positions south of Steinkjer in readiness for an assault on Trondheim to hook up with the troops from Aandalsnes and those that were due to be landed at Trondheim with Operation 'Hammer'. They had not taken any casualties, morale was good, but they could go no further for the time being. However, the troops had been harassed by dive bombers whenever they moved or were spotted. This did not bode well for the proposed operation against Trondheim and unless either the Fleet Air Arm, RAF or better still both, could provide protection and turn onto the offensive against the German Air Force then it was highly likely the mission would fail. Meanwhile, the French forces appeared in good spirits, despite losing most of their stores. They were currently positioned outside of the town. This assessment formed the basis of a signal sent back to England.

Nubian would now become a centre of Command and Control for the next few days with signals being sent and received from the cramped wireless rooms that had to be manned all of the time. These were not only signals which *Nubian* needed to make, but those on behalf of others, like General De Wiart and the French commander General Audet. In addition, Ravenhill needed to remain on top of the overall situation by having the wireless operators pick up signals from other ships or units in the area. All of these transmissions were cyphered and therefore required much work in decrypting or encrypting in readiness for transmission.

Communications were vital for operations at sea, *Nubian* had two Wireless Transmitting Offices, the Main located in the forward superstructure and the 2nd Office in the aft of the ship below the quarterdeck. The Main W/T Office housed a Type 49 High Frequency (HF) and Medium (MF) set for Long and Medium Range communications respectively. It could be set for Low Power and therefore shorter ranges if required. This set needed lots of power and therefore being a high energy device was located in a partitioned space with a wire meshed door that could not be opened when the set was operational.

A second Type 52HA provided High and Medium frequency capabilities that was primarily used for short range fleet communications or for fire control purposes. This, with its operators was located in the forward section of the Main W/T Office, whilst the Type 49 operators and decoders were to the aft of the office. A portable, battery powered Type 53 set was used for those times when boarding or shore parties were deployed, and more mobile communications required for ship to ship or ship to shore transmissions.

The second office was much smaller than the main office and being some way from the Main Office required a telephone link for inter office communication. Indeed, internal communications were as important as external ones and there were several methods employed to save the use of ships runners dashing about delivering messages. The most primitive was the Voice Pipe, and these connected the Main W/T Office to the Bridge, Transmitting Station and the Signal and Plotting Office. Then came the telephones, the main exchange located in the Main W/T Office. Most ingenious was the Pneumatic Message delivery. A written message would be loaded into a small metal case and fired with compressed air down a $1^1/_2$- inch brass tube between both the Main and 2nd W/T Office, the D/F Office and the Bridge Signal Office.

Staff positions numbered 9 in the Main W/T office and 2 in the Second and as a result, Ravenhill had to detail as many as 5 Officers and three ratings to assist in the workload at this time, utilising both W/T Offices simultaneously. Expertise that could be ill spared with the ship at a high state of readiness (for air attack), constantly on the move and having to be run as efficiently as possible. The whole crew had to perform at a very high level and with much more individual responsibility than normal if they were to get through the coming days unscathed.

As the discussion with General De Wiart came to a conclusion a Lieutenant was introduced to the two men. He had come aboard from the A/S Trawler Group, his name was Ferguson, and he had a report to make regarding the *Rutlandshire* and the groups present status. He looked most tired and somewhat distressed. The Trawlers had escorted Convoy F.P.1 in and out of Namsos delivering troops and stores. They had come under attack from the air, but the escorts had largely kept the aircraft at bay.

Rutlandshire was a 146 ft Trawler built in 1936, with a wooden wheelhouse in the centre of the ship in front of a single funnel from her boiler that could propel her 450 tons at a top speed of approximately 11 knots. She had 4 machine guns and a 12-pounder gun up front as well as her depth charges and ASDIC equipment for her primary role as an Anti-Submarine platform. Whilst one may consider the use of such a vessel as a bit of a joke, being so small and basic against such a modern piece of technology that the submarine represented, she and her class could be deadly. They packed quite a punch with their armaments, they were very manoeuverable and presented a small and therefore difficult target to attack with torpedoes. However, this advantage was very much lost within the confines of the Norwegian fjords and the Trawlers assigned to the campaign would pay a high price for their deployment.

Rutlandshire was commanded by RNR Skipper John Wilson who had served on trawlers in the first war, demobilised thereafter before being recalled for duties in August 1939. During the early hours of the 20 April, she was berthed in Namsos her crew of 30 hurriedly unloading stores before having breakfast at 08:00. Their Norwegian Pilot, Yngvar Ottensen had been helping them, and after breakfast he bade his farewell to the crew and headed home for some well earned rest.

As Ottensen was going to bed, 300 miles to the south at Aalbourg airfield in Denmark, the 15 Heinkel 111's of KGr100 had fired up their Juno engines to taxi out and take off for Namsos. Just before 09:00 they had almost completed their journey. The tolling of the church bell to warn the townspeople awoke Ottensen. He quickly got dressed and ran to the quay where the men of *Rutlandshire* were busying to cast off. The sound of the aircraft was getting louder and just after they moved away from the quay the first bombs began to detonate close to where they had just been moored. This was just the first air raid of the day that would see the town burning by the time *Nubian* arrived later.

With aircraft in hot pursuit, intent on sinking *Rutlandshire* the skipper began to weave the little ship back and forth at full speed in an attempt to throw the bombers off their aim hoping to escape to the open sea where she may gain more support from the escorts. Bombs began to fall with ever alarming frequency and accuracy, with as many as sixteen aircraft attacking from all directions simultaneously.

Below decks the noise was horrendous, above the gun crews fired with everything they had at their disposal. Eventually their luck ran out and whilst the ship was not hit, one bomb fell to starboard and exploded with such force that the stern was lifted clean out of the water. Ottensen wrote afterwards, 'The water poured into the engine room and the main steam pipe was broken. There was a loud bang in the engine, which immediately stopped. It was the crankpin that had broken.'[65]

They had been at full speed when the bomb had exploded so the ship had some momentum. As the rudder was intact the Skipper could still steer the ship the combination of the forward movement and wind over the water allowed them to make for the nearest shoreline. The aircraft kept coming, strafing with machine gun fire and bombs, but eventually the ship ran aground, her stern now sinking rapidly in the water.

Wilson gave the word to abandon ship and then ran below to pick up some matches and cigarettes. A lot of the crew did not have their lifebelts handy; they were locked away in cupboards by the lifeboat at the rear of the ship which was the being hammered with machine gun fire. As for the lifeboats the bullets had ripped huge holes in them making them useless. The men had no option but to jump overboard.

Petty Officer Thomas Graham RN from Ripon was still manning the machine gun and firing at the enemy aircraft as they repeatedly attacked the floundering *Rutlandshire*. He shouted at the men to get ashore, he would cover them. The men gathered quickly together and began to jump overboard either stripping their heavy clothing off beforehand or doing so in the water which was freezing cold and brought gasps from the men as they jumped from the ship. The shore was only 100 yards or so away but that seemed an awful long way in the icy cold waters of the fjord. Graham continued to fire at the aircraft until the men had made it ashore, and then as the *Rutlandshire* took on water she began to sink rapidly, so he also took to the cold water and swam ashore. Graham later received a D.S.M. for his efforts in protecting his crew mates.

---

[65] (Wilson)

Seaman Steward Roy Johnston was 26 years old also from Ripon, before joining up he had been a Purser aboard a P & O Line ship. Now he found himself swimming in a chilly fjord with bullets tearing up the water around him with his crew mates who were grunting and gasping in an effort to get ashore. Johnston had to kick off his boots as they were hampering his efforts, he also felt his Navy long johns become heavy and with each stroke they slipped further down his legs until he had to kick them free too. Ashore he met up with two crew mates and they struck inland, climbing the hill by the fjord to see if they could get help, despite being barefooted.

The depth of the snow hampered their progress and was exhausting to wade through, if they strayed into a gully or depression it went up to their necks. Now and again, they were fired upon, sometimes they crawled through the snow to avoid falling into what they thought may be a crevasse. On reaching the top of a hill they spotted a farmhouse some way off that was clearly inhabited. By the time they reached it all the men were in a bad way. One man had a bullet wound to the neck which was not too serious, but Johnstons feet were a particular concern, and a doctor was sent for. Johnston described his ordeal that was published in the Dundee Evening Telegraph on his return. 'My feet were in a terrible condition, and when the blood started to flow to them again the pain almost sent me crazy. Then as the circulation got going, the blood spurted from my feet onto the floor. The doctor attended to my feet and my companions wound.'[66]

Back on the shoreline the remaining crew had gathered together, all very cold and very miserable. The ship had by now disappeared, but beneath the waves her boilers blew and the explosion that ripped her apart on the bed of the fjord sounded a deep boom that roared and echoed across the water. A great wave rushed outwards from where the stricken ship had been, washing over some of the crew who were still at the water's edge, almost pulling them back into the fjord. Picking themselves up, they all trudged towards a beach hut where they tried to get warm. Sometime later, a small boat arrived sent by

---

[66] (Wilson)

the people that Johnston and his companions had found. They gathered up what gear they had and were ferried back to the farmhouse.

Lieutenant Ferguson requested arrangements to pick up the crew who were now being accommodated in a village close to the shore. He also stated that the situation with the remaining Trawlers was precarious. Fuel was running low, water and food in short supply. Whilst the locals were helpful there was little they could do for them. During the day they had to find shelter as best they could under the cliffs along the fjords, even camouflage the ships with branches in an attempt to hide from air attacks. Ravenhill secured permission to order the Trawlers to Skjel Fjord and out of harm's way for now, he also instructed Ferguson to make contact with Wilson and inform him and his crew to expect *Nubian* to pick them up when the opportunity presented itself.[67]

Sunday 21 April.

A few hours after De Wiart had left the ship Ravenhill received orders to rendezvous with the *Ville D'Alger* and escort her into Namsos and not to return to Scapa as planned. This placed him in an awkward position as he had specific instructions from the General commanding the land forces that under no circumstances could any more ships enter Namsos, and now he had received orders to do the opposite. Clearly De Wiart's signal had not been digested by those in the higher realms of command. In the meantime, the Sloop *Auckland* would come up the fjord and take over Anti-Aircraft protection from *Nubian*.

At 02:00 the weary crew of *Nubian* sailed the ship out of the fjord to sea, where Ravenhill decided to wait somewhere close to the expected location of the rendezvous but close enough to Namsos should the orders change as a

---

[67] The exploits of the 23rd A/S Trawler Group are from F. Wilsons Website of the same name.

result of De Wiart's signal. But, by 09:00 no counter order had been received and so they got under way to search for the *Ville D'Alger*.

Typically, the counter order came at 12:30 to return to Namsos immediately in support of *Auckland*. Being somewhat further away than he had originally planned meant there would need to be a tradeoff between speed in relation to their fuel which was running short. Despite shutting down No.3 boiler, *Nubian* could still make 26 knots and she arrived back at Namsos at 18:40. The aircraft had gone and so it appeared had *Auckland*.

Having received a signal earlier that *Auckland* was being bombed and strafed by the aircraft the crew thought the worst. It was a relief when *Auckland* appeared somewhat crestfallen having been forced to hide up a nearby creek during a snowstorm that had hidden her movements from her attackers between raids. The little ship had fired over 300 rounds of ammunition in retaliation during two raids, one in the morning the other in the afternoon. Her crew may have been forgiven for wondering what had kept *Nubian* from joining them.

One can imagine the trepidation that Ravenhill felt as General De Wiart came aboard *Nubian* once more. Thankfully he reported that despite the two raids there was little further damage to the town and no troop casualties. Ravenhill then had to reveal that he had been ordered to meet and escort *Ville D'Alger* into Namsos for unloading although he had been re tasked to return to Namsos before they could make contact with the freighter. De Wiart was almost apoplectic that his advice was being ignored and he insisted that a signal should be made to *Ville D'Alger* not to come down the fjord, which Ravenhill ensured was transmitted immediately. The last thing the General wanted was all those stinking mules unloaded and running loose about the place.

De Wiart gave another bleak appraisal of the current situation, much as he had done the previous day. He could not move the French forward due to lack of transportation and his own remained bogged down and under fire. He went further, suggesting that without air support or effective anti-aircraft defences it was becoming increasingly likely the troops would require evacuation. Ravenhill appears to have had a distinct feeling that De Wiart would not appreciate it if he suggested *Cairo* were to be brought into the mix to aid with the air defences. Indeed, the presence of De Wiart and what appears to have been his willingness to discuss the direction and objectives of the operation seem to have been awkward for Ravenhill who wrote in his subsequent report; 'In these and other discussions on the possibilities of the situation I found myself rather at a disadvantage. My rank and experience compared with that of the General made it difficult for me to effectively express my point of view on matters jointly affecting the Service and I was not in a position to propose any course of action by own service. Also, I had very little knowledge of the general plan and disposition of forces.'

The signal to *Ville D'Ager* had clearly been ignored as she soon arrived, escorted by the French Destroyer *Bison*. *Bison* was a large destroyer of the Guepard class at 427 feet length with 5 single 5.5-inch guns as her main armament, her crew was made up of 12 Officers and 224 men. On arrival she immediately received a signal from *Nubian* not to allow *Ville D' Alger* to land but to take her out again immediately. Despite this, *Bison* landed some officers who Ravenhill suspected were sent as a delegation to persuade General De Wiart to change his mind. They were seen to leave shortly thereafter no doubt with a flea in their ear for their troubles.

As tired and irritable as he was becoming, Ravenhill had to keep going and to be seen to do so by his equally tired Officers and men. The ship still needed running, the wireless room continued to send and receive signals and the visitors kept on coming with reports and demands. It was relentless pressure. As anyone who has been under continued duress when exhausted can attest that sometimes one feels you could just sit down and cry, or there is the urge to just say 'to hell with it' and walk away. But you don't, you pick yourself up, have a cup of tea and despite the pain behind the forehead that no end of rubbing of eyes will diminish, you carry on.

Yet another knock on his cabin door would come with a request to use his signal office or perhaps gain his opinion on a matter. For example, 'A sea transport officer to report the casualties to his colleagues…The British Liaison Officer to the French forces to ascertain information. A Norwegian Pilot to report the landing of German troops in Lovo Island and sundry people in search of food and clothing.' Then came Lieutenant A. H. Davies who had details of the whereabouts of the crew of the *Rutlandshire*. Ravenhill had the signals office inform *Auckland* that they were departing to pick the men up and would return shortly.

At 22:00 sharp the welcome shape of *Nubian* came into the expectant view of the *Rutlandshires* stranded crew. Seaman Steward Johnston and another man were lying on stretchers as their feet were too painful to walk, the remainder of the crew men were in good spirits, but exposure and the stress had taken its toll. Two motorboats approached managing to accommodate all of the men, who were soon aboard being well looked after by the galley staff with tea, kye and hot food. The skipper would receive a D.S.O, and many of the crew told the tales of their lucky escape to the newspapers on their return. *Nubian* was soon underway to return to Namsos.

Situation unraveling - Monday 22 April.

The He115 floatplane grumbled into view at around 07:30. It kept its distance for a while, skirting in and out of the hills and mountains before making what was obviously a photographic run over the port and the troops positions around Namsos, not to mention *Nubian* and *Auckland* as they trawled steadily around the enclosed waters, ready to accelerate away should they be attacked.

If the aircraft came close the ships guns opened up belching smoke and stinking cordite that hung in the windless air like coughs from asthmatic dragons. There were no shouts of 'open fire' now, the crews knew instinctively when they had a chance at scoring a hit. But none came. At one point the pilot of the 115 had clearly had enough made an attack run dropping a bomb that landed between the two warships simply making a nuisance and raining water onto the gun crews who no longer ducked at the sound of an explosion. There would no doubt be a follow up bombing raid later.

Ravenhill sent a signal party to the port to establish ship to shore communications that would save sending a boat. Meanwhile, a boat from *Auckland* was seen being lowered in order to carry out an inspection of the harbour. For now, all was quiet. The crews remained at readiness in their great coats and steel helmets, thumping fists into their mittens to keep warm, but there was a moment of peace.

Ravenhill sipped at a cup of kye and stamped his feet on the wooden grating of the Bridge, whilst he was quite warm overall his feet were bothering him, he could never keep them from getting icy cold, especially as they were often wet. An Officer came up from the signal room. 'Signal from shore station, Sir. General De Wiart instructs *Ville D'Alger* to disembark stores this evening.' Ravenhill could not help a smile, 'So the General will get his f'ing mules after all. Message *Bison* accordingly to bring *Ville D'Alger* inland confirm with shore that message received.'

As the signalman went below there was a shout from the lookout. 'Aircraft bearing Green three five!' Binoculars raised, Ravenhill shouted 'Fire at will, and signal *Auckland* in case she hasn't seen it'. The aircraft was alone, not the usual force of twin engine bombers, but a Focke Wulf Condor, a large 4 engined bomber and quite a formidable looking machine. For twenty minutes it flew in and out of range during which time a signal was received ordering *Nubian* to return to Scapa Flow, she would be relieved by the Sloop *Bittern*.

There was little time for the crew to gain any rest once the main engines were finished with in Scapa Flow at 22:30 the following day. The ship was a mess from having been at action stations for many days, as well has having the 30 odd guests aboard from *Rutlandshire* who had now been put ashore with fond farewells having been well looked after aboard by their new but temporary shipmates. There was rearming and refeulling to complete too, whilst Ravenhill had a report to file to the Commander-in-Chief of the Home Fleet aboard *Rodney*. He concluded.

> A very great strain is imposed on the personnel of these A.A. ships when employed on this type of duty. Owing to the high mountains, no warning can be obtained of the approach of hostile aircraft; and in ships who's entire is manned for A.A. fire it is essential to be in at least the second degree of readiness during daylight hours from about 0300 to 2100. Reversion to third degree readiness during the six hours of darkness does not provide much relaxation.

The following day *Nubian* put to sea. Over the ships tannoy their Captain announced. 'We are sailing back into Norwegian waters today with orders to patrol the approaches to the fjords around Aandalsnes for any enemy destroyer forces.' In order to carry out these patrols, *Nubian* would be joined by *Sikh, Ashanti* and her sister ship *Mohawk*.

Back in Namsos, General De Wiart was not getting anywhere fast. His troops were pinned down and with every hour that went by the ability to make an assault on Trondheim faded. It was quite clear that the Naval attack ('Hammer') would not materialise. It was becoming ever more likely they would have to evacuate but he was requested to hold the current positions for the moment. De Wiart had Peter Fleming contact the War Office for guidance, the reply was not helpful. 'He came back after a few days and told me that plans and ideas about Norway were somewhat confused and adding: 'You can really do what you like, for they don't know what they want done.'[68]

In customary fashion of the time, there followed an order to evacuate, then a counter order to stay which went on for a while. There was then a suggestion that they should march upon Moesjen which was a hundred miles to the north of Namsos. De Wiart had the route reviewed but he must have known that this was an impossible feat with the roads in dreadful condition and the

---

[68] (Wiart, 1950)

harassment they would receive from the air. Finally, on the evening of the 27 April, De Wiart was informed that the decision to withdraw the allied troops from Central Norway had been made. A withdrawal from Aandalsnes being scheduled on the 30 April and 1 May, followed by Namsos on the 1st and 2nd May. The Norwegian commander, General Ruge was clearly disappointed that his country was effectively being abandoned, in his words 'So, Norway must go the way of Czechoslovakia and Poland?'[69] His troops had been fighting effectively with his allied partners and he could not understand why the withdrawal was being planned when they were not technically beaten. However, they could not hope to hold out, without air superiority, which the Germans enjoyed, it would simply be a matter of time before the end would come.

All this while the German Mountain troops were pushing forward, indeed the German forces coming up from Oslo finally linked up with those at Trondheim and the writing was really on the wall. So much better equipped with skis and snowshoes they forced the British and French troops North of Steinkjer with air power, mortars and light artillery. Stienkjer was mercilessly bombed out of existence and left a burning ruin by countless incendiary devices.

The men fought a gallant rear guard action, sleeping in the snow at night, trudging waist deep through it during the day. One group of about 200 men became known as the 'Lost Company', only managing to escape through ingenious but simple deception. They were out in front of the main force when they found themselves surrounded by the enemy. Fortunately, a messenger had reached them with news of the withdrawal but for now they could go nowhere and were being fired upon from all sides. They first had to extricate themselves from this position climbing a steep 3000ft slope through waist deep snow which took them almost four and a half hours to complete. Once at the ridgeline they found they were looking down on the enemy below and here they decided to disguise themselves as a prisoner of war column. Two of the company went in front with rifles and fixed bayonets whilst the remainder

---

[69] (Captain Donald Macintyre D.S.O & 2 BARS, 1959)

formed a line, two abreast with their weapons slung butt upwards and concealed as best they could under their great coats. They began to march forward in sight of the Germans and simply walked out of the area unchallenged. Their ordeal had just begun as they now had 45-mile march which they managed to accomplish in 44 and a half hours with just a 2-hour break.

In the Namsen fjord the bombing continued. The Stukas were now being used much more effectively in an anti-shipping role. They had caused much damage at Aandalsnes where the Anti-Aircraft guns were so active that their barrels were shot through and as smooth as a 12-bore shotgun. The ships ammunition ran so low that they resorted to firing smoke and practice shells for effect more than anything else. Brigadier Clarke, who so aptly described the strafing of troops earlier, observed the way in which these aircraft were now being used to such great effect.

On one occasion we were treated to a grandstand view in brilliant sunshine of a Stuka attack on an anti-aircraft sloop in the fjord which was almost reminiscent of a 'set-piece' in an RAF display at Hendon. I think it was the *Black Swan* and she seemed to be the focus of every aircraft which visited Aandalsnes. This time they made a determined effort to get her. One pilot came out of the sun almost vertically and held to his course right down to mast-top height in spite of a mass of flak coming up from the ship. He went so low that for a moment it looked as though he were hit, but he dropped his bombs and zoomed up again, while spurts of water hid the Sloop completely.[70]

Captain Poland of the *Black Swan* gives us a vivid description from an alternate angle; 'For the hundredth time I shouted down the voice-pipe to the Transmitting Station, 'Open fire, pom-pom'. In the brilliant sunlight I could see the pilot clearly as the bomb was released at masthead height; then the aircraft zoomed away, surrounded by tracer bullets. I looked aft and my heart went cold. I gained a split-second impression of guns on duty at the after

---

[70] (Captain Donald Macintyre D.S.O & 2 BARS, 1959)

mounting, gazing open mouthed up at the descending horror, then I saw it hit the quarter-deck just below him. A little puff of smoke went from the wooden deck, and that was all.'[71]

The bomb was released too low (fortunately) and went right through the ship, detonating on the seabed without causing any further damage.

In Namsos the bombing continued with an intensity that was mind numbingly relentless. Lieutenant Richard Been Stannard R.N.R. was the skipper of the A/S Trawler *Arab*. His after-action report on 10 May tells how the bombers came over every hour from first light in waves of between 6 and 16 aircraft. The heavy bombers dropped from about 10/15,000 feet whilst the dive bombers came in from around 12,000 feet diving down to around 3000 feet to deliver their ordinance[72].

In an attack on Sunday 28 the French Ammunition ship *Saumur* was alongside the wharf at Namsos with some 40 tons of stores that needed off-loading. Stannard and his men began the unloading, ordering some British and French soldiers to assist, when an air raid began. A 500lb bomb detonated on the wharf some 50 yards from *Saumur* setting fire to the ammunition they had just unloaded. Smoke belched high into the sky and it was now imperative to get *Saumur* away, but she had a wire wrapped around her propellor and was aground. Another Trawler, the *Angel* managed to get *Saumur* in tow which left *Arab* to deal with the fire that if left out of control would render the wharf useless. In the typical understated style of an official report, Stannard describes his actions and those of his crew.

> Proceeded to run my bows into burning wharf, left engines going slow ahead and ran two hoses over her forecastle head to try and put out Ammunition Dump Fire. I signalled *Carlisle* that as *Angel* could manage the towing I would try and put out fire as *Arab* has good water

---

[71] (Captain Donald Macintyre D.S.O & 2 BARS, 1959)
[72] (Admiralty)

pressure and no water was obtainable from the shore. *Carlisle* answered, 'Carry on'.⁷³

The actions of her crew saved the wharf and Stannard was awarded the third Victoria Cross of the Norwegian campaign.

Bittern remained the constant attention of the dive bombers. They sought the little ship out remorselessly throughout the daylight hours but eventually her luck petered out on the 1 May. Around 17:00 three Stukas set upon her and despite her crews' best efforts a bomb hit her quarterdeck that on explosion set off ammunition stores ripping out her stern. There was no option but to abandon ship. Fortunately, the destroyer *Janus* was close by and helped take off the surviving crew. As the burning ship drifted away it looked like she would run aground and so in order to ensure her precious anti-submarine equipment did not fall into the wrong hands, she was sunk by a torpedo from *Janus*.

The last word on *Bittern* must go to General De Wiart, who was most amused by one of the Army Liaison officers who were by all accounts nothing but a nuisance to him. Of this man he wrote, '…he was so anxious that his plane should not go off without him that he thought he would like to go and site (himself) quite near it in a sloop which was in the fjord. A Hun promptly dropped a bomb on the sloop and sank it, but the gallant officer was not drowned and made a safe return to England, where his report must have been illuminating.'⁷⁴

---

⁷³ (Wilson)
⁷⁴ (Wiart, 1950)

Norway – 1940 Part 2

Evacuation 1 – 2 May

Admiral John Cunningham (no relation to 'ABC') was tasked to lead the evacuation that would comprise of both French and Royal Navy ships. On the 29 April, aboard his flagship *Carlisle* he discussed the plans with Commander Ravenhill and Captain Lees of the *Calcutta*, ascertaining that the wooden piers, although they had been patched up repeatedly, would be suitable for extraction. He also had assurance from Admiral Cadart of the French Navy that he could get all three of their troopships alongside the wharf together, these being the *El Kantara*, *El d'Jezair* and the *El Mansour*.

The overall plan was to load the troops over two evenings, however in Namsos they were in fact ahead of the game. After managing to put out the fires on the wharf the crew of the *Arab* had been placed under the orders of the French Destroyer *Brestois*. From here they were engaged to assist in the embarkation of a Battalion of the French Alpine troops aboard the S/S *Aminois*. This left 5400 troops to evacuate, and an opportunity.

On receipt of this information, Cunningham met with De Wiart and suggested that they get the whole force off in one night. However, De Wiart thought this impossible, not he hastened for any lacking in the abilities of the Naval forces, but simply because there were not enough hours of darkness to complete the task before the bombers returned. The plan therefore remained the same.

During the 1 May the ships gathered to form a convoy out to sea south of Namsos that included the French transports, *Nubian*, *Maori* and *Afridi* (Now commanded by Captain (D) Vian of *Altmark* fame) and *Kelly*, who was commanded by Louis Mountbatten. Additional warships included *Bison* the heavy Cruiser *York* and *Carlisle*.

Blue on Blue

Sub Lieutenant Guy 'Brock' Brokensha, Yellow Section, 803 Squadron Fleet Air Arm, eased the throttle of his Blackburn Skua forward creating enough thrust to move the aircraft towards the beckoning handler, aboard the flight deck of the aircraft carrier, HMS *Ark Royal*. In the back seat sat his Observer, Stan 'Andy' Andrews. It was 18:00. The smell of high-octane aviation fuel was almost overpowering in the cockpit as between both men, either side of the cockpit, were the aircrafts two fuel tanks. A volatile and ominous pair of occupants, not the greatest of travel companions when red hot tracer bullets were flying about.

Guy did a final check, full and free movement of the control surfaces. Stick fully over to the port, stick back against the chest and over to starboard, fully forward and then back to neutral. He checked that the flaps were lowered to the short take off setting, the trim tabs set to slightly aft before applying full throttle, glancing to his right with thumbs up. Ahead he could just make out the smoke flowing down the deck confirming the ship was into the wind, he released the brakes, the Skua was over the bow of the great ship in a moment, and they were airborne.

Guy was 19 years old when he decided that life as a Bank Clerk in Durban was not for him, and he would travel to England to pursue a dream; to be a pilot in the Royal Air Force. 1937 was a time of economic depression, and so Guy had to work his passage to the U.K. Once there he wrote home, telling how he had become an 'Eye and skin specialist' during the journey, having peeled so many potatoes.

On arrival, he immediately applied to the R.A.F and attended selection. He failed the medical, having answered honestly, that he had once contracted pleurisy. He must have been devastated, but still determined he sought out a physician, who told him that there were no lasting effects from the condition. Another possibility came in the form of the Fleet Air Arm, and this time, being prepared, he answered the medical questions to his advantage, and was selected for air crew.

Guy was well liked by his fellow squadron pilots. He had a vivacious smile and dashing looks that were well suited to the FAA flying kit and peaked cap. He was told that it was far more glamorous and interesting that the squadron had a pilot from Durban, South Africa, than some boring suburb of London. Besides, why should the RAF have all the South Africans?

A few days before (28 April), Guy and Stan had been in action over Norway, and been in the thick of the fighting. They had shot down a Heinkel 111 and were both confident in their abilities and their sturdy Skua. They had been regularly swapping carriers in the process. HMS *Glorious*, 803's home carrier, had been sent away for refuelling. They had first been aboard *Furious* and had ended up on *Ark Royal*. A temporary CO had been assigned to them whilst away from their normal home, and their quarters were makeshift camp beds where space could be found.

Their Skua climbed away, being joined by Petty Officer A. G. Johnson as Yellow Section, and with Blue Section formed up before splitting to independently patrol the area around Namsos. The patrol was uneventful, and as the sun was setting above a low cloud base, the two crews set course at 19:50 to recover on their home carrie*r, Glorious,* that had returned from refuelling.

The light was fading as the two aircraft let down over the position they had been given for *Glorious.* Below, the ships of the evacuation convoy detected incoming aircraft. They could not tell whether this was friend or foe, and as the Skuas had no radio, only an Aldis lamp for visual signaling, they could not confirm this either. At the same time, the Luftwaffe made their own appearance, and the sky became thick with aircraft.

Nubians gun crews were at full readiness, anyone that didn't need to be on deck was below. Soon the enemy aircraft began to appear, and attacks commenced. The gun crews began to get to work letting fly with a concerted barrage. A single engined aircraft appeared to be making an attack on them, and all fire was concentrated at this target. Black smudges popped, flashed and then sparkled as hits were scored on the airframe. Smoke trailed the aircraft as it began to fall away, the firing died down, and one of the crew shouted out 'Bugger, it's one of ours!'

In the cockpit of the Skua, tracer and all other manner of munitions came upwards, slowly at first then accelerating to lightning speed as they flashed passed the cockpit. Guy selected full power to climb away, shouting 'Bladdy hell', just as there was a huge bang, a reek of cordite, and the engine abruptly stopped. The propellor snapped to attention in front of him like an abusive finger. Silence, apart from the air over the airframe and whistling from a multitude of holes.

Guy's training kicked in; he was busy getting prepared to ditch. Ignition off, fuel off, harness tight. 'Stan, prepare for ditching'. The cloud began to break, they were barely a thousand feet up, but in a good glide descent. Below several ships slid under the wing but there was no power to select any kind of precision ditching area.

Guy was focused on the job at hand but felt that twinge of nervousness and a higher sense of responsibility for what he needed to do, to preserve his life for his immediate family and that of his crew mate, Stan. He scanned the instruments as he would on any landing. The sea looked hard as steel, but relatively calm. He needed to make sure that he did not lose too much speed and stall or hit the sea too hard, so he had to maintain a good scan of the instruments, it was one of those moments where everything other than flying the plane had to be ignored. But he had in is mind, that the Skua was a Navy designed aircraft, it was watertight and had an automatically deploying life raft.

The sea flattened out as the altitude dropped off, his trusty Skua flew straight and level, slower and slower, closer and closer to the waves. The ditching was textbook, but even so, within the cockpit it was like a sledgehammer had hit the underside of the aircraft and with harness throttling force it came to a stop. The only sound was the lapping of waves, and the deep breaths of relief from both men. 'Let's get out of here!'

They pushed open the cockpit and were overjoyed to see the raft had deployed, and thankfully still attached by its lanyard to the aircraft. Despite the fact that Guy had been a lifeguard back in South Africa, he was not keen to enter the Norwegian waters that were barely ten degrees Celsius and would kill anyone within an hour who was foolish enough to enter the water. Both men clambered into the raft and looked around for salvation. This came in the form of the whaler from HMS *Nubian* and a welcoming hand reached out to steady Guy and Stan aboard.

Recovered to *Nubian*, the airmen were taken swiftly down to the Wardroom and despite the obvious commotion as a result of their arrival and the ship getting back under way, a hot cup of kye was brought to them. The bulk of the Commander appeared in the doorway soon after and both men made to get to their feet. 'Please, as you were gentlemen' beamed Commander Ravenhill. 'Welcome aboard *Nubian*, a somewhat more pokey vessel than you have been accustomed to, no doubt. I am sorry that we managed to shoot you down, but we could not risk the convoy and we simply could not tell you from those blasted Germans, at least you are not harmed! There are some dry clothes on their way to you, please make yourselves as comfortable as you can. I am afraid you will be with us for a little while as we have to steam to Namsos to conduct operations to recover the troops there. It appears that we are pulling them out. We should head home directly we have embarked the troops. Now do excuse me, I have much to do,' With that, he was gone.[75]

Temperature inversion

When the air closest to the surface of the earth is colder than that above it, a phenomenon known as a Temperature Inversion is formed. Particles of moisture condense in the air resulting in mist and fog. Such was the case on

---

[75] (Brokensha)

the evening of the 1 May. A signal was sent to all ships in the convoy to abort the mission and head out to sea once more. For some reason, *Maori* did not receive the signal and carried on.

In Namsos, De Wiart had General Audet assemble his troops at the wharf in readiness for embarkation. He had previously promised the General that his troops would not be left behind. However, as the night wore on, De Wiart became more and more anxious as it became clear the Navy were not coming. The French troops, cold and tired were disconsolate as they realised, they would have to spend at least one more day in the vicinity of Namsos.

On board the *Maori* it was with some astonishment that they found themselves alone with a good position fix off the Kya Light, which would help them navigate into the fjord. She signalled the convoy to this effect. Mountbatten, aboard *Kelly* suggested they take two more ships and proceed with *Maori* up the fjord. They may at least get some troops off if they succeeded in reaching Namsos. The plan was approved.

It took some time even with additional lookouts posted to creep and grope their way up the fjord but around dawn they broke through in clear, brightening skies. Overhead Namsos, like vultures over a recent kill, circled the first wave of bombers that day. There was no way that they could risk embarkation, the only protection for the ships was to go back into the fog to conceal their presence. As they were embraced by the grey shroud, the crew resumed their lookouts and strained to listen for aircraft.

Maori's main mast was about 102 feet in height, of which a proportion now protruded above the fog as like a periscope on a submarine. The Stukas over Namsos had spotted the ships just as they disappeared from view, but now they fell with glee on the mast that betrayed *Maori*. Two bombs arrived without warning right next to her. One exploded by the bridge, the others beside the torpedo tubes. The ships boats disappeared in a mass of splinters that just added to the metal fragments of the bombs that shredded their way through the hull, the bridge and the funnels. 27 men were included in the damage inflicted by the fragments, 5 never made it back to England.

The only remaining option was to attempt what De Wiart had deemed could not be done. As he was later to admit; 'I thought it was impossible but learned a few hours later that the Navy do not know the word.'[76] Speed would be the name of the game. The Generals and Admirals met one last time ashore to finalise the plan. General Audet confirmed that his troops would be ready for extraction at 09:15 whilst De Wiart expected his last men no later than 01:00. The soldiers were instructed to leave with as little kit as they could, that meant guns and stores were to be abandoned.

By 09:00 *Nubian* and *York* were at Namsos and taking aboard the first troops ferried to them by the last two Trawlers of the A/S Group. Guy Brokensha later wrote home, 'The scene at Namsos was incredible, we stayed up all night. It never really got dark and the scene on the jetty was lit up by the remains of burning coal. Lorries and trucks powered in and at last we were under way...'[77]

Admiral Cadarts transports did indeed fulfil his promise and efficiently loaded the bulk of the troops from the wharf. Despite shivering in the cold and immensely uncomfortable the men boarded without panic or alarm. *York* and *Nubian* got under way whilst *Afridi* came in to remain until the last men were brought off. Admiral Vivian was informed shortly afterwards that there were men from the York and Lancaster Regiment still unaccounted for, about 780 in fact and quite likely some distance from the town. Vivian gathered together as many volunteers as he could to drive the few lorries left available and any other vehicles, they could find to fetch them. Fortunately, they were found, driven back to the pier and loaded by 02:20, but time was running out.

Now there was just the rear guard to wait for. They had blown the final bridge leading back to Namsos at midnight, but this was 10 miles away. The roads were by now mud and ice with deep snow facing anyone trying to take an alternate route. But finally, a lorry was heard gunning its engine in the distance, it got closer and picked up speed as it found better road conditions

---

[76] (Wiart, 1950)
[77] (Brokensha)

in the town. At the pier it came to a halt, the back flew open, and the Colonel shouted, 'Come on lads' as 33 men piled out to get on board *Afridi*. It was around 03:30, no doubt the Stukas were already being prepared for their first sortie of the day, there was no time to lose for the attackers or the hunted. *Afridi's* lines were cast, and she got on her way for England, Captain Vian ordered the guns trained onto the lorries and equipment left on the quay, tracer flashed towards the trucks, sparkled as it hit and soared into the sky as it ricocheted off the quay. The trucks caught fire, crackling and popping from the heat. There was some relief that they were under way. Just 16 days since they had landed full of hope and determination a stronger and better equipped enemy had driven them back to Namsos, but thankfully the remnants of the force had now slipped away in the nick of time. But it wasn't over yet.

The convoy was not out of danger. The Luftwaffe hit back with all their might, pitching raid after raid at the escaping ships with JU88 and JU87's, over 50 aircraft in each raid. Eventually a bomb found it's mark and hit *Bison*, but despite burning furiously her gun crews kept firing until a secondary explosion occurred in one of the forward magazines and blew off her bow. It was clear she was going to be lost so *Afridi* and *Griffin* approached her stern and began taking off the crew. Fuel oil began escaping from ruptured tanks spreading across the surface of the sea and catching fire forcing the two rescuers away. They lowered boats in an effort to bring off the last men, many of whom drowned or were burned in the flaming oil. Now came the familiar ruthlessness of the enemy, all the while the men were trying to escape from the burning *Bison* and the boats were picking up those in the water, the enemy aircraft dived again and again pouring gunfire at them. There were 69 French survivors on board when *Afridi* finally brought in her boat and fired the torpedo that put the *Bison* out of its misery.

Aboard *Nubian* there were tense moments as one of the transports got into difficulty. Guy Brokensha's Observer, Stan Andrews, an expert signal man, managed to read a message, flashed from one of the transports which Guy later included in his letter home. 'Stay with me engines broken down' followed by an anxious wait for 30 mins, scanning the sky for air raids, until the engines were fixed, and they got under way again.'[78]

It was likely this delay allowed *Afridi* and *Griffin* to catch up once more with the Convoy, but soon the Stukas returned, and all the ships were defending for their lives once more. *Afridi* had almost rejoined the convoy when two bombs from a Stuka caught her. One slammed into her deck behind her forward funnel the other landed right beside her forecastle and drove a huge hole in her side.

The explosion heeled *Afridi* over to starboard, she continued without losing pace, but the damage had been done. No.1 boiler room had taken the brunt of the detonation and soon she circled away from the convoy, losing headway and trailing a curving plume of yellow and grey smoke. *Griffin* and *Imperial* came at speed to her assistance, but it was soon apparent that *Afridi* would founder.

No.2 Boiler room had been plunged into darkness. Frederick Tandy, a young seaman at just 24 later told the Birmingham Mail. 'The light went out leaving us in pitch darkness. Two Stokers and I had to feel our way towards the ladder leading to the escape hatch. At last we found the ladder, however I was the last to go up on to the deck head.'

Seaman Walter Hall was a 21-year-old from North Shields, he was one of the gun crews assigned to A turret. He and his crew were ordered to begin throwing their shells overboard, whilst one of the forward magazines was flooded. Aft, the depth charge team began making these safe, whilst the torpedo crews were heaving the warheads from their weapons into the sea too. A secondary explosion from the ship's ordinance was something they could do without! He reported that the casualties were mainly located below in the mess decks and sadly they numbered about 100 in total.

---

[78] (Brokensha)

Fortunately, *Afridi* took some time to sink, 45 minutes in all. This gave the surviving crew some time to get off her and onto the destroyers that came to their aid. Eventually the large hole let enough water into her forward compartments that her bow went under, and she began her final journey to the sea bed.

The crew of *Afridi* were very young, many were under 25 but despite their youthfulness they performed the damage control and the evacuation of the ship with cool and calm efficiency. It cannot be escaped that many young men died that day. Added to the tragedy of *Afridi's* sinking was the fact that of the dead, 13 were Hallamshire Regiment soldiers from the rear guard and 30 crewmen picked up from *Bison*.

Nubian arrived back in Scapa Flow with the convoy on the 4 May, disembarking her various guests. News of loved ones was slow in getting out to those waiting anxiously at home, the telegram was the most expedient method available. For instance, Leading Seaman Cecil Knowles was an old hand from Gloucester. At 38 years old he had served his time in the Navy having gone through the Great War only to be recalled for round two. He had been assigned to *Afridi*. Back home his wife had not heard from him but knew *Afridi* was in Norway. As usual she tried to listen calmly to the One O'clock news on Monday 6, the day that the Admiralty released the news that *Afridi* had been sunk. It was not until Wednesday that she received the telegram. It simply said, 'I am safe'.

Afterwards

Nubians involvement in the Norwegian Campaign was drawing to a close. The ship received orders to escort the troopship *Royal Scotsman* to land Marines at Bodo on the 9 May, helping to ferry the men ashore and then carry out screening duties. She returned to Scapa on the 12 May where orders were received to proceed immediately to Devonport before deployment to the Mediterranean. There were personnel changes too. Lampard was to leave the ship to join the new Hunt Class Destroyer, HMS *Exmoor* that was being built by Armstrong Vickers in Newcastle, he would take Command of her and see her through final construction and commissioning whilst Lieutenant Commander Terry would also depart. Lt. Bush, despite being a junior officer had clearly made an impression on his Commander, as he was made up to 1st Officer.

Narvik was taken and operations to the south were successful, indeed the first successful allied operations in the war. However, events in Europe were overtaking those in Norway. The German advance that pushed the British Expeditionary Force to Dunkirk and evacuation that was so swift and surprising, not least to the Germans, meant that the British equipment was required back home. Operation 'Alphabet', the withdrawal of troops from Norway, was signed off in late May, and completed in early June. The Germans took Narvik on the 8 June and the surrender of the last Norwegian troops on the 10th.

Guy Brokensha left *Nubian* at Scapa and headed off for two weeks survivors leave. He went back to Norway aboard *HMS Ark Royal* and flew in the action against the *Scharnhorst*. He received the Distinguished Service Cross (D.S.C) for his contribution to the Norwegian Campaign. After seeing action in the Mediterranean, Guy joined 888 Squadron aboard HMS *Formidable,* which was tasked with convoy duties between Mombasa and Colombo. Sometime during the night of the 10/11 August 1942, Guy had been seen to go to bed, but in the morning, he was missing. It is presumed he fell overboard. His disappearance was both disturbing and a shock to all his fellow airmen who attested he showed no signs of stress or cause to take his own life. His loss was noted as a tragic, drowning accident, he was just 24 years old.[79]

263 Squadron returned to Scotland, reformed shortly afterwards and shipped back to Norway for the operations in May and June to take Narvik aboard H.M.S *Furious*. Mills was later wounded and hospitalised, returned to England to take over 87 Squadron. He survived the war and retired from the

---

[79] (Brokensha)

Air Force in 1956 a Squadron Leader. Craig Adams was killed in Norway when he purposefully rammed a JU88. The remaining crews from this first expedition returned to HMS *Glorious* with Hurricanes from 46 Squadron. *Glorious* made for home but did so with escort protection from the Destroyers *Acaster* and *Ardent*. They were detected by the Battlecruisers *Scharnhorst* and *Gneisenau*, which subsequently sank all three ships with the loss of 1500 men including the pilots of 263 Squadron.

General De Wiart returned to England and as we have seen, ended up a PoW in Italy following the engine failure of the Wellington bomber that was flying him to Yugoslavia. After two years and several escape attempts he was released and went to China as Churchills personal representative to Chiang Kai-shek. His association with Wellingtons continued whist in China. He required an aircraft to travel the long distances between the provinces and so requested one from the RAF. They were not forthcoming, suggesting it would take some months to deliver one. De Wiart wrote to Churchill who in turn wrote to the RAF 'You will provide General Carton De Wiart with a plane and report to me weekly until he gets it.'[80] He received a Wellington, which duly crashed landed with him on a return trip to India, it happened to be carrying very valuable whiskey in the bomb bay that was duly recovered. The second suffered a burst tyre and was wrecked, again no one was hurt, and the third crashed on takeoff when being ferried from India. He then received a Dakota which served him for the remainder of his stay.

De Wiart returned to England in 1946 before retiring to County Cork where he fished and lived a more peaceful life until he died in 1963, aged 83.

In 1940 HMS *Effingham* looked nothing like she did when we first encountered her on the South Railway Jetty all those years before. She had been modernised, her main armament was changed to accommodate 9, 6-inch guns, her Anti-Aircraft guns were updated and those torpedo tubes from under her waterline that caused so many problems were removed. Most notable was the single slab-sided funnel in place of the original pair. This gave

---

[80] (Wiart, 1950)

room for a catapult that was supposed to accommodate a Walrus floatplane which was never installed.

She had carried out a bombardment of Narvik along with *Warspite* and her old friend *Enterprise* before being loaded with 1000 troops, 10 Bren Gun carriers and 130 tons of stores bound for a landing at Bodo. She departed at 04:00 on the 17 May, the journey was not a long one and would be complete before nightfall. However, she managed to sail right into the Faksen Shoal at around 19:50, the rocks tearing long holes in her hull, so much so that the engine rooms were flooded, and she lost power. There was no likelihood of her being saved. The men were taken off her and despite all efforts, it was clear that she was a lost cause. To save any possibility of her being taken by the Germans, *Matabele* stood a little way off and fired a coup de grace of torpedoes that sank her. One wonders whether the framed letter from the Prince of Wales (now the King) was still hung in the wardroom, tilting to one side as the waters came in under the door.

Chapter 6

Eastern Mediterranean Fleet Destroyer

Admiral 'ABC' Cunningham was in Malta on 29 April when he received word from the First Sea Lord that the Admiralty were planning on rebuilding the fleet in the Eastern Mediterranean. Welcome news indeed, especially as it included the news that *Warspite* would be returning. The upgrading of the port of Alexandria had been going reasonably well and was almost ready to accommodate the fleet, with dredging works almost complete and the floating dock had arrived from Portsmouth. In Malta, things were better too, the 9.2-inch shore battery guns had been improved to provide a range comparable with that of any ships that would attempt to shell the island from out at sea. The monitor, *Terror* was incorporated into Malta's defence with her pair of 15-in. guns. However, Anti-Aircraft defences remained woeful and there were no fighter aircraft available from England as they were required there for defence, especially since Dunkirk and the likelihood of a German invasion.

Radar was a key component to enhance the eyes of the Navy but was still relatively infant in its capabilities. Reconnaissance from the air remained vital, but there were only a handful of flying boats stationed in Malta and Alexandria which were fine when there was no fighter opposition but at great risk when it appeared, this was especially so when they were required to operate close to the enemy coastline. Despite a request for more suitable aircraft, the protection of England and offensives against Germany took precedence.

At the western end of the Mediterranean, Force H took up station in Gibraltar from the middle of 1940. Its main tasks were to protect the Straits of Gibraltar, protect supply convoys to and from Malta and combine offensive operations with Cunningham's force in the east. However, it did, from time to time, operate out in the Atlantic, most notably in the hunt for the *Bismark* later in the war.

Force H was commanded by Vice-Admiral James Sommerville, described in Correlli Barnetts 'Engage the Enemy More Closely' as, 'Small of stature and with open, boyish features which belied his 58 years, Somerville was renowned in the Navy for his salty – some thought coarse – sense of humour and racy speech larded with foul language. Such ebullience manifested his derisive dislike of stuffiness and pompous consciousness of rank; it enabled him to achieve an easy rapport with younger officers and the lower deck.'[81] Under his command was the *Hood*, the battleships *Resolution* and *Valiant* as well at the carrier *Ark Royal* including a complement of cruisers and supporting destroyers.

Cunningham sailed to Alexandria on the 3 May, his arrival prior to that of the *Warspite* to which he duly transferred his flag on the 10th. Warships from around the globe began to arrive, the French of course were present, soon joined by the cruiser HMAS *Sydney* and the *Leander* from New Zealand. What was missing for now, was a strong force of Destroyers, but they were coming.

Departure

In Devonport there was a gathering of destroyers destined to join the Mediterranean fleet. *Nubian* and *Mohawk* would be assigned to the 14th Destroyer Flotilla, but first they had to undergo some important modifications which included the painting of a red over black band on their aft funnels to identify the ships as part of the 14th DF. The sinking of *Afridi* had shown that the fo'c'sle was difficult to escape from should bomb damage occur, many of *Afridi's* casualties had been trapped in this area of the ship. Modifications were made to provide simpler egress via the mess deck. In the boiler rooms,

---

[81] (Barnett, 1983)

rope ladders were added as alternative escape routes, as the blast from the bomb that struck *Afridi* had shattered some of the fixed ladders.

'An ideal leader of Destroyers in war. An unusually powerful personality whose vigorous and resolute outlook is an unfailing tonic to all serving with him.' A singular comment from Rear Admiral Glennie in 1942 endorsing the promotion of Philip John Mack to flag rank. For now, he had been given command of the 14th Destroyer Flotilla as Captain (D) in *Jervis*. He was 46 years old, a strong and fit character with a round but almost perpetual smiling face, as Cunningham wrote, 'At sea, whilst changing the destroyer screen, the *Jervis* often passed close down the side of *Warspite*, and Mack's large weather-beaten face and broad smile acted as a tonic to us all.'[82]

By the time Mack took charge of *Jervis* he'd had 8 ships under his command of which the majority were destroyers. He was born on 6 October 1892 in Paston, Norfolk, joining the Navy in 1905 at 13 years of age. During World War 1 his career was varied. Mack was on a troop ship during the Gallipoli landings and later took command of a Q-Ship, the *Result*. The development of Q-Ships came about when it was realised that U-Boat captains would generally surface and attack smaller craft with their guns, holding back their torpedoes for use on larger vessels. A number of small ships were requisitioned and armed but equipped with ingenious methods of disguising their guns. The idea was to lure the U-Boats to the surface when some of the crew, known as a 'Panic Party' would take to one of the ships boats as if abandoning ship. In some instances, one of the Panic Party would be dressed as a woman for added effect. Once the submarine approached, the remaining crew would deploy the guns from their hidden positions and fire on the submarine.

Clearly a dangerous business, and of course such a tactic only has a life as long as the surprise is kept from the enemy. Naturally the German Submariners became more cautious and eventually the use of Q-Ships was

---

[82] (Cunningham, 1951)

phased out. However, Mack used *Result*[83] to effect and damaged U-45 in September 1917 which earned him a mention in despatches.

In between the two wars he was promoted several times including time aboard *Hawkins* as Executive Officer whilst on the China Station between 1925 and 1927. He married Elizabeth Dawson in 1930 and the pair sailed out to Buenos Aires where Mack had been appointed Naval Attaché to South America. They stayed until 1938, clearly making an impression not only professionally but in the wider community too, as Viscount Halifax wrote in December 1938 'Captain and Mrs. Mack indeed made very many friends in Brazilian society, where they enjoyed a special degree of popularity, and they will be much missed in Rio de Janeiro.'

Mack was definitely the epitome of a Sea Captain; he smoked a large pipe and had the tattoos of coiled snakes on his forearms and around his chest. He was a strict disciplinarian with an ability to swear as well as any ordinary seaman, but this was counter balanced by his great humour, affection and care for the crews. These combined define a deep respect and loyalty that the men had for him. He was not infallible, he suffered dreadfully from sea sickness, but he did not make any effort to conceal this, indeed he sympathised and supported anyone who had a similar lack of sea legs.

Mack became Commanding Officer of *Jervis* in 1939 as Captain (D), 1st Division of the 7th Destroyer Flotilla based out of Immingham on the River Humber. Their task was to protect the FS and FN convoys which sailed to and from the Thames and the Tyne. However, *Jervis* was in dock when he was ordered to take command of the 14th Destroyer Flotilla which meant that he would command from one of the other ships until her return. On the journey down to the Mediterranean, Mack was aboard *Janus* as both *Nubian* and *Mohawk* had to remain until their refit was completed. However, Mack would use *Nubian* as Captain (D) for most of the remaining time until *Jervis* could join the Flotilla.

---

[83] *Result* is preserved at the Ulster Transport Museum, Cultra, N. Ireland

To have Captain (D) aboard was not always the most desirable of situations, certainly for the senior crew members and especially the ship's Captain. The Flotilla Commander would take over the Commanding Officers Cabin, which meant Ravenhill would have to move to his Day Cabin within the forward superstructure and command the ship from there. Mack would have brought some of his senior staff with him too, one of which would shadow *Nubians* Officer of the Watch and report any signals to Mack that he thought would be of interest. It meant some level of tact and understanding had to be adopted to avoid any friction. There were some perks though. There was a pecking order within the flotillas and as senior ship she would be first to enter port, refuel and re-arm. For all Destroyers first task on returning to port was to be in readiness to depart at a moment's notice.

The 14th DF arrived in Alexandria on the 23 May. According to John Davies in 'Lower Deck', 'Alex. Harbour is very exposed, and with it freshening up as it is now it may not be too easy to go to a buoy.'[84] The ships would have oiled and then berthed together in preparation for whatever task the Admiral had for them, which for the moment consisted of submarine patrols and convoy protection duties. They were in good company, as Cunningham wrote, 'By June 9th the fleet at Alexandria, on paper, was quite an imposing one. It consisted of the battleships *Warspite, Malaya, Royal Sovereign, and Ramillies*, the later in the floating dock. We had the 7th Cruiser Squadron: *Orion, Neptune, Sydney, Liverpool, Gloucester*; the 3rd Cruiser Squadron: *Capetown, Caledon, Calypso and Dehli*: some 25 destroyers…'[85] There was also the French Squadron that comprised of Vice Admiral Godfroy's battleship *Lorraine*, four cruisers and three destroyers.

Cunningham's main tasks in the coming months, indeed years, was to ensure that supplies reached Malta by protecting convoys that sailed between Alexandria, Port Said, Haifa and Malta usually designated MF (Fast) or MS (Slow) or Gibraltar and Malta, designated ME (East, Gib. To Malta) and MW (West, Malta to Gib.). There was the protection of allies, such as Greece and

---

[84] (R.N.V.R, 1945)
[85] (Cunningham, 1951)

the Island of Crete as well as Malta, while there would be offensive operations against the Italian Navy who it was hoped would be lured out of their bases by the convoys. Later, these offensive operations would extend to attacking Axis convoys supplying troops and materiel into North Africa. On a negative side, there would be the eventual evacuation and defensive operations in the withdrawal from both Greece and Crete.

The Regia Marina looked pretty good on paper too. With 6 battleships, 3 of which were the Littorio class of 45,000-tons, 15-in. guns and capable of 30 knots this was a formidable backbone for the 5th largest navy in the world. In addition, there were 21 cruisers, 52 destroyers and 106 submarines as well as smaller vessels (such as torpedo boats). However, the Italian Navy had her ships constructed to fight a 'limited' naval battle of a Jutland nature within the Mediterranean and the tactical thinking was based on this also. Whilst Radar and Sonar had been investigated and developed, the commanders did not have it adopted. The same went for the development of aircraft carriers, with the expectation the Regina Aeronautica would provide all necessary air support from their bases around the Mediterranean. There simply was no need for a sea going platform.

Supply of oil, however, was another achilles heel for the Regia Marina as was an ability to replace any ships lost in combat. Moreover, the commanders were hobbled by their centralised command, Supermarina, the commanders had little choice but to adhere to these orders, and even if they did provide alternative strategies they had to wait for revised orders before they could carry them out.

Like Great Britain, Italy had a Royal Air Force, The Regina Aeronautica. In many ways the Italian Airforce had come under criticism for its operations in the war, but one must wonder whether there was a reluctance to join with the Axis powers against former allies under the command of a man with such imperial and fanatical notions as Mussolini. This was just the start of their problems. However, there is no doubt that the pilots of the Regina

Aeronautica were highly skilled and brave men, as Admiral Cunningham pays tribute in his autobiography.

'It is not too much to say of those early months that the Italians high level bombing was the best I have ever seen, far better than the German. Later, when our anti-aircraft fire improved and the trained squadrons of the Regia Aeronautica came to be knocked about by our fleet fighters, their air work over the sea deteriorated. But I shall always remember it with respect. There was some consolation in realising that there was always more water than ship. Nevertheless, one felt very naked and unprotected.'[86]

From a strategic perspective, the Italian Air Force was very forward thinking, and it had been Giulio Douhet who had written a book in the late 1920's called 'Command of the Air' on future tactics. This book described how air superiority would win the wars of the future, with the bombing of industry bringing countries to their knees and to the negotiating table. So influential was this publication that his ideas were adopted by the Royal Air Force and the United States Army Air Corps.

As a continuation of these theories, another Italian, Marshal Italo Balbo developed the idea of the mass bomber raid that could deliver knock out blows to cities in large waves of aircraft. An idea that saw the development of Bomber Command and the strategic bombing by the United States. Even today, a large formation of aircraft is called a 'Balbo'.

In terms of aircraft, whilst they had on paper some 3000 at the beginning of the war their numbers were made up of far too many different types, although by 1940 the number of operational aircraft was more like 1000. This meant training requirements were more difficult to achieve, as was production and spares. Like the Navy, losses could not be replaced easily in a country without its own resources.

---

[86] (Cunningham, 1951)

Of the aircraft, most notable for their raids on shipping were the much loved (by their pilots) Savoia-Marchetti S.79, nicknamed 'Il Gobo' (The Humpback), indeed they made up some 40% of aircraft numbers in the Air Force. A purposeful looking medium bomber but one which like so many aircraft that Italy produced suffered from underpowered engines. So much so that the S.79, although designed initially as a twin engine aircraft, ended up with three (two wing mounted, one on the nose). This compromised the bomb load capacity drastically. However, the S.79 was converted to a torpedo bomber, of which it had some success. It could carry a single Whitehead 'Fiume' torpedo which at 4.5 meters long and almost 900 kgs packed a hefty punch.

Despite these shortcomings, the Regina Aeronautica attacked the Royal Navy with little let up and whilst not inflicting any substantial material damage, the effect on morale and energy was palpable. The Italians did eventually purchase some JU87's from Germany, and of course, the Luftwaffe did begin operations from 1941 onwards which tightened the Axis grip on air superiority over the Mediterranean. It took some time for this balance to be addressed but the attrition of aircraft and materiel that could not be replaced led to the inevitable.

With the fall of Paris imminent, Mussolini threw in his sword and had Italy declare war on Britain and France on 10 June (the Germans were in Paris on the 14th). Cunningham had his ships placed on two hours' notice to steam and the *Ramillies* was to be moved out of the floating dock immediately, her refit abandoned. For the destroyer forces there were a number of states of readiness. One Division would always be on patrol, with the others at 2 and a half hours' notice and the remainder on 4 hours' notice. The anti-aircraft guns on all the ships regardless of status were to be manned all of the time.

The following day *Nubian* sailed in support of *Warspite* on patrol with Captain Mack aboard as Captain (D). D14 now included *Janus, Juno* and *Hasty* to screen the force soon strengthened by the arrival of the battleship *Malaya* and the aircraft carrier *Eagle*. The Cruisers *Calypso* and *Caledon* joined them on the 11th. It was an offensive sweep out towards Crete, along its southern shores and then back along the North Coast of Africa, but the enemy was not sighted, nor was there any sign of the Regia Aeronautica, the ships returned to Alexandria on the 14th.

However, on the 12th, *Calypso* had been hit and sunk by a torpedo right under the noses of a destroyer screen. Therefore, there was no time to rest when *Nubian* returned to Alexandria. She and the Destroyers of the 14th, 2nd and 10th Flotilla's were sent out on a submarine sweep as a result, Operation MD2, which unfortunately did not bear any results and *Nubian* was once more in Alexandria on the 19 June.

Another bright sunny day at Alexandria, 22 June 1940, it is a Saturday, 'Make and Mend' day. The 14th Destroyer Flotilla were back in harbour, refueled and fully armed. At 06:30 the *Nubians* hands were awoken, and the ships day began with the normal scramble for the wash room. John Davies describes the bathrooms in HMS *Sikh* from his book 'Lower Deck'; 'This is a long, narrow compartment just aft of the mess deck on the port side. It has rows of tin basins across the foreward end and along the outboard side two taps, one hot and one cold, out of which water may sometimes be obtained, dependent upon the good graces of the engineers. A mirror at the forrard end, a couple of cans for carrying water, and a medium-sized hip-bath.'[87]

The crew were called to breakfast at 07:00. Each mess provided with credits with which to 'purchase' food from the galley over and above each messes ration of staple food such as bread and potatoes. This was known as 'Canteen' messing and was administered by the Leading Hand of each mess deck. Depending on how frugal or generous this hand was at his job determined what food the mess received. After breakfast the hands fell in for inspection and the day began with cleaning the ship after several days' operations.

It is now mid-morning and time for a cup of tea or a smoke during stand easy, just a ten-minute break and not always enough time to line up and get a

---

[87] (R.N.V.R, 1945)

brew. That is if you have a cup of course. John Davies tells how between the twenty men of his mess there were just three cups and only one of these had a handle. The Tribal's were issued with China cutlery which did not last long in heavy seas or would break whenever a gun was fired. As for the tea, Davies describes it as '…a thick sticky liquid, varying in colour from yellow ochre to burnt umber. It is made by putting an enormous quantity of tea in a teapot, adding boiling water, and pouring in a tin of condensed milk.'[88]

Back to work, then at 11:00 around the harbour it could be heard the call for 'Up Spirits' for the crews daily issue of Rum, or 'Grog'. The Leading Hands from each mess collect the 'Tot' for the men of their mess who partake in it. The Coxswain has a book which lists each rating and by each name is either a 'G' which means he can receive 'Grog', a 'T' for 'Temperance', in that he has elected not to receive a 'Tot' and will be remunerated with an allowance, instead or a 'UA' meaning the rating is Underage (below 20 years old) and not allowed to draw 'Grog'.

The 'Grog' is measured out at an eighth of an imperial pint, but then diluted with either one or two parts of water. 'Grog' could not be hoarded for use at another time, it had to be drunk fairly quickly. However, if a favour or debt needed paying to another then they could partake of either a 'Sipper' or a 'Gulper' of your 'Tot' according to the size of the debt.

Lunch comes and goes and there is a buzz that as the ship has been well tidied up, and the Commander is in a good mood, they may have the afternoon off rather than 'Make and Mend' aboard ship (This was the time when personal equipment was mended). However, despite the prospect of time ashore there is little enthusiasm. Alexandria harbour is a big open space that is a long way from the night spots of the town. Indeed, getting ashore is just one obstacle. If the ships boat is not available, which invariably it is not, then a trip ashore can only be made in a local felluca (small sailing or rowing boat). The frequently choppy waters of a windswept harbour would normally result in the occupants being rather wet through by the time they landed.

---

[88] (R.N.V.R, 1945)

Getting back had its challenges too. There was a liberty boat that went around the fleet but as Davies wrote, '…your ship is inevitably the last call, so that even if you come offshore at 22:30, you are lucky if you get aboard before midnight'.[89]

'We all feel dirty and ashamed…' - The French fleet at Oran and Alexandria

The armistice between France and Germany was signed on the 22 June 1940. Even today the implications in its words are chilling, especially as we have full knowledge of what was to come. The events that followed, in respect of the fate of the French Fleet relate directly to Article 8 in the document. 'The French war fleet is to collect in ports to be designated more particularly, and under German and/or Italian control to demobilise and lay up…' France could use its warships to protect its own interests abroad, but Article 8 states 'All warships outside France are to be recalled to France with the exception of that portion of the French War Fleet which shall be designated to represent French interests in the colonial empire.'

Article 8 also declares that Germany would not use the French Fleet for its own purposes, with the exception of guarding the coast and mine sweeping. Germany would not demand any action of the French Navy during or after the war, of which they clearly believed they would win. In all this suggested that all the larger warships such as battleships, cruisers and destroyers not required for coastal protection would have to return to France and fall under Axis control

It is little wonder the British Government were sceptical that Article 8 would hold over the coming months and years. Hitlers track record of honouring signed agreements was littered with documents torn to shreds and trampled under the jack boot. Indeed, it would have been most alarming that the powerful and modern naval materiel that France had built up could now

---

[89] (R.N.V.R, 1945)

be in the hands of the enemy. Plans were put in place to neutralise the French fleet either by having the ships combine forces with the Royal Navy or be destroyed.

What could the French Admirals do? They now had a new government, headed by Marshal Petain, who represented France and commanded the Navy. To ignore an order from the government or to hand their ships over to a foreign power but continue to fly the flag of France would be treason, no matter what the commanders' political views were. They certainly had no crystal ball to see into the future whether Germany or Britain would prevail in this conflict and what would be the consequences of any action they undertook now? They had little choice but to comply with their government or go against it.

In the Mediterranean there were two large French Navy forces present, one based at Mers El Kabir in Oran to the west consisting of two modern Battleships, the *Dunkerque*, which was a guest during the 1937 Navy Review and the *Strasbourg*, two older battleships, the *Provence* and the *Bretagne*, a Seaplane launch vessel, the *Commondant Teste* as well as 7 destroyers. Whilst at Alexandria, lay the Battleship *Lorraine* (although an older warship), the cruiser and flagship of Vice Admiral Godfroy *Duquesne*, three more cruisers and some destroyers.

Aboard *Warspite* on the 1 July, Admiral Cunningham was beginning his working day which had not started well. He had received a signal from the Admiralty that he had to read several times, during which he paced back and forth in deep thought. It would be the beginning of 5 days of intense stress that would test the nerve of the fleet at Alexandria and determine the fate of the French fleet. He called a meeting of his Captains and Flag Officers to brief them of the situation.

During the meeting, 'ABC' was once more pacing up and down the room (as he was custom to do), explaining that the Admiralty had major concerns around the French fleet falling into the hands of the Germans following the armistice. Both he and Sommerville (with Force H) had instructions to present ultimatums to the French Admirals. Join with the Royal Navy and continue the war together, sail to a British port and demilitarise their ships, sail to the West Indies and demilitarise their ships or go to sea with a reduced crew and scuttle them. If none of these were acceptable, the ships would either be taken by force or they would be sunk by the Navy.

'ABC' exclaimed that both he and Sommerville were appalled that it could be considered they should fire upon their own allies. Cunningham went on that he had written to the Admiralty to point out that he and his staff believed no good would come of this, only bad feeling, not only with the French but their allies all along the North African coast, and it could jeopardise their access to the Suez Canal. Besides, the French fleet in Alexandria was in a different position to that of the Atlantic Fleet in Oran. Here, the French were already hemmed in, within a Royal Naval base, they were going nowhere.

Cunningham had a meeting scheduled with Admiral Godfroy the following morning (3 July) at 07:00, where he would be given a revised ultimatum that included the option to render his ships unable to put to sea, manned by a skeleton crew who would be on full Navy pay. The final option was for Godfroy to take his ships to deep water and sink them. There would be no threat of military action, however there was a possibility that no agreement would be made. Therefore, all the battleships of the Royal Navy were being manoeuvered into a position where they could quickly fire a broadside on the French ships. As for *Nubian* and the other destroyers, they were to prepare men for a boarding party to take the French ships if ordered to do so, and should the French ships attempt to leave harbour they should be torpedoed as soon as they began to make way or if they opened fire. The meeting would occur simultaneously with operations that would be carried out by Force H.

The orders for Force H were somewhat starker, they were to deliver the ultimatum and if no agreement was made then the ships in Mers El Kebir would be sunk. Force H was scheduled to arrive off Oran by 06:00 on the 3rd and would consist of *Hood, Resolution, Valiant,* the *Ark Royal,* cruisers

Arethusa and *Enterprise* with a screening force of 11 destroyers. It would be called Operation Catapult.

At 07:00 on the 3 July, Admiral Godfroy (an honourable man, according to Cunningham) was welcomed aboard *Warspite*, the Royal Marines and the band piped him over the guard rail, before he and his Staff were invited to the quarterdeck and the after cabin for the meeting. This was according to Cunningham an informal affair. They sat in armchairs, not around a table, to review the signal from the Admiralty.

In short, Godfroy was receptive to the notion that the fleet should be contained at Alexandria, and he returned to his flagship at 08:30, no doubt under the gaze from a number of binoculars around the fleet. He had to respond by noon, which he did, but the answer was not what Cunningham had hoped for. Unless Godfroy should receive an order from his own government to render his ships inoperable, he would proceed to sea and sink them. There was no time for such a luxury, Godfroy was reluctantly granted 48 hours to reduce his crews to the minimum and prepare to take his ships to sea, for one last time, at noon on the 5th.

Meanwhile about 2000 miles away to the west, Force H was patrolling back and forth through what was becoming a blazing hot and hazy day off Mers El Kebir. From the crow's nest of the *Dunkerque* a French sailor could just make out the ships on the horizon, they had their guns pointed fore and aft, so no threat at the moment. He turned his gaze out to the harbour defence boom, HMS *Foxhound*, a Type F destroyer had been there since ten past eight that morning. It was now just before 17:00. Black smoke began to issue from her funnel now, men were bustling on deck, as she prepared to depart.

Captain Cedric Holland, was sent by Sommerville in *Foxhound* to meet with Admiral Marcel Bruno Gensoul to discuss the ultimatum the Admiralty had issued. Holland was fluent in French; he had been Naval Attaché to France in the late 30's and at the French Naval Mission at the outbreak of the war. He knew a number of the French Officers, loved France, its ways and customs and was therefore the right man for the occasion. Both he and Sommerville were deeply opposed to any military action against the French Fleet.

However, the French Admiral at first refused to receive him. Holland could not therefore, open face to face discussions in the friendly and conciliatory manner that he had hoped for. Not until 15:00 did Gensoul relent to a meeting, in which time the Admiralty had been frantically requesting information, blind to what was occurring so far from them and eager to determine what was going on. What is more, they were desperate to ensure the French Fleet would be out of the war or with them by the end of the day. Back in Alexandria, Cunningham's signal office was able to listen in to the communications and realise the gloomy possibility that Force H would soon be forced to open fire.

Indeed, during the morning it became clear the French were preparing to get under way as tell-tale whisps of smoke rose into the air from their funnels. This activity began to increase, especially in the afternoon when a French signal had been intercepted which read 'answer fire with fire', and that re-enforcements were on their way. The Admiralty were getting frantic and ordered Sommerville to get on with it or he would have company.

The French lookout noticed the Admirals boat heading towards the *Foxhound* as she continued to prepare for sea. Within the harbour, the ships of his own fleet were also nearing readiness to depart. Smoke was now issuing in larger clouds from the big ships, the awnings had been stowed and there were tugs manoeuvering into place behind *Dunkerque* and the other Battleships in readiness to guide them out to sea. More ominously, he noticed the Director Towers were now trained on the ships out to sea.

Foxhound was underway, and to his amazement the lookout noticed that she was mining the entrance to the harbour. There then came the call to 'Action Stations', he trained his binoculars back onto the ships at sea and saw a series of flashes, soon followed by the roar like a train of the 15-in. shells as they began to fall around the harbour. At first great plumes of water rose just outside the harbour, near the lighthouse, ranging shots. Moments later came the next salvo, this time they fell inside the harbour and in an instant, there was a colossal explosion as one shell landed directly onto *Bretagne*. A sheet of flame soared upward as one of her magazines erupted in a mushroom cloud of thick black and white smoke. In moments, she turned over.

Dunkerque began to move forward, but she too was straddled, and then grounded in the confines of the relatively small harbour. *Provence* was ablaze at the stern and already low in the water, she too was grounded whilst *Strasbourg* had begun to make way and out to sea, with 5 destroyers, avoiding the mines that *Foxhound* had deployed.

Catapult took little more than 9 minutes to execute from the first shot to cease fire at 18:04. The smoke flames and carnage was appalling. In the oil covered waters of the harbour the casualties still alive fought for their lives, but there were at least 1300 dead, the large majority in *Bretagne*. The French ships did attempt a reply, that was ineffective and short lived. The somewhat bemused sailors of the Royal Navy noted that the return fire, whilst unpleasant, was unusual as the waterspouts were of blues, pinks and greens from the marker dye in the shell cones to aid in observing the fall of shot.

In Alexandria, the mood was gloomy. Reports continued to come in that negotiations had not gone to plan at Mers El Kebir. Earlier in the day, when there was still all to play for Cunningham continued to pace about *Warspite* in deep thought. There was no need for Godfroy to sink his ships at this time, surely with more time to negotiate and slow up events the ships and certainly the lives of a number of French sailors could be saved. He was clearly the man on the spot, he had all of the information whereas the Admiralty did not, and information is 'king'. He had the conviction that it was wrong to have pushed Godfroy into a corner. There and then made the decision to take matters into his own hands in a last-ditch attempt to avoid disaster. He sat down and began to write a personal letter to Godfroy.

Cunningham suggested in his letter that the ships would be better spared to fight another day. Rather than completely demilitarise the ships, why not begin to remove the fuel oil and to remove the warheads from the torpedoes?

This would indicate that they could not put to sea, which should satisfy the Admiralty, and then the question of what to do with the crews could be thrashed out later. It would be a compromise that would save face on both sides, save the ships and surely save unnecessary loss of life? He sent the letter at once and requested an immediate response. He got one. This was Godfroys way out for now, and he agreed to begin discharging oil. By 17:30, the men on watch of the British ships noted activity around the French fleet, they were discharging their tanks. A feeling of relief that the situation was under control for now must have prevailed over Cunningham and his staff.

It didn't last for long. The Admiralty were not happy. The signal received was terse and to the point; 'Admiralty note that oil fuel is being discharged by French ships. Reduction of crews, especially by ratings, should however begin at once by landing or transfer to merchant ships, before dark tonight. Do not, repeat NOT, fail.'

A most unhelpful signal that simply poured pressure onto the situation, and this was further exacerbated when Cunningham received a further message soon after from Godfroy. Clearly the full news from Mers El Kebir had not yet reached him, but he was aware that an ultimatum had been made, and he had been ordered by his government to sail. He had requested confirmation that the signal was genuine, but he had to stop discharging oil.

Cunningham sent his Chief of Staff, Rear Admiral Willis over to meet with Godfroy, a meeting that was most awkward and forthright. Godfroy would not under any circumstances, resume the discharge of oil or send any of his men ashore. He would not be forced into submission and if necessary, he would scuttle the ships in the harbour, despite the order from his government to sail and fight his way out to sea if necessary.

At least the fleet was contained for now, and they would not force a conflict. That was a relief, but it still meant the British fleet had to remain in harbour until they could be sure that the French would not sail away into the hands of Germany. All operations against Italian and German forces were on hold, as was the protection of Malta. They had to make a decision, of which the options were to send boarding parties to seize the ships, sink them where they were moored or force Godfroy to surrender his ships and men, which would no doubt led to them being scuttled. The only option was the last one. There was no more they could do, one way or another, the fate of the French at Alexandria would be sealed the next day.

Of course, overnight Godfroy and his staff were fully appraised of the action at Mers El Kebir. They had lost valuable ships and lots of their ship mates, not to an enemy, but to an ally. Godfroy's letter the following morning effectively burned all the bridges from the day before. He would reserve the right to command his own men and ships and put to sea.

All of the British ships were at a high state of readiness, there was a strong possibility that they would have to fire upon the French, and they would in turn retaliate, resulting in a full scale Naval engagement right inside Alexandria harbour. It would be carnage. Whilst the British ships were, as we know, prepared for this eventuality, there would inevitably be casualties on both sides.

The French ships were clearly preparing to depart. The tell tale discharges from their funnels and the activity on deck indicated they were working up their engines and ominously they were clearing for action too. However, they would need time, quite a lot, at perhaps four to six hours before they could get underway. There was one last hope.

Cunningham gathered together his Flag Officers and Captains for one final push to bring the French around, they would go over Godfroys' head. In the first instance a message was flashed to each of the French ships, to all Officers and Men that there was no possible way of leaving harbour without a fight although this was not what anyone desired, and that there was an honourable way out of the situation. The message was also written on large blackboards which were taken around the French ships on boats.

Each French ship had a British counterpart, and the Captains of the British ships were then sent aboard to meet with the French Captains reason with them to stay within the harbour and demilitarise their ships. Captain Mack, still using *Nubian* as Flotilla leader (Jervis was in Malta and did not arrive in Alexandria until the 13 July) was responsible for all of the destroyers and no doubt his personality soon won them over. Captain Rory O'Conor was Captain of the *Neptune*, he went aboard the French Cruiser *Duguay-Trouin*, saying to her captain as he came over the rail 'When I saw the tompions[90] being removed from your guns, I immediately ordered the tompions to be placed in mine'.

As the morning wore on, the word clearly spread around the French fleet. Meetings were being held on the Forecastles and Quarterdecks where animated discussions between the crews were clearly taking place. In time, the Commanding Officers were seen to be visiting their Flagship and soon after lunch, Godfroy signalled to *Warspite* that he was coming aboard to visit Admiral Cunningham. During this meeting he conceded that there was overwhelming force against his fleet and as such as agreement was made to begin demilitarisation of the ships under his command. It was over. As Cunningham wrote, 'Never in my life have I experienced such a wholehearted feeling of thankful relief as on the conclusion of this agreement, and the same was felt by every officer and man in our fleet.'[91]

How the outcomes of both fleets differed as did the feelings too. Sommerville later wrote; 'We all feel thoroughly dirty and ashamed that the first time we should have been in action was an affair like this.' For the Germans this was a propaganda opportunity that was too good to miss, amid the equal condemnation from Petain's Vichy government. Operation 'Catapult' effectively took out the French Navy from the war and shifted the balance of Naval power in the Mediterranean away from the Royal Navy and handed it to the Italians. In hindsight it is easy to condemn everything about 'Catapult', but in a time where high speed communications is 'the normal' it is hard to think that at the heart of the issue was lack of information through poor communication. On the other hand, the actions of the Fleet under Cunningham at Alexandria demonstrate what can be achieved through taking the initiative and communicating well.

---

[90] A Tompion is a wooden stopper placed in the muzzle of a gun for protection.
[91] (Cunningham, 1951)

The Battle of Calabria

The morning of the 8 July was bright and warm, the sun already climbing high in the sky when the young boy ran down to the harbour to see the ships. He sometimes managed to catch a ride in the liberty boat and sail around the harbour and get very close to them. The sailors were always kind to him and often gave him sweets. This morning though, he was brought to an abrupt halt by the quay. The ships had all gone.

The young boy was not the only one to have come to the harbour that morning. In Alexandria there were many who spied for the Italians and Germans. The dock worker had an idea that the fleet would sail, the day before there was activity to suggest something was happening and indeed during the night, it had. The fleet had sailed, he would need to report this to his contact.

Aboard *Nubian* any thought of leave, or a trip ashore, vanished the day before. Commander Ravenhill had returned from a meeting of the Commanders aboard *Warspite* and the order had been passed to prepare the ship for sailing that night. Ravenhill was quite relieved that his cabin would remain his own as Captain Mack would command the 14th from *Janus*. The situation in Malta was bad, there had been many bombing raids, food and supplies were running desperately short. The entire fleet would sail that evening to meet with a convoy from Malta that was bringing out all non-combatants as well as some spares and equipment needed at Alexandria. The operation was called MA5, and consisted of two convoys, MF 1 (Fast) which included a small liner the *Knight of Malta* (aboard which were many Navy Staff families including Cunninghams), and two further transports, the *El Nil* and the *Rodi*. MS 1 (Slow) carried the spares and materiel, consisting of 4 ships, the *Zeeland, Kirkland, Masirah* and the *Novasli*.

Meanwhile, the Italian Army in Libya were also running out of supplies and a large convoy was put together to resupply through Benghazi. It consisted of 5 merchant ships taking some 2000 troops, almost 6000 tons of fuel and lubricating oils as well as trucks and materiel. This presented a very juicy target and therefore an equally if not larger escort force than that of MA5 was put together, consisting of close-in defence by four destroyers and 4 torpedo boats, a stronger protecting force stationed 35 miles out, consisting of almost 30 destroyers and 6 cruisers, whilst a Battlegroup of two Battleships with another 6 cruisers and 13 destroyer escorts were the distant protection. If these two forces were to meet, there would be a battle.

The British escort was split into three Forces, A, B and C. Force A consisted of the 7th Cruiser Squadron commanded by Vice Admiral Tovey from his flagship *Orion* in company with *Gloucester, Neptune, Liverpool* (which would rendezvous with the fleet from Port Said) and HMAS *Sydney* and the destroyer *Stuart*. The role of the Cruisers in this instance was to sail ahead of the main force and provide a surface reconnaissance role. Cruisers were of a size where they could defend themselves and defeat any other ship of similar size that they could not escape from, but fast enough to run away from anything bigger and more heavily armed than them!

Nubian was included in the destroyer element of Force B, protecting *Warspite* with her trusty Tribal sister *Mohawk* and the smaller destroyers *Hero, Hereward* and *Decoy*. They were ahead of Force C, the 1st Battle Squadron, made up of the battleships, *Royal Sovereign, Malaya* and the aircraft carrier *Eagle* which had 19 Swordfish at her disposal. These were protected by 11 destroyers of various classes, but included the 'J's', *Juno* and *Janus*.

The hands were called to stations after dark, and before long one could perceive she was moving away from her mooring. There were additional hands on watch this evening. With all ships running blacked out and the number of ships departing there was no room for error. *Nubian* made her way gingerly to the harbour entrance, passing the dark shapes of the fleet as they too began to slip quietly away from Alexandria. Eventually the calm waters of the harbour gave way to the rise and fall of the open sea, *Nubian* began to vibrate as her engines pushed her more eagerly through the water and her bow rose and fell as it pushed aside the rolling swell.

Ahead of the ships were the Submarines *Phoenix* and *Rorqual* who would provide covert screening protection for the convoy. *Phoenix* was a Parthian class submarine with 56 crew members commanded by Lieutenant Commander Gilbert Hugh Nowell. On that morning they had made out ships smoke on the horizon and dived to periscope depth to approach and investigate. Through his viewfinder, Newell could make out the two Italian Battleships, *Conte di Cavour* and *Giulio Cesare* along with 4 destroyer escorts. Aboard the *Cesare* was Admiral Arturo Riccardi, who Cunningham had met when the Italians had visited Malta in 1938. Cunningham had a chance to appraise the two newly modernised ships at the time, which he would no doubt be re-acquainted with soon. 'The two battleships were fine examples of old ships modernised, and the work had been most skilfully done. They had been rearmed with ten 12-inch guns and a good anti-aircraft armament. Some sixty feet had been added to their length and this, with modern boilers and machinery gave them a reputed speed of 26 or 27 knots as against the 21.5 when they were completed in 1915.'[92] Cunningham also noted that Admiral Riccardi had a copy of Robert Southey's 'The Life of Nelson' first published in 1813 on his bedside table, at all times.

Newell attacked the battleships with torpedoes despite the range being awfully long and therefore almost inevitable that these missed their targets. However, the intelligence was most important, and so he took *Phoenix* a safe distance away to make a report that reached Cunningham just after 08:00. It stated that they had spotted two battleships and 4 destroyers heading south indicating to Cunningham that the Italians were out in force, and they must be protecting a convoy.

There would be no dinner aboard *Nubian*, all hands had been at action stations since the first air attacks had been reported against Force C earlier in the morning. The crews were already tired, and this was compounded by the

---

[92] (Cunningham, 1951)

strain from the threat of attack. That attack came when they should have been at dinner. High level bombing was something *Nubian* had been subjected to in Norway, but this time the accuracy was far better despite the evasive action the ships were taking to avoid being hit. Naturally *Warspite* was the centre of attention which carried on until the evening.

Aboard *Janus* Captain Mack was watching the approaching S.79 bombers with some unease. The ship had opened fire, her guns booming trying to make an impression before they could no longer bear on the enemy aircraft. Close by was HMS *Gloucester* a Town-Class Cruiser, her Captain, 43-year-old Frederick Garside CBE. *Gloucester* was similar in design to *Belfast* that is moored by London Bridge as part of the Imperial War Museum collection. She too was hammering away at the enemy as the bombs began to whistle and rain down amongst them before exploding, shooting huge conical lumps of water into the air that were white on the outside and black inside, almost as if the bottom of the sea had been sucked up from below.

Mack watched as a stick of bombs fell around *Gloucester*, for some reason one caught his attention in its deadly purpose as it whacked into her bridge. There was a split second of what seemed like silence in which someone shouted, 'oh f...!' but his expletive was drowned out by the concussion filled crunch of the bomb exploding. Bits of the bridge flew into the air, the bomb having struck the compass platform and wiped out the Director Control Tower. Pieces of *Gloucester* whistled past and splashed into the sea and she seemed to judder and lose her way. Mack could see through his binoculars that cool professionalism was taking over, the wheelhouse was wrecked, medical and fire control teams were clearly rushing to contain the situation. In the meantime, the bombers had passed by and all was quiet once more.

Aboard *Gloucester* the damage had been quickly assessed, it was very bad, but they would not founder. Driving the ship was transferred to the aft wheelhouse, whilst fire and director control were transferred to this position also. Some form of order was being restored, but the butchers bill made sad and depressing reading. Stoker Bill Howe was one of the damage control party who attended the bridge following the attack. 'Most of the men appeared to have been killed outright by the blast, although we did find one young sailor, lying in a pool of blood, who was still registering a pulse.'[93] This was Able Seaman Fred Farlow, who survived and later recalled; 'When it happened I was on the bridge and heard what sounded like a steam train going through a railway station at high speed. After the explosion a young lad from South Africa, Lloyd Nolan, looked up and said to me that he was alright, then he died almost immediately.'[94] At the time the bomb hit there had been 23 Officers and men at station on the bridge. Only 5 survived.

Mack lowered his binoculars and spoke quickly to his Signals Officer, 'Send; to *Gloucester* from Captain D14, Have just noticed damage, have you any casualties' It took a few minutes before the response came. '*Gloucester* to D14, your 1226, Regret 17 killed including Captain and Commander and 9 wounded.' Mack rubbed his eyes trying to think of a suitable response to the awful news. What could he say? 'D14 to *Gloucester*, your 1230, I am very sorry.'

To the south, Sunderland L.5803 of 230 Squadron sighted the Italian fleet, reporting at 16:10 that it had almost completed an about turn onto 070 degrees. Cunningham realised that this could only mean the enemy had completed its operation of what he correctly guessed was convoy protection and was heading north to its base in Taranto. If his ships pressed on northwards, they could be in a position the following day to get between the enemy and his base, where they would be brought to action. Cunningham had the original plan placed on hold, the potential to engage the enemy fleet being far to big an opportunity to miss.

'Message from *Warspite* to all escorts. Steer 310 degrees and maintain 20 knots.' Came the signal report to Ravenhill. The intentions of the fleet and the outline plan to intercept the Italians was relayed to the escort Commanders. There were few general announcements to the crew, there usually was not

---

[93] (Otter, 2017)
[94] (Otter, 2017)

time for such luxuries and besides the bigger picture and strategies that were taking shape were of little consequence to the crew who were there to perform a duty. However, the crew generally did get to know what was going on through unofficial channels, namely the wheelhouse. For here the voice tube connection to the bridge was very short, and even when the covers were on, the discussions on the bridge were quite clearly heard in all their detail. Word then travelled fast.

The ensuing night passed uneventfully, the *Nubians* got some rest, as both fleets forged their way towards each other in the darkness.

The Battle – 9 July 1940

The equivalent to maritime satellite reconnaissance in the World War 2 era came in the form of aircraft, one type being the Shorts S.25 Sunderland Flying boat. It was a big aircraft, larger than a Lancaster bomber with a wing of 112 feet span some 32 feet above the water in a high wing configuration. It was powered by four Pegasus 1000hp radial engines with three bladed propellors that hauled the beast into the air. It certainly looked like a beast at its mooring, a huge squat toad sat in the water, its front turret jutting out like a prize fighters chin.

It was still dark on Malta before 05:00 on the 9 July when Flight Lieutenant David McKinley and his crew of 228 Squadron were gingerly stepping off the tender, tethered next to the forward hatch of Sunderland L5087. The crew made their way to their stations whilst McKinley and his second pilot slumped into the cockpit and began to run through their pre startup checks. One of these included setting the altimeters. These work on air pressure readings, which on land are given to the pilot relative to either sea level or the current air pressure at the airfield from which the aircraft is using. Air pressure is measured in millibars, each millibar representing roughly 30 feet in height. For the Sunderland crews the setting was very simple, as they would always be flying above sea level for a maritime reconnaissance. They simply turned the altimeter dial to zero feet before the flight and left it at that setting for the duration of the mission. There may be fluctuations in air pressure during flight, but they would have to live with that.

Behind and below the pilots the hatch door was closed and with a final bump the tender moved away. In those final moments of quiet the waters could be heard softly lapping against the hull, there was the dull thumping of the crew moving about, muffled voices and a laugh. One of the crew was in the galley already getting the primus organised for a brew once they were airborne. With a flick of the Master Switch the gyros began to whine and whir and shortly afterwards there was a cough and a bang as the outer engines were fired up followed by the two inner engines. The quiet had been ripped apart and would remain that way for the next 13 hours.

In the growing light, L5087 surged across the water at full power. The calm waters may appear to the untrained eye of the observer as perfect but for the Sunderland, the increased suction from a calm sea meant more power was required to lift the beast out of the water. At around 90 knots McKinley gently pulled back on the large, steering wheel like joystick and the beast took flight, the churning wake gradually grew less as the hull cleared the surface and the sea returned to its serene state.

McKinley kept L5087 at around 200 feet, gathering airspeed and raising the flaps before beginning a climb to their operating height. Once at 1000 feet the power was reduced to 2250rpm, which lessened the noise considerably, level flight was achieved and then the controls trimmed out. There was an autopilot available, but this had some form, it was known to shove the nose down unexpectedly which, when flying at low altitudes at several hundred miles an hour was unsettling! Their mission that day was to provide a reconnaissance service to the ships in the force protecting the two convoys. They had been ordered to cover the area to the northeast and the entrance to the Adriatic Sea, looking for any sign of the Italian Fleet returning to Taranto. They would be backed up by two more Sunderlands of 228 Squadron (L9020 and L5083) that would take off later in the day to provide continuous reconnaissance from dawn to dusk.

In general, patrols were carried out at relatively low level, usually around 1000 feet. Once airborne the distance one can see, especially over the sea where there are no obstacles to block your vision increases quite dramatically. At 1000 feet visibility in good clear air is around 30 miles, if you climb up to 4000ft this increases to just under 85 miles. On a brightly lit sea, especially in the Mediterranean, surface ships stand out quite clearly to the observer. That morning the weather conditions were perfect, clear skies, a slight wind and a relatively calm sea that shone like a mirror as the sun began to rise above the horizon.

At 07:32 the crew spotted the Italian fleet confirming 2 battleships, 4 cruisers and 10 destroyers sailing at about 15 knots towards Taranto, and a few minutes later, about 20 miles out on a roughly parallel course was another formation of 6 cruisers and 8 destroyers. Their position from Cunningham's ships was around 145 miles to the west, which would mean that initial contact should be made sometime during the afternoon.

Ahead of *Nubian* the 7th Cruiser Squadron could be seen by the lookouts some 8 miles distant (the visibility at sea level being between 15 and 20 miles). They would continue to range ahead probing for sight of the enemy and lead in the battleships to close within range of the enemy with their main armament. Just behind came *Warspite* and a further 8 miles back came the Battle Squadron, protected by their 10 destroyers. During the morning and early afternoon reports came in from the Sunderlands with the location of the enemy, but as the ships began to close the Fleet Air Arm took over localised reconnaissance to help the battlegroup pinpoint the Italian ships positions.

The Swordfish biplane is mostly recognised for its role as a torpedo bomber; however, it also had a role to play in fleet reconnaissance. This role versatility and an ability to accommodate a number of different weapons brought it the nickname 'Stringbag', after a ladies shopping bag that always seemed to hold much more than it was capable of. Simple to fly, and almost impossible to stall it was a very stable aircraft and although slow was much loved by the pilots who flew it. Indeed, it was so slow that it had a landing speed of around 40 knots. With just a 20-knot headwind across the deck of a carrier it could take off and land in conditions that many more modern aircraft could not. Indeed, with a reasonable headwind the take-off run was literally measured in tens of feet, and it would land at not much faster than walking pace! Clearly it did not require a catapult assisted take off from a carrier.

However, being so slow also meant that whilst a stable platform for munitions delivery, it also gave the opposing gunners plenty of time to aim at an approaching Swordfish. A strong headwind could mean that an aircraft could not make it back to its mother ship, an accurate approach was essential in windy conditions. It had been known for an aircraft to misjudge the approach and never make it back aboard.

The crew of three consisted of Pilot up front, Observer in the middle position and Radio Operator/Gunner in the rear, although the Radio Operator could be dispensed with if torpedoes were used or the aircraft was tasked on a bombing mission, especially if the target was at distance where the middle seat was replaced with an additional fuel tank. This necessitated the observer relocating to the rear seat. This in itself would be awkward being the narrowest part of the cockpit as the Observer, not only cocooned in his bulky flight suit was equipped with a Bigsworth plotting table for navigation. This was a 17-inch square wooden contraption to take an unfolded map, whilst a metal arm held a hinged Perspex ruler and compass for plotting purposes.

Upfront there was a single, Pegasus radial engine that proved very reliable and robust, known on occasion to continue to run even with a cylinder shot away. The engine was started by a handle, that had to be cranked by two ground crew from just behind the engine. The handle was rapidly turned to get a flywheel spinning enough to crank the engine. This was exhausting, especially when a misfire meant the process needed to be started all over.

Such was the handling characteristics, its folding wings also meant that it could be stowed away in relatively small spaces and coupled with its general robustness the Swordfish was flown off larger Cruisers and Battleships using a catapult. This was either installed amidships or off the top of one of the gun turrets. *Warspite* had three Swordfish aboard, all of which had floats instead of undercarriage so that they could land close by the ship and be winched back aboard by use of a davit. Failing recovery aboard, the aircraft would often leave the area of operation and land at a nearby base to refuel and rejoin the ship when the opportunity arose. The purpose of these floatplane Swordfish was twofold, general reconnaissance in being the 'over the horizon' eyes of the ships and, due to range of the main guns meant that the fall of shot was often beyond sight, so the reports from the 'eyes in the sky' assisted with the ship's gunnery accuracy.

During the morning, *Eagle* deployed a continuous patrol by Swordfish, relaying information on the dispositions of the enemy that added detail to the intelligence being gathered by the Sunderlands. The Swordfish were well suited to operations from *Eagle,* having been one of the first purpose-built carriers constructed back in 1912 she was small at just 670 feet long and rather slow. Eventually it was clear that there was an opportunity to launch an air attack. At 11:45 she began to turn into the wind, and as the steam indicator on her bow blew down the centre line of the deck, the Commander-Flying placed his green flag in its holder to indicate to the Deck Control Officer (DCT) that flying operations could commence. The DCT signalled 'chocks away' to the handlers and a split second later he dropped his green flag, and the first Swordfish was away.

With the first strike on the enemy away it would not be long before the cruisers would make contact, this meant the bigger ships needed to maintain contact and keep up. Whilst *Warspite* had the legs, *Royal Sovereign* and *Malaya* did not, the pace of the chase was determined by these two. *Gloucester* was clearly not fit to join in the main action so she was tasked to screen *Eagle* who would gradually be left behind the main force. The chase to catch up with the Italian fleet was coming to a conclusion, all ships were at full readiness. A fleet action was inevitable.

The Royal Navy does tradition in a manner that is wholly 'British'. The signals transmitted over the hundreds of years of Naval Action reflect this too and any chance of harking back to the era of Nelson and the epic battles of the Napoleonic era (especially in the Mediterranean) have to be taken. At 15:08 there came a signal from *Neptune*, 'Enemy Battle Fleet in sight'.

At a range of almost 13 miles from each other the cruisers began to exchange fire although quite quickly it became apparent there was a chance the 7th Cruiser Squadron may come off worse. They were armed with 6-in. guns, the Italians with 8-in. The difference in range, accuracy and punch favoured the Italians. The 7th would need some help from *Warspite*.

'The old lady's lifting her skirts!' declared Ravenhill to the men on the bridge of *Nubian*. Indeed, *Warspite* was increasing speed, as was *Nubian*. For that moment they were the cavalry, pressing ahead, cleaving the water once more. Looking across at *Warspite* it became clear something was about to happen, the crew of the Swordfish prepared for a flight off the catapult had got out of the aircraft, they and the handling teams had gone below. As the hatch door closed, *Warspite* opened fire with her main guns. The shells roared out towards the leading enemy cruiser like an express train, covering the 15 miles (26400 yards) in moments. *Warspite* fired ten salvos in total before check firing as the enemy cruisers began to lay down a thick smoke screen for protection.

The Swordfish crew were back on deck, and moments later, they were seen manhandling the aircraft over the side. It had been shredded by the concussion from the guns. They began to pull out a second aircraft from the hanger and prepare it for operations.

Signals came aboard *Nubian* that *Warspite* would make a 360 degree turn in order to allow *Royal Sovereign* and *Malaya* to catch up, followed by a gentle 'S' shaped course, both battleship captains were urged to make haste to join

Warspite. The 7th was signalled to make a 360 degree turn at the same time, which should bring the force together. Of which, *Neptune* had a similar issue with one of her Swordfish, which was also at readiness to fly and been damaged by a near miss that ruptured its fuel systems that leaked all over the deck. It too was pushed over the side. *Nubian* was then ordered with the rest of the screen to join up with the remainder of destroyer force in an effort to work around the smoke screen that had been put down by the enemy fleet.

Warspite thumped a further 4 salvos at a cruiser which appeared out of the smoke, and shortly thereafter the pilot of the second Swordfish increased the Pegasus to full power and the aircraft was shot off the catapult to begin a reconnaissance mission. The pressure was maintained on the Italians as *Eagle* launched a second strike with her Swordfish at 15:45. It had been barely half an hour for the first engagement to have been completed.

From above, the Swordfish pilots had a view like no other. The destroyer force was clearly converging, the *Royal Sovereign* was being left behind, she was just too slow, and the *Malaya* was coming on station, but painfully slowly. Ahead were the enemy ships including the two battleships. *Warspite* opened fire once more, this time at the *Giulio Cesare*, which returned fire with mixed results, although one grouped salvo straddled *Warspite* and came as close as 2 cables (about 400 yards) from her port bow. *Malaya* fired 4 salvos, but all of these fell short.

It took just 11 minutes for *Warspite* to fire 17 salvos, check firing at 16:04. She had fired at a range of 14 miles and managed one hit, observed to fall behind the funnel of the *Cesare*. This had been the one that had resulted in the smoke screen and the Italian ships had begun to retire at speed.

Nubian and *Mohawk* managed to make contact with *Juno* and *Janus* coming back under the umbrella of D14 and Captain Mack. The Italian destroyers began to make swift but half-hearted counter attacks from within the cover of their smoke screen. They would suddenly appear, loose off torpedoes and then dart back into their protective blanket. Many written reports and historical accounts mention a near miss by a torpedo as 'Passing harmlessly', well the crew of *Nubian* didn't think the pair of torpedoes that came hurtling towards their ship looked very harmless. For a moment, it looked like they would be done for, as the torpedoes aim was true, but fortunately the tin fish were too deep, and they travelled underneath the stern and away before their motors died and they sank to the bottom.

Attention now came from the air, and the Italian air force began high level bombing with S.79's from 16:40 which continued until 19:11 with concentrated attacks made on both *Warspite* and *Eagle*. The destroyers came under attack too, and despite there being no hits scored on any of the ships, there were many near misses that frayed the tired nerves of the men who had been at action stations almost constantly for 48 hours. Not being lured into the smoke and perhaps meet a counterattack from submarines or destroyers, Cunningham took the main force around the smokescreen and came within 25 miles of the Calabria coast before Cunningham called it a day. With the ships running at full power for so long, fuel was beginning to run low, they turned for Malta to resupply.

For the Italians, the day was not quite over. They were attacked by their own air force by mistake, twice on their way back to their home ports, but by 19:00 it was all over, and they were re grouping, having escaped in some disarray. With the damage control assessment complete, Admiral Riccardi quite likely went to his apartment in a reflective mood. Cunningham no doubt would like to have thought that as Riccardi sat his bed he pondered on the day and the upturned 'Life of Nelson' on the floor of his cabin.

In the early hours of the 10 July *Nubian* and the ships of D14 (*Mohawk* and *Janus*) arrived in Malta but were held off entering Valetta to allow those destroyers low on fuel to replenish, *Stuart* had just 15 tons of fuel left in her tanks (destroyers would burn fuel at around 2t/hr at their most economical speeds, about 12 knots). With the battle now over, attention had turned back to the two convoys for Alexandria and their safe passage. MF1 had sailed the evening before with *Warspite* and an escort of destroyers, whilst on *Nubian* a relatively quiet night could pass where just a little respite from the pace of war could be gained.

Of course, this didn't last long with the crew at a high state of readiness from the early morning. The inevitable first raid came at 07:40 when four formations of S.79's flew in from their base in Sciacca on the island of Sicily. With so many destroyers in Valetta refeulling, there was much consternation that at least one of them would be hit. Bombs soon began to fall and the barrage from the anti-aircraft defences boomed out across the water.

High above the S.79 crews from Squadriglle 192a (87 Grupo) and 195a (90 Grupo) were eager to get out of range of the murderous anti-aircraft fire from below. For three of the aircraft and their crews this was their last mission. Two were hit quite quickly, the crew members bailing out of their rapidly disintegrating and burning aircraft, but for one of the men, not even the parachute could save him. As the canopy began to open, it too caught fire, and in a moment its ability to carry the man's weight gave up.

A third aircraft took a number of hits, and it too began a long curving descent, trailing flames and smoke it rapidly accelerated towards the earth below, eventually ploughing itself into a defence post manned by the 1st Battalion of the Royal Dorset's, three of the men being wounded, the whole crew of the S.79 were killed.

For the remainder of the day there was little to do but wait until the destroyers had completed refeulling, but there was no letup in the state of readiness, men grabbed a nap here and there where they could, but it was a fitful rest that just made them feel even more groggy. The slow convoy crept out of harbour that evening at 21:00, with *Decoy, Vampire* and *Voyager* making up the escort signaling a cheeky goodbye to *Nubian*. Within an hour of their departure the sound of the air raid siren wailed from on shore, and shortly afterwards there is a roar of engines as two pairs of aircraft come in low, dropping bombs and strafing the harbour with machine gun fire. Almost as suddenly as it begun it was over, quiet descended once more and eventually the crew were stood down.

D14 pulled out all the stops racing at full tilt to catch up with *Warspite* and the slow convoy the next day. Many wondered why they had hurried to become a target for the Regia Aeronautica once more. The attacks came one after the other and with such an intensity that in some instances the ships disappeared in the dirty water kicked up by the bombs that fell around them. Whilst not in this particular convoy, Rear Admiral Pugsley gives some idea of the strain that the men went through during these attacks, even those who had to remain stoically silent throughout.

> This time, as the bombs left, I knew they must fall amongst the destroyer screen. To my intense inner fury, as I waited for them to arrive, I found it almost impossible to stop my knees knocking and I prayed that no one was noticing it[95]

After the bombers had passed, he continues. 'All round me on the bridge I heard breaths being suddenly expelled as I myself also sighed with relief and felt my heart thumping. It was all very well to remind oneself of the large area of water and the very small area of the ship that there was for the bombs to fall in. I knew I should never get impervious to being bombed.'[96]

The fact that the slow convoy and the almost 'top heavy' escort was being so heavily attacked was because it represented such as juicy target for the Italians. What it also achieved was to divert attention from the fast convoy that transported the families of the crews who were being evacuated from Malta which arrived in Alexandria on the 13 July.

With all the ships safely back in port, operation MA5 was at an end, as was the Battle of Calabrai, or as the Italians named it Punta Stilo. Time now to appraise the situation and the conclusions were worrying. *Warspite* had been the only one of the larger ships that had been able to make enough speed to keep any pace with the Italian fleet and guns that had the necessary reach to pose a threat to them. The Eastern Mediterranean fleet needed another ship

---

[95] (Pugsley)
[96] (Pugsley)

like *Warspite* if they were to effectively engage the Italians once more. The cruisers were equally under-gunned when up against the enemies 8-in. cruisers. Despite the fact that the Swordfish strikes had not been as successful as hoped, their potential was clear. The extended striking range provided by carrier born aircraft was encouraging. If only they had one of the new armoured carriers at their disposal, not only for their strike capabilities but fighter cover for the fleet too, which brought back into the argument the case for additional Anti-Aircraft Cruisers for added protection from the Regina Aeronautica. Cunningham wrote to the Admiralty with his requirements and held his breath for a response. Hopefully he would not have to hold it for too long. Whatever the shortcomings that were now apparent, the first major engagement had been settled by one very well aimed shot from *Warspite*.

Chapter 7

Illustrious

July - August 1940

The dilapidated, old Greek Hospital on Rue De L'Hopital had been the home of the Fleet Club in Alexandria since 1939. Set up by the Destroyer Flotillas Chaplain, Rev. Alan Spender, M.A., aided by Richard Dines, M.B.E. and a group of volunteers, the site was cleared of rubbish then painted and decorated with a grant of £100 from the Admiralty. A few weeks later, with a nice beer garden created within the grounds, the doors were opened for the first time.

The establishment of the Fleet Club was due to the high cost to visiting sailors of food and drink ashore, a lack of suitable accommodation for those on overnight leave and an almost non-existent night life for entertainment. The visiting ships officers noted that life in Alexandria had little appeal to the sailors, which meant they remained on board when the warships were in port. Too much time on their hands and boredom had a negative effect on morale and efficiency, not to mention the crews general health and well-being.

Despite the creation of the Fleet Club, the initial numbers of visitors were disappointing. It took some effort to raise the standard of the restaurant and bar facilities, and to lay on quality entertainment to entice the sailors ashore, but before too long word got around that the Fleet Club was indeed the place to visit. Its popularity took off. The number of visitors grew leading up to the beginning of World War 2, but as we have seen, the Mediterranean Fleet was much reduced during 1939 and the beginning of 1940. With the number of visitors dwindling to just a few as and when a ship visited Alexandria the Fleet Club would have folded if it had not been for the Greek Community reducing the rent of the building by half, and some careful cost cutting.

This all changed as the Fleet was built up once more and begun to use Alexandria as its Eastern Mediterranean base. The much larger force of ships swelled the number of visitors to the Fleet Club, which once more reverberated with music from bands, cabarets and the general hubbub of sailors enjoying themselves ashore, and quite frequently the cheers as someone got lucky on the Tombola. So large were the numbers the 4-acre site was becoming overcrowded on many evenings and another large area of ground was taken in hand to establish a Winter and Summer Beer garden that could accommodate about 2000 men.

Leave of any type would have been a common talking point. There was no hope that any of the ships of the fleet would be returning to England any time soon. Even if leave were granted, in any case there was no way of getting back. For the young crew members a trip ashore on the liberty boat was clearly a release and a chance to forget that tomorrow may be your last day on earth. For those like Herbert, family men for whom the lure of the bars and loud music had no further draw, it was most likely on-board ship that they spent their leave, playing cards, board games, reminiscing of home, or simply sleeping. However, for some the sins of the flesh could be accommodated and for the officers 'their' brothel was 'Mary's' whilst the Carlton and Monseigneur were popular nightclubs.

The Fleet Club was not exclusive to the Royal Navy, men from all services were welcome, although it became quite well known that if the Fleet was 'in' then the place would be swarming with Matelots. There would be almost no chance of getting a table or somewhere to sit and that would mean finding entertainment elsewhere in Alexandria, such as the bars and the cinema playing the latest films.

If the ships in harbour were sending a launch ashore these would be manned by a Coxswain and a Midshipman in overall command. Officers would be dropped off at the jetty by No.6 Gate, whilst ratings were delivered to No. 10 Gate, and picked up from the same at the end of the evening. Adrian Holloway was a Midshipman assigned to *Valiant,* he had joined the Navy at

13, attending Dartmouth for his schooling and then training for a Commission. He was just 17 when he was ordered to report aboard *Valiant* in 1940. In his memoir, 'From Dartmouth to War' he describes being in charge of the shore leave launch, assisted by a Coxswain who would be a rating. There was sound sense in this. Following a good night ashore most ratings were somewhat worse for drink and perhaps belligerent as a result. Taking an order from a teenage Officer was not always well received and therefore the Coxswains job was to ensure they did not come to blows, as this would result in a court martial for the offending rating.

Once aboard the launch, keeping the ratings in check continued. As Holloway describes: 'Running a boat was one of the finest character forming duties a midshipman could perform, and I loved it. Drunken liberty men would shout and sing on their return to the ship, but it was forbidden to take them alongside in that condition. Those singers of *Bless 'em all*, for which of course the copulative verb was submitted, soon learned that an extra cruise around the ship would keep them from their hammocks. Muted admonishments to their shipmates: 'Shut up you stupid bugger, or the pig (jack speak for an officer) will take us around again,' had their effect and made me smile in the dark of an Alexandrian night.'[97]

For those who ventured into town to visit the shops and bazaars the lure of the trinkets and presents that could be sent home for loved ones at a bargain price were like silver foil to a Magpie. But all that glitters is clearly not gold most of the items on sale were dubious in quality and either would not work or would fall apart almost immediately when one tried to use them. Getting into town could be facilitated by taking an open horse drawn carriage, called a gharri. The horses were generally in poor shape and their drivers of dubious quality who would often chance their arm at making a little more profit on top of their fare, as Adrian Holloway describes: 'Like many of his kind he would carry a supply of 'feelthy pictures' which would be produced en route. For some reason, all English officers had the rank of captain as far as the

---

[97] (Holloway, 1993)

Gyppos[98] were concerned. 'Eh, captain, you like come see my sister? All safe, very clean, all same Queen Victoria.'[99]

Holloway continues; 'A friend of mine swore that the following was ushered by his gharris driver after the initial invitation to visit his sister had been refused. 'Eh, captain, you like to fuck me?' Midshipman, drawing himself up haughtily, 'Certainly not, drive on.' Gharri driver in despair, 'O.K. captain, you watch, I fuck my horse, only twenty acker.' The journey was continued on foot.'[100]

Taking a gharri[101] by day through the French named streets of Alexandria was relatively safe, but at night it could be a different story with incidents of muggings occasionally occurring. Financial gain was not always the cause of these incidents. The Egyptians had some animosity towards the Allies, and this became more pronounced when the German advances were pressing closer to the city. It became unsafe to travel alone at night in Alexandria.

So, our shore leave would come to an end and officers would congregate at No. 6 Gate to be taken back to their ships. The powerful battleships' picket boats would jockey for position alongside the quay together with the fussy little motorboats from the destroyers. Shouts of *Valiant, Warspite*, would mingle with *Nubian, Orion, Gloucester*, all names steeped in naval history, many of the ships soon to lie at the bottom of the Mediterranean. Some officers (Warrant I suspect) could be heard calling in tipsy voices for *Scharnhorst* or *Gneisenau*![102]

During July and August, the ships of the fleet came and went on many tasks at sea, the work for the destroyers was varied. In between operations the ships had a day or two leave which meant a run ashore was available to the crews. In *Jervis* for example, the crews were split into two Divisions and

---

[98] "Gyppo" – slang for an Egyptian
[99] (Holloway, 1993)
[100] (Holloway, 1993)
[101] A small handcart
[102] (Holloway, 1993)

alternate leave where one Division would be able to go ashore for overnight leave, most likely to the Fleet Club where cheap rooms were available, whilst the other remained aboard to protect the ship.

Italian reconnaissance aircraft began to fly over Alexandria with regularity and almost impunity as there was no effective fighter cover available to see them off. This caused much consternation to Cunningham as he realised (and clearly let his superiors know) that the ships movements were almost continually observed. Before long the bombing raids on the port began, the first on the evening of the 16 July. Whilst the ships and the port were blacked out, the town was not, and the bombs soon began to fall around the moored ships. The aircraft were generally SM.81's and SM.79's of 92 Grupo that were based out of either Marizza or Gadurra air bases in Rhodes.

On one occasion a lone aircraft came in low over the breakwater, dropping what was thought to be two torpedoes before the aircraft flashed noisily over the fleet, its engine noise diminishing into the distance. Neither of the devices detonated, and it's thought that they buried themselves into the mud and silt of the harbour. Nevertheless, there was now a new and potential serious threat to the ships. Cunningham ordered that all ships, as soon as they moored, flew improvised kites that were equipped with explosive charges in a hope that the local enemy spies would report that the ships were well protected against low level attacks. These charges would occasionally be set off accidentally creating an ear-splitting explosion that rolled and echoed over the water, whilst on board cups of tea and kye were hurled into the air, men fell out of hammocks in dazed confusion and those awakened from hard earned blissful slumber shouted expletives at their Commander that would have them on a charge if he were in earshot.

Maintenance of the Fleet was becoming a worry. The destroyers had no depot ship, and the time cleaning their boilers was being cut to a minimum. Keeping the ships hulls free from barnacles, weed and algae of which the warm seas around Alexandria encouraged growth, was vitally important to keep under control. Just like icing causes drag on an aircraft wing, the efficiency of a ships hull and its ability to swim through the water its speed and fuel efficiency are all drastically affected by the buildup of foreign objects.

Having the floating docks available meant that the larger ships could be dealt with, the problem was when? In order to place a warship into the floating dock, all the ammunition needed to be first removed, no small undertaking where a battleship is concerned. What is more, the ship is now defenceless and vulnerable at a time when the enemy is bombing daily. Despite these risks, both *Warspite* and *Malaya* were dealt with during August when there was no moon, *Warspite* was also treated to a new camouflage paint job.

The ships engines suffered too, especially the condensers that returned the exhaust gases back to water which was re-fed into the boiler. *Malaya, Royal Sovereign* and *Ramillies* all suffered in varying degrees of severity that drastically affected their usefulness, the same condition was also present in the cruiser *Kent*.

With all the arrogance and posturing that was the persona of Mussolini it came as little surprise that he began to use the old Roman name for the Mediterranean, Mare Nostrum (our sea). It would now be the purpose of the Royal Navy to turn it into 'Cunningham's Pond'. For the moment however, Italy did indeed have much of the upper hand in both surface and underwater ships and of course, air power.

The Mediterranean is made up of two large basins, one in the east, the other to the west, bisected by the boot of Italy and the island of Sicily. Here the Sicilian Narrows are a mere 90 miles wide from the southern tip of the island to the North African coast. Almost halfway across is the little island of Penetralia. A little to the west is the island of Sardinia, again the distance between its southern port of Cagliari and Bizerte in Tunisia is just 140 miles. Through these points all the ships heading to and from Alexandria to Gibraltar via Malta would have to pass. It would become known as 'Bomb Alley'.

In the latter half of 1940 the Axis powers and Italy in particular, occupied much of the North African coast and the western Mediterranean. Algeria and Tunisia were in French hands but under the control of the Axis sympathetic Vichy government. Libya was occupied by Italy where there was a gradual buildup of troops and materiel in readiness for an inevitable assault on Egypt that threatened the British Fleet in Alexandria. The port was only 300 miles from the Libyan border and of course, the supply lines from the Southern Hemisphere and the Middle East through the Suez Canal. It became clear that Italy had designs on Greece, a neutral country under the control of yet another dictator, Ioannis Metaxas. Despite his authoritarian rule, this former General attempted to maintain Greece's neutral status and whilst suspicious of British intentions, joined with the Allies in October 1940 when Italy's intentions became all too clear. Of course, Malta was firmly in the sights of Italy too, its strategic position in the central Mediterranean was not lost on Mussolini and as such the continual bombardment of the island was seen as a prelude to invasion. Hence the convoys from Alexandria to strengthen the garrisons as well as provide food and fuel.

Italian air bases were numerous around the western basin which included those on Penetralia, mainland Italy and Rhodes. When the fleet were at sea therefore, Alexandria and Malta were all at high risk from airstrikes that could come within the hour after reconnaissance had been carried out. The reconnaissance flights were generally carried out with Cant 501 flying boats. These had a large Lagonda styled fuselage slung below a high wing configuration with a single engine power plant in front of a rear gun position that was accessed in flight by an external ladder!

The Cants would circle the ships, maintaining a safe distance from Anti-Aircraft fire, reporting back the numbers of ships, strength of escort, position, course, and speed. Within the hour the attacking force would arrive high overhead, out of the range of the fleets guns and the bombs would begin to fall amongst the ships. As we have seen, occasionally these attacks would result in a hit, but a ship was pretty unlucky to be seriously damaged as a result of these high altitude attacks. However, the nerves and constant vigilance required drained the ships crews there was little relief from stress when at sea and for now, no fighter cover to oppose the bombers. Perhaps Mussolini's claim that Italy was an 'aircraft carrier' and did not need to build one was justified?

Whilst this all seemed rather bleak, there was good news that filtered to the ship's crews. The destroyers *Hyperion, Hasty, Hero* and *Ilex* had come across two Italian 6-in. cruisers on the 19 July, the *Giovanni delle Bauda Nere* and the *Bartolomeo Colleoni* at just enough distance to stay out of range of their guns but close enough to encourage a 'catch me if you can' chase. What the Italians didn't know was the destroyers were leading them into the clutches of HMAS *Sydney*, to the north where an engagement was begun off Cape Spada. The destroyers disengaged whilst Sydney opened up, hitting the *Barolomeo Colleoni* midships and knocking out her boilers. She stopped dead in the water, smoke pouring from just behind the forward superstructure. A shot hit her forward of 'B' turret and caused an explosion in the forward magazine that blew her bow to pieces, it looked like someone had taken a meat clever to the ship and cut her nose off.

The destroyers returned and 525 of the crew were taken off before torpedoes were fired at close range to send her to the bottom of the sea. About 150 men died aboard the Italian cruiser that day, mainly from the forward compartments. Whilst still nowhere near parity, there was one less Italian cruiser to worry about.

Cunningham's letter requesting a carrier had also produced a result, *Warspite's* modernised sister ship, *Valiant* was being allocated to them, as was the armoured aircraft carrier, *Illustrious* and the cruisers *Calcutta* and *Coventry,* both modified for anti-aircraft duties.

Illustrious was one of the two new armoured carriers *Formidable* being the other. These ships could carry a compliment of Swordfish for their multiple capabilities and Fairey Fulmars as fighter protection, 35 aircraft in total. This was somewhat less than *Ark Royal,* which could carry between 50 and 60 aircraft, but the compromise in numbers of aircraft came in the form of the armoured deck and hangers that protected both the ship and her precious aircraft from aerial bombardment.

Valiant, Illustrious and *Coventry* were equipped with one more piece of modern technology that would give the Eastern Mediterranean Fleet a huge advantage over the Regina Aeronautica, R.D.F., or as it is now known, Radar. The Radar available to these ships could sweep about 40 miles ahead of the fleet. *Illustrious* would have a flight of 3 Fulmars airborne, providing what is now known as a Combat Air Patrol (CAP) with another 3 on deck ready as relief. On detecting an enemy presence, the CAP could be vectored directly towards the enemy aircraft and hit them a long time before they got to the ships.

The difficulty was getting these prize assets all the way from Gibraltar to Alexandria in one piece. A journey that as yet, had never been attempted during hostilities.

Operation HATS

Nubian was grubby, rust streaked and war weary as she entered Alexandria's defensive boom. The day before, 17 August, she and *Mohawk* had been involved in protecting a convoy into Port Said and then met up with *Warspite, Malaya* and *Ramillies* to head west, screening the big ships from Submarine and aerial attack whilst they pounded the port of Bardia with their 15-in. guns. It was a short sharp action that brought the usual response in the form of air attacks as they made their way back to Alexandria. The SM.79's kept on coming, bombs and shrapnel splashing all around the ships, but the response was effective. 12 of the SM.79's were brought down by Anti-Aircraft fire.

Herbert was very tired, the attacks had been relentless, the workload mind numbing as the crew tried to keep the ship operational. Apart from the clearing of the decks of shell casings and the detritus of actioning the guns as well as cleaning them, it was clear from what the Stokers were saying that the boilers were fouling, and the forced lubrication system was failing. This was causing the overheating of the propulsion systems and a danger that they would lose a critical bearing. *Nubian* was as tired as her crew and required attention, which was what she would now receive in a short break from operations, although the air attacks from Rhodes would continue to keep them awake, as would the exploding kites.

The break was brief, leave was cancelled after a couple of days, *Nubian* was being readied for sea again and a special mission. Ravenhill was briefed that he would take *Nubian, Mohawk, Hero* and *Janus* on a fast passage to Gibraltar on the 27 August to rendezvous with 'Force F' for passage to Alexandria. They would be escorted halfway by Sommerville's 'Force H', negotiate the narrows between Tunisia and Sicily then enter Malta to refuel the destroyers. They would then hook up with Cunningham's Fleet, which was escorting an inbound convoy of supplies into Malta with the dual role of appearing lightly escorted and therefore a tantalising bait to draw out the Italian Navy. Once replenished at Malta the fleet would return to Alexandria, and on the way, there would be a surprise for the Italians too.

Operation 'HATS' was the code name given to the escorting of 'Force F', which consisted of *Illustrious, Valiant, Coventry* and *Calcutta* that were finally being attached to the Eastern Mediterranean fleet. Herbert was immediately impressed when the ships of Force F came into view. Sure, he had seen cruisers and battleships before, even aircraft carriers, but nothing quite like *Illustrious*. Newly commissioned on the 25 May, she was 740 feet in length, 23,000 tons with a top speed of some 30 knots, she was a majestic, powerful looking ship. Whilst *Ark Royal* was impressive, *Illustrious* was both revolutionary and cutting edge. She simply oozed 'projection of power'. Whilst the older carriers had been built by adapting a heavy cruiser to take a flight deck, *Illustrious* had been designed and built as a carrier from the spars upward. Charles Lamb, a Swordfish pilot of 815 Squadron commented, 'The result was not just a masterpiece of planning and design, but a mighty ship of great beauty.

Comparing her with *Courageous* was tantamount to comparing her with Noah's Ark.'[103]

On board were 3 squadrons of aircraft, two equipped with Swordfish (815 and 819) and one squadron of Fulmars (806). The Fulmars could be launched by catapult (known to the pilots as 'boosting') whilst the Swordfish would almost always take off unassisted. There was an ingenious new recovery system employed on *Illustrious* too, this was the Safety Barrier, a large wire net that stretched across the flight deck at about its midpoint next to the Bridge, or as it is known on carriers, 'The Island'. On older carriers, an aircraft that had landed on would have its wings folded and then taken below to the hanger before the next aircraft could land. The advantage being the next landing aircraft had a free deck to play with and an ability to 'go around' if it missed all the arresting wires. Stowing the aircraft in this manner took about 2 minutes per machine to complete with some slick operating. Bearing in mind that a carrier had to sail into the wind to recover its aircraft, a squadron of 15 aircraft could take as long as 30 minutes to be recovered, in which time, if the wind were in the 'wrong' direction, the carrier could have sailed some distance from the rest of the fleet, and possibly into harm's way. With the new Safety Barrier, landing aircraft could be stopped and parked on deck beyond the barrier, allowing the next aircraft to land almost immediately. If the landing aircraft missed the wires it was caught by the barrier. Whilst it would invariably shatter the propeller there was usually little other damage. An inspection of the engine thereafter and any resulting repairs would normally have the aircraft airborne again in no time. The big advantage was the interval between aircraft landing; taxiing over the barrier to the next aircraft landing came down to about ten seconds.

As we have seen, all new warships (or those following a refit) have to go through a working up phase to become operational. Captain Denis Boyd was the Commanding Officer of *Illustrious* and he took her and the crew down to Bermuda for her working up period. Bermuda was a relatively safe environment, away from potential conflict that gave the crew a chance to

---

[103] (Lamb, 2001)

mould into the fighting unit that was so needed in the Mediterranean. It would be hard work, and it would demonstrate the dangers of air operations from a carrier, sometimes with tragic consequences. The Skuas of 806 Squadron landed on *Illustrious* on 11 June 1940, in preparation for the working up period which was not without incident. The Skuas arrived as the Swordfish were completing their landings, after which the more experienced pilots landed first, followed by the novices. One aircraft had an engine failure on final approach and had to ditch. The crew managed to retrieve their belongings and put them in the aircrafts dingy, they then got in the water and pushed the dingy around until they were picked up.

Youthful exuberance is certainly a quality that is part and parcel of the fighter pilot, and in every squadron or collection of young males with far too much bravado there is a tendency to make light of situations, even at the most inappropriate times. 'Stan Orr, having more hours flying than most, made an immaculate landing, catching the first wire but unfortunately raising the wrath of Captain Boyd by climbing out of his cockpit and combing his hair in full view of the bridge!'[104]

Flying an aircraft is a demanding skill that requires multi-tasking, a talent that is hard to acquire but can be taught through repetition and drills within the training of a pilot. Many find that in the early days of training the demands of concentration are so high that it becomes difficult to determine left from right or to carry out simple mathematics. All of this training leads towards times when things begin to go wrong, and flying the aircraft has to be second nature whilst the problem is dealt with. Getting lost is one such problem and in an aircraft, you cannot simply pull over to stop to look at a map.

During the passage to Bermuda 3 Skuas were detailed to practice dive bombing against smoke floats some 5 miles from the ship. The weather was unpredictable, with large storms muscling their way across the Atlantic. They completed their practice and then climbed away to return to the carrier, but it was nowhere to be seen. A big storm had crossed where *Illustrious* had been,

---

[104] (Galea, 2019)

it towered black and menacing from sea level to many thousands of feet. At first the pilots were not too concerned, but after two hours of trying to find their ship, it dawned on them that they were lost in the middle of a very large ocean. Gus Hogg was one of the pilots. 'When my clock showed that three hours had passed, I nearly went mad at the thought of a slow, horrible death in a dinghy in the cold Atlantic, but this feeling slowly changed to one of resignation - I was finished.'[105]

In the back of the aircraft, his air gunner was trying to raise the ship by continuous wireless transmissions, hoping that the ship may break its strict radio silence and come to their aid. As time went by this seemed more unlikely until at last there came a transmission from *Illustrious* giving them their relative bearing from the ship. However, mistaking this as a bearing to the ship in one of those moments where stress takes over Hogg turned onto this heading, and they began to fly even further away from the *Illustrious*. Fortunately, someone on board must have realised their mistake and gave them a bearing to the ship, but another 20 minutes had passed. A lack of fuel to get them back safely was now becoming the one factor between life and death. To their great relief, *Illustrious* came into view and they were able to land. 'We landed, having been in the air for five hours, with a few drops of petrol in our tanks. Stanley (pilot of one of the other Skuas) was so relieved to find that his time had not yet come that he crashed into the island structure, fortunately without hurt to himself. The CO gave us a strafing for losing ourselves, but we did not mind: better a strafing than death.'[106]

On arrival in Bermuda flying exercises for the Skuas were curtailed as *Illustrious* required some repair work which meant a week anchored in the roads. The Skuas needed a good headwind to safely get airborne and to land back on deck, so with no airfield available ashore they were 'grounded', however the Swordfish could continue to operate when the ship was not moving.

---

[105] (Galea, 2019)
[106] (Galea, 2019)

As the week progressed, there came a day where a tropical storm blew up and with the ship turning at her mooring into the wind there was sufficient headwind to launch all of the aircraft including the Skuas. The opportunity was taken, but on returning to the carrier the storm had passed and the winds had dropped to nothing. The Swordfish were recovered without too much difficulty, however for the Skuas, landing would be tricky, if not impossible with their high approach and landing speeds. Something was bound to give, either arrestor wires would break or more likely the arresting hooks on the Skuas would be ripped out. This was indeed the case, as one by one the Skuas attempted to land their hooks were torn off. Some aircraft managed to land on but could not stop and went over the side, others were deliberately steered into the island.

Lt. Nicolls and his burly, bearded air gunner made a stable approach, their hook caught but it too was disconnected from their aircraft. As they had made a relatively fast approach there was still enough speed available so when Nicolls slammed the throttles forward, they could lift off the deck once more. Their Skua surged forward under the power applied and before they knew it *Illustrious* was disappearing behind them. That was all well and good, but with the nearest airfield about 600 miles away in the United States and no means of landing on deck what on earth would they do now? The air gunner demanded they attempt a landing on the Belmont Golf course, which the pilot duly attempted on the 16th fairway, however the trees that lined it proved too tight and the Skua's wings were torn off. According to Charles Lamb, '…he ended up on the green having done a hole in one.'[107] For the observer, this was all too much, Lamb goes on; 'The air gunner leaped out of the rear cockpit and burst into tears. Nobody blamed him for this, but as he was a man who boasted an enormous black beard we all felt that his behaviour would have been less incongruous had he been clean shaven.'[108]

Fortunately, there were no injuries, but the effective strength of 806 Squadron had been reduced to one or two aircraft. Their participation in

---

[107] (Lamb, 2001)
[108] (Lamb, 2001)

flying exercises effectively ended there, and whilst it had been rumoured they would be heading to the Mediterranean once the working up had been completed, they would now need to return to England in order to re-equip 806.

As *Illustrious* was departing for home there was one final reminder that operations were hazardous. Charles Lamb was conducting some fighter evasion tests in his Swordfish, with a Skua piloted by Lt. Peter Dean and his air gunner Ken Jones. The tactic they practiced was indeed successfully adopted (or discovered) by Swordfish pilots thereafter and involved maximising the benefit of flying a very slow aircraft against a much faster one. On being attacked the Swordfish pilot would turn his aircraft towards the attacker, pulling up into a stall at the same time. The much faster attacker would then struggle to keep Swordfish in its sights and overshoot, it too stalling and diving away to gain airspeed. The Swordfish would dive towards the surface in an effort to fly at almost zero feet. This would force the attacking aircraft to either break off the attack or attempt to fly just as slow to set up for the kill. However, in doing so all advantage of speed was lost, the odds became much more even and gave the chance for the Swordfish gunner to fight back!

During this exercise Lt. Dean made several attempts to 'shoot down' Lamb's Swordfish, following it right down to the surface of the sea. Lamb could not believe it when Dean made one last attack, which at that height could only end in tragedy. It did, Dean's aircraft shot past and dived away inverted straight into the sea in a misjudgment of height. 'There was no chance of his survival after entering the water in an inverted dive, but in a hope of a miracle we flew around the spot for some time. The only thing to come to the surface was the Skuas tail wheel.'[109]

Back in England, 806 Squadron was re-equipped with Fairey Fulmar fighters. The Fairey Fulmar was one of the first attempts at providing the Fleet Air Arm with a deck operational monoplane fighter. Its origins were not promising, its forerunner, the Fairey Battle had arguably been the RAFs worst

---

[109] (Lamb, 2001)

aircraft ever to have come into service. A medium bomber by design the Battle, despite being powered by the Merlin engine used in the Spitfire and Hurricane was heavy and slow. During the German advance to Dunkirk, Battles had been pressed into action only to be shot from the sky in droves. Happily, the Fulmar was a far better aircraft, but still large and slow for a fighter aircraft despite its Merlin. In comparison to a Spitfire the Fulmar had two crew and was almost twice as heavy so therefore it was about 100 miles an hour slower. But it was well liked. Norman Hanson loved the Fulmar, and in his memoir 'Carrier Pilot', described its characteristics.

> 'Although somewhat underpowered, she more than made up for this deficiency by her complete lack of vices. She had to be kicked into a spin and, when it came, it was a leisurely sensation which was easily controlled. If she was involved in any incidents, they were certainly man-made, for the Fulmar, bless her, was the most gentle of aircraft and would never dream of embarrassing you.'[110]

Indeed, up against the equally slow aircraft of the Regina Aeronautica the Fulmar would hold its own in the skies above the Mediterranean.

On the 29 August there was no planning left to do, just the execution. In the east, Captain Mack brought *Jervis* (D) and the remainder of the 14th Flotilla out of Alexandria to join up and to escort 3 merchant ships to Malta. Sailing at the same time was Cunningham in the flagship with *Malaya* and *Eagle*, whilst the 3rd (*Orion* & *Sydney*) and 7th Cruiser Squadrons (*Gloucester*, *Kent* and *Liverpool*) also sailed.

The Convoy, designated MF2 consisted of the Royal Fleet Auxiliary *Plumleaf* (carrying fuel oil) and two merchant ships, *Cornwall* and *Volo* which would transport anti-aircraft ammunition and personnel. The captains of the two merchant ships had been briefed along with the Navy Commanding Officers aboard *Warspite* confirming suspicions why the Italians were so interested in them when they passed through Mombassa on their way to the

---

[110] (Hanson, 2016)

Suez Canal. Their destination was clearly well known as was their cargo, it was also apparent they were indeed part of a larger operation, and they were a target worthy of the attention of the enemy. They were the bait.

In the west, *Nubian* was at a high state of alert as the ships of Force H and Force F began to gather pace and head for Malta. Under Admiral Sommerville, Force H was going to make its presence known, again in an effort to draw out the Italians. On the 31st *Ark Royals* Skuas intercepted and shot down two Italian reconnaissance aircraft (Cant 508 and a 501), earlier in the day radio transmission interceptions indicated that the Italians had cruisers and destroyers at sea, perhaps the bait was attracting interest?

That night, the destroyers *Velox* and *Wishart* detached themselves from the main fleet, and at full speed they rushed northwards of the Balearic's in order to carry out Operation Squawk. They would transmit false information regarding the fleet positions and to cover the low frequency radio transmissions that *Ark Royal* emitted during flying operations which were about to commence. Operations 'Smash' and 'Grab' were conducted over the two nights of the 1 and 2 September. Swordfish launched from *Ark Royal* attacked Cagliari air base on Sardinia as diversionary raids whilst Force F quietly slipped away to the east towards Malta. *Ark Royal,* meanwhile, swung back towards the west, recovered her aircraft and returned with Force H to Gibraltar arriving without incident on the 3rd.

The morning of the 2 September began the same as any other aboard *Nubian*, the sea was flat calm, the sun rising through the mist and all the men at dawn readiness. This was the time when an attack could come any minute and the tension was normally palpable. But today there was a different air of expectation, for not far off cruised *Illustrious*, and she had just launched the first 3 of her Combat Air Patrols of the day, consisting of 3 Fulmars from 806 Squadron. It was time for some payback.

From the north, approached a Cant 501 at about 500 feet on a reconnaissance mission. On one leg of their sweeps, they flew a little further to the south, just enough for the crew to detect several smudges on the horizon. They flew on, realising that they had stumbled upon a group of warships, large ones at that, one of which looked like a carrier. Several pairs of eyes began to search the sky in case of fighters, the gunner began his lone climb to his gun position on the top of the wing behind the blaring engine.

Above, Blue Section could easily see Malta, just 35 miles distant, a beautiful morning for flying but trade was about to come their way. *Illustrious* had picked up some transmissions of morse code and they had got an intercept bearing for the aircraft to steer. As the fighters turned onto the correct heading, they spotted a Cant approaching and they dived down to position for an attack from astern.

Inside the Cant, one of the crew shouted in alarm as he spotted the Fulmars approaching. The pilot Ottavio De Martis attempted to evade his attackers pushing the nose down to fly about ten feet over the glassy surface of the sea. As the .303 bullets began to thump and bang into the airframe the radio operator managed to send off a signal with the position of the carrier and the number of ships escorting.

'Check Fire' came the order on board *Nubian*, as the crew watched the Fulmars close in on their prey. One by one they swooped into position to let off a burst of fire and for a moment it looked like the Italian would escape. Sub Lt. Ivan Lowe brought his Fulmar in close and pressed the gun button, he could see some tracer sparkle as it hit the Cant and moments later its wing dipped, touched the water and the aircraft cartwheeled away in a flume of spray and spinning components as it broke up in the water. The *Nubians* cheered, shouted, jumped up and down with excitement for the thorn in their side that was the constant harassment from the enemy had been, at least temporarily, dealt with, even though three brave Italian aviators were now dead as a result.

Having received the position of *Illustrious*, it was not long before the enemy sent out bomber forces to seek and destroy the carrier. Two waves of SM.79s, 10 from 60 Gruppo and 9 from 59 Gruppo were dispatched. 60 Gruppo did not find their target but 59 Gruppo did. Despite being at around

10,000 feet the ships crews could see the Fulmars go into action, two SM.79's were brought down to more cheers.

As Force F approached Malta, another raid of six SM.79's tried once more to attack *Illustrious*, three were shot down, one of which may have been hit by the ships Anti-Aircraft guns. Whatever the result, the aircraft of 806 Squadron had banged down a huge rubber stamp marked 'Carrier' on the table of the Italian Commanders. The Fleet Air Arm had arrived. As Charles Lamb wrote, 'No Fleet Commander can go into battle without his own air defence on the spot. A man without belt or braces can hold up his trousers for only a limited time; sooner or later his hands will be required for some other purpose and the resulting exposure could be fatal when fighting defensively, at close quarters. Without their own aircraft carriers, the Italian admirals were in that position precisely: their trousers were well and truly down.'[111]

Cunningham reflected not only his views, but the confidence that would prevail amongst the crews of the ships under his command on the arrival of *Illustrious* when he wrote, 'From that moment, whenever an armoured carrier was in company, we had command of the air over the fleet. By that I do not mean that the bombing attacks ceased. Far from it. But we felt that we now had a weapon which enabled us to give back as good as we were getting, and also gave us a vastly increased freedom of movement.'[112]

Late in the afternoon of the 2 September Herbert and the crew on deck of *Nubian* were part of the triumphant arrival of Force F into the Grand Harbour. *Illustrious* was not among them though, she was held off to the south to avoid bombing attacks on the harbour, but the escorting destroyers, the cruisers *Coventry* and *Calcutta* followed *Valiant* into harbour her decks lined with seamen and her marine band, welcomed by cheering and waving crowds.

Earlier that day Convoy MF2 had arrived almost intact. Whilst *Plumleaf* and *Volo* were already in the process of being unloaded. As *Nubian* passed

---

[111] (Lamb, 2001)
[112] (Cunningham, 1951)

her by the crew thought that *Cornwall* looked a very sorry sight indeed. She was listing to port very badly, her superstructures pockmarked, and smoke streaked from bomb detonations and extinguished fires. She had come under air attack en route, her engines momentarily disabled, and compartments flooded, her steering shot away. Despite this her crew managed to keep her afloat and steer a reasonable course using half revolutions on the port side and full revolutions on the starboard.

During the attacks, 9 members of her crew had been wounded, three very badly; 'The steward's boy had a femoral artery cut and a lump of shell in his thigh, an able seaman had a crushed foot, and a greasers chest was perforated by three splinters.'[113] Captain Mack could not consider stopping to transfer his surgeon, but instructions on their care were flashed by lamp and given to the chief Steward, Mr. J. Jesse. Later, under cover of darkness the convoy was stopped, *Juno* approached *Cornwall* and transferred her Surgeon Lieutenant Adnams, RNVR. All three men recovered and bore their wounds and treatment with admirable stoicism noted by Adnams; 'Their conduct…was of the best and never a murmur of complaint was to be heard.'[114]

Valiant, Calcutta and *Coventry* pulled alongside to begin offloading their cargoes of men and equipment that included Anti-Aircraft guns, artillery pieces and ammunition. *Nubian* found the oiler and refueled. Meanwhile, out at sea, the Fulmars were once more in action above Cunningham's fleet. Admiral Tovey and the Cruiser Squadrons had returned from the north, bringing with them a pair of circling Cant 501 aircraft. They were dealt with to the satisfaction of Cunningham; 'The Fulmars quickly tumbled both of them into the sea to the loud cheers of the ship's companies, who had had just about as much as they could stand of being bombed without retaliation.'

On board *Illustrious*, it is perhaps at this time that Charles Lamb, watching from the observation platform of the island noted; '…when one of the Fulmars succeeded in setting a Cant flying boat alight. Two of the occupants baled out

---

[113] (Woodman, 2000)
[114] (Woodman, 2000)

of the burning aircraft, but they had only one parachute between them, and the sight of those two wriggling bodies, like worms impaled on a single fisherman's hook, plunging to their deaths from ten thousand feet, was something I would rather not have seen. The mind boggles at what the rightful owner must have been saying to his unwelcome passenger.'[115]

With no time to lose, *Nubian* and *Mohawk* were sent off on a convoy protection duty with the cruisers *Gloucester*, *Kent* and *Liverpool* to protect 5 steamships to Port Said before returning to Alexandria. On arrival, the whole fleet was once more assembled, and what a sight it was. The harbour was crammed with powerful warships of all sizes, and they were jubilant too. They had muscled their way through the eastern Mediterranean on the second half of Operation Hats. 'All day the fleet in squadrons and flotillas entered, and it became a very crowded base with three battleships, two aircraft carriers, seven cruisers, 17 destroyers, the French demilitarised squadron, several fleet tankers and supply ships.'[116] As would be the mark of Cunningham from now on, the combination of ships and air power would be used to maximum effect in hurting the enemy, there was a parity in the opposing forces once more, perhaps in Cunningham's favour. During the return cruise the Swordfish from *Illustrious* and *Eagle* had hit back at those who had tormented them at their moorings in Alexandria. The airfields on Rhodes (Kalatho and Maritza) had been hit hard, hangers, aircraft were left burning with thick black smoke belching into the sky. Whilst sadly 4 crews had not returned, the fact that there was now a far more potent allied force in the Mediterranean was most evident. Operation Hats was complete, Force F had safely negotiated the 2000 miles to Alexandria, much needed supplies had been delivered to Malta whilst the Regina Aeronautica had been given a bloody nose. On the other hand, the Italian Navy had remained stubbornly at home, perhaps they would need a visit?

---

[115] (Lamb, 2001)
[116] (Connell, 1987)

Chapter 8

Relentless

Every man is not by nature a hero. He must be made into a fighter by training him to such a pitch that he is able and eager to overcome all instincts of self-preservation and to carry out his job to the limits of his mental and physical capacity - and this in situations in which he may be dead next minute.

Surgeon Lt. Commander Edward Benson McDowall D.S.C.

The Western Desert September 1940 to February 1941

In the final quarter of 1940 and leading into the first half of 1941 there were several events and operations conducted that shaped the course of war in the Mediterranean and the fortunes of the Royal Navy in that theatre. Of these, Operation Compass is a significant trigger for the rise of the Royal Navy's dominance in the coming months before the full weight of the Nazi War Machine came to bear on the region. Therefore, it is worthwhile pausing to look at the British Armies attack on the Italians in North Africa.

On 13 September 1940, following a number of skirmishes along the Libyan border with the British Western Desert Force, the Italian Army finally committed themselves to the invasion of Egypt. They were led by General Rodolpho Graziani, a fanatical fascist and ruthless man who did not hesitate in using all means of repression against his civilian opponents including concentration camps and gas attacks that earned him the nickname 'II mecellaio del Fezzan' (the butcher of Fezzan) from his time in Libya.

He was cautious in his approach to military strategy wishing to prepare thoroughly, attack and then consolidate his position before moving again. The preparation phase during August and September 1940 stretched the patience of Mussolini. Graziani's strategy was to invade Egypt at the same time as the German's were to initiate Operation Sealion (the invasion of Britain), hoping that the demoralised and battered British resolve in Egypt would soon crumble but Mussolini told him to get on with it whether or not the Germans invaded.

Ten Divisions of Italian Troops, backed up with tanks and artillery moved forward at about 12 miles a day before reaching Sidi Barani on the coast, some 60 miles inside Egypt. Here he stopped and began the consolidation process, creating a semicircular group of camps and fortifications, he even had a monument erected to their success. They had the sea to their left, and the desert to their right, in front lay the rest of Egypt, Alexandria and the oil fields of Iraq.

The Western Desert in Egypt was made for open warfare being almost devoid of people, farms, even roads. Perfect for the movement of armour and particularly tanks. It had gently undulating ground that allowed concealment and tactical surprise. However, the further that an army travelled the more reliant it became on re-supply. Hence Graziani's decision to consolidate, re-supply and prepare.

Graziani's opposite commander was Lieutenant General Richard O'Connor of the British Western Desert Force, his superior being General Wavell. O'Connor had his troops massed about 30 miles away to the east at Mersa Matruh. He had hoped that the Italians would extend their march towards him for he had a trap prepared, however this was not to be as Graziani had made up his mind to halt where he was. For the time being, O'Connor would prepare to send the Italians back from whence they came and for the next two months (October, November 1940) both armies waited and prepared.

In the meantime, Mussolini put into action his plans to invade Greece. This his armies did on the 30 October from Albania, but they were ill prepared with poorly equipped troops. The Greeks held on with a tenacity that surprised everyone who expected a swift capitulation, by stopping and halting the Italian advance just inside the Greek border. Churchill, still mindful of Britain's promise to come to the aid of Greece if attacked began to review which troops would be best spared to fulfil that promise and those troops would most likely come from the Western Desert Force.

Hitler too, was watchful of the situation in Greece. The Mediterranean was increasingly sucking in forces that really, he needed elsewhere. However, German forces were already in Romania and therefore in a position to assist the Italians who were increasingly looking like they were over promising and under delivering. Despite once declaring Germany would not spend one pfennig on North Africa and the Mediterranean theatre, it increasingly looked like Hitler would have to dip into his pockets. For Winston Churchill, the intervention of Germany into Greece would be a red line that could not be crossed.

By December, O'Connor was ready and on the morning of the 9th the assault on the Italian camps got underway. Operation Compass, planned to be a 5-day raid to drive them out of Sidi Barani, would end a staggering 10 weeks later in a rout that no one could have foreseen. The initial attack on Sidi Barani quickly drove the Italians back over the 60 miles they had taken in September to Bardia, where they re-grouped and attempted to hold their position.

The British attacks on Bardia began on the 2 and 3 January 1941 with massed artillery and tank barrages. In the morning of the 3rd, the Royal Navy fired a barrage from the sea until 11:00 and then the infantry went in. By the 5th, Bardia was taken. O'Connor's forces had by now destroyed 8 Italian Divisions and captured 70,000 prisoners.

Speed was the key, and to keep the Italians with their backs to the wall. But it was O'Connors supply lines that were growing worryingly long, with Mera Matruh now at least 200 miles away. They had improvised along the way with captured food, fuel and by cannibalising broken down equipment to keep moving, but that was not infinite. Re-supply would have to come from somewhere, that somewhere would be the port of Tobruk which would feature time and again over the coming Western Desert Campaigns. Despite its forthcoming fame during the next two years of the Western Desert Campaign as a place, Tobruk was pretty nondescript, as Correlli Barnett writes in his book, 'Desert Generals'.

> There was a small harbour, a scattering of white buildings rather like a transit camp on the flat, naked, sloping ground of the coastal plain. A hotel, a restaurant and a few shops made it an urban centre. It was treeless except for some battered palms in the main square. The narrow ribbon of the Via Balbia suspended it from the hazy horizons of east and west. Round Tobruk, over the barren hinterland, ran thirty-eight miles of perimeter defences similar to those of Bardia: an anti-tank ditch – which was incomplete – dense barbed wire, a double row of concrete bunkers each with its own ditch and wire, minefields. Tobruk seemed an easier proposition than Bardia: troops were fewer, the perimeter longer and the defences sparser.[117]

The attack was to be a repeat of that on Bardia. Artillery, infantry and tanks were all in position for the assault, Correlli Barnett describes it so: 'At five-forty on 2 January 1941, the assault on Tobruk was opened with O'Connor's customary bombardment by concentrated artillery, and the Australian infantry charged in to the accompaniment of red Very lights, the explosion of Bangalore torpedoes and an Australian voice bellowing: 'Go on, you bastards!''[118]

By now, Hitler had begun preparations for his foray into Greece, and Winston Churchill knew it. Pressure continued to grow from him to support Greece by re-assigning the troops under O'Connor, despite their successes so far. Indeed, he continued to press for intervention in Greece despite advice to the contrary. When he asked Wavell for his opinion, Wavell replied that if the Germans did invade, then whatever forces were sent would not alter the outcome. He would be proved correct. Hitler, meanwhile, was becoming more

---

[117] (Barnett, 1983)
[118] (Barnett, 1983)

exasperated by the Italian retreats from O'Connor's men and on the 11 January prepared the way to send German Troops to Libya.

O'Connor was running out of time on the political front even though Benghazi was now a firm possibility, and then perhaps Tripoli. The Italians appeared to be getting away and a decisive action was required to contain them before they could get beyond reach. This came at the battle of Beda Fomm, where O'Connor's forces finally annihilated the Italian Army on the 6 and 7 February 1941. The Italians made several attempts to escape, but 'They were caught in a flat but hummocky plain between Beda Fomm and the sea along fourteen miles of road. Low north-to-south ridges gave cover to the British armour'[119]

By 09:00 on the morning of the 7 February the battle was over, a complete success. When O'Connor heard of the outcome, he conferred with his second in Command; 'We'd better send a message to Archie. What shall we say?' Dorman-Smith suggested that Wavell would appreciate a hunting metaphor: 'Fox killed in the open...'[120]

Benghazi and Tripoli were both easily in reach now, despite the distance covered that was stretching supplies to the limit. But the Italians had been crushed and there were only token forces left to defend both of these objectives. Plans were drawn up for a combined operation that would kick the Italian army well and truly out of Libya. But it was not to be. Operation Compass was over, Greece was now the focus of attention.

Max Hastings writes in his book, 'Finest Years'; 'Churchill's decision to dispatch a British army to Greece in the spring of 1941 remains one of the most controversial of his wartime premiership.'[121] As for Correlli Barnett; 'Thus the Greek episode lengthened the campaign in North Africa by two years – a campaign that sucked in the major ground efforts of the British

---

[119] (Barnett, 1983)
[120] (Barnett, 1983)
[121] (Hastings, 2009)

Commonwealth, and left the Far East almost un-defended against the Japanese.'[122]

On the 12 February, looking every inch the Professional Commander that he was, Lieutenant General Erwin Rommel & the Afrika Corps arrived in Libya. Wavell and his staff believed that it would take Rommel some time to prepare for an advance, and in normal circumstances this would be true. But Rommel was no ordinary commander. The German's began an assault almost immediately and by the 13 April the Allied Forces had been pushed all the way back to the Egyptian border, whilst Tobruk was surrounded and under siege. So began two further years, where British and Axis forces chased each other up and down the North African coast until Bernard Montgomery's 8th Army began to roll back the Afrika Corps, beginning at the Battle of El Alamein and ending in the German Surrender in Tunis in May 1943.

Operation Compass had '…advanced over five hundred miles, destroyed an Italian army of ten divisions, taken a hundred and thirty thousand prisoners, four hundred tanks, one thousand two hundred and ninety guns, and two major fortresses, all for the cost of four hundred and seventy six killed, one thousand two hundred and twenty five wounded and forty three missing.'[123] But in the end, it was for nothing and O'Connor's name and his famous victory, the first major Allied Land success of the war, has all but been forgotten.

Rommel, perhaps, provides the bitterest pill. He stated, 'On the 8 February leading troops of the British army occupied El Aheila…Graziani's army had virtually ceased to exist. All that remained of it were a few lorry columns and hordes of unarmed soldiers in full flight to the west. If Wavell (sic) had now continued his advance into Tripolitania no resistance worthy of the name could be mounted against him.'[124]

---

[122] (Barnett, 1983)
[123] (Barnett, 1983)
[124] (Barnett, 1983)

Greece would fall, Crete would follow, HMS *Nubian* and her crew would play their part.

Of Insects - 11 September 1940

The regular, almost soothing pings that came from *Nubians* ASDIC were having a soporific effect on those on the bridge as another anti-submarine sweep was begun off the North African coast in Sollum Bay. A little distance away, closer inshore were the three odd looking ships that *Nubian*, *Jervis* and *Janus* were tasked with providing close submarine protection.

All three ships appeared to be sat very low in the water, to the untrained eye they almost looked like they have been sunk and were resting on the seabed. The two smaller vessels were Insect Class Gunboats, the *Ladybird* and *Aphis*. They were of just 625tons and a shade under 240ft long with two 6-inch guns placed fore and aft. They had been launched during 1915/16 for use in rivers like the Danube and later in the Yangtze or as close inshore gun batteries, their draughts allowing them to operate in shallow waters.

Rear Admiral Pugsley spent some of his early Naval career on Gunboats operating in China and for a short while on *Cockchafer*, seeing some action against Chinese Warlords. As an example of the perils of Gunboat diplomacy, Pugsley had been invited to dinner with Yang Sen, one of the warlords in Wanhsien (which incidentally is on the Yangtze River, some 1000 miles from the sea) during a particularly troubling period. He was concerned because Yang Sen had recently ousted one of his opposition having invited him to a similar banquet which he describes as follows; 'The invitation was accepted though the guest prudently arrived with a bodyguard of twenty-five soldiers, armed to the teeth, who stood guard round the banqueting hall while the two ruffians jovially feasted together. As the festivities drew to a close, at a signal from Yang Sen a number of his own men who had been concealed behind the hangings revealed themselves and covered the bodyguard with their weapons, while Yang Sen coolly drew his revolver and shot his guest neatly between the eyes.'[125]

The third ship in the trio that day was the much larger Erebus Class, Monitor, *Terror*.[126] Both she and her sister ship *Erebus* being named after the Bomb Ships used in the Franklin expedition of 1845 that never returned from their hunt for the North West Passage. This particular *Terror* was much larger than her pair of insects, being just under 8500 tons and 405 feet in length. She packed a huge punch with a pair of 15-in. guns mounted in a single turret. Extensively used for Naval Gunfire Support (NGS) during World War 1, she was now employed in similar activity that day, bombarding the Italian's who were attempting to form their bases along the coastal road that would take them deeper into Egypt.

In the morning the shelling began, the great guns of *Terror* booming out over the water, her shells falling amongst the Italians who were camped down the road. Great clouds of dust and smoke began to billow upwards into the warming air, and then the smaller but equally affective 6-inch guns of *Ladybird* and *Aphis* joined in.

Later in the afternoon, *Nubian* and her fellow destroyers moved close in and their 4.7-in. guns were trained inshore. They formed line astern, parallel to the coast. On all three bridges, binoculars were trained on the road, targets identified, their range and positions plotted and fed to the guns. The green firing lights came on in the Transmitting station and the Gunner placed his finger over the firing buttons. At that moment there came a signal from *Jervis*. 'Jervis signaling sir, Open Fire at will, plaster the bastards. Have fun!' Ravenhill ordered, 'Open Fire' to the TS, the Gunner pushed the firing button, the firing gongs chimed and the order 'Commence, Commence' was given. The three destroyers' guns boomed out joining in the shelling of the coast road.

---

[125] (Pugsley)
[126] (Connell, 1987)

Binoculars trained once more, a few moments past and then the shells began to fall. Lorries could be seen careering off the road to take cover, their canvas awnings flapping as the vehicles bounced off the road. One disappeared in a cloud of smoke, which as it blew gently away revealed the lorry, still moving but on fire. They could see men leaping from lorries, running in all directions, whilst others lay inert on the ground.

Much damage was being done to the encampments and stores that had been placed in readiness for the advance into Egypt. As darkness grew, the position of the ships was illuminated by the bright flashes of their gunfire, *Terrors* huge 15-in. shells continued to whistle over the bay until almost midnight when they finally fell silent, because she had exhausted her supply of 220 high explosive rounds. Likewise, *Ladybird* and *Aphis* had no more ammunition to fire.

HMS *Kent* - 14 September 1940.

Herbert sat sipping a cup of tea in what was a moment of quiet aboard *Nubian* as she rocked almost imperceptibly in the waters of Alexandria harbour. Mail had arrived, and he was reading a note from Doreen. The news from home appeared bleak. Above the skies of Hampshire there were battles raging almost every day. Portsmouth had been bombed, aircraft could be seen high overhead, occasionally gunfire could be heard to. Herbert ruefully smiled as Doreen described how she and her best friend Mini Spriggs had got a job at the laundry on Hayling Island. However, they often fretted when cycling over the bridge to the island as on several occasions German bombers had flown low and fast overhead and once or twice had dropped bombs that had exploded with great bursts of water not far from them. One time, Mini had almost reached home when a German fighter roared at rooftop level up the street where she lived. Sure in her heart that she was its intended target she leaped off her bike, ran up the garden path and jumped into a rose bush to hide. The family were fine but concerned that the rumours of an invasion were true and that it could happen at any time.

The moment was broken by the tannoy that barked preparation for sailing within 24 hours and all leave once again cancelled. They were going back to war, to support an air attack on Benghazi. The Italians were across the border of Egypt and the Admiral wanted to use *Illustrious* to give them a shakeup. Herbert finished his tea, put the letter in his ditty box, giving his horseshoe a little rub for luck, and went back to work.

On, Sunday 15 September, *Nubian* sailed with *Orion, Mohawk, Hasty* and *Hero* as the screening force for *Illustrious*. The crews, busy and intent at their work had no idea that back in England it would be a momentous day for the Royal Air Force and Britain as a whole.

> The tremendous air battles fought between Fighter Command and the Luftwaffe on this memorable Sunday represented the climax of the entire Battle of Britain…amounted to a crushing defeat of Goring's bomber forces. Thus the day can only be regarded as that on which the Battle of Britain was won and lost: for whatever qualifications may be added to the *degree* of damage done to Germany's principle long-range weapon, the *nature* of the defeat was uncompromising. It is logical therefore, that in Britain this date has been celebrated ever since as Battle of Britain day.[127]

Whilst there were clearly fears amongst many that an invasion was imminent, Cunningham for one, did not think it would happen as he wrote, 'Personally I was very sceptical about an invasion being attempted. With the home fleet in being, besides all the local flotillas, I could not see how the Germans could expect to obtain command of the sea for long enough to pass over the channel the enormous number of slow and defenceless craft that would be required to make a landing on any scale likely to be successful. Even if the enemy had command of the air, which they showed no signs of

---

[127] (Mason, 1990)

obtaining, our ships could still operate. We should have losses; but once among the invasion flotillas our ships would be comparatively safe.'[128]

By Monday the ships were off Benghazi when just before midnight the Swordfish of 815 and 819 Squadrons took off from the deck of *Illustrious*. 815's aircraft carried torpedoes and bombs whilst 819 were equipped for mining the harbour entrance. Two merchant ships were subsequently sunk in the mission that lasted 4 hours, whilst in the morning the Italian Destroyers *Turbine* and *Aquilone* departed, *Aquilone* made contact with one of 819's mines and sank.

Signals then arrived for *Mohawk* and *Nubian* to escort the 8-in. cruiser *Kent* to shell Sollum and the surrounding area once more. *Kent* was a County Class Heavy Cruiser and was built under the Washington Treaty restrictions displacing just under 10,000 tons. She arrived in the vicinity of Sollum on a clear moonlit night, the sea calm and glassy.

At El Adem airfield in the eastern coastal region of Libya called Cirenaica, 25-year-old Carlo Emanuele Buscaglia clambered aboard and fired up the engines of his SM.79. He had joined the 278 Squadriglia Sil which had been formed as a specialist anti shipping force. To one side of the fuselage a pair of stirrups held in place a single 876kg 'Whitehead' torpedo that was 5.46 meters in length and 450mm wide.

Taking off with another aircraft they headed at low level out across the water towards the position where they expected to find the enemy ships they had been instructed to attack. It took much concentration to fly low level over the water at any time, but the moon shone bright and made the task a little simpler by providing a horizon to fly straight and level for the duration of the relatively short flight. Soon the sight of tracer could be seen filling the sky from three ships that appeared to be racing towards them, an effect of their closing speed. Buscaglia made a small coarse correction to bring the nose of his 'Gobbo' onto the line of the largest ship and in few moments more the

---

[128] (Cunningham, 1951)

Whitehead was released causing his aircraft to suddenly jump up a few feet as the weight of the weapon was lifted.

On *Nubians*' bridge, at around 23:00, the sound of the approaching bombers was masked by their own gunfire, it was the huge splashes of the torpedoes hitting the water that got their attention. They could see the tracks of the torpedoes drawing a white line that terminated on *Kent*. One of the lines missed, the second didn't, and hit close to *Kent's* stern. In the distance, Buscaglia's aircraft could be seen banking around to the left and climbing away, before being obscured by a column of water, a flash from an explosion and black smoke. The sound and concussion hit them next, one of the lookouts was knocked to the ground. *Kent* seemed to buck like she had been kicked in the backside and then settled back into the water waves fanning out from her side as if trying to run away.

George Blundell was engineering officer on board *Kent*, he quickly realised that the electrical system had been damaged and requested permission to leave the bridge and investigate. As the steering motors were electrically operated, he had to ensure power was online for the ship to steer. By now the engines had been shut down and *Kent's* forward motion had ceased. Below decks it was dark and ominous, Blundell switched on his torch and made his way aft.

Despite intense heat and almost passing out from smoke inhalation, Blundell managed to reach the engine room and some order was restored. He then went to the Quarterdeck which was being machine gunned from the air. Despite being under attack he organised emergency steering cables installed and fed down to the steering room that was filling with water. After 3 hours hard work, the rudder, which had been jammed, was released and the ship was capable of maneuvering.

Nubian meanwhile received a signal from *Kent;* 'Incapable of steering, no power available, prepare to take in tow, please'. *Kent's* crew had already lowered a boat for the transfer of the hawser from her to *Nubian*. In normal circumstances the ship that is to be towed makes well-rehearsed and methodical preparations to pass the hawser to the ship that will be its appointed 'tug'. However, in hostile waters, and literally a sitting duck for any submarine that happened to appear speed and improvisation was called for.

At 01:30 a heaving line was thrown to *Nubian* from a boat manoeuvering parallel with *Kent* and the steel hawser pulled aboard and secured. The hawser was the heaviest they had on board, and the longest too. As the Manual of Seamanship states: 'A decided dip or catenary gives the same advantage in towing as a vessel derives when riding with a long scope of cable at single anchor, that is to say, the sagging bight acts as an elastic spring, preventing variations in the tension being not only on its length but on its weight; this sag does not in the least reduce the tension of steady towing, but it provides an elastic link between the two ships by which the forces arising in a sea-way are gradually absorbed, instead of acting with suddenness and jerks.'[129]

It took a further 4 hours before the situation was fully under control aboard *Kent* the fires were however, still burning, but contained in such a way that some normality was restored and breakfast was served at 05:30. Power was restored as well as the steering and *Nubian* was able to cast off the towing hawser as *Kent* got underway once more to limp back to Alexandria. *Nubian* remained at a respectful distance as the *Kent's* buried their dead at sea. George Blundell found himself the organiser of the burial proceedings, he wrote, 'I wept. So many of our shipmates'. Having been sewn into their hammocks and weighted, the bodies were slipped over the side of the ship, but the weights proved inadequate'. Blundell continues, 'About 12 of the bodies buried at sea yesterday washed up ashore during the night.'[130] The dead included Stokers from the engine room, Commander Cecil Hall, Paymaster Geoffrey Yelland, the ships blacksmith, Frederick Pringle and, to add to the sadness, Leading Steward Joseph Attard and his son, Anthony (Steward).

Admiral Cunningham praised the efforts of the Gunboats during the bombardment of the coast during the Italian offensives, and of the operations overall he wrote, 'Our bombardments from the sea certainly had some effect,

---

[129] (Navy, 1932)
[130] (Prysor, 2012)

for by 26 September we were able to report that all enemy concentrations had moved inland, and there was practically nothing left to be engaged.'[131]

RV Petrel

In March 2017 the RV *Petrel* was in the Mediterranean Sea, somewhere off Malta. A research ship dedicated to locating World War 2 wrecks, she was making a sweep of the seabed when her underwater radar returned a large object lying on the bottom at a depth of about 12,000 feet. Her remote-controlled submarine dived to examine the contact, and out of the darkness of those impenetrable depths, came into view the white paintwork of a ship. Her guns were pointing upwards, her empty torpedo tubes still in the position she had fired her last salvo. Traversing the very well-preserved wreck the cameras were able to make out the large red letters AR on her side. She was the Italian destroyer *Artigliere*, sunk 12 October 1940.

The Battle of Cape Passero

The fortification, protection and supply of Malta was well underway towards the end of September and the beginning of October 1940. Cunningham wrote to the Admiralty that by April they would need to have shipped some 400,000 tons of supplies to the island, equating to about 2 convoys per month, each would require fleet protection, but would perhaps draw out the reluctant Regia Marina. These convoys began in September by which time, in the usual sporting metaphors adopted by the military, the fleet had formed into two groups, the 'first eleven' being *Warspite, Valiant* and *Illustrious*, the 'second eleven' made up of *Malaya, Ramillies* and *Eagle*. In addition, the fleet would be bolstered by the arrival of an old friend, in the

---

[131] (Cunningham, 1951)

form of the battleship *Barham* and for the destroyers, the depot ship *Woolwich* was being assigned to Alexandria.

The 14th Destroyer Flotilla made up the screening and fleet protection forces for these convoys, that included the cruisers *Liverpool* and *Gloucester* which transported some 2000 troops to Malta at the end of September. On 11 October, having successfully arrived at Malta with one such convoy *Nubian,* along with the fleet was waiting about 100 miles southeast of Malta for the empty ships to come out of harbour to join up for the return cruise to Alexandria. The air was heavy and hot, in the distance there came the rumble of thunder and high above there came the drone of an aircraft. This was duly reported but there was no sighting that could confirm whether it was friend or foe. The aircraft in question was civilian, but Italian and the crew had spotted the fleet below. They immediately passed on the position of the warships to the Italian Admiralty.

At Supermarina headquarters there was some debate as to the authenticity of the report. This was a civilian source and could not be corroborated by the military. However, they decided to act upon the intelligence and determined to send out the 11th Destroyer Flotilla, consisting of four Soldati Class Destroyers, *Aviere, Geniere, Camicia Nera* and the Flotilla leader, *Artigliere* commanded by Captain Carlo Margottini. These ships were fast (capable of 35 knots) and quite potent, having two 4.7-in. guns mounted fore and aft, as well as two sets of triple torpedo tubes. The 1st Torpedo Boat Flotilla was assigned as support, consisting of the *Airone, Alcione* and *Ariel.* Not, as one may imagine small ships, they were of the Spica Class Torpedo boat and looked more like a small Destroyer at some 273ft long, 800 tons and capable of 34 knots. The two flotillas were ordered to strike out to the east of Malta in a hope that they would encounter the British fleet and, with an element of surprise on their side, engage the enemy successfully.

HMS *Ajax*, commanded by Captain E. D. B. McCarthy had undergone a refit at Chatham in July which included the fitting of a new Type 279 Aircraft Radar as well as four upgraded quick firing 4-in. guns to compliment her main armament of eight 6-in. guns mounted in four pairs. At just after 01:00 on the 12 October she was the northern most ship of the 7th Cruiser Squadron (*Orion* and *Sydney*) which were providing a ranging picket for the main fleet. The bridge was relatively quiet, cocoa was being handed around, the air was warm and above the sky was beginning to clear. Thunderstorms had ranged about during the day, but the sea state had remained relatively calm. In the dark distance there was a grumbling of thunder still and occasional flashes brightened the sky momentarily. Scudding clouds became discernible as the brightness of the moon began to penetrate through a thinning cloud base before it broke through. Not a full moon, but very bright indeed, gradually dropping towards the horizon, casting a silvery path leading to where it would finally disappear for the night. Having got to the southern point of her zig-zag course across the sea, *Ajax* turned north once more, the crew subconsciously leaning and bracing themselves from spilling their drinks as she commenced the maneuver.

Ahead and unseen, at about 01:35, the watchful eyes on the *Alcione* spotted *Ajax* heading towards them at a distance of some 11 miles. She signalled *Ariel* and *Airone* to follow, both ships picking up their target shortly thereafter. They closed at speed, there was no sign yet that they had been detected as *Ajax* continued on her course. *Alcione* was at a mile distant when she fired a half salvo (two torpedoes) towards her target, quickly changing course to position for a second attack. But both torpedoes ran wide and apparently, she remained undetected by the approaching cruiser. Meanwhile, *Airone* and *Ariel* positioned themselves to attack from either side of *Ajax* their combined approaching speeds eating up the distance in no time.

At 01:55 there came a shout from the watch. 'Two contacts bearing Green zero four zero and red three one zero, range two thousand!'. The Officer on watch called for the captain who was resting in his day cabin, he came quickly. 'Signal: What Ship?,' he barked. Meanwhile *Ajax's* guns began to revolve, bearing upon the two contacts. Unbeknown to all those on the bridge, both contacts had fired half salvos at the moment they had been spotted, but both missed. The reply to the 'What Ship' query came back. 'Contacts replying sir.

I'm afraid their signals do not make sense', came the puzzled voice of the signalman. McCarthy snapped, 'Increase to full ahead, hard a port'.

By now *Airone* was incredibly close and launched yet another half salvo of torpedoes at 750 yards, point blank range, but, yet again they missed! She then opened fire with four rapid salvos from her 4.7-in. guns that peppered *Ajax's* bridge and holed her close to the waterline. A fire was started in one of her storerooms. Any doubt that these were two hostiles vanished in an instant along with the command 'Fire as they bear!' *Ajax's* forward 6-in. guns crashed out, her shells taking but fractions of a second to punch into *Airone*, stopping her dead in the water where she burned furiously.

Ajax's turrets now turned their attention to *Ariel* and as soon as they came to bear the fire gong chimed once more. The resulting explosion, which was most likely the result of a hit on *Ariels* magazine occurred seconds after the report from *Ajax's* gunfire. Within minutes, *Ariel* had disappeared below the surface, leaving nothing but a few bobbing heads of survivors, oil, small flickers of flame and floating debris. When, about twenty minutes later, *Alcione* came back for what she hoped would be her second attack, *Ajax* had gone. *Ariel* was too, and *Airone* which was burning fiercely had settled low in the water. *Alcione* positioned herself to pick up survivors, oil covered, cold and in shock, *Airone* finally slipped beneath the waves to join *Ariel* at 02:35.

Aboard *Ajax* damage control was taking stock of their situation, the fire was being brought under control, they remained on a high state of readiness. It is argued that *Ajax's* radar did not contribute to the previous action (being fired at such close range) or perhaps the ensuing action, especially as it was essentially for the detection of aircraft. However, it seems probable that the ships radar did have a part to play in warning of the approach of the 11th Destroyer Flotilla which was steaming at full pelt to assist the Torpedo boats.

Whilst *Aviere* was the first to spot *Ajax* it was already too late as she was on the receiving end of a 6-in. shell which caused damage to her bow and she had to break off. Behind came *Artigliere*, her commander zig zagging his ship in an effort to avoid *Ajax's* guns which proved successful, managing to loose off several salvo's that struck *Ajax*. It was however a forlorn hope. Despite the fact that the moon had now dropped below the horizon, the resulting darkness was so brightly illuminated by the flashes from *Ajax's* guns that her crews were momentarily blinded (she had no flashless shells on board), a salvo of 6-in. shells found its mark. The blow was grievous to *Artigliere* and her commander, Captain Margottini. She was stopped dead in the water, all activity now concentrating on saving the ship, not fighting it.

The remaining destroyers continued to fire upon *Ajax* but with little effect. *Camicia Nera* began to lay down a smoke screen. At this point McCarthy decided to take advantage of the cover retiring his ship and making towards the protection of his own fleet and to take stock of their own casualties, 13 killed and 22 wounded. In what was just over 30 minutes of action, *Ajax* had damaged one ship, sunk two and seriously damaged a third. She had fired some 490 shells and 4 torpedoes in the action.

Very early next morning, a Sunderland of 230 Squadron (L5803)[132] was on patrol, being flown by Wing Commander Geoffrey Francis. The sun was beginning to brighten the morning sky when, shortly after passing over the fleet, he and his crew spotted two destroyers. These were the *Artigliere* under tow from the *Camicia Nera*. He attempted a closer look but came under fire from both. With the fleet close by, he turned back and signalled the ships position in morse code by Aldis Lamp. Both *Warspite* and *Illustrious* responded but indicated that he should remain close by. He later wrote; 'We flew at about 4000 feet and about eight Swordfish formed on us and with one third flap out we led them towards the destroyers.'[133] (the Sunderland, despite being a much larger aircraft, had a cruising speed of 178 mph, the Swordfish 143 mph, so the deployment of flap would allow the aircraft to fly slow enough for the older biplane). Admiral Cunningham described the scene as follows, although his numbers of Swordfish differ from the Wing Commanders: '…it

---

[132] (Hendrie, 1994)
[133] (Hendrie, 1994)

was a quaint sight to see the big Sunderland moving off with her three little chickens under her wing.'

Unfortunately, the 3, or 8, depending on the source, 'little chickens' did not fare well, they missed both Destroyers, although their intervention may have hastened the departure of the *Camicia Nera* who left *Artigilere* to fend for herself. However, the heavy cruiser *York* was detached to engage the Italians. *Nubian* and *Vampire* both received signals to break off from the fleet to join *York*, providing added support and protection.

When the ships finally found *Aritgliere* she was dead in the water. Some of her crew had begun to take to her boats, many were on deck waving white flags made of towels, clothing or anything they could do to ensure 'friendly' attention. Captain Portal of *York* instructed the crew of *Artigliere* to abandon ship within the next 30 minutes, at the same time carley rafts were dropped in the water to assist. *Nubian* and *Vampire* bustled carefully around the survivors and between all three ships they began to take on as many men as they could. But they could not and would not stop engines for fear of air attack or a lurking submarine. The survivors either bobbed in the water in their life jackets or were huddled on rafts or pieces of wreckage. The water stank of fuel oil that floated thick on the surface in large patches, some men were covered in it, their hair slick and black on their scalps. Of these who managed to climb on board there came a helping hand to be led away to be washed and cleaned up. Wherever they trod or laid their hands to steady themselves, there remained a slimy black imprint that would have to be cleaned away when time permitted.

Some men were injured, most in shock and these were attended to in the sick bay by *Nubians* Surgeon, Lt. Cooke and his Sick berth PO, Frank Harvison. Those lucky enough to get on board *Nubian* unscathed were taken below and given hot drinks and blankets or huddled together on the decks. Once bereft of their fighting ship, these were no more than ordinary men, sailors without a home, all they owned they were stood in. To the men of

Nubian, they were no longer the enemy, just shipmates in need of some help and compassion.

Before long the signal came from *York* to return to the fleet. The scrambling nets were hauled in from *Nubian,* much to the consternation of the crew as they realised that they could do no more for what remained a large number of the Italian men in the water. These men had a sad look of resignation and uncertainty of what their fate may be. Portal, knowing he had done all he could under the circumstance, had *York* fire off a single torpedo that struck the now abandoned ship setting off her munitions in an explosion that produced a tower of smoke hundreds of feet in the air and a brown cloud that puffed out across the sea like flour that has had an egg dropped in it.

As the sound of the explosion died away, the little flotilla of lifeboats gathered together whilst the three grey ships of the Royal Navy gradually receded over the horizon. Meanwhile the wreck of the *Artigliere* sank 12,000 feet with 132 of her crew to await the arrival of *Petrel.* It was not the end for the survivors. Cunningham had been impressed with the tenacity of the ships, so much so that he signalled in an unencrypted transmission to the Italian Admiralty their approximate position. About half of them were picked up the following day. For what was indeed a humane action, Cunningham was duly reprimanded for which he was unrepentant.

Nubian rejoined the main fleet, screening *Illustrious* on the night of the 13 October whilst she flew off a Swordfish raid on the airfield at Leros, before heading back into Alexandria to drop off the Italian survivors from the *Artigliere* and clean the ship up. It once more looked like a tip and smelled almost as bad. The crew were tired, and some tempers were frayed. With the addition of the Italian survivors what little space they had to relax had been taken over by their unexpected guests. Time ashore was looked forward to by some and perhaps a real bed in the Fleet Club. There were rumors that *Nubian* would require a refit soon, the Chief Stoker, David Chun, had been overheard down the voice pipe into the wheelhouse that she was developing a hot bearing and it would not take much more hard work before it would become a major issue. That could mean a good period of rest from operations.

But it was not to be. As they pulled alongside a signal was brought aboard ship. As soon as the survivors were taken off, *Nubian* was to make ready at haste to return to sea and assist in the escorting of the Town Class Cruiser *Liverpool* back to Alexandria. She had been torpedoed and had been taken in tow.

As the 7th Cruiser Squadron came into view, it was clear that *Liverpool* was in a sorry state. There were concerned and surprised looks amongst those who viewed the scene from *Nubians* bridge, one of the men let out an incredulous whistle. She was in tow from the stern by *Orion* and *Calcutta,* like a wounded soldier who is hastily dragged off the battlefield by his feet. At 19:00 the previous day the Squadron had been attacked by torpedo carrying SM.79's of 278 Squadriglia, out of El Adem in Cirenaica. *Liverpool* had taken a hit in the bow, which in itself did not immediately pose a threat, however the highly volatile fuel for her Walrus amphibian aircraft was stored forward in the bow section. This fuel tank was ruptured, and the stench of aviation fuel alerted the damage control teams of imminent danger. The forward 'A' turret was evacuated in the nick of time, before the fuel ignited, which appears to have detonated some of the munitions in the forward magazine. The resulting explosion blew off *Liverpools* bow, which hung down in the water as an injured limb might, being held intact to the rest of its body by muscle and sinew. The trailing wreckage acted as both a sea anchor and an unwanted rudder that hampered her recovery and caused the towing hawser to break. 'A' turret was pointing to starboard, its base structure quite visible like a bone exposed within the gaping wound, whilst its guns were pointed at various angles giving the ship an appearance of utter surprise, akin to someone who has unexpectedly been punched hard on the nose. During the tow back to Alexandria, *Liverpool's* bow finally parted company and sank to the bottom of the Mediterranean, not long afterwards the bodies of the 12 dead recovered from her wreckage made the same journey.

The battle-fleet brought the wounded ship back to safety in the small hours of the following morning, a brightly moonlit night that was perfect for the massive air raid that passed overhead Alexandria at 01:00, just as the fleet arrived. With a fear that amongst the raiders torpedo bombers may be lurking, Admiral Cunningham had the battle-fleet race as fast as possible to safety. He described the moment in his memoir; 'We made for the shallow water of the Great Pass – the entrance to Alexandria harbour – at high speed, firing a blind barrage on both sides with our guns flashing and the sparking of bursting shell over the horizon.'[134]

Later, once moored and secured the *Nubians* finally got some rest, but there was indeed work to be done to clear and clean the ship. This was made all the more expedient when a signal came to prepare for a distinguished guest. Commander Ravenhill addressed the crew over the tannoy, trying his best to remain upbeat not only in the knowledge that he was the bearer of unwelcome news, but by the fact that for the next few days he would have to make his quarters available to his guest and reside in his cramped sea cabin. 'Gentlemen, we have all been working most hard over the previous days with little rest, which I know we are all in desperate need of. Indeed, our ship is in need of some rest also as the Chief tells me she has a hot bearing that will require attention. However, before that we have one last task to perform, after which we can expect about a week for the repairs to be made and some time away from operations. We will expect Admiral Ulgin and his staff of the Turkish Navy aboard this evening, once he has dined with Admiral Cunningham. They will be located in my quarters for the passage to Mersin where we will drop them off. Therefore, we will clean ship today in preparation for their visit and look forward to a hasty return, hopefully on the 19th.'

This was indeed a most unwelcome addition to their workload. Cunningham had been compelled to entertain Admiral Ulgin, who, as Cunningham later explained in his memoir, made no secret of the fact that they had been detailed to observe and document the strength of the British

---

[134] (Cunningham, 1951)

Fleet in Alexandria. It was necessary to keep Turkey 'on-side' and so every courtesy was given to the Admiral and his staff whilst making sure that he and his entourage were removed from Alexandria as quickly and tactfully as possible aboard *Nubian*.

With their V.I.P. excursion complete there was once more the prospect of some rest from operations, and perhaps a chance to tie up alongside *Illustrious* which would allow the cooks to go aboard the carrier to make use of her kitchens and bakery in order to bring back fresh bread and whatever else they could scrounge. In return, *Nubian's* hull would provide some protection for the larger vessel should a torpedo attack manifest itself. Whilst some aboard *Nubian* would muse on the merits and vulnerabilities of being moored alongside a large warship in the confines of harbour there were others in high places who had indeed been contemplating this very seriously. Indeed, a plan to attack the Italian fleet at their main port of Taranto was first conceived and drawn up in 1935 following Italy's invasion of Abyssinia. Hostilities with Italy did not transpire, and the plan was shelved, however those plans remained among the secret papers locked away aboard HMS *Glorious* until Captain Lumley Lyster took command and found them in 1938. He was in turn asked by Sir Dudley Pound, to draw up an attack on the Italian fleet and therefore, Lyster had this original 1935 plan brought up to date. He initiated night deck operations with Swordfish to prove out the concept. At first, Pound objected, believing the Swordfish to be too obsolete and vulnerable for such an undertaking, envisaging heavy casualties. However, there was no alternative, and on arrival in the Mediterranean as Head of the Carrier Force, Lyster presented his plan to Cunningham. An attack on the Regia Marina was now a real possibility, and it was given a name, 'Judgement'.

Chapter 9

Operation Judgement

The original plan utilised both *Eagle* and *Illustrious,* with operations scheduled for the night of the 21 October, Trafalgar day. Events conspired against this date in two separate incidents. Aboard *Illustrious* there was maintenance and refuelling work being carried out below deck in the main hanger. In a closed environment with little ventilation, the fumes from evaporating aviation fuel filled the workspace. Whether it was indeed a screwdriver that fell from a fitters hand and touched a battery that caused the spark, or some other misfortune, is not fully understood. What is known though, is the resulting ignition of the vapour burnt out two Swordfish before the fire could be brought under control, quite quickly under the circumstances. The hangers water sprays indeed quenched the flames, but they also covered several of the remaining aircraft in salty sea water. They would have to be thoroughly stripped, cleaned, oiled and reassembled before operations could begin again.

Eagle, meanwhile, was having problems of her own. She was by now, a rather ageing ship. Her boilers had become unreliable, and the attention paid to her by the Regia Aeronautica had played havoc with her fuel systems, which became contaminated with water due to the incidental bomb damage sustained by near misses alone. 5 of her Swordfish were transferred to *Illustrious, Eagle* was stood down for the operation.

Despite the setbacks, morale was high. We have already seen that despite the Swordfish being obsolete, slow and somewhat vulnerable, the crews had great confidence in the aircraft's ability. There began a series of night flying exercises and in parallel some modifications made to the aircraft. A 60-gallon internal fuel tank was fitted to allow the aircraft to negotiate the 170 mile trip to and from Taranto from the jump off point, which meant that the crew would be reduced to the Pilot and Navigator/Observer.

432 Flight

Intelligence was now required in order for the mission to have maximum effect, all of the Regia Marina's Battleships would ideally need to be within Taranto harbour, individually identified and their positions marked so that they could be effectively targeted by the Swordfish pilots. Taranto is a large harbour with two distinct basins located on the southern 'instep' of Italy's 'boot'. The outer basin is called the Mar Grande, which is encircled by two large breakwaters that protected it from a seaborne assault whilst the smaller Mar Piccolo is land locked, apart from a short, relatively narrow channel for access. This meant that the larger warships (the battleships and some of the larger cruisers) would be located in the Mar Grande, and the smaller vessels in the Mar Piccolo.

In order to gather photographic intelligence, the Navy would require reconnaissance missions on a regular basis over the harbour. That would mean cooperation with the RAF out of Malta. The problem was, what aircraft would be suitable for such missions? The Sunderlands were far too slow and conspicuous. They would be easy prey for Anti-Aircraft fire or any marauding fighters that may be alerted to their presence. The answer was the Glen Martin Maryland and a group of pilots and crew who were up for low level, dangerous missions, one of whom would become one of the most successful reconnaissance pilots of the war.

The Maryland was a twin, radial engine medium bomber, designed and manufactured in America by Glen Martin. These aircraft had not been ordered by the RAF, but by the French Air Force. After the fall of France, the outstanding order was honoured by the RAF and a number were assigned to 22 Squadron. The Maryland was relatively fast with a maximum speed of just over 300 mph, somewhat slower than most of the modern fighters adding a level of vulnerability to operations. It had a crew of three. The pilot situated in a single seat cockpit behind a large all glass nose where the navigator was located. Behind the pilot sat a wireless operator to man the radios and to act as gunner to fire the guns from a dorsal mounted turret.

Australian 'Tich' Whitley was one of the senior flight commanders in 22 Squadron and he was given the task of forming 431 Flight which would consist of 3 Maryland's for operations out of Luqa air base on Malta. This was in some respects an odd choice of aircraft for such a task as the RAF pilots and engineers had no previous exposure to a type that had unexpectedly come into service. Indeed, there were very few, if any spares either, which could prove most inconvenient once operations were begun.

The initial problem 431 Flight had to overcome was actually getting the aircraft to Luqa from Thorney Island located on the South Coast of England, a distance of about 1300 miles. Whitley tasked Pilot Officers Paddy Devine and Adrian Warburton to plan the route. Whilst Warburton was indeed qualified as a pilot, his role within 431 Flight was that of a Navigator. Nevertheless, he and Devine got to work and plotted the route to Luqa, flying out over occupied France, then onto Sardinia, avoiding Sicily to arrive at Malta. They used as many of the navigational aids that were available to them at the time and so thorough was their work that this became the standard route out to Malta from then on.

Warburton, or 'Warby' to all who knew him, was 22 years old, blonde, blue eyed and of rather dashing good looks. Born in Middlesbrough in 1918, Warburton attended St Edwards School in Oxford at the same time as Guy Gibson (Commander of 617 Squadron, The Dambusters) and was proceeded by Douglas Bader (the legless Battle of Britain fighter ace). He joined the RAF in 1938 with a short service commission and was soon undergoing training. However, he was classified as a 'Below Average' pilot, which was the bare minimum pass rate. Warburton was selected as one of the crews for Malta, not because of his abilities as a Navigator, or because of his lack of ability as a pilot, but because he had married in secret to a girl (Beth) who was five years older than him, and he was quite broke with debts he could not possibly repay.

The flight arrived at Luqa early in September 1940. Tich Whitley did not delay in training the crews in aerial and photographic reconnaissance. Warburton was assigned Photographic Officer and he was given the task of training all the crews in ship recognition. As the training turned into operational sorties, the Italian ports of Taranto, Brindisi, Palermo, Messina and Benghazi were reconnoitered, as were Napes and Spezia.

Warburtons transition to Pilot came when two of the crews became ill with 'Malta Dog', a most unpleasant and debilitating stomach disorder. Whitley needed operational pilots, and so Warburton was given a chance to prove himself, despite having only some 35 minutes previous experience in twin engine aircraft! Indeed, according to Tony Spooner's autobiography 'Warburton's War', Warby had not flown in the previous four months, a long time for any pilot, let alone one whos aptitude was in question. Spooner described his take offs as follows; 'The Maryland is apt to swing sharply during take-off unless treated with respect. Almost as soon as Warby had slammed the throttles wide open the plane began to swing and career all over the airfield. Violent over-correction with the rudder hardly helped. Miraculously the undercarriage withstood these gyrations and the aircraft staggered into the air.'[135]

In respect of the pilot's ability to land the aircraft, Spooner continues; 'The 'arrivals' (to call them landings would be an overstatement) were as hair raising as were the take-offs. On one such 'arrival' the aircraft came back trailing strands of wire from the airfields perimeter fence.'[136] Warburtons lack of skill at this time did not go unnoticed and Whitley was berated for allowing a pilot of clearly limited ability to fly such a complex aircraft. However, Whitley continued with the training and when he questioned the crews, they responded that Warburton was improving and they would be happy to

---

[135] (Spooner, 1987, 1994, 2003)
[136] (Spooner, 1987, 1994, 2003)

continue flying with him, besides he was a gutsy and fearless flyer who showed more skill once in the air than either at the point of leaving the ground or becoming acquainted with it once more.

Warburton and Whitley began to fly regular reconnaissance missions over Taranto at the behest of the Royal Navy, with of course particular interest in the number of Battleships moored in the main harbour. Warburton came under air attack on several occasions, but he and his crew were not found wanting. They were attacked on two occasions by CR42 biplanes, which despite being obsolete by this time were still fast and very capable fighters when up against an aircraft as large as a Maryland. On the 7 November a more formidable opponent in the form of Macchi 202 fighters came into the fray. These sleek and powerful monoplane fighters were much more capable and on paper comparable with the Hawker Hurricane of the RAF. However, Warburton's crew managed to fend them off and shoot one of them down.

Of the flights that Whitley and Warburton made over Taranto it is 'Warby's' final sortie that is the most recounted. The weather on the 10 November was appalling. A deep low-pressure system resulted in very low layered Stratus that dripped misty rain and squalls at intervals. The cloud base was below 1500 feet with visibility just a few miles. Whilst flying in these conditions would be truly hazardous to the crew's health, the Italians would not be expecting any aircraft to be airborne that day.

The aircraft tasked for the mission could not have been more inappropriate. It had suffered minor bomb damage from the enemy raids on Luqa airfield and had been attacked in the air resulting in many holes of varying sizes around the airframe. So many that it had earned the nicknames of 'The Sardine Tin' and 'Whistlers mother'. Indeed, as Warburton increased the throttles to full power launching the Maryland into the inhospitable skies, the whistling and moaning of the air through those holes could be heard by all.

They flew direct to Taranto, flashing in at ultra-low level, Sergeant Johnny Spiers was the Navigator, and he would be required to plot the ships positions on a map to back up their photographs which, at such low level, may not provide the detail they required. The Wireless Operator, Paddy Moren would play his part by trying to read the names of the ships as they flashed past and shout them out to Spiers.

The first pass came a complete surprise to the Italians, and they only opened fire towards the end of the run. Having cleared the target, the crew discussed the intelligence they had gathered, it appeared there were six battleships in the harbour, not the 5 as expected. Warby decided this had to be investigated, they would have to go back and do it again. Not a happy prospect with the Italians now at full alert.

The second run was carried out even lower than the first. The barrage from the shore batteries was intense. Spiers was most likely using some poetic license when he later remembered; 'We were flying so low that the wing tips were cutting furrows in the calm water.'[137] The description certainly gives a vivid impression of the speed and height at which they were flying and if this were the case then they were certainly very lucky not to have cartwheeled into the harbour. Nevertheless, there was clear evidence of their operations height as the Maryland returned to base with one of the warships aerial's trailing from the tailwheel. It transpired that the 6th battleship was in fact one of the heavy, 8-in. Cruisers, quite an understandable mistake in the circumstances.

'Tich' Whitley made the final reconnaissance sortie, and this was the set of photographs that would initiate the operation. Beforehand, Boyd and Lyster needed to see the photographs for themselves which was more difficult than one may expect. Whilst inter service cooperation was becoming more common, there remained some barriers in particular the sharing of intelligence that one sometimes wonders who's side a particular arm of the services was working for! The photographs that 431 flight had taken were indeed the property of the RAF despite having been requested by the Commander-in-Chief of the Royal Navy in the Mediterranean. They were flown from Luqa to the RAF Headquarters in Cairo, where the Navy were

---

[137] (Spooner, 1987, 1994, 2003)

allowed just one person to view the photographs under supervision and the photographs were not to be taken from the building under any circumstances.

Fortunately, the Navy had a shrewd operator in former solicitor and graduate of Cambridge, Lt. David Pollock. He was the Navy Intelligence Officer who was given access to the photographs. He made much of marking the dispositions of the ships on his maps, whilst managing to surreptitiously slip the original photographs into his briefcase before making off with them to *Illustrious* so they could be copied. The photographs were duly returned without the RAF being aware they had been missing.

Using a Stereoscopic lens that transformed the 2D image into 3D, the 5 battleships could be plainly made out within the harbour, along with cruisers and destroyers, but to their great delight the 6th battleship had indeed turned up. White 'blobs' were seen to be lined either side of the battleship lines, which were determined to be barrage balloons. However, as they were assessed to be 300 yards apart it would be quite straightforward for the Swordfish to fly between the cables if they were deployed during the attack (which was almost certain to be the case).

'There was no option but to drain and refill every aircraft on board...' – Preparation for attack

Meanwhile, *Nubian* was on close support duty protecting *Illustrious*, which, whilst the planning for 'Judgement' continued, had to maintain regular reconnaissance and combat air patrols as well as the night flying exercises for the Swordfish Squadrons. On the 10 November, *Illustrious* made signal that she was turning into the wind to make a launch. From *Nubian* the sound of the Swordfish's engine could be made out as full throttle was applied, and the aircraft began to make its take off run along the deck. To those observing, it was always a sense of wonder how the biplane would get airborne at such a slow speed.

Aboard the aircraft the pilot kept one hand on the throttle that was pushed fully open in order to gain a safe speed and height. The deck slipped below them and then there was just sea. He began a steady turn to port, he could see the crew of *Nubian* looking up at him, the dirty smudge of the smoke from her funnel and the creamy white foam of the water as her bows carved through the water. The engine of the Swordfish suddenly spluttered, then caught once more. In the time that the pilot thought through the reasons this may have occurred the engine note died again, caught briefly and then stopped altogether.

There was little time to do anything, they were too low, ditching was the only option. 'Prepare for ditching!' he yelled to the observer in the back. Ditching at the best of times is not for the faint hearted, especially when there is a fixed undercarriage below the aircraft that, if not considered in the landing, will act as a sea anchor and flip the aircraft onto its back in a moment.

From the bridge of *Nubian* it was evident the Swordfish was in trouble; the blaring engine note went to nothing and then the aircraft began a glide descent to the sea. Lieutenant Bush called down to the Commander who was in his day cabin to inform him. Ravenhill ordered the ship to be slowed and the whaler launched to recover the crew. Meanwhile, those keeping a close eye on the aircraft noticed the pilot had dropped the nose a little to maintain the glide and then as he levelled out above the waves the nose rose once more as the pilot pulled back on the stick to flare the aircraft. The Swordfish hardly seemed to be moving at all as the pilot bled off as much speed as possible, he began saying over and over the phrase his instructor said when he was learning to land an aircraft for the first time; 'I don't want to land, I don't want to land' in order to get the flare right. Finally, the Swordfish stalled about ten feet above the sea. Despite his best efforts, there was still some forward momentum and as the wheels hit the water the induced drag stopped it dead, and the nose drove hard into the water. Fortunately, the aircraft did not somersault onto its back, but stood upright, the tail bobbing up and down as the waves created by the impact fanned outwards.

Nubians' whaler was in the water, its crew pulling towards the stricken plane which was by now just a hundred yards or so away. The crew were disembarking, the pilot last to extricate himself, standing on the trailing edge of the wing and almost stepping down into the little orange inflatable raft that had automatically deployed. His co-pilot helped him down so that he barely got his feet wet. As if his last step had been the final push needed, the weight of the engine took over and the remainder of the fuselage and tail gracefully disappeared beneath the sea, Having recovered the crew, *Nubians'* Signaller flashed across to *Illustrious* that the men had been recovered.

The day before a Swordfish had ditched after problems with its engine, and the day after *Nubian* picked up the crew of the second aircraft, a third suffered a similar engine failure that resulted in another ditching. This was a serious issue just hours before such an important and critical mission with the Italian Navy at their mercy. Was this really three individual engine failures, in as many days? Unlikely. As all three aircraft had been from 819 Squadron, attention began to focus on the fuel that had been transferred from *Eagle.*

The team effort to ensure the tanks were de contaminated was described by Leading Air Fitter Ted Whitley:

There was no option but to drain and refill every aircraft on board… The Fuel tank drains were inside a panel over the torpedo rack, so this meant all the 'fish' (i.e. the torpedoes) had to be removed. To ensure that all the fuel and, more importantly, water, was drained, the aircraft had to be put in the flying position. This required the tails to be lifted – with the wings folded – so bombs and flares had to be removed. It was a case of all hands to the pump: whoever was available was called in to lift the tails and move bombs, 'fish', flares jacking equipment etc. The aircrew were there as well, hardly the sort of thing to do with a night operation ahead. Eventually, all the aircraft were finished, drained, filters checked, carbs drained, everything replaced, and the aircraft all refueled through chamois leathers. We made it just in time![138]

In his comprehensive description of 'Judgement' from his book 'Stringbags in Action', Vice Admiral B. B. Schofield describes the investigation; '…it was found to contain water and sand mixed in with the petrol as well as a peculiar fungus type growth festooning the baffles in the tanks. Further inquiry elicited the fact that they had all been refuelled from the same supply point in the hangar and thus pointed to contamination of one of the ship's tanks.'[139]

The attack would go ahead as planned on the 11th, comprising of two waves of Swordfish. Both waves would consist of a section of aircraft armed with bombs and flares, whilst the main force carried torpedoes.

Dropping a torpedo from an aircraft was quite tricky. The Torpedo being cylindrical was connected underneath the Swordfish by a pair of inverted stirrups and retaining wires that had a quick release mechanism for final deployment. To ensure the correct angle of delivery there were two key components. An Air Tail, that acted as a simple elevator to control the pitch up/down of the torpedo in flight (this was made of wood and would break up on hitting the water), and a flywheel and pulley wire mechanism that prevented the torpedo rolling too much to the left or right. If this was not corrected, then the torpedo would shoot off course as it hit the water.

Aiming the torpedo was not (normally) just a case of pointing the aircraft at the intended target ship. Some form of deflection shot would be required to take into account the direction and speed at which the ship was travelling. The Swordfish (and later the Albacore) had a semicircular, bar torpedo sight outside the cockpit and in front of the pilot, with eight light bulbs attached, each representing about 4 degrees deflection. The estimated speed of the ship was input into the sight, and when the correct deflection was achieved one of the bulbs would illuminate and the pilot would release the torpedo. However,

---

[138] (Harrison, 2002)
[139] (Schofield CB, Reprinted 2011)

for Operation Judgement, the target ships were stationary, so aiming should be a simpler process, albeit under hostile enemy fire!

The torpedoes warhead had 450lbs of high explosive in the forward section, one of 6 compartments in total. These additional compartments included an air vessel, for compressed air that ran the gyro's and was mixed with the fuel for the 4-cylinder engine (in its own engine room compartment) which could drive the torpedo at speeds between 27 and 40 knots (which could be set prior to deployment). A Balance Chamber came before the engine compartment, where the depth regulating gear was housed that could be calibrated to ensure the torpedo would run at a set depth. Behind the engine compartment there came the Buoyancy Chamber that housed the gyros which ensured the torpedo would run on a straight course as well as the fuel and lubricating oils. Finally came the tail section with the gearing for the twin contra rotating screws that drove the torpedo forward (a single screw would simply spin the body of the weapon around its longitudinal axis), the stabilising fins and rudder.

For 'Judgement', the torpedoes were equipped with Duplex Firing mechanisms. These ingenious devices would detonate the warhead either on contact with the target vessel, or if it ran underneath the target, the magnetic effect of its hull would detonate the warhead. These devices were developed at HMS 'Vernon' before the outset of war and this would be the first opportunity to use them in anger.

The significance of such an important operation cannot have been missed by all the ships crews and aircrews on that Armistice Day. No doubt each ship held its own small ceremony and moments silence, whilst in London, The King and Queen, Queen Mary, the heads of the Armed Forces and Prime Minister Churchill laid wreaths at the Cenotaph. Next to Westminster Abbey there were two Fields of Remembrance dedicated to the civilians and civil defence personnel who had now given their lives in this war, especially since Herman Goering had commenced the Night Blitz of London and Industrial Targets since the end of October. Indeed, on the night of the 11th there were raids on London which fortunately were hampered by poor weather and thick cloud cover. They were over by 22:00 hours, but notable in the fact that it was the first time Italian Bombers had joined in a raid on Britain and that there were few casualties.

The *Illustrious* aircrews were detailed into two waves, the first would consist of 12 aircraft, 6 of which carried Torpedoes to attack the battleships, with the remaining 6 aircraft armed with Semi Armour Piercing (S.A.P), 500lb bombs. Of these 6, two were primary and back-up flare markers to illuminate the bombers targets consisting of the oil depots, ammunition dumps and of course any ships they could attack. The second wave was slightly smaller in number, it had 9 aircraft of which 5 carried torpedoes and the remainder were bombers, again with a pair designated as flare markers.

Illustrious was in position some 170 miles from Taranto soon after 20:00 on the evening of the 11 November. The first aircraft lifted off at 20:35, all 12 of the first wave were airborne by 20:40. They formed up some 8 miles from the ship before setting off for Taranto. A little later, at 21:28, the second wave began to depart with all bar one of the 9 aircraft aloft by 21:58. One of the second wave had to be hastily struck below deck for repairs to fabric on one of its wings. It managed to lift off at 21:58.

As Cunningham had put it, 'All the Pheasants had come home to roost' when he found out that all the Italian Battleships were in Taranto harbour. Now came the opportunity to alter the balance of naval power in the Mediterranean in favour of the Royal Navy by shooting those Pheasants whilst they were on their perches.

Force X

Earlier in the day, at 13:00, another component of Judgement was put into operation. Force X was detailed to depart the main force and head north into the Strait of Otranto. Its purpose was to make a separate raid into Italian waters, primarily to divert attention but also to add insult to injury if both attacks were successful. It would send a powerful message to the Italians; the Royal Navy could operate anywhere in the Mediterranean with impunity.

The particular target for this force was a convoy that was known to operate nightly across the Adriatic between the Italian Ports of Bari & Brindisi (to the North) and Otranto to the South, and the Albanian ports of Durazzo (Durres) to the North and Valona (Vlore) to the south. The trick was to find it at night, and with enough nighttime left to escape back to the south without being detected and attacked by the Italian Airforce in the daylight of the following morning.

Nubian and *Mohawk* were assigned to Force X as its destroyer escort, the main force consisting of 3 cruisers, *Orion* as the flagship of Vice-Admiral Pridham-Wippell, *Ajax* and *Sydney*. At 20:30 they were off to the southwest of Corfu, darkened for action and turning to north to begin a dash into enemy waters. There was a low, three-quarter moon on the horizon, the winds were calm, as was the sea. Ravenhill announced over the tannoy that they were going to make a nuisance of themselves that evening, just as the signal from *Orion* was given to increase to 25 knots. The change in engine note reverberated through *Nubian* as she surged powerfully forward.

Pridham-Wippell wanted to be sure he could get into their hunting ground undetected, and so had the ships of Force X in tight formation. The cruisers were in line astern, *Ajax* leading *Sydney*. *Nubian* was out to starboard, *Mohawk* to port. At 22:30 the ships were within their search area and were slowed to 20 knots. There was little noise aboard the ships, eyes strained through binoculars or at the glow of the radar screen. An hour passed by, then another, but there was no hint of the convoy approaching. Force X was now almost as far north as they dared to go, with the time approaching 01:00 the signal was made to turn back. There was some relief that they would go no further, but frustration that the convoy had yet to be detected.

Settled into a southerly course the men on *Nubians* bridge began to scan the horizon once more. Then, at 01:15 the Signalman shouted excitedly;

'*Mohawk* signaling. Contacts bearing Red zero six zero, am attacking, increase to 25 knots!' Ravenhill gave the order for course and speed, then quickly announced to the crew that the convoy had been sighted and they were attacking. Turning their gaze to the direction that *Mohawk* was engaging the men on watch picked out the target ships now silhouetted against the horizon. Almost at the same time, *Orion* signalled that she had spotted the convoy and ordered the cruisers to make a turn to port, line astern, to cut across the path of the enemy.

The Italian Convoy came on unaware of the impending attack, it had left Verona for Brindisi earlier that day and consisted of three freighters, the *Antonio Locatelli* (5,691 tons), *Capo Vado* (4,391 tons) the *Premuda* (4,427 tons) and they were accompanied by a passenger ship the *Catalani* (2,429 tons). Two escorts provided protection for the convoy, the Torpedo Boat *Nicola Fabrizi* built in 1918 and the Auxiliary Cruiser, *RAMB III*, one of 4 banana boats built in 1936 for the Regina Azienda Monopolio Banane (RAMB), now converted and armed for escort duties.

Giovani Barbini was the Commander of the *Nicola Fabrizi*, he and his crew may have spotted Force X before they came under attack. However, it is likely the first he and his crew knew of the dire situation they were in were the muzzle flashes from *Mohawk* and the scream of the incoming 4.7-in. shells fired at 13:25 from about 4000 yards (2 miles) away. 3 salvoes fell around their ship throwing up huge columns of water, the fourth was the one they didn't hear. The impact must have been deafening as heat and shell splinters engulfed the little ship. Commander Barbini was badly wounded in the leg, but despite beginning to lose blood rapidly and in much pain, he ordered the crew to deploy smoke and circle in front of the convoy in an effort to provide some parlance of protection.

On the *RAMB III*, the situation seems to have been a little different. One of *Mohawks* shells from her first salvo straddled *RAMB III*[140] without any

---

[140] RAMB III: The Italian Auxiliary Cruiser returned to duties after the loss of the convoy on 11 November 1940. However she had her bows blown off in the

resulting damage, however her Commander Francesco De Angelis, after firing 19 ineffective rounds, elected to turn and run for safety into the darkness.

By now *Nubian* had joined close astern *Mohawk*, who's guns continued to pour consistent fire on the enemy, straddling the second merchant ship in the convoy. In the next few moments both Tribal's had surged past the convoy. Now came the turn of the cruisers to rain down withering fire and complete the destruction of the convoy.

Orion fired simultaneously at the *Nicloa Fabrizi* with 4-inch shells and the third merchant ship in the line with her main 6-in. guns. Two torpedoes were loosed off, quickly followed by a star shell that arched high above the targets before exploding in a bright candescent light that illuminated the enemy ships. With the third ship now in flames, one of the two torpedoes found its mark and the resulting explosion sent it under the waves. *Orion* now traversed her main guns onto the fourth ship and soon there were hits being registered aboard the vessel that began to lose way and settle at the stern. Men were seen to be abandoning ship and when it appeared there were no further survivors, *Orion* fired a further torpedo that finished the job.

Meanwhile, *Ajax* also engaged the *Nicola Fabrizi* which soon drifted out of range. *Ajax* turned her attention back to the merchant vessels, three of which were now on fire, and in the confusion of smoke, star shell and the noise of battle it is uncertain which of the ships she was engaging.

---

port of Benghazi where she remained for some time, before being towed to Sicily and then Trieste where she was rebuilt. The Germans took her into service and converted her to a minelayer, operating out of the port of Rijeka. She was sunk by the allied whilst in the harbour in 1944, but after the war raised and taken into service with the Yugoslav Navy. Initially used as a training ship it became the residential Yacht of the Yugoslavian President, Marshal Josip Broz Tito. Having a distinguished career in his service, entertaining many political leaders if the time, even visiting London in 1953. The Galeb ended up back in Rijeka in the 1990's and is now being restored as a floating museum.

Sydney had actually spotted the convoy moments before the others in Force X, and her guns were also brought to bear on the hapless *Nicola Fabrizi*, however the gutsy torpedo boat was now making off and out of range of the cruiser's guns. Perhaps in desperate hope of scoring some form of morale victory, a torpedo was deployed by the Italian ship, which fortunately passed underneath the *Sydney*. The second merchant ship was now turning away hoping to make a run for it. Shells splashed all around it and before long both *Mohawk* and *Nubian* had swung around and were coming in for the kill.

By 01:50 it was all over, in less than 30 minutes, Force X had reduced the convoy to ruins, two wrecks remained barely afloat, burning, popping, roaring flames and billowing black acrid smoke. They lit up the sky revealing the gentle swell that was littered with detritus; bodies, oil, little clumps of men gathered in the water and lifeboats trying to rally the survivors together. There was the smell of burning oil and rubber whilst the thick tang of cordite came in wafts on the breeze. The *RAMB III* was gone, fleeing for home. Miraculously the *Nicola Fabrizi* was badly damaged but managed to reach port, she carried 11 dead and 17 wounded from her crew. Her Captain, despite refusing medical attention, remained in command until the ship was safely moored, he survived his wounds and was awarded the Gold Medal for valour. The following morning, two Torpedo boats picked up 140 survivors from the convoy, the remaining two ships had by then burned out and sunk.

At 01:53 Force X headed south at high speed, to rendezvous once more with *Illustrious* and the main battle group. It was imperative that the ships of Force X made their way south, away from their engagement before sunrise and the attention that must come from the Italian Airforce. The quicker they could get under the protection of the Combat Air Patrols deployed by *Illustrious*, the better for all.

By noon the next day, Force X met up with the main force. The CAP's proved most effective in staving off any reprisal attacks, in the main due to their ability to intercept and shoot down the Italian reconnaissance aircraft that were sent looking for the fleet. Three came in search of the fleet from their bases in Sicily but all they found was the Fulmars of 806 Squadron. The first to fall was a Cant 701 that was shot down at just before noon. The second was one of two, tri motor, Cant 706Bs, a more modern and slender float plane but no more potent in its own defence as the 701. As Lt. Vincent Jones wrote of these aircraft; 'These Cants of both versions made ideal targets as, apart from being almost defenceless, they were well within our capacity to catch and usually exploded and descended like Roman Candles.'[141]

On *Warspite*, the air action was watched by Admiral Cunningham; 'The last air battle took place over the fleet, and we saw the large bulk of the Cant (probably the larger 701) dodging in and out of the clouds with three Fulmars diving after her. There could only be one end, and presently a flaming meteor with a long tail of black smoke fell out of the sky and splashed into the sea just ahead of the fleet.'[142]

Over Taranto

The news of the previous night's actions was soon being passed around the fleet. Indeed, the night had been a long one for the staff aboard *Warspite* in the knowledge that the forces had now been deployed to do their work, and all that could now be done was to wait for the news of success or failure.

The Swordfish had indeed been successful, the crews were jubilant, the first aircraft landing back aboard at 01:20. They knew that they had hit several ships despite heavy but largely ineffective defensive fire from the harbours shore batteries. None of the crews were able to confirm what ships they had hit, but it was clear that considerable damage had been inflicted. They were so confident, they were keen to launch again the following day to ensure the job was well and truly finished, but the odds were considered too high for a second raid and fortunately a change in the weather made the decision a simpler one.

---

[141] (Galea, 2019)
[142] (Cunningham, 1951)

Also clear, was that two of the crews were missing. 815 Squadron's Flight Commander, Lt. Cmd N.W. Williamson and his Observer, Lt. N.J, Scarlet in Swordfish L4A were in the first wave, and, having descended to wavetop height began a run towards two Destroyers, the *Lampo* and *Fulmine* which opened up their Anti-Aircraft guns with murderous fire. In the next moment, the dark mass of a battleship came rushing out of the gloom. Williamson hit the release button and their torpedo sliced into the water and ran true to its target. Williamson then pulled a hard right hand evasive turn away, keeping some back pressure on the stick and right rudder to stop them side slipping into the harbour water. It was to no avail, machine gun fire pinged and banged into the airframe and control surfaces causing Williamson to lose control. The aircraft crashed into the sea with some force but both men managed to escape L4A. As the aircraft hit the water, their torpedo exploded against the hull of the *Conte de Cavour,* just aft of 'B' Turret.

The two men trod water and then made towards a floating dock some 150 yards away. There were dock workers aboard, that helped them out of the water and then set to roughing up the two crew men, before having them transferred to the *Fulmine*. Both men remained prisoners for the remainder of the war.

Swordfish E4H, 813 Squadron, was piloted by Lt. G.W. Bayley with his Observer Lt. H.J. Slaughter. They were in the second wave and followed their Flight Leader into the attack. What happened to their aircraft is not known, and indeed Slaughters body was never found. Bayleys was recovered and he received a full military honours burial in the cemetery at Taranto (his remains were later transferred to the War Graves Commission Cemetery Bari).

For the moment, the Italians were in some state of shock over what had occurred. The commanders had thought that an approach by an attacking force, especially a carrier-based force attempting to manoeuver to a launch position within 180 miles of any military port would be detected by air reconnaissance. This indicates that the success that the Fulmars of 806

Squadron enjoyed in thwarting these reconnaissance flights played a significant part in the success of Judgement.

As the damage control and salvage teams got to work to try to save those ships hit in the attack, the full enormity of what had occurred was evident to those in Command at Supermarina. Admiral Bernotti wrote; 'The success of the air attack against the Italian fleet in the outer anchorage of Taranto was the first example of the formidable potentialities of torpedo aircraft against large ships in strongly defended bases and confirmed in general the capabilities of aircraft carriers.'[143]

On the 14 November, Admiral Cunningham and his staff received the high-level photographic reconnaissance photographs from the Marylands of 431 Flight. They showed great plumes of oil spreading out across the harbour, and being carried away in the current, from three of the battleships. Salvage vessels crowded around the *Littorio,* the most modern Battleship in the fleet. She had taken three torpedo hits and would be out of action for months. The *Caio Duilio* had a 36-foot hole in her starboard side from a single torpedo and had been beached. However, the worst affected was the *Conte di Cavour.* Williamson and Scarletts torpedo had made a 40-foot hole in the forward compartments. In an effort to save the ship she had also been beached before being abandoned by her crew. She settled on the bottom of the harbour with a slight list to starboard, almost the whole of her upper decks awash. She would not sail again until after Italy sided with the Allies in 1943.

Of the peripheral damage, the cruiser *Trento* was leaking oil from bomb damage; luckily for that ship and its company, the bomb had failed to explode. Further bomb damage was being attended to by fire teams on the Seaplane hangars ashore.

Whilst Judgement was indeed a success and half of the Italian compliment of battleships were put out of action, this was only temporary. Both the *Littorio* and *Duilio* would be repaired. However, it was the future disposition

---

[143] (Schofield CB, Reprinted 2011)

of the ships and their threat to Allied shipping that was the long-term success of the operation. Admiral Bernotti wrote; 'By means of the aerial offensive the enemy had achieved results which obliged the nucleus of our naval power to move away from the southern waters, that is from the area where they were most likely to be employed, bearing in mind the necessity of disputing the movements of British naval forces between the two basins of the Mediterranean.'[144]

At a time when Britain stood much alone in the fight against Nazi Germany, and was very much still on a back footing, this was a welcome victory. Churchill was able to declare in the house of commons, that the action '…affects decisively the balance of power in the Mediterranean…'. In Germany, Hitler was furious, and as a result he would make a decision that would affect all those of His Majesty's armed forces in the Mediterranean and North Africa and would directly affect the fate of HMS *Nubian* and her crew.

Meanwhile, the fleet returned to Alexandria, and *Nubian* received her third Battle Honour, *MEDITERRANEAN 1940*.

December 1940

For the remainder of November and into December, *Nubian's* operational role within D14, was multi-faceted. This was due to a number of factors that were now in motion and led up to some significant events in the beginning of 1941. By now the Italians were well entrenched in their invasion of Greece and fairing badly. Their act of attacking Greece meant that Suda Bay on the north coast of Crete could be used as a Royal Naval base. In the past, when the Navy had tankers placed in Suda Bay for refuelling purposes, the Italians would attack them from the air prompting the Greeks to request their removal. The situation was now somewhat different. Whilst not an ideal port, it did give the Navy another option to refuel especially useful for the destroyers.

---

[144] (Schofield CB, Reprinted 2011)

Indeed, British and ANZAC (Australia and New Zealand) troop concentration began in both Crete and Greece and there were many convoy duties ferrying men and materiel into Suda Bay and the Greek Port of Piraeus. During one of these convoys, *Malaya* and *Ramillies* were escorted out of the Mediterranean for a refit back in England whilst arriving in their place was, *Barham*, and the cruisers *Berwick* (8-inch heavy County Class Cruiser) and *Glasgow* (4-inch light Town Class Cruiser), with three G-Class destroyers *Greyhound*, *Gallant* and *Griffin*.

At the beginning of December (1 – 7) *Nubian* was operating out of Alexandria, exercising with her fellow ships of D14 in the approaches to the port during the day and standing down during the night when her crews would get some needed rest. At sea on the 8 December with Operation Compass underway, D14, in particular *Jervis*, *Nubian* and *Janus* were providing anti-aircraft and anti-submarine duties for *Ladybird*, *Aphis* and *Terror*. Once again, these low draft gun platforms were getting close to the shore and hammering the Italian positions as they began their retreat from the British Army. The sea was rough, the crew very tired, and for some it cannot have been lost on them that it was two years to the day that they boarded *Nubian* for the first time and left their families behind *Nubian* gained yet another Battle Honour, LIBYA 1940.

In Germany, the Fuhrer was planning the invasion of Russia and how he may come to the aid of Italy without impacting on the first objective. Fuhrer Directive No. 18 began to outline these plans as Mussolini's forces were being pressured from all angles. The raid on Taranto was the last straw. Plans were afoot to move troops and aircraft onto bases along the Aegean Coast. This would not only give protection for the Romanian oil fields from aerial attack by British forces which could jeopardise Operation Barbarossa (the invasion of Russia), but would, if need be, provide a jump off point for an invasion of Greece, Crete and potentially North Africa.

As Operation Compass saw great gains against the Italians in North Africa, Hitler was faced with having to commit militarily to Italy. Directive No. 22

strengthened his commitment of air power to the Eastern Mediterranean with plans drawn up to deny the sea to the Royal Navy, attack and disable both the port of Alexandria and the Suez Canal which in turn would prevent any reinforcement from the south. In addition, came the formation of the Deutches Afrika Corps (DAK) under General Erwin Rommel destined for Libya. There was one more order given to the air forces destined for the Mediterranean. Sink the *Illustrious*.

Fliegerkorps X, with their Stukas had remained in Norway since the British forces had been ejected in May 1940, whilst in France the reputation of the Stuka, that had spearheaded the German advance to Dunkirk had been somewhat dented in the Battle of Britain during the long summer of 1940. However, this 'fall from grace' could be considered somewhat unfair, as it was the way in which the Stuka was utilised during the Battle, rather than the capabilities of the airframe and the skill of the pilots that was the main contributing factor.

During August 1940, it became obvious that the Stuka Squadrons could inflict devastating attacks on airfields and specific targets such as the Chain Home radar stations along the English coastline. Their reason for inclusion in the forces deployed against Britain during this time was to provide close aerial artillery support to the troops spearheading the intended invasion.

However, as we have discussed previously, the Stuka was terribly vulnerable to fighters, especially if they were left to fend for themselves. The losses of Stukas and their crews began to grow during August 1940, and whilst there were some spectacular results, such as the raid on Tangmere Airfield on the 16 August that set alight every one of the hangers on the base, the attrition rate was unsustainable. This came to a head on the 18 August as described by Mason in 'Battle over Britain'.

> Whatever material achievement was gained by either side on this day, 18 August must be recorded as the date of the first decisive defeat of the Stuka dive-bomber. Two weeks previously the number of these aircraft available for operations with the eight Stukagruppen based in France

amounted to 281, yet in the course of those weeks they had flown fourteen major raids and, according to Luftwaffe records had suffered the loss of 39 aircraft – all but a handful to the guns of fighters. In this one day's fighting, one Stukageschwader alone would lose seventeen more.[145]

The Stukas were thus withdrawn from operations, but not totally. They still played their part in specialist raids that required precision bombing, and they began to target merchant convoys that were trying to run between the southwest and northeast coastal ports of the English Channel. Tactics were being developed to target shipping and these methods would be continually adapted and honed, no doubt complimenting those that Fliegerkorps X had already demonstrated in Norway.

The formations adopted by the Stuka Squadrons were based on the 3 ship 'Ketten' where two aircraft would formate either side and just behind the lead aircraft. These two were known as the Kettenhunde (Chained dog) and they would simply follow whatever the lead aircraft did.

A 'Staffel' was made up of three Ketten (9 aircraft in total), the subordinate pair of Ketten following either side and behind the lead Ketten. This was the most favoured formation for anti-shipping operations, although the larger Gruppe formation of 30 aircraft would be used against larger ships such as cruisers and battleships. The largest formation that could be used was the Gruppe, and this at full strength would amount to 93 aircraft in total.

When approaching their target, the aircraft would split into either Ketten or Staffels and fly in staggered echelon formation, with the lead aircraft in the most forward position. When he was satisfied that the target had been identified and an attacking opportunity had come, the pilot would waggle his wings, and one by one the Stukas would peel off at intervals following their leader into the dive.

---

[145] (Mason, 1990)

Attacking formations would normally gather between 13,000 and 16,000 feet, with a dive down to anywhere between 1600 and 700 feet for bomb release, even lower perhaps if their bombs fuses were set for 'mV' or 'mit Verzugerung' (no delay). The Stukas usually carried a 550lb anti shipping and four 60lb bombs for attacks on merchant ships or a 1100lb armour piercing bomb for warships.

Attacking merchant vessels which had little in the way of protective arms, would mean a low-level attack from the rear was possible with little risk of being shot down. One way of determining bomb release was to strafe the ship on the final run, releasing the bomb when the splashes from the bullets could be seen in the water ahead of the ship.

Warships were somewhat trickier targets, especially destroyers. The speed and nimbleness of a well captained destroyer ensured that an attack from the stern was the preferred and most effective method. The pilot could better anticipate and have the time to react if the attack was spotted and evasive action was taken by the target ship.

By late October 1940, the inactivity and fighting effectiveness of the Stuka squadrons was beginning to become frustrating to the likes of Squadron Commanders such as Helmut Mahlke. He wrote.

> The sidelining of the Channel based Stuka units was, in fact, giving us real cause for concern. Whilst the rest of the Luftwaffe was locked in combat against England, we had been condemned to virtual inactivity. As our fighters lacked the range to escort the Kampfgruppen on their long missions in land, even our bombers had to abandon their daylight attacks. The growing strength of Britain's fighter defences was taking too heavy a toll of their numbers. Now they were being forced to operate under cover of darkness, flying one or more missions per night.[146]

---

[146] (Mahlke, 2013)

With the Royal Navy running amok in the Mediterranean, the British Army making great gains in North Africa against the Italians, it becomes obvious why the Stukas of Fliegerkorps X and those Gruppes almost idle in Northern France were ideally placed to be sent to aid the Italians. During the first two months of 1941, the Germans had deployed to the Mediterranean theatre some 120 JU88 medium bombers, 40 Me109 Fighters, 20 reconnaissance aircraft and 150 Stukas. This, against a few Fleet Air Arm Squadrons of Fulmars and Swordfish, supported by a meagre number of British Hurricanes in North Africa and from Malta. The odds were now firmly back in the Axis favour. Those aboard *Nubian* who had been involved in the Norwegian campaign would soon be re-united with the determined and deadly attacks from JU88s and the scream of the Stuka.

In the meantime, the ships of D14 entered Alexandria on Christmas eve, with the prospect of a day off for Christmas, but it was not to be a merry one for Herbert. He was on a Defaulters charge and due at the Captains Table. This was indeed a serious matter, for Herbert must have made a significant transgression. He would have been marched in front of Commander Ravenhill, ordered to remove his cap and stand to attention. His charge would have been read by the prosecuting officer, whilst another would provide some form of defence perhaps citing previous good conduct or some other positive aspects of his character and career. In any event, Herbert was guilty as charged and would have been given the option of accepting the Commanders punishment or facing a Courts Martial. Herbert chose the former and Ravenhill had Herbert's third Good Conduct badge 'Denied', which was duly marked on his record.

Denial (or taking away) a Good Conduct stripe indicates the charge was indeed serious. Such punishment was handed out for dereliction of duty, absent without leave, stealing from shipmates disobeying an order or a pattern of general disobedience as examples. The consequence of denial was financial as well as setting an example to others, the additional pay that came with the Good Conduct Badge was immediately withdrawn.

There is no record of what the charge was and looking at Herbert's service record this does appear the only black mark during his entire career. By December 1940, as previously noted, Herbert had been away from his family for two years. Adrian Holloway perfectly describes the situation Herbert and many others no doubt felt at the time. 'We were only one thousand, five hundred miles from England by direct route, but twelve thousand miles round the Cape. This was the only route open to us, had we been able to travel at all. With no telephone link, and these vast distances separating us from all those at home, we were indeed isolated.'[147] Herbert and the ship's crew had been on active service almost constantly and with little rest since the beginning of hostilities. Every day they faced attack, not only whilst at sea, but in harbour too. What is probably more significant is that there would have been no indication or prospect of heading back to England any time soon. Their presence in the Mediterranean was vital, the ship could not be spared. The only way out was to be sunk, killed or for the war to end, which was most unlikely for the foreseeable future. So perhaps this was perhaps what resulted in Herbert's visit to the Captains Table?

Christmas day arrived, a welcome moment of respite that the ships of D14 could take time out and relax. Each ship would have celebrated in their own way but by some improvisation using anything that resembled decorations, the mess decks and wardrooms would have been made festive for the day. The rum ration was served early, and the Commanders visited all the men to wish them a Merry Christmas. Ravenhill and his Officers of *Nubian* were invited, along with all the Flotilla Commanders as guests of Captain Mack aboard *Jervis* at 11:30 for drinks. *Jervis* had been decorated throughout with signal flags, whilst her Wardroom had been turned into '…a cross between an early Victorian conservatory. The harvest thanksgiving and the village on a carnival night.'[148]

Captain Mack was in fine form; he had already accepted a number of rum 'sippers' from his crew on his rounds that morning. His welcome was warm

---

[147] (Holloway, 1993)
[148] (Connell, 1987)

and convivial, with the good humoured banter that would be familiar to any group of people who have shared a dressing room or been together through good times and bad. By 14:00 all had returned to their ships, and dinner was served. It may not have been Turkey, but a meal most welcome all the same, made from whatever the mess caterers could find. The fare aboard *Jervis* gives us a good indication of what was available. 'The mess caterers and cooks had succeeded in converting the 'pussers' issue of pork and rather stringy chickens (obtained from the canteen manager) into palatable seasonal dishes, and some messes found ingredients which – liberally laced with illegally hoarded rum issues – became lethal Christmas pudding substitutes.'[149]

With 1940 drawing to a close, Operation Compass's success was evident, the Italians were effectively surrounded in Bardia and it would indeed fall on the 5 January. Cunningham had reason to write about his optimism at that time.

And so, the year 1940 ended in high hope. The Navy had a great degree of control in the Central Mediterranean and convoys were passing through both ways. We had carried out offensive strikes in the Adriatic and were taking a fair and increasing toll of the enemies convoys to Tipoli, upon which his army in Libya so vitally depended. Malta, though still rather lacking in anti-aircraft defence, was almost back to normal as regards repair work, while the RAF bombers working from the island were dealing heavy blows upon Triploi. Best of all, the presence of *Illustrious* gave us nearly as possible the command of the air over the fleet whenever it went to sea. We had the measure of the Regia Aeronautica, and the valuable help of the Royal Airforce had drawn its teeth.[150]

But, whilst the crews of D14 were nursing their hangovers on Boxing Day, and Cunningham was meeting with the C-in-C's of the Army and Air Force in Cairo,1/St.G1 (one Stuka Gruppe One) under Hauptmann Paul – Werner

---

[149] (Connell, 1987)
[150] (Cunningham, 1951)

Hozzel and 2/St.G2 (two Stuka Gruppe two) commanded by Major Walter Enneccerus arrived at Trapini Airbase, Sicily. They were soon followed by the remainder of Fliegerkorps X on the 10 January. Helmut Mehlke and his III./StG.1 were to arrive during February 1941.

Enneccerus was born on the 21 November 1921 in Mosel. He learned to fly in the Luftwaffe, as it was being secretly reformed in the late 1930's, gaining a commission in August 1933 before becoming an instructor. He later began flying Stukas, first going into action in Poland as Kapitan of 4./St.G77, being awarded the *Eisernen-Kreuz II.Klasse* (Iron Cross 2nd Class), in September 1939. Appointed to II./St.G.2 in January 1939 operating in France and Belgium as the Germans advanced on Dunkirk, gaining his Iron Cross 1st Class in May 1940. He then flew in missions against the RAF during the Battle of Britain in the summer of 1940, before the Stukas were withdrawn and redeployed to the Mediterranean. He was awarded the *Ritterkreuz* (Knights Cross) in July 1940, the citation (and reason for the award) listing his activities in leading the Gruppe during the Western Offensive.

Apart from attacks on columns, troop formations, batteries, fortified towns and railway targets, his *Gruppe* carried out attacks on the forts near Liege, near Maubeuge, near Givet, as well as parts of the Maginot Line near Weissenbuhl and on the Kaiserstuhl. The *Gruppe* sank four ships at Dunkirk, Le Harve and La Rochelle and badly damaged eight ships. The concentration of French armoured vehicles near Philippeville was disrupted by the Gruppe's Stuka attack and Evreux station was closed.[151]

Hozzel and Enneccerus were immediately tasked with making plans to neutralise the *Illustrious*. It was considered that four direct hits on *Illustrious,* would be enough to sink her, despite her armoured decking, her own defences and the protection of her escorts. A ship of her size with a huge, flat expanse of flight deck should be a relatively simple target, but they needed to practice. So, they had a mockup, to the exact size of the flight deck, marked off the shore

---

[151] Richard Meredith

using buoys. Then they began regular and intense exercises to hone their tactics and dive bombing accuracy. The day and the opportunity would come when their efforts could be tested, and this would come soon.

Chapter 10

Operation Excess 7 – 23 January 1941

'Then things started to go wrong.'

Admiral ABC Cunningham

08:34 Hours on Friday 10 January 1941, Position 36° 27' N, 12° 11' E, about 25 miles southwest of Pantellaria, the G-Class destroyer HMS *Gallant* is making 30 knots trying to regain position with the main Battle-Fleet, on board, 146 souls. Her bow wave spurts up and outwards as she powers through the water, on the Bridge Lt. Cmd Cecil Powis Frobisher Brown D.S.C is enjoying the ride as are his accompanying Officers and men.

Just below the surface, twisting in the current is a Pignone P200 Sea mine, ball shaped and armed with 441lbs of TNT explosive. It is tethered to the sea floor by about 1000 feet of cable and has been in the water some time. There is the odd limpet attached to its shell and fronds of green weed wrapped around its 'horns' waft gently up and down with the motion of the deadly device. The sea swell increases for a moment and gradually lifts the mine towards the open air above.

The last sound that those on the lower decks in the forward compartments of *Gallant* heard was the load thump in the moment the mine was struck by *Gallants* bow. One of the mines 9, Hertz Horns that protruded from its black metal outer case was compressed, opening an electrical circuit that fired a detonator. The resulting explosion caused a massive shock wave that blew off *Gallants* bow right up to the Bridge.

About 3 miles away on the Quarter Deck of *Illustrious*, Charles Lamb was enjoying a post breakfast smoke and a chat with Michael Torrens 'Tiffy' Spense (the CO of 815 Squadron), both men appreciating the fine looks and speed of *Gallant*. 'As we stood looking at the destroyer, she broke into two pieces and the fo'c'sle sank at once, leaving the bulk of the ship wallowing on the surface like an open-ended tin box. A second or two later we heard the dull thud of an explosion.'[152]

The whole fleet heard the explosion. 65 men lost their lives on *Gallant* that morning, 15 were injured, it was the moment that things began to go wrong.

This was the third day of 'Operation Excess', which began early on the morning of the 7 January when Force A, comprising of *Warspite, Valiant* and *Illustrious* left Alexandria, escorted by the destroyers *Jervis, Mohawk, Dainty, Greyhound, Gallant, Griffin* and *Nubian*. The objective was to meet with convoy 'Excess' which would be attempting to traverse the Mediterranean from east to west. Convoy 'Excess' comprised of 4, high speed merchant vessels. *Clan Cumming, Clan MacDonald* and *Empire Song* loaded with Tanks and other munitions, bound for Piraeus in Greece, whilst the *Essex* was bound for Malta with 4000 tons of ammunition, 3000 seed potatoes and on deck there were 12 crated Hurricane fighters. As was the norm, Force H would bring these ships out of Gibraltar towards the Sicilian Straights where, on this occasion, they would be met on the eastern side by the cruisers *Gloucester* and *Southampton* who would brave the narrow straights beforehand turning back as the initial escort. Accompanying 'Excess' for deployment in the Western Mediterranean was the brand-new Dido class cruiser, *Bonaventure*, equipped with the very latest Type 279 Radar for aircraft detection and range finding.

En route to their rendezvous, Force A would escort the oiler, *Brambleleaf* to Suda bay, protecting her through the Kaso Straight (to the west of Crete) and into the Anti Kithera Straight before arriving at Suda Bay. Here the escort Destroyers would refuel before heading out once more to meet with 'Excess'. In addition, a third convoy would head to Malta, out of Alexandria, consisting of the *Breconshire* and *Clan Macaulay* carrying Fuel Oil, petrol and other war materiel, with *Calcutta, Diamond* and *Defender* as escort. These three

---

[152152] (Lamb, 2001)

movements were the main components of the overall plan that consisted of a number of movements in a most complex set of operations.

Cunningham has come under some criticism for his deployment of *Illustrious* during 'Excess'. She was placed between *Warspite* and *Valiant* primarily for morale purposes. For those aboard *Illustrious* at the time, this was a tactic that was open to question even then. Torrens Spence held the belief, as did his superiors, that it would be far better if *Illustrious* were to hold off at a distance from the fleet and out of the range of the enemy aircraft but remaining close enough for the Fulmars Combat Air Patrols to provide effective cover. Indeed, Charles Lamb recounts that during his conversation with Torrens Spense on the morning of the 10th he confirmed that both Boyd and Lyster had made such a suggestion to their C-in-C but were effectively told to follow the orders given and get on with their jobs.

Cunningham makes no apology in his memoirs; 'As we swept on we passed close to the convoy, indeed some of the destroyer screen passed through it. We could just make out the figures of the troops in the merchant vessels, and I wondered at the time if they were thrilled by the sight of these three large ships steaming at full speed to the sound of the guns. It must have been a fine spectacle in the grey light of the morning.[153]'

When Lamb questioned whether the Italians were likely to attack that day, Torrens Spense gave him the answer that he probably was least expecting or wanted to hear. He revealed (without of course knowing the intelligence came from the breaking of German coded signals) that Fliegerkorps X was heading to the region. This was actually known as far back as mid-December but had not been passed onto the Admiralty. Indeed, Torrens Spense had only received this worrying news an hour beforehand! Now the ships were well within striking distance of the enemy bases. He could not understand how those in command did not appreciate that if *Illustrious*, their floating airfield, was lost then so was any form of air superiority over the fleet.

---

[153] (Cunningham, 1951)

'Well', said Tiffy, perhaps you can see why the mining we have just seen is only the beginning. This is a day you will never forget. You can thank your lucky stars that you are flying this morning, and not sitting in the hangar at action stations.'[154]

Some tea and bully beef sandwiches for a late breakfast were being eaten with gusto on the bridge of *Nubian*. They were discussing the action they had witnessed earlier as *Bonaventure* had engaged and apparently sunk an Italian destroyer, when the crump of the mine explosion stopped all chewing at once. A shout and an instinctive arm raised, pointing in the direction of the stricken ship had all heads turned and looking towards *Gallant*. Midshipman Hopper lowered his binoculars from his eyes and reported to Ravenhill, 'It's the *Gallant* Sir, she's either been torpedoed or mined. Her whole bow and fo'c'sle's gone, and she is now dead stopped.'

Yeoman of Signals Ellis Watson came for the Wireless Room to report, '*Warspite* has signalled for *Mohawk* to take *Gallant* under tow. *Bonaventure* and *Griffin* are to stand by her whilst *Hereward* and *Jaguar* will join us as screen.' *Mohawk* was already swinging around to take *Gallant* in tow from her stern section. Ravenhill ordered the ship to come to full readiness and be prepared for action at any moment.

At 50 feet above sea level the sense of speed was not lost on Capitano Orazi Bernadini, piloting his SM.79. The glassy water was rushing underneath the aircraft, and he could feel the sweat popping out of his body from the concentration required to stay alive. One slight mistake would plough them into the sea or a slight overcorrection could catch a wingtip and cartwheel them into oblivion. Not far out to his right, he perceived the presence of Tenente Angelo Caponetti's machine. Beneath both aircraft were slung Whitehead Torpedoes destined for *Illustrious*, more importantly both aircraft were beneath the sweep of the fleets radar.

---

[154] (Lamb, 2001)

At 11,000 feet Lt. Henley in Fulmar 6F and Sub Lt. Griffith in 6G were beginning another leg of their CAP. They were Red Section, one pair of 3 aircraft launched at 10:15 from *Illustrious*. Earlier they had dealt with an SM.79 which had been seen to dive into the sea in flames. It was now 12:10 when they spotted the two SM.79s approaching the fleet. Even at this height the enemy pair were unmistakable, like two tiny models skimming the silvery waves below. Henley tipped a wing and Red Section dove down to attack from astern.

The first that Bernadini knew of the approaching danger was a warning shout from the upper gunner followed by the unmistakable sound of his machine gun firing. Despite the gunners open position, the smell of cordite wafted back into the cockpit, thick, acrid and heavy. Then there came the sound of rounds striking the airframe, another sharp, angry shout and the gun went silent. Ahead the enemy fleet was coming into view, Bernadini hit the release button and the torpedo fell away. Out to the right Caponetti's machine sparkled as rounds from their attackers hit, the starboard engine suddenly belched a huge black cloud of smoke, the propellor stopped, then white smoke began to stream behind it.

The SMs were sitting ducks now, growing large and plump in the gunsight, rounds sparking off the airframe, but Henley's guns fell silent first, then Griffiths, they were out of ammo. The guns from both SM.79s were also silent but they were not out of ammo, their gunners were dead. The enemy had dropped their torpedoes that now streaked away towards the fleet, but none would find a target today, all passing astern of *Valiant*. Over the R/T, White Section was called down to give chase and before long all were over 50 miles from *Illustrious*. The attacks by the Italians had drawn the Fulmars away from the fleet, it would be the Germans turn next.

The alarm to 'Repel aircraft' was sounded just before 12:30 on *Nubian*. It was being sounded all around the escorts and of course on *Illustrious*. The x7 magnification binocular was deemed to be the best for aircraft spotting and there were many trained high above the fleet that morning. The eyes behind those optics widened with the realisation that these aircraft were not Italian high-level bombers, they were Stukas, and they were German.

At 14,000 feet the 43 Stukas of Stg 1 bobbed up and down in the warming air and the slipstream of the other aircraft. There were no fighters to meet them, the sky was clear and blue, the Mediterranean glistened, flat calm and serene on which the ships of 'Excess' were making their way east. In the middle steamed their target, just as they had imagined, right where they wanted her. Major Enneccerus moved the control column of his Stuka from side to side, his wings responding in a signal for his squadron to attack. The force would split, his Squadron targeting the carrier whilst the other two Squadrons would attack the battleships and harass the other escorts to draw their fire. Enneccerus peeled his aircraft off in a half roll and down they all went.

Charles Lamb (815 Squadron) had a relatively quiet morning, ranging ahead of the fleet on an anti-submarine patrol in his Swordfish Q-Queenie. His patrol had taken a surreal turn when it became apparent that his TAG was a certain Midshipman Wallington of 819 Squadron who had accidentally clambered aboard the wrong Q-Queenie that morning. A mistake that could well have saved the young mans life. With no contacts made, Lamb returned to a holding position ready for recovery onto *Illustrious*, when she was scheduled to turn into wind at 12:30.

Whilst holding, Lamb observed Swordfish and Fulmars being launched from the deck and then he was able to begin his own approach to land on, during which he noticed that the aft lift was 'down', but he calculated that it would be raised well before he would be making his final approach. For now, the first task was to jettison his payload of bombs, just in case they came off their mountings on board ship, should he make a heavy landing. As for the depth charge slung underneath the fuselage, this was confirmed by his TAG as set to 'SAFE' and would only explode if it fell overboard. It would automatically detonate at a pre-determined depth, and hopefully out of harms way.

Lamb begun his approach, down the wake of *Illustrious* whilst keeping an eye on the yellow bats of 'Haggis' Russell the Deck Landing Officer (DLO) guiding him down. Suddenly there was a huge cloud of smoke from one of the port 4.7-in. guns that enveloped the DLO. This was not unduly alarming or unusual as the pilots often landed whilst the defensive armament was active. However, this time, a large, grey aircraft flew across his glidepath, a huge red Swastika painted on its side. Instinctively Lamb pressed his gun button. What turned out to be a Stuka, jinked at that precise moment and his bullets passed harmlessly overhead. In the next moment it released its 1000lb bomb that '…looked like a GPO pillar-box, painted black.'[155]

Lamb had witnessed the four Fulmars of Yellow Section get airborne, along with 819's Swordfish. The Fulmars tried to gain height as fast as they could in order to get into the fight, but their slow rate of climb hampered their efforts. In Yellow 2, the climb out was all the more difficult as the port undercarriage would not retract, to make matters worse, when they engaged a Stuka, the Starboard wheel dropped down as well. The crew had no choice but to abandon the action and head back to Malta.

On deck another Section was desperately trying to get aloft. *Illustrious* was gradually turning into wind, but not fast enough. They would have to carry out a rolling launch partially into the wind without the aid of the steam catapult, there simply wasn't the time to position the aircraft for an assisted take off. The first aircraft due to launch was the Fulmar 6G of Pilot Officer Tallack and Sub Lt. Marshall. Its propeller turned with lethargy and a pathetic, almost asthmatic wheeze coughed out a small puff of exhaust. Behind in Fulmar 6A, Lt. Barnes was still going through some preflight checks as he started up the engine, in the back, Lt. Vincent Jones could see what was happening in front and knew the signs. He clambered up out of the cockpit and frantically waved the deck crews to move 6A out of the way. Time was desperately short; the Stukas were falling upon them and their forms were growing alarmingly close as they dived onto *Illustrious*.

---

[155] (Lamb, 2001)

In the next moments, Barnes opened the throttle and they passed by 6A to their starboard, no mean feat on the confined flight deck area and reduced visibility from the long engine cowling blocking the pilots forward view. In the next moment Barnes pushed the throttle fully forward, they accelerated down the deck which gave way to the sea as their Fulmar gained airflow over the wing that lifted them into the air.

> When we reached a few hundred feet we found ourselves surrounded by JU87s as they were pulling out of their dives and some of them were very close, one hundred yards or so and I could clearly see the rear gunners firing at us. Two bullets went through my plotting board and others lodged in my seat. I looked down and saw the poor *Illustrious* passing through huge columns of water, her guns blazing and a fire and smoke coming from the after end of the flight deck.[156]

Behind them, the deck crew manhandled 6A back to the rear lift, Tallack and Marshall visible in their open cockpits clearly frustrated at the situation, urging the deck handlers to get their aircraft back below as fast as possible in hope they may have another chance to launch once their machine had been looked at by the fitters. Both men watched the flight deck disappear as the aft lift dropped towards the hanger and the first Stuka struck. The 'black, pillar box' that Lamb observed coming off the rails of the grey Stuka flew with deadly accuracy straight into the aft lift, bouncing off it before exploding in the hangar below. Fulmar 6A, Tallack and Marshall were instantly vapourised in a massive explosion that ripped the length of the hangar.

At that time the hangar was divided into three sections by steel curtains that hung down to protect against a flash fire. These had no effect against the massive blast from a 1000lb bomb which crushed the air forward as well as up. The rear lift platform which weighed some 300 tons was blown clean out of the lift well, and fell back all askew, so that no aircraft could land back on. The

---

[156] (Galea, 2019)

forward Lift was bent almost straight down the yellow painted flight deck centreline to resemble the pitched roof of a barn.

Those trapped inside the hangar were faced with flying pieces of the steel flame curtain, exploding fuel and ammunition rounds that cooked off and flew in all directions. Some men lay flat in an effort to escape, others did not have the time. Charles Lamb describes the scenes in 'War in a Stringbag'.

> Poor Neil Kemp was killed by one of them (shrapnel from one of the flame curtains) immediately. He had been standing in the centre of the hangar talking to Jackie Jago when the first sudden explosion occurred. Jackie found himself facing a headless body, which was all that was left of a fine chap who would have made a wonderful Admiral had he lived. Even in death Neil refused to lie down, until Jackie gave his grim remains a little push.
>
> Mr Luddington, the Master at Arms, knew that the hangar was a raging inferno where men were dying in droves, and because he was a very big, tough chap, he must have thought that perhaps he could haul someone to safety. Whatever his reasons, his body was found in the hangar where no doubt he had never set foot before. He had been asphyxiated by the fumes and very badly burned.[157]

Captain Alan Sutton of 815 Squadron had been signed off from flying duties with an ear infection which meant that his alternate duty was to support the Commander of Air Operations on the Bridge. He was aft when the call to Action Stations came. The most expedient route to the Bridge was via the hanger, and it was as he was en route that the bomb exploded in the aft lift well. '…my only impression was that there was a mass of flame and smoke and that the ship was spinning 'round me' he later recalled. The blast had actually picked him up off his feet and flung him through two watertight doors that were mercifully open at the time. If they had been shut, or his trajectory

---

[157] (Lamb, 2001)

had been a little altered, he would have followed the way of many others that day and crushed against the ship's interior.

The Stukas continued to fall upon *Illustrious*, dropping bomb after bomb. Edward 'Ted' Whitley was a fitter with 819 Squadron. 'As the raid went on there was this rather unusual feeling as if the ship were lifted 2 or 3 inches out of the water and dropped it back in again and I realised that we had been hit and this happened again, and again, and again.'[158]

Around *Illustrious*, the escorts began pumping shells into the air with everything they had. Ravenhill had *Nubian* at full speed, shouting steering orders, hard over in both directions in an effort to avoid the incoming bombs and to spread effective fire over the carrier and the battleships. Together with the other escorts they were developing, on the hoof, what would become known as an 'Umbrella Barrage' by deliberately firing over the ships they were protecting.

Cunningham, aboard *Warspite*, watched as his prize asset was engulfed in a mass of bomb splashes that almost engulfed the great ship. He could not but admire the skill of the German pilots.

> 'One was too interested in this new form of dive-bombing attack really to be frightened, and there was no doubt we were watching complete experts. Formed roughly in a large circle over the fleet they peeled off one by one when reaching the attacking position. We could not but admire the skill and precision of it all. The attacks were pressed home to a point-blank range, and as they pulled out of their dives some of them were seen to fly along the flight deck of the *Illustrious* below the level of her funnel.'[159]

---

[158] From an interview with the IWM
[159] (Cunningham, 1951)

On *Valiant,* 18-year-old Midshipman Adrian Holloway described the attack on his ship.

'The first plane that came for us came from the port bow. It was the first time that I (or many others) had ever been dive-bombed. I could not help looking up as the plane came down to two thousand feet, and the bomb slowly swung out from underneath the fuselage. The nose of the bomb looked very oval as it came towards us, and then we were flattening ourselves on the turret top as the machine screamed overhead.'

This was the entry in his Midshipman's journal what he actually felt but could not write down at the time in fear his senior officers would read it, was how totally petrified he had been.

George Going of 819 Squadron could see very little in the now darkened carrier. He remembered that he had a torch in his cabin and headed there to retrieve it. In doing so he came across the aft Damage Control Party, who in his words appeared quite stunned. Most likely because their Officer had been killed. In what he termed an 'unwanted enthusiasm', Going took responsibility and found himself in charge of the Damage Control Party for the next two hours.

It is most probable that Alan Sutton also became one of the men assisting George Going. Sutton had found the repeated practice drills for this eventuality most tedious, following the routine of 'Close Ventilation, Put out the Fires, Rescue the Wounded, Apply First Aid'. On this day he appreciated those long, boring hours of practice as, despite being battered, bruised and in some shock, he and many others began to carry out their duties. However, before long, the next bomb hit, most likely the one that destroyed the Wardroom.

The Wardroom was meant to act as the Aft Field Dressing Station in times of action in conjunction with the Sick Berth which was in the forward section of the ship. As a consequence of this, the Quarter Deck, where Charles Lamb had taken his after-breakfast smoke not so long ago was now used for that purpose. Lamb wrote, 'One RAF Officer who had come with us as an interested spectator was unable to take any further interest: sitting in the anteroom, with all that hullabaloo going on outside, he must have thought himself reasonably secure from danger. Later he was found sitting in a scorched armchair, headless but still clutching an open copy of *The Times* in both hands.'[160]

Sutton was somewhat luckier than the RAF Officer, he was knocked unconscious by the blast. His next recollection was awaking, laid out on the Quarter Deck as someone had clearly rescued him! He quickly came to his senses, realising that around him, '…there were a whole mass of people with all sorts of burns and things being laid out on the Quarter Deck by various first aid parties'

It took cool heads and initiative to fight the new enemy that was pervading the ship. Fire could founder *Illustrious* if it were allowed to take a hold, and it was men like Arthur Sowman that stood up to the heat and flames. He was subsequently Mentioned in Despatches for, as Lamb once more comments; '…any number of people have told me how they were encouraged by Arthur Sowman, who appeared like some genie from a magician's bottle wherever a bomb exploded, saying: 'Come on chaps, man the hoses, let's put this fire out…' as calmly as if her were encouraging a rugby team from the touch line.'[161]

Having 'gone around' Lamb was now fighting for his life. The Stuka may have been little match for a modern fighter, but the Swordfish was definitely not modern. The Stukas fell on his Swordfish as they completed their bombing dive, firing bursts of machine gun fire at the biplane as it turned on a sixpence and dived away in the only effective evasive manoeuver that Lamb could employ. As for the Fulmars, they were beginning to recover at Hal Far airfield

---

[160] (Lamb, 2001)
[161] (Lamb, 2001)

on Malta at around 13:30 as instructed by Air Operations aboard *Illustrious*. Some had very little fuel, as little as 5 gallons in some cases. Not all made it.

The spent shells from *Nubians* four barrelled, 2-pounder pom-pom toppled gently but relentlessly forward clanging as they hit the deck below. The gun layer was turning his wheel slowly, tracking the Stuka above *Illustrious* at 4 degrees a second whilst the trainer did the same to traverse the gun on its mounting. The gun captain was firing in short, 8 round bursts to allow for the smoke to dissipate so that they could see, and more importantly remain eyes-on with target. The sound as each barrel fired consecutively was deafening when mixed with the 4.7-in. main guns and the .50 calibre machine gun that barked out in its own cry in similar bursts of fire.

The pom-pom crew were trying to maintain a deflection shot on the attacking Stuka as a gentleman shoots at a high pheasant. Estimating the speed and the angle of deflection required, the bursts from the gun ended in black puffs of smoke around the aircraft as the shells exploded in the air some 1000 yards away. The water was covered in little splashes as the shrapnel splayed out in all directions from the exploding shells.

The pom-poms were hungry, firing at a rate of 120 rounds per minute the stocks of shells in the port and starboard readiness boxes were running low. The loaders were waiting expectantly by the ammunition chutes that came up from below the quarter deck flat, shouting encouragement to their runners who were bringing up the fresh ammunition. But this was not easy. The magazine that held some 7000 pom-pom shells in metal boxes was right forward in the ship and had to be manhandled all the way from below deck and along almost half the length of *Nubian* to the chutes. There were 14 rounds connected by metal clips to form a link, the total weight of each link of shells was 45lbs.

The gun must not run out of rounds, and so to conserve what ammunition remained in the readiness locker the gun captain pushed the interrupter lever on two of the pom-poms barrels, cutting down the rate of fire in doing so. But now the ammunition came, and the loaders began clipping the first round of the new link to the last link of the one being fed into the barrels. This was a crucial moment as the warheads were prone to falling off the brass shell. If that happened and the shell casing was fed into the breach it was likely to be crushed and jam the barrel. The interrupters were reset, and all four barrels were back in action.

The barrels would get very hot if a continuous rate of fire was kept up, so they were water cooled by an outer sleeve. However, the water tended to get very hot too, so hot, that the cork stoppers used for filling or draining the sleeves could be forced out by the pressure that built up, sending a jet of boiling water bursting out that would badly scold any unsuspecting ratings in the way.

Illustrious had a total of 6 pom-pom guns, all octuple barrelled to compliment her 8, 4.5-inch multipurpose guns. Pom-Pom position S2 was just forward of the island, and its crew were firing for their lives. The pile of shells in front of their gun was growing almost exponentially as round after round was pumped into the sky. Firing forward of the ship, it is quite possible the gun crew was too engrossed in their job to notice the bomb that whistled down and struck the deck close by. The explosion wrecked the gun showering splinters that cut down all those in the vicinity without mercy. Ted Whitley, who would have been on deck if 819 Squadron were recovering, headed to the S2 position to help. The carnage was acute, and he caught the eye of Captain Boyd, who motioned for him to push the bodies of the crew over the side. Boyd later wrote of this, 'One of the ships best gunners was blown to bits by a bomb which hit the pom-pom in front of the bridge. He and all the crew were just in an awful mess but were killed instantly. I ordered them to be thrown overboard as these were dreadful sights. Arms, legs, heads and trunks going over the side were awful to see but were better than lying about the deck where they chilled the stomachs of others.'[162]

In ten minutes, *Illustrious* had been struck by 6 bombs and had a Stuka crash onto the flight deck, a portion of its wing lay mangled there. Smoke and

---

[162] (Prysor, 2012)

flame were rising around her and the black mushroom cloud that had billowed from the aft lift shaft following another hit began to drift behind the listing carrier. Charles Lamb was loitering in front of the ship, observing with sadness how the ship, now listing to port, was swarming with fire control teams trailing hoses to quench the fires that were raging below. Indeed, the fires were so fierce that the decks were beginning to glow with the heat and where water from the hoses touched, it instantly turned to steam. A Reuters correspondent described what Lamb clearly saw from above. 'The deck was covered with foam from the fire extinguishers. The flight deck was covered from end to end with debris from the bomb explosion. Further forward was a twisted crane, a heap of bomb splinters and empty shell cases.'[163]

Within the ship all electrical circuits aft had been melted, the fans used to feed air to the engines were simply sucking in toxic fumes and choking smoke to the engine compartments whilst the steering gear had been wrecked. Captain Boyd was amazed at the fortitude of the Stokers who stayed at their posts despite the hideous conditions in the engine rooms with temperatures soaring to a skin blistering 140 degrees Fahrenheit. Those working below untied and tucked their shoelaces into their footwear in case they had to swim for it, that was, if they could get out. Boyd realised he had to get to grips with the steering of the ship by engine revolutions alone. For the meantime the escorting ships observed the carrier flew signal flags indicating she was out of control, Boyd wrote.

> Fear came later when I realised, we must have more attacks before reaching Malta. I then felt utterly sick for a while and trembled from head to foot. I went down to my sea cabin, took a good hold of myself, offered up a prayer that I'd do my stuff and then went back and was waggling the engines to steer her for the next 8 hours and through two more attacks without any particular feeling other than an unsatisfied

---

[163] (Galea, 2019)

desire for food. From breakfast until 10 p.m. when we secured I only had a cocoa and a biscuit.[164]

Of the last section of Fulmars to launch, Lt. Lowe piloting, with Leading Aircraftsman Kensett in the back seat had earlier engaged a pair of JU87's. The rear gunner of one Stuka managed to fire a long burst, shells clanging into the airframe and puncturing the air cooler. Lowe got off some shots of his own which found their mark and the Stuka suddenly dived for one final time into the sea. However, the second Stuka had manoeuvered behind Lowe, and now its shells began to pour into the Fulmar, one hitting Lowe in the shoulder forcing him to disengage and try to run for home. However, the damage was done. The engine quickly overheated, seized and then the prop came to an abrupt stop. There was no reply from Kensett as Lowe dead sticked the stricken Fulmar into the sea. The violence of the ditching and the pain in his shoulder clearly disabled the pilot sufficient that he struggled to extricate himself from the cockpit. Lowe had received a large calibre bullet to his shoulder and perhaps he passed out for a short while after ditching. He had in fact come down close to *Nubian* but either they were unable to break off the from their operations or they did not believe anyone had survived as the ship did not stop to pick them up. When Lowe recovered, his attention turned to Kensett. By now the rear of the aircraft had settled low into the water, so much so that the cockpit was partially submerged. Lowe managed to open the canopy but this may have hastened the sinking of the aircraft, it didn't matter, poor Kensett was dead. Lowe could not release Kensetts body in time and the aircraft disappeared silently, almost gracefully, under the gentle swell. He trod water, for some twenty minutes in the open sea no doubt feeling very alone and frightened, before the welcome sight of *Jaguar* appeared, hove to and lowered a boat to pick him up.

Charles Lamb was not out of trouble either. He noticed that the starboard lower wing had actually separated from the fuselage and was literally being held in place by the wires and struts attached to the upper wing. However, the Swordfish was still under control, and they may just make landfall. A call to

---

[164] (Prysor, 2012)

the observer to plot a course for Malta was met with the reply that he couldn't do that. "I can't he said', almost in a whisper. 'The Bigsworth Board is floating about in Petrol."[165] Lamb checked the fuel level, which meant he had to peer through a hole in the dashboard to see the gauge which was far forward on top of the engine. It was clear they were leaking fuel badly and they had to ditch.

Lamb managed to bring the Swordfish down close to *Juno,* whom he had signalled his intention to ditch using the aldis lamp, receiving an 'R' signal indicating message received. *Juno* hove to and lowered a boat in readiness to pick them up. Lamb coaxed the aircraft around behind *Juno,* praying their wing wouldn't fall off, and despite taking care to stall the aircraft just above the waves, they made quite a violent ditching. The wheels struck the water and buried the nose into the sea, so hard that the Wireless Operator and Observer (who had released their harnesses) were catapulted out of the cockpit into the sea about twenty yards ahead of the aircraft.

Lamb managed to extract the life raft from the port wing, it had partially inflated as it was supposed to do on contact with the water, but as it was stuck in its recess, it only fully inflated once freed. Lamb climbed in, then hauled aboard his crew, noticing that the dingy was still attached to the port wing by a cord as the aircraft rapidly began to sink. He quickly tore the line away from the dingy and then remembered the depth charge that was still attached to 'Queenie'. It would explode fairly shortly, they had to get away!

Juno's Coxwain and crew were not rowing particularly well so Lamb made an effort to get aboard as calmly as possible and then took charge. "…I took over from the surprised man and stood up in the stern-sheets and said: 'Come on, row you silly buggers – pull together – in-out-in-out-in-out-one-two-pull together-in-out…' and I kept it up, all the way back, until we were under the scrambling net dangling over the ships side."[166]

---

[165] (Lamb, 2001)
[166] (Lamb, 2001)

With some composure, Lamb got all the whalers crew onto the scrambling net before he made a jump for it. 'The gallant old aircraft had held on for as long as she could, but her final death-throes erupted as I climbed up the net. I felt the ship heel over with the shock, and the ear-splitting cacophony behind me pushed me flat against the steel hull. Over my shoulder I saw a huge mountain of water cascading into the air, much too close for comfort.'[167]

Cease Fire! Cease Fire! Cease Fire!, came the order to all *Nubians* gun crews. The comparative silence following the intense firing in support of *Illustrious* was almost as overwhelming as the noise had been. The drone of the Stukas as they headed back to their bases slowly faded. For a moment the whole crew were silent, some removed their helmets and wiped their foreheads of sweat, exhaling through puffed cheeks. On the bridge there were exchanged glances of relief and an unspoken appreciation that this was Norway revisited in spades. The black crosses on the undersides of the swooping JU-87s had not gone un-noticed. Binoculars were trained on the stricken carrier whose magnified image shook in the eyepieces as the adrenaline found its way to the hands of those holding the optics. Smoke and flame were evident, as were the men on deck dealing with the fires and attending to the wounded or the dead. *Illustrious* was listing and clearly not in control, a similar but different perspective than the one that Charles Lamb had from his high vantage point.

Ravenhill broke the silence. 'They will return. We need to be ready.' With that he began to issue orders to ensure that *Nubian* would be prepared. The gun crews began to clear the spent shells that rolled around the deck and threatened to turn an unsuspecting ankle. Many were just kicked over the side, some were gathered up by the ship's boys in large wicker baskets. Replacement ammunition was brought up from below and before long the ready lockers were full once more. More sandwiches appeared and were gratefully washed down with tea or water. It had taken less than fifteen minutes for the Stukas to have stamped their authority, but it had seemed like an hour.

---

[167] (Lamb, 2001)

The engagement of *Illustrious* was the first of what would be many setbacks until the Afrika Korps finally surrendered to the Allies in May 1943. There would be victories, but for now this was the beginning of some dark and relentless days in the Mediterranean. Of the deployment of *Illustrious*, there have, as stated earlier, been many critics of Cunningham, but perhaps none more measured than that of Adrian Holloway, and his comparison of the latter stages of 'Excess' with the Falklands conflict many years later.

'With the benefit of hindsight and the events of the Falklands war, the question should be posed as to why Cunningham placed our only modern aircraft carrier in such jeopardy. For by placing her in such jeopardy, he also endangered the fleet. Down in the Falkland's, the carriers' role had been learned and they kept out of range of enemy aircraft whilst at the same time providing a CAP for the rest of the Task Force. Cunningham, a brilliant surface admiral, knew nothing of the air, and like so many of his contemporaries looked down on the Fleet Air Arm as a rather common necessity forced upon him.

Agreed, the Mediterranean is in no way comparable to the South Atlantic. The former is landlocked, the latter wide open. But even if Cunningham had anticipated an attack by Italian capital ships he should have kept *Illustrious* separate from the main body. He could have interposed the battle-fleet between her position and the Italian mainland from which an enemy sortie might have come. Perhaps he had been lulled into a false sense of security by only having the Italians with which to deal. The arrival of Fliegerkorps X and their aircraft changed the whole ball game.'[168]

On the 'ground', so to speak, whilst possibly a broad-brush perspective, it is hard to dismiss that the thoughts of Marine Arthur Jones, of the Royal Marines aboard Warspite, were perhaps representative of the fleet.

There were plenty of near misses and somehow, we were lucky, but it was very wearing. You looked at what happened to the *Illustrious* and

---

[168] (Holloway, 1993)

wondered how long it might be until it happened to you. Everybody became a bit bomb happy. In fact we were getting so ragged on *Warspite* it became a punishable offence to slam a hatch because it jarred the nerves so much.[169]

Boyd signalled that his intention was to take *Illustrious* with all speed into Malta. He had his work cut out to do so. Problem after problem confronted him and his team. Most serious was the advice that the magazines should be flooded. This would have truly made the great ship impotent and so Boyd decided not to do so. It was a risk, but the ship must be able to defend herself from any further attack.

That attack came at around 16:00. Whilst the Stukas were re-arming the Regina Aeronautica made a softening attack from upon high, 12,000 feet to be more precise. The bombs fell predictably short and inaccurately, simply killing fish, not ships. The Fulmars had also been re-arming on Malta, and despite being unfamiliar to the ground crews at Hal Far, they returned to the fray along with the few Hurricanes that were available. In the meantime, some 25 Stukas returned, and battle was re-joined.

Once again *Illustrious* was targeted, one Stuka managing to get through the barrage and deliver yet another bomb onto the deck of the carrier. The Germans had hoped that four bombs would sink 'Lusty', they had delivered seven so far, but she still swam. *Warspite* and *Valiant* had been the attention of two Ketten apiece, the intensity of their defence and that, no doubt similar aboard the destroyers was described by Adrian Holloway. 'Every time there was a lull, men came up on the turret top, festooned with 'necklaces' of ammunition, whilst we literally waded about amongst the spent shells.'[170]

---

[169] (Ballantyne, 2001, 2013, 2014)
[170] (Holloway, 1993)

On *Warspite*, Admiral Cunningham found himself a reluctant spectator, with heart firmly in his mouth as the Stukas once more attempted to deliver the coup de grace.

> My heart sank as I watched her, wondering how with all her heavy damage, she would stand up to it. I need not have worried. As the attacks developed, I saw every gun in the *Illustrious* flash into action, a grand and inspiring sight. Moreover, her Fulmar fighters, which had flown onto Malta when their parent ship was damaged, had refuelled and come out again.[171]

The Fulmars and Hurricanes were not in time to prevent the attack, but they had some success shooting down two of the returning Italian SM.79's and a further 6 Stukas claimed 'down'. As the day came to a close, *Illustrious* gradually approached Malta. Lt. Vincent-Jones, who was in the rear seat of one of the Fulmars of 806 Squadron wrote, 'Ammunition expended, we returned to Hal Far and as we flew in over the coastline, I got a glimpse of poor old *Illustrious* rounding the point only a few miles from the entrance to the Grand harbour of Valletta. Smoke was still pouring out of her hull.'[172]

At around 21:45 *Illustrious* limped into the Grand Harbour, listing badly where she was gently secured alongside the dock. Gathered alongside the dock there formed a long, sad looking queue of ambulances and volunteers to take off the butcher's bill. 91 wounded bound for hospitalisation and 126 killed, they would be buried at sea over the coming days. She may be down, but she was not totally out, yet. She may have reached Malta, but she remained in range of the Stukas and in her present condition, a large, stationary target. If she were to survive, she required urgent maintenance to make her seaworthy, and thus a means of getting her back to Alexandria and then onto America for repairs.

---

[171] (Cunningham, 1951)
[172] (Galea, 2019)

Meanwhile, the violent, high-speed manoeuvers that *Nubian* had undertaken in order to protect the fleet had not come without a price. Spent of much ammunition with a worn-out crew, her fuel status was now of some concern. She had to break off from Force A, as did *Juno*, and escort the remaining 3 ships of 'Excess' Convoy at what was a more sedate and ultimately fuel-efficient pace to Pireaus arriving there on the 12th. *Mohawk* towed what remained of *Gallant*, stern first into harbour in the early hours of the 11th. *Gallant* was beached and was gradually repaired over the coming months, but the following year she was damaged in another air aid after which she was written off before being towed out to St Pauls Islands and sunk as a blockship in 1943.

The 11th was to be another day of significant loss. *Mohawk* and *Griffin* came out of Valetta at 05:00, escorting the cruisers *Southampton* and *Gloucester* in order to rejoin the main fleet. In the afternoon they were surprised by the Stukas of Fliegerkorps X led by Major Enneccerus. A 500lb bomb hit the roof of *Gloucester's* Director Control Tower and then penetrated through 5 deck levels before coming to rest in the ships Met Office. Mercifully it failed to explode, but on its way, it had killed a Royal Marine Bandsman, 'Sticks' O'leary. The sinister object was taken on deck, where a young NAAFI assistant named William Black straddled the bomb to prevent it rolling around the deck, before it was thrown overboard.[173]

Southampton was not so fortunate. She was hit by incendiary devices, and before long she was ablaze. The timing of the bombing coincided with a stand down period and many of her officers were present in the wardroom which received a direct hit. As the fires took hold, *Gloucester* and the *Diamond* attempted to come to the aid of the sailors who were rapidly losing the fight to contain the fires and there were many who were trapped below decks. Telegraphist Richard Garner wrote, 'It was one of my worst experiences in the Royal Navy. I shall never, never forget seeing *Southampton* a mass of flames.

---

[173] (Otter, 2017)

We were trying to get alongside her to take off survivors when I heard the screams of men trapped down below, banging on the ship's hull.'[174]

To get some idea of the horror of the situation, G. G. Conell describes the sheer helplessness of one who is above decks with men trapped below in 'Mediterranean Malestrom', when he describes the flooding of HMS *Jervis* after she had been struck by a merchantman.

A quick muster told us that five stokers were missing, and we probed the dark waters that were rising in our mess deck for signs of life. The waters were three-quarters of the way up the bulkhead when we heard Micky shout for help. His Irish voice entreated us from the dark depths and drove us frantic at our inability to succour him. The water was only one foot from the hatch when he began to scream; it was then they closed the hatch to keep the sea at bay. I could still hear him when the officer ordered us aft.[175]

What wounded could be brought aboard were laid on the upper flats (decks). Another Telegraphist, Maurice Conquest noted with sadness; 'I was very distressed by the sight of so many men lying around with their faces blackened from the horrendous burns they had sustained.'

At about 19:00 it was becoming clear that *Southampton* could not be saved, and so *Gloucester* and *Orion* stood off at a safe distance, to finish the stricken ship with torpedoes. As Hugh Mulleneux of *Jervis* described, *Southampton's* end was dramatic; 'We arrived, about 200 miles east of Malta, at 21:30 and found *Southampton* blazing and abandoned with *Gloucester* and *Diamond* in attendance. When we arrived, *Diamond* had taken off all the survivors and transferred them to *Gloucester*. We circled round while *Orion* finished *Southampton* off with a torpedo. The fire had got such a hold that any hope of saving the ship had to be abandoned. She blew up with a simply gigantic

---

[174] (Otter, 2017)
[175] (Connell, 1987)

explosion which if it hadn't been so tragic, must have been the best display of fireworks on record, a truly Wagnerian funeral.'[176]

The fleet was back in Alexandria on the 13 January but without their carrier. However, Cunningham had by now received news that *Illustrious* would be replaced by her sister ship, *Formidable*, en route from the Atlantic via the Suez Canal, although she would not be expected on station until March at the earliest. On land, Operation Compass was in full flow and plans were afoot to take Tobruk on the 20th. Therefore, D14 had little time to re supply before heading out once more on the 17 January. It may have seemed a blessing as the harbour could be particularly inhospitable at this time of year. 'In Scapa Flow they had mist and fog. In Alexandria we had sandstorms. The sand blanketed the harbour, swirling around and around for hours. It was impossible to see even the ships moored nearby, and the melancholy sound of their bells ran out across the harbour.'[177]

The Mediterranean Sea, whilst often benign, can throw some awful conditions from time to time, this was one of those times, perhaps going to sea was not preferable to Alexandria! High winds not only created huge seas that battered and buffeted the ships, but they also whipped the sand from the North African coast into a stinging curtain of a blinding sandstorm with visibility reduced to zero. The signal from *Orion* was made by ship-to-ship radio, Ravenhill was required to take *Nubian* closer in shore to stand by *Aphis*, which was having difficulties in the conditions. Indeed, they all were, and the bombardment of Tobruk had to be postponed until the 22nd, when *Ladybird* and *Terror* supported the Australians advancing on Tobruk with sea based artillery fire. The weather did not improve and the ships of D14 retired to Suda bay to refuel before returning to Alexandria, being tasked to intercept and escort *Illustrious* out of Malta on the way.

Making a good 25 knots *Illustrious* had slipped away from Malta on the 23rd and quickly gathered speed giving the slip to her cruiser escort (Force B)

---

[176] (Connell, 1987)
[177177] (Holloway, 1993)

who had not expected her to make such a good turn of foot. *Nubian* and *Mohawk* were part of Force C, which included *Barham* and *Valiant*, that came out to provide further cover. The large black smoke trail was the first sign of her on the horizon and as her form became more defined there appeared little outward sign that she was badly damaged, inside was a different matter though.

In Alexandria, *Warspite's* band was on deck to play her in, the officers and men of all the ships in the harbour came on deck to cheer and wave whilst the ships sirens sounded, creating a huge wall of sound to welcome the carrier home. It had been a trying time in Malta for the carrier as she had come under constant attack whilst the Maltese dock hands tried to make her ready for an escape. This time came to be known as the 'Illustrious Blitz', and whilst she was hit once, and had several near misses, the Stukas could not finish the job. The toll on their crews had been equally distressing, as Lieutenant Colonel Paul Werner Hozzel recounted for Charles Lamb. They had been ordered by Goring to sink *Illustrious* in Valetta harbour, and they had come up against the furious fire from the ground and air defences.

> So began the heavy missions against La Valetta. We had no losses during the attacks at sea. We now lost our best crews in the following attacks. When I rose in the morning, I knew with certainty that by the sinking sun, some five of six crews would have gone. One day, after the last mission, the leader of my 2nd squadron, who was a very hard chap, could not report to me for tears: he was the last of his squadron, all his old chaps he lost.[178]

Charles Lamb re-boarded *Illustrious* on her arrival and went below eager to inspect the damage for himself. What he found shook him badly, and was much worse than he had ever expected.

> She had been such a beautiful ship inside, with quiet passages and neat cabins, nicely furnished. The hangar had always been the showpiece of

---

[178] (Lamb, 2001)

the ship and the squadrons had vied with each other to keep it spotless. Now it was no longer there. There was no trace of its deck – just a gaping void surrounded by grey tangled metal, and the ships sides visible to a height of some fifty or sixty feet. Wherever one looked there were the signs of violent death in an open space of twisted disorder. I took one fearful look and fled.[179]

Despite the extensive damage, 'Lusty' would return to action in the spring of 1942, the fact that she was still afloat was a testament to her design and build quality that did not go unnoticed, not the least by the C-in-C of the East Mediterranean fleet. But she was deeply wounded. *Gloucester* needed repairs whilst poor *Southampton* was now scattered over the seabed. The effectiveness of the German Stukas and their threat to continued sea operations effectively handed air superiority back to the Axis powers. It was a depressing thought.

For the actions in January, *Nubian* was awarded the Battle honour: MALTA CONVOYs 1941.

Ravenhill called down to the engine room, 'Finish with main engines.' Soon after, *Nubian* fell silent and ceased to vibrate. The beginning of a two-week refit program which would give the officers and men some time away from an almost relentless period of active service. Some of the officers would find digs ashore, whilst the remainder of the crew lived aboard. It would not be a bed of roses though. Air raids continued which meant a state of readiness had to be maintained but for some, the tiredness was overwhelming, and those that were not on watch soon found they slept through the night time raids.

Receiving of mail, and an opportunity to write home now presented itself and it can be hard to recall, or for some to imagine, a time before mobile communications and internet video calling that gives us such instant access to loved ones in far off countries, common place in modern times. However, even in a time of global conflict in the 1940's the mail did get through, and

---

[179] (Lamb, 2001)

there were developments to rationalise what was becoming a service that was hard to fulfil.

As we have seen, the buildup of Naval personnel grew during 1940 with the deployment of an ever-increasing number of ships joining the Eastern Mediterranean fleet. Then there came the deployment of troops in preparation for Operation Compass. Notwithstanding the combat ready servicemen there were support and logistical staff as well as a growing number of civilians converging on Alexandria and the Middle East. The demand on the mail service increased, especially as both service men and women and their loved ones back home, were encouraged to write as often as they could to maintain morale.

If the direct route across the Mediterranean between Gibraltar and Alexandria was effectively cut off, then the only route left was by sea via the Cape of Good Hope and the Suez Canal. Notwithstanding the distance, the volume and weight of the mail prohibited any faster means of getting it through. The passenger and freight aircraft of the time were simply not large enough, and there were not enough of them. Indeed, pilots were required for fighting ahead of delivering mail. Delivery times began to range from between 3 and 6 months.

'Airgraph' was the key. Introduced during April 1941 (in America a similar system was introduced called V-Mail, or Victory Mail) it used a Kodak developed system that was comprised of a standardised form that would accommodate a letter of 100 to 200 words. This was photographed and reduced to a negative, known as compression in today's digital photographic terminology. Letters could be miniaturised into a format (microfilm) that was incredibly light and of little volume which meant that thousands of letters could easily be transported by one aircraft rather than a few hundred. At the receiving end, they were developed to about a quarter of their original size and then passed onto their recipients. The British Overseas Aircraft Corporation (BOAC) began to use their flying boat services to deliver the mail into Western

Africa, and then forward onto Egypt for delivery to the armed forces and of course as a reciprocal service.

A downside to this form of communication was loss of privacy. The forms could not be folded and so any letters were open to scrutiny by those who handled them prior to being photographed. This would certainly curtail some of the more private written conversations that may have occurred in the traditional sealed letter, but one must not forget that censorship of letters at this time was a necessary evil. The letters written home by the service personnel could not contain any information that may compromise operations, deployments, military or civil information that may aid the purposes of the enemy. Therefore, it usually fell to a ships Chaplin, one of the senior officers, or the Educational Officer ('Schoolie') on larger warships, to read the mail and censor as appropriate. A most unpopular job.

With *Nubian* in dock and her crew trying to relax or write letters home, it is appropriate to review the current political and strategic situation. On the 29 January 1941, General Metaxus, the Greek Dictator and ally to Great Britain passed away. He was replaced by Alexander Korizis, who had been governor of the Bank of Greece. He was sworn into office by King George VI and almost immediately requested military assistance should the German Army invade. This provided Churchill with an opportunity to re-enter the war in Europe, despite all the protestations to the contrary from his military leaders and advisers. The forcefulness of Churchill's conviction is illustrated by Correlli Barnett in 'The Desert Generals.'

> 'On 11 February 1941, General Dill, the Chief of the Imperial General Staff, told Churchill that all troops in the Middle East were fully occupied and none was available for Greece. Churchill replied: 'What you need out there is a Court Martial and a firing squad…"[180]

On the 7 February, the forces under General O'Connor had effectively annihilated the Italians at Beda Fomm, and were poised, despite very long and

---

[180] (Barnett, 1983)

stretched supply lines, to kick the Axis forces out of North Africa through Tripoli. This was not to be. Rommel and the Afrika Korps arrived on the 12 February and the following day, O'Connor was ordered to cease further offensive operations and to disband his fighting forces for re-deployment to Greece.

For General Wavell, in overall command of the British forces in North Africa, this was a headache he could do without. He had to be mindful to provide sufficient fighting forces for offensives in Greece whilst retaining enough strength to counter any advance by the Germans out of Tripoli. He considered that as it would take some time for Rommel to build up his forces for an offensive, his armoured defence could remain relatively weak for the time being. As for air cover, there really was none. Everything was stretched far too thin, and the writing was on the wall for those who could see it.

An inability to stifle German Air operations was concerning Admiral Cunningham too. The concern had always been that the Germans would attempt to block the Suez Canal and cut off the supply lines to Alexandria from the south. The dropping of Magnetic Mines into the canal began on the 30 January, by the 7 February there had been some 16 magnetic mines discovered and dealt with, regrettably there had been casualties in the process. No doubt these were not the only mines lurking in the canal, so efforts were stepped up to find and neutralise these too. Cunningham received the grim news that it may not be until the 18th that the canal would re-open, and then only to ships no larger than 15,000 tons. In real terms, that meant neither *Illustrious*, due to depart for repair in the U.S.A, or *Eagle*, being redeployed to the Far East, could sail. More importantly, *Formidable* was now languishing uselessly in the Red Sea. It would not be until 10 March that *Formidable* would reach Alexandria.

Of the wider military situation, Cunningham succinctly outlines this in 'A Sailors' Odyssey'.

There has been much discussion and controversy as to whether we were right or wrong in sending troops to Greece. We, the naval element, thought roughly as follows. We were bound by treaty to help Greece if she were threatened, so there was no question at all that it was, politically, the right thing to do. On the other hand, we had serious misgivings if it was correct from the military point of view. We doubted very much if our Naval, Military and Air resources were equal to it. No doubt our opinions were somewhat influenced by the fact that we were in possession of the Libyan coast as far west as Benghazi. From the Navy's point of view this facilitated the supply of Malta and the passage through the Sicilian Narrows, and conditions would be better still if the advance were continued towards Tripolitania. We had no illusions that the help we could send the Greeks would enable them to stem a really serious German invasion. Indeed, when the decision to send troops was finally taken, we started at once to think of how we should bring them out.[181]

That last sentence is most enlightening. It was to prove most fortuitous that Cunningham and his staff were preparing for the worst. Almost as soon as the troops were deployed in Greece in early March, they were being pulled out again. Before we reach that point, there are sea battles to fight.

A new Surgeon for *Nubian*.

At Catania airfield, the twin engine JU88's of Lehrgeschwader 1 (LG.1) belonging to Fliegerkorps X had been in country since their arrival from France on the 26 December. Their initial action had been over Malta as components of the Illustrious Blitz, and they had lost aircraft and crews in the process. They had also endured serval bombing raids on their airfield by Wellington's out of Hal Far.

Within LG.1 there were 5 Gruppe, identified by a roman numeral, each Gruppe, had 3 Staffel (Squadrons) which at maximum strength (although this was rarely achieved) consisted of 12 aircraft. LG.1 had started life as a training

---

[181] (Cunningham, 1951)

and tactical evaluation wing, with each Gruppe equipped with different aircraft types There were two bomber Gruppe, a fighter Gruppe one with Zestorer aircraft (ME110) and one with Dive Bombers, which would either be JU87 or JU88 aircraft.

II/LG.1 and III/LG.1 had been assigned the twin engine JU88 for use as medium level and dive-bombing operations. With the arrival of German units into North Africa these two Gruppe began harassment missions along the coast, targeting British positions and supply lines, notably the port of Benghazi where the delivery of supplies was being brought in by convoy. On the 18 February the crew of one of the JU88's noted two large warships in Benghazi and reported their presence on return. One of these was HMS *Terror* the other *Coventry*.

As we have seen, *Terror*, along with *Ladybird* and *Aphis* had been supporting the rolling back of the Italian forces during Operation Compass as part of the Inshore Squadron. *Terror*, in particular, with her twin 15-in. guns had been providing offshore H.E. artillery throughout the operation as well as water supplies for the advancing troops. She had expended some 500 tons of explosives at Tobruk and 600 tons at Benghazi, now her barrels were in a sorry condition and the rifling was all but worn away reducing her accuracy of fire considerably. Her role was thus being reduced to an Anti-Aircraft platform. Despite being a 25-year-old ship and an odd looking one at that, (she was known in the Navy as 'Old Flat Iron' as that was exactly what her profile looked like), *Terror* had outperformed expectation, which had not gone unnoticed by German High Command, and they ordered her to be sunk. They could not risk having her following them back up the coast and harassing their every move.

On the 22 February, Surgeon Lieutenant Edward Benson McDowall R.N.V.R. was in a thoughtful mood. He had just finished talking to his Commanding Officer, Commander Henry Haynes who had requested some pain relief for his lumbago, that had almost seen an end to his career in the 1930's. Haynes was 48 years old and had been in the Navy since he was 13, attending Britannia and then Dartmouth. He had been a Lieutenant in World War 1 and received a D.S.C. in 1918 for services in destroyers. He had commanded the V-class Destroyer *Vanquisher* between the wars, during which he took the blame, but with no more than a caution, for a collision with *Campbell*. In 1938, with the war looming, he had requested retirement, but this had been refused and he ended up as CO of *Terror*.

McDowall was pleased that his Commander had come to him to talk about his problem and been quite open in their discussion. He was concerned that they may be attacked from the air that morning, as the Germans had attempted to do so 3 days earlier when 5, JU88s from III/LG.1 had dive bombed them without scoring a hit. The AA gunnery from *Terror* and a single Hurricane had managed to beat them off, but they would be back. He was also mindful that his crew were tired and worn out. They needed a rest like everyone else. McDowall could see that too, and he was beginning to make notes on the behaviour of the men. His particular interest was how they maintained their morale, as well as their composure under the stresses of combat. He would later write, 'The strain of a sea fight leaves its immediate mark on the crew, they are keyed up, more emotional; they become talkative, irritable, boastful, quarrelsome and are given to harmless exaggeration, merry drinking, and easy laughter. Furious arguments, maddening remarks, petty annoyances sweep the wardroom.'[182] Just a few days before, *Coventry* had left Benghazi, almost as soon as she had arrived. On departure, *Terrors* crew had jeered at *Coventry*, 'Windy, can't take it' amid much laughter.[183]

It was not long before the Commander was proved correct. The alarm for an air attack came over the tannoy, followed by the thumping of many boots as the gun crews went to their action stations. McDowall began to prepare the sick berth to receive any wounded whilst the ships guns roared as they opened up on the JU88s, this time from II Gruppe. In the next moment there came two enormous explosions that felt as if they lifted the old monitor out of the water. McDowall's medicine bottles jangled in their cabinet, and then the door

---

[182] (Moran, 2007)
[183] (Moran, 2007)

popped open spilling several onto the linoleum floor, where they shattered on impact.

On the bridge, Commander Haynes had ducked instinctively as the stick of bombs had straddled his ship. Great plumes of water shot up either side, towering over them before depositing themselves on the deck. It had been such a shock that he hardly registered the noise. In the next few minutes, damage control parties were reporting flooding in several compartments, it appeared the bombs had missed *Terror*, but only just. As a result, her hull plates were compromised, and she was taking on water. It was very clear that *Terror* was a priority target.

With the situation under control, Haynes spoke with his leading signalman. 'Make to C-in-C from Commanding Officer, *Terror*. Near miss by two 500lb H.E. bombs, ship taking on water in number of compartments. Request air cover with immediate effect. I consider it only a matter of time before the ship receives a direct hit.'

Cunningham could not provide air cover, there simply wasn't any. However, he did appreciate the danger that his ships were now in and had to take the difficult decision to withdraw all of his assets in Benghazi. If they could not be protected, then they had to be extracted. The army were being left to defend the port themselves, and to make matters worse for them, their Anti-Aircraft batteries had been removed for use in Greece.

The following morning, *Terror* sailed from Benghazi escorted by the *Hunt* Class minesweeper *Fareham*, and the Flower Class Corvette, *Salvia*. As they progressed down the channel, *Terror* triggered the detonation of two magnetic mines, fortunately they were at a safe enough distance not to cause major structural damage, but their explosive force hastened the flooding. Hugging the coast she had to be taken in tow and the majority of the crew, including McDowall, were transferred to *Fareham* and *Salvia*. In Alexandria, Ravenhill received orders to make all speed to assist *Terror* by escorting her back to the safety of port.

Progress was slow, but by 18:22 *Terror* was 15 miles off Derna, *Nubian* was still some way off but travelling at all haste to assist. They would not make it. From 10,000ft five green and black camouflaged JU88's of III/LG.1 spotted *Terror* and attacked.

> Terror immediately opened controlled fire at the centre bomber and was attacked by four aircraft. The firing was accurate, speed was increased to full, and as the planes commenced their dive course was altered to starboard. The 4-in. guns were put into long range and the Breda guns opened fire. Three machines attacked from different bearings on the starboard side, the fourth made an almost vertical dive from overhead; its bombs fell wide. Each aircraft released three bombs. One stick fell about 200 yds. on the port bow, another over the port beam and the third stick fell very close to the starboard side. The last bomb of this stick fell just alongside the bridge; the explosion was violent and appeared to lift the ship at least a foot.[184]

Luck had appeared to be on the big ships side, but this time the proximity of the explosion tore at the hull plates to an extent that the damage control parties could not contain the flooding. Haynes listened gravely to the damage reports and realised that the ship would founder. It was the end for the 'Old Flat Iron'. Water had poured into the engineering spaces and extinguished her fires. All steam power was lost which subsequently killed her pumps. The engineering crew quickly realised that they would not be able to raise steam once more, and with that all hope was lost.

> At 2330 it was decided to abandon ship. In order to increase the rate of sinkage so that escort vessels could be well clear of the position by daylight, the Commanding Officer ordered depth charges set at 50' to be dropped as close as possible to the starboard side.

---

[184] (Admiralty, 1941)

Terror turned slowly over to starboard, capsized and sank at 04:15.[185]

In August Haynes would receive a D.S.O, whilst there were 11 of the crew awarded a D.S.C, and a further 15 Mentioned in Despatches; 'For courage, skill and devotion to duty in operations off the Libyan coast'. In 1943, Haynes was retired from the service due to his age with the rank of Captain.

McDowall alighted in Alexandria and was almost immediately given a new posting. He was to report to Commander Ravenhill as Surgeon Lieutenant aboard His Majesty's Destroyer, *Nubian*. These two postings, *Terror* and *Nubian*, would provide McDowall close contact with men under combat conditions. Their reactions and in particular their ability to maintain their composure and morale under fire would lead him to publish a paper that, according to the *'The Naval Review'*, Vol. LIII No. 1 January, 1965[186] was confidentially issued to all ships in the Mediterranean Fleet in 1942 as a Battle Order. The paper was also referenced by Lord Moran in his book, 'The Anatomy of Courage', first published in 1945.

Perhaps for Commander Ravenhill, this was a time that his resolve was shaken. He had been in command of *Nubian* for over two years, responsible for the ship and the conduct of his crew in all manner of stressful situations, under duress from almost constant high and low level bombing every time his ship left any port. He would not have been alone in the ships company to feel the strain, and the news that HMS *Exmoor* had been sunk by E-Boats in the north sea on the 25 February, and that their former XO and then Captain of that ship, Robert Lampard was missing presumed dead. It would have hit them hard. *Nubian* had been a lucky ship, so far, how much longer though, before it was their turn?

---

[185] (Admiralty, 1941)
[186] (Koppes, 2006)

General Adrian Carton De Wiart

Admiral "ABC" Cunningham

HMS Formidable

Fairey Albacore's being readied for a mission aboard Formidable

Captain Philip J. Mack leaving HMS Jervis for the last time.

Tribal Destroyer HMS Nubian.

Chapter 11

The Battle of Matapan 27 – 29 March 1941

RADAR

There were many factors that led to what was a resounding victory at the Battle of Matapan for the Royal Navy. One of these was the utilisation of Radio Direction Finding (RDF) as it was originally called, or RADAR (Radio and Direction Finding, which became the recognised acronym) as the Americans called the detection of land or man-made objects using radio waves.

Lord Lewin, in his foreword to Derek Howes book, 'Radar at Sea' describes how the basic rule of seamanship relied on the three Ls, Lookout, Log and Leadline. That basically means a good seaman should know exactly where he is (and has been) as well as the depth of water he has between the bottom of his ship and the seabed. He says, '…even so the most experienced navigator could miss an important discovery just out of sight over the horizon or come to disaster on an unknown coast in fog, while in war whole fleets could pass in the night, each unaware of the other's proximity. The outcome of the Battle of Jutland, the last great battle-fleet action, depended on visibility.'[187] The advent of RADAR changed all of that. Indeed, Howse, in the preface of his book, echo's the words of Commodore Deny (Chief of Staff to the Home Fleet), that he made in 1943 when saying. 'There is no doubt that the development of radar during the short period from 1938 to 1945 had a greater impact on naval warfare than any other development since steam replaced sail.'[188]

So, what is RADAR? Howes describes the system in the simplest terms.

Radar is the electronic system that uses radio waves to detect objects that may be invisible to the naked eye because of distance, darkness and

---

[187] (Howse, 1993)
[188] (Howse, 1993)

cloud. Radar can also determine the position of an object, its distance from the observing station – on land, sea, or in the air – and, of the object is moving, its speed and direction of travel.[189]

The main components of a radar system are the radio transmitter and an associated mechanism to generate the wave pulse. An aerial (or antenna as it is commonly called today) to transmit and receive the pulses, this may be fixed or moveable in order to direct the beams at a specific target. Finally, a receiver that is connected to some form of display to provide the operator with the results of the radar 'sweep'.

The greater the wavelength used, the larger the aerial is a basic rule of thumb. This is coupled with the power used to generate the waves, therefore the greater the power, the greater the range of the system. This posed several challenges for the use of radar in ships. On land, the RAF developed the Chain Home system of radar stations around the coast of Britain. These were large complexes with tall masts that had the luxury of almost unlimited power sources to give the ranges required for the system to be effective. On a ship, the conditions are much different, the antennas have to be small enough for practical installation and there are limited power sources available on-board ship.

The operational uses of radar differed between the two services as well. The RAF needed 'bigger', longer range systems for fighter interception purposes. It takes some time to scramble an aircraft, get it airborne and in position to intercept any incoming enemy strikes, so the further out the enemy can be detected the more time is available for positioning the defences. On a ship, it takes just a few minutes to come to action stations and close up a gun to a state of readiness, so the distance required in time to achieve this came down quite considerably.

In August 1935 the Admiralty instructed the HM Signal School, responsible for all radio and wireless equipment development, to begin work as soon as possible on the radar detection of aircraft, suitable for installation in His Majesty's ships. By July 1936 an installation at Eastney Fort East, on the grounds of the Royal Marines barracks overlooking Spithead had begun

---

[189] (Howse, 1993)

testing and trials of what was designated the Type 79 set, simply named because within the Signal School this was the next number due to be allocated to a new wireless set.

The initial requirements were very rough as this was a totally new development. The outline specification was a warning approach of 60 nautical miles for aircraft and 10 nautical miles for shipping with a precision fix of 10 nautical miles for aircraft and 5 nautical miles for shipping.

For the first two years, progress was slow, but development accelerated in the two years before the outbreak of World War 2 when new ships (such as *Valiant, Illustrious* and *Formidable*) and those ships scheduled for a refit had Type 79 Radar sets installed. The Type 79 was a Ship to Aircraft device (SA), however once integrated with the Army's GL (Gun Layer) Mk I ranging radar its effectivity was increased to an accuracy of 50 yards at 14,000 yards, but its bearing accuracy was $+/.10°$. This version was designated the Type 279 and was soon fitted as standard on warships as an SS (Ship to Ship) system albeit a stop gap for a true Ship to Ship system.

Work on the type 281, a specific SS design began with three principal requirements. It would have a long range (early) warning capability, and an Anti-Aircraft (AA) range finder which could be slaved via Fire Control to the main guns, but it would not handle both operations simultaneously. For the fire control of the main armament, the indicated range from the radar system could be fed into the Fire Control Table, rather than using the 'True' range that came from the Director Control Tower optics. Finally, it incorporated 'Beam-switching' which was a method of verifying the bearing in a similar manner to triangulation by rapidly switching the direction of the beam onto the target. This improved the accuracy of the bearing down to $+/.^1/_2°$.

The fitting of radar in ships was initially prioritised to battleships and cruisers in particular as their role as a shadowing force was best suited to the use of radar for keeping a close contact with, but out of sight of enemy forces. There was a need though, to install radar in smaller vessels, destroyers in particular and so the ASV (Air to Surface Vessel) 286 & 286M radar, that was used in aircraft, was adopted. The disadvantage here was that the aerial was 'fixed' and forward facing. It was housed in a rectangular frame that gave an arc of coverage down the Port and Starboard side of the ship to somewhere near abaft (before the stern). This meant that when a target was located the ship would have to steer towards it to maintain contact.

As we have already seen, the use of radar revolutionised the operations of carrier born aircraft. Fighter Direction was indeed in its infancy, and two forms of Fighter Direction came into being. The 'Informative' method, which *Illustrious* used when working up in the Bahamas, relied on position reports from the screening ships that provided by wireless (morse), the estimated location, height and direction of an attacking force. The Controller, who was based on the bridge of the ship near the w/t office, would then plot the contacts onto a Bigsworth board before relaying the information to the wireless operators aboard the fighters, again in morse. The fighter's observer would then plot and pass the intercept course to the pilot.

With the introduction of radar, the 'Directive' method was adopted where the Fighter Director could now plot the positions of both his own fighters and the enemy aircraft. He could provide the observer with a course and speed at which to intercept the enemy, and sometimes even the height at which they were operating, reducing the cockpit workload which is vital in fast moving and stressful situations when in the air and especially in combat.

So, the radar situation at the beginning of 1941 in the eastern Mediterranean was as follows, *Valiant, Illustrious*[190], *Ajax & Coventry* were equipped with 279 radar, as was *Formidable* that joined the fleet in March. *Carlisle* had a 280 set (shorter wavelength than the 281), whilst *Berwick, Orion, Manchester* and a few Destroyers had the 286M.[191]

As for the Italians. They had not developed or adopted radar in their warships. It would be their undoing during Matapan.

---

[190] The 279 radar aboard *Illustrious* was transferred to *Gloucester* before she left for repairs in America
[191] (Howse, 1993)

Lustre

Operation 'Lustre' was the name given to the transportation of men and equipment from the Northern ports of Egypt to Greece, the convoys being given the prefix of AG (Alexandria to Greece and GA, Greece to Alexandria) and numbered consecutively. The outline of the plan was detailed in a despatch from Admiral Cunningham and sent to the Admiralty in December 1941. It was published by the London Gazette in May 1948. The opening paragraphs cannot be bettered and provide a backdrop to events that led to the Battle of Matapan, possibly the last great sea battle since Trafalgar.

Be pleased to lay before Their Lordships the following report concerning Operation 'Lustre' the move to Greece of some 58,000 troops with their mechanical transport, full equipment and stores. The operation commenced on 4 March and ceased on 24 April when the evacuation from Greece commenced.

The operation was carried out in accordance with the outlines contained in the Commander-in-Chief's Operation and Order and, in general, went according to plan.

The passage from Egyptian ports to the Piraeus, virtually the only port of the country, led past the enemy bases in the Dodecanese from which his air and sea forces were in a good position to operate against our lines of communication. Cover had also to be provided against interference from enemy surface forces from Italy. In consequence it was desirable to move as many personnel as possible in warships whose high speed would take them quickly though the danger zone. In the event the movement of personnel in H.M. Ships became a necessity owing to the mining of the Suez Canal which prevented sufficient troopships being available.

This policy proved successful and during the whole period of this complicated operation no men or equipment were lost at sea – except for a few casualties from bomb splinters in one merchant ship. The losses sustained were either in ships proceeding in the convoys but not connected with 'Lustre' or in ships returning empty.

During the greater part of the move a proportion of the Battle Fleet was kept at sea to the westward of Crete to provide heavy cover for our forces. In addition, Operation M.C.9, running a. Malta Convoy, was carried out between 19 and 24 March whilst 'Lustre' still proceeded.[192]

In respect of the Axis powers, a Naval conference was held in Merano on February 13th and 14th between Admiral Riccardi and Admiral Raeder supported by their staff officers. The Italian Navy was lacking in fuel supplies, and may indeed run out by June, the Germans required support for their build-up of forces in North Africa out of Sicily. The prospect of an invasion of Malta and perhaps Gibraltar, in order to completely deny the Mediterranean to the Royal Navy was reviewed and there was indication from the Italians that they expected a battle with the Royal Navy was inevitable, perhaps on a similar scale to Jutland. Raeder insisted that more needed to be done to protect the convoys to North Africa and that this was clearly the priority. Fliegerkorps X was a huge asset that could be utilised, but the Regia Marina would need to play their part. In Italian terms, Fliegerkorps X had been designated X Cat (X Corporo Aereo Tedesco).

Supermarina had indeed been making plans for large scale operations that would include their battleships and cruisers, escorted by destroyers to draw the Royal Navy into a decisive battle. It was the timing that would be important. This was named Operation 'Gaudo'. The combined pressure from Raeder that included the protection of the German transports, and the disruption of 'Lustre' became the opportunity for its instigation, the trigger to commit came from two erroneous intelligence sources.

The first of these originated from Fliegerkorps X, who reported that their aircraft had torpedoed and sunk two Royal Navy battleships, which was uncorroborated and indeed incorrect. The German Naval Liaison Officer in Rome subsequently wrote up a report outlining the 'Naval Strategic Situation in the Mediterranean' which was then passed to the Italian Naval staff, its content was the finger that pulled the trigger on 'Gaudo'.

---

[192] (Gazette, 1948)

The German Naval Staff considers that at the moment there is only one British Battleship, '*Valiant*', in the Eastern Mediterranean fully ready for action. It is not anticipated that heavy British units will be withdrawn from the Atlantic in the near future. Force H is also considered unlikely to appear in the Mediterranean.

Thus, the situation in the Mediterranean is at the moment more favourable for the Italian Fleet than ever before. Intensive traffic from Alexandria to the Greek ports, whereby the Greek forces are receiving constant reinforcements in men and equipment, presents a particularly worthwhile target for the Italian forces.

The German Naval Staff considers that the appearance of Italian units in the area south of Crete will seriously interfere with British shipping and may even lead to the complete interruption of the transport of troops, especially as these transports are at the moment inadequately protected.[193]

In the meantime, at 10:30 on the 10 March HMS *Formidable* entered Alexandria and with her an ability to defend the fleet from the air. She would become the floating airfield for the Fulmars of 803 Fighter Squadron (supplemented by the remaining Fulmars of 806 Squadron from *Illustrious*), and two Squadrons of Fairey Albacore's, 826 and 839, Fleet Air Arm, in torpedo bomber and reconnaissance roles. The Albacore was the successor to the Swordfish, and it is fair to say that its career has always been in the shadow of its predecessor. It had several things in common with the Swordfish, it was obsolete by the time it became operational, it too was a biplane and could accommodate two crew for its torpedo bomber role and three for the reconnaissance missions. The distinct feature that differed from the Swordfish was the enclosed cockpit that afforded much improved protection from the elements for the crews.

S.W.C. Pack was aboard *Formidable* when she arrived in Alexandria and wrote; 'In the harbour were *Warspite*, *Valiant*, and *Barham*, the submarine parent-ship *Medway*, the damaged *Illustrious*, the old aircraft carrier *Eagle*, long overdue for a refit, and many ships of various size and class, including

---

[193] (Pack, 1972)

the immobilised French warships. We passed *Warspite* and saluted the flag of the Commander-in-Chief. We were given a welcoming cheer from *Illustrious*. We felt rather like a new batsman walking to the wicket, and we could imagine the remarks: 'I wonder how long she'll last'. 'I give 'em six weeks at the most.'"[194]

In the days leading up to the 27 March it was noted that there was an increase in Italian reconnaissance flights to the south and west of Crete. The number of Italian overflights of Alexandria ramped up too, along with many coded Enigma transmissions intercepted, flashed between the Italians and the German forces. All this indicated that something was about to occur, and that something could well involve the ships of Regia Marina. Operation 'Gaudo' had begun.

Following the raid on Taranto, the Italian fleet had been dispersed around the southern coast of Italy. On the 26 March, from those Italian naval ports came four groups of Italian ships that would converge to make one large force on the western side of Crete.

The main force comprised of the battleship and Flagship; *Vittorio Veneto* escorted by 4 destroyers of 13a Squadriglie Cacciatorpediniere under the flag of Admiral Iachino. She sailed from San Vincenzo near Naples, taking a southerly route through the Strait of Messina where she would join up with the 3rd Division heading from their base at Messina. This Division comprised of the two Trento Class 8-in. cruisers *Trieste* and *Trento* accompanied by the *Bolzano*, also an 8-in. cruiser that whilst built after the former two ships, had similar design flaws that made all three vulnerable. A desire for speed meant that weight and therefore protective armament were sacrificed and in the case of *Bolzano* she became quietly known as '…a perfectly executed mistake.' Whatever the flaws, all three ships were, in typical Italian style, graceful in appearance. The 3rd Division was escorted by 3 destroyers.

From Brindisi came the 8th Division of two, light 6-in. Garibaldi class cruisers, the *Luigi di Savoia Duca degli Abruzzi* and the *Giuseppe Garibaldi* (hereafter referred to as *Abruzzi* & *Garibaldi*) escorted by 2 destroyers. These two cruisers, whilst of lighter firepower than those of the 3rd Division, were a

---

[194] (Pack, 1972)

much-improved design, having thicker armour protection and a sleek profile that reflected the high speeds (31 knots operationally) that these two ships managed to achieve. So effective was this design that *Garibaldi* remained in service for 34 years before decommissioning in 1971.

Finally, from Taranto came the 1st Division of three, Zara class, 8-in. heavy cruisers, the *Zara, Fiume* and *Pola*. These ships were an improved design of the Trento class having much improved armour protection that allowed them to be placed front and centre of any naval action. Some clever weight saving designs had been incorporated to ensure the hull remained within the 10,000-ton limit of the Washington treaty and crucially ensured that operational speeds of 30 to 31 knots remained achievable. Their purposeful and almost majestic lines meant they could and were on occasion mistaken for battleships. The 1st division was escorted by 4 destroyers of the Oriani Class, the *Alfredo* Oriani, *Giosue Carducci, Vincenzo Gioberti* and the *Vittorio Alfieri*.

This was a formidable set of forces, which for the first time in the war, was being committed to an operation at some distance from the safety of their home ports. *Vittorio Veneto* and the 3rd Division would head south towards Gaudo whilst the 1st and 8th Division would enter the Aegean to locate and harass British convoys heading to and from Greece and perhaps engage with the Royal Navy on their own terms. For protection, Operation Gaudi was promised air cover by X Cat to the west and the Regia Aeronautica on the eastern flank.

Deception - Thursday, 27 March 1941

The short, stocky man in civilian clothes, with a suitcase in hand slipped through Gate 6 of Alexandria Harbour with little fuss, it was a warm evening, and all appeared calm and serene. His steely eyes surveyed the warships in harbour, their white awnings spreading cool shade on the decks beneath suggesting they were at rest and not going to sail anytime soon. He was quietly satisfied. By the jetty, a small boat bobbed gently in the water the sound of the little waves lapping at its side reaching him as the hubbub of Alexandria diminished behind him. The boat came from one of the Royal Australian Navy ships attached to the fleet, and the man hailed the coxswain and asked him if he was free to give him a lift. 'Where to mate?' the Coxswain asked, looking the man up and down. 'Could you take me to *Warspite* please?' the man replied. 'I've just come from playing a round of Golf and need to get back in time for dinner.' The Coxswain agreed, thinking that this man was probably the Canteen Manager aboard the great ship. 'Mate, you'll have to hop on to one of the gangways as we pass her. I've a problem with the clutch and can't run her astern, are you good with that?' The man nodded, and so stepping aboard, they set off for the battleship. As they came alongside *Warspite's* centre gangway, the man athletically jumped onto it, suitcase in hand, giving a wave to the coxswain as he took to the ladder at the double. Once back aboard his own ship the coxswain was told there was a signal waiting for him. Curious he went to the w/t office where to his astonishment he had a message from the C-in-C of the Mediterranean fleet, thanking him for the lift.

The previous tale has been attributed to the time of Matapan but whilst a nice story it cannot, it seems, be corroborated. However, what is certain is that Cunningham did go ashore on the afternoon of the 27th to play golf, and he did have a suitcase with him. This was just one part of a simple set of ruses aimed at confusing the local spy fraternity and in particular, a rather large and rotund Japanese consulate who was suspected of passing information to the enemy and often frequented the Alexandria Country Club and Golf course.

Early that same morning, a Sunderland from 230 Squadron, based out of Scaramanga on the Greek coast had spotted one of the Gaudo Battle fleets and reported it back to Alexandria. This information dovetailed in with the increased reconnaissance flights and enigma traffic that appeared to indicate some form of Italian naval operation was underway. The question was, how large was that operation?

Cunningham acted straight away. There were two convoys operating in the area, AG9 was already en route to Greece with troops and equipment, a juicy target that may be too tempting for the Italians to pass on. So, Cunningham ordered AG9 to continue to sail north until darkness and then double back away from potential trouble. Convoy GA9 was still in Piraeus and so was ordered to hold. Vice Admiral Light Forces (VALF), Admiral Pridham-Wippell in *Orion*, with *Gloucester, Ajax, Perth* and 4 destroyers was told to proceed to the southwest of the island of Gaudo to rendezvous with the Battle-Fleet the following morning at 06:30.

In Alexandria, Cunningham decided to execute further plans of deception, and to depart under darkness that evening without anyone but the fleet knowing his intentions. All the ships in the fleet would leave up their awnings until the last possible moment, whilst quietly making ready for sea and operations. Invitations to a drinks party aboard *Warspite* were issued to the officers of the ships in harbour so that it would appear the fleet would not be sailing for at least another 24 hours. Cunningham, as we know, went ashore and pretended he would be away for the night. In the afternoon, around 14:00, a lone Italian reconnaissance aircraft flew over Alexandria and reported the fleet in harbour and 'at ease'.

Meanwhile, a second Sunderland of 230 Squadron had picked up one of the Italian squadrons of 8-in. cruisers, heading in what appeared to be the direction of Taranto at speed, and the smaller squadron of 6-in. cruisers. Piloted by F/Lt. Alan Lywood the crew began to report back the position of the ships during the remainder of the day. Flying at just 70 feet above the waves, Lywood was concentrating on flying the aircraft, an error at this height could dig a wingtip into the waves and send the big aircraft to oblivion in a moment. In the right-hand seat, the co-pilot was keeping a close eye on the distant ships, when he suddenly announced, 'That's funny, they seem to be signalling to us'. Lywood took a very brief glance at the distant ships and sure enough there were a series of flashes that looked like morse signals. At the back of the aircraft, the rear gunner almost jumped out of his skin as huge plumes of water rose behind them and way above the height of the aircraft. He called over the R.T., 'Rear gunner to pilot, we are being shelled, shots falling behind us but too close for me!' They were not being signalled after all.

As darkness enveloped Alexandria the party invitations were cancelled, the awnings hastily stowed away, and the ships crews were ready for departure. Rumour and conjecture were abound, Adrian Holloway aboard *Valiant* wrote in his journal a pretty accurate assessment of the situation; 'The general rumour going around the ship is that the Italian fleet has at last come out of harbour and this is the reason for our crash departure.'[195]

---

[195] (Holloway, 1993)

No doubt fuelled with similar rumours, *Nubian* was provisioned of stores and ammunition earlier in the day, ready for action when she slipped her moorings at 16:00. She, along with *Mohawk, Hotspur* and *Havock* were heading out to sea on a bright spring day with little wind and just a whisp of high cirrus cloud, a beautiful day for flying. That indeed was part of their task that afternoon, she was to form up with *Formidable*, whose aircraft were landing on from Dekheila airfield. Later, after dark, the tannoy announced that their little force was now in company with Force A, their C-in-C in *Warspite* with *Jervis* (D14), *Janus, Mohawk, Stuart, Greyhound, Griffin, Hotspur* and *Havok as the* destroyer screen for, *Barham, Valiant* and the carrier *Formidable.* Now clear of the harbour the crew had confirmation that the Italian fleet had been reported at sea, and they were going after them.

The interception and interpretation of military signals was not confined to the intelligence services of the British. Admiral Iachino had sypher experts aboard *Vittorio Veneto,* so he did not have to rely on information passed to him from Naval Headquarters. His intelligence 'picture' was not good. The intercepted communications from the Sunderlands of 230 Squadron were sketchy but they had reported the Italian Navy was at sea in some shape or form. He also knew the weather had conspired against any reconnaissance flights over Alexandria in the late afternoon of the previous day, and that the last flight of the day had simply stated that the fleet remained within the walls of the harbour. However, although they could not be decoded in full, there were British signals of an 'Immediate' nature that would suggest the Royal Navy was on alert. He would have to wait until these messages were properly decoded by Naval Headquarters, but surely if these did indicate the British were on the move his fleet would be recalled? He deduced that with the Royal Navy on a high state of readiness it was unlikely any convoys would be at sea in the Aegean. He was correct. Supermarina decoded the signals and at 22:00 they ordered the 1st and 8th Divisions to turn about, sail south and form up with Iachino. A decision that would place the cruisers of VALF outgunned and slap in between the faster *Vittorio Veneto* with its 15-in. armament, the 8-in. cruisers of the 3rd Division with the 1st Division approaching fast behind and the British fleet still some 100 miles away by dawn.

'What battleship is that over on the starboard beam' - Friday, 28 March 1941 - Morning

150 miles to the south of Crete, light was seeping slowly from the eastern horizon forming a pencil line in the distance. An early morning sea mist had been breaking up and lifting into broken cloud, assisted by a brisk north easterly breeze. Upon the sea Force A of the Royal Navy sailed purposefully westwards, the crews at action stations, as they always were at dawn. Progress had been slower than hoped as on leaving Alexandria, *Warspite* had come too close to a mud flat and sucked up enough silt and mud into her condensers to reduce her speed, and that of the Force to a mere 20 knots. The ships of VALF were in a similar situation, *Gloucester* also had engine problems and as a result she was at the rear and struggling to make 22 knots at best. Despite this, her captain announced to the crew; 'We expect to be going into action against the Italian fleet in about one hour. The ship's company will take breakfast in two watches and whilst at breakfast, change into clean clothing and clean underwear. Good luck.'[196]

Iachino now had visual contact with the two cruiser components of his force, both at about 10 miles distance off to Port, converging from the northeast to meet with the *Vittorio Venetto*. Closest, and on course to intercept VALF was the 3rd Division, whilst further out was the 1st and 8th Division who, if VALF had to make a run for Alexandria, would be in a position to cut off their route of escape.

For both commanders, intelligence was needed. As daylight was breaking the crews of the Swordfish on reconnaissance duty clambered into their cockpits, had the engines turned over and launched into the morning sky. Iachino did not have an aircraft carrier at his disposal, but he did have a small Ro43 biplane that could be catapulted off his ship to reconnoitre ahead of the fleet or spot any fall of shot, but it was in no way ideal for the task. It had a limited range and time in the air, around 5 hours maximum. It could not be recovered by the parent ship either, so the crew were required to land ashore once the mission was complete which cut down their search time considerably. This little aircraft was instructed to range to the southeast, some

---

[196] (Otter, 2017)

30 miles off Crete and as far as one hundred miles distant at the extremity of the patrol. Iachino was still unaware that the fleet had sailed, but what he was looking for, was any sign of a convoy that could be attacked. He doubted that they would make contact, so he made the decision that if the Ro43 had not sighted anything within the first hour of its flight he would turn the fleet back towards base.

Once airborne, all the reconnaissance aircraft faced the same issue. The cloud was now broken, which meant there was more cloud cover than gaps through which the sea was visible, and in some places patches of mist stubbornly remained at sea level. Any errors in position or sightings were therefore more likely to occur.

Within the hour before 08:30, the Swordfish began to report a force of cruisers and their destroyer escorts. Any early excitement was dampened on the British ships when it became known that VALF was of a similar disposition in numbers and supposed to be in the vicinity. This force was likely to be VALF. On board *Orion*, the reporting of this force was received with the same apathy, the Swordfish crews must indeed have been reporting the position of Pridham-Wippells force, but they were wrong.

Suddenly one of the Swordfish revised an earlier report increasing the number of ships they had sighted. This had to be some other force, not VALF after all! *Trieste* had already sighted the British informing Iachino that the ships were clearly heading towards Alexandria and the impression was formed that this was a convoy protecting force. The ships of 3rd Division opened fire, their shells beginning to fall close to *Gloucester*. Pridham-Wippell, realising that he was confronted by superior forces in both firepower and speed sent an emergency signal to the Fleet to this effect. He ordered the ships in his force to head at all speed towards the Fleet primarily to gain protection, but to also lure the enemy to within the sphere of the carrier's air component and into the range of the fleet's guns. Iachino could only rue the fact that his promised air cover never materialised.

Gloucester began to take evasive action, twisting and turning, 'snaking the line' to avoid the falling shells, the range was coming down to a mile and she could now open up with her own 6-in. armament. No hits were scored, but soon thereafter the Italians ceased fire and turned about. Iachino, somewhat puzzled that the British cruisers were running (and still unaware the Fleet was at sea), decided that they had travelled far enough south, and he should now return to base. S. W. Pack, in 'Night Action off Matapan' quotes Commander R. L. Fisher who was aboard *Orion* during this exchange of fire.

> First thing in the morning I was on the bridge off Gaudo and we saw a small aircraft of a type which somebody said could have come from an Italian cruiser. Pretty soon after that we saw the Trento lot and ran away for all we were worth, our four cruisers in line abreast zig zagging and making smoke and the four Australian V & W destroyers scattered around us. We were shot at for quite a long time and lots of salvoes came close – close enough for us to get some splashes on deck – but nobody hit.
>
> During this run away I was mostly in the plot, but whenever I did come out I couldn't see the enemy for smoke. After a time shells stopped splashing around and we went on running away making smoke.[197]

The breaking of contact by the Italians, and their withdrawal now gave Pridham-Wippell the ability to use his cruisers for the purpose for which they were employed. He would shadow the Italians from a distance as they repaired westward. What he did not know at the time, was that just over the horizon was the *Vittorio Veneto*, and now he was the one walking into a potential trap.

During this first phase of the battle, *Nubian*, along with *Mohawk*, was instructed to proceed with *Valiant* (she was the fastest of the battleships at that moment) as her anti-submarine screen to catch up and support *Orion* and the ships of VALF. Adrian Holloway noted that their normal cruising speed was fifteen to sixteen knots, during the hour that the three ships powered northwards to support VALF they maintained 23 knots. 'The thrumming of the propellors made sleep in the Admiral's flat almost impossible, whilst the foam of our wake came right up to the quarterdeck.'[198] However their dash was short lived, a counter order was issued, they were to return to the fleet. *Orion* was under fire, she had run into the Italian Battleship, it was now about 11:00 in the morning.

---

[197] (Pack, 1972)
[198] (Holloway, 1993)

Pack once more quotes Commander Fisher aboard *Orion*.

> We now steamed westward again, feeling braver and braver as we recovered from our first plastering. It was sunny and the sea was void of the enemy; the turret crews were sitting on the roofs of their turrets, and action bully beef sandwiches arrived on the bridge. The Commander (T. C. Wynne) came on the bridge and, with a mouthful of sandwich, nudged me and said 'What battleship is that over on the starboard beam? I thought ours were miles to the east of us.' As I took my binoculars to examine a vessel hull down to the northward there was a whistling noise and the first salvo of 15-inch from the *Vittorio Veneto* landed somewhere around. We made a hurried turn to the south (I think without waiting for our turn signal to be answered), and did another hurried retreat, making smoke.[199]

'Sorry…haven't seen them for some time.' - Friday, 28 March 1941 – Afternoon

The emergency signals to the ships of VALF from its commander were picked up by the main Fleet, they indicated VALF was in some trouble. He had ordered an about turn, to proceed at all speed and to make smoke. Shells began to fall as the Italian battleship groped towards the cruisers like the paw of a huge cat playing with a mouse. *Gloucester* was in trouble, she was barely making 23 knots as the accuracy and fall of shot got ever closer, surely an accurate salvo would have them done for? Ken Otter quotes Signalman Les Thomas; 'Once the shells started coming over, I ducked beneath a canvas screen for protection. It was daft really but somehow it made me feel safer.' He also quotes Petty Officer Yeoman, Bob Wainwright; 'I had a grandstand view as they started to send the shells over us. When they came over the top of us it was like the sound of a tube train approaching.'[200] The hotness of the situation may have galvanised the efforts of the engine room staff as very shortly full power was miraculously restored and *Gloucester* managed to escape into the relative protection of the smoke screen. The trouble was, they

---

[199] (Pack, 1972)
[200] (Otter, 2017)

were now heading towards the cruisers of the 3rd Division, that Iachino had ordered to pull around to port and gain a position on VALFs starboard quarter. It would mean the destruction of VALF.

On the *Vittorio Veneto* a lookout spotted approaching aircraft, radial engine biplanes that looked like CR42's, hopes were raised that the promised air cover had finally arrived. This was soon shattered when the aircraft assembled and turned in to attack. They were not Italian after all; they were British Albacores from 826 Squadron. Iachino ordered the guns to cease fire and his ship to turn away in order to comb the incoming torpedoes, none of which found their mark. The appearance of these aircraft indicated a carrier was in striking range of his forces, and so Iachino decided to head westward to base, whilst VALF headed east, unaware that he was no longer being chased and the gap between him and the enemy was increasing by the minute. When the smoke screen finally cleared, the horizon was devoid of the enemy.

The intervention of 826 Squadron certainly saved the ships of VALF from almost certain annihilation, but it also put the chances of sinking the battleship out of reach. VALF had no choice but to head towards the main Fleet coming up slowly from the east, but the two opposing forces were now, effectively on divergent courses, with the Italians having the upper hand where speed was concerned. Cunningham was, of course being frustrated by the reduced speed of *Warspite* following their encounter with the mud bank, the opportunity to hit the Italians hard must not slip from their grasp. Cunningham wrote afterwards.

> At about noon the air striking force returned and reported one probable hit on the battleship, which was the *Vittorio Veneto*. A few minutes later a Royal Air Force flying boat reported a further enemy force consisting of two 'Cavour' class battleships and some further 8-in. cruisers. The battleship attacked by the Fleet Air Arm was alone except for a destroyer screen; but there was another force of cruisers 20 miles to the south eastward of her. The air reports showed that all the enemy forces were retiring to the westward.[201]

---

[201] (Cunningham, 1951)

The light cruisers of the 8th Division were now returning to base, the 3rd Division and 1st Division with their accompanying destroyer screens were what had been sighted, however the two 'Cavour' class battleships were clearly a case of mistaken identity, they quite possibly were two of the Zara's of the 1st Division.

As *Orion* re-joined the fleet at maximum signalling distance and almost breathless from their escape, a flash signal from the C-in-C was received. 'Where is the enemy?', *Orion* could only reply, 'Sorry don't know. Haven't seen them for some time.'[202] The reality of the situation was beginning to dawn on Cunningham and his staff that the chances of a naval gunnery action were slipping away. They had to slow the enemy down, and air assault was likely to be the only way of achieving this. They also needed an accurate assessment of the course and speed of the enemy, they had to have 'eyes on' the adversary. Fortunately, they had an expert Observer Lt. Commander A. S. Bolt, on board *Warspite* who could get aloft in the ships Swordfish to make aerial contact. They also had fast ships of their own, and so the cruisers of VALF were once more turned around and sent with all speed back westwards to try and make visual contact once more, that was of course, their job. Once in contact, then perhaps a classic torpedo attack from the destroyers could be made, crippling the enemy enough to allow the battleships to come up and finish the job with their big guns.

Formidable had already dropped away from the fleet, she needed to sail into wind in readiness to recover 826 Squadron but before that she had to launch 829 Squadron that was clearly ranged on the after part of the flight deck. The squadrons three Albacores, and a couple of Swordfish were armed up with torpedoes, the flight crews busying preparing them for launch whilst the aircrews stole themselves for action, no doubt butterflies and pre mission nervous excitement gripping their stomachs. In the lead aircraft, the Squadron CO, Lt. Commander John Dalyell-Stead waved away the chocks and as the smoke on the ships bow fluttered and drifted straight down the deck he was waved clear for take-off. The big Albacore thundered down the centreline, the second strike on the *Vittorio Veneto* was underway.

---

[202] (Woodman, 2000)

Amidships of *Warspite* her Swordfish 'Lorna' floatplane K8863[203] of 700 Squadron, sits comfortable on a catapult cradle. In the cockpit Pilot Officer Ben Rice is going through his power checks, the Pegasus engine running smooth and eager, the airframe shuddering in happy anticipation of carrying him aloft. Behind him is TAG Maurice Pacey and Lt. Commander Bolt, who is busily arranging his code books, ensuring his maps were in order and his pencils stowed safely. Through the speaking tube Rice asked, 'all set?', Bolt replied, 'Yes, we are ready when you are.'. Rice smoothly applied full power and gave a thumbs up to the Directing Officer who dropped the blue flag he has been holding aloft indicating a readiness to launch. In a moment the Control Worker pushed the launch lever forward firing the cordite cartridge which forced the catapult ram home. The cradle, gently holding the Swordfish, shot forward on its tracks, a 2g force on both crewmen pushing them back in their seats as the Swordfish was released into the air. It dipped slightly towards the sea in a snappy crosswind that Rice anticipated, and in a moment, he could feel the controls respond nicely to his command as airspeed built. He climbed away in a gentle curve from the mother ship. Bolts orders from the Commander-in-Chief were as follows; '… to obtain a visual link between the fleets as soon as possible and then report generally on the tactical situation as seen from the air.'[204]

Out of Menedi in Greece now came one of two forces of Blenheim bombers, which made for the *Vittorio Veneto*, they commenced high level bombing in two waves from 14:20, which whilst not scoring any direct hits, managed to keep the Italian anti-aircraft gunners in employ. Looking on were the aircraft of 829 Squadron which used the cover of the bombers to attain a height of 5000 feet and to position themselves with the sun behind them. At just after 15:10 Dalyell-Stead took the three Albacores down into the attack.

The escorting Fulmars attacked first, coming in low and strafing the bridge. Bullets zinged, sparkled and ricocheted as they impacted the ships superstructure. Her gunners dived for cover, some were transfixed by the sudden attack, so soon after the bombing had ceased. It gave 829 a little time, and before the recovering gun crews regained their composure, the Albacores were upon them.

---

[203] (Simmons, 2011, 2012)
[204] (Simmons, 2011, 2012)

The battleship grew rapidly in size against Dalyell-Steads torpedo sight, the little light bulbs blinking as at 1000 yards the aiming point was reached. The huge warship had now opened up with everything she had, her sides sparkling with muzzle flashes, tracer came at them in all colours, slowly at first before flashing passed as they got closer. The aircraft began to take hits, the controls suddenly felt unresponsive. Dalyell-Stead shouted, 'torpedo gone' to his crew, Lt. Cooke (Observer) and PO Blenkhorn, (the air gunner), and he banked over to port in an attempt to cross the ships bow to escape the murderous fire. They never made it. Their Albacore presented a side on target to the gunners at point blank range, shells thumped into the airframe which appeared to shudder with each impact. Dalyell-Stead was either already dead, or simply lost control through severed control lines, for his Albacore just cleared the bow and then smashed into the sea about 1000 yards away. Iachino, whilst ordering his ship to turn violently to avoid the torpedo that now sped towards them, could only admire the courage displayed. He later wrote; 'And so died a brave pilot without the satisfaction of knowing that his attack had indeed been successful.'[205]

The crew had indeed been successful. The torpedo exploded close to the port propellors, tearing off the outer propellor disabling the inner and creating a hole in the ships underside that allowed thousands of tons of water into her stern compartments. Her engines stopped; she was dead in the water with the British fleet coming up at 25 knots. Somehow, the Italians managed to get her engines started once more, creating several large black smoke rings which belched forth from her funnels happily observed by the shadowing aircraft. They reported back that although the battleship was underway once more, her speed was greatly reduced, perhaps to a mere 8 knots.

Meanwhile Lt. Commander Bolt had been periodically reporting their aircrafts fuel status to *Warspite* without reply. PO Rice was equally aware of the dwindling fuel, they had been aloft over four hours, with possibly 45 minutes at best left in the air, Suda bay was over an hour away. They would need *Warspite* to recover them. Bolt made one last report that they had just 15 minutes of fuel remaining, he got a reply. They would be recovered, but *Warspite* would not stop for them.

---

[205] (Pack, 1972)

Normally a float plane would land within the 'slick' of calm water that was created behind the bow wave of a slow-moving ship, and then 'taxi' up to a crane that was ranged out of one side of the parent ship. One of the aircrafts crew would help direct the pilot to come below the crane, whilst the other crew member climbed onto the upper wing and fasten the aircraft for hoisting aboard. Even in relatively calm conditions a float plane taxiing on the sea looks like a trout flapping and thrashing on the end of a line, trying to return to the environment it belongs to. On this occasion, the normal procedure was not practical, *Warspite* was giving chase to her enemy and could not afford to slow down from her 20+ knots. Rice had to land ahead of *Warspite*, then wait for her to catch him up. At over 30,000 tons displacement her great bows pushed aside the ocean with ease, a bow wave of hissing foam and disturbed water catching up the little floatplane that, but for some skilled manoeuvring would have been swamped. The crew worked together to bring 'Lorna' under the crane and safely secured, she was lifted back aboard. Bolt later recalled; 'We had never practised this method of recovery and were a good deal disturbed by the bow wave. However, I was able to con PO Rice to a position under the grab hook and Lieutenant Commander Copeman with whom I had a good understanding in the recovery operation hoisted us quickly clear of the water as soon as I gave the hooked-on signal.'[206] *Warspite* had barely slowed during the recovery and had lost less than a mile in the process.

Whilst the Swordfish was being replaced onto the catapult and refuelled, Bolt began to try and unravel the various reports and plots they had from the previous patrol, and it became apparent that there were many discrepancies in the size of the force, it's possible intentions, course and speed. What was more pressing, was to ascertain if the *Vittorio Veneto* was indeed in trouble and her speed reduced. They catapulted off once more at 17:45.

An hour earlier, Cunningham had ordered VALF to make all speed in one last effort to catch up with the Italians and gain a visual sighting, hopefully before darkness which would occur at about 19:15. This would take him out of visual with the fleet, so *Nubian* and *Mohawk* were tasked to break away from their screening duties and with all haste position themselves between VALF and the fleet to maintain visual contact. The pair surged forward at full

---

[206] (Pack, 1972)

revolutions, two eager spaniels, let off their leads, galloping forth desperate to please.

By 17:00, with only her starboard engines driving her remaining propellors, her rudder hard a starboard and steered by hand, listing to port and down at the stern, the *Vittorio Veneto* managed to regain a creditable 19 knots. Directly in front and behind were her attendant destroyers, whilst she was flanked and protected on the starboard, some 1200 yards away, by *Zara*, *Pola* and *Fiume*, then a further thousand yards out 4 destroyers provided the outer screen. This was mirrored on the port side by the *Trento, Trieste* and *Bolzano* with their three destroyers also screening a thousand yards to port. They had 420 miles at least to go, steering 300 degrees, until they would reach the safe refuge of their home port.

This was how Bolt, and the crew of 'Lorna' found the Italian fleet at 18:20, shortly thereafter he was able to transmit a report accurately detailing the disposition of the Italian force. As Pack states in his book on the action; 'To reduce the fifty miles gap to twelve miles, so as to bring the Italians within gun range, would take four hours or more. Everything seemed to rest now on the torpedo attack by the destroyers immediately Pridham-Wippell's cruisers regained visual contact, but in *Formidable* we had high hopes of success from the dusk air attack with torpedoes.'[207] Bolt continued to methodically report the position of the Italians, to such good effect that he was later awarded a DSM. The Swordfish remained on station until after dark, before flying on towards Suda Bay to land. This was not as straightforward as one may think. There was no visible horizon for a start, the sky and the sea seemed as one. With spares at a premium, most of the 'Lorna's' instrumentation had been removed before the flight, PO Rice had nothing but his turn and bank indicator to give him an artificial horizon. When close by, they made a low level run so that Bolt could drop a line of 3 flare floats giving Rice a reasonable approach point to land on the water. On landing they had a 5 mile 'taxi' to the harbour, which Bolt described as 'interminable'. Little wonder, they had been in the aircraft for over 7 hours.

Formidable's crew had not been idle. The wind had dropped off in the afternoon, allowing her to catch up with the fleet but more importantly, the

---

[207] (Pack, 1972)

change of wind meant that she no longer needed to turn about to launch her aircraft. This had become increasingly annoying for Cunningham as the battle fleet had to continually weave in a lazy 's' formation to allow *Formidable* to stay in touch and catch up after launching her aircraft. 826 Squadron consisting of 6 Albacores and 2 Swordfish from 829 Squadron were now refueled and re-armed. They would be joined in the attack by more Swordfish from 815 Squadron out of Maleme. 'Well done. Give him another nudge at dusk'[208] had been the suggestion from Cunningham, Rear Admiral Boyd would oblige.

'It almost seemed an act of god' - Friday 28 March 1941 – Twilight

At 19:45 and at 8000 feet the sun still blazed a trail across the sea belying the fact that below it was already twilight. Down at sea level the last vestiges of light were seeping away, turning from orange to violet. Admiral Angelo Iachino glanced at his force of steel that now protected the flagship. He was about to turn 51 the following week. Born in the seaport of Sanremo on the 4 April 1889 to a school teacher, he, like many career Naval Officers, had joined the service when he was 15. He entered the Livorno Naval Academy in 1904, graduating in 1907. His career was varied. He had served on Motor gunboats during the First War before taking command of a destroyer and then a cruiser between the two wars. By 1940 he was already an Admiral and had served for a spell as the Commander of the Livorno Naval Academy and then, during the same year he was appointed commander of the 2nd Naval Squadron with his flag aboard the *Pola*. Then, on the 8 December 1940, Admiral Campioni was fired from his position as Commander of the Regia Marina, his apparent lack of willingness to commit his Navy to decisive action and the humiliation of Taranto contributing to his removal. Iachino replaced him the following day, raising his flag on the *Vittorio Veneto*.

Now he could perhaps in those dying moments of the day take stock of the situation. The light was fading fast and with darkness the threat of aerial attack

---

[208] (Woodman, 2000)

would diminish. The fleet was making good speed, despite the damage his flagship had sustained. By daylight tomorrow his ships would be that much closer to friendly airbases, and almost permanent aircover from X-Cat, but how he must have felt let down by the lack of support he had received from the air so far. Out to starboard his eye fell on his old command, the *Pola,* her sleek lines slicing the water, guns pointed fore and aft, a symbol of the might of the Italian Navy. Leading her was the *Zara*, on which he had served during the Abyssinian war and at the rear, the *Fiume*, from which he had once commanded the 1st Cruiser Division. Traversing his binoculars to port he began to pick out the formation of enemy aircraft, gathering beyond the range of his guns; they could yet alter the outcome of his day, he thought. For indeed they were clearly positioning for one last attack on his precious fleet, as he wrote after the war. 'These were the planes' whose job it was to give us the coup de grace at nightfall.'[209]

From the ever-growing darkness the six Albacores of 826 Squadron were joined by two Swordfish of 815 Squadron that had flown out from Maleme in Crete. The sun was setting behind the Italian fleet, silhouetting them perfectly against the horizon. The rearmost destroyer began to make smoke as the final light began ebbed away and the aircraft turned in for the attack.

The Albacores went in first, attacking together at wavetop height at little more than 90 knots airspeed. The Italian ships began to lay a huge smoke screen from within which they poured out Anti-Aircraft tracer fire. They also turned on their searchlights in an effort to blind the attackers, the combination of which split up the initial attack and forced the aircraft to make individual assaults on their enemy. The Observer in the lead Albacore wrote of the attack.

> When we eventually went into attack from the dark side with the Italians silhouetted against the last glow of light in the west, we found that we had been spotted at long range and were met with an impassable barrage of fire. We were forced to withdraw and split up and came in again individually from different angles. The barrage of fire put up by the Italians was immensely spectacular but not very effective. A good deal of hose-piping went on which resulted in a

---

[209] (Pack, 1972)

number of their ships hitting each other but little damage to our aircraft.[210]

There is some speculation which aircraft scored the one vital torpedo hit that day. Commander Pack states in his book 'Night Action off Cape Matapan' that it was Albacore 5A from *Formidable* piloted by Sub. Lt. C.PC. Williams, whilst other historians believe it was the Swordfish of 'Tiffy' Torrens Spence from 815 Squadron. Whichever it was, a torpedo struck the *Pola* amidships at about 19:45 and immediately all power to the great ship was lost. She hove out of line whilst the fleet sailed on, oblivious to her situation. Grattan M'Groarty, a U.S. journalist who was aboard *Formidable*, later interviewed *Pola's* Captain, 42-year-old, Capitano di Vascello Manilo Piba who had been with the ship for two and a half years years. 'I have never seen anything like the pilots' daring. One came down within two yards of the sea and loosed off his torpedo at not less than 250 yards. We were struck between the forward engine room and the after boiler, with the result that we were unable to move. I have never seen anything like that attack. It almost seemed an act of God.'[211]

The Albacores and Swordfish, their torpedoes spent, headed for home. *Formidable* could not land them back on, so they were ordered to head for Crete. With a surface action almost certain, the recovery aboard would hinder preparations and overexpose the aircraft from damage or destruction if caught under fire and ranged on deck. Not all of the aircraft made it, some ditched but mercifully their crews were picked up.

It was over half an hour before Iachino realised the *Pola* was 'missing'. The first sign of trouble came when signals between the *Zara* and *Fiume* were picked up by the flagship. It soon became evident that something was wrong with the *Pola*, as *Zara* was now requesting a situation report from her sister ship.

By now the fleet were several miles ahead of *Pola*, for Iachino and his staff, the evidence suggested she had been torpedoed during the last attack. Knowing that she was of sound construction, Iachino believed she could be

---

[210] (Pack, 1972)
[211] (M'Groarty, 1941)

salvaged if taken in tow. But *Pola* was a large ship, with a significant number of crew aboard, it would require more than one or two destroyers to take them off, should she be beyond recovery. Iachino ordered Admiral Cattaneo to double back with the *Zara*, *Fiume* and the Destroyers of the 9th Destroyer Flotilla, to assist their wounded comrade. There was a caveat, they would abandon *Pola* if they ran into signification opposition. At this time, Iachino was still unaware that Force H was close by, despite having received intelligence that the British were at sea; 'That we were within a relatively short distance of the entire British Force never occurred to me. I thought the British Cruisers had decided to turn back leaving only two destroyers to deal with us.'[212]

Night Action - Friday, 28 March 1941

Admiral Cunningham had his own, difficult decision to make. The reports from the final airstrike suggested that one of the large warships, perhaps the *Vittorio Veneto* had been hit and was dead in the water. If he sent his cruisers and destroyers from D14, they could run smack into the enemy ships and come off worse, indeed as they pursued the fleet deeper into enemy waters, they would subsequently come into range of the enemy air component. In committing the light forces, *Warspite, Valiant, Barham* and *Formidable*, whilst a potent force, would be left with just 4 destroyers as their screen.

Of the Italians, Cunningham thought that they were aware of his presence, and so surely, they must commit their own light forces and cruisers which also had torpedo capabilities? They could well be on course to intercept Force H at that very moment. Cunningham conferred with his staff; all were of the opinion that to take up the chase would court with disaster. Not what he wanted to hear. The Fleet Gunnery Officer, Cmd G. Barnard, later quoted Cunningham's response; 'You're a pack of yellow-livered skunks. I'll go and

---

[212] (Pack, 1972)

have my supper now and see after supper if my morale isn't higher than yours.'[213] It was.

20:37 IMMEDIATE

14th D.F. 2nd D.F. from Commander-in-Chief.
Destroyer flotillas attack enemy battle-fleet with torpedoes.
Estimated bearing and distance of centre of enemy fleet from Admiral 286° 33 miles at 20:30.
Enemy course and speed 295° 13 knots.

The orders were clear to Philip Mack, he must take the two flotillas, attack and sink the Italian ships with torpedoes and gunfire. This was what the destroyer forces were built and trained for. Mack's task was to build the plan of attack, relay this to his Destroyer Commanders and execute it. The first Lieutenant aboard *Jervis* described the plan of action.

Destroyers were spread, speed increased to about 28 knots and course set to intercept. The picture presented by the plot in *Jervis* showed the battleship many miles ahead steaming at about 12 knots to the north westward, flanked by the two cruisers about five cables on each beam, and two destroyers a farther five cables away on each side. Captain Mack's intention was to work around ahead and then, dividing his force into two divisions, to come down on opposite courses, each division to pass between the battleship and the cruisers, one division passing at a range of 500 yards each side. Thereby it hoped that the enemy would be thrown into confusion and might fire on its own side.[214]

With orders given the crew of *Nubian* prepared for action, the ships engines took on a note of urgency as she and the two divisions raced forward into the night. The earlier winds had died away, the clouds had dispersed

---

[213] (Pack, 1972)
[214] (Pack, 1972)

although there was a slight haze that brought down the range of visibility. The sea conditions were described from aboard the *Stuart*; '... as flat as a river. Above the masthead the stars hung countless in a luminous haze. The moon had not yet risen, and the faint starlight seemed only to accentuate the darkness which fell wide and dense on all sides.'[215]

There must have been some apprehension within the crews of the British destroyers mixed with the excitement of a battle to come. Their opponents could out gun and outrange them, with the potential to decimate the smaller ships with their heavy guns. However, the Italian Navy had neglected training for night action, unlike the Royal Navy. The Regia Marina expected a 'Jutland' type daylight engagement which did not necessitate the need for the sophistication of radar, nor did they believe that aircraft carriers were necessary with the strength and numbers that the Regia Aeronautica possessed. It would be their undoing. For now, the crews on board those racing destroyers had to believe they had the element of surprise and the night fighting skills to win the day.

The last known course and speed of the Italians was based on Bolts final report. What neither Mack or Cunningham knew, was in the meantime, Iachino had turned to a more northerly route towards port and that his speed was nearer 19 knots putting him much further north than expected. When Mack's force reached the point that in theory was ahead of the Italian fleet, he turned onto a reciprocal heading in readiness to attack. Mack had, in fact turned behind his target as it continued north and into safety. It was probably for the best that the expected engagement never occurred. With some indication of what the outcome may have been, Commander Scott noted; 'It was a bold plan, and, in keeping with the Commander-in-Chiefs known views that the nearer you got to the enemy the better. What the result would have been if contact had been made it is quite difficult to think, but it certainly would have been a short and very sharp engagement.'[216]

---

[215] (Simmons, 2011, 2012)
[216] (Pack, 1972)

Earlier, VALF, sailing westwards, had his ships fanned out at 7 mile intervals in an attempt to pick up the Italian fleet, had observed the flashes of the searchlights, smoke and tracer lighting up the ever darkening sky from that final air attack of the day. He ordered his ships to reform into line astern and proceed with some caution. At 20:14 Commander R. L. Fisher, Staff Officer (Operations) aboard *Orion*, received a report from Ordinary Seaman A. B. Craig who was working *Orion's* fixed aerial 286M radar. Having just turned onto a heading of 310° the radar screen had revealed a contact at a distance of about 6 miles and out of visual range. Craig began to read off the ranges, and relative bearings of the contact, he also estimated the size of the ship to be some 600 feet long. It soon became apparent that the ship was stationary, but what ship was it? The size suggested that perhaps this was the Vittorio Veneto, but it was in fact the crippled *Pola*.

VALF reported the contacts position and now content that the Battle-Fleet was coming up to meet it, and D14 on the loose to help finish the job, the ships of VALF were able to concentrate on catching the remainder of the enemy fleet. If the stopped ship was not the *Vittorio Veneto*, then at least they would have a chance of regaining contact and perhaps prevent her escape.

As the battle-fleet approached the position of the *Pola*, *Valliant's* 279 radar was set to short range and was sweeping ahead of the fleet. Communication between the radar station, the Transmitting Station and the range finding equipment had been established prior to *Valiant* sailing. This allowed the accurate laying of her 15-in. guns on a target. Now those guns were moving onto the *Pola* some four and a half miles ahead.

At his battle station deep in the bowels of *Valiant*, Adrian Holloway heard the unmistakable click from the tannoy that indicated an announcement was about to be made. 'Alarm, Alarm, Alarm'. In Holloways words, this was an 'electrifying' moment, as they had surely come across the enemy. Another announcement came quickly, 'Enemy in sight. Salvoes, Salvoes, Salvoes.' The men braced themselves for the 15-in. gunfire that must surely follow any moment, however, there came almost immediately the order to 'Check fire.'

That order was to hold off firing but be in readiness to open-up on the next order, which came seconds later. The gun blasts were so violent that Holloway thought his ship must have been hit. 'So great is the concussion from guns of such huge calibre as ours that my mistake was a legitimate one – it was our own guns which were shaking the ship as though some giant hand had hold of us.'[217]

To understand this sequence of events one must refer to The Searchlight Control Officer that night who was Prince Philip of Greece and Denmark, later to become The Duke of Edinburgh and husband of Queen Elizabeth II. The Gunnery Officer had been about to fire on the *Pola*, but some instinct (according to Holloway) stopped him doing so. In the next few moments, both the *Fiume* and *Zara* were spotted. A bearing was quickly given to Prince Philip in which direction to train the huge searchlights under his command. This was followed by the order to 'Illuminate'. Caught in the beam, only some 2000 yards away was one of the two Italian 8-in. cruisers, so close it was within the narrow portion of the beam that lit just a small part of her hull. Neither of the enemy ship's companies had an inkling that they had run into the British Fleet. The ships guns were facing fore and aft, their ensign's fluttering in the breeze from their forward motion. The lack of radar had them blind whilst a naïve belief that they needed no training in night manoeuvers was about to cost them very dear indeed.

The guns of *Valiant, Barham* and *Warspite* were immediately trained on the two cruisers. Cunningham was on *Warspite's* bridge and recalled the moment. 'In the dead silence, a silence that could almost be felt, one heard only the voices of the gun control personnel putting the guns on the new target. One heard the orders repeated in the director tower behind and above the bridge. Looking forward, one saw the turrets swing and steady when the 15-in. guns pointed at the enemy cruisers.'[218]

---

[217] (Holloway, 1993)
[218] (Cunningham, 1951)

'Director layer sees the target' announced from the director tower, indicated that the guns were aimed and ready to fire, this was followed by the 'ting, ting, ting' of the firing gongs and then the roar and flashes from the big guns as they were fired. According to Holloway, *Valiant* had fired at just after 22:20.

Hits quickly registered on the two cruisers. *Warspite* fired two full broadsides at *Fiume*, 30 seconds apart. *Valiant* at first fired on the *Zara* and then, because her 'X' & 'Y' turrets could not come to bear, switched aim to the *Fiume*. *Barham* meanwhile had engaged the destroyer *Alfieri*, setting her ablaze before turning to the *Zara*. Flames now engulfed both cruisers from bow to stern. *Fiume* began to list and gradually dropped out of line to sink half an hour later.

The *Zara*, like the *Fiume*, had her electrical systems shot away, and therefore neither ship could return fire. Even if they had, they did not have the necessary techniques or flashless charges to engage effectively at night. Admiral Cattaneo was still alive and ordered the *Zara* scuttled, with fires out of control and finished as a fighting force. He would go down with his flagship. Sub Lieutenant Giorgi Parodi made his way to the side of the ship and jumped into the water, which he claimed was very cold. He swam away from the ship as the scuttling charges blew, triggering the secondary explosion of the *Zara's* magazines. He wrote. 'When the flames died down the *Zara* seemed to be trying to lift herself out of the water. Then she began to turn over. A few minutes later there came a succession of huge waves… Then all was dark.'[219][220]

In the melee of that encounter, Cunningham's destroyer screen came close to as fiery end as their enemy. *Griffin* had attempted to cross ahead of the battleships early in the engagement, she was the first to be straddled in error

---

[219] (Simmons, 2011, 2012)
[220] This description of the *Zara's* sinking is contradicted by many accounts of the battle where *Jervis* is attributed with her demise by torpedo.

by *Warspite*. Cunningham quickly signalled to the little ship, 'Get out of the way you bloody fool.'[221]

Havock had not illuminated her fighting lights[222], which would have helped identify her as a 'friend'. From *Warspite*, having already seen the enemy Destroyers attempt a retaliatory torpedo attack, the *Havock* appeared a legitimate target and the big ship fired two broadsides that straddled *Havock* but mercifully did no damage.

As the guns fell silent the destroyers were sent off in pairs to do their cleaning up work. *Greyhound* and *Griffin* were assigned the task of chasing down the Italian Destroyers, whilst *Havock* and *Stuart* would complete the destruction of the Cruisers with torpedoes. However, it was *Havock* that came across the *Carducci* and began to give chase. She fired four torpedoes that scored a hit and stopped the hapless destroyer in her tracks. One of the seamen aboard *Havock* stated that they were so close when the torpedo struck that '…the explosion from our torpedo lifted us out of the water.'[223] *Havock* circled the *Carducci*, pouring gunfire into the now stationary target, which at 23:15 blew up and sank.

The action had lasted just 6 minutes. Pack, aboard *Formidable*, which had sensibly turned and stood off from the action (her 6-in. guns were of no use in a full-scale naval engagement), recalled that he had not long having gone to sleep when he was suddenly awoken. 'There were mighty explosions at which the *Formidable* shuddered violently. The view from the compass platform was

---

[221] (Pack, 1972)
[222] Fighting Lights are often mentioned in WORLD WAR 2 RN engagements, what they were is difficult to ascertain. However, John Roberts provides a detailed diagram from the National Maritime Museum of the Tribal, HMS Cossack in his book, 'Destroyer Cossack' (Seaforth Publishing 2020). Across the main boom of the forward mast, two pairs of Fighting Lights are shown and annotated as such. One pair is Green, the other Red, which suggests Starboard and Port respectively. These would indicate (to another vessel), which direction and rough relative bearing the ship burning them was travelling. Most useful in a night action, not only for identification purposes but to avoid collision and friendly fire situations occurring.
[223] (Osborne, 2017)

almost indescribable. The night scene was lit by vivid flashes of 15-inch guns, bright beams of searchlights, and an orange glow of huge fires that broke out in the ships under fire. It was breathtaking.'[224]

There was now a danger, that with both British and Italian destroyers running amok, one of the battleships, or even the *Formidable* could end up damaged or worse, sunk. A signal was sent to all ships to sail to the northeast where they could form up safely. Whilst the signal had the right intentions, it was, as Cunningham later stated, a mistake. VALF and his light forces now shadowing the Italians, broke off their pursuit and so ended any likelihood of further action. This was not the case for Captain Mack and the ships of D14.

Earlier, some 60 miles to the north, the only source of light on the bridge of *Nubian* came from the dull glow of the compass. She was in one of the two Destroyer columns, 6 cables apart (about a half mile) cutting through the water at 28 knots still looking for the Italian fleet. Ahead, the wake of *Jervis* foamed white, betraying her position as did her fighting lights. A great flash to the south lit up the sky like a distant storm, quickly followed by many more in very quick succession. Heads turned in their direction, the Star shells could be made out curving at the top of their trajectory before falling slowly back to the surface. The flashes seemed to go on for some time before fading out and the darkness returned once more before to those with a keen ear heard low and deep rumbles from their source.

Soon thereafter Captain Mack received the signal for the forces to repair to the northeast, but at just after midnight another signal was intercepted, this time from *Havock*. She had come across what she thought was the crippled *Vittorio Veneto*, it was of course, the *Pola*. Mack, sensing that now was the moment to act, flashed orders to the ships under his command to form in line astern and full ahead to *Havocks* position.

At 02:00 the Destroyers of D14 arrived in the vicinity of the earlier conflagration. In the water were many Italian survivors either swimming or in

---

[224] (Pack, 1972)

boats who cried out for help as the ships passed by. Illuminating the scene were the last fires burning aboard the largely abandoned *Zara*. Captain Mack ordered his ships to begin picking up survivors before instructing his Gunner to fire a salvo of torpedoes to finish off the *Zara*. At 03:11, Mack made a signal to VALF, by now aware that *Havock's* earlier signal was in error, 'Have sunk *Zara* and am about to sink the *Pola*.'[225]

Whilst many historians have commented on the Nelsonian qualities of Andrew Brown Cunningham, one cannot escape those of Captain Philip Mack of D14 and His Majesty's Ship *Jervis*. As *Jervis* approached the stricken *Pola*, now low in the water but still a valuable prize, he ordered a boarding party, made up of the 'A' Gun crew, assembled to go aboard. He had briefly considered taking the disabled ship in tow, but with a risk of aerial attack that could place the remainder of the fleet in jeopardy he favoured taking off the *Pola's* crew and then sinking her with torpedoes. The boarding party were duly armed with cutlasses and pistols, and when brought smartly alongside a heaving line was thrown by the captain of the foc's'le who shouted, 'Catch hold of this you buggers!'[226]. Once secure the boarding party leaped, yelling and screaming onto the decks of *Pola* to take her. But the fight had long gone from her crew.

Once *Pola* had been torpedoed in the 'Act of God' that Captain Piba called the attack on his ship, all power had been lost and the great vessel had stopped dead in the water. Not only had propulsion been lost, but all electrical power to train and fight her guns too. A quiet finality of their situation fell upon the ship's crew as the ship gradually began to settle in the water, her guns facing impotently fore and aft, her ensign fluttering gently in the evening breeze. Then came the tumult of the night action that sunk her sister ships and the defeat was clear and close to completion. There would be no rescue. Captain Piba later wrote; 'I signalled my position and when 2 hours later I saw the battle I told my men that those who wished to do so could abandon the vessel.

---

[225] (Connell, 1987)
[226] (Connell, 1987)

About 700 men did so. I was contemplating sinking my vessel, for I could not fight her, when the *Jervis* came up and rescued us.'[227]

It was likely that this 'every man for himself' instruction from the *Pola's* Captain resulted in a breakdown of order, for it appears that a number of the 257 men left aboard, had decided the best course of action was to get drunk, no doubt included in this number, were some of those who, having been in the water for some time, had decided to return to the ship. As Pack writes, 'The officers' cabins had been looted by the ships company of the *Pola*, and empty Chianti bottles lay everywhere. Verification of this came when a number of the prisoners showed unmistakable signs of inebriation.'

Having set up a brow[228] between the two ships, the Italian prisoners filed in orderly fashion onto *Jervis* before she cast off from the cruiser and then stood off to finish *Pola* with a torpedo. However, this was ineffective and so, with no torpedoes left, Mack had to request assistance to complete the task.

'Signal from Jervis sir. Out of torpedoes, stand off and sink *Pola* at will.' Ravenhill requested the presence of the Gunner, Frank Miller, to issue him with his orders. Miller was born 6 July 1900, the son of a Lace Dresser from St. Ann's in Nottingham and one of seven children from his mother Annie. St Ann's was at the centre of the Lace Industry, where the sprawling Victorian housing was home to the Lace factories working men and women. It looked like Miller would follow his mother and father into the factories, as he was employed as a Warehouse boy, but in April of 1916 he joined the Royal Navy instead, signing up for 12 years. His training began as a Boy Seaman aboard *Powerful* before he was assigned to the cruiser *Aurora* and then *Gloucestershire*. Relatively short at 5' 3 inches, with dark brown hair and unusually, one Hazel eye, the other Grey, he was clearly an intelligent young man who was determined to do well within the service. He became a Leading Seaman in 1922, he studied hard and passed his Higher Education Certificate the following year before entering 'Vernon'in May 1925. Advancement to

---

[227] (M'Groarty, 1941)
[228] A brow is a gangway between two ships

Petty Officer came in 1928 and by 1930 he was acting Gunner aboard the 'S' Class Destroyer *Sesame*. His was a classic example of how life in the service could advance someone who otherwise had few prospects.

Now, as Gunner aboard *Nubian*, Miller was preparing to fire their first live torpedo in anger at an enemy ship. *Nubian* had a set of quad torpedo tubes located directly forward of the quarterdeck. In peacetime the live warheads were stored below, however right now, those live warheads, containing 810lbs of high explosive Torpex, were attached, armed and ready to fire on all four of the 21-inch, Mark IX torpedoes contained in their tubes. Each had a range of 11,000 yards when their speed was set at 41 knots, or 15,000 yards if set to 35 knots. However, it was very rare for a ship to launch a torpedo at such a distance, accuracy diminishing appreciably with distance. The Mark IX was not without its problems. The compressed air used in the propulsion system was pressurised to 3100lb/sq in, which meant the casing had to be free from any flaws. It had been known for such flaws to cause the torpedo to explode, and one such explosion resulted in the loss of the *Khartoum* on the 23 June 1940. Christopher Langtree describes the extensive damage that occurred; 'In *Khartoum's* case the flaw was near the fore end of the vessel and blew the warhead through the aft deckhouse setting fire to the gravity oil feed tank on the No. 3 gun deck. The resulting fire set off the aft magazine causing the loss of the ship. Interestingly, the torpedo warhead did not explode...'[229]

The searchlights from *Jervis*, slowly circling the *Pola*, illuminated the target for Miller. He could fire the torpedo from either the bridge, or from the tubes themselves, and one suspects it was from the later that he carried out the final act of the battle. The torpedo launched into the black water, and for those watching, the trace of bubbles that marked the progress of the deadly weapon would have been visible. Moments later the explosion of the warhead cracked open the night sky and the *Pola* was swiftly on her way to the bottom of the

---

(Langtree, 2002)[229]

sea.[230] Miller would receive the Distinguished Service Cross from the King the following year for his work that morning.

With daylight not far away, Mack gathered his flotilla together and they made for the rendezvous with the battle-fleet. Once re-grouped the fleet set a course for Alexandria, passing back over the area where the battle had been fought. The larger ships were unable to stop for survivors, that was left to the more manoeuverable destroyers. Adrian Holloway described the view from *Valiant;* 'There were many small boats, carley rafts and pieces of wreckage in the water, some of them with occupants. It was a pathetic sight, the remains of proud units of the Italian fleet now reduced to so much flotsam in Mussolini's so called 'Mare Nostrum''[231]. Whilst aboard *Gloucester,* Ernie Evans recalled; 'There were hundreds of bodies and also some survivors in the water. I looked down and saw bodies bumping against the side of the ship. As we watched we couldn't believe what we were seeing, and I remember someone saying it looked like the sea of the dead.'[232] Ken Hopper, also aboard *Gloucester* recalled; 'It was a beautiful day and as the fleet went back into formation, we must have been a formidable sight. There were hundreds of white bodies floating in the sea and I think most of them must have been killed by blast because they didn't appear to have any injuries. Many of the survivors were on chairs, doors, or mess deck tables although some were in carley floats. They waved to us to be rescued. It was an awesome sight for a youngster like me.'[233]

It is difficult to comprehend the assault on one's senses and emotions when confronted with such a scene as the ships crews witnessed. As the ships passed by, the voices of the men in the water could clearly be heard so anyone with an ounce of compassion must have felt pity for the men left behind whose chances of being picked up were small.

---

[230] Some accounts state that *Nubian* fired two torpedoes, the first being ineffective. It could be the first was in fact the one fired by Jervis.
[231] (Holloway, 1993)
[232] (Otter, 2017)
[233] (Otter, 2017)

The destroyers did stop for survivors, however this was no place to dally, for they were within range of enemy air attacks. For an hour the destroyers slowly manoeuvered amongst the wreckage, both human and material, accounting for some 900 men plucked from the oil covered sea before approaching enemy aircraft were detected, it was simply too dangerous to remain any longer. It did not matter that there was a rescue in progress, in wartime, whilst the ships remained afloat, they were a legitimate target, even if they were saving the lives of their enemy. Cunningham had a signal sent to the Italian High Command, informing them of the survivor's position and the following day an Italian ship picked up several hundred more, but despite such efforts, some 2400 Italian sailors were unaccounted for.

The fleet now proceeded to Alexandria, shadowed by JU88's which concentrated their attacks on the carrier. They were driven away by umbrella barrages and the Fulmars from *Formidable*. Approaching Alexandria, a submarine contact was picked up, the remaining Destroyers, *Nubian* included, peppered the sea with depth charges that generated huge plumes of water and stomach punching, concussion laden booms that drew cheers, even from the Italian prisoners.

From 17:00 the ships began to arrive back in harbour on what was a fine spring evening. They had gained a notable victory over their enemy, 5 ships in total sunk at the cost of one Albacore and its brave crew. The next morning, all the ships of the Mediterranean Fleet held a service of thanksgiving for the Victory at Cape Matapan.

The Battle of Cape Matapan was the last major sea action between large capital ships that was reminiscent of the Napoleonic era and of course in particular the Battle of Trafalgar. It demonstrated the projection of power using aircraft from both land bases and of course, the sea in the form of the Aircraft Carrier. The battle also illustrated the vital importance of accurate reconnaissance, concise communications and an effective use of modern technology in the form of Radar.

In researching this component of the narrative, it is clear how those first two topics were major contributors to the outcome of the battle and how both sides made errors. From the Italian perspective, their great strength was in excellent aerial reconnaissance that was blatantly missing during Operation Gaudo as well as being woefully let down by X-Cat. Indeed, the indication that British forces were 90 miles distant, when they were actually half that distance away gave Iachino a false impression that he could afford to send his prize cruisers to the rescue of the *Pola* as well as an Admiral, of whom he could rely on to make the correct judgement on whether *Pola* could be saved or not.

Tactically, we have already discussed the lack of Radar equipment and thus a nonexistent night fighting capability, *Fiume, Zara* and their Destroyer escorts literally walked blindly to their destruction because the main gun crews were not at their stations and the reliance on the Mark 1 eyeball to detect an enemy at night.

The Royal Navy, whilst the victors, perhaps did have an opportunity to take out more ships if the reconnaissance had been more accurate. As we have seen, there were instances of mistaken identity and errors in the estimation of speed and direction that allowed the *Vittorio Veneto* to retire from the scene of action and, despite being quite badly damaged, make her home port safely. Nevertheless, it was a resounding victory for the Royal Navy, resulting in the containment of the Regia Marina to its home ports for the remainder of the war. Admiral Cunningham wrote.

> Looking back on the engagement which is now officially known as the Battle of Matapan, I am conscious of several things which might have been done better. However, calm reflection in an armchair in the full knowledge of what actually happened is a very different matter to conducting an operation from the bridge of a ship at night in the presence of the enemy. Instant and momentous decisions have to be made in a matter of seconds. With fast-moving ships at close quarters and the roar of heavy gunfire, clear thinking is not easy. In no other circumstances than in a night action at sea does the fog of war so

completely descend to blind one to a true realisation of what is happening.[234]

From the perspective of my armchair, perhaps the mistakes made were already behind the Royal Navy by the time of the night action, and that if it had not been for the one torpedo that took out *Pola's* engine room and electrical power, maybe the battle would not have occurred at all?

---

[234] (Cunningham, 1951)

Chapter 12

Strike Force Malta

'Our job is to nip out and attack the Tripoli convoys by night'

The Battle of Tarigo

At dawn on the 6 April 1941, Operation Marita, the German invasion of Greece began. Attempting to hold the northern, mountainous border of Greece were the 6th Australian Division, the 2nd New Zealand Division and the British 1st Armoured Brigade. In essence, with Rommel's Deutches Afrika Corps (DAK) now on the offensive in North Africa, the allied armies were spread far too thin on two fronts. The attacking Germans deployed armour as well as infantry, supported by the Luftwaffe, they would prove to be unstoppable.

Operation Lustre continued to supply men and equipment to the expeditionary force in Greece, mainly through the port of Pireaus, which came under attack by Hajo Herrmann's JU88's of 7.KG 30. They approached the port from the direction of Corinth at 2100 hours, initially dropping mines into the harbour before falling upon the ships. One of these was the *Clan Fraser,* a munitions ship of 7529 tons, carrying 350 tons of TNT. Some 100 tons had already been unloaded onto the dock when she was straddled by 250kg bombs from the attacking bombers. Explosions tore through the dockside cranes and buildings, some exploded close to the ship literally lifting her from the water and in the process set her on fire, snapping her mooring lines and casting her adrift.

Attempts were made to bring the *Clan Fraser* under some control, if she were to hit a mine, then she may block the harbour entrance. Like a fireship from the age of sail, *Clan Fraser* became a menace to the other ships awaiting unloading and not long thereafter she set alight the *City of Roubaix* (7000 tons), and she too contained munitions.

All efforts came to nothing, when in the early hours of the following morning, *Clan Fraser* exploded quickly followed by the *City of Roubaix*. The result was cataclysmic in proportions. A large number of ships (almost 100 in total) were damaged or lost and the whole of the harbour complex was destroyed. The master of one ship described Pireaus being 'in a state of chaos caused by the explosion of *Clan Fraser*, which had been hit while discharging ammunition. The ship had disappeared and blown up the rest of the docks, and pieces of her were littered about the streets.'[235] The port was closed for 10 days, stifling the supply of much needed supplies to the defenders, but in the long run it would not matter.

In North Africa, the DAK had been rolling back the British and Commonwealth forces as far as Benghazi and were now pushing towards Tobruk. Whilst Rommel's staggering progress was to create an aura of invincibility that would cement his reputation as a master tactician and aggressive leader, the German High Command were very worried. The faster and further the DAK advanced, the longer and more stretched became their supply lines. Rommel had already considered this and had determined to take Tobruk before he could attack Egypt. If captured, Tobruk, a strategic port, would give the Afrika Corps the ability to shorten the supply line considerably and land the necessary supplies to facilitate the next phase of the campaign.

From the 13 to 16 April the Germans began to attack Tobruk, but resistance was strong everyone knew the significance of either capturing or defending the port. The defence was so strong that Rommel requested the transportation of the 15th Panzer Division for support. Of this unit, the 33rd Signals Battalion, a reserve reconnaissance Battalion, began loading onto ships in Naples, bound for Tripoli. The 33rd was made up of 3 Motorised companies, consisting of Signals, Radio and a Light Signals Supply Column as well as supporting vehicles for all three companies amounting to some 300 vehicles

---

[235] (Weal, 2009)

in total. 3000 troops with their officers would embark along with, fuel, ammunition, and stores.

Allocated to the convoy were four German vessels, *Adana* (4205 tons) accommodating the personnel. *Arta* (2452 tons) with 3500 tons of general stores, *Aegina* (2447 tons) and *Iserlohn* (3704 tons) transporting the vehicles and fuel. A fifth, Italian merchantman, the *Sabaudia* (3704 tons) carried the ammunition.

Providing escort cover for the convoy were three Regia Marina destroyers, led by the Navigatore Class, *Lucia Tarigo*. She was 350 feet long and displaced 2600 tons fully loaded with her compliment and associated stores. Like all her sister ships in the class she was typically flamboyant in design, having a long, fo'c'sle, two raked funnels and armed with three pairs of 4.7-inch guns mounted fore, aft and amidships. However, all the Navigatore class suffered from a top heavy construction that, whilst they were fast ships capable of 40 knots, required modifications to improve stability. These modifications included a clipper bow, but whilst this complimented her appearance, it actually reduced her top speed to about 28 knots. Commander Pietro de Cristoforo was *Tarigo's* commanding officer, born in Naples in 1900 he became a Midshipman at 19, a Capitano di Corvette in 1932, joining the *Tarigo* in November 1936.

Accompanying *Tarigo* were two Foglore Class destroyers, the *Lampo* (Capitano di Corvetta Marano) and the *Baleno (Capitano di Corvetta Arnaud)*. Smaller in size than *Tarigo* they were built as part of a second batch of 4 ships designed around the Freccia Class, being 315ft in length and 2,200 tons fully loaded. These classes also suffered from stability issues and despite modifications the problems persisted with a degradation in overall performance being the only result. Both ships were armed with two pairs of 4.7-in. guns fore and aft and distinguished by a single funnel.

The safest passage to Tripoli for such a convoy was to cross the Mediterranean to the west of Sicily over to the North Coast of Africa at Tunis, and then hug the coastline southwards passing to the west of Pantelleria, the

Kerkennah Islands and Sfax towards Tripoli all the time under the protection of air cover from X-CAT and the Italian Air Force.

The successful supply of the German forces with men, armour and general supplies with convoys was clearly a huge cause of concern for the British Commanders and their disruption became a priority. Desperate times required desperate measures, Cunningham was authorised to use *Barham* to block and then bombard the port of Tripoli along with the C-Class Cruiser, *Caledon* even if both were lost in the process. However, Cunningham had grave concerns; to man both ships in order to achieve their aims would require some 1000 seamen who were highly unlikely to return. Just to get in position, both ships would have to sail at speed, during daylight hours, inevitably coming under strong air attack, it was unlikely any of the sailors would survive. Fortunately, the plan was shelved. But the Navy would still be required to bombard Tripoli in due course, and if a battleship were damaged, then Cunningham conceded that it would be forced into the harbour and sunk as a block ship. Nevertheless, Cunningham received the following, personal and terse communique from The First Sea Lord.

> H.M. Government has given instructions that every possible step must be taken by the Navy to prevent supplies reaching Libya from Italy and by coastwise traffic even if this results in serious loss or damage to H.M. ships. The army's difficulty to stabilise and improve will be increased with every convoy reaching Libya and any coastal transportation of supplies. Failure by the Navy to concentrate on prevention of such movements to the exclusion of everything not absolutely vital will be considered as having let the side down.[236]

The challenge for Cunningham was how to build and operate a strike force in order to effectively attack the convoys. The destroyers available were limited in number, still greatly overworked and a mixed bag in their capabilities. He would have to pick out some of his most capable ships in order to make up a creditable force whilst losing their valuable fleet protection

---

[236] (Cunningham, 1951)

services. They would have to operate out of Malta in order to be in reasonable striking distance of the enemy convoys and to be on call at very short notice when a convoy was detected at sea. The problems in operating from Malta were the daily air attacks by the enemy and the counter reconnaissance which would quickly detect when the strike force was putting to sea. Therefore, the ships would need to be dispersed in separate berths, only joining up when sailing out on operations which to avoid detection and subsequent air attack would have to be at night. The disadvantage of night operations was fuel, which on Malta, was in short supply. In order to be effective and to get into position, the ships would have to sail for most of their time at high speed and so consume vast quantities of fuel. But problems are there to be overcome.

On the 8 April the one man in the Eastern Mediterranean that could lead such a force was Captain Philip Mack of D14. He was ordered to form and take command the Malta Strike Force from *Jervis*. He would be joined by the two most experienced and capable destroyers in the fleet, *Nubian* (Commander R.W. Ravenhill) and *Mohawk* (Commander J.W.M. Eaton). The last ship in the quartet was *Janus* (Commander J.A.W Tothill). In 1941, most of the smaller ships of the Navy fitted with radar were protecting the North Atlantic Convoys, however *Janus* had not long been refitted and she was now equipped with a Type 286 set, which would be most valuable in any night operations.[237]

Meanwhile *Nubian* had been quickly put back to work following the Battle of Matapan. She was at sea with Convoy ANF24 on the 2 April, bound for Pireaus, when attacked by high level bombers, during which the S.S. Devis was hit, starting fires in No.4 hold, killing 7 and injuring another 14. The following day (3 April), the bombers came again, but this time it was a Dive Bomber attack which fell upon them. The ammunition ship, *Northern Prince*, paid the

---

[237] In some accounts of the battle it is suggested that all of the ships in the strike force, with the exception of *Jervis*, had radar. I have been unable to corroborate this, and indeed there is no mention of radar installed in any of the ships with the exception of *Janus* either within the after action reports or during the inquiry into the sinking of *Mohawk*.

price, bombs setting her on fire, which eventually got out of control forcing abandonment of the vessel which exploded later that day.

On the 4 of April, a suspected submarine contact was picked up, *Nubian* and the Flower Class Corvette, *Hyacinth* were detailed to locate and attack the U-Boat. *Nubian* was equipped with 30 Mark VII Heavy Depth charges. These devices weighed some 440lbs, with 350lbs of TNT or amatol explosive encased in a barrel like steel case, detonated by water pressure which activated hydrostatic pistol that could be set to explode at depths down to some 300 feet below sea level with a rate of sink of about 16 feet per second. Depth Charges (dc's) were most destructive to a submarine if they detonated within 25 feet of the hull but could inflict serious enough damage to force the submarine to the surface if they got within 50 feet of the target vessel. To be on the receiving end of such a device would have shaken the nerves of the bravest of men. Akin to being trapped in a steel drum that is being hit with multiple lump hammers may get close, but the fear of being drowned by a massive inrush of water or trapped hundreds of feet at the bottom of the sea in pitch black, freezing conditions to die a lingering death from oxygen starvation or hypothermia is beyond comprehension.

The dc's were 'delivered' by two methods. A rail over the stern could handle 3 dc's at one time and was fed by two racks placed to Port and Starboard (3 dc's per rack), with a further 3 in reserve behind. These were lifted onto the stern rail by a small davit (crane). Above the aft superstructure there were a pair of dc Throwers (dct's), facing abeam, (at 90° angles to the ship). The dct's could launch a dc some 150ft from the side of the ship and thus, coupled with the stern rails, *Nubian* could fire a 5 dc pattern in one salvo. However, on this occasion, the submarine remained elusive, and having not fired a dc in anger, Nubian received orders to make for Suda Bay and await the arrival of *Jervis* and Captain Mack to receive further instructions.

The four ships joined up and refueled at Suda Bay on the 8 April. Captain Mack met with Ravenhill, Eaton and Tothill to discuss the deployment of the Malta Strike Force. They would sail on the evening of 9th, passing through the

Kithira passage under the protection of *Perth* and *Ajax*. On reaching Malta (which they reached at 06:00 on the 11th), they would disperse. *Jervis* would be moored in Dockyard Creek, *Nubian* and *Mohawk* at Mersa and *Janus* in Sliema. Once berthed, a daily routine began, as described by Hugh Mulleneux of *Jervis* in Connells, 'Mediterranean Maelstrom'.

> Our job is to nip out and attack the Tripoli convoys by night – during the day presumably we remain in harbour and provide a target for the bombers. One of us (D's Staff) has to go to the operations room at 1600daily to get the latest reconnaissance reports. If anything good comes through we sail out to attack at about 1900. I was the duty officer today and duly sat about the operations room from 1600 until 1830.[238]

The Tarigo convoy (named after the lead destroyer, *Luca Tarigo*) left Naples at 23:00 on the 13 April, and at noon, two days later was spotted by a Maryland from 69 Squadron (formerly Warburton's 431 Flight, having been given Squadron status in January 1941) passing Cape Bon off the Tunisian coast. The report correctly identified 5 Merchant Vessels with 3 Destroyers in escort on a southerly course for Tripoli. Mack ordered the ships prepared for sailing at 18:00 that evening, with the expectation to meet and engage the convoy somewhere near the island of Kerkennah that night. In 'Mediterranean Malestrom', G. G. Connell quotes CPO Wheeler, an Able Seaman aboard *Mohawk* as she and her crew prepared to depart. No doubt the atmosphere was similar across all 4 ships, which of course included Herbert aboard *Nubian*.

> We slipped out of Sliema creek that evening, we knew that something was definitely on that night, you could sense and smell it. At the first turn of the screws the older hands rolled their paper money carefully into thin rolls and placed them into condoms which had been drawn from the sickbay on the last run ashore and then stowed the packets in our belts...Night action - ship to ship was a hell of a lot different from the constant air attacks which were the normal daily routine at sea. This

---

[238] (Connell, 1987)

was the Navy against Navy, and we were confident. We were battle wise we were good and we knew it.[239]

At 18:36 the following signal was sent to the Strike Force from VAM (Vice Admiral Malta).

IMMEDIATE

To ... D14, Nubian, Mohawk, Janus

From... V.A.M.

Enemy position, course and speed 036° 12' North 011° 16' 180° 8 knots at 1665B. Disposition line abreast extended two miles, two destroyers ahead and one on port bow. Visibility four or five miles improving.

(1836/15)[240]

HMS Jervis - D14

At 01:00, Captain Mack sat back in his chair on the bridge of *Jervis*, tipped back his cap and rubbed his temples in contemplation. *Jervis* was leading the strike force, followed by *Janus, Mohawk* and *Nubian* which snaked the line in the rear. They were reaching the No.4 Buoy off the Kerkanah Bank, where they were expected to overtake the convoy, but there were no ships in sight. So, what had happened? The moon was appearing to the southeast, through the breaking clouds revealing in the dim light the moderate swell that was felt in the rise and fall of the ships passage. A little earlier it had been pitch black, and perhaps the convoy had sailed on unnoticed? Or could it be that the appearance of the Maryland the previous day had sent the convoy scurrying back towards Pantellaria? Alternatively, perhaps, the Maryland's crew had

---

[239] (Connell, 1987)
[240] (The Admiralty, 1941)

overestimated the speed of the convoy? That would mean Mack was in position too early. He chose the latter and turned onto a reciprocal, northerly heading, to meet the convoy head on.

30 minutes later, Telegraphist Hague reported from the w/t office that he had picked up a number of transmissions from the convoy, so many that he could get a reasonable fix to give an intercept track. After a few more minutes Mack decided to swing closer into the shore and perhaps within the southerly course of the convoy. He was right. On board *Janus*, her 286-radar shone back a clear set of contacts on a westerly bearing at a range of some 12,000 yards. Many pairs of eyes strained through binoculars, their owners trying to breathe slow to hold the optics steady, but the excitement made it almost impossible.

'Contacts bearing One Seven Zero Degrees, approximately six miles!', came the call from *Jervis'* port watch. Mack ordered, 'Make, Enemy in Sight signal to the flotilla, alter course to one four zero degrees, ring full ahead'. As the range began to close on the convoy, reports and orders were given calmly and professionally.

01:58 – 02:20 16 April 1941

Mack: 'Use night torpedo firing signal to the flotilla and signal, train torpedo tubes to starboard.' *Mack was contemplating their disposition even as he spoke the words, and soon decided that it would be better to position his force so that the convoy would be between his ships and the moon.*
Mack: 'Alter course to two, one zero and signal flotilla to, train torpedo tubes to port.'
Lookout: 'Five ships confirmed visual. Sir', followed a few minutes later by, 'Enemy bearing one four zero at 4 miles, now visual with 7 ships.'
Mack: 'Alter course to one seven zero.'
Lookout: 'Enemy bearing between one three five and one five zero, range two and a half miles.' **Mack:** 'Alter course one six zero degrees, stand by to fire.'
Lookout: 'Enemy confirmed 5 merchantmen, one large destroyer Navigatori Class ahead and to Starboard of the Convoy, a Foglore Class to the rear Starboard Quarter and another Foglore on the Port forequarter.'

Mack: 'Alter course to one five zero.'

Lookout: 'Enemy bearing one four zero.'

Mack: 'Engaging Foglore Class destroyer, bearing one zero zero degrees, Stand by.'

Signals: 'Signal from Janus, range zero two four (two thousand four hundred yards).'

Director Control: 'On target'.

Mack: 'Fire continuous (Each gun team is given freedom to select and fire independently of each other and the Director) ... 'Commence Firing, Commence Firing.'

At 02:20 *Jervis* engaged the *Balerno* but at point blank range, *Jervis*' shells flew over the top of the destroyer, it was just a moments reprieve. Almost immediately shots from *Janus*, using her radar range finding to its full effect, crashed into *Balerno*, wrecking her forward superstructure and killing Captain Arnaud and all the officers and men on the bridge. *Balerno* began to drift, coming under fire from the other British ships. Her crew frantically fought the fires that were raging about her as well as trying to fend off her attackers. She eventually grounded and began to sink on a sandbank.

The scene around *Jervis* was now complete mayhem as she, and the flotilla opened up on the convoy with everything they had. *Jervis*' three, twin mounted 4.7-in. guns were blasting everything at sight, at will, whilst her pom-poms and machine guns added a staccato backdrop to the booms of the bigger guns. Mack describes the targets as being at ranges of 2000 yards down to as little as 50 yards.

Suddenly there was a shout of alarm and bearing down on *Jervis* came one of the larger merchant vessels, clearly intent on slicing the destroyer in two. Mack bellowed 'Full Ahead!' The engine room responded, Jervis shooting forward and out of the path of the merchantman. The situation was clearly one of confusion and danger, Mack ordered Fighting Lights turned on in an effort to prevent a friendly fire situation.

Captain Cristofaro in *Tarigo* now turned about, leading the *Lampo* at full speed back down the line of the convoy and in-between the attacking destroyers. Hugely outgunned and with one of his escorts already out of action, he must have known that his chances of saving the merchant ships was a somewhat forlorn hope. It certainly was for the *Lampo*. As she came down the line, *Jervis* illuminated her with searchlights, *Lampo* did the same to *Jervis*, much to the consternation of two men who were up her main mast trying to disentangle the radio aerials that had come adrift due to her violent manoeuvres. The men somehow scrambled down as *Lampo* poured fire into *Jervis*. 'We were targets for all kinds of small arms; red, white, and green tracer came uncomfortably close. I shouted to Bob, 'Are you a bloody hero' and to this day neither of us can remember coming down the masthead ladder, we must have done for we picked up the loose ends of the aerial and scampered aft to attach it.'[241]

The gunnery control officer aboard *Jervis* had by now, resumed control of his three 4.7-in. batteries, directing a concentrated broadside into *Lampo* as she passed by in *Tarigo's* wake. *Jervis* fired off two torpedoes of her own, one at the *Tarigo*, which Mack thought may have hit her aft the other at a merchant vessel that was stopped, but this missed. Just 1500 yards away from *Jervis*, the *Sabaudia* finally succumbed to her fires and a torpedo from *Janus* which set off the ammunition stores in her hold. The resulting explosion literally blew the ship to pieces. Mack described a 2000ft ball of fire and smoke above the wreck, before pieces of wreckage (some he estimated at being 20lbs in weight) began to shower *Jervis*, turning the sea around her to a boiling cauldron. On later inspection, the ammunition was identified as German. Hugh Mulleneux from *Jervis* described the explosion.

> We were too close for it to be at all pleasant. There was a gigantic explosion, conflagration and blast effect, the latter knocking everyone on the bridge down except for the pilot and myself and it blew our tin hats off. Then for what seemed an eternity it was like living in an inferno and one got also a good idea of how unfortunate inhabitants of

---

[241] (Connell, 1987)

Sodom and Gomorrah must have met their end. We were entirely surrounded by fire, and directly above our heads ammunition was blowing up like so many Chinese crackers. The sea boiled and sizzled as all the bits started to come down - some white hot - and at the same time reflected a fiery glow. Great lumps came pattering down from the sky and harmed no one.[242]

'Signal from *Nubian*. *Mohawk* torpedoed and sunk, picking up survivors.' With all of the enemy ships on fire and effectively out of action, Mack responded to *Nubian*. 'Burn masthead lights and we will come to assist.' Moments later a torpedo track was sighted, apparently coming from the burning *Tarigo*. Those who could see the deadly weapon heading directly for them must have held their breath, for it would hit right underneath them. But underneath *Jervis* it passed, much to the relief of all.

Jervis approached the upturned hull of *Mohawk*, her lights picking out men in the water, many covered in cloying, thick, black oil. Some men were clinging to her keel. Mack called out for the men on the keel to swim across, but they appeared too distressed to leave the comparative safety of their steel island. Mack had *Jervis* pick her way carefully between the men in the water to close on the wreck and get these men off.

Stoker George Morel of *Jervis*, had been at his action station for the duration of the battle, one of the aft ammunition supply party. He had not been aloft since they had gone into action, his only perception of the previous hour had been trying to remain standing as *Jervis* twisted and turned whilst manoeuvring. There was too, the thrumming and changing engine tones, the great cracks from the 4.7-in. guns and the rattle of machine guns. Now sight was restored, and a different view of the world came. There were fires raging that lit up the sky behind them, the odd explosion still rolled across the water, whilst illuminated close by were the men and the wreck of *Mohawk*. Morel swung a leg over the side of *Jervis*, and down to the water using the scrambling

---

[242] (Connell, 1987)

nets on which some of *Mohawks* survivors were already clambering up. Morel entered the water to lend a hand to those who were beginning to struggle.

'Some of them were so bemused and shocked that I swam out a few yards to help them inboard quickly. I remember thinking that if the ship had to shove off quickly, I would be left behind.'[243]

Having picked up all the survivors, Mack ordered a position fix of *Mohawks* wreck taken from the position of the Nos. 3 & 4 Kerkanah light boys, 34° 56. 5'N; 11 42°.4'E. As the fix was being made, one of the merchant vessels was seen to turn over and sink. Mack then ordered *Janus* to sink the floating wreck of poor *Mohawk*. According to *Jervis'* log, it was 04:03 when they set a course 080 degrees, *Jervis* leading *Janus* and *Nubian*, zig zagging 10 degrees either side of their track and soon making 29 knots for Malta.

HMS Janus

Commander John Anthony William Tothill hailed from Bradford upon Avon, joining the Royal Navy on the 15 May 1919 and made a Lieutenant on the 30 April 1928. He took command of *Janus* in November 1938 when she was commissioned, he was 36 at the time. Whilst a Midshipman he was involved in a serious accident that it appears to have stalled his progression, but whatever the disability he sustained, he was able to overcome it and continue as a cadet.

Tothill was not one for sports, perhaps because of his accident but he could ride (horses) well. He was assessed as, 'quiet and rather diffident personality with good social qualities but should turn out well' and was 'excellent socially'. Despite being 'prone to moments of extreme sloppiness', his peers thought he could become a 'good officer', but he would 'need watching'. By now, of course, he was a capable and reliable commander. In the coming minutes he

---

[243] (Connell, 1987)

and his crew would fight their ship in a manner that all destroyer commanders lived for.

'On Target' was indicated to the bridge, quickly followed by the order to 'Shoot'. *Janus* had a good firing solution using her 286-radar giving a range of 2400 yards to *Balerno* and her guns opened up a split second after *Jervis* at 02:20. The 4.7-in. shells from *Janus* tore apart *Balerno's* bridge superstructure creating a huge fire. It was quite clear that she was disabled and no longer a fighting force. The 286 radar now demonstrated its limited capability where multiple, and cluttered targets were concerned, and so for now her guns were aimed using her Advanced Fire Control Clock (AFCC) in the Transmitting Station (TS). In the Director Control Tower (DCT), Leading Seaman Robert Wills (J115277) was Director Layer. A former Page Boy from West Ham, he joined the Royal Navy in 1928 (on his 18th birthday), signed up for 12 years, took his educational exams in 1934 and now found himself in a key position during the attack, for which he would be awarded a D.S.M. Wills picked out a merchant vessel at 4000 yards, the 4.7-inch guns swivelled on their mountings towards the target, the TS lights shone green, the firing gongs sounded, and *Janus* opened fire once more. The first salvo missed but with some adjustments for range hits were scored on the second salvo, and by the fifth there were fires observed on the target vessel. The guns were now retrained onto a second vessel and once that was on fire, the order was given to 'Check Fire'.

With a momentary lull in the action, Tothill decided to try and finish off the *Balerno* with a torpedo. This was initiated from the bridge, but the torpedo ran wide of the target. With the leading three merchantmen now providing clear targets, *Janus* opened up with her main armament once more, concentrating on the lead ship. Hits were obtained when Tothill altered the attack to torpedoes. There was some disappointment that no hits were observed from the bridge, however the launcher crew were adamant that one had found its mark.

Lampo now steamed fast into view, coming between *Janus* and *Jervis,* and in doing so her crew launched a pair of torpedoes at *Janus,* which, fortunately missed astern. There was little that *Janus* could do in retaliation as none of her guns could come to bear on the fast moving enemy, however her pom-poms could, and tell tale sparkles appeared along the enemy ships side as the shells hit home.

Having been taking evasive action which had momentarily taken her out of position, Tothill brought *Janus* back into the fray. The *Sabaudia,* now on fire and 'on-target' for the torpedo crew would be their next victim. Ascertaining the position of *Nubian* and *Mohawk* from their fighting lights, and that they were not likely to be hit by mistake, one torpedo was sent on its way, causing the explosion that showered *Jervis* with wreckage. However, as the torpedo sped towards its target, Tothill was informed that *Mohawk* had, herself, been torpedoed. Moments later the *Lampo* was spotted once more, making smoke, trying to protect what was left of the convoy. Tothill ordered *Janus* full ahead to 30 knots, turning hard out to port to try and bring the main guns to bear. As soon as the bows of *Lampo* were spotted appearing from the smoke, a firing solution came from the TS and three hits were observed with the first salvo before the ship disappeared once more into the smoke.

Attention now turned to the *Luca Tarigo,* and *Janus* began to give chase with high speed manoeuvres at speeds from 16 knots up to 30 knots. The range was now so short that any computed fire solutions were unnecessary, the guns were aimed simply using their fixed sights. *Tarigo* fired back, but as Tothill wrote in his report, 'The Italian gunnery was poor, their tracer could be seen going high and wide.'[244] Whilst the guns did their damage, three more torpedoes were fired, one initiated from the bridge, the other two from the launchers local control. None found their mark.

At 02:59, Tothill ordered 'Cease Fire!' *The Luca Tarigo* was, he considered, no longer a threat and 'in a sinking condition'. Her guns were finally silent, she was on fire and dead in the water. Tothill then began to retire towards

---

[244] (The Admiralty, 1941)

Jervis but received a signal from Mack to finish off the stricken destroyer. From 2000 yards, *Janus* opened fire once more with many hits seen to strike home. Another fire broke out amidships as the gallant destroyer began to list to starboard.

Half an hour later, with the 286 radar once more online and effective, a large contact was detected on a bearing of 330°, 10,000 yards away. *Janus* made course for the contact, but Tothill soon realised he was in the vicinity of the sand back and in danger of running his ship aground. He hauled off to the eastwards, whilst the lookouts reported that what was thought, from the radar 'picture' to be a single ship was in fact two ships aground and less than 1500 yards apart.

Returning to meet up with *Jervis* & *Nubian* revealed that *Mohawks* surviving crew had been picked up, whilst *Mohawk* lay overturned, an air pocket within the forward part her hull exposing 100 feet of her length with her inverted bow about 6 feet out of the water. A signal came over from *Jervis* instructing *Janus* to finish off what was left of Mohawk. The crew of 'B' gun were ordered to fire one of the guns at quarters (i.e. at their discretion). After 4 hits were observed the air was released from *Mohawks* hull which slipped below the surface of the sea.

As *Janus* prepared to get underway for home, one lucky survivor from *Mohawk* was spotted in the water and picked up. Tothill then ordered full ahead in an effort to form up astern of the departing *Jervis*, with *Nubian* soon joining at the rear. A small group of rafts was passed as the three ships began to pick up speed, their bow waves hissing and forming large wakes aft. From the rafts came the distinct hail of 'Heil Hitler'. Tothill noted that an Able Seaman who was standing forward, observing the rafts as they passed, gave what Tothill described as 'the service reply of 'passing''. As this signal is normally made as a series of blasts from the ships horn, it must be left to one's imagination what signal the Seaman actually gave.

HMS Nubian

Ravenhill had his ship closed up for action, all watertight doors shut, the ship darkened with the men at their battle stations and the damage control parties on standby. Earlier, Ravenhill had taken to the ships tannoy, outlining their intentions that evening to locate and engage a convoy of merchant ships which included three destroyers. They were to sink, burn and destroy.

At 00:45, CPO Leonard Stephen Morris (J100124) was steering the ship, snaking the line astern of *Janus*, his hands gripping the wheel, bare forearms taught and bronzed, revealing the tattoo of a bird on his left arm. Hailing from Fareham, he had been an Apprentice Turner before the sea had beckoned, and he had joined the Navy in 1921 on his 19th birthday. He was promoted to Petty Officer in 1934, and Chief Petty Officer whilst aboard *Nubian*. He would be a Lieutenant before the end of the war.

At 01:20, from what he could hear down the voice pipe from the bridge, he was about to steer *Nubian* into action. A sighting was made of some dark shapes on the horizon, which was initially thought to be land, but then it became clear these were indeed the ships of the convoy. Leonard smiled to himself as he thought how busy his shipmate and Yeoman of the Signals, Ellis Watson (JX133088) was going to be in the coming minutes. True enough, the signals appeared to be coming thick and fast. *Jervis* had ordered torpedo tubes to starboard and then moments later a counter signal to train to port which indicated to him that he would soon be required to turn the ship about. Sure enough, the order came, and Leonard spun the wheel, to bring *Nubian* onto the required course. Moments later he could hear someone call out 'Convoy Red 20, inclination 10° to the right', followed by his Commander ordering, 'Increase speed to 25 knots.' *Nubian* was attacking.

On the bridge, Midshipman Peter Hopper was tasked with relaying his Commanders firing orders to the Director Control Tower (DCT) behind the bridge. Within this small, cramped, revolving tower were four crew positions for the Layer, Trainer, Gunnery Control Officer and the Range Taker. When required for High Angle, or HA operation (air attack, long range bombardment) all four positions were manned. However, for the expected surface action this night the DCT was crewed for LA (Low Angle) operation which meant that only the Layer and the Gunnery Control Officer were required.

Like Leonard Morris, Petty Officer Walter Wynne (J94813) had been with *Nubian* since her commissioning in 1938 and promoted to PO in June 1940. This evening, the 38 year old, ex Grocers Assistant would be the Director Layer in the DCT alongside the ships 1st Officer Lt. Bush who was acting as Gunnery Control. They had voice links to the Bridge and down to the TS, in particular to PO Walter Keens (J113646) who was heading up the team inputting the information from the DCT into *Nubians* 'brain', the AFCC. Keens, 31 years old at the time, from Petersfield in Hampshire, was another of *Nubians* originals.

Just after 02:00, Midshipman Hopper relayed the first target to Bush in the DCT, a merchant vessel at the rear of the convoy. Wynne and Bush passed the target information to the Transmitting Station down on the forward upper deck, where the course, speed, range and relative bearing of the target was fed into the AFCC. The AFCC was also fed with the current barometric pressure as well as *Nubians* speed and course so that the guns could be correctly trained on the target

At 02:10 the ting of the firing gongs sounded, followed by the flash, smoke and loud report from *Nubians* 4.7-in. guns. The first salvo, in normal Naval gunnery procedure, was aimed 200 yards short of the targets estimated range and bearing, the second, 400 yards beyond. The third salvo was brought back by 200 yards and with that the target should be 'bracketed' or 'straddled'. Once this was achieved, the guns could be instructed to 'fire for effect'. In this instance, it was not necessary. Two spouts of water rose up either side of the merchantman before the third struck home. A large explosion erupted aft of the target, and a fire broke out on her decks.

Ravenhill ordered *Nubians* guns to bear on the second ship from the rear and then to a third, and smaller ship (probably the *Sabaudia*) that was angling away from the convoy to port. The flash of accurate hits was observed before smoke began to obscure the targets. 'Check Fire!' came from Ravenhill, he needed the smoke to clear before the guns could be brought effectively to bear once more. Then he issued new steering orders down to Morris and a reduction in speed to 20 knots in order to bring them back around to the head of the convoy and clear of the smoke.

'Destroyer starboard beam, 1000 yards, reciprocal course!' All heads turned to the right, 'Mr. Hopper, have that ship targeted please and instruct the point five machine guns to open fire at will.' barked Ravenhill, who then called to Sub Lieutenant Kirkland Lacey, 'Mr. Lacey, have your Pom-pom crew target the oncoming destroyer, fire for effect.' In the confusion of the action, and from some conflict in the reports, it is not clear which destroyer was being engaged, but it was most likely the *Luca Tarigo*. Hits were observed flashing below the bridge superstructure as well as aft, and she was seen to return fire. However, the order to 'Check Fire!' came once more as *Mohawk* crossed in between *Nubian* and the target.

Out of the smoke there suddenly appeared the towering form of the leading merchantman. Ravenhill ordered 'Full ahead!' which allowed *Nubian* to clear away in the nick of time and avoiding what appeared to be a clear intent to ram her. 'Signal from *Mohawk* Sir. 'Have been hit by torpedo."' There was a moment of shock written across all the faces of those who had heard the signalman. No one, it appeared, had heard an explosion, besides, which ship could have fired on *Mohawk*? All of the enemy destroyers appeared to be disabled. Ravenhill called up Ellis Watson to communicate *Mohawks* misfortune to D14 (Mack) aboard *Jervis*.

Now the *Lampo* came into view off the port quarter, and once more Peter Hopper was instructed to have the DCT engage. The firing gongs sounded for what would be the last time, shells from several salvoes repeatedly found their mark bringing the little Foglore destroyer, reeling from the onslaught, slowly to a halt, mortally crippled. She began to drift towards the sandbank to join *Balerno*, her crew broken and bleeding upon her decks.

After a hasty wild goose chase to close with the contact that *Janus* had reported from her radar, *Nubian* returned to the site of her stricken sister ship and between 03:13 and 04:05 she gingerly picked her way around the forlorn scene, picking up survivors. At 04:10 Nubian was under way and just 13 minutes later, she was making for Malta on a heading of 080°, at 29 knots.

HMS Mohawk

Commander John William Musgrave Eaton was born 3 November 1902 and educated at Temple Grove prep school in Eastbourne before joining the Navy and attending Osborne and Dartmouth, being promoted to Lieutenant in 1925. A keen rugby player and one who kept himself in shape at all times, fitted well with required attributes of an officer cadet. In his initial years it was commented upon that he was of 'dubious personality, very sensitive, inclined to be a little sure of himself and does not relish the advice of those older than himself.' His records state that he lacked 'sea sense' but was keen and reliable and it was fortunate that, although seen as an error of judgement on his part, he was not blamed for the loss of a ships anchor in a subsequent hearing in January 1927.

However, his leadership qualities improved with time, and by the end of 1929 he was an 'above average leader, keeps ship in beautiful condition, knows his men and was a considerable personality.' In the Officers mess he was very popular being 'charming socially and a clever entertainer' with an ability to play the Piano, Guitar and he was a good singer. Eaton, an 'Officer with a marked ability' was therefore the right man to take over command of *Mohawk*, that when launched, was the epitome of how a Destroyer should look and perform.

Right now, *Mohawk* was trailing *Nubian*, which had slowed to 20 knots in order to reposition alongside the convoy. In doing so, the two ships dropped out of formation with *Jervis* and *Janus*. During the initial phase of the engagement, Eaton had conserved his ammunition as the lead ships had already caused much damage. Once a target was selected, accurate and deadly fire was laid down by Petty Officer Walter Whitehorn (K58933) in *Mohawks* DCT, striking several merchantmen before turning the guns on the *Luca Tarigo*. Hits were observed amidships *Tarigo* where fires had broken out, the flames roaring and showering sparks into the dark sky.

Aboard the *Luca Tarigo*, the bridge had been smashed to pieces. Captiano Cristofaro lay bleeding profusely on the shattered deck, one leg had been torn off by shell splinters. He managed to pull off his belt to use as a tourniquet whilst beside him, his Executive Officer Pietro Dante Radaelli was breathing his last. The shots from *Mohawk* had hit the forward gun director, and since the bridge was destroyed he knew that his ability to direct any sort of counter fire was very remote. Shortly thereafter, his engineering chief, Cap Luca Balsofiore who had a serious headwound that had blinded him, was assisted to the broken bridge to deliver his engineering report before he too succumbed to his wounds. Cristofaro had no doubt already guessed that the ships engines were out of action, as was gunnery control and steering. However, despite the dire situation, they could still fight.

As his leg wound was being crudely bandaged, using a sailor's smock, Cristofaro set out his final orders to what remained of his officers and men who were gathered around him. The ship could be steered from the aft wheel position, and it may be possible to fire the aft gun, and perhaps even the aft torpedo tubes could be deployed. STU Ettore Bisagno was to take charge of ship and make his way aft with haste as the ship was foundering, mercifully it appeared that the enemy ships no longer saw the *Tarigo* as a threat as their incoming fire had ceased.

Once he had made his way to the stern of the ship, Bisagno ascertained from Sub Lt. Espedito Fantasia[245], the Deputy Chief Engineer, that the ship could indeed be steered. Bisagno, with the help of some able seamen and Chief Adriano Marchetti managed to swing outboard the rear, twin torpedo tube whilst instructing Fantasia to try and position them with what leeway and steerage they had to fire on *Mohawk*. By now, *Tarigo* was beginning to sink by the stern, and her fires were so fierce that the men at the torpedo tubes would not be able to remain there long, but gradually, *Mohawk* came into view, about a mile away, and the first two torpedoes splashed into the water. The men somehow managed to load a third and that too entered the water and sped on its way towards *Mohawk*. With that, the order was given to abandon ship.

Soon after *Mohawks* final salvo flew towards *Tarigo*, a lookout reported torpedoes had been launched by the enemy ship, but Eaton was not overly concerned as it appeared these had been aimed at *Jervis* and *Janus*. For now, Eaton and the men on the bridge of *Mohawk* were watching *Nubian* turning to port and just ahead of the lead merchantman which, in the next moment made its intentions clear as it turned hard over, heading straight for *Mohawk* in order to ram her at full speed. The merchantman missed Mohawk astern by what Eaton later considered no more than half a cable's distance (about 100 yards). He quickly ordered the helmsman to bring them around to starboard on a parallel course and for all guns to bear on the merchantman. As *Mohawk* began to turn, the first of *Tarigo's* torpedoes came streaking through the water, impacting just below Y turret (it is possible the second torpedo was the one that passed under *Jervis*).

The resulting explosion completely blew away *Mohawks* stern and in an instant, there was no trace of Y turret, indeed anything or anyone that was behind it. Eaton shouted, 'All engines stop!' *Mohawks* forward motion, still under the helm, began to decrease whilst she continued to cut a turn to starboard. Eaton was thinking hard and fast now, his experience and training taking over he quickly began issuing orders to continue the fight. 'Guns, target

---

[245] (ILR22)

and engage that merchantman, fire at will. Miller: (P.O. James Miller, Telegraphist, J110977, once a rivet heater from Yorkshire, born in 1908), signal *Nubian*. "We have been torpedoed", then be ready to remove all secret code books in case we have to abandon ship.' Eaton picked up the telephone connected to the quarterdeck and in particular his engineering officer, Lt. Cmd John Russell de Meza Warren, 'Damage report as quick as you can please Mr. Warren'.

Forward of the ship, both A & B turrets were training onto their target. Below Petty Officer John Bains (K76925) began to galvanise the forward supply parties to deliver shells up to guns that were hungry for ammunition. The shells were loaded into a set of 3 parallel rails, slanting at about 45 degrees through the decks to the gun turret. The shells were lifted by a simple pulley with a T-bar that, as pulled downward (similar to a weight training pulley), propelled the shell up the rails. In the film 'In which we serve', a similar mechanism can be seen in operation. During action stations, those Stokers that were not on duty in the engine compartments were tasked, along with the Stewards, to supply shells to the guns from the ships magazines. Shortly after the target order had been given, both A & B guns began rapid fire on the merchant ship, gaining hits almost immediately and setting her on fire.

At the stern of the ship and in the engine rooms, the damage control parties were hard at work making sure she stayed afloat and could continue to fight. E.R.A. Basil Briscoe (DMX61563) was one of the aft ammunition supply teams feeding shells up to 'X' turret. He was above the wardroom when the first torpedo struck, and it was a miracle that he was still alive, all of *Mohawk's* stern behind him had simply vanished. He quickly gathered his damage control team and began plugging holes that were letting in water by hammering home wooden shores. He also found that one of the 5' Downton Suction Pump pipes was broken and needed repairing. The Downton Pump was a hand pump, located on the upper deck just ahead of the aft funnel. The pump connected to 5-in. pipes which terminated at the bottom of each watertight compartment where a straining box prevented any rubbish being sucked into the pipework. Despite being hand powered it was very effective and could pump out water at a rate of between 4.5 and 7 tons per hour, critical in preventing the loss of the ship if the portable pumps were knocked out or there was no power.

Below Briscoe, Thomas Alfred Read (J87611), supervising 'X' magazine, may have been excused for wishing we had stayed in Eastbourne to become a Blacksmith. At 41, he was another of the older hands and one with a cool head when needed, which was certainly the case right now. The bulkhead between X and Y magazine was buckled in towards him, on the other side, where Y magazine used to be, was just open sea. Thankfully the bulkhead appeared to be holding for now. Several of the men were down with shell splinters, but they were all alive, they just needed to get out of there fast. Read helped the men up the ladders, before closing the watertight hatches and sealing the room. He then located Lt. Cmd Warren to report the damage, then packed the wounded off to the sick bay before reporting to the damage control party.

According to Eaton, it was barely three minutes after he requested a damage report that the telephone on the bridge rang. Eaton snatched the receiver from its cradle and listened intently to his engineering officer, the news was better than he had hoped. There was no immediate danger from fire, but the stern had been blown away, including Y turret, her crew and supply party. Despite this, the bulkheads were holding and therefore the ship was unlikely to founder. Miraculously it appeared one of the propellor shafts was intact and they may get the ship underway. Warren hung up his telephone having completed his report, checked the damage control parties had the situation in hand before heading down to the boiler rooms to supervise getting *Mohawk* underway once more, sadly as a consequence, he would go down with the ship.

Ordinance Artificer Samuel Corsie (P/MX 51465) was busy trying to repair 'X' gun and whilst the activity was keeping his mind off what was going on around him, it looked like he would be hard pressed to get it operational once more. He deduced the stokers of the ammunition supply party would be of more use in helping their shipmates to get *Mohawk* underway and reported as such to damage control. So it was that Stoker Walter Purkis (K58933) came to be making his way from the stern of *Mohawk* to assist in Boiler Room 1. He walked down the starboard side towards the bow past the motorboat and at the whaler took a left turn between the funnels to see if he could ascertain the damage on the port side before going below. A seaman was busy attending to the whaler, apparently getting it ready to launch. That did not bode well.

A & B turret guns continued to pour rapid fire into the convoy, the gun teams and those on the bridge preoccupied with fighting the ship, whilst the damage control teams continued their efforts at the aft end of *Mohawk*. Consequently, no one spotted the tracks of *Tarigo's* third torpedo, not that they could have done much about it. As *Mohawk* slowly drifted to starboard, she presented a beam-on target for the onrushing device. Just five minutes after the first torpedo struck, *Tarigo's* last torpedo penetrated *Mohawks* hull six feet below the waterline almost dead centre of No.3 boiler room, where it exploded, ripping a huge hole in her side. Martin Brice in his book 'Tribals', describes the catastrophic result of the explosion. 'No.3 boiler burst, scalding people on deck. The centre line of the upper deck split open, plunging all standing on the spot into the bottom of the ship. The torpedo tubes fell into the engine room, crushing most of the watch below.'[246]

Stoker Perkis had reached the port side when the torpedo hit. Naturally turning around to the sound of the explosion, he saw a great water spout rising up above the ship, on top of which was the poor seaman who he had seen attending the whaler.

In Boiler Room 1, Stoker P.O. William Thomas Taylor (KX75075), born in Gosport in 1907, was on watch when the first torpedo hit, he later recalled that he hardly felt a thing, but the second explosion threw him from the port side of the boiler room, right across to starboard. Shortly thereafter water began to flow in from the bulkhead on the port side, between Boiler Room 1 & 2.

---

[246] (Brice, 1971)

Mohawk was mortally wounded, and her end would come quickly. For a moment, Eaton thought they may get away with it, as she seemed to settle low in the water but on an even keel, however his hopes were quickly dashed. No.3 boiler room had flooded almost instantly causing *Mohawk* to rapidly list to port with her stern now submerged as far as the torpedo tubes. There was nothing for it but to order all hands on-deck, and abandon ship.

Down in No.2 boiler room, Stoker P.O. James Robb (KX77374) and Stoker George Brown (P/KX92164) began to shut down their boiler as the lights flickered and the water rose rapidly around them. As the ship began to list, Robb, who had 15 years in the service, was no doubt trying to keep himself and Brown calm under what would have been terrifying circumstances. The fact that the ship could heel over at any second, trapping them within the hull would have been obvious to both men. As *Mohawk* leaned over further and further, their only means of escape was the ladders to the deck hatches. But they had to shut the boilers down. With the ship listing over the ladders were canted over at such an angle they may prove impossible to ascend. It must have seemed an eternity to the men, but they succeeded in their task and with great difficulty, they clambered up the ladders to safety.

Once the two men reached the deck there appeared little alarm. Lt. Peter Dixon RNVR was supervising the launching of six Carley life rafts with ex milkman, CPO Ernest Lethridge (J104458), it was all they had, *Mohawks* whaler was little more than splinters, whilst the other boats could not be deployed due to the angle of the ships list. That meant many men were taking to the water with either a life vest or nothing at all. Able Seaman George Akehurst from Worthing[247] was just 19 years old, a bakers roundsman before the war, he had been one of the bridge lookouts when *Mohawk* was hit. He dived into the water when the order to abandon ship was called. Fortunately, he had been a keen swimmer at school, and after 15 minutes found a float to cling to; it would be 2 hours before he was picked up.

---

[247] (Wor22)

In *Mohawks* dying moments, there was one last important task to perform, the destruction of her Confidential Books (C.B.s). The task fell to P.O. Telegraphist James Miller who ordered his team to throw overboard all those documents that were already weighted, from the W/T Office and from their lockers on the bridge. In the W/T Office there stood a safe which contained a number of important documents that were not weighted, so the simplest way of dealing with these was to manhandle the safe out onto deck and overboard. Not at all easy in a sinking ship that was listing badly, but somehow Miller managed it. Once complete, Miller went over the side of the ship, and as is custom, Eaton, *Mohawks* Commanding Officer, followed being the last man into the water.

Some two hours later, once the fighting was over *Jervis, Janus* and *Nubian* arrived to pick up *Mohawks* survivors. Both ships had to gingerly approach the mass of bobbing heads, Carley floats ringed with men clinging to their ropes, and the little lights from those who had managed to put on a life jacket. One of those with a lifejacket (although he said it was 'a bit knocked about'), was 20 year Able Seaman George Albert Wheatland. He was interviewed by the Bognor Regis Observer when he was back in England on leave. Having been blown into the water he observed that there was fuel oil all over the sea, and worse, he was in the middle of a large patch. It is perhaps a hint of the trauma of such a situation that the correspondent wrote, "Its nasty stuff,' said Mr. Wheatland meditatively, 'and I inhaled a lot of it."[248]

Nubians scrambling nets were lowered to receive *Mohawks* survivors. C.P.O. Thomas Edgar Tribe (J97508), another former Milkman from Brighton, had joined the navy in 1922 when he was 18, a strapping lad, standing nearly six feet tall. He served aboard *Barham* and *Effingham* for 3 years following her stint in the East Indies. One must assume that he had many discussions about his time aboard with Herbert. On this night he would earn a DSM, 'For coolness and efficiency under fire, and energy and resourcefulness when recovering survivors.' He was not alone in his efforts, Sick Berth P.O. Frank Harvison (MX48091) was recommended for a Mention

---

[248] (Bog22)

in Despatches by his CO, 'For carrying out his duties as Sick Berth Petty Officer with great cheerfulness, and showing unusual initiative and efficiency in the emergency treatment of many survivors from MOHAWK.'

The final word from the crew of Mohawk must come from CPO Wheeler, quoted in G.G. Connell's 'Mediterranean Maelstrom'.

We started to sink by the stern and also listing heavily to port. The captain ordered abandon ship; my station was the starboard whaler, but it was so much matchwood now. So it was over the side and swim for it. I had a lifebelt on and uninjured too, I wasn't too badly off, at that moment after a few minutes in the water I spotted a Carley raft ahead of me and made for it. There were about eight of the crew onboard it, mostly to my surprise stokers; how the hell did they get out of that flaming inferno? One stoker petty officer was badly injured but managed a grin and said 'You damned near missed the last boat young Wheeler.' I remember chaps calling for their oppos hoping to find them safe and well... About two hours later the fight was over and *Jervis, Janus* and *Nubian* turned to pick us up. The Carley raft I was on bumped alongside *Nubian* and we were soon scrambling up the nets to the safety of *Nubians* deck. The hospitality of *Nubian's* ship's company was overwhelming, we survivors were treated like long lost brothers.

There were a dozen of us *Mohawks* washing each other down in *Nubian's* ship's company bathroom. Suddenly in steps my oppo H.G. Fleming covered in blood and oil fuel but with his cheeky smile on his face. 'Anyone want to buy a battleship?' he asks. His smile was short-lived however for when he started to strip he took off his service belt and undid the pocket to take his money out. Then with a look of horror and disbelief he held up the oily soggy mess. The pocket had been slashed by a piece of shrapnel during his escape from 'X' gun and the waterproofing condom had been torn to shreds. 'I was keeping this for

Carmelita,' he said as we all howled with laughter, for his Carmelita worked in the 'Lucky Wheel' down the 'Gut' and she was fifty if a day.[249]

Aftermath

Returning to Malta at 10:00 on the 16th, *Jervis, Janus* and *Nubian* were flying their battle ensigns, but it must have been a bittersweet moment, especially for *Mohawks* survivors spread across the three ships, they had lost everything. There is no doubt that the sinking of the convoy had been exactly the type of operation the strike force was set up to achieve, but it had come at the cost of a valuable destroyer and 43 members of her crew. The remainder of *Mohawks* experienced and battle hardened company would now be broken up and dispersed to new assignments. The admiralty and government were over the moon, as was Admiral Cunningham, who shrugged off the regrettable loss of *Mohawk* as bad luck and not to be unexpected in such a confused action.

However, there were 5 enemy merchant ships and 3 Italian Destroyers that had been sunk or put out of action, not to mention the destruction of the 33rd Signals Battalion, its equipment and some 1700 personnel. Of the destroyers, *Lampo* was eventually recovered, towed back to Italy, repaired and put back into service in May 1942. She was sunk by air attack in 1943. *Balerno* was sunk, as was *Luca Tarigo*. Of *Tarigo*'s crew, just 36 survived from the 230 aboard[250], Capitano Cristofaro was one of the dead, both he and Cap Luca Balsofiore would receive a posthumous Gold Medal for Valour. STU Bisagno survived, and was awarded the Silver Medal, but was killed later in the war when serving in fast motor torpedo boats. A memorial plaque listing the Officers of *Luca Tarigo* is located in the Chapel of the Military Academy in Livorno, whilst *Tarigo's* battle flag, saved from the sinking ship by a survivor, is kept at the Shrine of the Flags, Vittoriano.

---

[249] (Connell, 1987)
[250] (Poggiaroni, 2022)

The manner of *Mohawks* loss appeared unusual. She had been hit by two torpedoes, one to starboard, the other to port, which at the time may have suggested that one of these could, in the confusion of the night action, have been fired from either *Jervis, Janus* or *Nubian* So a court of inquiry was convened and the Commanding Officers from the Task Force were invited to attend.

You are to assemble on board HMS 'St Angelo' at 09:30 on Friday, 18th April, 1941, as a Board of inquiry whereof Captain Edward Conyngham Denison, M.V.C., of HMS 'St. Angelo' is to be the president, Royal Navy, and hold a full and careful investigation into the circumstances attending the loss of His Majesty's Ship 'Mohawk'.[251]

Office of Vice-Admiral, Malta. 17th April, 1941.[252]

This was not a Courts Martial, and indeed there appears to be no inference that anyone was to blame, but each Captain was required to prepare a written report, detailing the action from the perspective of their own ship (the transcripts and notes taken at the inquiry being the basis for the accounts above). Eaton was accompanied by key representatives of his crew to assist in describing the action and the attempts to save *Mohawk* from sinking. The men would answer a series of questions from the board, consisting of 3 Officers, chaired by Captain Denison, and Lt. Commander Arthur De Winton Kitcat, the 37-year-old Commanding Officer of *Imperial*, (which in turn would be lost scuttled following bomb damage on the 29 May 1941) and Commander (Acting) Masters Norman. At 09:30 on the 18 April, the board convened, at St Angelo, Malta.

A reconnaissance flight brought back photographs of *Mohawk*, clearly visible lying on her starboard side in 7 fathoms (42 ft) of water and this would be used as evidence during the board of inquiry on the 18th. The photograph betrayed the gaping hole in the starboard side below her waterline and this, it

---

[251] (The Admiralty, 1941)
[252] (The Admiralty, 1941)

concluded was '…severe enough to cause immediate flooding of No.3 Boiler Room and rapid flooding of No.2 Boiler Room and the engine room. This, combined with the damage aft, would cause the ship to capsize.'[253]

The inquiry concluded *Mohawk* was sunk by two torpedoes fired from the *Luca Tarigo*, but more importantly for Eaton and his crew the following was recorded. 'It is considered that no blame is attributable to the Commanding Officer and ship's company of HMS 'Mohawk' for the loss of their ship. The conduct was worthy of the highest traditions of the Royal Navy.'[254]

However, there is the question of *Mohawks* Confidential Books, and their recovery by the Italian Navy that some have attributed to the success of the audacious and successful attack by Italian frogmen on Alexandria Harbour on the 18/19 December 1941. On that night, three pairs of Italian frogmen, astride submersible 'chariots' managed to access the harbour and place mines under the Battleships *Valiant* and *Queen Elizabeth*. Their story is well told in Adrian Holloway's memoir 'From Dartmouth to War.' This singular attack inflicted such serious damage it put both ships out of action for many months and as Holloway states (he was aboard *Valiant* at the time of the attack); 'At the cost of six men taken prisoner the Italians had dealt a devastating blow to British sea power in the Mediterranean. Taranto and Matapan had been avenged.'[255]

During the inquiry into *Mohawk's* loss, Eaton does indicate his concern over the possible compromising of these documents, and it must have been on his mind that his ship was vulnerable to inspection by enemy divers having sunk in such shallow waters. He states in his report: -

> The weighted W/T and signal books were all thrown over the side, the unweighted W/T books being locked in the safe in the W/T office, the Bridge Confidential Books were locked in the steel perforated boxes on the bridge itself, but I regret that it was not possible to destroy two

---

[253] (The Admiralty, 1941)
[254] (Admiralty, 1941)
[255] (Holloway, 1993)

weighted Signal Publications and a copy of the Fleet Tactical Instructions which were contained in the signalman's steel locker on the bridge. This locker does not lock but fastens with a spring catch.[256]

Indeed, later in July the admiralty noted that; 'In view of the clearness of the air photographs of the wreck and the depth of water (7 fathoms), there may be some doubt as to the security of the C.B.s, particularly those in the signalman's locker on the bridge.' However, this was effectively dismissed a few days later; 'The possibility that books carried by HMS Mohawk were compromised was appreciated at the time and any steps possible to mitigate the results were taken.'[257]

It is of course, probable that these documents did aid in the planning and execution of the attack, however it is worth noting that Holloway attributes the success to a lack of security, especially in respect of the harbour boom defences which were opened many times that night allowing the attackers to enter the harbour unchallenged. 'The Boom Gate was opened no less than three times that fateful night and was open for a total of no less than six hours ten minutes for traffic to pass in and out.'[258]

To conclude this chapter, perhaps the words of John Davies, from 'Lower Deck' are fitting. They illustrate the thoughts of his shipmates following the sinking of the Tribal Destroyer *Sikh,* of the same class as both *Mohawk* and *Nubian.*

> And *Skye* (Davies used pseudonyms for all the ships in his narrative), has gone. At last, we are beginning to accept the fact. The ship herself has gone, but, more than that, her ship's company has vanished forever as a unit, that strangely composite yet united body of men which through trial and tribulation and triumph took on a character transcending that of the individuals of which it was composed. What

---

[256] (The Admiralty, 1941)
[257] (The Admiralty, 1941)
[258] (Holloway, 1993)

remains? New ships, new crews. The beginning of a new life of mutual hardship and experience out of which another ship's company will gradually be evolved.[259]

---

[259] (R.N.V.R, 1945)

Chapter 13

Operation Demon, the evacuation of Greece

Mohawks injured were disembarked in Malta and taken to hospital whilst preparations were made to return to Alexandria with the remainder of the men. For the two days that the Strike Force remained in harbour they became the target for almost constant bombing raids by the enemy. Meanwhile the battle-fleet sailed from Alexandria escorting the tanker *Breconshire* (which had fuel for the destroyers) to Malta. They would then turn about on the pretext of escorting back *Breconshire* and four empty merchantmen accompanied by *Jervis, Janus* and *Nubian* (designated Convoy ME7). However, en route *Diamond* and *Nubian* (with *Mohawks* crew aboard) would proceed to Alexandria, whilst the battle-fleet would break off and bombard Tripoli.

The bombardment of Tripoli was a success, and Cunningham was clearly relieved that the Luftwaffe had not made an appearance, more importantly, he had not lost any of his ships in the operation. Lack of air cover continued to cause frustration for Cunningham as his requests to increase combined offensive operations with the Royal Air Force continued to fall upon deaf ears. Clearly the resources were lacking, but he argued that the bombardment of Tripoli could have been accomplished in one night with a force of heavy bombers rather than the 6 days and high risk to important naval assets. It was quite clear that the Axis air forces had, effectively, air superiority in the eastern Mediterranean.

During the middle of April 1941, it was all too clear that the Germans had the upper hand in their invasion of Greece. An evacuation of the British and ANZAC forces was now inevitable, with the 28 April set for what was to become Operation Demon, the third evacuation of troops by the Royal Navy in retreat from the German Army within two years. The situation developed rapidly, so much so that Operation Demon was brought forward to the 24 April. The Greek army was at the point of collapse through exhaustion from constant defence against a sustained attack, as stated in the report published in the London Gazette in 1948.

> The deterioration in Greek Army morale and the sudden collapse of the Greek forces in Epirus were due largely to the hopelessness of the military situation after the German attack, to the demoralising effect of the lack of air support, to exhaustion to which Greece had become subjected after many months of fighting against an enemy materially and numerically superior, and to the dispiriting effect on the front line units of having to withdraw from positions which they had previously won by dint of many months of hard hand to hand fighting.[260]

In respect of air cover, what resources the RAF had at their disposal was minute, whilst their forward airfields were continually being over run by the advancing German Army. The Luftwaffe, therefore, were at will to harry the retreating troops and make their means of withdrawal arduous by bombing roads and railways ahead of them. Radio communications, vital at all times were hampered by the mountainous regions which blocked wireless transmissions to such an extent that the General Headquarters were often blind to the military situation on the ground for between 24 to 48 hours after the troops had moved.

With the main port of Piraeus destroyed during the landings, there remained very few ports available for the berthing of large ships. So, a number of beaches were selected for the embarkation of the troops which would be facilitated by the fortunate arrival of two Glen ships, the *Glengyle* and *Glenearn*. These were Landing Ship Infantry (L.S.I.) of the Royal Fleet Auxiliary, converted in 1940 from fast merchant ships for a specific task, the landing of seaborne forces. They accommodated shallow draft craft that were used to ferry the troops ashore, and these could also carry lorries, jeeps and heavy armament such as tanks. For the evacuation, all three types of landing

---

[260] (Gazette, 1948)

craft were utilised, (the number of troops given in brackets), Landing Craft Tank (L.C.T. 900), Landing Craft Assault (L.C.A. 60-70) and Landing Craft Mechanised (L.C.M. 150). In order to maximise the number of troops per craft, all materiel was to be left behind. Just as at Dunkirk.

Along with a number of merchant vessels, all available Destroyers were assigned to Demon to ferry the troops out of the fighting area. As a generalisation, most of the British soldiers went to Alexandria whilst the ANZAC's were ferried to Crete via Suda Bay. The use of the destroyers meant that the Battleships and *Formidable* could not be called upon, as they could not be screened. With the heavy forces stuck in Alexandria, the ships involved in the evacuation would be vulnerable to attack from the Italian Navy. Fortunately, this did not occur.

This still left the threat from the Axis air power, clearly enjoying air superiority over the region. Therefore, the evacuations would be carried out from the hour of darkness until 03:00. This had a twofold advantage, the evacuations were unopposed from the air and, to an extent it did not reveal which beaches were being used.

Having dropped off the Mohawks at Alexandria, *Nubian* was directed to Suda Bay arriving there on the 26 April. In the harbour was the sorry sight of the cruiser *York,* badly damaged in a Motor Torpedo Boat raid by the Regia Marina on the 26 March, she had been run aground in the hope that she could be saved, but this was not to be the case. Amassed around the harbour were the ships readying to depart for their evacuation duties around the coast of Greece the prospects for success were not good, on the 21 and 22 April some 23 ships had been sunk in the operation, including the Greek destroyer, *Hydra*, which precipitated the decision to embark the troops at night.

Nevertheless, the ships sailed with the following dispositions, which gives one an idea of the size of the operations each night: -

Raphina: *Glengyle, Nubian, Decoy and Hasty.*
Raphtis: *Salween, Carlisle, Kandahar, Kingston.*

Nauplia: *Slamat, Khedive, Ismail, Calcutta, Isis, Hotspur.*
Tolon: *Glenearn, Diamond, Griffin and Havovk.*
Kalamata: *Dilwara, City of London, Costa Rica, Phoebe, Defender, Flamingo, Hero, Hereward.*

At Raphina, *Glengyle* had to stand off over a mile from the shore, whilst the landing craft busied themselves between the port and the ship. They managed to get 3500 troops out that evening, during which *Nubian* was detached to pick up some troops from Zea island, but when she arrived there were only three left, the remainder had managed to get an LCT to Raphtis where they embarked on *Ajax*. *Nubian* caught up with the departing *Glengyle* and headed back to Suda Bay. 18,000 troops were embarked overnight, but the *Slama*t (with 500 soldiers aboard) and the destroyers *Diamond* and *Wryneck* were sunk.

Over the following days the evacuation went at a pace with no let up, the crews enduring very little sleep, constantly at a high state of readiness through the night and subject to air attack during the day. *Nubian* had just completed escort and evacuation duties returning to Suday Bay when she and her fellow destroyers were ordered out to escort incoming Convoy GA14. David Thomas illustrates the workload of the destroyers at this point in his work, 'Crete 1941: The Battle at Sea.'

> Just how hard worked these light forces were at this time is demonstrated by this timetable: nearly all these ships had arrived at Suda Bay at about 19:00, they discharged what troops they had collected the previous night, refuelled, then at 20:30 – just ninety minutes after arrival – many of them sailed again to escort the convoy.[261]

Many of the small landing craft and support ships were lost during the operation but according to Cunningham some 50,672 [262] troops were

---

[261] (Thomas, 1972)
[262] According to David A. Thomas in Crete 1941: The Battle at Sea, 'The figure is undoubtably wrong, but it is accepted by the Admiralty as the nearest approximation to the truth'.

evacuated from Greece, about 80% of the original force, 14,000 of which came out of ports with wharves or jetties that could accept the larger ships, the remainder came off the beaches in the smaller craft. On the 27 April the German forces reached Athens, at which point the Headquarters in Alexandria received their last call from the allied wireless station in the city. 'Closing down for the last time, hoping for happier days. God be with you, and for you.'[263] Then at 03:00 on the 29th, the final troops were embarked on *Ajax* and 'Demon' was effectively over.

Convoy GA15

With all eyes now on the future of Crete, Convoy GA15 was hastily assembled at Suda Bay to ensure that as many troops as possible were moved to Alexandria and (hopefully) out of harms way. Sailing at 11:00 on the 29 April it comprised of six transport ships, carrying some 10,931[264] souls, its route would take it through the Kaso strait (between the eastern end of Crete and the island of Kasos), as far as possible from any enemy air bases. *Nubian* and the cruiser *Perth* had been assigned to the First Battle Squadron which with the freeing up of destroyers available for screening (now Demon was over), sailed from Alexandria and consisted of *Barham, Valiant* and *Formidable*. However as often happened, the two warships were almost immediately reassigned to assist in the close protection of GA15.

It is quite likely that the dawn of the 29 April was like the one John Davies describes in his book 'Lower Deck'.

> There is a strange, ethereal quality about these Mediterranean mornings, The sea is velvet smooth, undulating gently with an easy, sinuous movement. The surface of the water, wrinkled like crepe, takes on a deeper blue as the light strengthens, except around the ship herself, where there is a whole gamut of pastel colour, from the snowy white

---

[263] (Cunningham, 1951)
[264] (Thomas, 1972)

beneath her forefoot, to the turquoise sliding down her side, dotted still with dim phosphorescent lights, to be engulfed in turn by the great while turbulence of the wake.[265]

The day had begun the same as any for the crew with the call, 'Hands to Dawn Action Stations! Hands to Dawn Action Stations!'. The clattering of boots on gratings, the clang of watertight doors came before the confirmation that the ship was closed up and ready for action. Two and a half years had almost passed since *Nubian* had been commissioned. The happy times cruising the Mediterranean before the declaration of war were very dim and distant memories, for almost ever since that day, the ship and her crew were on active duty.

Nubian carved her way through the clear blue waters of the Mediterranean, her wake an enormous wedding dress train of white water from her propellors at maximum revolutions. As a component of the destroyer screen for the cruisers, *Nubian* was stationed some 3000 yards off the nearest cruiser, ready to effect what was known as an Umbrella Barrage. Her main guns were trained upwards and over the top of the cruisers and merchant vessels the shells in her breaches had their fuses set to explode at a fixed altitude and rain down shrapnel to dissuade or destroy any enemy dive bombers that dared attack the bigger ships. Meanwhile, the Cruisers had their guns levelled just above the wave tops and pointing directly outwards towards the destroyers. Their shells were set to explode at 2500 yards, inside the destroyer screen to take out any low-level aircraft that got past the destroyers' light weapons. There was, of course, a high risk that a faulty or incorrectly set fuse would travel further than 2500 yards, causing a friendly fire incident, which did on occasion occur.

Low on the horizon a lone JU88 circled, just out of range of the ship's guns, but close enough to observe and report the disposition of the convoy and her escorts. As the aircraft manoeuvered between the ships and the sun, it suddenly turned and climbed, its engines taking on a higher note as the

---

[265] (R.N.V.R, 1945)

throttles were pushed forward, now heading straight towards *Nubian* and the convoy.

The guns of the screen opened up *Nubian's* included. Black puffs of smoke from exploding shells appeared around the dark green, twin engine aircraft, the dull thump, thump, thump of the pom-pom assaulting the senses followed quite clearly by the tinkle and clatter of its shells as they tumbled into the collecting trays, white splashes in the water as the shrapnel fell like storm rain but the JU88 kept on coming. 'Aircraft approaching, sir', declares a lookout, the JU88 climbed to 1000 feet before it begun a shallow dive towards *Nubian* releasing four 250kg semi armour piercing bombs that tumbled towards the ship. 'Hard a starboard, full ahead!' comes the order from the Commander. *Nubian* lurched forward and heeled over, the bombs straddling her, one missing just 20 feet ahead, the other 10 feet off the port bow and the remaining two off the starboard quarter by 15ft[266]. The eruption of blackened water, concussion and noise are shattering, but they have missed, thanks to the cool handling of the ship by her CO.

The JU88 continued on its course, towards the cruisers and to its end. A series of flashes twinkled across the port wing, its engine suddenly engulfed in a plume of flame that quickly ate away the spars, the wing detached, and the aircraft plunged into the sea. There were no parachutes, just an ever increasing ring of white water where the aircraft went in, like someone had lobbed a big rock into the sea.

It had been a very close call. The damage report came, there were no injuries, although *Nubian* was taking on water forward, the damage was very slight, but she could continue operations for now, she would require repairs when she next put in. It cannot have escaped the crew that they had been lucky, very lucky.

---

[266] (Admiralty, 1941)

Chapter 14

Crete – 1 May to 1 June 1941

Operation Tiger

Nubian returned to Alexandria on the 1 May where she would undergo a long awaited boiler clean and the repairs to her forward seams sustained in the air attack on convoy GA15. It would be a welcome rest for the crew. Elsewhere, Tobruk had been surrounded and was effectively under siege. Ultra-intelligence pointed towards an invasion of Crete by the Germans whilst all of the tanks and artillery that had been sent to Greece remained in enemy hands following the eviction of British and Commonwealth troops from the country. It had become imperative the armoured forces in Egypt were re-supplied with tanks as soon as possible.

At this time, a large Convoy (WS7) was about to depart from the Clyde and Liverpool bound for Suez via the Cape of Good Hope with the much needed tanks and ammunition. Churchill correctly realised that this would take far too long and ordered the 5 fast merchant ships containing some 270 tanks (mainly Cruiser tanks) and 53 crated Hurricanes, split from the main convoy and diverted on the more expedient, but dangerous route, through the Mediterranean via Gibraltar. This would be designated WS8 and re-named Operation Tiger. Accompanying the merchant ships to deploy with the Eastern Mediterranean fleet was the battleship *Queen Elizabeth* and the cruisers *Naiad* and *Fiji*, they sailed from Gibraltar on the 8 May. As had become standard practice, Force H escorted these ships through to Malta where Cunningham's forces would rendezvous to provide onward escort to Alexandria. On their way, a convoy of supplies bound for Malta, including 24,000 tons of fuel would be escorted, and the bombardment of Benghazi would take place.

Despite the loss of the *Empire Song* after she hit a mine and exploded, taking 57 tanks, 10 Hurricanes and assorted munitions with her, the ships of Operation Tiger arrived in Alexandria on the 12 May and was deemed a success. That was not necessarily the case according to Cunningham, as when the tanks and hurricanes were offloaded, initial inspection found they had not been fitted with the necessary engine filters to combat the desert sands. Whilst air attacks had materialised, unseasonal weather, in the form of low cloud, mist and fog, had largely grounded the enemy air forces, allowing the convoy a relatively unhindered passage through the Mediterranean. Cunningham quietly fumed that the detractors back in England were inclined to think that he and his staff had over exaggerated the threat from the air. They would soon be put firmly back in their box.

Allied & German perspectives

Indeed, Cunningham was right to be worried about the coming weeks, particularly how an attack on Crete would manifest itself, and how the Royal Navy could defend the island with little, if any air support. What was equally worrying was the rapidly depleting stocks of ammunition, especially of Anti-Aircraft type. He wrote;

> '…on May 13th had to inform the Admiralty that since April 20th between one-third and one-half the main items in the Mediterranean Fleet had been expended.'[267] Moreover, what meagre air cover there was, was being whittled down by an enemy air force that enjoyed almost complete air superiority. Of course, this was not only a degradation in aircraft numbers, but the pilots too. Cunningham wrote that on 15 May seven Hurricanes had been downed within three days and most of them took their pilots with them. 'The result of the attacks was that no less than twenty-seven Hurricanes, four Beaufighters and

---

[267] (Cunningham, 1951)

two Glen Martins had been badly damaged on the ground, while one Blenheim had to be wiped off.'[268]

The problem of airframe availability was not confined to the Royal Air Force. During Operation Tiger, *Formidable* had provided fleet protection with her Fulmars, but their attrition rate was high, as Pack (who was aboard *Formidable*), tells us in his book,' The Battle for Crete'. 'Tragically the poor visibility which prevailed for so much of the time was responsible for the loss of many of *Formidable's* fighters, a feature which was to be irremediable before the battle for Crete. As she steamed into Alexandria once again, on 12 May, just two months after her arrival in the Mediterranean, during which she had covered thousands of miles and seen much action, she was down to her last four Fulmar fighters.'[269] With no reserve fighter aircraft available, *Formidable* was all but useless, except for a handful of Albacores and Swordfish.

As a result, the Luftwaffe began mining operations, almost unhindered. Very soon both Alexandria and the Grand Harbour were almost off limits, the destroyer *Jersey* was sunk in the entrance to the Grand Harbour, whilst *Gloucester* (which had become part of the Malta Strike Force) was often bottled up inside the harbour because of the mines, or forced to lay offshore, until the channel into the harbour was cleared. A lack of minesweepers meant that the only practical way of sweeping a channel was to drop depth charges regularly through the channel in an attempt to either disrupt the mines firing mechanisms or set them off.

On Crete, the remnants of the forces evacuated from Greece combined with the garrisons that were already stationed there amounted to some 32,000 troops. However, their numbers were almost meaningless due to a lack of equipment. As we have seen, the heavy weapons, including anti-aircraft guns, artillery and tanks, (just as at Dunkirk) had been left behind in Greece. What tanks they did have were old and worse, unreliable. Most likely to break down

---

[268] (Cunningham, 1951)
[269] (Pack, 1972)

at any moment. What made their position equally precarious was the lack of communications (telephony and radio equipment) exacerbated by little means of transportation which even when available, had to travel on unpaved tracks and roads. Pack writes in 'The Battle for Crete'; 'There were no railways, and only one good road full of hairpin bends which ran along the northern coast; south of this was the mountainous volcanic range running like a backbone throughout the whole length of 150 miles, and rising in places to 8000 ft.'[270]

Once again, air support would be almost non-existent. Maleme airfield, about 10 miles west of Suda Bay, had been expanded since the British arrived during 1940, with the FAA taking residence alongside the RAF. 20 miles away there was a small landing strip at Retimo whilst a further 65 miles to the east was another airfield at Heraklion. The Axis forces began softening up the island from the 15 May, at which time the airframe resources were pitiful. According to Cunningham, at Maleme there were just three Gladiators, three Fulmars and three Hurricanes of the RAF serviceable. In a matter of days, the strength was reduced to one Gladiator and one Fulmar, the FAA fighter crews then combined with the RAF pilots to keep the Hurricanes in the fight. But this was short lived. Despite being completely overwhelmed, they managed to shoot down six enemy aircraft before they too were taken out.

Of the naval assets, Suda bay, sheltered by the Akrotiri mountain range, provided a sheltered harbour for the refuelling of the Navy's ships, but it was small and was not capable of handling large quantities of men and equipment. Pack states: 'Facilities for unloading the British supply ships which arrived at Suda Bay were limited and were subjected to ever-increasing bombing attacks during daylight hours. Between April 30th and May 20th, fifteen supply ships arrived, of which eight were sunk or damaged while in harbour. It was possible to get only 15,000 tons of stores ashore during this time.'[271] He describes the alternatives, which had little to encourage optimism. '…there were two other ports on the north coast; Heraklion which could take a destroyer, and Retimo

---

[270] (Pack, 1972)
[271] (Pack, 1972)

which could accept only small coasters. On the south coast, about 20 miles from Suda Bay as the crow flies, was the fishing village of Sphakia, but the rough road leading towards it stopped abruptly in the mountains several miles short of the village.'[272] Cunningham's view of Crete is telling. 'From the point of view of defence it would have suited us much better if the island could have been turned upside down.'[273]

Whatever the geographical challenges were, Cunningham still had the job of organising the Naval defence of Crete, which would necessitate him remaining at his Headquarters in Alexandria rather than his preferred desk on board *Warspite*. From his HQ he could see the disposition of his ships, plotted hourly on a large chart in the war room, whilst communications between his forces should remain unhampered. There was a lot of sea to patrol in search of any approaching invasion forces, staying vigilant in case the Italian fleet made an appearance and to support the landing of reinforcements and supplies to the island. So, Cunningham split his fleet to cover the four compass points around the island. These forces could interact and support each other depending on the threats or the operational requirements as they evolved. Operating so far from Alexandria and with the likelihood that Suda Bay would no longer be available, the problems of fuel and ammunition supply would be critical. Destroyers, constantly operating at high speed would need their fuel tanks topping up regularly, and so replenishment at sea from the battleships was inevitable.

Following the varied movements of each force is complex but by the 20 May, these forces comprised of the following ships: -

Force A: *Warspite, Valiant, Napier, Hereward, Decoy, Hero, Hotspur. (Admiral Rawlings on Warspite))*
Force B: *Gloucester, Fiji, Greyhound, Griffin. (Captain Rowley on Gloucester)*
Force C: *Naiad, Perth, Kandahar, Kingston, Nubian, Juno (Admiral King, on Naiad)*

---

[272] (Pack, 1972)
[273] (Cunningham, 1951)

Force D: *Dido, Orion, Ajax, Isis, Kimberley, Imperial, Janus (on Glennie, on Orion)*

Meanwhile the Germans had not been idle. Goering had given assurances to Hitler that the operation to take the island could be mounted from the air, completed in just a few days and would not affect the Luftwaffe's capability to support the forthcoming invasion of Russia. Hitler took Goering's word, General (Luftwaffe) Kurt Student headed up Germany's airborne, paratroop forces (Fallshchirmjager) that were now gathering in southern Greece. Airfields such as Milos, Molaci, Scarpanto, all within an hour's flight time of Crete were upgraded to accommodate the Stukas, Junkers bombers and ME109 fighters (about 700 aircraft in total of which some 50 were reconnaissance), that would bomb and harry the ground and naval forces in support of their airborne troops, some 13,000 being mustered for the drops. The paratroopers would be delivered by tri-motor JU52-3m transport aircraft (approx. 500) which could either carry 12 paratroopers or tow up to three DFS-230 gliders (about 70 within the invasion force). The German paratroopers would drop into the battlefield equipped with only a sidearm, their automatic weapons and ammunition dropped separately in canisters. Their method of parachuting had the chute lines terminated to the back of a shoulder harness, which meant the soldier had no means of steering or controlling his descent, approaching the ground in a peculiar stance, his body angled head forward, feet behind. The advantage in using gliders meant a 10-man team could arrive with their MP40, 34 or KAR 98K automatic weapons, but being built from fabric and aluminium tubing, the gliders airframe provided little protection. The pilot (who would become a rifleman once on the ground) and five of the troopers were forward facing, whilst the remaining four faced the rear (they could be substituted for additional equipment), all were seated on a single bench. The pilot had basic instrumentation, an ASI (airspeed indicator), Altimeter, VSI (Vertical Speed Indicator) and Turn & Bank Coordinator that could be used as a basic Artifical Horizon. The gliders were released at a maximum height of 5000 feet, some 2 – 5 miles from their target. Up until supplies from the sea could be established, the JU52s would continue to supply the ground troops with between 200 and 240 sorties per day.

Hitler Directive number 28, issued on the 25 April 1941 outlined Operation Merkur (Mercury); 'As a base for air warfare against Great Britain in the Eastern Mediterranean we must prepare to occupy the island of Crete.' The German airborne plan split the force into 3 sectors, Group West attacking Maleme, Group Central would drop into Chania and Suda whilst Group East would attack Heraklion. Due to the interception and decoding of Luftwaffe Enigma signals, the British High Command knew all about it.

In London, Churchill was stating that Crete must be held at all costs. Another defeat was unthinkable, but the bare facts were pretty clear, Crete would be difficult to defend but moreover, if the defence was successful, how long could it be held and at what cost? Max Hastings writes in his book 'Finest Years', describing Churchill's time in office during World War 2; 'Strategically the fall of Crete was a much less serious matter for the British than would have been the loss of Malta. Admiral Cunningham believed that if the island had been held the British would have paid a heavy price for continuing to supply it, in the face of overwhelming German air superiority.'[274] On the ground in Crete, the New Zealand General Bernard Freyburg was in charge of the defence of the island. His view remained that the main attack would come from the sea with support from the air, and not the other way around. He based his defensive tactics in this respect, believing his forces could fight off any supporting attacks coming from the air. His after action report is candid in its admission of his lack of situational awareness.

> The main defence problems which faced me in Crete were not clear to me at this stage. I did not know anything about the geography or physical characteristics of the island. I knew less about the condition of the force I was to command. Neither was I aware of the serious

---

[274] (Hastings, 2009)

situation with regards to maintenance and, finally, I had not learnt the real scale of attack which we were to be prepared to repel.[275]

However, Peter Ewer is not alone when he suggests that actually, Freyburg did have access to Ultra information that could, perhaps, have swung the battle to the defenders advantage, he writes in 'Forgotten ANZAC's'; 'Ultra' informed Freyberg on the 13th May that attempts to seize the aerodromes by paratroop landing would be followed by a seaborne invasion; from this the defenders could have concluded that if they could hold the airfields, Merkur must fail. Given the availability if this information, Freyberg's preoccupation with the threat from the sea was unfortunate."[276]

Looking at these challenges, it is little wonder that Churchill, Cunningham and Freyberg were pessimistic. Perhaps most telling is what Pack (who, as we know was on *Formidable* at the time) states in 'The Battle for Crete'; 'It is of interest to record that a widespread feeling prevailed at that time among service personnel, that having been kicked out of Greece, mainly because of enemy superiority in the air, it could not be long before British and Imperial forces were driven out of Crete.'[277]

Invasion

In the early morning of 20 May the Germans began to bomb the anti-aircraft guns and fortified positions that they had identified from aerial reconnaissance. This was followed by the JU52's, coming in as low as 100m (about 350 ft) to drop the paratroopers making the aircraft very vulnerable to small arms fire. The same situation applied to the paratroopers themselves. Having no means of steering due to their parachuting technique, and being at

---

[275] (Ewer, 2008)
[276] (Ewer, 2008)
[277] (Pack, 1972)

their most vulnerable during their decent, many were killed before they touched the ground.

Next came the gliders, whose quiet descent would have been most unnerving. Gliders make a gentle swishing noise or a mournful whine as the air flows across the control surfaces. A calm comes before the crunch as the glider makes contact with the ground, a swirl of dust and the machine skids to a halt. Then the guns open up, the troops inside have little protection and in many cases are cut to pieces before they have even opened the doors. Peter Ewer quotes one of the men there, 19-year-old Frank Sherry, who witnessed 5 gliders approach his signals unit on that first day; 'Even a .303 made the gliders jump visibly in the air,' he recalled. This flight of Germans had landed successfully within 50 meters of Sherry's billet but, according to him, 'out of those five, not many came out alive.'[278]

During the first day, the Germans came over in several waves, making landings at Retimo and Heraklion, but their casualties were severe. They had landed amongst determined troops, who were not a beaten force following a humiliating retreat, they were battle hardened men that whilst only equipped with small arms would put up a strong fight. But by the end of the day, despite a gallant defence, ground had been lost at Maleme. They would re-group in the morning, planning a counterattack to retake the airfield on the 21st and 22nd.

It was not to be. The weight of numbers, bravery and determination of the German paratroopers was overwhelming. They began to crash land the JU52's on any flat ground they could find, wrecking many aircraft in the process, just to get the men into the fight. At Maleme, the aircraft simply begun to land amongst the incoming fire from the 27th NZ Battery. One aircraft managed to land, unload and take off once more despite the shelling. But many were wrecked in the process, their torn and twisted carcasses littering the airfield. According to Heinz J. Nowarra, there were over 150 JU52's wrecked across the airfields of Crete by the 27 May, so many that; 'The Luftwaffe use the term

---

[278] (Ewer, 2008)

'aeroplane graveyard Crete'.[279] As the Germans consolidated their position, so the number of reinforcements increased, the outcome was inevitable.

Despite determined defence, by the 26th it had become all too obvious that evacuation was once more on the cards. The allies were being pushed eastwards, General Wavell informed London that Freyburg's hold on Suda Bay was slender, German air superiority precluded any chance of reinforcing the island, the situation on Crete was literally, untenable. The response was immediate. Evacuate.

The British and the ANZACs would have to be lifted from Heraklion, and Sphakia which meant for some, a retreat to the south over the mountains fighting a rear guard action all the way, to be plucked once more from the iron fist of the German war machine by the Royal Navy.

---

[279] (Nowarra, 1987)

Chapter 15

12 days in May 1941

At 3 p.m. on May 27th the fateful decision was taken, and we wearily turned to planning another evacuation with fewer ships, far less resources and in circumstances much more difficult. Our seamen and our ships were worn to the point of exhaustion, and now they were asked for more.

Admiral Cunningham

Operation M.A.Q.3 – Prelude

At 12:00 on the 25 May 1941, HMS *Nubian* slipped her moorings in Alexandria and headed out to sea as a screening component of Force A, Operation M.A.Q.3 consisting of *Queen Elizabeth, Barham, Formidable* with the destroyers *Jervis, Janus, Kandahar, Hasty, Hereward, Voyager, Vendetta* (Royal Australian Navy). Since the invasion of Crete began, the fleet had been subjected to daily attacks from the Luftwaffe, deploying combinations of high and low level bombing from JU88s and JU87 Stuka dive bombers respectively that had been spectacularly successful over the previous week. M.A.Q.3 was literally the last counter offensive throw of the dice for *Formidable* and indeed the air assets available to the allies, its purpose was to attack the airbase on Scarpanto.

But before we concentrate on M.A.Q.3, we need to look back earlier in the month. Following her boiler clean and repairs, *Nubian* had been sent out almost immediately on operations. On the 15 May she was included in Operation M.D.8, the shelling of El Fateyah airfield near Derna on the Libyan coast. The outcome was a failure, much to the crew's disappointment. The location of the airfield could not be identified and not a shot had been fired. The ships of M.D.8 fell in frustration upon the harbour of Derna, intent on destruction, but the harbour was empty of shipping. So, there followed patrols of the Kaso straight in search of any seaborne forces headed for Crete before the softening raids on Crete by the Luftwaffe began. It had been a fruitless exercise. *Nubian* was back in Alexandria on the 18 May, refuelling and rearming before heading back to the Kaso Straights once more. The landings on Crete began on the 20th, and *Nubian* was involved in the repulse of an attack by Italian high speed torpedo boats that same night. Then things began to get very bad.

On the 21st the Stukas arrived in force and attacked Force C, (*Naiad, Perth, Nubian, Kandahar, Kingston* and *Juno*) in great numbers, initiating attacks from 09:50 to 13:50. But it was Italian SM.79's from 30 Gruppo BT, out of Sicily that did the damage. At 12:49, despite increasing speed and heeling over to port in an attempt to evade her attackers a stick of 5 bombs straddled *Juno*, 3 of which hit aft of the bridge. The first two exploded in her engine and boiler compartments, the third in her aft magazine which blew out the ship's sides, the resulting secondary explosion was catastrophic and broke the ship in half. *Juno* sank within two minutes and despite the continued attacks from the air, *Nubian, Kingston* and *Kandahar* came on hand to pick up 97, oil soaked, cold and exhausted men from the water (6 Officers and 91 seamen).

'I came to dread every ring on the telephone' - Thursday 22 May 1941

On the morning of the 22nd the Luftwaffe was free of its obligation to protect the landing forces. Reconnaissance missions could not fail to spot the allied warships, their sightings of the fleet massed to the north and west of the island was greedily digested by the crews of the JU87's, 88's, ME109's and 110's based in northern Greece at Argos, Eleusis, Molai and Myli, over 700 aircraft in total. They took off in Gruppe formations of over 30 aircraft, an airborne force eager to get into the fight with the mighty Royal Navy, brimming with confidence that the day would be theirs and ships would be left burning and wrecked around the coasts of Crete.

From the north came a convoy of Greek caiques (local fishing boats, trawlers and small craft to the waters of Crete), bound for Heraklion with German troops. They were often commanded by skippers and crews pressed unwillingly into service by the Germans. The convoy was protected by the small Spica Class Torpedo board, *Sagittario,* a wholly inadequate escort for some 30 small steam ships and caiques, but one that would fight its corner. These ships ran smack into Force C at 08:30 and a general chase by the cruisers *Perth*, *Naiad* and *Carlisle* quickly ensued followed by *Nubian* and her fellow destroyers which rapidly overtook the cruisers who were forced to remain at a paltry 21 knots, as this was all that *Carlisle* could maintain. The force began to get spread out, which went against the tactic of ships sticking to close formations for mutual protection from air attack and indeed air attacks came on in relentless waves.

With ammunition running low, Admiral King, commander of Force C in *Naiad*, called his forces back together whilst the convoy, still protected by the little *Sagittario* escaped to the north and made for Piraeus. This large invasion force had been forced to retreat, and so could not initiate a substantial part of the German seaborne invasion, but Admiral King later came under criticism from Cunningham and Churchill for not pressing home his attack.

The pressure from the skies never gave up that day. When the mass formations that gathered at the beginning of the day landed having completed their first mission, they still had plenty of time for another. The crews, so eager to get back into the fight in the knowledge they had complete command of the skies, had their planes refueled and re-armed immediately, taking off in twos and threes to get back into the fight. As David Thomas states, 'The consequence was that German aircraft were in the air over the ships for hour upon hour committing the British crews to man action stations for seemingly endless hours and inflicting upon them an almost unbearable, ceaseless pressure which drove them close to breaking point.'[280]

That breaking point must be examined. Each man aboard ship would have harboured and controlled his own fears in his own way, gradually drawing on that inner strength of courage, as Lord Moran compared to a bank account, in his book, 'The Anatomy of Courage', whereby one drew from reserves until all 'credit' was used up and no more strain could be endured. Captain Charles McMoran Wilson, a Doctor in the Royal Fusiliers during World War 1, gained a Military Cross for his part in the Battle of the Somme, becoming Dean of St.Mary's Hospital Medical School for twenty years. In 1940 he became Winston Churchills personal doctor, whilst from 1941 to 1950 he was the President of the Royal College of Physicians. He was created 1st Baron Moran of Manton in 1943. In 1945 he had published the first edition of 'The Anatomy of Courage' which drew from his experiences on the front lines during World War 1 exploring courage, fear and cowardice in the fighting man whilst the second edition included chapters on the effects of combat stress within the Royal Air Force and the Royal Navy. General Sir Peter de la Billiere wrote in his introduction to the book; 'When Commanding Officer of the Special Air Service, I instructed every new recruit to purchase a copy of this eminently readable book, so that they might take Moran's experience into battle with them.'[281] Most notable within this work is the inclusion of a passage by Surgeon Lieutenant Edward Benson McDowall R.N.V.R., of whom we met earlier. With his inclusion, we get a firsthand account from someone who was aboard *Nubian*, and in particular, of her Commanding Officer, as we shall see shortly.

Moran wrote of the Mediterranean, and destroyers in particular.

> And this war is grimmer and tougher still, in a closed sea like the Mediterranean, bombing from the air has given the sailor no peace. Moreover the rating nowadays is often not a professional sailor. In

---

[280] (Thomas, 1972)
[281] (Moran, 2007)

three years of war the Navy has grown threefold; of the officers who broke down in 1940 only a sixth were sailors in peace. There is another reason why so little is heard on a battleship of cruiser of the ravages of war. It is the drawn out strain of service on a small ship rather than the sharp stress of a naval action which ends in defeat. Three-quarters of those who were broken were serving in small ships.

Of the younger sailors, Moran wrote, 'Youth – it is a young sailors' job – nine times out of ten is undefeated by this battle with man and nature. But sometimes in the smaller craft ratings who have lost the resiliency of their early years are asked to meet the same calls on mind and body…'[282] Whilst of the older sailors he gives an example of a Minesweeper crewed, in the main, by older sailors, but neglected by their officers.

Nine out of a crew of fifteen were more than forty years old. They had been kept too long on the same run – like keeping a battalion too long on the Ypres salient – and the enemy knew this run. They could neither look forward nor look back to any cheerful prospect. No one had ever shown interest in them or in their craft: they felt their isolation. They had no hope of leave, they wanted to sleep once without being called for a watch. And then, when the nerve of the captain and the senior rating had gone, there was no more fight left in the rest of the crew.[283]

Clearly, if the crew were likely to be cracking under the strain, it was so much more important for the Commanding Officer to set an example to his officers and his men. To fail in this respect would inevitably lead to an unhappy ship that would quickly become ineffective as a fighting force. Indeed, this goes for operational uncertainty too. John Davies described a time when *Sikh* was part of the Malta Strike Force. The ship was permanently at readiness for operations and there had been a succession of cancelled departures during which the CO and his 1st Lieutenant's air of impending danger and uncertainty pervaded the crew. 'The constant mounting and

---

[282] (Moran, 2007)
[283] (Moran, 2007)

relaxation of tension is having a disastrous effect upon the nerves of almost everyone aboard'[284]. The effects of which were all too evident; 'There is a noticeable change amongst the hands working on the quarter deck. They move reluctantly to their tasks, and there is no laughter or good humour. They go slowly about the business of re-securing *Skye* (*Sikh*).'[285]

Davies recalled a time when he tried to make light of a very heavy air raid to one of the Stokers in his Fire Party; 'This sort of thing must take years off your life,' I said. But when I turned to look at him he was grovelling on the deck in an abandonment of terror.'[286]

But at the time, Post Traumatic Stress Disorder (PTSD) or Battle Fatigue was frowned upon, and mental issues seen as some kind of weakness. There were glimmers of understanding and some who had been front and centre for extended periods were indeed rested where possible or withdrawn from frontline duties all together. In a ship of the Royal Navy, especially a small and intimate community such as a destroyer it would be very difficult to admit a failure of nerve, but equally very public if one did. What is more, there was no escaping the trials of daily exposure to danger, as a sailor, you were stuck aboard ship with little chance to 'get off the bus'. As Moran put it; 'Small wonder the Navy refuses to countenance nerves; in conversation you do not hear that this man is not wearing well or that another needs a rest.'[287]

For the Commanding Officer, the drive and resolve to retain a 'stiff upper lip' in the face of adversity, to set an example to the rest of the crew in order to maintain an effective fighting ship would eventually sap the reserves of the most courageous of men. Roger Hill is most candid in his description of his own struggles with fear, and his eventual nervous breakdown, despite of which he returned to active duty after some rest. He wrote in Destroyer Captain; 'As I stood on the bridge keeping station astern of *Penn* I had a violent reaction. My knees shook so hard I had to hold onto the bridge rails. I felt sick and

---

[284] (R.N.V.R, 1945)
[285] (R.N.V.R, 1945)
[286] (R.N.V.R, 1945)
[287] (Moran, 2007)

utterly terrified. The thought of going back over the thousand miles to Gibraltar, without another friendly ship or aircraft, appalled me. I felt sure the Italians would be waiting for us at daylight. Our speed was twenty-five knots and their cruisers went well over thirty. I wondered if the others on the bridge saw the state I was in and, as soon as we were clear of the Grand Harbour, I went down to my cabin and was violently sick.'[288] Whilst Surgeon McDowell stated of his time on *Terror* and *Nubian*, 'There were more than five hundred men in the two ships and of these only two came to me about their nerves.'[289]

Just as Lord Moran wrote in 1945, Hill realised that he had a finite number of 'points' that made up his account of courage. As the dangers came and went, so he used up his points, until he had no more. As these diminished, his character began to change, and he became more and more unreasonable and intolerant of his crew. 'The sad thing was that, as a captain more nearly approached a breakdown, or operational fatigue as it was called, so he became increasingly impossible to serve and live with. As a man on the verge of a nervous breakdown takes it out on his wife and children, so the captain suffering from or on the verge of operational fatigue takes it out on his long-suffering officers and bridge staff.'[290]

Returning to *Nubian* once more, she did come under intense attack on the 22 May, Surgeon MacDowell was aboard, and it is on this day, during one of the dive bombing attacks on the ship, he observed something extraordinary. He is quoted in Lord Moran's book as follows.

> I saw the Captain[291] of a ship drinking a cup of tea on the bridge in the course of dive-bombing attacks that had gone on all day. While he was drinking the look-out reported 'Aircraft on the starboard bow, sir.' He

---

[288] (Hill, 1979)
[289] (Moran, 2007)
[290] (Hill, 1979)
[291] It is reasonable to accept that the Captain in question is Ravenhill, and the ship is *Nubian*. We know that MacDowell served on two ships, *Nubian* and *Terror*. He describes two instances aboard these ships, one from Benghazi, which can only be *Terror*, the other as stated in this quotation, which therefore, has to be *Nubian*.

did not even look up. 'Aircraft diving, sir,' the Captain glanced up only. 'Bomb released, sir,' and the Captain gave the order 'Hard a-starboard,' and went on drinking his tea until the bomb hit the water nearby. The reaction to this episode was a kind of schoolboy hero-worship on the part of everyone who saw it. When the bombing had ceased the captain went down to his cabin and when he was alone he wept.[292]

Returning to the morning of the 22nd, Cunningham's fears in respect of ammunition supplies was becoming a reality. The night before, Force D had been in action against an invasion convoy, during which a large amount of ammunition had been expended. Indeed, both the cruisers *Gloucester* and *Fiji* were dangerously low in stores. David Thomas quotes the following figures for remaining ammunition onboard the ships, *Dido (25%), Orion (38%), Ajax (40%), Gloucester (18%)* and *Fiji (30%)*.[293] A perilous state of affairs with the Luftwaffe in complete control of the air and so the cruisers of Force D were recalled to Alexandria, whilst surprisingly *Gloucester* and *Fiji* remained on station, with tragic consequences.

In the meantime, Force A, which included *Warspite*, had come to the aid of Force C. At about 13:00 both groups of ships were inundated by Stukas and bomb carrying ME109's, three of which came in low at no more than 800 feet upon *Warspite*. Two of the 500lb bombs missed as the great ship heeled hard a-port, a third didn't. Iain Ballantyne quotes Jack Worth, who was manning one of *Warspites* pom-poms; 'Then this blob came away from beneath the German plane and hurtled my way. It was a bomb and it got bigger and bigger and bigger. But it didn't hit my position, it took out the 4-inch gun beneath me.'[294]

To state, simply, that a warship has suffered damage, does not convey the sheer destruction that occurs. In a single moment, *Warspite* had one of her 4-inch guns and its crew literally thrown overboard, some 100 feet of her

---

[292] (Moran, 2007)
[293] (Thomas, 1972)
[294] (Ballantyne, 2001, 2013, 2014)

decking was blown out and a gash of fifty feet along her side torn open like a tin can. That is not to mention the crew who were now burning as fires quickly raged where the bomb had struck. David Thomas quotes the scene described by *Warspites* Executive Officer, Commander Charles Madden (later made an Admiral), who took charge of the fire control teams. 'We had great difficulty in opening the door (to the 6-in. battery decks) and had to use a sledgehammer. Finally, it gave, to display a gruesome scene, The starboard battery was full of flames and smoke, in among which the cries of burned and wounded men could be heard. This was very unnerving and I remember thinking how accurate were the descriptions in C.S. Forester's books of the carnage on the gun decks in Nelson's day.'[295] The human damage was 38 men killed (most were unaccounted for) and 39 wounded, whilst the ships damage was so extensive that she had to retire from the Mediterranean for repairs in the United States, she would be out of the war for at least 6 months.

The Destroyer *Greyhound* was next to be attacked, having been detached from *Gloucester* and *Fiji* to intercept and sink a caique off Antikithera, which was successful. However, *Greyhound* was in turn, set upon by dive-bombers at 13:51, which scored three direct hits, sinking the ship in minutes. The destroyers *Kingston* and *Kandahar* were dispatched to pick up survivors, but they too were soon under pressure from the air. The enemy aircraft gave no quarter as they strafed the life rafts, killing many of the men who had taken refuge in the carley floats. Not long afterwards Admiral King, clearly unaware of the cruisers lack of ammunition, ordered *Gloucester* and *Fiji* to assist.

Gloucester was targeted first at 15:30, her guns managed to shoot down two aircraft but before long, she had only practice ammunition left to fire, it was all over for her. Hits were registered, quickly rendering her without power or steering, steam belched forth from her funnels, fire and smoke from where bombs had created great holes in her decks, whilst near misses create great circles of disrupted water around her.

---

[295] (Thomas, 1972)

Fiji rallied round the stricken ship, dropping her own carley floats into the water as the *Gloucesters* began to abandon ship. She was circling at full speed, trying to keep out of harm's way, her own crew cheering the poor *Gloucesters* as she began to settle in the water and list to port. In the end, *Fiji* had to leave, there was little more she could do, her own ammunition was depleted to just a few rounds. She had to retire to fight another day or go the same way as *Gloucester*.

Ken Otter provides many accounts of the sinking in his book HMS *Gloucester*, Victor Parsons, only 19 years old jumped into the water without a life jacket, and on turning to watch his ships final moments recalled.

> The ship looked as though a giant had hit her with a hatchet; the gun turrets were hanging over the side; the funnels were split and the upper deck was smashed. I could see a big black mass of survivors near the bows of the ship and then a dive bomber came down and dropped his bombs right in the middle of them. He didn't attempt to hit the ship. When the ship sank the explosions from the boilers sent shock waves through the sea and I thought my lower body would fall off. Then I got onto the carley float and there were about forty men in the sea clinging to the raft, or to each other. Then we were strafed by the Luftwaffe's machine guns.[296]

Ted Mort was another, just eighteen years old at the time, he witnessed the ship sink. 'I was about half a mile from *Gloucester* when she went down. She turned over for some time, then stood on end before she finally sank. It was a horrible feeling, watching my home going down and being alone, floating on the canteen door.'[297]

In the end, *Fiji* would not last much longer, harried by bombers for the remainder of the day, she too expended her last live ammunition, resorting to firing practice shells in a futile act of defiance. But her end came unexpectedly.

---

[296] (Otter, 2017)
[297] (Otter, 2017)

At 18:45 a lone ME109 out of Molai spotted *Fiji* through broken cloud, the pilot dived, releasing a single 500lb bomb at low level which missed close to the port side about amidships. The bomb must have been set with a minimum delay fuse as it exploded just below the waterline. The explosion tore out a large section of her bottom, water flooding one of her boiler rooms. She soon began to list to port, coming to a stop all power to her engines gone no ammunition to fight with, impotent. About 30 minutes later she was spotted by another aircraft, three more bombs finished her off, at 20:15 the water reached critical mass, rolled her over and sank her.

As darkness began to fall on the Mediterranean that day, one can only imagine the relief that the ships crews felt for the respite from attacks the night would bring. It had been a very bad day indeed. In Alexandria, Cunningham was clearly shaken by events, he wrote, '…as the afternoon gave way to evening, and evening to night, our hearts were heavy as the news of our casualties kept coming in. In my office ashore close to the war room where the positions of all our ships were plotted, hour by hour on the large-scale chart, I came to dread every ring on the telephone, every knock on the door, and the arrival of each fresh signal.'[298] But, of course, it was not over. Tomorrow, the 23rd would be another day, and the attacks would come again.

As we have discussed, poor communications can quickly lead to disaster in times of action. The radio communications and transmission of information in the 1940's was primitive with much of the equipment in early stages of development. As many consumers know in this 20th century age of telecommunications, low bandwidth equals slow communications speeds, especially at times of contention, when many users are attempting to use the same service. This was very much the case with the equipment used in Royal Navy ships in 1941, long delays and complex coding of signals for secure communications meant signals were prone to errors. During a 'most immediate' transmission from Admiral Rawlings, in command of Force A, to Cunningham, the loss of *Gloucester* and *Fiji* was reported as was the ammunition status of the ships at sea, which now was a source of concern for

---

[298] (Cunningham, 1951)

Cunningham. In the receipt of the signal, the status of the battleships anti-aircraft ammunition (pom-poms) was read as 'empty', when it should have read 'plenty'.

As a result, Cunningham had to make a decision, but one based on erroneous information. Recall those ships that required replenishment, leaving a fragmented, scattered and weakened force at sea, or bring in the whole fleet? He decided on the latter. At 04:00 on the 23rd, the general recall of the fleet to Alexandria was given.

HMS Kelly - Friday 23 May 1941

The 5th Destroyer Flotilla, under the command of Captain Lord Louis Mountbatten, had recently replaced the 14th DF in Malta as the Malta Strike Force. It consisted of the J & K destroyers *Kelly* (D), *Kashmir*, *Kipling*, *Kelvin* and *Jackal*. They had been ordered to sail from Malta to support Force A, departing on the 21st to arrive on the 22nd. Their initial operations included the shelling of Maleme airfield and the searching for survivors from *Gloucester* and *Fiji*, before being recalled to Alexandria. On the morning of the 23rd they were steaming at full speed westwards from the region of the island of Gaudo. There was a long way to go before they would be safe.

Earlier, *Kipling* had developed a steering problem; initially intending to join up with Force A, her crew had managed to make the necessary repairs, so she sailed to the southwest of Crete in order to rejoin the 5th DF in the morning. No doubt her crew spotted the high level Dornier bombers that at first light had found and were now bombing the 5th DF. It could lead to only one thing, Stukas. Sure enough, when 13 miles south of Gaudo at 07:55 they arrived, 24 of them from I/St.G.2, led by Maj. Hubertus Hitschold. *Kipling* increased to full ahead to close and give assistance, but it was too late.

The destroyers were zigzagging at high speed in a vain effort to avoid their antagonisers, but the numbers were too many and the skill of the pilots too good. *Kashmir* took the first hit, a bomb hitting her amidships and just forward of her funnel, which broke her back and she went down within two minutes. *Kelly*, now at 30 knots was desperately trying to escape, but as she turned hard over to port she was hit, the explosion ripping out her port side. The sea immediately poured in, the rate of ingress exacerbated by her speed, pulling her even further to port so that she went beyond the point of return and flipped over. Somehow, a number of her crew managed to escape, taking to whatever they could find to keep them afloat, but they were strafed by their assailants. *Kelly* remained hull up for some 30 minutes before she sank.

Kipling came to the rescue and despite the repeated attacks, she managed to pick up 128 crewmen from *Kelly* and 153 from *Kashmir*[299], including both of their captains. According to Cunningham; 'Between 8:20 a.m. and 1p.m. she was attacked by forty aircraft which dropped more than eighty bombs; but emerged undamaged.'[300] Having got aboard all she could, and still under attack, *Kipling* made for Alexandria, but ran out of fuel 70 miles from port, and had to be towed in by *Protector*.

'It was as if the surface of the water had been swept clean.' Saturday 24 May 1941

Take off at first light for armed reconnaissance of the sea areas en route to, and around the island of Crete. Destroy all enemy ships sighted, particularly troop transports sailing to or from Crete. You are free to attack *all* vessels within areas specified, as no friendly shipping in vicinity. If no ships found, alternative target enemy troop positions at Canea.[301]

---

[299] Figures from S.W.C. Pack, The Battle For Crete.
[300] (Cunningham, 1951)
[301] (Mahlke, 2013)

These were the orders that Stuka Pilot, Helmut Mahlke and his crews were given on the evening of the 23 May. When he took off the following morning, the weather was perfect. A clear blue sky with visibility for miles.

> From our altitude of 3,000 meters (around 10,000ft) we could scan a vast area of sea. But that didn't help us much today. It was as if the surface of the water had been swept clean. Despite all our searching, not a single ship came into view. The whole way to Crete there was not a ship to be seen. In the entire sea around the island, not a ship to be seen. After nearly three and a half hours spent staring fruitlessly at the sun-dappled water, I was finally forced to opt for the alternative target, which we bombed to considerable effect at 08:45 hours.[302]

Cunningham had a moment to take stock of the situation. He argues that whilst the mistake in the communication regarding the ammunition status was a factor in the loss of the *Kelly* and *Kashmir*, perhaps they would have been lost in any case? Or could they have lost even more ships, at a greater loss to the fleet, if they had been sent to assist? He did, however, acknowledge that the loss of *Gloucester*, *Fiji*, *Greyhound*, *Kelly* and *Kashmir* were down to the fundamental mistake that they had been tasked away from the main forces, and their mutual protection from air attack. A rule the fleet had written themselves but clearly forgotten during the heat of battle.

On Crete, that battle was, as we know, not going well. The Chiefs of Staff in London, still preoccupied with protecting Crete from a seaborne invasion (whilst it was evident to all in the Mediterranean that all German forces were being sent in by air), asked Cunningham for an appreciation of the situation.

He responded that the weight of enemy air power over the seas around Crete (and the Aegean) now restricted any fleet operations to the hours of daylight. The chiefs were not swayed, they wanted the Navy to respond to any aerial reconnaissance that detected seaborne forces bound for Crete, whatever

---

[302] (Mahlke, 2013)

the time of day, whatever the cost, only time and experience would prove otherwise. Cunningham was clearly incredulous. He wrote to the Chiefs:

> It is not the fear of sustaining losses but the need to avoid losses which will cripple the fleet without commensurate advantage which is the determining factor in operating in the Aegean. As far as I know, the enemy has so far had little if any success in reinforcing Crete by sea.
>
> The experience of three days in which two cruisers and four destroyers have been sunk, and one battleship, two cruisers and four destroyers severely damaged shows what losses are likely to be. Sea control in the Eastern Mediterranean could not be retained after another such experience.[303]

Whilst he was writing this, Operation M.A.Q.3 was at sea, and under attack.

M.A.Q.3 - Sunday 25 May 1941

> What do you think on a morning like this? Do you think 'A lot of people are going to be killed today.' Or even, 'Shall I be killed today?'? No, not a bit; not once the game is on. Before you sail, waking in the dark of your cabin and alone, you are scared stiff, and after it is all over you have, probably, a bad reaction. But with all the things to attend to on the bridge, all your young men around you and dependent on you, and all the other ships in sight, you never think anything will happen to you. Worry about the merchant ships, yes, and the carriers which

---

[303] (Cunningham, 1951)

will always be the object of the enemy air attack, but your own little ship – no.[304]

Commander Roger Hill

Quite likely there were many mixed feelings aboard all the ships forming up outside Alexandria on the 25 May. News would have been filtering through to the ships, that at 06:00 on the previous day, far to the north in the Denmark Strait, HMS *Hood* had been sunk by the *Bismark*. It was shattering news. Whilst here in the Mediterranean, over the past few days, they too had witnessed the loss of familiar ships that had been part of their fleet for so long, now lying torn and tangled masses on the bottom of the sea. They had picked up the bedraggled, exhausted survivors, retching up sea water or worse, heavy, black fuel oil that not only covered their bodies, but sat heavy in their lungs and stomachs. Others had burns to varying degrees, or wounds that left dark stains on the decks which would remind those who had to clean them up of the trauma these men had been through. Some were cheerful, relieved they had survived, whilst others just stared, with a bewildered look of the refugee who has lost everything. To the men of the ships departing that morning, many must have wondered if it would be they who were next.

There was some hope though, they had with them two battleships in the form of *Queen Elizabeth*, and although a little long in the tooth, dear old *Barham*, to accompany them, moreover, there was *Formidable* with her own aircraft, about to strike back at the enemy who had caused so much grief lately.

The crews had all been awakened early for a lunchtime departure, the day would be bright and warm, temperatures in the mid 70's (22+ °C), with a light breeze. *Formidable's* crew were awakened early in order to clean ship at 06:00 before they were required on the flight deck at 09:10 for a church service and briefing. Dismissed they prepared the ship for sea at 10:30, slipping her buoy at 12:15. By 15:00, with her attendant destroyers close by as the aircraft were landed on, and the fleet could set course for Scarpanto. Aboard *Nubian* it was

---

[304] (Hill, 1979)

no doubt noted by the more experienced hands, that the number of aircraft flown on that afternoon was very few in number. They must have hoped that she already had aircraft stowed in her hangers.

In reality, the numbers of serviceable aircraft and crews aboard were pitiful for a raid on such a large airfield. Possibly the most accurate figure on airframe numbers comes from Brian Cull and Frederick Galea's history of 806 Squadron FAA: 'The carrier had aboard 12 Fulmars, crewed by a hotchpotch of whoever was available from 803, 805 and 806 Squadrons: some of the aircraft were of doubtful serviceability but all that could be made available, plus 15 Albacores and Swordfish. One of the pilots to join 806 Squadron was Lt.(A) Pat Massy, who had been flying Sea Gladiators from *Eagle* the previous year.'[305] It is quite clear that fighter cover would be minimal, the attack on the airfield would have to be made by Albacores, whilst the Swordfish were of no use with the exception of anti-submarine patrols.

Barrage! Barrage! Barrage! - Monday 26 May 1941

Oh Lord God
Thou knowest how busy
I am going to be this day
If I forget thee
Do not thou forget me

Jacob Astley, 1ˢᵗ Baron of Astley, Reading 1572 - 1652

A clear sky meant that in the early hours of the 26th there was plenty of light to fly visually, the winds were light from WSW, the sea calm. *Formidable* was sailing a northerly course of 325° at a steady 17 knots, about 100 miles from Scarpanto. Earlier, *Formidables'* crew had walked the flight deck to clear away any foreign objects that may cause damage to the aircraft. Ranged

---

[305] (Galea, 2019)

towards the stern of the carrier, just four Albacores were bombed up ready for their mission, behind which were four Fulmars. The Albacore crews clambered aboard as *Formidable* altered course to 290° and into the wind. The smoke from the bow gradually fluttered its way towards the flight deck centre line as the first Albacore taxied forward before the pilot applied full throttle and the first of the raiding party was aloft. This was soon followed by the remaining three aircraft, that circled above the carrier to form up before heading north for Scarpanto for an arrival at first light.[306] An hour later, at 05:00, the Fulmars were airborne, their higher cruising speed would allow them to arrive on target at the same time as the Albacores.

The raid caught the airfield unprepared. The crews reported rows of Italian CR42's and JU87's bombed and strafed by the raiding party, but in truth there was little damage done, as once more, we can refer to Brian Cull and Frederick Galea for a detailed appraisal; '…there is no record of any JU87s being damaged, although one JU88 was recorded as destroyed and two more damaged, damage also being caused to one SM81 and six CR42s. One Luftwaffe airman was killed, the only casualty.'[307]

At 06:20 the aircraft started to return, *Formidable* sailed into the wind once more so that at 07:10 they began to land on. By 09:05 all aircraft were recovered, there were no losses. But the wasps nest had been well and truly poked and they would have to get away before the retaliatory raids could get to them, on what was another perfect day for flying operations. The fleet turned about onto a course of 150° at 19 knots on a race to put miles between it and the Luftwaffe. As they did so, the Fulmars were re-armed, and Combat Air Patrols launched. But it was not from Scarpanto, that the fleets antagonisers would appear.

Several hundred miles to the south, on the coast of Libya and 50 miles to the northwest of Tobruk was the landing ground at Tmimi. The airstrip was

---

[306] Brian Cull and Frederick Galea state that 6 Albacores launched that morning, with two returning to the carrier with technical problems. However, *Formidables* log states for 04:00, 'Flew off 4 Albacore for attack.'
[307] (Galea, 2019)

flat, with a sandy but firm surface, sparsely vegetated area of about 1510 x 1005 meters (1650 x 1100 yards). Ranged about the landing ground were the Stukas of II./St.G.2, who had been deployed there a few days before. Their primary task was to support Rommel's DAK in the siege of Tobruk, hampering any inbound shipping or attacking the defenders.

For the flight and ground crews, the living conditions were more akin to the infantry than a bomber squadron. They were in tented accommodation, with the most basic of cooking and sanitary facilities. The air was hot and dusty, the fine sand finding its way somehow, into everything, including the airframes of the aircraft. On takeoff, great plumes of dust and sand billowed behind the departing planes prop wash, creating mini sandstorms that billowed and hung in the still air for some time, coating everything in fine red dust.

In command of II./St.G.2 was Major Walter Enneccerus, or 'Ennec' as he was known to his men, who, we will recall had successfully attacked *Illustrious* and *Southampton* earlier that year. No doubt that morning, his first task of the day was to check his boots, a healthy habit he had picked up, and imparted to any new crews that joined his squadron, as Helmut Mahlke recalled when he met Ennec; 'Having taken our boots off, he warned, never put them back on again without first thoroughly checking for scorpions. A warm boot was a favourite hiding place for these venomous little creatures.'[308]

On this day, he would be leading 30 aircraft as a Gruppe, that included Staffels 4 (Oblt. Eberhard Jacob), 5 (Oblt. Bernhard Hamester) and 6 (Oblt. Fritz Eyer). Their aircraft were dark green Stuka JU87 Rs (*Reichweitenausführung*), the long range version of the aircraft, with an external fuel tank under each wing, and a single SD-500 bomb slung along the centre line of the fuselage. The fuse was almost certainly set with a minimum delay. The sortie would take them out over the sea, looking for shipping heading inbound for Tobruk. Ennec was a cautious flyer, and like any pilot of a single engine aircraft of today, flew over the sea with caution, especially

---

[308] (Mahlke, 2013)

operating out of an inhospitable airstrip such as Tmimi. As Mahlke described of Ennec, 'I could well understand Ennec's distaste for over-water missions. Flying over the open sea in a single-engined aircraft was no rest cure at the best of times. But to do it in Africa, where you could almost hear that one engine choking on the sand it had swallowed, was a real test of nerves...'[309]

By early afternoon, Ennec's Gruppe was high above the sea, some 150 miles to the south of the Kaso straight, almost the limit of their patrol. Flying over the sea was much less stressful than over land, despite having one engine. The air was so much smoother than over the desert, where turbulent air or updrafts from the hot surface would cause the aircraft to buck or sink unexpectedly, making it difficult to fly at a constant altitude let alone stay in formation. At just after 13:00 the Gruppe spotted the ships, heading south. To Ennec's delight, there were two very large warships, most likely battleships and surprisingly the unmistakable flat top of a large carrier, whilst clustered around these large vessels fussed their attendant destroyer escorts. The intelligence they had been given was that *Formidable* was still in Alexandria, so this was a welcome development, and Ennec had been here before. It was another chance to cripple or sink a British carrier.

The 4.7-in. gun crew of 'Y' turret, at the stern of *Nubian* were quite a typical mix of older hands looking after the younger, inexperienced men, all from different walks of life before the war, and from across the counties of England and Scotland. Of the older men, Francis Hayter, married to Nellie back in his hometown of Southampton, was senior at 40 years of age. He had joined the Navy in June 1929 after working on the farm once he had left school, using his agricultural background to pass a butchery exam in 1932. His job this day was supplying the shells to the gun crew with George Scicluna, from the aft 4.7-in. magazines up through the wardroom to the gun above. Most likely assisting was 20-year-old Eric Scott from Hucknall, Nottinghamshire.

---

[309] (Mahlke, 2013)

Manning the gun itself were 7 lads, John Anderson from Larkhall in Lanarkshire and William Hill from Edmonton, Middlesex, had turned 21 in the past year as had Raymond Germany from New Tupton in Derbyshire who joined the Navy at 16 after a spell at Williamthorpe Colliery. Cyril Jones from Birmingham, Frank Neall from Lincolnshire and Ronald Thain of Low Fell, County Durham were 20 years old. Thomas Coupland the youngest at just 19, was a farmer's boy from Timberland, Lincolnshire. Of the older men, John Kitching, 28, and Matthew Gibson, 25, came from County Durham, and Kenneth Sharrock, Ainsdale Lancashire. Finally, Leonard Bradford, from Neath near Port Talbot South Wales, whose age is not recorded.

Formidables radar picked up the incoming Stukas at 13:20 and raised a red flag, signaling an imminent attack from the air. In the next few moments, the crew of 'Y' turret received the order that they were expecting, 'Barrage! Barrage! Barrage!' as all four of *Nubians* guns opened up to provide covering fire over the fleet. Any pre-action nerves were immediately cast aside as the gun crew, so well-practiced, began to slam shells into the breeches followed almost immediately by the guns report, the shell was ejected to bounce onto the deck, a coil of expended cordite smoke whisping from the casing, a larger waft of smoke from the gun itself before another shell is loaded and fired. The barrage was described by S.W.C. Pack from Formidable; 'The sky was full of white puffs and brown blobs of smoke. Jagged bits of steel rained into the sea like gigantic hailstones. We were hurtling along at maximum speed, but the noise of the ship's vibration was out-rivalled by the roar of gunfire and the blast and cackle of pom-poms.'[310] Then comes the order to Check fire!

On *Nubians* bridge it had suddenly become clear that the twin engine JU88's (from I.LG.II) were making to attack the screen, and there was nothing for it, but to break off the umbrella barrage, and take avoiding action. The view from 'Y' turret canted over as the ship turned hard away from the fleet, the ensign fluttered and flapped madly, making a whip cracking sound. *Nubian* heeled hard over, the great wake hissed and bubbled, spent shells clattered around the deck whilst the smell of cordite was joined by that of burned fuel

---

[310] (Pack, 1972)

oil as the smoke from *Nubians* funnels belched thickly from her new exertions. Several huge water columns appeared either side of the ship as bombs near missed, the dull crump of their detonation clear above the noise of the close range fifty calibre machine guns and pom-poms as they opened up.

The leading aircraft had succeeded in their aim of drawing the protective fire away from the larger ships so that Ennec's JU87's could have a better chance of sinking *Formidable*. Ennec attacked first, scoring the initial hit on *Formidable*, he was followed by the Staffels of Hamester, Jakob and finally Eyer. Pack's description of the attack on the carrier cannot be bettered.

> Now we could see the swarm of Stukas in the clear blue sky silhouetted against the bright sunlight. They were already peeling off undaunted by the gunfire. Their target was obviously the carrier. Violent avoiding action was now taken in answer to the captain's order for 'Hard a-port' followed next by 'Hard a-starboard'. The *Formidable* responded instantly, heeling sharply to starboard as her head turned to port then seconds later to port as her head came back again. But all of us on the bridge could see the relentless approach of the Stukas. And now we could hear the whistle of the bombs. A mountain of filthy black water shot up close on our starboard bow and rose to eighty feet. Five seconds later there was another mountain, even closer and higher. Millions of crystals of water glittered in the sunlight as they fell. Then there were two in quick succession. We continued to weave. The next one hit. We were immediately on fire on the starboard side forward. A bomb had penetrated one of the 4.5-in. gun turrets. The explosion had blown out the ships starboard side below the fo'c'sle causing damage, and the fire appeared to be spreading. The sea was calm, and the hull was still sound below the waterline, so little water was being shipped into the great gaping hole as we tore along. The firing from the fleet continued; and still the bombers peeled off to dive. There were near misses, and then a gigantic jolt in the *Formidable* when the whole ship seemed to lift from aft. A 1,000lb bomb had gone under the starboard quarter. It was an

uncanny sensation feeling the stern violently lifted and then falling, shuddering like a tuning-fork vibrating about its fixed end. It was all terrifying but in some odd way exhilarating.[311]

Whilst the Stukas were completing their attacks, attention to the screen continued.

The beginning of the end – 26 May 1941

HMS *Nubian* weaved hard to port at 26 knots, a racehorse's power with the nimbleness of a polo pony, her engines turned the screws faster carving a huge wake in the Mediterranean waters that foamed and sparkled in the sunlight. On the bridge Commander Ravenhill, his Officers and men of the watch swayed and steadied themselves trying to maintain their view through raised binoculars at the JU88's and JU87s that were swarming like flies above. The noise was deafening as *Nubian's* pom-poms and 4.7-in. guns thumped shells into the sky re-initiating the umbrella barrage over the carrier. Smoke billowed from *Nubians* funnels as her engines powered her into yet another turn that drew a dirty black curve that mirrored their wake.

Somewhere behind *Nubian*, a pilot of St.G.2 tightened the harness of his Stuka and ran his eyes over the instruments for one last time. He was on this occasion flying at low level, unusual for a dive bomber. His hunch that the crew of the British destroyer were totally focused on protecting their prize asset (the *Formidable*) was proving correct as now a number of JU88's were flying low down one side of the ship, drawing off *Nubians* close range weapons. Levelling out and slightly obscured by the smoke from *Nubian*, he pulled up to 1000 feet about a quarter of a mile behind and then began a shallow dive towards the target.

The thundering sound of the low level JU88's passing close down the ships port side got the attention of everyone on deck. That close and that fast, it was hard to train any of the close range weapons into effect, the tracer rounds arched behind their targets in a vain effort to catch them. These violent,

---

[311] (Pack, 1972)

evasive actions and the thunderous noise were not lost on those crew below either. Trying to put a stopper on fear was personal. Some crossed themselves or said a Hail Mary, some whispered a quiet prayer, some screwed their eyes tight shut willing it all to stop, whilst some simply gripped tight to anything solid to stay on their feet as the decks canted from one side to another.

Back on the bridge, there came a shout from one of the lookouts who was frantically pointing towards the stern. A lone Stuka was now in a shallow dive and at about 600 feet released the black, deadly SD-500 kilo bomb that flew as if on rails towards *Nubian*. Ravenhill shouted 'hard a-starboard!', but it was too late.

The 'Y' turret gun crew frantically tried to bring their 4.7-in. to bear. The call 'Y Gun Ready' was immediately followed by the 'ding ding' of the fire gong and the concussion of the gun as it hurled a shell towards the target. 'Barrage, Barrage, Barrage!' the frantic order to concentrate fire on the approaching enemy was yelled at the gun crew. There was no time to think, no time to be afraid. The young gun crew were now intent only on their job. Just the loaders and tray-workers could see the lone Stuka bearing down on them, but they ignored it and kept up the tempo.

A shell appeared on the loading tray and almost immediately it was rammed into the breech which was slammed shut and the gun fired. There was a great cloud of smoke, the spent case ejected, and a fresh round slammed home. "Bang!" goes the gun again and yet another ejected shell hits the deck with a hollow "gong" and a clatter as it rolled away with the turning of the ship.

But *Nubians* luck had finally run out. Moments later the bomb slammed into 'Y' turret with a shattering explosion that indiscriminately tore the bodies of the gun crew to shreds. Metal splinters, some as large as 6 x 3 inches scythed through everything in all directions with no regard for what or who they ripped through. Fragments were later discovered as far forward as the Sick Berth. But the destruction did not end there.

At the rear of the quarter deck, and just in front of 'X' turret, there were 6 barrel like objects. These were floating gas canisters containing Chlorosulphuric Acid (C.S.A), which when it came into contact with air or water created a dense white smoke. Most warships created a smoke screen by adjusting the operation of the boilers to pour black smoke from the ships funnels, however the C.S.A. floats were another method of generating smoke, but it appears, rarely used. The gas was irritating to the eyes and caused respiratory problems if inhaled. When the bomb went off, it ruptured the canisters which instantly obscured the stern of the ship, blinded and filled the lungs of all those who were still alive in that part of the ship. Damage control would be severely hampered, as would any visual assessment of what had occurred ascertained from the bridge.

In fairly short time though, the Engineering Officer, Lt. J.E.C. Costello, reported that 'Y' turret had been carried away, a fire had broken out and that his recommendation was to flood number 3 and 4 magazines. However, the smoke from the C.S.A. canisters was preventing this action for the moment. What was surprising was that there were few electrical warnings sounding, although there was a steering alarm. In the meantime, the 1st Lieutenant suggested he hand over gun control to Lt. Round Turner whilst he would venture aft to assess the situation. As he left, Lt. Costello reported that no.4 magazine was now flooded and requested he continue to flood no.3 magazine, to which Ravenhill consented.

As Lt. Bush was approaching the quarter deck there came a secondary explosion that Ravenhill described in his after action report.

> This explosion occurred about four minutes after the first and was much more spectacular due to the fact that it was freely vented (A large column of flame and smoke rose to a height of about 200'). I do not think it caused as much damage as the actual explosion of the bomb, but it is difficult to say as the whole scene was clouded with C.S.A. smoke throughout. I think this second explosion was caused by depth charges or cordite in the ready use lockers, there were four depth charges primed in the trap but I think if all four had exploded the explosion would have been rather worse that it was.[312]

As the C.S.A. smoke began to clear, the wounded were sent to the sick berth, where Surgeon Lt. McDowell began to deal with the men brought to

---

[312] (Admiralty, 1941)

him with burns and splinter wounds. After a time, they found the badly wounded George Scicluna from the gun crew of 'Y' turret. What remains there were of the gun crew dead were brought forward and prepared for burial at sea when time and safety permitted. Lt. Bush and Costello began to assess and report the damage, whilst detailing the damage control parties in keeping the ship afloat.

What quickly became clear, was that *Nubian* was grievously wounded. Her stern had been completely blown away, including 'Y' turret and her crew. There lay a huge gaping hole, filled with water mixed with fuel oil and detritus where the wardroom had once been. The decks had collapsed jamming the rudder, but miraculously the propellors and shafts were still intact and on-line. The electrical systems and fire control systems continued to function, and whilst 'X' turret was indeed still able to operate, the structural integrity of the ship was in doubt, effectively putting the turret out of action.

Ravenhill ordered the Not Under Control (N.U.C.) flag raised as *Jervis* closed to assist. However, damage control ascertained that *Nubian* could be steered by her engines, she began to make headway, and a course was set for Alexandria under escort. Getting *Nubian* back to safety, intact, was now their only concern. Whilst her stern was indeed missing, the flooding had only just reached the aft oil tanks (No. 7 to Starboard, No. 8 to Port) ahead of the aft magazines. Whilst No. 8 was flooded with water, No.7 was intact, and so with careful fuel management and by connecting No. 3 boiler to the aft tank, the ship could be kept in trim. In addition, Ravenhill ordered the torpedoes, remaining depth charges and any unused ammunition in the ready lockers jettisoned overboard to lighten the ship. He also ordered any items deemed superfluous to the running of the ship thrown overboard to which Ravenhill noted with perhaps a note of irritation tinted with some humour; 'Some expert threw overboard the officers' laundry which was in the after flat.'[313]

With the ships condition stable, her forward main guns operational, *Nubian* in company with *Jervis* was able to maintain 25 knots in a race to safety. But inevitably, they were being hunted down. At 14:35, high above there droned, possibly to the crew's relief, a number of Italian SM.79's (rather than German JU87's!). Their bombs began to fall, and it looked like they

---

[313] (Admiralty, 1941)

would be close. Ravenhill ordered the starboard engine stopped, and as the ship turned the bombs fell off to port, the closest by a mere 70ft. It was a close call. *Jackal* then relieved *Jervis* as escort and having her positioned a quarter ahead and into the sun, Ravenhill had an object on which to steer the ship and have forward warning of any shipping, enemy or otherwise, ahead. At midnight, with no doubt a sigh of relief for all, *Nubian* entered the Great Pass, and the safety of Alexandria.

Nubian was out of the war for now, and once safely berthed, the process of clearing away and assessing the damage, both physical and human could commence. The sight of ambulances lines alongside the dock made it clear to all that the crew had not escaped unscathed. But before we continue with her story we must return to the Battle of Crete and its conclusion. The evacuation of troops from the island began in earnest from the 27 May, but with a depleted fleet and the Luftwaffe still in command of the air, success was not a foregone conclusion. There were many challenges ahead for the Navy.

Estimates indicated there were 22,000 troops remaining on the island, but this inaccuracy just gave the Navy a planning headache. How many men would they expect to evacuate per night, and therefore how many ships would be required to achieve success but minimise the risk to the remaining Naval assets? The lifting of the troops would have to be made at night, between midnight and 03:00. This would give the ships enough time to clear the island and get far enough away to minimise the effect of air attack.

The evacuation beaches posed a separate set of issues. Heraklion to the north of the island was a small harbour, but it had jetty's that smaller ships could use to lift the soldiers. However, it was that much closer to the Axis forces and there was a threat from motor torpedo attack and perhaps even the Italian Navy. Fortunately, the majority of troops being evacuated would be from the southern port of Sphakia, which had its own set of problems. It was tiny, for a start, only 200 yards of shingle beach that could only be approached by small craft or Landing Ships. It was ringed by hills and cliffs, some 500ft high, the only paths down to the beach narrow and windy.

Nevertheless, over the coming nights the evacuations took place in a race against time as rapidly strengthening opposition on the ground was gaining the upper hand. Attacks on the ships from the air continued, and on the last day of evacuation, 1 June, the cruisers *Calcutta* and *Coventry* sailed from Alexandria to rendezvous with the final convoy. They were attacked just 85 miles from Alexandria, a stick of bombs narrowly missing *Coventry*, but two struck *Calcutta* and within minutes she sank.

The Battle of Crete was over. In evacuation terms, Pack gives a brief overview in 'The Battle for Crete' as follows; 'The defending army in Crete, including last minute reinforcements, amounted to about 32,000. Of these, in rough figures, 1,800 had been killed, 12,000 taken prisoner, and 17,000 evacuated; about 1,000 escaped after the evacuation of the island.'[314]

For the Germans, they had taken the prize, but at a cost. Whilst the island had been taken by airborne forces, their losses had been grave. So many killed and transport aircraft lost, that apart from special operations, German Paratroops were never deployed in numbers from the air again. But they had Crete.

Cunningham's summary from his dispatch printed in the London Gazette[315] is often quoted, he even includes this, in whole, in his memoir 'A Sailors Odyssey'. Of his men, he wrote in the final paragraph; 'More than once I felt that the stage had been reached where no more could be asked of officers and men, physically and mentally exhausted by their efforts and by the events of these fateful days. It is perhaps even now not realised how nearly the breaking point was reached, but that these men struggled through is the measure of their achievement, and I trust that it will not lightly be forgotten.'[316]

Of his own thoughts, written in his memoir, he wrote; 'So ended the Battle of Crete, and a disastrous period in our naval history – a period of great tension and anxiety such as I have never experienced before or since.'[317] So affected was Cunningham that he effectively tended his resignation. It was refused.

---

[314] (Pack, 1972)
[315] (Gazette, 1948)
[316] (Gazette, 1948)
[317] (Cunningham, 1951)

However, on reflection Cunningham pondered, as have many, whether the loss of Crete was such a blow as it felt at the time, indeed back at home the defeat was tempered by the fact that HMS *Hood* had been avenged with the sinking of *Bismark* on the 27 May, the day the evacuation began in earnest. The prolonged defence of the island may have stretched the Navy even further and put the more strategically valuable island of Malta in jeopardy. Besides, the defence of Crete had tied up Axis forces in the Mediterranean and in delaying Hitler's invasion of Russia may have contributed to their defeat in the east?

Of the Eastern Mediterranean Fleet, it had been sorely ravaged. A month afterwards, Hugh Mulleneux of *Jervis*, as quoted from his diary in Connell's 'Mediterranean Maelstrom', wrote on the 30 June 1941; 'Arrived at Alex; to find a sadly depleted fleet. Practically all the works except *Formidable* have gone, which leaves the mighty Med fleet represented by *Valiant, QE (Queen Elizabeth), Ajax, Pheobe* and one or two destroyers besides the Force B at Haifa. How the mighty have fallen – a month ago we wondered what we were going to do with all the ships at our disposal. The problem has unfortunately been solved by the Luftwaffe.'[318]

The Navy's butchers bill at Crete was as follows. Ships sunk: *Gloucester, Fiji, Calcutta, Juno, Greyhound, Kashmir, Kelly, Imperial* and *Hereward*. Lightly damaged and out of action for a few weeks at most were *Naiad, Carlisle, Napier, Ilex, Havock, Kingston* and *Nizam*. However, due to extensive damage, and laid up for the foreseeable future was the only carrier in the Mediterranean, *Formidable*, the Battleships *Warspite* & *Barham*, the cruisers *Ajax, Orion, Dido* and *Perth* along with the destroyers *Kelvin* and *Nubian*.

The damage assessment on *Nubian* made it clear she could not be repaired locally, not only would she require a whole new stern section but the complete renewal of her steering gear as well. She would be patched up, made watertight, with a rudder, jury rigged on a stem to give her steerage. The work would be carried out at Port Tewfik, before making passage to HM Dockyard in Bombay, India for her complete repair. It was estimated she would be ready to sail via the Suez Canal in August. Of the crew, the majority of hands would

---

[318] (Connell, 1987)

be re-assigned, whilst the remainder would take the ship to Bombay, before they too, would be re-assigned. In the end, she did not sail from Aden until the 20 September, arriving in Bombay 7 days later. It would be almost a year before she would return to action.

Among the human cost of 2000 Officers and men lost during the battle of Crete, *Nubian* had 14 men killed from 'Y' turret, their bodies buried at sea. On arrival in Alexandria on the 26 May, the wounded, Able Seamen Brown, Goulty, Wilmore and Leading Stewards Cassar and Scicluna were immediately transferred to the hospital ship *Maine*. But the following day, 27th, at 05:10, poor George Scicluna succumbed to his wounds and died. He was buried in the Alexandria (Chatby) Military and War Memorial Cemetery, plot 39.

The notification of George Scicluna's death is held at the National Archives and reads.

Admiralty C. in C. Mediterranean N.O.I.C. Malta H.M. Hospital Ship MAINE principle M.O. HMS NUBIAN Capt. (D)14th D.F. HMS ST. ANGELO. IMPORTANT.
661. Regret to report death of George Scicluna leading Steward E/LX 20618 HMS NUBIAN Religion R.C. on board H.M. Hospital Ship MAINE at 0510 Tuesday 27 May from wounds received in action next of kin wife Mrs Scicluna 83 Mostahope Street Malta.

The process of informing of the next of kin now began using a list of actions prescribed within the Navy, 'Casualty Action Sheet'. The names of the men killed were confirmed by the 4 June, with the go ahead given to proceed, initially informing the casualties Navy depot (Portsmouth, Chatham etc.). From that depot the confidential letters were written to the next of kin, telegrams sent off, phone calls made and once complete, the press may have been informed. These actions were completed on the 16 June and the dreaded telegrams, calls and letters dispatched to wives, mothers and fathers.

In Southampton, Nellie Hayter received the telegram she never believed, but dreaded would find its way to her door. Whilst in Gillingham, Kent the postman, telegram in hand, trudged reluctantly up the hill to the corner of Longfellow Road where Leonard Bradfords mother lived. It was a similar situation around the country where the consequence of that one bomb snuffed out the friendships forged aboard ship, the joyous promise of a homecoming, a future for lovers and took everything from the men it killed.

The final action listed on the Casualty Action Sheet. Royal Condolence Sent.

'The Queen and I offer you our heartfelt sympathy in your great sorrow. We pray that your country's gratitude for a life so nobly given in its service may bring some measure of consolation. George R.I.'

Postscript

Nubian

July 1948 and once more *Nubian* lies forlorn in still waters not a basin within Portsmouth, but Loch Striven on the east coast of Scotland. Her engines long silent her bridge deserted all armaments removed the voice tubes on the bridge open but mute. A gentle breeze blows through her wires, softly whistling a mournful tune to the officers and men who have served aboard her. High above, an eagle gracefully circles the loch, her cries carried away on the wind. *Nubian* has been assigned as a target ship for the testing of new munitions, there were no guns to defend her, nor indeed men to man them. Rust streaks like running sores from her anchors and the bare metal where her paint has peeled away, exposing her steel hull to the weather. Inside, condensation runs in rivulets within her once crowded crew spaces and pools on the linoleum floors. It is a lonely end for a proud lady.

When *Nubian* had returned to the Mediterranean in October 1942, the situation was much different than when she had left. Operation Pedestal, the relief of Malta by convoy, at the cost of many ships and men of the Royal Navy, had been the high-water mark for the Germans in terms of air supremacy, but Malta had been relieved. In North Africa, the tide was turning too, the second battle of El Alamein was under way on the 23 October, beginning the rolling back of the DAK by Montgomery's 8th Army to the shores of Tripoli and into Tunisia by March 1943. In the meantime, the allies, including forces from the U.S.A. (having entered the war following the Japanese attack on Pearl Harbour in December 1941), had landed in Morocco under Operation Torch back in November 1942, and were about to link up with the approaching 8th Army.

Convoy duties and aggressive patrolling became the norm for *Nubian* until the invasion of Sicily (Operation Husky). She was involved in the bombardment and capture to the islands of Pantelleria and Lampedusa in July

1943, followed by offshore artillery support during the Salerno landings in August. In October she was sent back to England for a major refit between December and June 1944 which included the upgrade of her radar systems.

Assigned to the Home Fleet she either patrolled the Western Approaches or was sent to the Arctic with the fleet to sink the Tirpitz. In the end, it was the Lancaster's of 617 and 9 Squadron that turned the great ship turtle which allowed the reassignment of the Home Fleet to the conflict in the Far East. *Nubian* sailed to Alexandria for another refit before heading to her area of operations, participating in the Burmese campaign before the war ended.

Nubian gained 13 Battle honours during her war career (and this is counting her three Mediterranean Battle honours as one), just one less than *Warspite*. Of the first batch of ships of her class, she alone out of the 8 built, survived beyond 1942. One of her Commanding Officers, Admiral Sir Deric Holland-Martin wrote the Foreword for Martin Brice's book 'The Tribals' and commented; 'Although the Tribals were ships of a class and outwardly looked alike, each developed, as in a family, a personality of her own. They lived dangerously in a war that took a heavy toll of overworked destroyers and their crews, but, serious as were the casualties, the enemy suffered even greater loss at the hands of the Tribals.'[319]

Nubian returned to Portsmouth via the Mediterranean and for some time was used as an accommodation ship, moored off Whale Island, before she headed north to the quiet of Loch Striven.

On the 25 June 1949, a tug entered the river Neath estuary in Swansea bay, towing what was left of *Nubian*. On these last few miles to the breakers yard at Briton Ferry, perhaps one could see the reluctance in both ships sad journey, like an old, wise horse being gently led to the knacker's yard by a grateful handler.

---

[319] (Brice, 1971)

Battle Honours

Norway 1940
Calabria 1940
Mediterranean 1940, 1941, 1943
Libya 1940
Malta Convoys 1941
Matapan 1941
Greece 1941
Crete 1941
Sicily 1943
Salerno 1943
Burma 1945

Note: HMCS Haida is the only remaining Tribal Class Destroyer in existence. Designated a Canadian National Historic site, she is moored at Pier 9, near Bayfront Park, Hamilton, Ontario, Canada.

The Men

Rear Admiral Philip John Mack D.S.O

'Then at 10:00 a stunned ship's company became aware that Captain Philip Mack was being landed as a sick man, sent to hospital by Doc.'[320]

So writes G. G. Connell in Mediterranean Maelstrom of the moment that Mack left *Jervis* on the 22 February 1942. He returned briefly on the 15 March, to visit his old ship and to say goodbye to his staff officers and men and those of the other ships in the 14th DF. He was returning to London. Connell does not divulge why Mack was admitted to hospital, or why he was being sent back to London, although knowing the stress and strains of command that we have witnessed through Roger Hill, 'Tony' Pugsley and Richard Ravenhill one cannot rule out exhaustion as the root cause. On his leaving, John Mosse, who

---

[320] (Connell, 1987)

according to Connell had just joined the staff of D14, wrote; 'Captain Mack was a giant among men. He simply exuded confidence among all who met him and did much to foster in the destroyer command a spirit of dedication that can only be compared to Nelson's celebrated Band of Brothers.'[321]

Mack was perhaps rested, hopefully with time to visit his home, Paston Hall in Norfolk, and spend some time with his wife Elizabeth. He was appointed Commander of the battleship *King George V* as Flag Captain to Admiral Sir John Tovey who was C-in-C of the Home Fleet, in May 1942 and remained in the *KG V* until he was promoted to Rear Admiral in January 1943. At this time, preparations were being made for Operation Husky, the combined forces invasion of Sicily scheduled for the July of that year and Mack was given the task of preparing the Naval aspect of the operation.

On the morning of the 29 April 1943, Mack was at RAF Hendon, north London, to take a flight to Algiers for a planning conference discussing Operation Husky, with Captain Sir Thomas Lubbock Beevor R.N, Major General Harry Leonard Nowell Salmon M.C., Canadian Army, Lt. Colonel Charles Francis Jeffrey Finlay, R.C.A.S.C. and Lt. Colonel Guy Gervers Holmes Wilson of the Royal Artillery.

The aircraft for the flight was a Lockheed Hudson, F.H.307 of 24 Squadron, the pilot, a volunteer replacement (as the original pilot had reported sick) being Canadian born Flight Lt. Gordon Leslie MacIntyre, D.F.C. who had come to England to join the RAF in 1939. MacIntyre was an experienced pilot and had seen action with Coastal Command that had earned him a D.F.C. in September 1942. His three crew members were Flying Officer Frederick Ford, who was Navigator for the flight, WO Percy Laver, Wireless Operator and Aircraftman 1st Class Harold Newton who was a Steward and would be looking after the passengers for the flight.

The route to Algiers would be via Portreath, on the north coast of Cornwall then down to Gibraltar and onwards to Algiers. However, the weather was foul. Low dark clouds, at barely 1000 feet scudded across the country accompanied by rain and drizzle. Portreath called to suggest the flight should be cancelled, however this was an important meeting, and these men were

---

[321] (Connell, 1987)

required to attend. The alternative was to fly to Chivenor on the north Devon coast, a little closer to Hendon with marginally better flying conditions at present.

The Hudson lifted off from Hendon at 11:00, quite possibly taking a route down the Bristol Channel to avoid the hills over Exmoor, which were likely to be covered in cloud. At 12:15 MacIntyre approached the airfield from the north to join at base leg of the west-east runway. The cloud cover was almost complete and down to 1000 feet, it was drizzling rain but the visibility good at 12 miles, the winds were light and from the southeast.

MacIntyre would have been aware that the Hudson was prone to stalling at low speeds, but a taxing flight in poor conditions, with an important group of passengers may have affected his mental capacity. One primary cause of air accidents is 'press-on-itis', where outside factors and pressures force a pilot to undertake a flight that really should be cancelled, this flight has all the hallmarks of such a situation. MacIntyre would have made a plan in his own mind how to make the approach, and he would have decided to either deploy landing flaps, allowing him to approach in a stable attitude at a lower airspeed, or without assistance from flaps, in which case he would need more airspeed on the final approach so as not to stall the aircraft.

As he turned the aircraft onto finals, he was much too low, estimated by observers to be no more than 300 feet, when he should have been at about 700 feet. The aircrafts flaps had not been deployed and his airspeed was far too low, perhaps he had simply forgotten to lower them but continued as if he had? Shortly thereafter the aircraft stalled and entered into a spin, clearly MacIntyre attempted to recover, and for a moment the Boston did level out, but a full recovery requires an increase in airspeed and the only way to do that is to push the nose down. There simply was not enough height to do so, and the Boston, still in a stall, crashed into the ground, bursting into flames. Everyone aboard was killed. The accident report concluded.

From the evidence available, coupled with detailed inspection of the wreckage, it is clear that in spite of the extensive experience of the Pilot his circuit and approach was carried out at a slower speed and lower altitude than is usually associated with aircraft landing on the particular runway in question. After the final turn-in to land the aircraft appeared to 'stay still in the air' and it can reasonably be assumed that a stall was encountered which developed partly into a spin, from which recovery was not made.

The cause of the accident, therefore, must be attributed to an error of judgement on the part of the pilot.

That would seem somewhat unfair with the clarity of hindsight. Whilst the meeting was clearly of importance, was it necessary for the flight to have taken place? Perhaps it was the passengers themselves who insisted on making the flight that just maybe, in the back of his mind, MacIntyre, as an experienced pilot, was not comfortable with undertaking? Of course, we will never know, and the result was the loss of a group of highly experienced men and perhaps one of the most capable naval commanders, Rear Admiral Philip Mack, D.S.O.

'Tony' Pugsley wrote of Mack; '...I think Mack was my ideal of what a destroyer leader should be. A superb ship-handler, an inspiring leader and, with it all, an air of modesty and great charm, he had severe standards by which he judged destroyer captains in time of war. One by which he measured them all was 'How many enemy ships has he sunk?'[322]

Admiral Cunningham was a great friend of Mack's, and it would be easy to quote the whole of his appreciation of the man from his memoir. If we can extract a fitting quote of Mack, then perhaps this is it.

'Everyone was fond of Philip Mack and went to him for advice if in difficulty or trouble. I am not unduly sentimental; but few men have inspired in me such admiration and personal affection. In all respects he was a grand man and a fine officer, fighting seaman of the very finest quality with the supreme knack of making himself loved, respected and trusted.'[323]

Rear Admiral Philip Mack, D.S.O. is buried in St Margarets Church, Paston, Norfolk.

---

[322] (Pugsley)
[323] (Cunningham, 1951)

Captain Richard W Ravenhill, CBE. D.S.O

Ravenhill remained with *Nubian* until 23 October 1941, during which time his crew were being either re-assigned or retained to sail her to Bombay for her repairs. In that time, he re-instated Herbert's third Good Conduct Stripe. He returned to England to become Deputy Chief of Staff (Operations) at Western Approaches Command, based in the top-secret Royal Navy headquarters in Derby House, within the Exchange Buildings, Liverpool.

Within the H.Q. the Operations Room, spread over two storeys there was a huge map of the Atlantic and the Western Approaches, which displayed the positions of the convoys as they sailed to and from England, in the main, landing their cargoes at Liverpool docks. The purpose of the Western Approaches Command, in particular the Operations team was to ensure the safe and timely arrival of convoys. There was of course the constant threat from U-Boat attack and from the air by the big, 4 engine Condor aircraft, not to mention the adverse weather and sea conditions that could be treacherous. The operations team also reviewed the performance of the RN ships and crews, developing new tactics to fight the enemy. Although closed at the end of the war, the bunker remains open to the public, whilst a good idea of what the place was like was recreated in the film, 'Sink the Bismark!'

Of Ravenhill's time there, his Commanding Officer, Admiral Horton, wrote; 'Highly intelligent with a cool, balanced judgement which makes his opinions invaluable. He has a vigorous outlook, is never flustered in emergencies or under pressure and is resourceful to a degree. Completely trustworthy and reliable and fearless of responsibility. Health and enduring but owing to the long hours worked in this sedentary job with little opportunity for exercise he may not be at his physical best at the moment.'[324]

In February 1941, Ravenhill travelled to Boston, where he took command of the cruiser *Newfoundland,* which had just completed a refit. Ravenhill and her crew worked up to operational status in preparation to join the 4th Cruiser Squadron as Flagship under C-in-C, Admiral Sir Bruce Fraser within the British Pacific Fleet, using Sydney, Australia as the primary base.

---

[324] (Admiralty, 1945)

Newfoundland remained in the Pacific until the end of the war, being present in Tokyo Bay when the final Instrument of Surrender was signed by the Japanese on 2 September 1945 aboard the USS *Missouri*. Ravenhill left *Newfoundland* on the 7 October 1945.

Clearly Ravenhill had an interest, if not a flair for navigation and in December 1945 he became the Director of the Navigation Division, a post he held until 1947 after which he spent a year at the Imperial Defence College before travelling to Melbourne, where he was assigned Naval Chief Staff Officer. In 1950 he and his wife Enid celebrated their Silver Wedding anniversary, before returning to the U.K.

Enid at just 59 years old, died in 1955, but Ravenhill remarried on the 27 July 1957 to Marjorie Gilley. Having retired from the Navy he found an appropriate position with The Sperry Gyroscope Company, who manufactured precision navigational equipment, before his final retirement when he and Marjorie moved to Worthing in Sussex. He died on their wedding anniversary in 1978 at the age of 76. Marjorie lived on until 1986. Ravenhill left no children from either marriage.

The Crew

It would appear that of the older Nubians whose service record is accessible, almost to a man, were sent to shore establishments around the Royal Navy for the remainder of the war. Some were assigned to training positions, some simply clerical, others went on to serve in other ships. The older hands had done their bit, it was now time for the hostilities only sailors to finish the job. It is almost uncanny that *Nubian* should be put out of action almost two and a half years since her commissioning, the length of a tour of duty in the Navy at that time. In researching this book, it has been impossible to identify all the crew members of *Nubian*, however of her Officers and men (excluding her Commanding Officers), I identified 40 crew from the ship who were aboard at the same time as Herbert Leeder, and I was able to track down some of their service records within the National Archives. I also identified a further 11 crew members who served on her after Herbert had left but may have been drafted in after her refit.

Unfortunately, I have not been unable to locate much personal information of the crews time aboard *Nubian*. Like most servicemen who were in the armed forces during World War 2, their experiences were rarely shared in written or spoken word. However, I was astonished to find the recording of an interview with John Duyland Bush from the Imperial War Museums archive. It was poignant listening to a man who served with my Great Grandfather, and indeed I was able to correct a few small but important facts from the interview, and pleasingly, confirm that for the most part, my research was correct!

Of the younger members it was sad to find that Sub Lieutenant Peter Hopper, who was transferred to *Intrepid*, was killed on the 5 March 1942 during arctic convoy PQ12, which attempted to lure the *Tirpitz* (the *Bismarck's* sister ship) into action. The weather conditions on those particular convoys were appalling as would life aboard a small destroyer been most uncomfortable and dangerous. I could not ascertain how Hopper was killed, but it was either a tragic accident aboard ship or god forbid he was washed overboard. He was the youngest of two sons and just 21 years old when he died.

Herbert Leeder

On the 14 September 1945, just 12 days after the Japanese surrender, Herbert Leeder walked through the Unicorn Gate for the last time as a serving member of His Majesty's Royal Navy. He had spent much of the remainder of the war in North Africa at the shore establishments of 'Hasdrubal' and 'Hannibal'. 'Hasdrubal' was located at the port of Bizerte and Herbert was present there as the allied forces prepared in great numbers for Operation Husky. Perhaps these postings reflected the time he had spent on operations? It is quite likely that he would have been mentally affected by the almost constant bombardments the injuries and deaths of his crewmates and of course the distinct possibility that it would be his turn next. In the final chapter I hoped to convey the exhaustion of combat that came during the fall of Greece and Crete. I found the writing of those final pages, as I have named one of the preceding chapters, 'Relentless'.

Herbert returned to England to live out his life with Kathleen and his growing family in their small home near Southsea (Doreen married in 1943 and had two girls, Jacky and my mother, Josephine). Motorbikes became a passion for him, and he brought a sidecar so that he and Kathleen could tour around the lanes of the Hampshire countryside. Like many young men who had left the land or the factories to join the Senior Service, Herbert had made himself a career and despite the war had come through to raise a family, in his own home and to live a peaceful life in the country.

One has to reflect, how did a man who was entering middle age at the beginning of World War 2, who should have been at home raising his family, perhaps sat by the fire with his pipe and slippers cope with the danger, carnage and distinct possibility that he could be killed at any moment? How did any of the men involved in that conflict that was World War 2? I find it humbling that Herbert Leeder was one of those men and was my great grandfather. I don't know whether I could have done it.

Herbert died in 1965, the year that I was born, from respiratory complications that dogged him throughout his later life. Apparently, he claimed his condition was due to the coal used to fire the ships, and his time abroad, but one has to wonder whether the C.S.A. gas explosion aboard *Nubian* may have been closer to the truth?

As I conclude his story it is saddening to think that if I had realised sooner that his career was so unique then maybe I would have pressed my grandmother and indeed my own mother to know him a little better? Perhaps the fact that they could provide no more than his service record and a few notes written in the margins of a book is an indication that, like many veterans, he simply never spoke about his time in the Navy? These are questions that I must resign to the fact I will never know the answer. What I do know, is that I have been able to place his presence amongst some of the most incredible naval operations. I hope in doing so I have brought these actions to readers who are perhaps not so familiar with the sea war in the Mediterranean during 1940 and 1941 and may wish to learn more about the period as a result. At the very least, my family now has a record of a man who served to protect our futures.

A Sailors daughter.

I finish with some words from my grandmother Doreen written for me, that in part led to the writing of this book.

'My fathers ship was called HMS Nubian. He was 40 years old and about to end his time in the Navy, war came so he had to go all those war years!

He joined the Navy at 17 and a half years old and saw the last few months of the 1st World War.

Your Grandmother was 15 years old when war came, I gave him a lucky keep sake, a shoe. He kept it all through the war years and kept it with his money, it was very much worn. He said it saved his life. HMS Nubian was blown in half and my father came back to Portsmouth at 46 years old. He was very kind and had a good word for everyone. I loved him very much.

My sisters and I would tease him dreadful, telling him he had a cold coming saying his eyes looked watery. He would look in the mirror and go to bed with a dish of boiled onions. He got very chesty with a cold as he was in the Far East before the war on 2 and a half year commissions, he said it was very damp up the Yellow River.'

Doreen McFall

Appendix I – Awards – Battle of Tarigo Convoy, 16 April 1941

Bar to Distinguished Service Cross

Captain Philip John Mack, D.S.C., HMS Jervis

Distinguished Service Cross

Commander Richard William Ravenhill, R.N., HMS Nubian
Commander John William Musgrove Eaton, R.N., HMS Mohawk
Commander John Anthony William Tothill, R.N., HMS Janus
Lieutenant Commander (E) Sydney Vincent Parode Capper, R.N., HMS Janus
Lieutenant James Barry Laing, R.N., HMS Jervis
Lieutenant John Fitzroy Duyland Bush, R.N., HMS Nubian
Lieutenant Lionel Robert Patrick Lawford, R.N., HMS Janus

Distinguished Service Medal

Chief Petty Officer Thomas Edgar Tribe, P/J 97508, HMS Nubian
Chief Engine Room Artificer Edwin Jenkins, P/M 38356, HMS Janus
Petty Officer Walter Wynne, P/J. 94813, HMS Nubian
Petty Officer Harry John Whitehorn, P/J 102361, HMS Mohawk
Stoker Petty Officer James Robb, P/KX. 77374, HMS Mohawk
Petty Officer Harold James Quick, C/LX. 20349, HMS Jervis
Stoker Petty Officer William Ernest Sargant, C/KX. 79218, HMS Jervis
Petty Officer Telegraphist James Miller, P/J. 110977, HMS Mohawk
Engine Room Artificer George Thomas Foy, P/MX. 50866, HMS Nubian
Ordnance Artificer George Ernest Hesford, C/M. 35343, HMS Jervis
Leading Seaman Robert Charles Wiills, P/J. 115277, HMS Janus
Able Seaman Thomas Alfred Read, P/J. 87611, HMS Mohawk
Able Seaman James Robert Arthur, P/JX. 149078, HMS Janus

Posthumous Mention in Despatches

Lieutenant Commander (E) John Russell de Meza Warren, R.N. HMS Mohawk

Mention in Despatches

Engineer Commander James Anthony Ruddy, R.N. HMS Jervis
Lieutenant Walter Scott, R.N., HMS Jervis
Lieutenant Peter John Dixon, R.N.V.R., HMS Mohawk
Lieutenant Shirley Elliston Jagger, R.N., HMS Janus
Probationary Surgeon Lieutenant Walter Fitzgerald Fraser, M.R.C.S, L.R.C.P., HMS Jervis
Sub-Lieutenant Kenneth Kirkland Lacey, R.N.V.R., HMS Nubian
Midshipman Peter Nelson Hopper, R.N.R., HMS Nubian
Commissioned Gunner (T) George Douglas Packham, R.N., HMS Jervis
Chief Petty Officer Ernest Edward Lethbridge, P/J. 104458, HMS Mohawk
Chief Petty Officer Cook Percy Frederick Hayles, P/MX. 45408, HMS Janus
Chief Engine Room Artificer John Henry Hathaway, C/M. 34525, HMS Jervis
Chief Yeoman of Signals Charles Wilfred Harris, C/J. 93211, HMS Jervis
Chief Stoker David Chun, P/K. 35434, HMS Nubian
Chief Ordnance Artificer Charles Aubrey Wilson Freeman, P/MX. 47568, HMS Nubian
Petty Officer Arthur Burns, D/J. 105778, HMS Mohawk
Petty Officer Herbert Samuel James, P/J. 90925, HMS Mohawk
Petty Officer William Sutton, P/JX. 125326, HMS Nubian
Petty Officer Robert Stewart Gibbs, P/J. 113023, HMS Janus
Acting Petty Officer John Smith, P/JX 143247, HMS Nubian
Acting Petty Officer Arthur Edgar Perkins, C/JX. 108322, HMS Jervis
Acting Petty Officer Osred Miles, C/JX. 136977, HMS Jervis
Stoker Petty Officer John Charles Baines, P/KX. 76925, HMS Mohawk
Stoker Petty Officer Charles Everitt Smith, P/K. 56516, HMS Mohawk
Stoker Petty Officer Albert Edward Wardell, P/KX. 80164, HMS Janus
Stoker Petty Officer Jack Beauchamp, P/K. 305209, HMS Jervis
Engine Room Artificer Basil Briscoe, D/MX. 61563, HMS Mohawk
Yeoman of Signals George Ernest Westgate, C/J. 113517, HMS Jervis
Ordnance Artificer Samuel Corsie, P/MX. 51465, HMS Mohawk
Leading Seaman Benjamin Hurst, P/J. 108492, HMS Mohawk
Leading Seaman John Bikerstaff, P/JX. 138899, HMS Nubian

Acting Leading Seaman Walter John Davies Ridgeway, D/J. 110805, HMS Jervis
Ordnance Artificer III Richard John Evans, P/MX. 54309, HMS Janus
Stoker George Brown, P/KX. 92164, HMS Mohawk
Able Seaman Frank Whitaker, P/SSX. 15458, HMS Mohawk
Able Seaman Harold Rodney Reed, P/SSX. 18636, HMS Nubian
Able Seaman Arthur William Thurley, C/J. 45803, HMS Jervis

Appendix II Casualties H.M.S Nubian 26 May 1941

ANDERSON, John S, Ordinary Seaman, P/JX 190462, killed (21)
Son of John Reid Anderson and Isabel Millar Bennet Anderson, of Beith, Ayrshire.
Portsmouth Naval Memorial, Panel 50, Column 1

BOYD, John, Able Seaman, P/SSX 18417, killed (23)
Son of James and Janet Perrie Boyd, of Larkhill, Lanarkshire.
Portsmouth Naval Memorial, Panel 47, Column 2

BRADFORD, Leonard V, Able Seaman, C/JX 154067, killed
Chatham Naval Memorial, 42/2

COUPLAND, Thomas J, Able Seaman, C/JX 154656, killed (19)
Son of Frank and Martha Jane Coupland, of Timberland, Lincolnshire.
Chatham Naval Memorial, 42/2

GERMANY, Raymond, Able Seaman, P/SSX 24940, killed (20)
Son of Archibald and Kate Germany, of New Tupton, Derbyshire.
Portsmouth Naval Memorial, Panel 48, Column 1

GIBSON, Mathew, Able Seaman, P/SSX 18967, killed (25)
Son of John G. and Ellen Matilda Gibson, of Broom, Co. Durham.
Portsmouth Naval Memorial, Panel 48, Column 1

HAYTER, Francis, Able Seaman, P/J 49379, killed (40)
Husband of Nellie K. Hayter, of Shirley, Southampton.
Portsmouth Naval Memorial, Panel 48, Column 1

HILL, William, Ordinary Seaman, P/JX 182268, MPK (21)
Son of William and Daisy Hill, of Edmonton, Middlesex.
Portsmouth Naval Memorial, Panel 51, Column 3

JONES, Cyril W, Able Seaman, P/JX 154105, killed (20)
Son of George Thomas Jones and Sophia Jones, of Birmingham.

Portsmouth Naval Memorial, Panel 48, Column 2

KITCHING, John J, Able Seaman, P/SSX 24649, killed (28)
Son of John R. and H. M. Kitching, of New Brancepeth, Co. Durham.
Portsmouth Naval Memorial, Panel 48, Column 2

NEALL, Frank, Ordinary Seaman, P/JX 190731, killed (20)
Son of John William and Caroline Jane Neall, of Brigg, Lincolnshire.
Portsmouth Naval Memorial, Panel 49, Column 1

SCOTT, Eric G, Stoker 1c, P/KX 96215, killed (20)
Son of George and May Scott, of Hucknall, Nottinghamshire.
Portsmouth Naval Memorial, Panel 55, Column 2

SHARROCK, Kenneth W, Able Seaman, P/SSX 17187, killed (27)
Son of Thomas Edwin and Mary Sharrock, of Ainsdale, Lancashire.
Portsmouth Naval Memorial, Panel 49, Column 2

SCICLUNA, George, Leading Steward, E/LX 20618, DoW

THAIN, Ronald, Ordinary Seaman, D/JX 217066, killed (20)
Son of Albert and Christina Thain, of Low Fell, Co. Durham.
Plymouth Naval Memorial, Panel 48, Column 3

Appendix III Abbreviations

AFCC	Advanced or Admiralty Fire Control Clock
AFCT	Advanced or Admiralty Fire Control Table
ASI	Air Speed Indicator (aircraft cockpit instrument)
Boom	Harbour entrance
Cable	Unit of measure, distance. Equivalent to 200 yards or 182.9m
CAP	Combat Air Patrol
Captain 'D'	Captain Destroyers. Senior Officer of a destroyer flotilla
Carley Raft	Lifesaving raft
Cmd	Commander
Commission	Period of service
Cordite	Propelent explosive
CPO	Chief Petty Officer
C-in-C	Commander-in-Chief
dc	Depth Charge
dct	Depth Charge thrower
DCT	Director Control Tower
DF	Destroyer Flotilla
Director	Gunnery control position
Ditty box	Wooden box with lock, for personal possessions
D.S.C	Distinguished Service Cross
D.S.O	Distinguished Service Order
ERA	Engine Room Artificer
Fathom	Unit of measure, depth of water. Equivalent to 6ft or 1.8m
Fish	Torpedo
Flashing	Signalling

Flat	Deck
Foc's'le	Forecastle. Forward part of the upper deck
Galley	Kitchen
Green	On the Starboard (right) side
Gun Layer	Member of gun's crew controlling gun's elevation
HA	High Angle
Hand	Sailor
HMAS	His/Her Majesty's Australian Ship
HMCS	Her Majesty's Canadian Ship
HMNZS	Her Majesty's New Zealand Ship
HMS	His/Her Majesty's Ship
Kye	Cocoa
LA	Low Angle
Lt.	Lieutenant
Lt. Cmd	Lieutenant Commander
Make and Mend	Period when duties are suspended
MID	Mentioned in Despatches
NCO	Non Commissioned Officer
Number One	First Lieutenant
Oblt	Oberleutnant
PO	Petty Officer
Pompey	Portsmouth
Pom-pom	Close range automatic weapon
Port	On the left side
Red	On the Port (left side)
Quarter Deck	Deck space astern
Quartermaster	Rating responsible in harbour for piping daily routine. At sea assumes helmsman's duties.
Run ashore	Shore leave
Scran-bag	A 'pound' or place where articles left lying around are stowed. Traditionally these may be redeemed with a piece of soap.

Scuttle	A type of port hole.
Ships company	Crew
Stand easy	Short period of rest.
Starboard	On the right side
Stripey	Long service man
Swept channel	Clear passage, usually into harbour.
Tot	Daily allowance of rum.
TS	Transmitting Station. Centre of communication.
VALF	Vice Admiral Light Forces
VSI	Vertical Speed Indicator (aircraft cockpit instrument, displays rate of climb & descent)
WO	Warrant Officer
WT	Wireless Telegraphy

Sources

Shields Daily News 01/05/1940 – Seaman Walter Hall – 'Afridi' sinking
Birmingham Mail 10/05/1940 – Frederick Tandy – 'Afridi' sinking

Bibliography

[Online] // Malta War Diary, Story of a George Cross. - www.maltagc70.com .

Admiralty The Action off SFAX, April 1941, ADM/267/104 [Report]. - [s.l.] : The Royal Navy, 1941.

Admiralty The After Action Report Arab ASM 199/476 [Report].

Admiralty The Bomb damage, May 1941, ADM/267/103 [Report]. - [s.l.] : The Admiralty, 1941.

Admiralty The Ravenhill, ADM 196 94 18 [Report]. - [s.l.] : National Archives, 1945.

Association The Fisgard The Fisgard Association [Online] // Home Page. - 2022. - May 1, 2021. - https://www.thefisgardassociation.org.

Ballantyne Iain Warspite, From Jutland Hero to Cold War Warrior [Book]. - Barnsley : Pen & Sword Ltd., 2001, 2013, 2014.

Barnett Correlli The Desert Generals [Book]. - London : Pan Books Ltd., 1983.

Bognor Regis Observer - Saturday 25 October 1941 [Online] // The British Newspaper Archive. - Findmypast Newspaper Archive Limited. - August 22, 2022. - https://www.britishnewspaperarchive.co.uk/viewer/BL/0001922/19411025/003/0001?browse=False.

Brice Martin H The Tribals [Book]. - Shepperton : Ian Allan Ltd., 1971.

Brokensha David Guys Story [Online]. - http://www.brokiesway.co.za/guysstory/.

Bush John Fitzroy Duyland Bush, John Fitzroy Duyland (Oral history) [Interview]. - [s.l.] : IWM https://www.iwm.org.uk/collections/item/object/80026859, 2005.

Captain Donald Macintyre D.S.O & 2 BARS D.S.C., R.N. (Retd.) Narvik [Book]. - London : Evans Brothers Ltd., 1959.

Captain John G. Wells C.B.E., D.S.C., Royal Navy Whaley, The Story of HMS Excellent 1830 to 1980 [Book]. - Portsmouth : HM Stationary Office, 1980.

Carter Geoffrey The Royal Navy at Portland since 1845 [Book]. - Liskeard : Maritime Books, 1987.

Connell G. G. Mediterranean Malestrom, HMS Jervis and the 14th Flotilla [Book]. - London : William Kimber & Co. Limited, 1987.

Cunningham Andrew A Sailor' Odyssey [Book]. - [s.l.] : Hutchinson & Co. (Publishers) Ltd., 1951.

Dowie John A Largo Bay Maritime Log & The Methil Convoys [Online] // Scottish Fisheries Museum. - The Scottish Fisheries Museum Trust Ltd., 2012. - 2021. - www.scotfishmuseum.org/perch/resources/largobaymaritimelog.pdf.

Dunning Chris Courage Alone, The Italian Airforce 1940 - 1943 [Book]. - Aldershot : Hikoki Publications, 1998.

Ewer Peter Forgotten ANZACS, The Campaign in Greece, 1941 [Book]. - Melbourne : Scribe Publications Pty Ltd, 2008.

F 540 - ITS Pietro de Cristofaro [Online] // Seaforces.org. - May 23, 2022. - https://www.seaforces.org/marint/Italian-Navy/Corvette/F-540-ITS-Pietro-de-Cristofaro.htm.

Fenwick Kenneth H.M.S. Victory [Book]. - London : Cassell & Company, 1959.

Galea Brian Cull and Frederick 806 Naval Air Squadron [Book]. - Stroud : Fonthill Media Ltd, 2019.

Gazette The London Transportation of the army to Greece and evacuation of the army from Greece, 1941 [Article] // Supplement to The London Gazette. - London : H.M. Stationary Office, 1948. - 65-38293. - 38293.

Gazette The London Transportation of the army to Greece and evacuation of the army from Greece. 1941 [Journal]. - London : The London Gazette, 18th May 1948. - 38293.

Hanson Norman Carrier Pilot [Book]. - London : Silvertail books, 2016.

Harrison W. A. Fairey Swordfish and Albacore [Book]. - Ramsbury, Marlborough : The Crowood Press Ltd., 2002.

Hastings Max Finest Years [Book]. - London : Harper Press, 2009.

Hendrie Andrew Short Sunderland in World War II [Book]. - Shrewsbury : Airlife Publishing Ltd., 1994.

Higginbottom Peter [Online] // The Workhouse, The story of an institution.... - https://www.workhouses.org.uk.

Hill Roger Destroyer Captain [Book]. - St. Albans : Granada Publishing, 1979.

Holloway Adrian From Dartmouth to War [Book]. - London : Buckland Publications Ltd., 1993.

Howse Derek Radar at Sea, The Royal Navy in World War2 [Book]. - Basingstoke & London : The Macmillan Press Ltd, 1993.
IL R. Cacciatorpediniere "Luca Tarigo" [Online] // libero Digiland. - August 20, 2022. - https://digilander.libero.it/carandin/tarigo.htm.
Jacobsen Alf R. Death At Dawn [Book]. - Stroud : The History Press, 2011, 2016.
Konstam Angus Hunt The Bismark (Audio Book) [Book]. - [s.l.] : Audible, 2019. - Vol. Audio Book released Audible 17 Sept. 2019.
Koppes Hans Houterman & Jeroen Royal Naval Volunteer Reserve (RNV) Officers 1939 - 1945 [Online] // World War II unit histories & Officers. - 2006. - 21 March 2022. - https://www.unithistories.com/officers/RNVR_officersM2.html.
Lamb Charles War in a Stringbag [Book]. - London : Weidenfeld & Nicolson, 2001.
Langtree Christopher The Kelly's, British J, k & N Class Destroyers of World War II [Book]. - Rochester : Chatham Publishing, 2002.
Mahlke Helmut Memoirs of a Stuka Pilot [Book]. - Barnsley : Pen & Sword Books Ltd., 2013.
Mason Francis K Battle over Britain [Book]. - Bourne End, Bucks : Aston Publications Ltd., 1990.
M'Groarty Grattan Formidable New Hero of Naval Battle [Article] // Belfast Telegraph. - Belfast : Belfast Telegraph, 1941. - 6.
Monsarrat Nicholas The Cruel Sea [Book]. - London : Penguin Books, 2009.
Monsarrat Nicholas Three Corvettes [Book]. - London : Cassell & Co, 2000.
Moran Lord The Anatomy of Couragge [Book]. - London : Constable & Robinson Ltd, 2007.
Museum Orkney Orkney Museum [Online] // The Scuttling of the German Fleet: 2019 Summer Exhibition at the Orkney Museum. - orkneymuseum, 2021. - 2022. - https://orkneymuseum.wordpress.com/2021/03/09/the-scuttling-of-the-german-fleet-2019-summer-exhibition-at-the-orkney-museum-panel-4-eyewitness-accounts/.
Navy The Royal Manual of Seamanship Vol. II [Book]. - London : H.M. Stationery Office, 1932. - Vol. II.
Nowarra Heinz J JU52, aircraft & legend [Book]. - Sparkford, Yeovil : Haynes Publishing Group, 1987.
Osborne David Goodey & Richard H Destroyer at War. The fighting life and loss of HMS Havock. From the Atlantic to the Med 1939 - 1942 [Book]. - Barnsley : Frontline Books, 2017.

Otter Ken H.M.S. Gloucester, The Untold Story [Book]. - Barnsley : Pen & Sword Books Ltd., 2017.
Pack S. W. C. Night Action off Cape Matapan [Book]. - London : Ian Allan, 1972.
Pack S.W.C. The Battle for Crete [Book]. - [s.l.] : Ian Allan, 1972.
Parliament UK Navy Estimates 1939. (Hansard, 16 March 1939) [Online] // HANSARD 1803–2005. - 2021. - https://api.parliament.uk/historic-hansard/commons/1939/mar/16/navy-estimates-1939#S5CV0345P0_19390316_HOC_448.
Poggiaroni Giulio The Battle of The Tarigo Convoy [Online] // Comando Supremo, Italy in WW2. - June 15, 2022. - August 20, 2022. - https://comandosupremo.com/the-battle-of-the-tarigo-convoy/.
Pruszewicz Marek WW1: The letter that reveals a brutal day at Scapa Flow [Online] // BBC News. - BBC, June 19, 2015. - October 16, 2022. - https://www.bbc.co.uk/news/magazine-33152438.
Prysor Glyn Citizen Sailors [Book]. - London : Penguin Books, 2012.
Pugsley Rear Admiral A . F. Destroyer Man [Book]. - London : Weidenfield and Nicolson. - Vol. 1957.
R.N. Commander E. D. Webb H.M.S. Vernon A Short History from 1930 to 1955 [Book]. - [s.l.] : The wardroom Mess Committee H.M.S. Vernon, 1956.
R.N. Commander E. D. Webb H.M.S. Vernon, A Short History from 1930 to 1955 [Book]. - Portsmouth : The Wardroom Mess Commmittee, H.M.S. Vernon, 1956.
R.N.V.R Lieutenant John Davies Lower Deck [Book]. - London : Macmillan & Co. Ltd, 1945.
Rea W. E. Nil Desperandum [Book]. - Frome : Printed for Private Circulation, 1935.
Roberts John Destroyer Cossack [Book]. - Barnsley : Seaforth Publishing, 2020.
Rohwer Jurgen War at Sea 1939 - 1945 [Book]. - [s.l.] : The Caxton Publishing Group, 2001.
Schofield CB CBE, Vice Admiral B. B. Stringbags in Action [Book]. - Barnsely, South Yorkshire : Pen & Sword, Reprinted 2011.
Simmons Mark The Battle of Matapan 1941, The Trafalgar of the Mediterranean [Book]. - [s.l.] : Spellmount, 2011, 2012.
Spooner Tony Warburton's War. The life of Maverick Ace Adrian Warburton [Book]. - Manchester : Crecy Publishing Ltd, 1987, 1994, 2003.

Squadron 263 Operational Record Book AIR 27/1548 [Online] // 263 Squadron. - 2007. - October 16, 2022. - https://263squadron.weebly.com/about.html.

Taylor Bruce The End of GLory, War & Peace in HMS Hood 1916 - 1941 [Book]. - Barnsley : Seaforth Publishing, Pen & Sword Books Ltd., 2012.

The Admiralty Royal Navy ADM 1/11299 // Boards of inquiry and disciplinary courts: Loss of HMS Mohawk. - Malta : National Archives (U.K.), 1941.

The Herald Scapa 100: School trip witnessed scuttling of German fleet [Online] // The Herald. - https://www.heraldscotland.com/news/17608869.scapa-100-school-trip-witnessed-scuttling-german-fleet/.

The launch of HMS Nubian. - British Pathe, 1937.

Thomas David A. Crete 1941: The battle at sea. [Book]. - London : Military Book Society, 1972.

Unknown H.M.S. "Effingham" [Book]. - Colombo : Private, 1927.

Vigors Tim Life's Too Short To Cry [Book]. - [s.l.] : Grubb Street, 2008.

Weal John Junkers JU88, Kampfgeschwader, In North Africa and the Mediterranean [Book]. - Oxford : Osprey Publishing Ltd., 2009.

Wiart Sir Adrian Carton De Happy Odyssey [Book]. - Barnsley : Pen & Sword Books Ltd, 1950.

Wilson F. Home Page [Online] // 23rd A/S/ Trawler Group. - October 16, 2020, 2022. - http://www.royal-naval-reserve.co.uk/trawlers/default.htm.

Woodman Richard Malta Convoys 1940 - 1943 [Book]. - London : John Murray (Publishers) Ltd., 2000.

Worthing Herald - Friday 01 August 1941 [Online] // The British Newspaper Archive. - August 22, 2022. - https://www.britishnewspaperarchive.co.uk/viewer/BL/0001920/19410801/001/0001?browse=False.

Wragg David Stringbag, The fairy Swordfish at War [Book]. - Barnsley : Pen & Sword Books Limited, 2004, 2020.

Photographs

Cover © IWM
P99 – J Carter Personal Collection
P100 – 101 © IWM
P375 – 378 © IWM

Ingram Content Group UK Ltd.
Milton Keynes UK
UKHW012210080523
421345UK00001B/2